W9-BNQ-143

THE COURTYARD

THE COURTYARD

ARKADY LVOV

Translated by Richard Lourie

DOUBLEDAY

NEW YORK LONDON TORONTO SYDNEY AUCKLAND

All of the characters in this book are fictitious,
and any resemblance to actual persons,
living or dead, is purely coincidental.

Published by Doubleday, a division of
Bantam Doubleday Dell Publishing Group, Inc.
666 Fifth Avenue, New York, New York 10103

DOUBLEDAY and the portrayal of an anchor
with a dolphin are trademarks of
Doubleday, a division of Bantam Doubleday Dell
Publishing Group, Inc.

Library of Congress Cataloging-in-Publication Data

L'vov, Arkadiĭ.
The courtyard.

Translation of: Dvor.
1. Odessa (Ukraine)—Fiction. I. Title.
PG3549.L86D913 1989 891.73'44 88-20204

ISBN 0-385-23113-X

Translated from the Russian by Richard Lourie

BOOK DESIGN BY MARYSARAH QUINN

Printed in the United States of America
September 89
FIRST EDITION

BG

To the people of Odessa

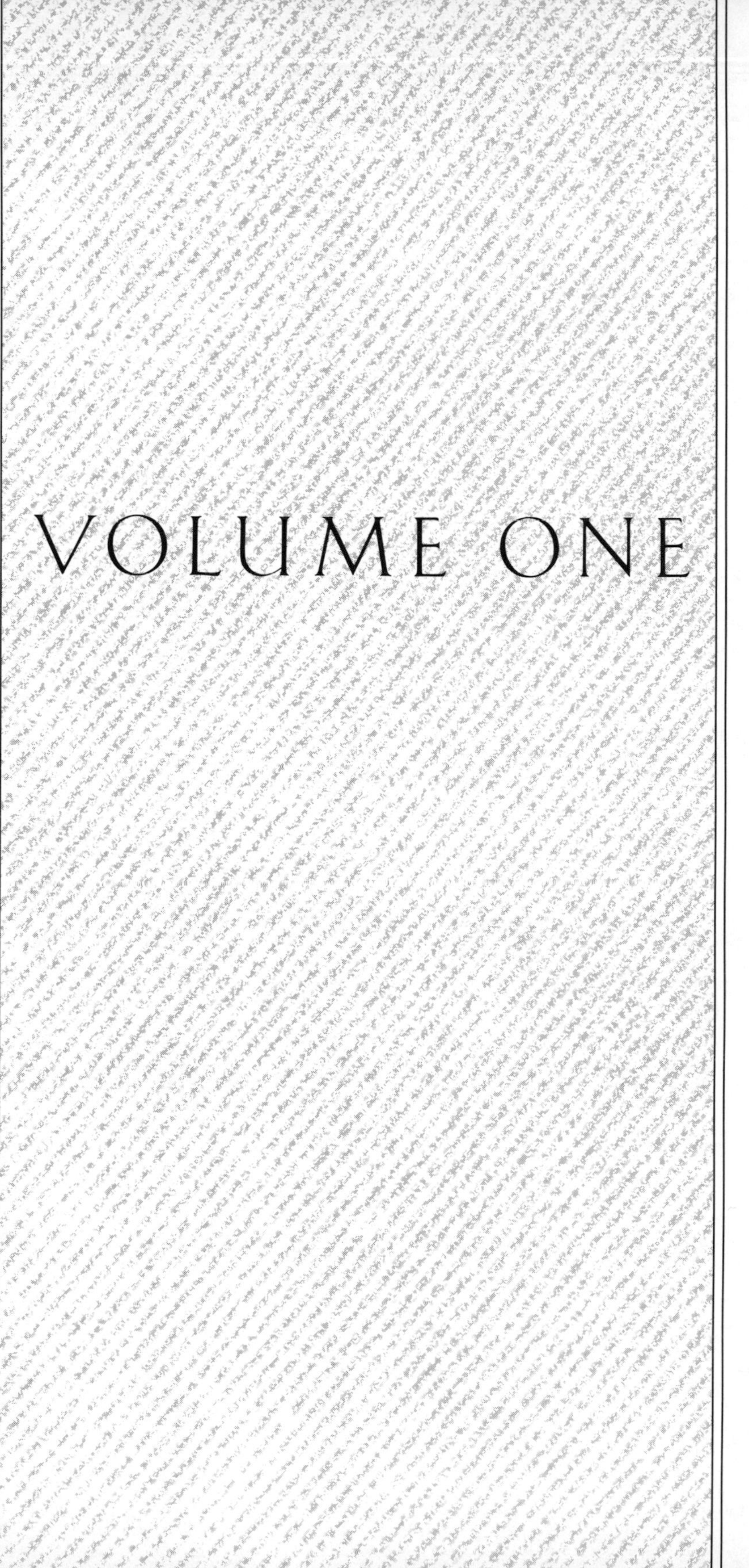

VOLUME ONE

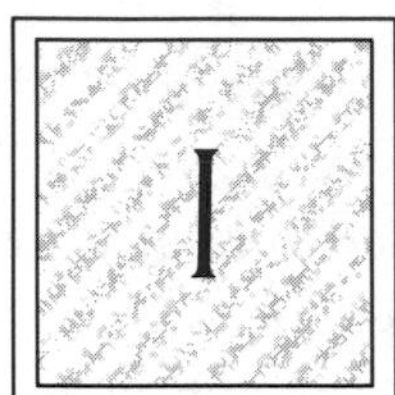

In the evening, after work, people lit torches and set off for Lieutenant Schmidt Avenue. There they formed columns that headed for Commune Square via Roza Luxembourg Street, formerly Police Street.

Even spaces separated the columns, each of which was headed by three people—one from the party organization, one from the union, one from management.

Iona Degtyar was at the head of one column and the two people beside him, one from the union, one from management, were lagging back a little, a half step or so. When that column passed the building where Comrade Degtyar lived, the people in the gateway smiled with joy and nudged each other with their elbows so that no one would miss a glimpse of their neighbor leading a column that must have numbered a thousand. Efim Granik, a house painter who everyone said had a hundred times more talent than any artist, made a megaphone of his hands and shouted for the whole street to hear: "Three lumpen-proletarian cheers for Iona Ovseich!"

Degtyar did not bat an eye. Granik placed his hands by his mouth again because he could not endure going unnoticed, but he wasn't given a second chance to shout. Stepa Khomitsky, the building administration's plumber, spoke first, to explain Granik's error: a lumpen proletarian was an unemployed person who didn't even look for work and just wanted to eat and drink at the expense of others, but a proletarian was a worker, even if he was unemployed.

"And maybe that's just what I want, to eat and drink, and not work!" retorted Efim Granik.

The people standing by the gate broke into laughter because Efim Granik was the kind of person who would slander even himself to avoid appearing foolish or ignorant.

The columns bearing torches and portraits of the leaders, framed in red cotton, moved slowly past the Alexandrovsky Gardens. The people responsible for maintaining order shouted words of encouragement, their voices husky from the December cold. There were thousands and thousands of others behind these marchers who wanted to keep moving and not mark time.

Suddenly Granik ran in front of the others and again began shouting: "Three lumpen-proletarian cheers for Iona Ovseich! Long live the Constitution!"

At that very moment the column seconded him with a loud cheer, and when Degtyar raised his hand and cried: "Long live the Soviet socialist Constitution!" the entire column raised an even louder cheer.

Madame Malaya, Osoviakhim's assistant in the building, pointed to Efim and said, "He has won his point. We all feel the same way he does."

When Granik returned to the gateway, it was as a hero and everyone wanted to say a warm word to him so that he would respond to them just as the column had responded to his words.

"Fima," called Madame Malaya, stepping out in front of the others, "you might make a decent public speaker."

Efim smiled like a man who knew an exaggeration when he heard one and flatly stated that he would never make a good public speaker: first, because he didn't have enough background and, second, because he didn't have the perseverance to read everything the Soviet leaders wrote.

"He's right about that," agreed Madame Malaya, "a public speaker needs perseverance and a good brain."

Stepa Khomitsky replied that Granik had a good pair of hands and not everyone needed a good brain: a good brain wouldn't pull a plow or clean a grain separator, that was hands-on work.

Everyone standing by the gate, including Madame Malaya, laughed again. Efim Granik gave Stepa a firm, workerly handshake and modestly asked everyone else not to provoke Stepa.

The columns had been on the move for about an hour by then, and people were exclaiming over the size of Odessa and its population. "Before the Revolution Odessa was the third largest city after Petersburg and Moscow, but now it is fifth, after Kiev and Kharkov," Stepa announced to the group.

"Would you prefer the capital to be smaller than Odessa?" Madame Malaya asked, waving her arms as she spoke.

"Madame Malaya, you're getting yourself excited for nothing," Stepa said, "I am entirely satisfied with the present state of affairs. I was simply stating a fact."

"But Kharkov's not the capital," interjected Granik. "All right, Kiev's the capital, but what does Kharkov have to do with anything?"

"What do you mean?" said Malaya in surprise. "Just two years ago Kharkov was the capital and Comrade Petrovsky was headquarted there, and he's asking what Kharkov has to do with anything!"

"But that was two years ago!" Efim countered. "And if you go back further, Russia had a tsar, Germany had a kaiser, and Austro-Hungary had Franz Joseph. What of it?"

Stepa Khomitsky made a dismissive gesture but Madame Malaya said that Fima's mind was as disorderly as a bordello and Stepa should help him tidy it up. Coming from someone else, those words could have been offensive but no one took offense at Madame Malaya because she had been born in the building in which they all lived. Moreover she had a son who was an aviation engineer. He had graduated from an institute in Moscow and, before that, had been a pilot. He came to see his mother every year when he was on leave.

"Madame Malaya," said Granik, squinting as if aiming a rifle, "if my mind is what you say it is, then Stepa shouldn't be involved, because with his tool he'll make things even worse."

Remarks about Stepa's tool were always good for a chuckle but this time it was so apt that they all laughed out loud as if they were tickling one another under the arms and no one wanted to be the first to stop.

The columns continued to pass by and no one could tell when it would end. Even though the people standing by the gate had plenty of work waiting for them at home, they stayed where they were and continued watching so that they wouldn't have to ask other people about it later on, and be irritated by their own foolishness at not staying. As Madame Malaya had quite rightly remarked, it wasn't every day that a new Constitution went into effect, especially one personally written and signed by Comrade Stalin. She didn't say anything about the Special Eighth Congress of Soviets or about Comrade Stalin's speech. There was no need to speak of these things any more than there was to say to a passenger who had bought a ticket and boarded a steamship: "Comrade, you bought a ticket and boarded a steamship."

Everyone knew about the Special Eighth Congress of Soviets, Stalin's speech, and the new Constitution which gave everyone eighteen and over the right to vote. The children in the courtyard shouted to Madame Orlov and old man Kiselis: "Even you get the right to vote returned to you!" Old man Kiselis brandished his cane at them, calling them little bastards and monsters. Many people were of the opinion that it was a mistake to give the vote to people like old man Kiselis, who had been a shopkeeper under Tsar Nicholas—he wouldn't change as long as he lived. But because he was already so old and the Soviet government was becoming stronger all the time, other people were entirely in favor of the article in the new Constitution conferring the right to vote on everyone. Stepa Khomitsky added that old man Kiselis had not chosen his father and mother, and so then why needle him about his origins for the rest of his life? Stepa's argument could only draw laughter—it sounded odd to say about a person with one foot in the grave, "Your parents are to blame for everything." Still, on the other hand, it wasn't all that laughable either.

"Stepa," said Madame Malaya in surprise, "you went through the whole Civil War with Kotovsky—have you really forgotten that the Whites never asked who your father and mother were?"

Stepa rubbed his chin. "On the contrary, the Whites were very much interested in a person's social origin."

Madame Malaya seized on this point with even greater surprise in her voice. "Yes, they were interested, but why? Why, I ask you? To put you up against a wall, not to give you the right to vote because you didn't choose your own parents!"

There was no objection Stepa could make to that so he referred instead to the Soviet Union's current situation. It had conquered one sixth of the globe and shouldn't fear its enemies, as it hadn't earlier, during the Civil War.

"That's true," agreed Madame Malaya. "We don't have to be

afraid now. But tell me, who would pat someone's head when he should get a kick in the ass?"

Stepa concurred, but still he could not entirely agree with her any more than he could object to what she was saying either.

It was dark by then but the torches, though very smoky, shed considerable light, and it was no problem to read the slogans on the banners the marchers held high. Of course, there was no real reason to read them because every two or three minutes first one voice, then hundreds would shout out those slogans, ending with an obligatory rousing cheer. Most of the slogans were about the Constitution and the leaders, and when caricatures of Franco, Hitler, or Mussolini were carried past, people would shout: "Long live republican Spain! Death to the fascist rebels! Down with world imperialism! Down with the bourgeoisie!"

"You hear that? 'Down with the bourgeoisie!' " said Madame Malaya to Stepa. "That means Kiselis."

Stepa did not reply but it was plain from his face that he didn't like the connection Madame Malaya was making between the world bourgeoisie and old man Kiselis.

"Klava Ivanovna," interjected Granik unexpectedly, "I'm no student of politics, but that's too much. I'm a hundred percent on Stepa's side when it comes to old man Kiselis. Yes, Kiselis was a parasite before the Revolution, a bloodsucker, no one's arguing that, but I'd stake my head that he wouldn't have been capable of picking up a rifle and shooting a person."

"He'd stake his head!" said Madame Malaya indignantly. "Everyone knows you've got golden hands but your head is less than pure gold."

People laughed, and Efim laughed along with them. Then he frankly admitted that he wasn't a good businessman when it came to politics, unlike Degtyar.

"Efim," said Madame Malaya with a frown, "you should remember some things can be joked about and some can't. I can see that it's not only your brain that gives you problems but your teeth."

"My teeth?" said Efim in surprise.

"That's right," seconded Stepa. "They can't keep your tongue where it belongs."

"Oh!" said Madame Malaya, wagging a finger.

Some people laughed, others remained silent. To extricate himself from a ticklish situation, Efim gave his word of honor to brush his teeth every day and keep them ready for action.

"That's another subject entirely," said Madame Malaya approvingly. "And do me a favor—don't make me run up three flights of stairs every day for you when you're supposed to be at political studies. Degtyar has already asked me twice why you haven't been there."

"You know why," said Efim, shrugging his shoulders. "I'm looking for work."

"That's no excuse," replied Madame Malaya. "In the first place, all offices are closed in the evening; in the second place, until you start working, you have to show up for political classes without being reminded. We don't have the wherewithal to be sending special messengers after people. And the fact that you don't like studying with housewives and old people is your own business. You shouldn't keep skipping from one job to another."

Madame Malaya's remarks were fair enough: everyone knew that Granik was a drifter and lucky to stay at a job six months. On the other hand, there was no malice in what she said—it was just his nature, he couldn't sit still very long.

When the last torch-bearing column had passed and there were only stray passersby on Lieutenant Schmidt Avenue, Madame Malaya told Efim to drop by the reading room with her and make a sign, announcing tomorrow's meeting, which was for all the building's residents, both those who were working and those who were not. The bakers' club was letting them use their premises. The meeting was for everyone and the children should come too.

Granik said that he would make the announcement at home; he had his paper, paints, and brushes there and was used to working at home. But Madame Malaya declared, "No, better you use poor paper and ink instead of paints. The announcement has to be posted at once, so that later on no one can say that he didn't see it because it hadn't been posted in time."

Now Granik agreed with Klava Ivanovna's view of the matter but immediately posed another objection—his professional honor did not allow him to do a slipshod job on such an important announcement.

"Fine," conceded Klava Ivanovna, "you can make it at home, but I'll go with you and I'll stand over you until it's all done."

Granik thought for a moment, searching for other objections, but, finding none, he was finally forced to give in: all right, Madame Malaya could stand over him as long as she wanted.

Efim lived in an enormous room, almost twenty meters square, with his wife Sonya and his two children, Oska and Khilka. The room had an entry hall that was no less than five square meters. The hall could easily have served as a kitchen but, house painters being what they are, every corner was so crammed with pails and jars that a person could scarcely make his way through. A kitchen was out of the question.

There was also nowhere to turn in the room itself, which contained a trundle bed in addition to a regular bed, four chairs, and a dining table: both windowsills and the floor, not to mention the table and chairs, were piled with paints, paper, and small squares of glass on which various people's names, initials, and instructions on how many times to ring the bell had been written in brown paint. Madame Malaya picked up one and asked: "Who are these orders from? Private customers?"

"What do you mean, private customers?" asked Efim in reply. He waved his arm at the stacks. "Just people who wanted a plate on their door so other people would know who lived there."

"Who do you think you're fooling? I'm not asking you what people wanted those plates for, I'm asking you whether you received these orders officially as a temporary cottage industry worker or whether you received them from private parties?"

"When a person asks me to paint him a door plate," said Granik with a smile, "should I ask him for his passport? If he wants his name painted on one way, we paint it on like that, if he wants his bell rung once, we paint what he wants, and if he wants it rung a hundred times, then that's what we paint."

"Listen to me," said Klava Ivanovna, losing her patience. "Do you receive money for those door plates? Or do you do it for a thank you and a smile? Give me a straight answer."

"What do you mean, a straight answer?" said Granik, smiling again. "If a person wants to show me his gratitude for some trifle like, say, a door plate, I'm no slob, I don't spit in his face and say, 'Keep your dirty hands off and keep your dirty money too.' First of all, we're not talking about dollars here, but good Soviet money with pictures of workers on it, and, second of all—"

"Second of all," said Madame Malaya, stomping her foot, "stop acting like a fool and answer me in plain Russian: have you told the Revenue Department that you're taking private orders or haven't you?"

"Whether I did or I didn't," said Efim, shrugging his shoulders, "what difference does it make? If the Revenue Department needs to know something, it knows it, and if it doesn't, that means it's not interested. Why should I try to take them in?"

"Oh, finally, he's answered like a human being. The Revenue Department doesn't know anything about his private business."

"One minute," said Efim in surprise. "Who told you that the Revenue Department doesn't know about it? What I said was that, if the Revenue Department doesn't know, it's because it's not interested, and, if it's interested, it knows. In the last ten-day period a man came by here and counted all the plates. Then he took a stick and started tapping the whole floor and the walls. I said to him, 'Why tap them? Let's just pull them down.' 'Don't get excited,' he said, 'if we have to pull them down, we will.' I brought over an ax and said, 'Here, take it, chop the walls down.' Then he got all worked up and ran for the door where he says: 'Chaim, I'll make you shit blood for that!' Chaim's my name on my passport."

"Fima," said Madame Malaya, slapping her hands together, "why are you trying to wriggle out of it like an idiot, why aren't you giving me a straight answer? Your late mother was a working woman and your father was a craftsman like you can't find today, and nobody could say a bad word about them, but you—you're like the wind in the field: first you blow one way, then the other, and you live your life like the whole world was already Soviet. And we still have as many internal enemies as you have kopecks, not to mention the ones encircling the country. I'm in my fifties and I have a good, clear memory of the old regime. In 1919 my husband, Boris Davidovich, lost his left hand and half a leg, and in 1930 they brought him to me on a sleigh from Tsebrikovo from the German colonists who were for Soviet power but without kolkhozes and collectivization. Efim, I'm asking you like your own mother—is your mind so messed up you can't live a normal life?"

"Klava Ivanovna," said Efim, placing both hands over his heart, "I swear by my children, I give you my word of honor—"

"Fima," interrupted Madame Malaya, "why can't you live like everyone else, so nobody can criticize you, so people only say good things about you—'You should follow Efim Granik's example!' "

"Klava Ivanovna," whispered Granik, "I give you my word of honor—"

"All right," said Madame Malaya with a dismissive wave of her hand, "let's make the announcement before people start coming home from work."

One after the other, the letters took such elegant and beautiful form that they seemed not the creation of a human hand but of some special machine. Klava Ivanovna could not restrain her delight and sighed: "Oh, Fima, what golden hands you have!" Then, so as not to praise him too much, she immediately switched to another subject—his wife and children—asking why they weren't home yet when it was so late.

"Why aren't they home?" said Efim, spreading his hands wide. "Sonya said she was planning on going to temple today."

"But what about the children?" asked Madame Malaya.

"She took the children with her. But they don't go in, they stay outside and wait."

"That's bad. Not a pretty picture," said Madame Malaya. "I don't want to interfere but, if I were in your shoes, I wouldn't allow her to take the children along. Personally, I haven't been in church in twenty years and your Sonya's half my age. But if she's ignorant enough to be religious, let her pray to her Yaweh, but she shouldn't confuse the children's minds, the children are our future and we're responsible for them. You should forbid it."

"I already have, a million times."

"So?"

"She says, 'Would you rather have the children running around the street like homeless waifs?' "

"No, we know all about those tricks. If she doesn't want her children running around like homeless waifs, she should bring them to the reading room, there's always something to do there."

"Madame Malaya," said Efim, his hand on his heart, "I tell her the same thing: 'Take the children to the reading room.' And what she answers is, 'And how would you like it if everyone starts saying we're dumping our children on other people?' "

"Efim," said Madame Malaya indignantly, "you're so smart, but she twists you around her little finger like a total fool. Do the children's teachers know about this?"

Efim said that he didn't go see his children's teachers, Sonya did that. But why should the teachers know that the children's mother took them to the synagogue?

"What about the other children?" exclaimed Madame Malaya. "They make a laughingstock out of your Osya. No, Efim, I'm going to be blunt here: you're not acting like a man but like a mattress with springs—as soon as your wife sits down on you, all you can do is squeak. It looks like I'll have to stop by the school myself."

"No," said Efim, suddenly raising his voice, "I give you my word of honor that I'll have a talk with her, and I'll give her a talking to she won't forget for the rest of her life!"

"Easy," said Klava Ivanovna, "calm down. I think it's better that I have a little talk with her. God only knows what will happen, the way you fly off the handle."

"I won't fly off the handle," said Efim, whacking the table with the palm of his hand, "but I want things to be done my way at home, not hers! She's disgracing me in front of the neighbors, Odessa, and the whole Soviet Union. Not only will the children stop going with her, she won't set foot inside there herself."

"All right," agreed Madame Malaya, "we won't intervene. You talk with her. But don't forget it's results that count, and if there aren't any . . ."

"What do you mean?" Granik raised his hand and made a tight fist. "There'll be results!"

"Calm down," said Klava Ivanovna. "An artist should be calm when he's painting."

They left the apartment together. Granik took his hammer and a few nails with him to hang the announcement in the front entrance. They chose a place in the exact middle of the entry hall where the announcement would be equally visible to those entering and those leaving. Efim leaned against the wall, made a mark above his head, smoothed out the announcement, and nailed it to the wall. Madame Malaya took a few steps back to check that it was easily readable from a distance. Impressed again by what a beautiful and elegant job Efim had done, she promised him that he would have Comrade Degtyar's personal gratitude.

"You're very welcome, Klava Ivanovna, you have my word on that," said Granik, striking his chest with his fist. "But I'll tell you something else. It's not well attached. There should be a slat at the top and the bottom to keep the wind from blowing it at night. There's always a draft here in the hall."

Madame Malaya objected that he was being too fussy but, after a moment's thought, changed her mind. Efim ran to his apartment and was back in no more than a minute.

The slats diminished the poster's elegance but they also lent it an air of greater significance: it was immediately apparent that this was no mere hastily posted piece of paper people could safely ignore.

The very first to read the announcement was Stepa Khomitsky and Dina Vargaftik, and, though their tastes varied, this time they both agreed that it was as beautiful as if it had been done for May Day or the anniversary of the Revolution. They were followed by Olya Cheperukha, who read the announcement intently, then burst out laughing. At first, spotting the large poster from a distance, her heart had missed a beat; she thought that one of the leaders had died but then realized that if the country was in mourning the letters would have been black, not red and gold.

"Olya," said Madame Malaya, frowning, "this is no laughing matter."

"I swear I wasn't thinking anything bad," said Olya.

The meeting had been called for seven, figuring it would start at eight: people would have time to eat dinner and change their clothes after work. Of course, the meeting could have been called for an hour earlier but that would have made people hurry and worry, and people had to be cared for. Comrade Degtyar himself, however, arrived at seven o'clock on the dot, just as the radio was giving the time, and took a seat at the table next to the rostrum.

The rostrum had been knocked together from pine board and was usually painted crimson or red, but today it had been draped with a piece of red calico which everyone agreed looked much more elegant and imposing. The table had also been covered with a piece of red calico cloth that almost reached the floor. These details betrayed a woman's touch. And it was no secret that the touch was Madame Malaya's. Still, even when hearing that fact yet again, people could not refrain from exclaiming over a woman who, without any money and simply because of her political consciousness, was able to accomplish more than people with money. As for Klava Ivanovna's political consciousness itself, people no longer gave its origins the slightest thought, any more than they asked themselves why they breathed air and drank water.

Iona Ovseich turned the pages of his note pad, making short one- or two-line notes. He would suddenly narrow his eyes, support his forehead on a bent finger, then make further notes, no longer on the same page but on the page ahead, or, the other way, on one, two, or three pages back. At seven-thirty he stood up, intently scanning the hall, which was about a third full, people having come from other courtyards as well. He announced that it was now seven-thirty Moscow time, and the meeting had been called for seven on the dot—also, by the way, Moscow time. Though not everyone got the joke, people did understand that Iona Ovseich was joking and they laughed amicably. He smiled with one eye, patiently waiting for people to calm down.

"Well, now that you've settled down," he said, "I can ask you whether we should start the meeting or wait a little while longer?"

There was no unanimity on the point: some people thought they should wait a while longer since people weren't late out of malice, while others believed that people's reasons for being late were irrelevant—late was late—and they demanded the meeting begin. However, those in favor of waiting were a clear majority, so Degtyar proclaimed: "We'll wait."

The meeting finally began at eight on the dot and this time people were unanimous: Degtyar took a formal vote and anyone wishing to object could object but there were no objections.

A motion was made to elect a workers' presidium consisting of five persons: Malaya, Khomitsky, Dina Vargaftik, Dr. Landa, and Degtyar. People applauded loudly after each name but when Iona Ovseich said his own name, Degtyar, the applause grew even louder, and many people noticed that Degtyar's name had come last, though it had every right to be at the head of the list, the very first.

When the workers' presidium had taken their places, a new motion was made: to elect an honorary presidium consisting of the Politburo and headed by Comrade Stalin. The entire audience rose to its feet as a man; the walls shook from the power of the applause, and the ceiling seemed about to collapse any minute. Then Efim Granik jumped up onto his seat, filled his lungs with air, tensed his every muscle, and cried wildly: "Three cheers for the great genius, Comrade STALIN!" and the hall roared with new energy, the cheers breaking from one person to the next like ocean waves. At moments it even seemed that people had to gasp for breath but then there would be a fresh surge of energy and the whole thing would start over again. Finally they quieted down and Comrade Degtyar requested permission to consider the applause as a sign of the audience's complete approval. The audience responded to this with another ovation, a surf of thundering cheers, but it did not last as long this time though it was every bit as intense as it had been before. People had given their emotions free rein and needed to catch their breath now.

Iona Ovseich withdrew his watch from his watch pocket, placed it on the table, and announced the decision of the workers' presidium to have Klava Ivanovna Malaya chair the meeting. So that no more time would go to waste, Madame Malaya rose and at once gave the floor to Iona Ovseich Degtyar, who would make a report.

Iona Ovseich looked all the members of the presidium in the eye, tossed his head back a little, and then stated that the Special Eighth Congress which had opened in the city of Moscow on November 25 of this year had, in its evening session of December 5 of this same year, unanimously ratified the new Constitution and resolved that December 5 be made a national holiday and that coming elections be conducted in accordance with the new electoral system.

There was nothing new about this information but, then and there, with all of them assembled, it acquired fresh power, and people rose to their feet in unison and applauded. The workers' presidium also stood and applauded, their hands stretched out in front of them as far as they would go. An outsider might have thought the presidium was welcoming the audience while the audience in turn was responding with doubled, even tripled, intensity.

When this storm too had passed, Iona Ovseich took a sip of water and addressed a question to the audience: "What changes in Soviet life were carried out in the period between 1924 and 1936? And what is the essence of those changes?"

The audience was well aware that the question required no answer, and in fact had a single purpose: to focus their attention. Iona Ovseich would answer the question himself, after a short pause, by reminding the audience that in 1924 they were in the first NEP period, in which the Soviet government allowed a certain resurgence of capitalism. At the time socialist industry accounted for eighty percent while the NEPmen had a good twenty percent of their own. The situation was even worse in agriculture. True, the landowning class no longer existed—it had been liquidated—but, on the other hand, there were agricultural capitalists, the kulaks. As the saying goes, it was six of one, half a dozen of the other.

The audience rippled with jolly laughter, and the speaker said that now, of course, they could laugh, but back then, in 1924, the kulaks were powerful and the collective and state farms were weak, and people didn't talk about liquidating the kulaks but only about limiting them. It was the same story with trade, the socialist sector amounting to about sixty percent, with all the rest in the hands of merchants, speculators, and other private parties.

Today the picture was entirely different: agriculture had been totally collectivized and the capitalist element had been driven from industry. Moreover, who could belittle the fact that today's socialist industry was over seven times more productive than its prewar counterpart? No, there was no belittling that fact. And there was another fact that could not be belittled either: that today the collective and state farms had four hundred thousand tractors with seven million five hundred and eighty thousand horsepower, if not more. And, as far as the country's commerce was concerned, the merchants and speculators had been driven out once and for all.

"To take our own courtyard for an example, everyone can see for himself that Citizen Kiselis, who formerly was a licensed haberdasher with his own store, now works in that same store as a salesman and is paid a fixed salary, on a par with everyone else's. Citizen Orlov, who, under the old regime and for a while after the Revolution, led a nonproductive life by selling that which should never be sold, is now employed in the packing department of the tobacco factory that formerly belonged to Popov, and she fulfills her work quotas one hundred percent and more. Dr. Landa, who once had his own practice in dermatology and related ailments, renounced private practice himself and is a member of our presidium here today.

"So, from all this, we should draw the conclusion that the class structure of our society has changed and there are no more exploiters among us. But people's minds have a way of lagging behind reality. Many of those present here tonight yesterday witnessed Efim Granik running alongside the marchers and shouting a slogan that was illiterate from the political point of view, addressing the workers as lumpen proletariat. And what does that demonstrate? That demonstrates that, in the concrete case at hand, Efim Granik's mind is lagging behind reality. Not only has it been a long time since we had a lumpen proletariat, so well described by Maxim Gorky, we no longer even have a proletariat. What we have is the working class as its own master!"

This remark elicited loud applause. Klava Ivanovna took advantage of the moment to refill the speaker's glass. After a sip, Iona Ovseich returned to the subject of Efim Granik.

"What was the root of Efim Granik's mistake? Was this simply a slip of the tongue, something that might happen to anybody? No, of course not, because Efim Granik, by dint of his profession, leads a cottage industry type of life and has never worked at a factory or plant. And that was the direct cause of a backward mentality. In the U.S.S.R., the working class is not only its own master, it controls all the means of production and, in addition, is free of all exploitation, but our very own Efim Granik has not noticed that little difference which took place right before his very eyes."

Iona Ovseich, Madame Malaya, and all the others smiled at Efim Granik, and he smiled himself, realizing that he had made a fool of himself in public and that it was better to laugh at himself along with everyone else than to be isolated.

"And now," said Comrade Degtyar, "let us move on to the next question: What are the fundamental characteristics of the new Constitution? First and foremost, a constitution should not be confused with a platform because, while a platform speaks of what is lacking and must be fought for in the future, a constitution, on the contrary, should speak of what already exists. In other words, a platform concerns the future, and the Constitution the present. In other words, the Constitution should not reflect what we would like to have happen—for example, complete communism when everything will be from each according to his abilities and to each according to his needs—but that which already exists in reality, that is, the first or lowest phase of communism, meaning—"

"Socialism!" cried Efim Granik from his seat.

"Absolutely right," confirmed the speaker, "socialism. And so the new Constitution is not a platform but a summation of the road we've traveled, and that is its primary characteristic.

"Comrades," asked Iona Ovseich all of a sudden, "is everything I said clear to you all or not? There's no reason to be shy about asking questions—this is very complex material, and it's better to be safe than—"

"Sorry!" exclaimed Granik again.

Madame Malaya reprimanded Granik but Comrade Degtyar noted that such replies demonstrated a high degree of active participation and there was no need for people to suppress them.

He did not dwell very long on the Constitution's second and third characteristics because to understand them in depth required a knowledge of political economy, and political economy was not the sort of thing you just leaped into headfirst—it could cost you your head. All the same, everyone should make a mental note that all bourgeois constitutions, without a single exception, were based on a capitalist foundation whereas the U.S.S.R.'s new Constitution was based on the fact that capitalism had been abolished in the U.S.S.R.

"Not only that, bourgeois constitutions proceed from the tacit assumption that society consists of antagonistic classes whereas our Constitution once again does just the reverse, proceeding as it does from the assumption that there are no longer any antagonistic classes in our society.

"Comrades," said Iona Ovseich, interrupting himself, "is there any special need for me to interpret the concept of class antagonism or can we keep going?"

"We can keep going," replied Madame Malaya. "Everyone should know what that means, and anyone who doesn't can ask afterward."

Degtyar went on to say that the new Constitution's fourth characteristic was of primary significance and had an even more important role in the Transcaucasus and Central Asia.

"And why is that? It's so because that fourth characteristic is the complete equality of all races and peoples, regardless of their language or the color of their skin, and this applies in all spheres of life: the economy, the government, and culture. Here in Odessa the tsarist government poisoned one ethnic group against another and launched pogroms against the Jews, but now all that remains of those nightmares is the memory of them, and our children can study in Russian, Ukrainian, Jewish, Bulgarian, or Polish schools. And, in addition, there are two German schools, one in the center of the city and the other in Lustdorf, which can be reached on the number 29 trolley that goes to Tiraspolsky Square. The stop's just three blocks from there."

People shouted from the audience that it was even less than three, only two and a half. The speaker accepted the correction and moved on to the next point, the fifth characteristic.

The fifth point was that, unlike the bourgeois', the new Constitution made no distinction as to a person's sex, that is, between men and women, nor did it make distinctions between those who were well off and those who were not, the settled and the nomadic.

"But do gypsies get the right to vote?" asked Efim, jumping from his seat, remembering halfway that he was supposed to raise his hand.

"Sit down," ordered Madame Malaya. "Don't interrupt the speaker!"

The speaker, however, took a different attitude toward the question and replied that the example of the gypsies was a very interesting one since, on the one hand, they weren't registered and no one knew where to find them, while, on the other hand, the local branches of the Soviet government were offering them both registration and permanent work. At the same time, many gypsies had already joined collective farms where they worked as blacksmiths and stablemen, since they'd been dealing with horses their whole lives and knew them well.

"And from this we can directly conclude that equality exists not only in word but in deed. Anyone who has seen the movie *The Last Gypsy Camp* starring the famous actress Lyalya Chernaya has seen for himself that our Soviet gypsies are not the same beggars who existed before the Revolution or in the first years after it. It is true that a few gypsies still stroll about with their accordions or violins on trolleys and trains, begging for alms, but, as they say, every family has its black sheep, and in the case at hand the exception only proves the rule."

The speaker's last remark met with unanimous applause because everyone, especially those who could remember the old days, knew from experience that there were now fewer and fewer gypsies on the trolleys and streets, though near the market, at the Starokonny Bazaar, and even on the corner of Deribasovskaya and the Tenth Anniversary of the RKKA, formerly Preobrazhensky Street, fortune-tellers still sometimes grabbed passersby by the sleeve, and, if someone wasn't interested, the fortune-tellers dashed up ahead of him and blocked his path until he gave in.

Moving on to the next characteristic, the sixth, Iona Ovseich said with complete assurance that, as opposed to bourgeois constitutions, the new Soviet Constitution's center of gravity was the question of guaranteeing people's rights.

"For example, if people are given the right to work, that right is upheld due to the fact that our country experiences no economic crises; people are not only given freedom of expression, they are also given access to printing presses and paper, and have a place to live and work. You don't have to go far afield for a good example. Yesterday, anyone so wishing could participate in the demonstration, and today everyone can speak his mind here in front of the residents of this building and of other courtyards, and tomorrow he can write a notice for the newspaper, and it will be read by the entire nation, not just Odessa, Nikolaev, and Kherson, but the entire U.S.S.R., because that notice can also be broadcast over the radio, and radio is the fastest means of communication, distance is no obstacle to it."

"And can it go abroad too?" cried Granik.

"Yes, it can," replied Iona Ovseich. "And so, Granik, you have a chance of becoming world famous, like David Oistrakh."

Everyone laughed and Efim honestly admitted that he had never once held a violin in his hands.

"That doesn't matter," retorted Comrade Degtyar. "There's a first time for everything and there was a day when David Oistrakh was holding a violin for the first time. And, if the need arises, we can furnish the Stolyarsky school with a certificate stating that you're a prodigy, and in a few years Oistrakh will be happy to be greasing your bow strings. Of course, that is, if you allow him to."

"If he asks me nicely!" cried Granik, but he was heard only by those beside him because the whole audience was roaring with laughter.

Since the new Constitution had six main characteristics which had all been elucidated, the speaker announced that he would now allow himself to pass to the final point, namely, the bourgeois criticism of the projected Constitution, which was now past the project stage and was a fact of life.

Iona Ovseich took a sip of water, turned the page, and began with the first group of critics, who had found no more intelligent approach than to pass over the new Constitution in silence as if it did not even exist.

"Some people might think that passing something over in silence is not criticism, but that's wrong, because approval is one thing and silence quite another. Of course, this is a foolish and ridiculous form of criticism, but all the same it's one form criticism can take. But how did the silent treatment work out in practice? It was a total flop, and so that particular group of critics, the fascists and reactionaries, were forced to turn up the heat."

"They should drown in their own you know what!" shouted Granik. The audience and the speaker burst out laughing, and this time Madame Malaya raised no objections, laughing louder than anyone herself.

The second group of critics proved a little smarter than the first, but only a little, since, on the one hand, they acknowledged that the Constitution existed as a fact of life but, on the other, called it a mere tactic, a meaningless scrap of paper, designed to deceive. Strange as it may seem, a typical representative of this group was the German newspaper *Deutsche Diplomatisch-Politisch Korrespondent,* which proclaimed for all the world to hear that the U.S.S.R.'s Constitution was a "Potemkin village" because the U.S.S.R. was not itself a country but, at most, a geographical concept.

This revelation by the German newspaper *Deutsche Diplomatisch-Politisch Korrespondent* so tickled the audience that the speaker was forced to halt until they were done laughing. And then when Iona Ovseich explained that a similar fool had already appeared in the works of the great Russian writer Shchedrin—that fool was a petty tyrant of a bureaucrat who didn't like America and proposed a resolution to "undiscover America"!—the audience laughed so hard that the speaker was forced to pause again.

Then he said that, no matter how great a fool Shchedrin's bureaucrat had been, he was less a fool than the one who wrote for the *Korrespondent* because at least he understood that you could undiscover a country on paper but that this had nothing to do with reality.

"As far as the facts are concerned, these are the facts: above and beyond the lands that the peasants had before the Revolution, the collective farms have now given them an additional five hundred million hectares, and today's Soviet agriculture produces a yield one and a half times that of the old days. Not only that, we have no unemployment, work is a right here; we have no pariahs, as they call India's forgotten people, the right to vote by secret ballot is a universal, direct, and equal right here.

"Those are the facts, and facts are stubborn things. But the *Korrespondent* might say, 'So much the worse for the facts.' And to that our response could be, 'You can't teach an old dog new tricks.' "

"But there's no reason even to answer someone like that!" exclaimed Madame Malaya, pounding her fist on the table. "They're all bark and no bite."

As for the third group of critics, the speaker immediately warned that they were much smarter than the second group, not to mention the first. But to be smarter than a fool is not the same thing as being intelligent. And that was true of the third group of critics: though they were smarter, they were still a world away from true intelligence.

"This group of critics says: 'Yes, the U.S.S.R.'s Constitution is a positive achievement but just you try to put it into practice.' And what is our response to that? First and foremost, that we have already encountered such skeptics before, back in 1917 when we took power. There were plenty of big mouths back then telling us that the Bolsheviks weren't bad people but they couldn't run the country and failure was inevitable."

"They made their bed, now let them lie in it," interjected Madame Malaya.

"Absolutely right," Iona Ovseich seconded her, "and there's no reason to doubt that the skeptics will fall down this time too."

Before dealing with the fourth group of critics, the speaker requested permission to cite an example from literature. "Every schoolboy has heard of the famous writer Nikolai Gogol, and there's even a Gogol Street near the water, just past Deribasovskaya Street. And so, in Gogol's novel *Dead Souls,* Pelageya wants to give the coachman Selifan directions but gets confused and ends up in trouble because she can't tell right from left."

"Maybe she was left-handed?" suggested Granik.

"No," said Iona Ovseich, "she wasn't left-handed. She was completely normal. But the fourth group of critics are claiming at the top of their lungs that the Bolsheviks have lurched to the right. To translate that from political terms into ordinary language, that means that the Bolsheviks have renounced the dictatorship of the proletariat and are in favor of Soviet power but without Bolsheviks—that is, without themselves."

Madame Malaya was the first to laugh, followed by the workers' presidium and then by the entire audience because laughter was the only way of reacting to the fourth group's idiotic criticism.

"They should each get themselves fifteen kopecks and take a ride on number 15!" suggested Granik, increasing the merriment: the number 15 trolley went to Slobodka where the provincial hospital and insane asylum were located.

"What do they need money for?" said Dr. Landa, opening his arms wide. "We can dispatch ambulances for them, one, two, three, as many as needed."

"We will note Dr. Landa's suggestion in the minutes of the meeting," announced Madame Malaya. "All those for?"

As if on command, everyone instantly raised his hand. People kept them in the air even though the speaker and the chairman called for order, the joke having lasted too long.

"Comrades!" Iona Ovseich was forced to raise his voice. "The fourth group of critics is not the last, there's one more. We wouldn't have to pay them any attention whatsoever if they weren't claiming that the new Constitution will be the ruin of democracy in the U.S.S.R. Of course, it's ridiculous to have to prove that something is an elephant by saying it has a trunk in the front, but sometimes you just have to. The last group of critics is screaming for all they're worth that only one party is still allowed in the U.S.S.R. and so where's the democracy? 'Yes,' we answer, 'one party, the Bolsheviks' Communist

Party, and you, gentlemen, would you like us to have liberals, conservatives, monarchists, and, let's be blunt, fascists? That's not going to happen, and you people in the top hats should know that! We have no hostile classes here, we have workers, peasants, and working intelligentsia, and so what need do our people have of parties that would walk all over them and drink their blood? No, gentlemen, one party is enough for us, the party of the Bolsheviks, we don't need any others!' "

Iona Ovseich pronounced that final phrase so resoundingly that people had the impression that he had concluded. The presidium and the audience applauded, still seated at first, but when Klava Ivanovna rose to her feet, the presidium and everyone else followed suit, and the room reverberated with enthusiastic cheers.

After the ovation Madame Malaya, as chairman of the meeting, opened the floor to questions but it turned out that she was rushing things a little: the speaker still needed to shed some light on the first article of the third amendment to the new Constitution. The authors of that article had proposed that the words "working intelligentsia" be added to the "government of the workers and peasants."

"Is this right or isn't it? No, it isn't, or, to be even more precise, it's absolutely wrong and profoundly mistaken. In their opinion the intelligentsia should rank on a par with the workers and the peasants. But anyone who has read Marx carefully knows that the workers and peasants are classes whereas the intelligentsia is only a social element, and never was a class and never will be. To put it in personal terms, Stepa Khomitsky is a class but Dr. Landa is an element, because Stepa Khomitsky is a plumber, that is, a worker, and creates material values with his own hands, whereas Landa is a doctor and his task is to provide people with medical services."

"And what am I?" said Granik, jumping to his feet. "That's what I want to know."

"You're a big mouth, that's what you are," replied Madame Malaya to the laughter of all. "Now sit down on your seat."

Stepa Khomitsky and Dr. Landa, who had just served as the stuff of specific examples, now exchanged glances, Stepa's a bit condescending. Stepa was clearly restraining himself against his own will, being human about it, when he would have preferred to display pity for Landa. A minute later, however, the situation reversed itself when the speaker announced for all to hear that, although the intelligentsia was not a class but an element, its members still enjoyed the exact same rights as the workers and peasants, in all spheres of the country's life, economic, political, and cultural. Now Dr. Landa was free to take revenge on Stepa and no one would have blamed him for it but he continued to conduct himself as he had before the explanation, quietly and modestly.

There was a second and very important point in the third category of amendments concerning the right of every republic to withdraw freely from the U.S.S.R. The authors of the amendments had proposed excluding Article 17 from the Constitution on the grounds that it granted every republic the right to secede but that had no practical significance because no one would ever wish to secede from the U.S.S.R.

"On the contrary," interjected Madame Malaya, "other countries will be requesting permission to join."

"That's true," said Iona Ovseich, raising a finger and smiling, "but genuine democracy requires that you be given every right you have coming, and whether or not you want to make use of it is your own affair."

"No," disagreed Klava Ivanovna, sticking to her guns, "once you're given something you don't need, you can end up thinking it might come in handy for something."

"No," Comrade Degtyar retorted flatly. "Only an individual could reason like that but an entire republic, with a population of a million or ten million people, can't reason like that. Consequently, we must act the way genuine democracy requires because a million or ten million people can't all go mad at the same moment."

Comrade Degtyar's reply met with total support and Madame Malaya said that of course she yielded the point but that she would return to the issue later as it applied to individuals.

Now the speaker indicated that he had reached the conclusion and all that remained was to note the world historical significance of the new Constitution.

"Something that millions of people in the capitalist countries have dreamed of and are still dreaming of has already been put into practice in the U.S.S.R. and, in that regard, it is a source of great satisfaction to know that the blood our countrymen have shed so abundantly has not been shed in vain."

When delivering these final words, Comrade Degtyar began clapping loudly, his hands extended toward the audience. Efim Granik placed his hands beside his mouth and cried, "Bravo! Bravo!" but was immediately drowned out by a mighty "Hurrah!" as if the audience were soldiers launching an attack.

When the ovation had abated, Madame Malaya announced that there had been a motion to send a telegram with salutations to Moscow, the Kremlin, Comrade Stalin. These words met with another storm of applause and need not even have been said because they were in everyone's heart even before Madame Malaya had said them aloud.

The applause signified complete approval of the new Constitution and the motion concerning the telegram. So now they could move on to the next point on the agenda: questions and remarks on the speaker's report. "As far as the questions go," said Klava Ivanovna, "they can be of every possible sort since the Constitution embraces all aspects of the U.S.S.R., international and domestic."

Efim Granik was the first to rise to ask a question and, though there was nothing especially funny about that in and of itself, people laughed because they had known beforehand he'd be the first.

"Comrade Speaker, the new Constitution and the law also allows individual and collective farmers to keep a cow and domestic fowl. And for that purpose they have various structures—barns, chickens, cattle sheds, and so forth. But do I have the right to keep a cow? And if I do, who's supposed to provide me with a cow shed?"

Iona Ovseich paused for half a minute, then, convinced that the question had been fully posed, he shrugged his shoulders and said: "What do you want to live in a cattle shed for? You have a nice sunny room and a hallway."

People exchanged merry glances and Landa said that, as a doctor, he could not sanction his neighbor's living in a cow shed.

"I don't mean that the cow shed's for me," said Granik indignantly. "The cow shed's for the cow."

"We didn't know you had a cow," said Iona Ovseich in surprise. "Have you registered it with the Finance Department? Or are you going to drink the milk free and let other people pay the taxes?"

"Efim's no fool," said Stepa with a wink. "If his cow wants to give milk, let it pay the taxes."

"But he didn't register the cow in his own name," objected Iona Ovseich.

"What nonsense!" said Granik, still indignant. "How can I pay taxes on a cow which I don't even have?"

Iona Ovseich bent his head and narrowed his right eye. "And so why do you need a cow shed for a cow that you don't even have?"

"All right," said Madame Malaya, "sit down, Granik, and don't be jumping up to ask foolish questions. Go buy yourself a cow and we'll build a shed for it in the attic. Are there any other questions, comrades? If they're like Granik's, they're better left unasked."

Stepa Khomitsky objected to that statement, saying that when you wanted to find out where a pipe was clogged you had to force a piece of wire through it or hold it up to the light. It was the same thing with questions: first you had to drag them out into the light and only then could you see if they were smart or stupid.

It was a very apt comparison and people's approval could be heard in their merry animation, but Klava Ivanovna called the audience to order, reminding it that they were there for serious purposes and not an evening's entertainment.

Granik blew Stepa a kiss but this time no one paid him any attention, for everyone had realized that laughter which interferes with serious purposes is no longer just laughter but something else again.

Dr. Landa took the floor.

"Comrades," he said, "if we compare what organized medicine was like in Odessa before the Revolution with what it is now, then to speak in terms of the proverbial differences between night and day, heaven and earth, black and white, will tell us absolutely nothing at all. What's needed here are facts and figures, figures and facts. As you know, I work in the area of skin diseases. I'm a dermatologist and specialist in venereal diseases, to put it in professional terms. And in that regard I can speak with complete authority, and so if I were to say that certain diseases have been reduced by a factor of five, you would be entirely within your rights to multiply that figure by three and in some cases by five. But if we take the figures in percentage terms, the results would be so meager that you couldn't see them under a microscope in the daytime, and a microscope is a thing that allows you to see with one eye, in an area no larger than a kopeck, a million microbes all at the same time." People gasped at the figure which, after a slight pause, Dr. Landa repeated: "Yes, a million. And there's nothing surprising about that because in the Soviet period science has made such progress that we're no longer satisfied to see a million—we want to see ten million, a hundred million!"

People gasped again and Dr. Landa was about to present other examples from the world of medicine but was interrupted by Iona Ovseich.

"Dr. Landa, please tell people in detail how and why you gave up your private practice."

"Why did I give up my private practice?" the doctor repeated automatically.

"That's right," said Degtyar. "Someone might think that it was because of a sharp decline in the number of patients requiring treatment in your area of specialization and not something you yourself desired."

"That impression," said the doctor, "would be radically mistaken. In the first place, though there are ten times fewer patients in my field than there were before, it should not be forgotten that there is still a shortage of specialists, a shortage we inherited from the old regime. In the second place, statistics were of no interest to me when I gave up my private practice: by that time I had fully realized that medical services should be free and a private practice would only help preserve the old view of medicine, namely, that the more expensive the treatment the better it was. And that would have meant preserving the old inequality among patients: if you can pay, you'll be cured, if not, go find yourself a priest or a rabbi, whatever you prefer."

This last remark was met with laughter and applause and Madame Malaya made no secret of her approval: "Well said, Landa. You may continue."

"Before the Revolution, Odessa had a mayor by the name of Tolmachev—the older people will remember him. I'll tell you what Count Witte, no mean exploiter himself, said about Tolmachev." The doctor took his eyeglasses from his pocket, wiped them, but did not put them on. "He said that Tolmachev failed to carry out the law, that he only scoffed at the law. And he meddled in everything, not only things concerning government and society, but private affairs as well. Why am I saying this? I am saying this because at that time the Peresyp district, to take one example, was entirely without running water, and when fifty thousand rubles were needed to lay the pipe, the Municipal Council turned it down cold. The situation was even worse with lighting, but the head councilman, Dontsov, replied without the slightest twinge of conscience: 'Peresyp doesn't need streetlights, only workers live there.' And that is how our so-called city fathers treated the workingman, not to mention anyone else."

"Comrade Chairman," said Iona Ovseich, raising his hand, "may I have permission to ask the speaker a question? Dr. Landa's father owned a two-story house on Treugolny Lane, and he also had a store on Alexandrovsky Street. I'd be interested to hear where that real estate went after the Revolution."

"Where could it go?" said Khomitsky, shrugging his shoulders. "It's still where it used to be."

"Khomitsky," said Iona Ovseich with a frown, "we don't need an interpreter here. Dr. Landa understood the question."

"Yes, I did," said the doctor, nodding. "As for the house, I can tell you right off that when the officials came to transfer it to the city my father agreed without a second's hesitation."

"What you mean," interrupted Comrade Degtyar, "is that he offered no resistance to those representatives of the Soviet government."

"That's right," confirmed the doctor. "However, he wasn't thrown out into the street. On the contrary, even though they were very old people, my mother and father were given a beautiful room, about twelve square meters, in the center of the city, near the Protestant church. After the pogrom of 1905 my father had converted to Lutheranism and so, for him, being moved there was a sign of special grace. Of fate, I mean. As for the store, he worked there for another few years. But both my brother, Boris Alexandrovich, and I kept telling our father that he needed that store like a hunchback needs his hunch."

"When words can do some good," said Iona Ovseich with a smile, "the right words come to mind. And did your words do any good?"

"To be honest," said the doctor, joining his fingers, causing a slight cracking sound, "not right away. My father, who had been instilled with prejudices from every side his entire life, could not rid himself from them all at once."

"By the way," said Iona Ovseich, "people were ridding themselves of those prejudices back in the time of Tsar Alexander II; that is, long before the Revolution, people attacked with plots and bombs when tsarism was at the height of its power. Not to mention the underground literature and leaflets."

As far as leaflets and underground literature were concerned, everyone in the courtyard knew that, from 1911 on, Iona Ovseich had been active in distributing them at the Gen factory, now the October Revolution factory. This was particularly dangerous then because the tsar's minister, Stolypin, had erected gallows throughout the country, "Stolypin neckties" in common parlance.

"My esteemed Iona Ovseich," said Dr. Landa, finally putting on his glasses, "your words are golden words, and if everyone thought and acted like you, I dare say we'd already be past the first and lowest phase of communism, we'd be a good bit higher than that."

"Do you mean full communism?" said Iona Ovseich, seizing on the point. "If that's so, I must tell you straight out, Dr. Landa, that you are very much mistaken, extremely mistaken. It is impossible to build full communism in one country today when we are encircled by the capitalists. It would be a different matter if revolution were to erupt in the countries around us, but meanwhile the U.S.S.R. is alone and there are no other U.S.S.R.s. And so, I repeat, Landa, you are very much mistaken there."

Stepa Khomitsky broke into laughter—what could you expect from a person if he was only an element? There were gusts of laughter in the back rows as well. Iona Ovseich said that he saw no cause for laughter and demanded that it cease at once before the meeting turned into a feast in time of plague.

Instead of supporting Comrade Degtyar, Dr. Landa did the exact opposite, introducing an example that was neither here nor there: in medicine, he said, there was a special term—hyperdiagnosis, meaning that a doctor, worried about what the final results might be, makes a diagnosis more serious than need be.

"No," said Iona Ovseich, striking the table with his fist, "we're not doctors, we're not medical men, but we know exactly where the pain is!"

"Degtyar is right," asserted Madame Malaya. "It's like they say—when a man has a nervous illness, he doesn't know what the problem is and neither does the doctor."

"And when it's gonorrhea," said Khomitsky, shaking with laughter, "the doctor knows and the patient knows, but his wife doesn't."

"Stepa," said Klava Ivanovna, wagging a threatening finger at him, "lucky for you you're on the presidium."

Stepa lowered his head and clearly was about to apologize but he was convulsed by laughter. Now the audience was infected with it. Klava Ivanovna picked up a glass of water and extended it to Stepa but was unable to say what she had intended—laughter had now seized her too. Finally even Iona Ovseich lost his self-control. When people had calmed down a little, he said that their eruption of laughter had been a good thing because laughter, when it was not out of place, could restore people's energy.

Dr. Landa confirmed the fact that laughter was able to restore people's energy and he also frankly admitted his mistake about communism's highest phase in one country, saying he was in full agreement with Iona Ovseich.

Comrade Degtyar addressed the audience: "Is everything clear on that count or should we go back a bit?"

There was no need for that—people were well aware that, given the complete capitalist encirclement of the country, it was impossible to build full communism today though they could pursue that goal in dead earnest. Just so long as a war didn't break out, that was all. As for the plans for building communism within the U.S.S.R., there was every reason to look to the future with confidence: the first Five-Year Plan had been fulfilled ahead of schedule, in four years, and the January Plenum of the Central Committee in 1933 had stressed that this was the most significant event in contemporary history. Now the second Five-Year Plan was almost completed, though they still had a whole year to spare, and if they really tried, people could do a year and a half's worth of work in that year. All in all, given those rates of speed, there was every possibility of completing four Five-Year Plans in the time allotted for three, thereby saving an entire Five-Year Plan.

"From this it follows," said Comrade Degtyar in summation, "that, though the highest phase is still a good distance away, people will soon feel they've achieved full communism because abundance will have become a fact of life. However, I repeat, this is no basis for drawing the sort of deeply mistaken and untimely conclusions about the highest phase that Dr. Landa drew."

"Landa," said Madame Malaya, "do you have anything to add?"

Dr. Landa said that he had nothing to add.

"Do you have any proposal to make, or were you just informing us that in the old days your father switched from the synagogue to the church, and that was all?" asked Madame Malaya with a tone of surprise in her voice.

No, said Dr. Landa, he did have a concrete proposal—that a list of the reading room's books be posted so that anyone wishing to could make a copy of it.

"Comrade Chairman," said Iona Ovseich, "allow me to inform you that a list has already been made and will be posted tomorrow."

"Landa," said Madame Malaya, "sit down. A list's already been made and will be up tomorrow."

After Dr. Landa spoke, the floor was requested at the same time by two people—Efim Granik and Stepa Khomitsky, Granik beating Khomitsky by half a second. Madame Malaya, however, flatly informed Granik that he had already said more than his share and would now only be wasting people's precious time. Efim was indignant. On Comrade Degtyar's proposal that the question of what democratic centralism dictated in a case like this be put to a vote, there were a few scattered chuckles but the majority was for allowing Granik to speak. Efim was already on his way to the speaker's stand but Klava Ivanovna stopped him halfway there: she declared the results of the vote null and void on the grounds that people had not displayed a serious attitude and had laughed while voting. It had to be put to another vote.

The results of the second vote were the exact opposite of the first: the majority, which had just been for Granik, was now firmly against him. Indignant, Granik announced that he was going to lodge a complaint with the authorities at being silenced and would now leave the room and just let anyone try to stop him. The threat was unnecessary because no one made any attempt to restrain him, whereas he, when he had reached the entrance, turned abruptly around, perpendicular to the presidium, and froze as motionless as a guard on duty. The people in the back rows yelled at him to sit down because he made a better door than a window, but Efim stood there for the time he had set himself, one minute. Then he announced for all to hear that it was only his personal regard for Comrade Degtyar that compelled him to return and he demanded this be noted in the minutes of the meeting.

"All right," said Madame Malaya, "write up your own version and don't forget to post it with a nail. But right now it's Comrade Khomitsky who has the floor."

Stepa gave immediate warning that he had no skill at public speaking and for that reason would not beat around the bush but grab the bull by the horns. He said that Dr. Landa had pointed out that before the Revolution there was no running water in Peresyp. And that was true, there hadn't been any in Peresyp, though there had been in the center of the city where the rich people lived.

"And now it's us who are living in the center of the city, Deribasovskaya Street is only a five-minute walk. But what of it? Do we make proper use of our running water and sewage system? No, we do not. This morning, when it was already light, Olya Cheperukha emptied her garbage down in the courtyard, bones and all. And she's got a drain right nearby. And what's the drain for? To catch anything that's too large and could clog up the pipes. But no, she empties it without thinking."

"Olya Cheperukha, stand up," ordered Klava Ivanovna. "Is he telling the truth or making it up?"

Olya lowered her head. Everyone was looking at her, those sitting in front of her having turned around and remaining in that position until Madame Malaya ordered Olya to sit back down.

"And what's the upshot of it?" continued Stepa. "The upshot is that we're tossing out crap on our own heads. Cheperukha has part of an apartment, there's no toilet in her half, and she has to use the one in the courtyard, but no, she tosses it out the window. That's not all. Two days ago a pipe got clogged at Joseph Kotlyar's. He lives on the third floor and so he had to hop down all the way on his one leg. I went up to his place and started checking. I put a wire down the pipe —you wouldn't believe it, more paper there than in an office. But in his case it's forgivable—it's just been six months since he moved here from Nikolaev, and out there a honey wagon with a barrel goes around the courtyards. On the other hand, I gave him a good warning back in the summer. I told him he's throwing paper in there for a month or two and he thinks he can go on forever like that. But gradually it builds up and finally backs up."

"Kotlyar," said Klava Ivanovna, "did he warn you last summer or didn't he?"

"He did, but I thought that, if it didn't clog the first month or the second, why should it clog in the third?"

"Is the janitor here?" asked Madame Malaya. "Nastya, stand up so I can see you. Stepa, draw up a report and you and Nastya sign it. Kotlyar and Cheperukna will pay for the cleanup, they'll think twice the next time. And if it happens again we'll raise the issue in a different way and in a different place."

Comrade Degtyar asked for the floor, saying he had a motion concerning the issue at hand: no report need be written up since both Cheperukha and Kotlyar had admitted their mistakes; the matter should be limited to a warning and the presidium would see how well they kept their promise. Klava Ivanovna replied that Comrade Degtyar was displaying excessive liberalism; still, when voted upon, the motion received a clear majority, and the chairman had to resign herself, though she did add a few words of her own:

"I'll say it again, this sort of problem should be solved administratively, this is not what democratic centralism's for. Continue, Khomitsky."

"They don't treat the plumbing properly," said Stepa, "and they don't treat the faucet in the courtyard right either. Often water doesn't reach the third floor and it has to be brought up in buckets from the courtyard. So one woman puts down her bucket and keeps turning the handle to make the water run faster but it can't go any further. Another one uses all her strength on it and some people have even tried using a brick or a piece of iron. What we did in Grigory Ivanovich Kotovsky's brigade was to post watchmen where they were needed; maybe we should do the same thing with the faucet in our courtyard."

The audience, as well as the speaker himself, burst into laughter. Everyone was well aware they had to use their own resources to solve this painful problem, not those of a watchman.

"For your information," announced Klava Ivanovna, "we've taken this up with the building administration. And if the situation continues, we'll draw up a schedule for building residents to stand duty by the main faucet, and we'll fine anyone guilty of damaging the faucet. What's your reaction, Comrade Degtyar?"

Iona Ovseich supported Madame Malaya fully and completely and, in regard to Comrade Khomitsky's remarks, he allowed himself one small but important criticism: the speaker had named names where the plumbing was concerned but had not been specific about those involved with the faucet.

"That makes everyone guilty, from which one might conclude that nothing but low life live in our building. But to draw that conclusion would be radically wrong, from both the legal and the political point of view. Furthermore, is it even appropriate to raise such subjects today when we've gathered to discuss the new Soviet Constitution, or could it have been postponed to some later date? Of course, it could have, not to mention the fact that every issue, whether large or small, should be raised in the context of the state and people shouldn't wallow in the . . . muck."

Everyone knew what Iona Ovseich really meant to say and his choice of words met with applause. Joseph Kotlyar put his hands beside his mouth and yelled: "You tell 'em, Degtyar!"

Iona Ovseich raised one hand, enough time having been spent on applause as it was. He said that Comrade Khomitsky's remarks were entirely worthy of a positive response, both because of the principles he based them on and because they were in the genuine interest of their courtyard, which had already accomplished a good deal but could accomplish a good deal more. Not only could but must.

Those final words drew renewed applause and a roar of approval. Klava Ivanovna also clapped but warned that those words had to be justified or else Comrade Degtyar would have to take them back. Since Stepa had been interrupted he was still standing by the rostrum. Now Madame Malaya told him to be seated, that he had used up his time, but Stepa declared that his time had been taken by others and now he wanted to reply to the accusation Degtyar had made. No, said Madame Malaya, that would mean a whole new speech. Here Comrade Degtyar intervened in the skirmish, demanding that the chairman observe democratic centralism and allow Stepa to speak; otherwise, they would stray too far. "No," said Klava Ivanovna stubbornly. "Let's put it to a vote." Exclamations of support for Comrade Degtyar rang out from every side.

"All right," said Stepa, "let's move on. We've been told that all issues have to be raised in the context of the state. But what does that mean—in the context of the state? The entire U.S.S.R. all at once or just all of Odessa? The state is like a locomotive—everything can be just where it belongs, except for one wheel, and that can screw up the whole train!"

"Khomitsky," reprimanded Klava Ivanovna, "this isn't the market."

"No, it isn't," replied Stepa, "other words are more popular there. But a train won't go with a wheel missing, and that's a fact. We can check that ourselves, we can turn off all the toilets and faucets in the building. What'll happen then? Will you go to another courtyard? But what if I turn them off in that other courtyard and in the whole rest of the city, where will you go then? To another city? I'll turn them off there too. I'll turn them off everywhere!"

"Bravo!" shouted Granik. "Bravo!"

"So I ask, should we raise that issue today or should we wait until we're up to our ears in shit and only then realize what we've done and shake our heads for not acting in time?"

"Oh," exclaimed Iona Ovseich, "now you're presenting the issue in the context of the state!"

When Stepa left the rostrum, Comrade Degtyar gave him a firm handshake and then turned to face the audience. For a moment it seemed that they would hug and kiss each other in front of everyone. Expecting this to occur, people were preparing to applaud but Stepa quickly returned to his seat.

"Don't worry, Khomitsky," said Madame Malaya encouragingly, "none of your neighbors are going to try and get back at a plumber like you. They'd just be cutting off their noses to spite their faces! Dina Vargaftik has the floor."

"Yes," said Dina, "no one wants to cut off his nose. But people have different ways of going about things. One person'll say, 'This doesn't have anything to do with me,' and sit there with his hands folded, another person'll say, 'This has something to do with me,' and he'll squeal so loud they'll hear him in Moscow and end up in a heap of trouble for that. Let's take an example. Joseph Kotlyar, who recently moved here from Nikolaev. Every evening after work and every morning before work he's up there using his nail-making machine. Where he got the machine and where he gets the wire is none of my business, there are people who specialize in that, let them look into it, but meanwhile the machine is making the whole building shake."

So what was Dina supposed to do—keep quiet about it or squeal at the top of her lungs? But if the whole building was shaking and the premises were being destroyed, then who had the right to keep quiet? Nobody. And she'd already let Kotlyar know ten, twenty, a hundred times that she and Grisha didn't give a damn about the noise from his machine, but they did give a damn about the destruction of the building and no one was going to change their minds about that. Of course Grisha said that they shouldn't get mixed up with Kotlyar, they still didn't know what kind of a person he was, but she told Grisha that *he* could lie on the couch and read the newspaper but *she* wasn't going to take it lying down when that sort of outrage was happening right in front of everyone's eyes. And so what happened? The other day she had another talk with the nail maker. At first it seemed like he understood her but then in the end he spat and told her where to go!

"Comrade Degtyar spoke beautifully today about our new Constitution, that all people are equal, but our Constitution isn't there for Kotlyar and his nail machine, there must be some special law that gives him the right to drive people crazy and tell a woman where to go. Since when? Where's the limit?"

Everyone expected Kotlyar to speak in his own defense but instead Comrade Degtyar rose to his feet. "As far as the machine and the wire are concerned," he said, "we know that Joseph Kotlyar, a former Red partisan, whose lung was pierced by a bullet and who lost one leg —in other words, a disabled Civil War veteran—has a license from the Finance Department. It's another matter if the machine is hammering away day and night, as Dina Vargaftik put it. That machine is not a sideline but Kotlyar's main source of income, and what we need to know is where he's getting all the raw materials."

Iona Ovseich did not say that the raw material in question, wire, was in especially short supply but everyone was well aware of the nail shortage and could draw the proper conclusion.

His enormous belly supported by two army belts, Joseph Kotlyar walked to the rostrum, wiped his bald spot with the palm of his hand, smiled gently, and said:

"Comrade tenants, comrade neighbors, that woman said that I am destroying the building. How can I answer that? I can only answer that she does ten times more damage when she hits her husband with a chair so hard it makes my chandelier sway. I don't want to interfere in her personal life—if she likes hitting him, fine by me, and if he likes getting hit, fine by me too—but it hurts me when someone says I'm destroying our building. And now as to the raw materials. Where do I get them? I'll give you the address if you want, and you can get some too—it's not black market, it's scrap wire that's slated for smelting because it's not worth the factory's while to deal with it. On the other hand, these are half-finished goods, and a capitalist like me doesn't turn up his nose at half-finished goods that are on their way to be scrapped."

From his seat Efim Granik shouted that people should kiss Kotlyar's hands because he was economizing on state property, but Dina Vargaftik said people could kiss Kotlyar wherever they wanted, to each his own, but they weren't little children and he shouldn't feed them all that dreck about where he got his half-finished goods. The same was true for the building, they could cut her into little pieces but she'd never stop telling the truth, which was that every time the machine shot out a nail the building shook and shuddered. A committee should be appointed to look into it.

"What do you mean, a committee?" said Granik, springing to his feet. "The man's a Red partisan, not some criminal. He lost half a leg and part of a lung for the Soviet system!"

"Sit down!" ordered Madame Malaya. "Back in your seat, or I'll give you two demerits."

"Please don't shout at me," replied Efim. "You can't scare Granik!"

Khomitsky was given the floor. "The truth is the truth," he said. "The machine makes noise. But the cars and carts going by on the street make ten times more and the building's still standing, still in one piece, because every building has a built-in safety margin." Their building had one too and so Dina Vargaftik could sleep in peace with her Grisha, even face up, or wherever else she liked to put her face, because the ceiling wouldn't be collapsing on them.

Dina was outraged. "Save your idiotic hints for your own wife! And a committee should be appointed to see who's right."

Iona Ovseich leaned toward Chairman Malaya and whispered a few words to her. Klava Ivanovna nodded in reply, then ordered everyone to be silent and announced:

"There has been a motion to appoint a committee. I'll put it to a vote."

"Why vote?" Kotlyar asked. "You want a committee, form a committee."

"No one's asking you," said Klava Ivanovna. "We don't need to be told what to do. And whether you want a vote or not is your own private little business. We want one."

Everyone, including Kotlyar himself, was in favor of a committee; the only one against it was Efim Granik. He had risen to his feet and raised his hand high enough so everyone could see it and held it there until Madame Malaya ordered:

"Sit down and stop trying to make people laugh."

The meeting charged the presidium with drawing up a list. Comrade Degtyar rose immediately and made a motion to select a three-man committee with Lapidis, the engineer, as its chairman, and the plumber Khomitsky and Dr. Landa as members. Klava Ivanovna Malaya would oversee the committee. The vote could either be for all three at once or on an individual basis, whatever people preferred. Klava Ivanovna said there were no strangers there, everyone knew each candidate by sight, and so there was no point in voting on an individual basis.

They voted on the list as a whole. This time everyone voted in favor of the motion, with one person abstaining, Efim Granik.

Since the committee had been appointed and the hour was late, the chairman, after conferring with Comrade Degtyar, made a motion to close the floor to debate and allow Iona Ovseich to make his concluding remarks. He had already walked over to the rostrum but just then Lapidis, the engineer, shouted from his seat that he was withdrawing as a candidate.

"Listen to him!" said Klava Ivanovna indignantly. "You can withdraw from your wife if you want, but the people have placed their trust in you and you should be grateful for that."

"Trust's not the point!" shouted Lapidis in response. "I'm away traveling all year round on business and sometimes I don't spend the night at home for weeks on end."

"Where you spend the night is your own personal business, but once the masses have placed their trust in you, you should be proud of it," said Madame Malaya, and the entire audience supported her because each one of them had his own private business and, if you followed Lapidis' line of reasoning, you'd end up hiring outsiders to run your own building.

"Your withdrawal is not accepted," repeated Madame Malaya, and she warned Lapidis that people's patience was growing thin and a report might be lodged where he worked. This was an unnecessary waste of time and did no one any good.

Lapidis lowered his head like a feisty steer but it was clear that the time to withdraw had already passed. Now obstinacy could cause only protest and righteous indignation.

"All right," said Lapidis. "You win."

Klava Ivanovna nodded with approval but her words were somewhat guarded: "But actions speak louder than words."

"He'll come through!" said Iona Ovseich happily. "Lapidis is not the kind of person to shirk his duty. And now, allow me, on behalf of the building administration, the activists, and the courtyard community, to express our gratitude to Efim Lazarevich Granik for the conscientious job he did in making the announcement and also to express our confidence that in the future he will also participate in the artistic presentation of all other such measures connected with the political education of the masses."

Comrade Degtyar beckoned Granik to the rostrum so he could personally shake his hand. However, excited, and completely at a loss, Granik headed in the exact opposite direction—to the exit. People laughed, letting him take a few steps toward the door before grabbing him by the shoulders and turning him around. Then, when he was beside the rostrum and Comrade Degtyar extended both his hands to Granik, everyone saw that Efim had tears in his eyes and they only laughed all the harder and clapped their hands.

"My word of honor, my word of honor!" said Efim, and Iona Ovseich grasped his hand firmly with both of his and would not let it go.

"And where's your wife Sonya?" asked Madame Malaya. "When you spend the whole day at home or in the synagogue and talk with God more than with people, you don't know what's going on in the world around you. She should be here now to see for herself what kind of a man she's married to."

Efim wiped away his tears, turned toward the audience, and said: "My papa was a house painter. When he was painting the pediment on the fourth floor at number 3 Ekaterinskaya Street, he fell off the scaffolding to the stone sidewalk and never got up again. I was working with my father that day and saw it all with my own eyes. And now the audience is grateful to me for a piece of paper which anybody could have drawn up as well as I did. My word of honor, you can stop by to visit me any time, night or day, and I'll be glad to see any of you."

Comrade Degtyar stepped forward and shook Efim's hand again, followed by all the members of the workers' presidium—Madame Malaya, Dr. Landa, Stepa Khomitsky, and Dina Vargaftik.

"And now," said Iona Ovseich, "let us move on to our conclusion. In fact, what our comrades have said this evening and what we've all seen with our own eyes tonight is the best possible conclusion but we'll do a last summing up. As they say, a little extra butter can't spoil the kasha. Today we have a new Constitution. This document of world historical importance is simple and compact, its style like a diplomatic protocol, so that it can be understood by any worker or peasant, not only in this country but abroad as well, so they can understand that the working people of the U.S.S.R. have been liberated from capitalist slavery and also that the most highly developed and consistent form of democracy has triumphed in the U.S.S.R. Now, when the troubled wave of fascism is splashing the socialist movement of the working class with spit and mud, the U.S.S.R.'s new Constitution is the most formidable indictment of fascism and perfect proof that socialism and democracy are invincible!"

Though no one had given any command, they rose as one man and began to applaud. Comrade Degtyar proposed three toasts—to Comrade Stalin, the party, and the people—and the applause, which had begun to die down, rose again to its initial height, and even higher.

Klava Ivanovna walked over to Stepa and whispered in his ear. He bent down, withdrew a blue box from under the table, pulled its handle out from its side, and handed it to her. Now everyone could see that it was a gramophone and yet they were startled when it began to play because the sound was so powerful. Klava Ivanovna and Stepa smiled because they were the only ones who knew about the microphone and loudspeaker; even Degtyar and the other members of the presidium had not been told.

People only listened at first to the song about the black baron and the White armies, then they began moving their lips, finally breaking into song themselves, so loudly that at the very end their voices drowned out the gramophone and the loudspeaker. When the record was over, Madame Malaya began gesturing like a conductor and people repeated the final words without music: "And nothing must stop us from that final life-and-death battle!"

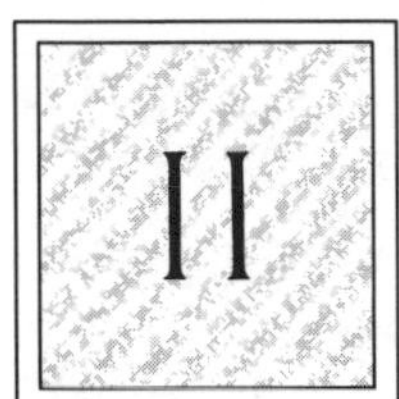

The committee chaired by Lapidis, the engineer, conducted a thorough examination of Joseph Kotlyar's apartment and of the detrimental effect his nail-making machine was having, as alleged by Dina Vargaftik, on the building's structure. It was the committee's unanimous opinion that the nail-making machine in question was having no destructive effect whatsoever, either on the adjacent apartments or on the building as a whole. Given that, the disabled Civil War veteran and former Red partisan, Joseph Kotlyar, could continue his domestic manufacture, on one condition: he was to place under the machine a layer of felt or some other shock-absorbing material sufficiently thick to reduce the vibrations to a minimum when the machine was expelling finished nails. As for the raw material, no violations were discovered, apart from the fact that the manufacture itself was based on a nonprofit recycling of waste products.

"What does nonprofit recycling mean?" asked Comrade Malaya, who was supervising the committee.

Lapidis, who held two degrees, one in engineering and the other in economics, said that the question of profitability and nonprofitability was very complex, and a calculating machine was required to solve it. For that reason, the committee had not gone into details.

"Let's say that's so," said Madame Malaya with a frown. "But did you inform the right people there at the factory or did you simply tell them what they needed to hear?"

No, said Lapidis with a grin, he hadn't done that. But he didn't get any thanks for it either. On the contrary, they told him to get out, they had more smart alecks around than a gypsy had lice.

"And they were right," Madame Malaya was quick to respond. "It's not talk that's needed. A paper has to be drawn up and put on the table."

"What's written with the pen can't be hacked out with an ax," said Lapidis.

"No," said Madame Malaya, tapping a foot, "you can't smooth-talk me. We don't need things done just for the sake of form. If everyone thought the way you do, Lapidis, we still won't have built communism in twenty years. I can see that the two of us have to sit down together. The way you go about things, it'll get drawn out to Judgment Day."

"The two of us working together, that's a good idea, more efficient," said Lapidis.

"All right, all right," said Klava Ivanovna mischievously. "Don't brownnose me. We all know how good you are at that."

Lapidis was not insulted: everyone, Madame Malaya included, was well aware that Lapidis was incapable of that.

Six days later Lapidis went to the building committee office himself and reminded Madame Malaya that she had promised that the two of them would sit down together.

"Oh," exclaimed Klava Ivanovna, "I knew that you'd come at the very wrong time! I don't even have a minute for your problem right now."

"My problem? Why is it mine?" Lapidis shrugged his shoulders, turned immediately around, and waved good-bye.

"Wait a minute," called Madame Malaya. "Sit down and listen to what I have to say. There are instructions to reduce the size of the laundry room in the courtyard so that the children will have somewhere to play and not run around like a bunch of homeless waifs. We have to take down the main wall, put in a window, and set up ventilation. You are to draw up a plan for us to approve within ten days."

"Me?" said Lapidis with surprise. "Why me? Let someone who makes his living at it do it."

"And meanwhile our children will be running around in the streets!" said Madame Malaya, astounded. "I know that you personally don't care because your son Adya goes to music school. But the Soviet system is still too new for all children to attend music school, and the Building Department will waste six months on a trifle like this."

"That's true. But where do I come in?"

"The Soviet system has granted you two higher degrees and now it wants you to repay your debt to it," said Klava Ivanovna. "Just don't think you can bang out such plans one-two-three. Don't waste time, get right to work. Tomorrow I'll start looking for the building materials."

"Go ahead," said Lapidis with a grin, "who's stopping you? But do you have an estimate of what kind of materials you need, and how much?"

"Doesn't matter," said Klava Ivanovna. "There won't be any estimate for the time being. We'll take what they give us."

"What about workers? Where are you going to find skilled workers who'll do the job out of the goodness of their hearts?"

"We'll do the work ourselves," said Klava Ivanovna. "Everything's not as complicated for some people as it is for you. If the cement is delivered tomorrow, can we throw it in the laundry room or will the dampness there be bad for it?"

"Don't count your chickens before they're hatched," replied Lapidis. "First get the cement."

"That's not your problem," said Madame Malaya angrily. "Just answer the question."

"As for the question," said Lapidis, "the cement has to be thoroughly heated first, to remove all moisture."

"Are you mocking me or what?" Klava Ivanovna asked indignantly. "Where are we supposed to get coal and firewood?"

Lapidis seized his head and began laughing like a madman. Angry, Klava Ivanovna slapped him on the back and demanded that he get hold of himself at once or else she would call an ambulance for him.

"Klava Ivanovna," said Lapidis, finally regaining his self-control, "you're an intelligent woman, can't you see that the simplest thing would be to put the cement in people's apartments?"

Madame Malaya hit her forehead with her palm.

"You're right. I'm a fool. And not only the cement, but the lime and the boards too. Cheperukha's place would be best—it's right off the entrance. Everyone will take a portion of the nails and iron to his apartment and take personal responsibility for it. Otherwise it'll all be stolen before the first nail goes in."

"Why get everything all at once?" said Lapidis, furrowing his brow. "Why not get the materials as you need them?"

"What an idea," said Madame Malaya, bursting into laughter. "You have to get them while the getting's good. You think all it takes is having a degree."

"To get them all at once or not, that's the question!" interjected Lapidis.

"It takes more than two degrees," said Madame Malaya, narrowing her eyes. "All right, enough shooting the breeze. Get to work and draw up the plans."

Five days later Lapidis brought Malaya the plans. The lumber arrived the same day and was tossed in the entry hall. Olya Cheperukha said they should take it back, her apartment was for people, it wasn't a woodshed.

"What do you mean, they should take it back?" said Madame Malaya. "Do you realize what we had to go through to get this lumber?"

"I do," replied Cheperukha, "but what if, God forbid, someone has to run to the drugstore or call an ambulance—are we supposed to jump over the lumber?"

"No problem," said Klava Ivanovna. "It'll be good for you to shake your fat a little."

"Oh, Klava Ivanovna," groaned Olya, "a person's got to be tough to argue with you. My husband is right when he says that Madame Malaya could raise a dead man and convince him to walk behind his own coffin to make things easier on the horses."

"Fine," said Madame Malaya, "thank him for the compliment, but we need him to carry wood right now. And you too. The hallway has to be kept clear."

An hour later the lumber had been neatly stacked in Cheperukha's hallway, and half an hour after that Olya's son Zyunchik, Kolka Khomitsky, and Osya Granik had made it into a steamboat for themselves, its stern jutting out into the entrance hall. As soon as they had given the hoot, signaling departure, the anchor chains began to rattle, and people, saying good-bye for a long time, or perhaps forever, shouted wildly. Black clouds of smoke streaked with sparks flew from the funnel, all three of the captains spitting nonstop overboard.

Madame Malaya was first to smell the smoke and shouted out the window: "Cheperukha, your place is on fire!"

But Cheperukha did not hear the warning because fifteen minutes before she had gone with her husband to the trolley workers' club, which included people who worked in draft or rail transportation.

Madame Malaya ran posthaste downstairs, a pail of water in hand, and poured it on the vessel, ordering the brats to take the boat apart at once and to put the boards back in the hallway the way they'd been before, and saying that when the Cheperukhas returned from having a good time she'd give them a talking to they wouldn't forget. First Zyunchik, then Kolka and Osya said that they weren't servants or lackeys who had to carry heavy things.

"You mean you can drag the wood one way but you can't drag it the other?" said Klava Ivanovna indignantly.

But all three of the children kept repeating in unison that they weren't servants or lackeys, and they weren't for hire either.

"You bourgeois kids!" said Madame Malaya even more indignantly now. "You're not for hire!"

"I'm not bourgeois," answered Zyunchik. "I can't be bourgeois."

"We're not bourgeois," said Kolka. "Kiselis is bourgeois, he didn't have the right to vote, but our parents did."

"No," insisted Madame Malaya, "you are true bourgeois children. You want to eat white bread and jam every day, but you don't want to work, other people are supposed to do the working for you. I'm going to go to your school tomorrow and tell the principal to call a general assembly, and there in front of everyone he should take your red scarfs away from you because bourgeois children cannot be Pioneers."

"Children aren't supposed to lift heavy things," said Zyunchik. "That can cause hernias."

"Hernias!" said Madame Malaya, brandishing her fists. "What about Pavlik Morozov! He didn't worry about hernias, he gave his life!"

"His father was a kulak," said Osya, "but we're the children of workers and peasants."

"You?" said Madame Malaya, stunned. "You are exploiters. You are bourgeois. A person isn't bourgeois if he loves working like he loves breathing. But all you want to do is eat and drink and make caca all day long."

"All right," said Zyunchik, "we'll put the boards back. The way they were before."

"That's not enough!" said Klava Ivanovna, shaking her head. "I also want Osya to give his Pioneer word of honor that he'll never set foot inside a synagogue again."

"I'll do it," Osya agreed at once, "except you can't give your Pioneer word of honor when you're not wearing a Pioneer scarf, and I'm not wearing mine."

"Zyunchik," said Klava Ivanovna in a tone of command, "you live the closest, go get your scarf, but make it snappy."

He didn't make it snappy but that wasn't his fault: the door opened out and so first they had to clear the boards away. Kolka said it was a bad job—first you carried them out and then you carried them back.

"Get out of here," ordered Madame Malaya, "you good-for-nothing brats!"

Kolka did not leave but immediately grabbed the top board, shouted, "Let's go!" and began dragging it away. Zyunchik grabbed the other end of the next board and the one after that. Klava Ivanovna publicly acknowledged her mistake in calling them bourgeois, and then began loudly singing the Pioneers' favorite song: "We're young children and we love to work. These minutes pass like pleasant dreams!"

When the stack was repiled, Zyunchik ran and got his elegant Pioneer scarf, which was made of pure silk, and put it over Osya's head. There was no tie clasp and, so as not to wrinkle the scarf by tying it, Klava Ivanovna took a safety pin from her bodice and pinned the scarf from underneath. Then she arranged the children in line by height, told them to pull up their socks straight, and ordered them to stand at attention. She gave Osya a signal, then stood at attention herself.

Osya raised his right hand above his head, checked that his thumb was in the right position to his forehead, and loudly announced that, in the presence of his comrades, he made a solemn promise never again to set foot inside a synagogue, an Orthodox church, or the Catholic one on Lutheran Lane. And if he broke his word, he should be thrown out of the Pioneers and no one in the courtyard should play with him again.

"And may I be disgraced!" said Klava Ivanovna.

"And may I be disgraced!" repeated Osya.

"At ease!" ordered Klava Ivanovna. "You've all heard the oath. The person who breaks it has only himself to blame. And now I'm turning personal responsibility for the boards over to you. If anyone objects, let him step forward and say so right now so we all can see and hear."

No one stepped forward. Klava Ivanovna announced that the motion had passed, and from that moment on the three of them would have full responsibility for the boards, and for the rest of the construction materials as well.

Klava Ivanovna did not explain what the rest of the construction materials entailed, but the next day two cartfuls of sand were delivered to the courtyard, as well as a pile of lime and four bags of cement on which there were black non-Russian letters and, beneath them, huge numbers, also in a foreign language. Zyunchik said that numbers were the same the world over. Kolka and Osya agreed but pointed out that beside their numbers there were also Roman numerals, but theirs were a thousand times better.

"We use Arabic numbers," said Zyunchik. "But in Italy they use Roman numerals. Rome is the capital of Italy."

"That's right," said Kolka. "Rome is the capital of Italy."

"And New York," said Osya, "is the capital of America. New York is the biggest city in the world."

Zyunchik spit on the ground just like his father did and rubbed it in with his foot: didn't matter, Moscow would catch up with it soon. "And when the workers have won everywhere and Soviet power is everywhere, Moscow will be the capital of the whole planet Earth."

"When Earth is a name," said Kolka, "you have to write it with a capital *E.*"

"The name of what?" asked Osya.

"You're stupid," laughed Zyunchik and Kolka. "Earth is the name of earth, and Odessa is the name of Odessa. Got it?"

"But why does Odessa always have a capital letter and earth doesn't?"

Zyunchik and Kolka laughed again and told Osya anyone could see he'd done well at school. They explained that the names of seas, rivers, lakes, and cities were written with capital letters, and Odessa was a city. Or wasn't it?

Osya agreed that Odessa was a city and that the names of cities were written with capital letters but then he thought of the sun, which was a million times bigger than the earth and was the only sun in the heavens but still its name was written with a small *s*.

"There's not just one sun," said Kolka. "There are as many suns as there are stars because every star is a sun. And furthermore there aren't any heavens."

"That's true," said Osya, "there are no heavens. The sky is just air. But we don't write 'the sun of socialism' with a capital letter. And it should be because there's only one sun of socialism, the U.S.S.R."

This time Kolka and Zyunchik agreed—if you were going to follow the rule, then of course it should be written with a capital *S*.

That evening, when the sun had set behind the bell tower of the Uspensky Cathedral, Anya Kotlyar ran out into the courtyard with a pail to get some sand. Zyunchik, Kolka, and Osya joined hands, barred the way, and informed her that they were personally responsible for the sand and for all the construction material.

"You sniveling little brats," said Anya Kotlyar with indignation. "A person needs a pailful of sand and they're supposed to ask some snot-nosed kids' permission?"

"Madame Malaya!" shouted Zyunchik. "She's stealing sand!"

Osya dashed up to the second floor and started pounding on Madame Malaya's door as if the building were on fire.

Klava Ivanovna came running out with her apron slung over her shoulder and rubbers on her bare feet. Her gout gave her so much pain that she would have been happy to go around barefoot. She grabbed Osya by the arm and asked:

"What's going on here? Why are you running around like a chicken with its head cut off?"

"She's stealing sand! We're not letting her take it but she's stealing it anyway!"

"Who's she?" said Madame Malaya, brandishing her fists, and taking the stairs at a run.

Anya Kotlyar was already at her own front door but she couldn't go through it: Zyunchik was hopping back and forth in front of it, barring her way, and, whenever the situation started to look dangerous, Kolka would grab her pail.

"You little monsters!" Anya shouted wildly. "You little horrors!"

"Hold on there," ordered Madame Malaya. "I want to know what's going on here."

Anya Kotlyar began explaining that she had just popped out with her pail for a little sand and these three healthy bulls, who should have been married a long time ago, attacked her as if she were stealing food from their mouths.

"All right," said Madame Malaya, "but did they warn you that the sand wasn't to be touched?"

"What kind of sand are we talking about?" said Kotlyar with surprise. "I didn't take any more than a baby would use."

"Don't try to smooth-talk me," said Madame Malaya. "Give me a straight answer: did they warn you not to touch the sand or not?"

"You call that a warning!" said Anya, growing suddenly heated. "Three bandits attack a woman and start tearing her to pieces, some warning! Where we used to live in Nikolaev—"

"If you don't like it here in Odessa," said Madame Malaya, taking her down a peg, "go back to Nikolaev."

"Don't you tell me where I should live!" cried Anya. "I'll live wherever I want to."

"I'll say it again: go back to Nikolaev and you can start making your rubber raincoats there again."

"What rubber raincoats?" said Anya, turning pale.

"Rubber raincoats for men," said Klava Ivanovna. "You know what I mean. Let's not talk about it in front of the children. The only question is where you got the rubber to make those vile things."

"My husband was a Red partisan and he lost half a leg," said Anya, bursting into tears. "Aren't you ashamed of yourself?"

"That's true," agreed Madame Malaya, "your husband was a Red partisan. But we don't need partisans who become petty tradesmen under Soviet power and make all sorts of vile and nasty things to sell to NEPmen and their sluts. Children, there's no reason for you to be here. Leave."

The boys walked ten steps away and stopped—Osya's shoelaces had become untied.

Anya wiped her tears on her sleeve and kept repeating to herself, "What a disgrace, what a disgrace!" Madame Malaya watched in silence, then suddenly asked Anya how much sand she needed, then told her to go get a regular-sized pail and fill it to the brim, and if that wasn't enough she could go back for more.

"Thank you," said Anya, shaking her head, "thanks a lot, Madame Malaya. I don't need that much. All I need is a little for under the window. A piece of the stone fell out after the last rain."

Klava Ivanovna said that she knew that window, the one that looked out on Troiskaya Street. There was salt-shell rock there and it soaked up water like a blotter. And it would be like that till summer and the hot weather came, and in October it would be soaking wet again. "But that's no problem, God let that be our biggest worry."

"Yes," sighed Anya, "it's no problem, and anyway why argue, why quarrel? People should be nice to each other, it's better for the health and easier on the nerves."

"Well," said Klava Ivanovna with a bitter smile, "why did you have to take things into your own hands? Couldn't you have just come by and asked the way a person should?"

"I didn't think I had to ask. It was sand, not bread," said Anya, chewing on a finger. "But those boys shouldn't have gotten so mad at me. Children shouldn't get angry, children should be lighthearted."

"You have two sons," said Madame Malaya. "Why did you leave them in Nikolaev? Why didn't you bring them straight to Odessa? Isn't one of the boys from Joseph's first marriage to your older sister who died?"

Anya blushed deeply and said that among Jews it used to be a custom for a widowed brother-in-law to marry his late wife's younger sister. As for her sons, she informed Malaya that they were studying at a technical school, they needed to transfer but, in the meantime, were living with their grandmother.

"Listen," said Klava Ivanovna, nudging Anya's chest affectionately, "you're so pretty, so young, what do you need that old fogy for? He's twice as old as you are."

Anya blushed again, looked all around, then burst into laughter though her eyes were fearful.

"God forbid Joseph hears, he'd cut my throat on the spot! He tells everyone we're only fifteen years apart in age."

"Naw," objected Madame Malaya, "he's not fool enough to kill a juicy beauty like you."

Confused, Anya covered her face in her hands as if she had heard an indecent remark. Madame Malaya warned her not to misinterpret what she was being told. And when her own late husband, Boris Davidovich, was still alive, especially when he was still a young man, they'd wear each other out so much during the night, they could barely walk the next day.

"Oy," said Anya, deeply embarrassed now, "please!"

"You don't have to say please to me," said Madame Malaya, shrugging her shoulders. "Let your husband Joseph say please to you. Don't be a fool, he should ask you nicely at the beginning. We're always giving in to them."

"That's true," said Anya. "I curse myself a lot for that. But he takes me for granted. One time, when I wasn't in the mood, he flew off the handle like a wild animal, grabbed his saber off the wall, and shouted, 'I'm going to cut you up into little pieces!' "

Madame Malaya sighed. "Don't take it personal, that's just a partisan joke. He loves you a lot."

Anya shrugged her shoulders. "Why take it personal? It's just life."

"Wait a second," said Madame Malaya, remembering something. "We'll need two kilos of nails for the play area. Tell your husband to make them for us. And remind him there's a meeting tomorrow. You come too."

The notice for the meeting had been posted three days ago. Iona Ovseich's instructions were that after reading the notice everyone should sign in the notebook hanging beside it. But, judging from the list, it would appear that a good number of the building's residents had not been out of their apartments for the last two days.

"Kotlyar," Madame Malaya shouted after Anya, "come back here for a minute. I'll give you a list of people to call on. Have a little talk with them so that this doesn't happen again."

Anya said that she would be happy to perform the task but she'd like to put it off for a day if that were possible: she was expecting guests and had to clean and cook.

"No," Madame Malaya refused categorically, "do it today, right now. Your guests can wait or can come some other time. Guests are no excuse."

Despite the measures taken, a hundred percent attendance was not achieved. Although at least one member of each family attended, that did not alter the fact that certain of the building's residents were making a point of their opinion that the building of the Pioneer outpost was the private business of Degtyar and Madame Malaya.

"Comrades," said Iona Ovseich, "I think I will be expressing the general view of all the building's residents if I propose that everyone absent from today's meeting be given an additional day's work on the outpost. Who is in favor?"

People had already begun raising their hands when Stepa Khomitsky interrupted to introduce an amendment: he agreed to the extra day, but those who had a valid reason should be separated from those who did not, otherwise it wouldn't be fair.

"When a person has a valid reason," said Degtyar, "he should inform us of it beforehand. But if the majority is in favor of your point, there will be no objections."

The amendment passed without a formal vote: the din of approval made it clear that the majority was behind Khomitsky.

"Comrades," said Iona Ovseich, "the idea is this. People who don't work the first shift should come down to the courtyard in the morning, and those who do should come down in the evening, after work. What is the opinion on this subject?"

Dr. Landa, who was given the floor first, remarked that Comrade Degtyar's motion took account of the building residents' differences as well as the time factor, but one clarification needed to be made: apart from the first and second shift, there was also a third shift, and many people worked staggered hours, and what about them?

"Comrades," said Degtyar, "allow me to make a point: Dr. Landa did not make a clarification but raised a question. All the same, it's very timely and must be examined with all seriousness."

"I don't see any problem," said Madame Malaya. "If a person has the third shift, the night shift, his whole day is free. He can choose for himself which time is more convenient for him, afternoon or evening. If a person works the second shift, it means he's at work in the afternoon and evening, and morning is the only time he has to work on the outpost."

Dr. Landa leaned toward Iona Ovseich and said a few words in his ear. Nodding in Madame Malaya's direction, Iona Ovseich drummed his fingers on the table, closed his eyes, and stood up.

"Comrade Malaya is proposing too narrow a framework for people who work the second and third shifts. This makes for a certain carelessness in dealing with people. In that regard there is the following opinion: that conditions on the construction work done on their day off should be fixed for representatives of all the categories and, at the same time, in cases of special exception, members of the person's family can work off the time allotted him. I am requesting that this motion be weighed carefully so that disciplinary measures won't prove necessary later on."

Chairs began creaking, voices buzzed. Many people were clearly dissatisfied because, instead of one version in which everything was clear and simple, now, because of those who worked the second and third shifts, people had to rack their brains and try to please everyone.

"Comrade Lapidis," said Degtyar, "I think you wanted to say a few words as a specialist."

Lapidis shrugged his shoulders and stated that he couldn't say anything definite at the moment since it wasn't clear which work fronts were to be secured; in other words, was there a specific task for everyone during construction?

"Comrade Lapidis," said Degtyar, releasing his lapel and cleaving the air with the edge of his hand, "your thinking is wrong: whether or not everyone will have a specific task at any one time is a secondary issue. The main thing is that a person be here, along with everyone else. In any case, the problem has two aspects—an economic aspect and, last but not least in importance, an educational one. Did I make myself clear, Engineer Lapidis?"

Lapidis did not answer directly as to whether it was clear to him or not but repeated his argument about the different work fronts because that was precisely what interested him most as a specialist—the various work fronts. He saw no reason to discuss the issue as put forward.

"I understand you very well, Engineer Lapidis. And if you've understood me as well as I have you . . ." said Degtyar with a smile.

"And, just think, we didn't need an interpreter to communicate. However, we are allowing ourselves to continue this futile discussion because, from our point of view, it is far from futile. As the saying goes, there's a time and a place for everything."

"You tell him, Degtyar!" shouted Iona Cheperukha.

Iona Ovseich raised his hand with his thumb pointing at Lapidis.

"Our esteemed specialist has reproached us and given us bad marks. He says that, under the pretext of raising an issue, we're trying to involve people in a discussion on whether or not Soviet people are able to carry out a project with their own forces. But we don't need any discussion, this isn't the English Parliament, and our answer is: in the future, if our highly esteemed specialist would please keep his opinion to himself, awkward moments can be avoided. History can furnish many examples here."

"What does history have to do with it?" retorted Lapidis. "What we're talking about are specific construction problems."

"Engineer Lapidis," said Iona Ovseich, narrowing his right eye, his torso inclined slightly forward, "history always has something to do with it!"

"Bravo!" cried Granik, applauding and darting out into the aisle. "Bravo!"

Others began clapping as well but Lapidis only shrugged his shoulders as if he were surprised that everyone supported Comrade Degtyar and he was alone with his educated opinion.

Malaya's and Degtyar's motions were then voted on in the order in which they had been made. Some people tried to vote twice—for both her motion and his—and the process had to be repeated. Comrade Degtyar received the overwhelming majority and a count was not even necessary.

The next morning two one-hundred-twenty-liter boilers were removed from the laundry room. Stepa Khomitsky said that the boilers had lasted fifty years and were still good for three times that. Yes, agreed Efim, things outlived people, technology was making great advances, and something new was invented every day, and soon they'd be up to their ears in things. On the other hand, they didn't have master craftsmen today like there used to be. "Before, a man could remain an apprentice till the day he died but nowadays they take all kinds of courses, and one-two-three they get a diploma and they're full-blown masters. Anyway, soon everyone will have a higher education. So who's going to work then? There won't be anyone to work —everyone will be busy wagging their tongues."

Stepa laughed and said that in that case Efim could be said to have three degrees already. No, objected Efim, he personally had no degrees but he could outdo any specialist.

"You don't have to," said Stepa, "just leave them alone and they'll screw up all by themselves."

"Like Lapidis!" replied Efim. "They think that everything can be put down in a book. But there was a time when people couldn't read or write but they still did everything so well the scientists are racking their brains to this day trying to figure out how."

"And they'll rack their brains another hundred years," said Lapidis.

"A hundred!" said Granik with a laugh. "Another two hundred, another thousand years! And they still won't be able to figure it out. Yesterday I stopped by the Historical Museum, near Feldman Boulevard. They have a mummy there, a pharaoh. His face looks like old man Kiselis', just a little darker. How old do you think he is?"

Stepa said that he didn't know exactly and didn't feel like guessing.

"Come on," pressed Efim, "it doesn't have to be exact. Approximately."

Stepa repeated that he didn't feel like guessing but named a figure anyway: five hundred years old.

"Five hundred!" chuckled Efim. "How about one thousand five hundred! Or two thousand five hundred! Or five thousand!"

Stepa admitted his mistake, then asked just how old was the pharaoh who looked like old man Kiselis.

"Two thousand one hundred and thirty!" said Granik, raising a finger. "If Jesus had actually existed, he could have been that pharaoh's great-grandson. But where is Jesus Christ now? Has anyone seen his bones, his boots, his pants? And yesterday I saw a pharaoh with my own eyes and I can go again today if I want. He's been lying there five hundred years, a thousand years, fifteen hundred, two thousand, and no problem. He's been lying there two thousand one hundred and thirty years, and there's no problems, and the scientists are racking their brains to figure out why he doesn't rot and they're not a millimeter closer to the truth!"

"They haven't understood it for a thousand years," said Stepa, "but tomorrow they'll grab hold of the problem and figure it out."

"You're naïve!" said Efim, beside himself. "They couldn't do it in two thousand years and then they'll do it in one day? For us this secret is like bread or like water. Our leaders should be embalmed so that our grandchildren can also see them with their own eyes. Look, Madame Malaya just arrived."

"No, I haven't just arrived," said Klava Ivanova. "I've already been hanging around here half an hour. Why don't you give your tongues a rest and put your hands to work? The wheelbarrows are standing empty in the courtyard while Granik and Khomitsky swap fairy tales about pharaohs."

"Pharaohs?" said Efim in surprise. "What do you mean, pharaohs? We're discussing contemporary science. It can't embalm our leaders, but five thousand years ago people could."

"What do you mean, they can't?" said Madame Malaya indignantly. "What about Lenin? He's there in the mausoleum, looking alive as could be. I've been five times, and he's always the same."

"But what about Dzerzhinsky? Frunze, Kirov, and Kuibyshev!" said Efim, bending back four fingers. "And Maxim Gorky! I want a look at Maxim Gorky."

"Are you serious about that?" retorted Madame Malaya. "According to you, mausoleums should be built for everyone."

"No," said Granik, "there should only be one mausoleum. But we should have sarcophaguses with glass lids you can see through. I want to see Kirov, I want to see Maxim Gorky, I want a look at Maxim Gorky."

"You want to see Kirov?" said Madame Malaya. "You want to see Maxim Gorky? Who's stopping you? Go to the Frunze theater. You'll not only see them, you'll hear them speak and laugh and address the people. You'll even forget that they're no longer alive. And so tell me now, can you compare that with a sarcophagus, even one made all of glass?"

"Malaya's right," said Khomitsky. "The movies are better than a sarcophagus."

"The movies are better than a sarcophagus!" said Efim, exasperated. "The movies are just pictures, but a sarcophagus is part of life. If you want a look, you can look, if you want to touch it, you can touch it."

"Efim," said Madame Malaya, "you said that you wanted to look through glass but now that's not enough for you, you want to touch them too."

"Oh! So what's better then—the movies or a sarcophagus?"

"All right," yielded Madame Malaya, "if you like sarcophaguses so much, the courtyard will take the trouble to obtain one for you when the time comes, and we can even write your epitaph today: 'Here lies Efim Granik, the number-one rowdy in all Odessa.' "

No, said Efim, he couldn't write his own epitaph because he didn't know hieroglyphics. Didn't matter, replied Madame Malaya, he should write it in Russian, maybe people would be able to read it then.

Stepa burst out laughing. Efim tried to find an apt reply but, as if to spite him, his mind went blank. Madame Malaya said there was no hurry, even pharaohs had a little free time in their sarcophaguses.

"Pharaohs do," Efim responded, "but workers don't!"

Madame Malaya admitted that this was tit for tat but said straight out that the Granik-Khomitsky twosome had to be broken up before their bad example proved infectious.

Stepa remained in the laundry room with Anya Kotlyar as a helper while Efim was put to work carting out construction debris because Iona Cheperukha was on a swing shift that started before lunch.

"Take care, Malaya, be well!" shouted Cheperukha from the entry hall. Klava Ivanovna wished him the same and reminded him not to be late; the sooner he was back, the sooner he'd be finished with his share of the evening work.

Dina Vargaftik said that Cheperukha would work the evening shift when hair grew on the palms of your hands or when the market's wine stalls were transferred into the courtyard.

"My dear woman," said Granik, "a person should be a little more compassionate. If Cheperukha likes to stop by the market after work and have a look at what color the wine is today, where's the harm in that? It gives him pleasure. You can keep him company if you want, but it's ugly to sling mud at a person."

"You want me to go drinking with that *shikker*?" said Dina, becoming worked up. "You go drinking with him yourself and let your wife pull off your drawers and smell the puke on your breath!"

Efim had already lifted the end of his wheelbarrow and was about to start pushing it but Dina Vargaftik's words had cut him to the quick. He lowered the wheelbarrow and turned to the people there to ask if they had heard what that woman had said to him. People had heard and said so, but Madame Malaya ordered Efim to shut his mouth at once or else she would treat his actions as deliberate sabotage. All right, said Efim, he'd shut up, but at the same time he demanded a Comrades' Court for the personal insult he'd received: two years ago he had had a resection on his stomach and the doctor had ordered him to drink vodka like a bird and this woman was saying that his wife had to pull off his pants while he was reeking of drink.

"Liar!" Efim tore open his shirt. "Look at the scar on my stomach!"

"Granik," said Madame Malaya, losing all patience, "cover your stomach and get back to work, or you'll be given a work load that would make a draft horse on the White Sea Canal drop dead!"

Efim said he would yield out of personal respect for Madame Malaya, but he was still going to submit a petition in writing for a Comrades' Court and would demand that it be in effect as of this moment.

"It could even be an hour earlier," said Klava Ivanovna. Efim said that he didn't need any favors, he would go find out the exact time. He had turned to walk away when Madame Malaya grabbed him by the collar and shouted:

"You lousy good-for-nothing, they can send me to Solovki, but if I don't kill you, my name isn't Klava Ivanovna!"

Efim was horrified—only kulaks, thieves, and prostitutes were sent to Solovki. Fine company for Madame Malaya!

Klava Ivanovna wound up to smack Efim in the mouth but just then Anya Kotlyar came running out of the laundry room followed by Stepa Khomitsky, both of them soaked from head to toe. Stepa shouted that he had turned off the water but some bastard had gotten into the crawl space and turned on the main valve in the rear courtyard.

Stepa, Madame Malaya, and Efim set off at a run while Anya Kotlyar remained behind to wring out her clothes. The other women gave her a hand and kept marveling at how strong the pressure was when you didn't need it, and then, as if by agreement, they all began to laugh in unison. Anya said that now it was funny to her too, but when it happened she thought it was the Deluge.

"Thank God you weren't by yourself," exclaimed Dina, "and that Stepa was there with you. Your husband's away at work and he doesn't have the slightest idea that you were just fighting for your life with your neighbor."

Anya blushed, and the women laughed till they cried, pinching themselves under the arm to make themselves stop. Just then Olya Cheperukha walked over, saying she wanted to know what the joke was, and the whole thing started all over again. Olya got the hiccups and she asked the women to hold her firmly or otherwise something bad would happen. Something bad did indeed happen and the women shouted "Phew!" and laughed all the harder.

This foolish laughter reached Madame Malaya in the rear courtyard and she shouted that you needed a policeman to talk to people like that but she would manage without one somehow. Then, seeing Olya Cheperukha, her indignation reached its height because it was none other than Zyunchik, Olya's son, who had incited Kolka to climb into the crawl space and open the valve.

Stepa had found the two of them, his own son Kolka and Zyunchik, in the crawl space. His first impulse had been to close the cover and let the two of them stay there till the next morning. Klava Ivanovna said that this could cause the children to stutter for the rest of their lives and ordered him to let them out. Stepa grabbed one, then the other, by the scruff of the neck, knocked their heads together, and ordered them to crawl out. Zyunchik obeyed the order at once but Kolka burst into tears and said that he wasn't coming out and would stay in there until he died of hunger. Madame Malaya went for Zyunchik and demanded that he honestly admit that he was the ringleader or else there'd be nothing left of Kolka.

Yes, admitted Zyunchik, he had been the first to climb in and Kolka had stayed up on top and hadn't wanted to climb down. Then Zyunchik repeated his story in front of his mother, who grabbed him by the forelock and began yanking him to and fro. But after five or six pulls her son suddenly ducked and leaped off to one side and all Olya could do was yell after him that he should come back of his own free will because otherwise it would be even worse when his father came home. Klava Ivanovna also warned him that he'd better come back but Zyunchik knew from experience that there was no way of telling whether it would be worse later on or not—the main thing was that it wasn't worse now.

At one o'clock Klava Ivanovna reminded Olya that it was time for Zyunchik to be off to school but that his briefcase with his schoolbooks was at home.

"Oy," said Olya, clutching her head and setting off at a run for her apartment.

"Hold on," said Klava Ivanovna. "He's too afraid to go into the apartment. Put his briefcase by the door and then go away. No tricks, don't hide, kids can smell it when something's up."

Olya burst into tears: she had so many problems with him, he was such a touchy boy, you always had to be nice to him but how could you be nice to him all the time when he was up to some nastiness every day?

"Stop crying," ordered Madame Malaya. "He shouldn't have any idea how much this costs you or else you'll never have him off your back."

Yes, nodded Olya, that was true. When Zyunchik saw her suffering, first he felt sorry for her and promised to be good, but half an hour later it all went flying out of his head and he was off his leash again, so to speak.

"That's all right," said Madame Malaya. "Children shouldn't be downhearted for too long, there'll be plenty of time for that."

After lunch Lapidis, the engineer, tore himself away from his work for a minute and ran down for a look at how things were going. In the laundry room Khomitsky and Anya Kotlyar were dismantling the heater. There was dust everywhere. Lapidis advised them to splash some water on the brickwork, open the flue all the way for the strongest possible draft, and to open the windows wide.

"Aren't you the smart one!" said Anya. "In your office you worry about all those fat women catching cold from a little draft but people's health doesn't matter to you here. Who cares if they come down with sciatica or pneumonia?"

"Comrade Kotlyar," said Lapidis with a laugh, "in the first place, the women in my office are no fatter than they are here, and, in the second place, we don't work in an office, and, in the third place, it's my job to give advice and it's yours to disregard it."

"Anyway," said Anya with a grimace, "you're an educated person and you can always outtalk anybody."

"Stepa, I won't say anything, you tell her," said Lapidis.

Khomitsky replied that there was nothing to say, women were women, and as for Lapidis, he added, God should make all educated people like him, then you could stand to have them around.

"All right," said Anya, yielding, "probably I was wrong. He's special, he's not like the others."

"Thank you," said Lapidis with a bow. "Hearing a testimonial from a woman with eyes like that, well. . . ."

"Stop laying it on," said Anya, flaring up. "Everyone says that I have horrible green eyes like a cat."

"By the way," said Lapidis, "Balzac wrote a novella called *The House of the Ball-Playing Cat.*"

"A ball-playing cat?" said Anya in surprise.

Mixing a bucket of cement, Stepa began to sing a vulgar song.

"Foo!" said Anya with a grimace. "What a terrible song!" Lapidis seconded the opinion and suggested they go have a look at his copy of Balzac.

"Why should I go to your place!" said Anya, flaring up again. "If I want the book, I know where the library is. But, if you really want to, you can write down the title on a piece of paper for me."

Lapidis tore a page out of his notebook, wrote down the title, and handed it to Anya. Through the window Klava Ivanovna could see that Stepa was the only one working and that Kotlyar and Lapidis were exchanging notes. She flung open both doors, extended her arm, and demanded that the piece of paper be placed in the palm of her hand.

"Klava Ivanovna," said Anya, automatically slipping the paper into her bra, "we were just kidding around."

"I know you were just kidding around," said Madame Malaya, "and so I'm asking you nicely: give me the piece of paper."

"Don't give it to her," interjected Lapidis. "The right of private correspondence is guaranteed by law in the U.S.S.R."

"All right," said Madame Malaya, giving both Anya and Lapidis an angry look, "you can keep your secret to yourselves, but anyone who thinks that Malaya has sclerosis of the brain is sadly mistaken."

"Good God!" Anya took the note from her bra. "Here, go ahead, read it."

"No." Madame Malaya categorically refused. "I don't read other people's notes. You take it and hide it where it was before, in your tits."

"Klava Ivanovna," said Lapidis, scratching the tip of his nose, "you're a great psychologist. Stop getting the woman all riled up."

"A person doesn't get riled up when there's no reason," said Klava Ivanovna, "and when a person gets riled up, that means there's a reason."

Anya wiped her eyes on her apron and demanded that Lapidis be made to leave, his talking just distracted people and he wouldn't let them work.

"Get him out of here, out of here!" shouted Lapidis good-naturedly, then, suddenly becoming serious, he said that it was precisely for his straightforwardness and his principles that people admired the new Soviet man.

"Lapidis," said Madame Malaya, stamping her foot, "your tongue's running away with you."

"Oh, wicked tongues are more frightening than pistols!" said Lapidis, striking a pose as if he were an actor in the Ivanov Theater of the Russian Drama.

Anya walked over to the window and placed the note so that Klava Ivanovna could read it but Lapidis snatched it at once and shoved it in his pocket. Then he waved good-bye and walked past Madame Malaya. He pulled out the note and tore it neatly into sixteen pieces, counting aloud as he did.

"You're a good counter," praised Madame Malaya. "But we can count too."

"It's like school!" blurted Lapidis without rhyme or reason.

Madame Malaya waved a threatening finger at him, saying: "Lapidis, I'm warning you, you'll go too far."

Iona Ovseich arrived late that evening. There had been an open party meeting at his factory. People had been unanimous in demanding that the NKVD apply the strictest measures to Reznik, the head of planning, and Khais, the head technician, who had for a long time been consciously and deliberately undermining all the collective's efforts to increase productivity.

He hadn't had a minute to himself all day. There hadn't even been time for a quick bite but, without stopping at home, Degtyar had first asked to be shown how much progress had been made on the outpost that day. He asked questions about the boilers in the laundry room—had safety procedures been followed when dismantling them? He picked up two bricks from the ground, struck one against the other, causing some clay to chip off. Degtyar said that gigantic construction projects, the likes of which the world had never seen, were under way in their country from one end to another, and bricks were worth their weight in gold.

"Degtyar," said Madame Malaya, placing her hand over her heart, "I swear on my life that I've said the same thing a thousand times."

"Saying it is not enough," said Iona Ovseich. "You have to give a good explanation and keep a close watch on things, otherwise they'll start to slide."

"Things won't slide here," replied Klava Ivanovna, "though Lapidis did spend half an hour on idle talk."

"What does that mean?" Iona Ovseich frowned. "And what were you doing at the time, catching flies?"

Klava Ivanovna said that, no, she had not been catching flies at the time; on the contrary, if she hadn't taken steps right away, Lapidis would have spent another two hours hanging around that beauty with the size thirty-eight bra.

"Thirty-eight?" asked Iona Ovseich. "Who do you mean?"

"Oh," said Madame Malaya, slapping her sides, "you're all hot for the same one!"

Iona Ovseich stopped, turned his face to Malaya, and looked her right in the eye. "Don't compare me with him. We can hear what he says but we still don't have a real idea of what he thinks. Don't compare me with him."

"Did you visit Polina in the hospital today?" said Klava Ivanovna, changing the subject.

"Malaya," said Iona Ovseich angrily, "don't ask stupid questions. You know I couldn't get to the hospital today."

"How about tomorrow?" asked Klava Ivanovna.

Tomorrow, replied Iona Ovseich, his schedule would be even tighter. First thing in the morning he was going to a party activists' meeting at the District Committee.

"A fine thing!" cried Klava Ivanovna. "And who's going to bring your Polina her package?"

Degtyar stood for a moment in silence as if made out of stone until Klava Ivanovna said that she could go herself or send someone, Anya Kotlyar for example.

"Kotlyar? Maybe," agreed Iona Ovseich, "but Polina is in the tubercular hospital and people are afraid to go there."

"Don't talk nonsense!" said Malaya indignantly. "The most any disease can do with a woman like her is to kiss her you know what."

Degtyar narrowed his eyes to a squint. Klava Ivanovna sighed deeply and repeated that all men only had one thing on their minds, especially if their wives were ill. Then she asked how he was managing with meals and offered to cook him enough food for two or three days, which he could heat up on his Primus stove.

No, said Degtyar, he didn't need to be cooked for: he took care of meals at work—he'd bring a bottle of milk and a loaf of bread with him and that would last him the day. After work he'd buy a hundred grams of sausage and fifty of butter and that would take care of breakfast and dinner.

Madame Malaya shook her head: if a person wanted to give himself a cold or an ulcer, that was his own business of course.

She didn't have to worry about him getting ulcers, said Iona Ovseich, he'd gotten them in 1920, in Lustdorf Road Prison. He was in there the whole fall and winter, until his comrades from the outside helped him escape.

"Ah!" said Madame Malaya with indignation. "You're a real cannibal. With an ulcer like that and you don't take any hot food all day long! Dr. Landa wouldn't let himself do that. And neither would Lapidis."

"Listen, Malaya," interrupted Iona Ovseich, "let's get back to business: we should post a socialist competition graph on the building of the outpost in the front hall. Granik should stop by and see me in the morning at the factory and I'll give him a sheet of good plywood. He can contribute the paint himself and we'll take a little off his work time."

No, said Klava Ivanovna, she wouldn't send Granik, he'd never make it to the factory and he'd be nowhere to be seen around the building all day either. She'd send Zyunchik and Kolka. Iona Ovseich frowned. It wouldn't look good, sending kids. On the contrary, objected Malaya: the boys would wear clean clothes and their Pioneer scarfs and be a pleasure for people to see.

"All right," agreed Degtyar, "let's do it like that, but the sign has to be posted tomorrow, no excuses, so that everyone can see who's doing what. That's the great strength of socialist competition."

"Yes," said Madame Malaya, "but how can you figure who gave a hundred percent and who gave less, or more?"

Degtyar shrugged his shoulders. "What's the big problem? Everyone should be given a quota. If he does it, that's one hundred percent, if he does more or, the other way around, less, that means it's a hundred plus or minus X percent. There's no other way it could be."

Madame Malaya admitted that he was right and that she hadn't given the matter real thought. Degtyar said there was no harm in that, anyone could make a mistake, the main thing was not to cling to your mistakes but to correct them as you went.

"Easier said than done!" said Malaya, hitting her knee. "It helps to have someone like you around."

Iona Ovseich frowned. "There's always someone around."

"What we need is a leader, a locomotive!" exclaimed Malaya. "And what if the only person around is Efim Granik?"

"Only Efim Granik?" said Degtyar. "Then you will correct him and he'll correct his wife Sonya, and she'll correct her son Osya. Besides, people are always correcting each other, there's always someone around, we don't live in a void."

A large red sign hung in the entry hall the next evening. Last names had been painted in light blue and people's initials in brown to make them stand out from each other. The totals had been entered in chalk.

That day everyone had fulfilled his quota one hundred percent and Granik was the only one to receive a hundred and ten because the making of the chart had required special skill. Efim walked through the entry hall several times and each time there was someone else in front of the chart who would call out to him and offer loud congratulations. Efim, however, only listened and refused to accept the congratulations and kept saying that he had not done anything so special; on the contrary, anyone could have done it better than he.

Only Lapidis was surprised that Granik had received a hundred and ten and said so to Malaya.

"And how much would you have given him?" she asked.

"One hundred ninety-two and eight tenths."

"Why exactly one hundred ninety-two and eight tenths?" said Madame Malaya in surprise.

"Why exactly one hundred and ten?" replied Lapidis.

"You know what," said Klava Ivanovna, grimacing, "you're too smart, you know too much, I can't tell you anything."

That same evening when Degtyar returned from his activists' meeting at around eleven o'clock, Klava Ivanovna dropped by to see him and to tell him about her conversation with Lapidis.

Iona Ovseich listened closely and without interrupting, then suddenly said: "Enough, I understand it all now. The conversations Lapidis engages in are unhealthy conversations. Nevertheless, stop in and see him at work tomorrow, better in the morning, and hear his point of view on the subject of the chart, and you and I will discuss it in the evening."

Klava Ivanovna suggested not putting it off until the next day but going to see Lapidis right away but Degtyar was categorically against this: "If a person's home at midnight he's not obliged to take part in a production conference. A person's home is his home and that shouldn't be forgotten."

"Degtyar," said Klava Ivanovna, "you work night and day but Lapidis can loll around when he feels like it, is that it? I'm completely at odds with you on this point and you can't convince me otherwise."

Iona Ovseich replied that he had no intention of doing so, she could keep her opinion, but that was nothing to get up in the clouds about, both feet on the ground was what was needed here.

"That all depends," said Madame Malaya, shaking her head. "A kneeling person's feet are on the ground too."

Iona Ovseich replied with a Polish proverb: *"Co zanadto—to nie zdrowo* [There can be too much of a good thing]."

"No," said Malaya, continuing her polemic, "there can be too much of a bad thing but not of a good thing."

"Klara Tsetkin was an important person too," said Iona Ovseich, "but she talked less than you do."

Madame Malaya had found another objection but Degtyar did not let her voice it. "By the way," he said, "Papanin and his team are supposed to arrive at the North Pole tomorrow."

"No!" said Madame Malaya, clasping her hands. "How do you know that?"

Iona Ovseich repeated it: "Papanin and his entire team are supposed to arrive at the North Pole tomorrow and don't ask me any questions."

At noon the next day there was a radio report that Papanin, Shirshov, Krenkel, and Fyodorov had landed at the North Pole. The entire courtyard had been waiting all morning for news and all the loudspeakers had been turned on. When the news was confirmed, many people went running to Madame Malaya and asked her to tell them her secret, how she could have had advance knowledge of information known only to the government. Madame Malaya frowned slightly as if the question were out of place and answered everyone the way children are answered: "Knowing too much will make you old before your time."

They finished work around eight o'clock in the evening and put one large one hundred on the graph because on that day no one wanted to stand out from the rest.

Before the shift Madame Malaya had a conversation with Lapidis. Actually, it wasn't so much a conversation as an exchange of words because Lapidis declared that he needed a standard, a point of departure, to measure anything, and to just pluck one from the air wasn't his style. Klava Ivanovna asked how they were supposed to conduct a socialist competition if no one knew who was ahead and who was behind. Lapidis burst into foolish laughter and said: "If no one knows who's ahead and who's behind, then it isn't a socialist competition."

Klava Ivanovna grew seriously angry: "A fine thing for someone here to laugh about!"

When Degtyar learned about Lapidis' foolish laughter and foolish remarks, he withdrew into himself for a minute or two and only drummed his fingers on the table. Klava Ivanovna asked him to stop twice because it was getting on her nerves but Degtyar paid her no attention, as if she were not speaking to him. Suddenly he stopped and said: "Malaya, there's something to what he says. But his behavior is another matter entirely. Tell him for me that he should come here and put his theory to work in practice."

"And what if he doesn't want to?" said Madame Malaya with a shrug.

"Don't worry, he'll want to."

It turned out exactly as Degtyar had foreseen: Lapidis didn't even so much as think of refusing. In tandem with Malaya he took a sampling of the work done during the shift by Stepa Khomitsky, Dina Vargaftik, Olya Cheperukha, and Anya Kotlyar. Then Lapidis spent a long time putting figures down on paper, translating them into percentages, and said that Khomitsky had done approximately forty percent more than Vargaftik and she in turn had done twenty percent more than Cheperukha and Anya Kotlyar.

"Wait a minute," interrupted Madame Malaya. "Can you explain to me who did a full hundred percent?"

"If you wish," said Lapidis. "It was Stepa Khomitsky and, if you like, Cheperukha and Kotlyar."

"What about Dina Vargaftik?"

"Her too," said Lapidis, his grimace deepening. "As I told you—if you wish."

"Listen, Lapidis," said Madame Malaya, losing her temper, "you're still talking to me like I was a greenhorn. Someone tries to talk to you like a human being but you treat people like they were idiots."

Lapidis looked at Klava Ivanovna with blank, expressionless eyes. She pounded him on the back to snap him out of it. He cleared his throat, shook his head like Punch, and said that Anya Kotlyar should be given a mark of one hundred percent.

Klava Ivanovna asked what about Khomitsky? Khomitsky, replied Lapidis, should be given a hundred and seventy and Dina Vargaftik a hundred and twenty.

"How can that be?" said Madame Malaya in surprise. "Everybody's overfulfilling the plan and there's no one lagging behind?"

"Yes," agreed Lapidis, "that's the way it came out in this variation."

No, said Malaya, that variation didn't suit her: let Dina Vargaftik be given a one hundred and then Khomitsky would be a shock worker, and Kotlyar and Cheperukha would be laggards.

"Klava Ivanovna," said Lapidis, crinkling his face again, "why do you need any laggards? Let everyone be shock workers. They'll like it and you'll like it too."

No, Madame Malaya categorically refused, it was never that way, that everyone was a shock worker. Then who would the real shock workers be in that case? "To make a long story short, let Dina Vargaftik get a one hundred and whoever did less will get less."

When they tallied up the sums for the day and entered them on the socialist competition graph, Sonya Granik turned out to be in last place with Olya Cheperukha and Anya Kotlyar right ahead of her. Sonya Granik suffered from asthma and no one blamed her for finishing last; on the contrary, many people even said that she'd done a great job for a person with her health, but, as for Olya Cheperukha and Anya Kotlyar, all you could do was throw up your hands. The most interesting thing of all was that both women had the nerve to complain to Madame Malaya as if she had forced them to do a poorer job than the others. Klava Ivanovna had every reason to be indignant but instead she calmly explained that she had not make up the figures but had worked them out along with Lapidis.

Anya flared up as soon as she learned about Lapidis: "He has too high an opinion about himself, that bald dirty old man!"

This surprised Klava Ivanovna, who said: "Why are you calling him bald?"

Anya grew even more incensed and said that people like him should have all their hair plucked out so they couldn't flaunt their head of hair in front of women.

Though no one had asked him to, Zyunchik ran upstairs and called out to Lapidis to come quick, Madame Malaya wanted to see him.

Klava Ivanovna said that she did not want to see him but, since he was there, he should speak with the women: Cheperukha and Kotlyar were very upset at being given such a low percentage that they ended up in last place.

"Comrades," said Lapidis, hand on heart, "Klava Ivanovna will attest to this: I wanted to give you each one hundred percent but she wouldn't agree."

“Ah,” exclaimed Anya, “you poor boy, his feelings were hurt! How old are you, boy?”

Lapidis burst out laughing. Kotlyar shouted that she could see right through him and could not wait to see Lapidis’ wife publicly disgraced the way he had done to them. Lapidis stopped laughing. Anya suddenly burst into tears because she felt hurt and insulted by this injustice: now the whole courtyard would be saying that she and Joseph were selfish people who only did things for themselves and didn’t give a damn about other people.

“My dear Anya,” said Lapidis, “tomorrow you’ll have every opportunity to be a shock worker like Stepa Khomitsky and have a little red flag by your name. The flag will be so bright that it will be visible from every street, from Karl Marx and Lenin Street to Franz Mering and Klara Tsetkin Street. And the whole courtyard will be proud of you.”

Anya turned her back to Lapidis and said that he was a loathsome type and disgusting to deal with and Klava Ivanovna should kick him out.

“Why is that?” Lapidis threw his head back as if looking down from above. “A person should leave on his own so he’ll be asked back again.”

“Oh, oh!” cried Anya. “Hold me, I’m fainting!”

Lapidis immediately grabbed Anya from the back, slipping his arms under hers and around her solar plexus. Anya was so staggered that at first she could not utter a single word. Madame Malaya and Olya Cheperukha both laughed as if there were something truly funny about it. Anya shoved Lapidis with her behind and his hands slid down to her stomach. Anya froze for a moment, then gave Lapidis a good hard pinch. Lapidis jumped away. Her first impulse was to smack him in the mouth but in front of everyone Lapidis asked Anya to have mercy on him, especially since he had meant no harm, he was just trying to be of assistance to a woman who had fainted.

Klava Ivanovna told Lapidis that that was enough, there were limits, but she herself continued to laugh. Anya grew even more offended and for some reason attacked Olya, who gave as good as she got, saying there was no reason to let every shithead get on your nerves.

"Olya," said Lapidis, crossing his arms over his chest, "I didn't expect that from you!"

"That's right," said Olya, twisting her lips, "you can do whatever you like and we're supposed to take it, like servants."

Lapidis replied that since there was now complete equality between men and women, everyone could vote and be elected. Saying this, he made a crude upward gesture with one finger and laughed out loud. The women were on the verge of indignation but just then Dr. Landa put his new SVD-9 radio out on the windowsill and the whole courtyard reverberated with the song from the film *Seven Brave Men:*

Let the song go far and wide!
Don't be sad, don't cry, my wife:
The country's sent us to ride
Out the storm on a distant sea!

"Oy," moaned Olya, "some people, some people in this world!"

Klava Ivanovna whacked her on the hip—there was nothing to feel so bad about! But in fact she understood Olya very well: her husband had come home at midnight yesterday and was so drunk he smashed all the dishes in the house. Last year he had to go before a Comrades' Court and he had promised to mend his ways, but afterward went back to his old habits and was even worse than before. He reviled her every day as if she were to blame for their neighbors becoming fed up with his pranks. On the contrary, Klava Ivanovna herself had proposed taking him before another Comrades' Court but Olya had fought tooth and nail against it, making excuses for her husband—he did such hard work, chasing all over town with his wheelbarrow from morning till night.

The next day Stepa Khomitsky was in first place again. And though Anya Kotlyar was given a full 100 percent and could look people in the eye, she said very crudely of Khomitsky that people like him exceeded the norm only to get in good with the higher-ups.

Her remark even reached Degtyar and that same evening he called a meeting and made his warning perfectly clear: no one was allowed to undermine socialist competition, and all ambiguous attitudes and remarks would be seen for what they were. At the same time, in order to further develop socialist competition, the building committee was offering a prize for shock work: a cotton suit and two pairs of shoes, one made of leather, the other of rubber.

Three weeks later Lapidis, accompanied by a technician from the building administration, inspected the premises of the former laundry room and concluded that they could now proceed with plastering. Iona Ovseich declared the first phase of construction was concluded and the second phase was beginning, one no less, indeed even more, important than the first.

Efim Granik shouted from his seat: "That's absolutely right, it's easier to tear something down than to build something."

Iona Ovseich replied that you had to use your head when tearing something down too or else even the Devil himself couldn't figure out what to do with it. Not only that, they should also proceed with the painting of the interior of the outpost, a task that would be entrusted to Efim Lazarevich Granik. Overall construction had to be speeded up, especially since a special government decision on elections to the Supreme Soviet was expected in the very near future.

"Degtyar," interrupted Iona Cheperukha, "how do you know what our government intends to do when Moscow is nine hundred miles from here?"

Degtyar narrowed his right eye and a smile flashed over his lips as he said: "There's no reason for you to know how I know that. And as for the factual aspect of the matter, you have a legal right to ride herd on me and, if there's a mistake, to say loud enough for everyone to hear: 'Degtyar doesn't tell the truth, he tricked us.' "

People laughed. Klava Ivanovna asked Cheperukha to exhibit some patience, if only for a while, and in honor of the elections to forget the way to Pushkin Street between Kirov and Lekkart streets. The laughter became ten times louder after Madame Malaya's request because the Odessa Agricultural Institute's wine cellar was located on Pushkin Street between Kirov and Lekkart, formerly Bazaar and Bolshoi Arnautsky streets.

Cheperukha did not have to wait long: in July the radio and all the newspapers and posters pasted all over town announced that the Central Executive Committee had issued regulations signed by Comrade Kalinin concerning elections to the Supreme Soviet of the U.S.S.R. Henceforth, and for the first time, elections would be held in the place where the citizens resided. Anyone who was eighteen years of age on election day was eligible to vote or be elected.

"Degtyar," Cheperukha shouted for the whole courtyard to hear, "your name's Iona and my name's Iona and I want you to be our deputy. Do you have anything against that?"

Degtyar answered that he didn't but advised Cheperukha to choose other subjects to joke about, otherwise people might put the wrong interpretation on them.

"No," said Cheperukha, sticking to his guns, "give me a straight answer: on behalf of the entire courtyard, I'm going to nominate Iona Degtyar for election to the Supreme Soviet—and so, will you be elected or not?"

Now Iona Ovseich came out and explained that, since the courtyard was neither a factory nor a social organization, it could not nominate candidates for election as deputies. But the transport union, of which Cheperukha was a member, could.

Cheperukha thought for a moment, then shook his head: nothing would come of that, they had their own people like Degtyar there.

"I could have guessed," said Degtyar. "Now answer a question for me: did you, an old transportation worker, read the paper today?"

How could he have read the paper, said Cheperukha, spreading his hands, if he'd spent the whole day running around Odessa with his wheelbarrow? This one needed coal, that one needed a wardrobe delivered, and someone else wanted a couple of coffins.

"All right then," said Degtyar, "passenger ships and naval vessels have been using the Moscow-Volga Canal since July 19. The new dams and locks near Rybinsk are nearing completion. Now all that remains is to build the Volga-Don Canal and Moscow will be a five-sea port."

"Good God!" said Cheperukha, clutching his head. "Who'll need us then? Odessa with her port and me with my wheelbarrow!"

"As far as Odessa is concerned," said Degtyar, "one can assume that it will still be of use, though I'm not so sure about your wheelbarrow. But tomorrow you'll have a chance to do something of importance: bring two milk cans of drying oil and two of paint to the outpost or otherwise Granik won't be able to work."

"Comrade Brigadier General," said Cheperukha, saluting, "your order will be executed!"

Early the next morning Cheperukha wheeled the four cans into the outpost, got a receipt from Madame Malaya, read it aloud, then pretended to wipe himself with it and threw it away.

"You bum!" said Malaya, brandishing a fist. "I'll show you!"

There was a short meeting that evening: as a response to the Central Executive Committee resolution on the elections, the courtyard assumed the obligation of finishing the construction of the outpost ahead of schedule and to have it in operation no later than the thirty-first of August, a good present for the children at the start of the new school year. The second question concerned the elections themselves since preparations for the election campaign were already under way everywhere, in town and country. Madame Malaya proposed that Dr. Landa's wife be excused from working on the outpost. She knew how to type and could be used entirely for the preelection campaign.

"Malaya," replied Degtyar merrily, "we accept your proposition."

After the meeting Degtyar told Malaya that now the order of the day was to supply every family with a copy of the resolution about the elections so that everyone could study it properly. As for old man Kiselis and Lyalya Orlov, who had the right to vote for the first time, careful thought should be given to organizing individual study with them.

"Kiselis," said Madame Malaya, "went to the hospital yesterday with angina."

"And so," said Degtyar with a frown, "does that mean he counts for nothing?"

"No, a person always counts for something even if he's dead," replied Klava Ivanovna, "but the question is whether individual study with him is appropriate at the present time."

"Malaya, you're worse than Efim Granik."

"By the way," said Madame Malaya, "Granik took second prize today, finishing behind Khomitsky. But the day before yesterday a man from the Revenue Department came by the courtyard, wanting information about how many clients Granik has."

"And what did you tell him?"

"I told him that Granik's been working on building the outpost from dawn till dusk and has been a shock worker."

"Malaya," said Iona Ovseich with a smile, "was that man asking whether Granik was doing a good job or a poor one on the outpost?

He was asking about Granik, who lives in the same courtyard you do, asking how many clients he has."

"When you're busy all day on one job," said Klava Ivanovna, "there isn't much time left for other work. How many clients could he have?"

"That's just what the man from the Revenue Department was asking you about—how many clients could Efim Granik, who possesses a registration certificate, have?" said Degtyar.

"You know what?" proposed Madame Malaya. "The next time the man from the Revenue Department comes here, I'll send him to see you and the two of you can talk it over."

"Malaya," said Degtyar, smacking the table, "we're not playing soccer here—you kick the ball to me and I kick it back to you. A person from a state agency asks his questions of the right people and not just anyone off the street."

"That's true," agreed Malaya, "the right people. All the same, I'll say it again. Granik has as many clients as Degtyar has warts on his nose. It's surprising how Sonya puts up with him."

"Whether she can put up with him or not," said Iona Ovseich, "is her headache. The Soviet government has its own interests and won't let anyone rob it. Make a mental note of that."

"I will," promised Madame Malaya, then changed the subject. Yesterday she had sent Anya Kotlyar with a package to the tuberculosis hospital. Polina complained that Degtyar had not been to see her for three days. "She's getting all sorts of ideas in her head even though she's fully aware they're nonsense and shouldn't be paid any attention."

Iona Ovseich grew angry. "Any nonsense she thinks is her own business. And Kotlyar should be told not to meddle in other people's business."

"Where's the meddling?" said Klava Ivanovna indignantly. "A sick person spoke to her, was she supposed to just sit there like a stone?"

Degtyar's eyes were slits. "If a person has all sorts of nonsense in her head, where is it written that she'll feel better by having it supported and sympathized with?"

"No," objected Malaya, "sympathy does make a sick person feel better."

Iona Ovseich grinned. "If sympathy can make a sick person feel better, that means the pain's not fatal and they can bear it."

"Don't measure everyone by your own standards," countered Madame Malaya. "Take that, Degtyar!"

"All right," said Iona Ovseich with a dismissive flick of his hand, "that's enough of that. Now, as far as old man Kiselis is concerned, someone has to drop by the hospital—the man has no relatives and so there's probably no one who knows about him." Malaya should go herself.

Klava Ivanovna told Degtyar that she was only one person and couldn't be everywhere at once but, if she had to go, she had to go.

The next day after lunch she left Stepa Khomitsky in her place and went to the therapeutic section of the Stalin District Hospital. Old man Kiselis was a bit surprised to see her and asked if someone in her family was sick. Klava Ivanovna told him that she had come to see him, and had brought him a jar of fruit compote and a half kilo of apricots and tomatoes. "The tomatoes are especially good," she said.

"I can't eat the tomatoes, they make me swell up terribly: the gas makes pressure on my diaphragm, my diaphragm presses against my heart, and I have trouble breathing."

"I have the same problem, which I solve by puréeing the tomatoes. I'll run by the cafeteria and get a strainer."

"Madame Malaya," Kiselis said, taking her by the hand, "I swear, it's not worth the effort. How much time do I have left? Somehow or other I'll make it without puréed tomatoes."

She was taken aback by this remark. "Kiselis, this year you'll be voting for the first time and eighteen-year-olds will be voting too. Who thinks about death when he's eighteen?"

"Madame Malaya," said Kiselis, shaking his head, "I'm four times eighteen."

"That's just the point. We'll give you four votes, and you can vote to your heart's content. And don't try to stop me, I'm going for the strainer."

On the way Klava Ivanovna stopped by the house surgeon's office.

"Doctor," she said, "I don't like how the patient Kiselis looks."

The doctor replied that he didn't like the way Kiselis looked either but medicine could do only so much and no more.

"That's no answer," said Madame Malaya. "When is the hospital planning to release Kiselis and let him go home?"

"Home?" said the doctor in surprise. "That depends."

"What does that mean? Can he go home or can't he? Give me a clear answer."

"My good woman," said the doctor, taking her by the arm, "I think you know as much as I do about this."

Klava Ivanovna suddenly felt weak in the knees and sat down on a stool.

"Is he a relative of yours?" asked the doctor.

She did not answer the question and, still weak in the knees, rose with effort and set off to the cafeteria.

In the cafeteria she was told she would not be given a strainer; she could bring the tomatoes and purée them there. Madame Malaya told the kitchen workers that they were stone-hearted sticklers for rules but she wasn't going to waste time arguing. They shouted after her that this wasn't a restaurant and if people brought food to a patient they should be thinking about him.

When Madame Malaya handed old man Kiselis a jar of tomato purée, he ate a few spoonfuls, smacked his lips, and admitted that the tomatoes *were* particularly good.

"Summer in Odessa," said Klava Ivanovna, opening the top buttons on her blouse to let a little fresh air in. "That's something you have to experience yourself, summer in Odessa."

"I was born in Odessa," said Kiselis. "I was born ten years before Colonel Kotlyarevsky's father built our house. Kotlyarevsky wasn't a bad person."

"They were all good to themselves," said Madame Malaya.

"Kotlyarevsky knew his business," continued Kiselis. "He was considered a decent merchant. He did business with people in London, Hamburg, Lyons. Everyone respected him, poor people too. When a person couldn't pay his rent, he didn't throw him right out onto the street but gave him an extension."

"Kiselis," interrupted Madame Malaya, "there's no need for you to be thinking about that. You're better off thinking about something else, something more pleasant."

"Kotlyarevsky had another building, on Ekaterina Street. That's where my brother lived. He used to take his textiles from Kotlyarevsky's warehouse, where the municipal market is now. Blomberg's warehouse was across the street. Blomberg was pretty good at his business too."

"Kiselis," said Klava Ivanovna, shaking her head, "someone might think you miss those people."

"Blomberg did business with people in London, Hamburg, Lyons, and Lodz. Blomberg had warehouses on Troitskaya Street and at the old market. I used to get up every morning at four-thirty because the store on Alexandrovsky Street near the old market had to be opened every day at the same time—six o'clock. When I was four years old I had the measles, then whooping cough and scarlet fever, then all the other children came down with them. Then I studied at the Faig Business School. The Faig School was on Nezhinsky Street where the venereal disease clinic is now. My mother hired a tutor to teach me French; people thought that a businessman should be an educated person. I used to speak French like you speak Russian, you can take my word on that, Madame Malaya."

"Kiselis, please, eat an apricot. They contain a lot of glucose and that's good for your heart."

"They hired a music teacher, the violinist Tsunets, for me when I was seven years old. My mother never thought I'd be a Jascha Heifetz. There was no Jascha Heifetz then. She just wanted her son to be able to play the violin for himself when he was feeling bad."

"Kiselis"—Madame Malaya leaned forward to whisper in his ear—"I've been here a long time. Is there any place you want to go?"

"No," said Kiselis with a smile, "they give me everything I need—a plate, a cup, a bedpan. I can go whenever I need to."

"It's a good hospital," said Madame Malaya with a sigh. "Good specialists here. Where could a person get treatment like this before at no cost? A person can just lie in bed and not have to worry about where he's going to get the money for the medicine, the doctor, and the food. They give you your medicine on the hour, the doctor comes to see you himself, your food is brought to you, and they're also concerned that you eat all your food. Tell me, where could a person get all this before?"

He never had, said Kiselis. After the measles, whooping cough, and scarlet fever, he hadn't come down with any other diseases and a healthy person has no need of doctors.

"That's not very nice of you," said Klava Ivanovna, wagging a finger. "When something's good, a person should honestly admit that it's good. Anyway, get better quick, there's no reason to stay around here long. And when you come home we'll give you a present—a new outpost. And you can teach the children French there; why shouldn't our children know French too? Your name will go up on the roll of honor, everyone who walks by will read about you."

"Well," said Kiselis, narrowing his eyes in pleasure, "a coffin is small. You only put what's necessary there or there won't be room for yourself."

Before leaving, Klava Ivanovna stopped to see the house surgeon again.

"Doctor, is there any medicine Kiselis needs that's in short supply? Tell me the name of it and I'll write to my son, who lives in Moscow."

The doctor shrugged.

That day Granik finished putting the primer on the outpost. Accompanied by Malaya and Lapidis, Iona Ovseich inspected the walls and all three of them agreed that the paint on walls primed like that would last two hundred years.

After Klava Ivanovna had told Degtyar of her conversation with Kiselis, Iona Ovseich said bitterly: "The past never lets go. The man already has one foot in the grave, you'd think he'd take a good look around and finally see the truth. But no—he keeps thinking of the past, beginning with his childhood, as if that were all life had to offer. Not only that, to listen to him, all the people on earth were happy back then, not just him. Karl Marx and Lenin were constantly reminding us of the inevitable narrowness of the class position of the petit bourgeois, and they were a thousand percent right. It enters a person with his mother's milk and he can never entirely free himself of it."

While Degtyar was reasoning aloud, Lapidis stood by and said nothing. Then, when the time for a response had long since passed, he suddenly said that history could furnish quite a few other examples since the grave-diggers of capitalism had emerged from the ranks of the exploiters and the same was true earlier of feudalism. Henri St. Simon, to take but a single example.

"Engineer Lapidis," said Comrade Degtyar with a smile, "feudalism, which was an exploitative system, was replaced by capitalism, which is also an exploitative system, and so there wasn't much of a difference."

"Not much of one," objected Lapidis, "if looked at through our eyes, but from the point of view of people back then, it was a very big difference, otherwise there would have been no need for a revolution."

"I think we ought to look at everything with our eyes," said Degtyar, narrowing his own, "and anyone who thinks differently is obviously looking at things with eyes different from ours."

"Ovseich," said Lapidis, "I wouldn't trust you as far as I could throw you."

"Talk is cheap," said Madame Malaya, "but you should try to find someone who would dare say aloud that Degtyar is an egotist and cares only about himself."

Lapidis laughed.

Iona Ovseich grinned. "I can see that courage is not your strong suit. Don't criticize me and I won't criticize you. We know that philosophy."

"As the proverb says, you go your way and I'll go mine," said Lapidis with a pious gesture.

At Malaya's suggestion, the old outpost was painted yellow: when a room's bright yellow, it feels like the sun is out even on the cloudiest days. Granik decorated the ceiling in his own style with a young moon flanked by a dirigible and an airplane. The top of the pilot's body stuck out of the plane and he held an open book in his hand.

Klava Ivanovna said she had never seen anything more beautiful and was now entirely in favor of giving Granik first prize. Degtyar shared that opinion and promised to find the wherewithal for two first prizes, one for Efim and one for Stepa, whose percentages were almost twice those of everyone else.

At the end of July, Anya Kotlyar gave notice that she and Joseph would be spending the month of August in Nikolaev. Klava Ivanovna said that it was all right for Joseph to go, he was as much use there as a three-legged goat, and Anya could join him when work on the outpost was done.

"What do you mean?" asked Anya in surprise. "What if the

outpost isn't finished by the thirtieth, which is when his vacation ends?"

"That means," said Madame Malaya, "that this year he'll go to Nikolaev and you won't."

Anya said that she absolutely had to go: the children were there and their grandmother was old, she couldn't deal with everything all by herself.

"Kotlyar," said Madame Malaya, clapping her hands, "you astonish me! They spent the whole year there without their mother or their father, and their grandmother was able to deal with them. But now, when your husband has his vacation, all of a sudden the old woman can't deal with them anymore. Do you think you're the only one with a brain and everyone else is a fool?"

Anya swore by the health of her children that was not what she thought but it was her husband's vacation, and he got one vacation a year, that had to be taken into account.

"Yes, one vacation a year," said Madame Malaya, "but we only build an outpost for our children once in twenty years. Or are you prepared to take a free ride from the Soviet system?"

God forbid, said Anya, clutching her temples, might she be struck dead if she wanted a free ride from the Soviet system, but on the other hand . . .

"There you go again!" said Klava Ivanovna angrily. "If you don't want other people doing your work for you . . ."

"Madame Malaya," said Anya, her hand on her heart, "this isn't a job, this is a social obligation."

"What!" said Madame Malaya, dumbfounded. "Get out of here! Get out of here right now. I didn't hear what you just said, and let that be the end of it."

The next morning, before work, Anya and Joseph went to see Degtyar. Joseph wanted to explain the situation but Iona Ovseich said that wasn't necessary, he was up on it. Malaya was one hundred percent right, there could be no other decision. And if the decision didn't suit them, an activists' meeting could be called, the community could decide.

"The activists!" said Joseph. "What are they without you? What you say goes."

"No," said Iona Ovseich, "the masses are not there for Degtyar, he is there for the masses, let there be no mistake about that!"

"Ovseich," said Joseph, taking a stand, "wait a minute—"

Degtyar said there'd be no waiting: he would give his order at once, the activists would assemble, and they could resolve the issue.

Joseph Kotlyar and Degtyar were drinking tea on the balcony that evening, when the sun was setting behind the bell tower of the Uspensky Cathedral. Joseph supported Degtyar entirely, "Women are like horses: before obeying the whip, they first have to mark time a little."

Iona Ovseich poured his tea into his saucer, blew carefully on it to keep it from splashing over the edge, then took a sip. After another sip, he remarked to Joseph how difficult it was to arrive at a correct decision even in trifling matters. And why was that so? It was so because everyone took his own parochial view in the belief that it was superior. "They say that a person can't jump higher than his own head. But that's not right. A real person should be able to do so."

"Ovseich," said Kotlyar with a loud sigh, "not everyone can do that. And everyone shouldn't be required to."

"Not everyone can," agreed Degtyar, "but everyone is required to keep the goal in view. Otherwise, he'll never get out of the swamp of middle-classness until it's up to his neck."

After her husband had left for Nikolaev, Anya was free of all domestic duties and devoted all day to working on the outpost. Now Madame Malaya could not praise her enough and held her up as an example for everyone else. When she had to be away at the District Soviet Council for a few hours' work on the election campaign, Klava Ivanovna was able to entrust the outpost to Anya with an easy mind. In front of everyone the engineer Lapidis said twice that Anya Kotlyar was a born leader and was capable of managing the giant blast furnace operation at Magnitogorsk. "All she needs is a diploma from an institute."

Anya was somewhat offended by Lapidis' remark because at her age a diploma was something she could only dream of, but all the same those words did give her pleasure—the truest things are said in jest.

Lapidis came to the construction site every day in August. Dina Vargaftik was the first to notice this and explained it by saying that Lapidis had decided to follow Anya Kotlyar's example. Anya was as tanned from working in the open air as if she had been at the beach; her arms and legs were the color of peaches and looked good enough to eat.

"Dina," said Anya Kotlyar indignantly, "the way you talk about me, someone might think I was as beautiful as Lyubov Orlova!"

"If I were a man," replied Dina, "Lapidis, for example, I'd rank you above her, and if anyone was envious, let them eat dog shit."

"Feh!" said Anya with a laugh. "You should be ashamed of yourself!"

Other people laughed too, but Dina grimaced as if she had a toothache.

Someone began playing the piano in Lapidis' apartment on the second floor. The sound was so strong that the piano seemed close by. Dina said that Adya, Lapidis' son, was a prodigy and would be world famous one day. She just felt bad for his mother: every year she would spend up to three months at Slobodka and return home quiet as a candle. It wasn't easy on Lapidis either, and you had to wonder where he found the strength to joke and laugh. You had to respect a man like that.

Anya Kotlyar suddenly felt the blood rush to her head and she became faint.

"What's the matter?" asked Vargaftik. "You're still too young for menopause."

Adya Lapidis was playing a Chopin waltz, but not as loudly as he had at first, and the more softly he played, the greater their fear that something strange was about to happen.

Anya burst into tears and, though no one asked, she explained that she had no idea what those stupid tears were about, but she felt hurt and unhappy.

Olya Cheperukha said that it sometimes happened to her too: it was as if someone you loved had died. "It's nothing, it comes and it goes. Crying makes it better."

Stepa Khomitsky had finished plastering the new outpost and had also added a sink not called for by the plan so that the children could have somewhere to wash their hands. Comrade Degtyar said that such spontaneous contributions could only be welcomed and made particular mention of the fact that an ordinary worker, if given scope for initiative, could improve on any engineer. Because of their psychology, engineers clung to outmoded technical norms and barred the way to the new. But a worker, the most revolutionary force of all, had an inborn class hatred for all stagnation. That was the source of the Stakhanovite movement, and that was also the source of our Stakhanovs, Busygins, and Vinogradovs, who had fully mastered the tools of their trade and surged ahead.

Lapidis too approved of the plumber's initiative but at the same time expressed surprise at Degtyar's luck.

"What do you mean by that?" asked Iona Ovseich. "Speak plainly, without all those fancy turns of phrase."

"What fancy turns of phrase?" said Lapidis, raising his tone of voice. "Yes, engineers are reactionaries. A group of specialists from the Ministry of Railroads, the NKPS, had to be given a little punch in the teeth and sent packing, but didn't you ever run into any conservative workers at your shoe and sandal factory?"

Iona Ovseich recoiled as if about to be struck. "Yes, I have. I have run into workers who are—if I may call things by their proper names—hangers-on and stooges to those specialists and intellectuals from the various ministries who strive to sling mud at our working class."

"Lapidis," said Klava Ivanovna, taking him by the sleeve, "for God's sake, get out of here before I lose my temper entirely."

"Malaya," said Iona Ovseich, stopping her, "you shouldn't be kicking him out. He's just quoting Comrade Stalin on the specialists from the NKPS."

Four Primus stoves were set up to make the walls dry faster. Anya Kotlyar kept an eye on the stoves, adding kerosene every two hours. Kerosene was in short supply in the city and Degtyar had obtained an entire canister, twenty liters, from his factory.

Granik had selected a light blue for the ceiling of the outpost because that was the color of the sky. And the sky was—the air force, aviation. The words from one of the Pioneers' favorite songs had been written in large red letters along the top of the wall: WE WERE BORN TO MAKE DREAMS COME TRUE! Everyone knew the song by heart and it was enough to read the first line of it for the rest of the stanza to come to mind all by itself, with its words about wide-open spaces and the intelligence which gave us wings for arms and a fiery motor for a heart.

At first the walls had been a pure yellow. Klava Ivanovna was for keeping it that way but Iona Ovseich said that it seemed to need pictures of compasses, pencil boxes, globes. And when Efim had painted a globe and, on either side of it, open pencil boxes, everyone could see that Degtyar had been quite right. In addition, a map of the hemisphere had been hung on the large wall opposite the door and the combination of dark and light blue against the yellow walls lent extra beauty to the room, as if the sea and the sky had come together in the outpost.

"My God!" said Klava Ivanovna, bursting into tears. "It's more than anyone could have dreamed of! It's a palace, it's Count Vorontsov's palace!"

Lapidis said that it was ten times more beautiful than Vorontsov's palace, considering that under the old regime this had been a courtyard laundry room for lowlifes and right beside it a bathroom that was still serving the courtyard to this day.

Lapidis had not yet reached the end of his thought when Dina Vargaftik came running in demanding that everyone come at once to see the poem those two little bastards, Zyunchik and Kolya, had written in the bathroom and, as for the drawing they'd done beside it, it was too terrible for words.

Madame Malaya automatically read the poem aloud:

"This was an office for the tsar
And a bedroom for his wife,
A lunchroom for his ministers,
But it's where the workers shit."

Lapidis said that it was a good poem for where it was but since there was a Pioneer outpost next door, and not the baths at Pompeii, the drawing should be erased.

"Malaya," said Degtyar, stamping his foot, "I want Khomitsky and Cheperukha to come here at once so they can admire this along with the rest of us!"

Instead of obeying the order, Madame Malaya burst into giggles and was completely unable to restrain herself. Lapidis picked up a brick and scraped off the drawing, first the man, then the woman, but he left the poem.

"Enough of your jokes!" shouted Degtyar. "Since you've started, finish!"

"Here," said Lapidis, handing Degtyar the brick. "You do a little work."

Klava Ivanovna seized the brick and gave the poem a thorough rubbing until all that was left was an orange stain and a few of the letters showing through. Then Degtyar took the brick and finished the job and there were no traces left.

When the two of them were alone, Degtyar said to Malaya that children will be children, but the grown-ups were the ones in charge, and it was time to think a little about Lapidis.

Klava Ivanovna shrugged her shoulders. "What's there to think about? The man is a big mouth, he's got a loose tongue. On the other hand, you can understand: half the time his wife is home, half the time she is at Slobodka. Lapidis has to take care of his son, do the cooking and cleaning, and, on top of that, he puts in a full day's work. So sometimes he feels like making a joke, saying what he thinks."

"Be quiet!" ordered Degtyar. "You're talking nonsense and you know it!"

Later that evening Madame Malaya dropped by to see Lapidis in order to warn him: "Keep it up if you want your son to be an orphan." Lapidis jumped to his feet like a madman and said they could all go straight to hell. Then he regained his self-control and apologized, but he still looked angry. Klava Ivanovna bent toward Adya and stroked him; the child was sleeping soundly. She left without saying good-bye.

Two people, Stepa Khomitsky and Efim Granik, had finished first in the socialist competition for the building of the outpost. Iona Ovseich had managed to acquire a second cotton suit and so the fact of two winners presented no problem. Second prize was awarded to Anya Kotlyar—a pair of men's canvas shoes and a box of "Carmen" face powder. The powder had been added because it had been thought a man would take the prize but things had taken a different turn.

Anya was congratulated even more heartily than Granik or Khomitsky, and people quoted Lenin, who said that once women were freed from domestic slavery they would catch up to men in no time. Anya herself shared that opinion: if she could have had another couple of weeks, she could have taken first place but it had turned out very nicely all the same: when Joseph, whose legs pained him visibly in the summer, came back and found out that she had won a pair of leather-soled shoes that were just his size, he wouldn't regret that his wife had spent the whole month of August in Odessa and not accompanied him. On her last day off there had been shoes like that for sale on Deribasovskaya Street. Anya had stood in line for them for five hours, but speculators and dealers had slipped in from every side and she had gone away empty-handed. Now she had been given those shoes free, all she had to do was sign her name. The prizes would be presented tomorrow but, since the drugstore was open till midnight today, she was going to go there at once to buy five cans of tooth powder so that the shoes would always be white as snow and so that later on she wouldn't have to go running all over Odessa like a madwoman for tooth powder.

Third prize—rubber-soled women's shoes with a leather instep and cork heels—was won by Dina Vargaftik. The shoes were two sizes too big for her but there was a simple solution to the problem—place a few wads of cotton batting in the toe and more could be added when the wad became too compressed. But, in the presence of everyone, Iona Ovseich gave his word that he would exchange the shoes at the factory—no easy task. Madame Malaya said there was nothing so terrible about Dina wearing shoes two sizes too big and that he shouldn't go to all the trouble. Iona Ovseich raised both his hands, palms forward, but that did not mean he was surrendering; on the contrary, he was demanding that discussion on the subject be closed, a decision had been made and had to be put into effect.

The opening of the outpost and the awarding of the prizes was scheduled for August 30, that is, one day ahead of schedule. The walls had dried well, only one was still a little sticky. Efim explained that the siccative made it sticky but that the siccative was necessary to make the walls dry quicker. "Just to be on the safe side," said Malaya, "we'll post a sign not to touch it." No, Degtyar refused categorically, no signs: let Granik touch up those spots. People should not have to worry, people should feel free, that's what a celebration was all about.

The children from Pokrovsky Lane were invited to the opening. For years in the past relations with Pokrovsky Lane had been bad; once every six months war would be declared on Pokrovsky Lane if

Pokrovsky Lane didn't declare war first. And war was war—meaning sticks, stones, and blood. An ambulance would take the wounded to the hospital from which they would return on crutches, with casts, or minus an eye. And sometimes they never returned.

But today the children from Pokrovsky Lane were all dressed up, wearing white T-shirts and their Pioneer scarves and clasps. The grown-ups patted them on the head, asked them who their parents were, and how the water was at the beach, sighing sympathetically because school would begin again in another few days.

Klava Ivanovna had ordered Lapidis' piano brought down for the opening. Adya would play. Lapidis had no objection, but moving the piano proved a headache: first it got stuck in the apartment door and then the door to the outpost turned out to be too narrow and neither brain nor brawn could solve that problem.

The piano was left out in the courtyard. Lapidis demanded that it be brought back to his apartment immediately. It was a Becker and money couldn't buy a replacement for it now, but Madame Malaya replied that he could curse to his heart's content but there were more important things that needed doing at the moment than bringing Lapidis' piano back.

It was much easier carrying down Dr. Landa's upright, even though it had to go down three flights. Gizella, Dr. Landa's wife, kept dashing from side to side imploring the men carrying it to keep it away from the iron banister. The movers found it easy going and twice, once on the third and again on the second, they had joked that the weight was too much for them and the piano would drop any second. Both times Gizella covered her face with her hands and a second later laughed along with everyone else, then again begged them to keep it way from the railing, otherwise she'd have a heart attack and they'd be responsible. Granik said that hearts didn't matter, everyone had a heart but not everyone had a piano.

"Efim," said Gizella, "a person can live without a piano but just you try it without a heart."

"Madame Landa," said Cheperukha, "don't mislead us or else when you cry for help people will think your heart is in the piano."

Cheperukha stumbled, followed by Stepa and Efim, one pedal clanking loudly.

"Slobs!" said Gizella in despair. "They're wrecking my beautiful instrument on purpose!"

Cheperukha was the first to regain his balance; he readjusted the strap, waiting to give the others a chance to do the same, then said:

"Madame, I don't like your tone of voice. I could smash your beautiful instrument and no specialist in venereal diseases could be of any help."

"Cheperukha," said Gizella indignantly, "you're giving my words a whole other meaning!"

"She gave them one meaning," said Cheperukha with a laugh, "and we gave them a whole other one. Madame, in our day, we've seen many people who wanted to let the cock do all the work."

Gizella stuck her fingers in her ears and turned away.

The upright passed easily through the door of the outpost but, once inside, the question arose of where to place it—in the new room or the old.

Degtyar said there was no reason to create artificial problems—wherever they put it was fine.

"You're a genius, Ovseich!" cried Cheperukha. "On my next day off I'll drive you all the way to Duke Richeleaux and all Odessa will envy me my luck."

"In my opinion," said Degtyar, "you could be envied today. I'd bet you've already had a minimum of a pint, I'd stake my life on it."

"Ovseich, you're a real man!" said Iona with great delight. "You didn't tell me to can it. You took me at my word, because everyone should have one day in his life where people take him on his word from morning till night. Ovseich, let me give you a kiss!"

Before Degtyar was able to respond, Cheperukha had grabbed Iona Ovseich's head, pulled it toward himself, and kissed the top with a loud smack. Madame Malaya said kisses like that could cause a concussion and Iona grabbed her by the shoulders and kissed both her cheeks.

"You drunk," said Madame Malaya with tender indignation, "you poor boozer."

Dina Vargaftik and Tosya Khomitsky were on the first and second floor in charge of rounding up tables and chairs. Accompanied by Zyunchik and Kolka, Anya Kotlyar went from one apartment to the next looking for platters large enough to hold the *piroshki,* grapes, and watermelons for the children. The watermelons had to be sliced beforehand to avoid having to give the children knives. Madame Landa brought jam dishes. She said that she would have brought teaspoons too but, as bad luck would have it, she only had silver ones and strangers would be coming to the opening, they could be anybody.

"Shut your mouth, my fine lady," said Madame Malaya. "To listen to you, there's nothing but thieves around here."

Iona Ovseich said that it was time to stop haggling and for the guests to be seated at the table. He ordered Adya Lapidis to play a flourish. Those who were already seated rose and those who were standing stood at attention, their faces becoming stony. When the music was over, Iona Ovseich said that people did not have to rise for a flourish; only for the "Internationale" was it obligatory to rise.

"And now," said Comrade Degtyar, "on behalf of the builders of the outpost and on behalf of the activists and the entire courtyard, I would like to extend the warmest welcome to the representatives of the District Party Committee, the District Committee Komsomol, Osoviakhim and MOPR, and to all our guests as well!"

Adya was signaled to play another flourish and, despite the explanation, people rose again but this time it was not a mistake, because it was proper to respond to a greeting by standing.

When people had resumed their seats, Degtyar requested permission to pass immediately to the day's agenda and to cite some concrete information on how the activists and the courtyard's residents, along with the rest of the nation, were building socialism.

"We used to say that technology is the solution to everything. But now we say that people are needed, the cadres are needed in order to set technology in motion and extract maximum benefit from it. We didn't import such people, such cadres, from abroad, we didn't invite them here from other cities like Moscow, Kiev, or Kherson, or entice them here from the neighboring streets, we found them right here in our own courtyard and spurred them on. The Trotskyite-Bukharinite scum, those White Guard pygmies, those puny gnats, have forgotten that the Soviet people are the masters of the Soviet Union and that all those Rykovs, Bukharins, Zinovievs, and Kamenevs are no more than temporary government servants who can be thrown from their offices at any moment like useless trash. Those paltry lackeys of fascism have forgotten that all the Soviet people have to do is to lift a finger for all trace of them to vanish. A Soviet court sentenced the Bukharinist-Trotskyite scum to the firing squad and the NKVD has executed the sentence. The Soviet people approved the crushing defeat inflicted on the Bukharinist-Trotskyite gang and have moved on to other matters. While carrying out the construction of the outpost for our children, the activists and the residents of the courtyard were also involved in the election campaign and assumed the obligation of completing construction no later than August 31. It is with pride that today we inform our comrades from the Stalin District Committee that we have fulfilled that obligation and the outpost has been completed!"

Adya Lapidis played a flourish, the comrades from the District Committee and the guests applauded loudly, and the representatives of Osoviakhim and MOPR raised clenched fists in salute.

"From the very outset," the speaker continued, "the construction was marked by socialist competition, arising from the grass roots, even though the people involved were not fully aware of it. The more politically conscious among them, simply, without any ado, tried to work well today, better tomorrow, and even better the day after tomorrow. It is true that at the beginning there were some laggards among us but, later on, in the course of the socialist competition, those who had been behind moved to the forefront, catching up with the others and overtaking them. We all remember the situation with Anya Kotlyar in the initial phase but today she has proven her merit and the building committee has awarded her a second prize."

After a flourish and applause, people began to demand that Anya Kotlyar come forward so that everyone could see her. Anya refused flatly but the people sitting beside her forced her to stand and bow to the masses. Embarrassment made her more beautiful than ever and people openly admired this young woman, finding it difficult to believe that she had two sons, both of whom were already in a technical school.

Just as Anya sat down, an astonishing, miraculous event occurred: all of a sudden Joseph Kotlyar, her husband, who had been away the entire month, came walking into the outpost and the applause exploded with renewed force. Joseph was at a complete loss as people began shouting: "The prize! the prize!" Submitting to the will of the masses, Degtyar announced, "For her great success in the socialist competition Anya Kotlyar has been awarded a pair of leather-soled shoes and a box of 'Carmen' face powder. In a slight change of schedule, the prize is being awarded to her first, ahead of Stepa Khomitsky and Efim Granik." Anya accepted the prize and, keeping the powder for herself, passed the shoes down the row to Joseph. When the shoes reached him people demanded that he try them on then and there. Joseph Kotlyar put on the shoes and they fit as if they had been made to order. Then he was asked to come forward and stand closer to Degtyar. Instead he took five or six steps between rows, stamping his real foot once and his prothesis once, and there was practically no difference.

"Bravo!" shouted Granik, and the guests picked up the cheer because Iona Ovseich had already explained to everyone who didn't know that Joseph Kotlyar had lost a leg in 1919, when serving in a partisan detachment.

Then Joseph stamped his feet twice again but still you couldn't tell which leg was the real one and which the prothesis, and once again the guests cried: "Bravo!"

The people sitting beside Anya moved aside making room for Joseph. Iona Ovseich waited until Joseph was seated, then said that the awarding of the first prize would now take place. Since two people had won first prize, he announced their names in alphabetical order: Granik, Efim, and Khomitsky, Stepa. Adya played another flourish. Iona Ovseich shook the two winners' hands and ordered Klava Ivanovna to present the winners with their prizes. The red tin seals on the suits were torn off right there before everyone's eyes and the prizewinners tried on their jackets. Iona Cheperukha shouted out that they should try on their pants too and Efim pretended to start unbuttoning his fly. The women gasped and Iona Cheperukha shouted still louder: "Come on, Efim, come on: the women are only pretending, they can't wait to see!"

The jackets fitted Khomitsky and Granik perfectly. Everyone said that soon private tailors would be out of business because the factories were making better clothes than they could and five times cheaper to boot. A father could wear a suit like that for a minimum of three years, then have it altered to fit his son and it would still be in good condition when the time came to throw it out.

While people were speaking, Klava Ivanovna walked over to Khomitsky and opened one side of his jacket to show its lining—it was genuine serge, and not sateen made of rice paper. There were problems finding serge in the stores; for a few yards a person had to stand in line all night waiting for the store to open and so everyone was able to appreciate the high quality of that factory-made suit all the more. Efim and Stepa were told that one of them should be sent at once to the Japanese consulate on Feldman Boulevard and the other to the Italian consulate so the foreigners could see how simple painters and simple plumbers dressed here.

Third prize—the rubber-soled women's shoes with the cork heels—also caused admiration, but what counted most was that Degtyar had kept his promise and had succeeded in obtaining a pair two sizes smaller. In her own words, Dina Vargaftik said the shoes were lighter than air on her feet, as if all her corns and callouses had been removed.

"All right," said Iona Ovseich, "since the prizes have been presented and Stepa and Efim have returned from their diplomatic mission, allow me to give the floor to our children."

The applause and laughter exceeded all bounds and even Iona Ovseich himself laughed and clapped his hands because none of it was for his successful joke but for the children whom Klava Ivanovna and Gizella Landa had lined up beside the piano. Klava Ivanovna raised her right hand but people were unable to quiet down. She gave the command for the children to begin.

Adya Lapidis played the prelude and Zyunchik and Kolka began singing in two-part harmony:

"On the grass in central park
A mignonette grows in a dark flower bed.
You can wear a bright, bright tie
And be a hero of labor in the mines."

Gizella flung up both her hands and a second later the other children joined in:

"Is that true—a mignonette and hero of labor?
How can that be? Explain?
Because everyone is young now
In our beautiful youthful country!"

Klava Ivanovna signaled the audience, who now sang the refrain along with the children:

"Because everyone is young now
In our beautiful youthful country!"

After eight o'clock when it had already started growing dark, the benches were carried from the outpost to make room for the tables. At first Klava Ivanovna was worried that the children would spit watermelon seeds and throw the rinds at each other but her fears were groundless: children knew when some things could be done and when they could not.

Then everyone went out into the courtyard. Two boys from Pokrovsky Lane played a Caucasian dance song on the mandolin and balalaika while a girl wearing her Pioneer scarf danced.

"What children we've got!" said Klava Ivanovna, weeping openly, "what children we've got!"

The celebration lasted until midnight. Iona Ovseich said that was long enough, tomorrow was a workday, and the children had only one day left before school started. Before leaving, he reminded Klava Ivanovna to begin drawing up a list of the building's residents for the elections.

"Now we have our own outpost and a place where we can work with people."

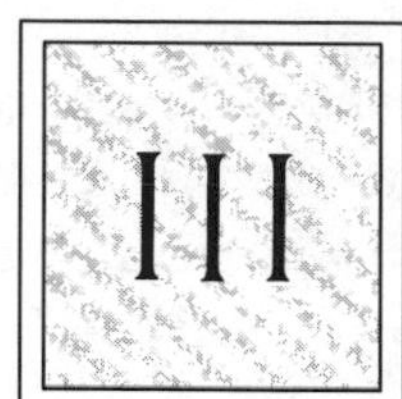

Old man Kiselis' condition grew worse with each passing day but he didn't complain. On the contrary, he argued that a person couldn't feel good his whole life: there had to come a time when he felt worse than he had ever felt before and it was then that a person started wanting to die. Klava Ivanovna told Kiselis to put those stupid thoughts out of his mind and that he'd yet lay flowers on her grave. Then Klava Ivanovna sighed bitterly, saying she could see right through Kiselis—he'd rather take a young girl to the movies than bring flowers to an old woman's grave.

No, objected Kiselis, this time Madame Malaya was mistaken: it would be easier for him to put flowers on her grave if she was buried at the international cemetery where Jews and *goyim* lay side by side—she'd be right near him.

"All right," said Klava Ivanovna, adopting a more serious tone, "enough talk about the next world, we should talk about this one now. Is there anything I can bring you?"

Kiselis shrugged his shoulders: he didn't need anything, he had everything.

"Listen, Kiselis," said Madame Malaya, "don't be so gallant with me and give me a straight answer. What do you need, and we'll get it for you."

Kiselis shrugged his shoulders again: he didn't need anything, he had everything.

"All right," yielded Klava Ivanovna, "then we'll figure out what you need. But get rid of those stupid ideas. The living should think about life, let the dead think about death, they've got plenty of spare time. Yesterday the Central Executive Committee issued a resolution that elections are to be held on the twelfth of December. That's just two months away, so don't dawdle here too long. The government has given you the right to vote and we want you to tell the young people what life was like under the old regime. Did you have the right to vote for elections to the Municipal Duma?"

"No," said Kiselis, shaking his head. "I did not have that right. By and large I took no part in political life."

"Oh!" exclaimed Malaya, "you were a store owner, a businessman, and you didn't have that right! The young people need to hear that otherwise some of them will think that everything they have hasn't been given to them but has just fallen from the sky."

"In July 1914," said Kiselis with a smile, "I was supposed to receive a consignment of Lyons braid through Colonel Kotlyarevsky. Now braid is only popular for the tassels and fringe on flags but back then it was used on aiguilettes, gold braid, galloon . . ."

Kiselis raised his eyebrows, his eyes grew round and happy as if he had had a drink of cherry brandy and vodka. Then he suddenly hiccuped, opened his mouth, and emitted a long crackling sound that was not unlike a snore. His eyes stopped moving and became glassy.

Klava Ivanovna ran for a doctor to give Kiselis an injection but when the doctor picked up Kiselis' hand he said that no injection was needed. Klava Ivanovna sat down on a stool, stroked Kiselis' hair, kissed his forehead, then suddenly burst into tears. She tried to hold them back, blocking her mouth and scratching her cheeks with her fingernails but the pain did not help.

A nurse brought a sheet and the doctor himself placed it over the dead man and ordered everyone to leave the room. Klava Ivanovna felt weak in the knees. She stopped by the door, walked back to the bed, lifted the sheet, stroked Kiselis' cheeks, and kissed him on the lips.

"He was all alone in the world," she moaned, "he had no one. He was all alone in the world."

Kiselis was brought home the next day. He had had a large, sunny room, about ten square meters in size: when the coffin was set in the center of the room and chairs placed on both sides, the room seemed smaller but, as Dina Vargaftik remarked, for one person to have a room like that was something many people could only dream of.

"Dina," said Madame Malaya, shaking her head, "that's ugly—in the home of the deceased."

Kolka, Zyunchik, and Osya were assigned by Klava Ivanovna to go from floor to floor and inform people that the coffin would be carried out at three o'clock. The boys kicked at the doors and hollered so the people inside could hear. But they shushed the boys and in muffled voices demanded decent behavior from them, at least on a day like that.

The children were not allowed to go up to the coffin right away: there'd be plenty of time for that. The boys stood in the hallway until Kolka brought three candles and then, candles in hand, they walked to the head of the coffin.

Old man Kiselis looked alive. His face was peaceful and calm, not at all like it had been before when they used to shout out to him, "You've got the right to vote back!" He'd brandish his umbrella at them and now it seemed impossible that they used to run away from him.

"He's come and gone and it's like he never existed," whispered Anya Kotlyar. "And while he was alive it seemed like he'd live forever."

Osya cried and so did Zyunchik and Kolka. They kept looking at Kiselis and trying not to see him at the same time.

At three o'clock he was carried out into the courtyard and the coffin was placed on chairs and covered with sackcloth. People waited in silence until Iona Ovseich arrived.

"Comrades," he said, "today we accompany on his final journey an elderly resident of our building who knew this spot before the stones we're standing on were here, before the roof we live under was here, when there was nothing but bare earth here. For the greater part of his life Abram Kiselis lived under tsarism, and today we will not recall that everything about the deceased's life was not to our liking. The Soviet system took no vengeance on him; on the contrary, it gave him a sunny room and a job in a haberdashery, which was his line of work, a store which at one time had been his own property, in other words, when he had been a member of the exploiter class. But a year ago, the Soviet system restored all his civil rights to him so that there was no difference between him and all other working people. He was all alone in his old age: his only brother, Lazar, fled the country to

America in 1919. But that did not matter to anyone, on the contrary, Comrade Malaya visited him right up to the end and he died in her arms. He was not a forgotten man, he was aware that people cared for him, and he was ready to respond to that concern but death prevented him. When he had literally only seconds left to live, this former businessman recalled with bitterness that he had not had the right to vote for elections to the Municipal Duma. In the instant before death a person understands more than he does during his entire life. Farewell, good neighbor. Farewell, Kiselis."

Klava Ivanovna smoothed out the black covering decorated with a silver six-pointed star, the men lifted the coffin to their shoulders and set off toward the gateway where a small black cart was waiting. It had black wheels, was drawn by black horses, and its low sides would keep the coffin from sliding.

The procession set off down Karl Marx Street for the cemetery. When crossing Lieutenant Schmidt Avenue, they encountered a company of Red Army soldiers. The company was headed for the garrison bathhouse, formerly known as the Isakovich, and the soldiers were singing about hot cabbage soup but they stopped upon seeing the funeral. Then the only sound was the soldier's heavy boots on the cobblestones.

"God let there never be another war," whispered Anya Kotlyar.

Dina shook her head and said—if it only depended on the U.S.S.R. After looking around her, she bent close to Anya and added: "By the way, Isakovich, who was a Karaite, owned more than a bath house. They say he also had three or four bordellos, one on Red Lane. The whole block was nothing but bordellos, the entrance was right from Deribasovskaya Street."

"That's horrible!" Anya covered her mouth with her hands. "Right next to Deribasovskaya and people weren't ashamed to go there!"

"And how about our Madame Orlov," said Dina with a shrug.

"Stop!" said Anya indignantly. "I don't believe it."

"Oh, you don't believe it," said Dina, nudging Anya in the side. "Who gives a damn if you do or you don't. Red Lane was called Red Lane before the Revolution too—there was a red light next to every gateway."

The space for Kiselis was in the left corner of the cemetery; to the right of it was the monument to the writer Mendele Moikher-Sforim of the Odessa Province Executive Commitee; a mass grave for the victims of the anti-Jewish pogrom of 1905 was about six hundred feet from the wall.

They carried the coffin along the main path past the graves of many rabbis and the grave of Kangun, the twenty-year-old commander of the Red Guard.

They bade Kiselis farewell in silence, a heavy sadness in their souls. On the way back Cheperukha stopped by the Odessa Agricultural Institute wine cellar. Then he spent the entire evening in the outpost arguing that Kiselis was to be envied—he'd been able to smile up to the last moment and to converse with Madame Malaya. Not only that, he'd been given a good spot in the cemetery and didn't have relatives wailing over his grave. His brother Lazar, who they say opened his own haberdashery in New York, would now have one less heir. What else was there to say, other people, himself for example, could only dream of a death like that.

"Bite your tongue," said Klava Ivanovna angrily. "Better think about your own son and your wife, you poor *shikker.* We'll take measures if you don't get hold of yourself."

"Malaya," said Cheperukha, bursting into drunken tears, "don't shout at me or else I'll get scared and start hiccuping like a child. I want to offer you a bribe: get in my wheelbarrow and we'll go for a ride down the Potemkin stairs. All Odessa will come running to see us, we'll be the envy of the city."

On Friday, before the first stars of the Sabbath were out, Sonya Granik was on her way to the synagogue with Osya and Khilka to make an offering in memory of the deceased. At the large double cast-iron gate, Oska suddenly tore free and ran home. Later on, back in their apartment, there was an unpleasant conversation, complete with shouting and tears, that could be heard in the hallway. Efim took his son's side because these days it was hard to look people in the eye when your own wife spent her time with rabbis and ignorant Jews from Gaisin. You tried to make her see what was plain as day but she was like a brick wall.

Klava Ivanovna praised Oska and said that now she could see that she was dealing with a person who kept his Pioneer word of honor and did not treat it lightly. She promised to enroll Oska in the percussion band where he'd play the triangle and, if they found that he had a good ear, he'd be given a balalaika or a mandolin.

"One with a pick?" asked Oska.

"No, you can manage without one," Klava Ivanovna answered.

The next morning Oska cut up Khilka's celluloid doll and made himself ten fine picks for the mandolin. He flushed what was left over down the toilet, the most reliable method—the sewer emptied far away in the sea, no one even knew just where.

Khilka cried all day. Her mother ran around looking for the missing doll and Oska did everything he could too but the doll did not turn up. Sonya said to her husband that it was as if the doll had fallen into the ocean. For a moment Oska was frightened but then his fear passed and he had a strong and sudden desire for some bread and butter with jam on top. That made his mother happy because the child had not asked for food for quite a while.

"The Chinese," said Efim, "eat a bowl of rice a day and the Koreans eat soybeans. They never see any bread there."

"The poor children," sighed Sonya. "But doesn't the International Alliance of Supporting Workers send them anything?"

"IASW can't help everyone, it doesn't have its own bank," said Efim, becoming angry with his wife. "IASW aids striking mine workers."

"But don't other people have to eat too?" said Sonya, sticking to her guns.

"What an idiotic argument!" said Efim, becoming even angrier. "When you can't feed everybody, the first people you should feed are those who are on the barricades fighting—and not for themselves alone but for the whole working class, the whole world proletariat."

The man from the Revenue Department came to see Madame Malaya again on the thirtieth, the eve of the new month. He said they had information that Efim Granik was concealing a portion of his taxable commissions.

"Comrade," asked Klava Ivanovna, "do you have a horse?"

"What do I need a horse for?" he replied in surprise.

"I'll tell you why. A horse has a large head so go and turn the horse's head, not mine. Let's go to Granik's together. I'll open his wardrobe, his bureau, and all the sacks where he keeps his suede shoes."

"My good woman," said the revenue agent in a tone of offense, "I wasn't born yesterday and there's no reason to make me out more of a fool than I am. You have your work and I have mine. Today you're obliged to help me and not the other way around. So let's not argue, shall we?"

"Listen," said Klava Ivanovna, "I'll tell you again in plain Russian—you're barking up the wrong tree."

"You're sticking out your neck for him?"

Klava Ivanovna answered that, yes, she was. Then the revenue agent told her in confidence that his office had received a letter from someone in their courtyard. He didn't have the right to tell her from whom—that was an official secret.

"And you're going to trust some lousy informer more than me!" said Klava Ivanovna in astonishment. "Any more of that and I won't even let you in my door. Go."

The revenue agent did not say good-bye and slammed the door behind him but, before he left, he did say that she, Malaya, needed a good looking into as well, to see if she wasn't recruiting customers for Granik. For a percentage.

"You fool!" Klava Ivanovna shouted after him. "You're the biggest fool in all Odessa."

The revenue agent caused Klava Ivanovna and Degtyar a harsh exchange of words. Degtyar made a firm promise that the Revenue Department would be kept informed as to Granik's actions. He told Malaya that she, as a representative of the troika, should also remember her position and give priority to her obligations to the Soviet system and not to her own arrogance. That did not mean that in the specific case at hand, Malaya had been a fool, although there were still plenty of fools around, but no one had given her the right to forget that the agent had been performing a task entrusted to him by the state. "If you don't like the way he does his job," said Degtyar, "inform the proper people. But you must not take matters into your own hands: the Soviet system is powerful enough to rap any knuckles that need rapping."

Klava Ivanovna replied that she was not going to attempt to justify herself but asked Degtyar to imagine for a moment that he was at a train station and saw the last train leave with his own eyes and, an hour later, when the train had already reached Razdelnaya, some fool with a ticket in his hand started pestering him, saying maybe Degtyar only thought he had seen it leave, maybe it was leaving an hour later today?

Iona Ovseich admitted that this was a good analogy but still did not yield his own position: all parallels, historical and otherwise, were equally dangerous—at first they seemed to make things clear but in fact they only obscured the facts and distracted the attention. Klava Ivanovna opened her mouth, clearly about to raise an objection, but Iona Ovseich said that was enough idle talk and he moved on to the next issue—the list of voters.

Compiling the lists had uncovered complications that had been difficult to foresee: names didn't match up, some Jews had changed their names to make them sound Russian, dates of birth were incorrect. In some cases the priest hadn't noted the date, in others it had been added later on, and in still other instances, people, especially women, had made up their dates of birth.

"Why would they do that?" asked Degtyar in surprise.

"What do you mean? The voter lists will be displayed under glass and be visible from the street. Some women will be ashamed if everyone knows their true age."

"That's true," said Iona Ovseich, rubbing his hands and twisting his fingers together. "There's something everyone dislikes about his life, everyone would like to change a little something, erase a little something."

"That's not surprising," said Klava Ivanovna. "People had masters over them their whole lives who did as they pleased without once asking the workers."

"Malaya," said Iona Ovseich, closing his eyes, "sometimes you've got a real mess in your head. I ask you about Ivan and you answer me about Pyotr."

"All right," sighed Klava Ivanovna, "Ivan, Stepa, Pyotr, but we started with Granik and got lost along the way."

"Malaya," said Iona Ovseich, opening his eyes and closing them again, clearly a tired man, "they need a specialist in the art studio on Greek Street. I put a call in there."

"Ovseich," Klava Ivanovna exclaimed, "I was just about to ask you to do it and it's already done! I'll go get Efim and you can have a little talk with him."

"No," said Degtyar, "don't. Better he goes right to the studio tomorrow morning. If he has time to think about it, he'll start waiting for something else to turn up. He's been a cottage worker since his youth and he's used to that, not to a collective. We should be done with this throwback. At any cost. He should come by the outpost in the evening, I'll be there. Dr. Landa and Lapidis should be there too."

The next day reconfirmed Degtyar's insight into Granik: Efim went to the studio and couldn't say anything bad about it. On the contrary, he had only good words for it but still he asked for some time to think it over so it would not be an offhand decision.

"Efim Lazarevich," said Degtyar politely, "you've been thinking for a year and a half now and nothing has come of it. What basis do you have for thinking the next year and a year will produce any different results?"

"What basis do I have?" said Efim pensively; "I'll tell you: life doesn't stand still, there are changes every day."

Now it was Degtyar's turn to become pensive. Klava Ivanovna was on pins and needles; then all of a sudden she could no longer restrain herself and said: "Efim, stop with your idiotic jokes, take the job, so you'll be employed like everyone else!"

"Wait a minute," interrupted Degtyar. "Let him answer this question first: was it only today that life stopped standing still or was that also true a year and a half ago?"

"Uh-uh," said Granik, wagging a finger. "Degtyar's trying to catch me out but what I'm saying is that yesterday and tomorrow are two different things, you can't compare them."

Degtyar pounded the table, "No, you have to compare them and we will. If a person doesn't give a damn about the elections to the Supreme Soviet and wants to live today the way he lived yesterday and yesterday he wanted to live like he did the day before, and who the hell knows where it all will end, that person should think very hard before he says anything aloud. Acts and deeds begin with words, that we've seen a thousand times, and we're immune to it."

"Good for you," said Efim, "but I don't want anyone telling me how I should live. The Stalin Constitution gives me the right to live and work where I want, and I spit on that studio."

"Efim," said Madame Malaya, "I can see that talking nicely with you gets us nowhere. If your father were alive, I'd advise him—Lazar, get out a long stick and tell your son to point his behind at the sky."

"My father did have a long stick," said Efim with a laugh, "and it haunts me to this day."

"He understands life," said Degtyar, in exasperation, "but pretends that he doesn't see a thing!"

"You're right, Ovseich," said Madame Malaya. "He sees everything ten times better than we do. Let's wait till tomorrow."

Dr. Landa arrived, followed by Lapidis. Iona Ovseich gave Granik permission to leave and added a final note, saying that starting tomorrow his life should make a hundred-and-eighty-degree turn. Though no one had asked for his opinion, Lapidis announced with a laugh that to make a hundred-and-eighty-degree turn, you had to turn your butt so it was facing you.

"Why have I called you here?" said Iona Ovseich to Landa and Lapidis. "I've called you here to say a few words about the campaign post. The election campaign has extended all across the country from one end to the other but we haven't seen or heard anything from you."

"It depends where you mean," interrupted Lapidis. "Where I work, at the Marti factory, I was given my work load quite a while ago."

"Let's say that's so," said Iona Ovseich, "but that's there, at the factory. What about here?"

"What absurd sophistry!" said Lapidis, waving both arms. "Here, there, what's the difference, it's all the U.S.S.R.!"

"That's true," agreed Iona Ovseich, "but people are different and now everyone in the courtyard is saying that you couldn't find Lapidis and Landa at the campaign post with a flashlight in the daytime."

Lapidis waved his arms again: what did he care about all those big mouths and gossips!

"Lapidis," said Iona Ovseich softly, "why is there always something out of joint with you? You and I have been neighbors for many years. You work and I work, you have a wife and I have a wife, you have a son and I had two children, but that's a different story. Why is it so hard to come to any understanding with you? If I was the only one, you could say that Degtyar has a rotten personality. But you want your own way with everyone, you want to follow your own line—the Lapidis line."

"Listen, Ovseich," said Lapidis, blanching with anger, "I'm no Efim Granik. So let's just forget these little talks, all right? I've got plenty of gray matter and can loan you some, if you need it. But let's just forget these little talks!"

"Comrade Lapidis," said Dr. Landa with a laugh, "I swear, you're as touchy as a rooster. We all play the psychologist a little but not everyone speaks openly and out loud. Iona Ovseich speaks openly, right to your face. I don't want to play any games: yes, it's true, we're not at the campaign post very often."

"You!" said Lapidis, jumping up. "How do you know about me if you're not there often yourself!"

"My wife is in charge of the children's choir at the outpost and she sees who comes to the campaign post and who doesn't."

"To make a long story short," said Iona Ovseich, summing up, "I'm not trying to catch you at anything, Lapidis, but it should be clear to you now that you can't fool everyone, people have eyes and they use them. Now to the matter at hand. Tomorrow we have to begin consultations for the voters at the outpost so that people can be given advice by specialists. Dr. Landa will consult in his field, and Engineer Lapidis in his. My wife will be returning from the hospital in a short while—she'll work with the children who are behind in their math. We're not going to assign you any fixed hours: give it some careful thought and choose them yourselves, but afterward they can't be changed."

The room became still for a moment. Klava Ivanovna looked over at Lapidis and Landa, then her lips grimaced bitterly as she recalled old man Kiselis:

"He was a hair's breadth from death when he remembered with bitterness that he lived his whole life outside of politics. A businessman and the owner of his own haberdashery, and he hadn't had the right to vote for elections to the Municipal Duma! And just what was the Municipal Duma, what power did it have? To count how many pails of water the Cossacks' horses drank and figure out how much to fine somebody for spreading his lice in the public baths. Bah!"

"Madame Malaya," said Lapidis with a smile, "if you were thirty years younger, not even thirty, say, twenty-five, I would stand under your balcony with a guitar all night long."

"Lapidis," replied Klava Ivanovna, "now I can see how lucky I am."

They all laughed, Lapidis included. When they were done laughing, Iona Ovseich pointed out that there was only one simple announcement on one of the outpost's four walls: Elections to the Supreme Soviet—December 12!

Klava Ivanovna looked around in surprise and promised that in a few days there would be no cause for complaint.

"And I would also request," added Iona Ovseich, "that no later than the day after tomorrow, there be signs for the voters informing them at what hours Landa, Lapidis, and Degtyar will be available for consultation. I'll fix my hours later on, to make things more convenient for Landa and Lapidis."

"Oy," said Madame Malaya, shaking her head, "Ovseich, you work like a horse; the years are passing and no one's getting any younger."

Dr. Landa took the first shift. He arrived at seven o'clock on the dot, sat down at a table which had been allotted for consultations in the small outpost: the preschoolers and pre-Pioneers had been temporarily switched to the large outpost. Madame Malaya was sitting beside Landa.

They talked about one thing and another for half an hour, then Olya Cheperukha peeked in the door, her eyes darting back and forth as if desperately searching for someone. Klava Ivanovna guessed at once that Olya was simply shy and needed a nudge or simply to be taken by the arm and led to the table.

And that was exactly what Klava Ivanovna did. At first Olya swore on her life that she didn't need anything, that she was just looking for someone but, when she was taken by the arm and seated across from the doctor, she made no further effort to conceal the truth: she'd been intending to go see a doctor for a long time now but there was always a line at the polyclinic and you could waste a whole day there. Her heart was giving her pain at night, as if it were being burned from underneath, from her stomach, by a match; sometimes there was a burning sensation under her shoulder blade but that was probably a different problem.

"Don't tell the doctor what's a different problem," interjected Klava Ivanovna. "That's his business, not yours."

Dr. Landa pointed out that he was a dermatologist, a specialist in diseases of the skin, and that Madame Cheperukha's complaint was internal. He prescribed a bromide and tincture of valerian, saying she could still get it filled today at the drugstore. Tomorrow morning he would send her to a specialist in internal medicine. Personally, he thought it was no more than a minor nervous disorder.

"Excuse me, Doctor, I don't know how this can be, but sometimes I have an unbearable itch between my fourth toe and little toe on my right foot," said Olya, stroking her hip.

"Show me your foot," said the doctor. "You have to take off your shoes and stockings, I'm not a clairvoyant."

Olya turned red as a beet and cried that she had left dough in the oven and it had probably burned to a crisp by now.

"No," said Klava Ivanovna, taking her by the shoulders, "you're not going anywhere until the doctor has examined you. A person's health is more important."

"Klava Ivanovna," begged Olya, "please let me go. I'll come again, I'll do whatever the doctor orders."

"Olya," said Landa, wagging a threatening finger, "there may not be a next time."

When Cheperukha had left, Klava Ivanovna explained to the doctor what it had all really been about: the big toe on Olya's stocking had a little darn on it and the next time she came she'd be wearing brand-new stockings. That was how aristocratic ways got started.

Yes, agreed Dr. Landa, but, on the other hand, Olya was a young woman, it was understandable. He wasn't saying that to defend her but—

"No," interrupted Madame Malaya, "to say it's understandable is one step away from excusing it. A person should be ashamed of dirt and rags but a nice, clean patch is nothing to be ashamed of."

Dr. Landa paused for a second's thought, then raised both his hands, saying: "I surrender."

Efim Granik arrived when there were no more than five minutes left of the two hours assigned to Dr. Landa for consultation. He was there for one reason only: to inform them that he would be starting his new job next week. But, while he was there and the doctor was still there, maybe Landa should have a look at his hands: lately his skin had been as dry as grass, and when you ran a finger over it, it simply squeaked.

Dr. Landa said that in the course of a month everyone's epidermis was replaced entirely and that was perfectly normal but that in the case of Granik, who no doubt used too much gasoline to wash the paint off his hands, the process had been somewhat accelerated.

"What can be done?" asked Efim. "Does that mean there's nothing that can be done?"

"Hold on," said Klava Ivanovna. "The doctor hasn't finished yet and you're already asking him questions and answering them yourself."

"To make a long story short," said Dr. Landa, glancing at his watch and frowning, "you have to rub glycerin on your hands twice a day: at night before going to sleep, and in the morning before you start work. And it would also be a good idea to bathe them in milk."

"Milk? Pure milk?" said Efim, astounded. "How are you supposed to get milk in the store every day?"

Dr. Landa snapped his briefcase shut, said a general good-bye, and was about to leave when Granik reminded him that he hadn't written out a prescription for glycerin.

"You don't need a prescription for glycerin. If they ask for one, I'll be consulting here again next Monday. And I'd like to thank you personally, Klava Ivanovna. Every doctor should have a nurse like you."

"Landa," Madame Malaya shouted after him, "don't forget to bring some posters and booklets on health to the campaign post."

Consultations on construction and economic matters were scheduled for the next day. The consultant, Engineer Lapidis, arrived a full hour late and Madame Malaya was beside herself.

"Finally!" she cried when Lapidis walked in the door. "You're lucky that Degtyar was detained at work."

Lapidis said he too had been detained at work—they were tallying up the final figures for the third quarter.

"You were doing the figures for the third quarter today?" said Klava Ivanovna. "And where were you before?"

"The same place I was today," said Lapidis with a laugh.

"Oy, Lapidis," said Madame Malaya, "one day those stupid jokes of yours are going to land you in trouble."

"Malaya," said Lapidis, "do you think Anya Kotlyar will have any questions for me on economics or construction?"

"That depends, on what kind of economics," said Klava Ivanovna, pitching her head to one side, "and what kind of construction."

"Socialist economics, and socialist construction," said Lapidis, "that's the only kind that interests me."

Klava Ivanovna warned Lapidis not to be wagging his tail around Anya, adding that she could see right through him, and right through his jacket and pants. He'd better watch his mouth, Anya's husband Joseph could still give him a good punch.

"But our armored train is standing at the ready!" said Lapidis, bursting into song.

The children on their way to the large outpost looked at Lapidis and twirled their fingers by the sides of their heads. Lapidis winked merrily to them and twirled a finger by the side of his own head in reply.

Anya Kotlyar was the first to arrive for a consultation. She had a book under one arm. Klava Ivanovna asked if it was a serious book or just some novel. "It's just a trifle; *Père Goriot* by Honoré de Balzac. I'm reading it for the fourth or fifth time." That surprised Klava Ivanovna: why read one book five times when you could read four others instead?

Madame Malaya's remark caught Anya off guard because deep down she had been counting on a different response: when a person said that he was reading Balzac for the fifth time people were usually surprised at his patience.

"You're mistaken there, Comrade Malaya," said Lapidis.

"That's your opinion!" parried Klava Ivanovna.

"Not just mine," said Lapidis with a sly wink, "but Marx's as well. In a personal letter to Engels he said that you could acquire a better and deeper knowledge of life from Balzac's novels than from the works of scholars and economists."

"Do you have that letter?"

"Not on me," answered Lapidis, "however, it can be found in any library. But, wait a second. Anya, give me the book."

Lapidis ran a finger quickly down the first page, turned to the next and began reading in a loud voice: "Marx wanted to write a separate book on Balzac but never managed to."

"All right," yielded Madame Malaya, "let's say Lapidis is telling the truth and that such a letter does in fact exist, why didn't you say something at once about Marx's attitude toward Balzac, Anya?"

Anya shrugged her shoulders: Karl Marx was mentioned in the foreword and she saw no need to read forewords.

"And so who's going to read them then?" said Klava Ivanovna in astonishment.

Anya did not reply. The prolonged silence became uncomfortable and, as if addressing the audience at a circus, Lapidis said in a jolly tone of voice:

"Ladies and gentlemen, let's move on from economics to construction! Are there any questions on construction?"

Anya said that she had one question about construction: she wanted to install a faucet in her own apartment so that she could have her own independent water supply but she didn't know if she had the legal right to do so.

"Are you being serious here or not!" said Klava Ivanovna, astonished again. "This is a campaign post, the man is consulting on the elections to the Supreme Soviet of the U.S.S.R. and you're worried about installing a tap in your apartment."

"Wait a moment, Malaya," interrupted Lapidis, "any sort of question whatsoever may be asked here, what matters is the answer. As far as the plumbing and a separate faucet are concerned, Citizen Kotlyar should be aware that in this case we are dealing with major construction, which requires the permission of the District Executive Committee, and past experience indicates that the District Executive Committee does not give its permission for such things."

"What can be done then?" asked Anya.

"What can be done?" said Madame Malaya, spreading her hands. "A person might think that you and your mother always had your own private bathtub. If you don't have a good enamel basin, you can get one at the store on Preobrazhenskaya Street, corner of Privozny. Ask the salesman approximately when the goods will arrive but then don't go home and lie on the stove waiting for it to be delivered but keep dropping by the store every day."

"I have a six-gallon enamel basin," said Anya.

"You do?" said Klava Ivanovna. "Then I don't understand at all. What more do you need? What is it you want?"

"I want my own tap," answered Anya, lowering her head. "But if I can't, I can't."

"Anya," said Klava Ivanovna softly, "you're not a stupid woman but Lapidis could think he was dealing with an utter fool. Is that what you want?"

Anya lowered her head even further. Finding it difficult to breathe, Anya unbuttoned her jacket. Lapidis was entirely on her side and said straight out that a woman who was so concerned about her home was worthy of great respect.

"Cut the gallantry, and stop trying to turn the woman's head, you bald old devil!" Klava Ivanovna put an arm protectively around Anya's waist.

Anya resisted a little but it was quite clear that she welcomed Madame Malaya's protection, and Anya pressed closer to her.

"Well," said Iona Ovseich right from the doorway, "now it's clear where economics ends and construction begins. And I sit on the factory committee like an old fool but all my thoughts are here. I think we forgot to say hello, and so, hello, comrades."

Iona Ovseich shook each of their hands, beginning with the most senior in rank, then sat down beside Lapidis, requesting that they pay him no attention and proceed with the consultation.

"You're not disturbing us," said Klava Ivanovna. "On the contrary."

"Thank you," said Iona Ovseich; "then allow me to join in. I have a question for you, Kotlyar."

Anya shuddered and pushed Klava Ivanovna's hand from her waist. Degtyar pulled his chair up closer to the consultant and repeated: "I have a question for you, Kotlyar. I know that you live in two places. Your sons are in Nikolaev with their grandmother, but Joseph doesn't make a bad living at the Lenin factory working his press, isn't that so?"

"It's more than not bad," replied Anya. "I think it's a good living. I'm satisfied."

"All the more so," said Iona Ovseich, laying the palms of both hands on the table. "Then why is it that everyone points a finger and says Joseph Kotlyar makes nails at home, and that Joseph Kotlyar is in business for himself."

"But we have permission from the state," said Anya, covering her heart with her hands, her fingers trembling slightly.

"If you didn't have permission," replied Iona Ovseich, "this would be another conversation altogether. The elections are just around the corner, the country has been seized with unprecedented enthusiasm, but Joseph Kotlyar is home making nails. A person who was a Red partisan in the past should understand that times are changing: today a person can't live the way he did yesterday, today we have to live differently, otherwise we'll sink in the mud before you know what's happening."

Lapidis grasped his chin with his fingers and looked from Iona Ovseich to Anya, then to Madame Malaya, who kept shifting her gaze back and forth from Iona Ovseich to Anya Kotlyar.

"Degtyar is right," said Klava Ivanovna, "the elections are just around the corner, and what we need are deeds, not fancy talk. When Joseph finishes work this evening and climbs in bed with you, explain to him that every wife not only wants to love her husband but to be proud of him as well. And how can a person be proud of someone who does cottage industry work?"

"Klava Ivanovna," said Anya softly, "you know that no one has ever said a bad word about Joseph at the Lenin factory."

"Kotlyar," said Iona Ovseich with an affectionate smile, "imagine for a moment that you work in a school. A pupil named Sidorov has a good memory and can memorize all of Pushkin's poetry but in arithmetic he doesn't know how much two times two is. What grade would you give him in arithmetic, a good one because he can memorize Pushkin's poems, or a bad grade because he doesn't know the multiplication tables?"

"I'd make him learn the multiplication tables," said Anya.

"That's right," said Iona Ovseich in approval, "because if a person is good in one area he should be good in another too. Otherwise, how can we know if he's really good? Is everything clear now?"

Yes, nodded Anya, everything was clear, but Joseph wasn't a crook; after a whole shift at the factory, he did another shift at home —what was the harm in that?

Degtyar squinted for a moment as if from bright sunlight. While

Lapidis butted into the conversation, saying: "Your example about Sidorov was a good example but what does that have to do with Joseph Kotlyar? The man is not deceiving anyone, he knows Pushkin by heart and the multiplication tables too—and so give him the mark he deserves for each subject."

"Lapidis," said Iona Ovseich, shaking his head, "we didn't put you here for that sort of consultation. And people have to be given the grade they deserve for that sort of consultation too. And so let's call a spade a spade."

Lapidis crossed his arms over his chest and said that he was calling a spade a spade, but questions had to be posed clearly without any biblical parables and poetic devices.

"Fine," said Iona Ovseich, slamming the table, "from now on, you will be consulting only on construction, and I'll do the economic consultations myself."

"Ovseich," said Lapidis, bending forward and propping his hands on his knees, "I have nothing against that. What matters is that the right thing be done. But don't you think you should discuss that with the other activists first?"

"You can be sure he already has," interjected Klava Ivanovna. "And you should be grateful to someone who has just taken a load off your shoulders and onto his own."

"Malaya," said Iona Ovseich frowning, "that's not the point. Everyone does what he should and if Lapidis is having trouble then we have to help him. And if our help isn't enough, then others will pitch in too. We don't live in a desert, as I'm always telling you."

"Listen, Ovseich," said Lapidis, rising from his chair, "I have a favor to ask: when I'm consulting, there's no reason for you to be wasting your time here, and when you are here you can do the consultation yourself and I'll find something else to do."

Iona Ovseich narrowed his eyes again and replied that as a citizen he, Degtyar, had every right to consult on matters of construction here in the campaign post. But if the specialist prefered to go against the election regulations and divide voters into those with full rights and those with less, well, that was a horse of another color.

While Iona Ovseich was speaking, Lapidis stared intently at him even though Degtyar kept his eyes closed. Then Lapidis tugged at

Degtyar's sleeve and said that it was impolite to talk to someone with your eyes closed.

"I'm a little bit tired," replied Iona Ovseich. "Don't attach significance to trifles."

Lapidis said that he didn't but asked how Degtyar would like it if he turned his back to him.

"How would I like it?" said Iona Ovseich, opening his eyes and smiling happily. "We thought it was a good sign during the Civil War when the enemy turned his back on us. We took it to mean he was retreating. But these are different times, of course, and we won't make any such comparisons."

Anya Kotlyar, who had been listening intently to the conversation between Iona Ovseich and Lapidis in an effort to understand what they were saying, now suddenly burst into laughter: she said that when Joseph couldn't convince her of something by talking, he too would bring up the Civil War.

"Your husband," said Degtyar, scratching his Adam's apple with one finger, "sometimes says some very intelligent things."

Lapidis laughed too though his was a little more peppery.

"You make good jokes, Iona Ovseich, but your logic is like iron. It does not bend."

"There's something to that," admitted Degtyar. "They can't take that away from us."

At twelve-thirty that night Joseph turned off his nail-making machine, turned down the wick on his kerosene lamp, and got into bed. The room smelled of fumes. Anya moved over toward the wall at once.

"You're starting up again," said Joseph.

Anya remained silent and tried to move even further away but there was no more room between her and the wall.

"What's the matter," said Joseph in surprise, "why are you acting up again?"

Anya answered that she didn't want to talk to him and that he should just leave her alone.

Though it was hard to swing his hand under the blanket, Joseph gave his wife a smack on the bottom and laughed: if Anya said she didn't want to talk, that meant that she was dying to talk.

"Yes," said Anya, "I don't feel like talking, and I won't, because the people in the courtyard won't let me pass without shouting in my face, 'How's your nail-maker doing!' "

"And what do you say back to them?" asked Joseph.

"I don't say anything," said Anya, beginning to cry. "I cover my face and run away so as not to hear them. It makes me feel so ashamed!"

"It's shameful if a person steals," said Joseph, "but what's shameful about honest work? I'm not ashamed."

"He's not ashamed!" said Anya, flying off the handle, as if the night were over and day had come to the courtyard. "But I am! Yes, I'm ashamed, and Degtyar couldn't be more right when he says that if a person is good in one place he should be good everywhere, otherwise he's wearing a mask and pretending."

Joseph gave his wife another whack and told her not to raise her voice to him. Degtyar, that was another story. Degtyar had his own life and he, Joseph, had his. He had to think about feeding his family himself and not wait for Degtyar to bring him food.

"What's the way out?" said Anya, beginning to cry again. "We're living today the way we did yesterday and tomorrow we'll live like we did today, and the day after tomorrow it'll start all over again from the beginning. People are getting ready for the elections, something new happens every day, but nothing changes for me, and still people envy me—she's so young, she's so beautiful!"

Joseph moved away to the very edge of the bed where he lay in silence for a while, then asked in a soft voice: "What is it you want? I could give up making the nails and then no one would criticize you anymore. But then where would we get the money to send to Pinya and Sasha? Not to mention your mother."

"Petya and Sasha will be getting a stipend next year."

"And with that money you can buy a ticket to the movies and treat a girl to a roll, but Pinya has already had pneumonia twice, he has to eat properly."

"Stop calling him Pinya!" said Anya angrily. "That name is all right for Gaisin but in Nikolaev, and especially in Odessa, he'd be teased for it at every step."

"All right," said Joseph, "but you didn't answer my question: where are we going to get the money to send to him and Sasha?"

For a long while Anya did not reply, then she said: if a husband couldn't feed his family, a wife didn't have the right to sit home but should work too and tomorrow she was going to go out looking for a job.

"Hold on," said Joseph. "Are you telling me that you and your children are going around barefoot and hungry?"

"Just what I thought," said Anya with a bitter laugh. "Now he's going to begrudge me a piece of bread!"

"Anya, may a rock fall on my head if I begrudge you your bread."

"No," groaned Anya, "he doesn't begrudge it, he only says that his wife and children walk around with their bellies full wearing fancy clothes while he works like a mule. Lapidis doesn't talk like that to his wife even though she spends the whole year in a mental hospital. And Lapidis discusses Balzac with your wife, and I have to pretend that my husband and I read *Père Goriot* out loud to each other. Oh, God, why am I so unhappy! Why is everyone else so happy and cheerful and I have to be ashamed that my husband is a cottage worker. In Nikolaev he made condoms from rubber, in Odessa he makes nails. Then it'll be condoms again, then nails! My God, when is it all going to end!"

"Anya," said Joseph, "I didn't know that Lapidis discussed foreign writers with you."

"You don't have to worry. We only talk during consultations at the outpost and Madame Malaya is there the entire evening."

"The entire evening?" said Joseph in surprise.

"Don't pick at every word I say!" said Anya furiously. "The two of them sit there the entire evening, I just run over for a minute because I have to wash my cavalryman's puttees and have to give you fresh, hot knishes from the oven every day."

"All right," said Joseph, "I'll have a little talk with Degtyar tomorrow."

Anya moved from the wall almost to the center of the bed, rested her head on her husband's shoulder, and said softly, as if someone else might hear: "Give him your word of honor that you won't go near your machine until the elections are over, but that you'll still keep paying for your license so that the state doesn't lose any money."

Joseph kissed his wife under the arm, his lips tarrying there for a while: Anya's underarms always had a fresh smell to them like hay after rain. Then, thinking of Lapidis, he said that Lapidis was a loudmouth, even though he did have two higher degreees: he'd had his fill of big mouths like that back in the days of the Civil War. They all liked to show off but all you had to do was give them a taste of their own medicine and they'd fall to their knees and tear out their hair and say, I didn't mean it, you've got me all wrong.

Anya was snoring softly and Joseph too began to doze off but just when he had fallen asleep, she suddenly tugged at his arm: "If a person's no good that doesn't make you any better and, anyway, there's no reason to sling mud at people."

Joseph did not reply. Anya pressed her back to him and laughed. Of course, it was true that Lapidis was a big mouth, but she always found it interesting to hear him argue with Ovseich.

"Let him argue," mumbled Joseph sleepily. "See where it gets him."

It was after midnight when Iona Ovseich returned from the factory the next day, the party meeting had run very late, and Kotlyar had to postpone seeing him until his day off. That worked out quite well in fact because Degtyar had scheduled additional consultations for voters on that day.

Degtyar sat at the table, pencil in hand, as he leafed through the pages of his notebook. The children walked past on their way to their half of the outpost, greeting him politely and closing the door carefully behind them. Klava Ivanovna shook her head and exclaimed with delight how civilized the children could be when they wanted to.

"Malaya," said Iona Ovseich, "remember—the way you are with the children is the way they'll be with you. It's all up to us."

Dina Vargaftik appeared in the doorway, stared at Degtyar and cried: "Oh, if he only came late once. But no, he won't give anyone that pleasure."

"Dina," interrupted Madame Malaya, "sit down here beside me and compare how the children go into their room and how you came into this one."

"Malaya," replied Dina Vargaftik, "you have to remember the world we grew up in and the world they're growing up in."

Even though it was already dark, Zyunchik Cheperukha and Kolka Khomitsky began hollering like drunks:

"Mama, I love a pilot!
Mama, I'll marry him!
Pilots fly high
And earn lots of money—
Mama, I love a pilot!

"Mama, I love a driver!
Mama, I'll marry him!
He drives a big car
and he'll screw me in the front seat—
Mama, I love a driver!

"Mama, I love a doctor!
Mama, I'll marry him!
Doctors do abortions
and send you on vacations—
Mama, it's a doctor I want!"

At first, when they were singing about the pilot, Degtyar simply listened, but when they reached the part about the driver and the doctor, his mouth opened as if he were gasping for air. Klava Ivanovna and Dina giggled and winked at him. Someone was banging on his window with all his might on the third floor, and Gizella Landa shouted that it was nighttime, people wanted to rest, and the son of that drunkard Cheperukha was singing obscene songs and corrupting the other children.

"She doesn't like it because they're singing about doctors," said Dina, shaking with laughter.

Gizella leaned out of her window and swore that she was going to call the police right away and have the paddy wagon come and take those hooligans off to a labor colony.

"Doctors do abortions, and send you on vacations!" hollered the boys all the louder.

"Malaya," said Iona Ovseich, "do you see what's going on?"

Klava Ivanovna replied that she did indeed see what was going on but she wasn't going to intervene to help that bourgeois doctor's wife.

"Malaya," said Degtyar, shaking his head, "you're making a mistake. Let's say they do think of her as an aristocrat even though she does work with the children's choir, we have no right to accept this sort of behavior. I want this to be the first and the last time for this."

"That's what we all want," said Klava Ivanovna with a shrug of her shoulders.

"Malaya," said Iona Ovseich with a frown, "if I didn't make myself clear enough for you to understand me, I can can say it again differently."

No, replied Klava Ivanovna, she had understood it all, but there was no reason to exaggerate: children will be children and there was no shutting them up.

Iona Ovseich looked her right in the eye and said in a soft voice: "Malaya, it's no good when the kasha is overcooked and no good when it's undercooked either, and so the right conclusion is that the proper measure has to be found, then both the cook and the customer will be happy. And children, who are the most important thing in Soviet society, children, who are our future, must be treated with the same kind of care so they turn out right. And you shouldn't think that the election campaign is just something that lasts two months and then people can go lie on the stove and write letters to their grandfather in the village, like that boy Vanka in the Chekhov story."

Both Degtyar's examples, the kasha and the Chekhov story, were right on the mark and Dina said straight out that when a man has a head like that, it didn't matter what he looked like, and she was ready to give Degtyar a kiss in front of everyone.

"First you have to find out," said Klava Ivanovna, "if Degtyar will let you or not."

No, said Iona Ovseich, he wouldn't, and she shouldn't even ask.

"What about Anya Kotlyar?"

Iona Ovseich began to narrow his eyes, clearly wishing to imagine that possibility when the door opened and Joseph Kotlyar shouted for the whole courtyard to hear that while they were sitting there calmly drinking their tea, Kolka and Zyunchik were running down Troitskaya Street and hollering about Murka, abortion, and that bandit Gopsosmyk.

"Who's drinking tea!" said Madame Malaya indignantly, but in reply Joseph shouted in his cavalryman's voice: "Yes, it makes you wonder why we built the outpost, and what all that time and effort went for!"

"What's wrong with you today?" said Klava Ivanovna in surprise. "You're not acting like yourself."

"No," said Degtyar, "he's a thousand percent right, and Malaya should openly admit that this is her own personal oversight. Do you agree with me, Kotlyar?"

Joseph shrugged his shoulders: "What a question!" Then he shook hands in greeting with Degtyar and Malaya, nodded to Dina Vargaftik, and sat at the corner of the table so that his prothesis could hang freely, otherwise it would rub against the stump. The room remained in silence for half a minute as if they were all waiting for someone else to start first. Then Kotlyar asked in a loud voice: "Ovseich, do you know why I'm here?"

"As far as I know," said Degtyar with a smile, "today is my day to consult with the voters. Or am I wrong about that?"

"Ah, what a memory the man has!" exclaimed Joseph.

"And ah, what a memory you have," exclaimed Degtyar in response. "You didn't forget that I'd be consulting."

"What a comparison," fumed Joseph. "How many people do I have to remember about compared to you!"

Klava Ivanovna laughed and recalled her old dance classes, back in the days of Tsar Nicholas II, where they taught you how to curtsy and bow but they wouldn't have accepted Kotlyar with that belly of his.

"Malaya," said Joseph with a cunning look in his eyes, "from the outside it sometimes seems you regret the old days are gone."

"Why sometimes?" said Klava Ivanovna in surprise. "I always regret they ever existed in the first place."

"Malaya," said Joseph, utterly delighted, "you deserve an A-plus for an answer like that. And I want you and Ovseich to be the first to know that as of tomorrow at six o'clock, I'm going to stop making nails."

"No, you're wrong there," said Degtyar, pounding the table. "There should be other people here so they could hear with their own ears the way the December 12 elections should be marked!"

Iona Ovseich paused for thought: it was one thing to propose doing something and quite another to put it into practice. Outside the window Olya Cheperukha was shouting plaintively for Zyunchik to grab a sack immediately and run to Tiraspolsky Square where the grocery store was selling granulated and lump sugar. He must hurry the line had already stretched to Franz Mering.

"Malaya, you and Vargaftik call Cheperukha in here," said Degtyar, snapping to. "And then the three of you go around to people's apartments and remind them that a day off is not for lolling in bed from morning till night."

Thirty minutes later there were a dozen chairs in front of the consultant's desk and nevertheless some people had to sit two to a chair. The children had also been called over from the large outpost, so they could hear about matters of state.

"My dear neighbors," said Iona Ovseich, "today is an ordinary day, but in our times even an ordinary day is an extraordinary day. Just five minutes ago, Joseph Kotlyar, whom you all know well, came by here and informed us that he had his own personal present to give to the elections of December 12. What's the present, or is it a secret? we asked him. His answer was that it was no secret—he had decided to renounce once and forever his cottage industry work even though as a disabled Civil War veteran he has a legal right to that work. Then another question arose: Joseph Kotlyar lives in two places, his children are with their grandmother in Nikolaev, sixty miles from Odessa, and so perhaps was he in too much of a hurry? But no one even had time to ask that question because Kotlyar, a former Red cavalryman, was way ahead of us: he'd already thought the whole thing through and his decision was final."

Iona Ovseich was the first to begin clapping but everyone else was right behind him. Then someone suggested that Kotlyar himself say a few words.

"My dear neighbors," said Kotlyar, "I only did what my conscience dictated, and in the Soviet era there's a little conscience to be found even in the most conscienceless man."

The grown-ups responded to that remark with laughter but the children began clapping their hands boisterously.

"Comrades, neighbors," Joseph continued, "it happened in the middle of the night. I couldn't fall asleep and kept tossing and turning. Anya woke up too and she said: 'Joseph, I know why you can't sleep, there's something on your conscience.' Well, who likes hearing that? I got angry and answered her the way a partisan answers, but she stuck to her guns and let me have it point-blank: 'The country is moving toward the elections, people are celebrating, and you're still living the old life, the dust is coming out of your seams.' Yes, yes, it's funny to you, but to me it wasn't funny at all. All of a sudden I knew that Anya was right, you can't spend your whole life on your duff worrying about keeping it warm."

Efim Granik laughed and was about to make a remark when Klava Ivanovna, who was laughing herself, told him to keep his remarks to himself.

"Well," said Joseph, "now I feel as pure as if I were just born."

"And where's Anya this late at night?" asked Klava Ivanovna.

"Malaya, I'll tell you a secret," interrupted Iona Ovseich. "Not every woman likes to hear her man showered with praise."

"Who's praising him?" said Klava Ivanovna in surprise. "He's just doing what he should have done three years ago."

"Beautifully said!" cried Joseph. "Malaya, I want to put my arms around you."

"Oh, now we all can see why Anya's not here."

Everyone laughed. Iona Ovseich waited for them to calm down and then reported the latest news: the Stalin electoral district had nominated the well-known stevedore leader Comrade Aron Abramovich Khenkin for election to the House of Nationalities'!

There had been talk about Khenkin before but Degtyar had also learned some further information and people wanted details about their deputy. Although the elections had not been held yet, people began referring to Khenkin as their deputy from the very first day it became known he was on the ballot.

"Comrade voters," said Iona Ovseich loudly, "allow me to report certain facts to you. It was a sunny, spring day in 1933. A tall thin man was standing on pier nineteen beside the steamer *Jean Jores* and he was delivering a speech to the workers and the stevedores. People listened and wept because that tall thin man was Maxim Gorky. Gorky himself was also weeping as he recollected his youth when he used to work sixteen to eighteen hours a day running up and down with huge packing bales on his back, then spend the night in doss houses that were damp all winter, and airless and reeking in the summer. Because of his broad shoulders and iron muscles one man stood out from all the rest of the workers and stevedores. He wasn't crying. On the contrary, he had clenched his teeth and was vowing to himself as a former Red Army soldier to work with all he had and be unsparing to himself. A foreign steamer arrived in Odessa a year and a half ago and that stevedore took a good look at it and said to his team: 'Comrades! Let's compete to finish the work in record time. Don't anyone let us down! Let's show that captain and his crew that his ship is being unloaded in a Soviet port!' The first record was set that day. Their usual quota was a hundred and one tons. But working like Stakhanovites, they unloaded two hundred and fifty-five tons, and the next day, they set a mind-boggling record of three hundred and ten tons. I won't tell you how amazed the captain of that foreign ship was to see all this with his own eyes!"

"Why would we envy them?" shouted Dina Vargaftik. "They should all drop dead!"

"Comrade Vargaftik," said Iona Ovseich, extending his hand forward, palm first, "what you say is right but I want to ask you a question: who ever died of a curse and who was ever cured by fancy talk? No, Dina Vargaftik, we have to work like the Stakhanovite Khenkin, fancy words aren't needed. And now we want to ask Olya Cheperukha a question: how is it that she's sitting home while her son is out running around the city singing dirty songs like a homeless waif?"

Olya blushed red as a cooked crab, then looked at the children who were sitting along the wall and said that there are lucky parents and unlucky parents.

"Cheperukha," said Klava Ivanovna, wagging a finger at her, "a person makes his own luck, and shouldn't blame other people for his troubles."

"I'm not blaming other people, Klava Ivanovna," said Olya, with another look at the children, "but your husband doesn't come crawling over to you drunk and demanding you do things, and your son doesn't threaten to run away from home."

"Malaya," said Iona Ovseich, "she's right. And we should make a note today that—and this will be your personal responsibility—that, on the eve of the elections, the building's activists assume the obligation of involving all the children in the outpost. People can unload two hundred and fifty-five tons, or even three hundred and ten when their norm is one hundred and one, and we're acting like a bunch of blind baby goats in a washtub. It's shameful, comrades!"

Joseph Kotlyar raised his hand. "Give me the floor, Ovseich."

"What do you want to say?" asked Degtyar.

"I want to say that we should buy mandolins and balalaikas for our children so that they can have their own band."

"With what money?" asked Degtyar.

"Let everyone just reach in their pocket and chip in," said Joseph, pulling out his wallet and extracting three rubles, which he then threw on the table. "Actions speak louder than words."

Degtyar stared in silence at the money and at first it seemed that he was confused but then he ordered Joseph to take back his money and stop acting like he was in the marketplace. A genuine grass-roots initiative was one thing, and one that was always welcome, but merchant ways were something else again. There was a roar of approval. Kotlyar sat back down with a pitiful smile. Iona Ovseich had clearly decided to spare him and, not waiting for the room to become completely quiet, he announced that he had a small piece of news to report even though it didn't quite belong at the moment. When Kiselis died, one of the building's residents, Idaliya Orlov, had applied to move into the space which had been freed since she was living in a semibasement room through which the plumbing ran and was constantly leaking. A building committee commission, a troika consiting of Comrade Malaya, Comrade Khomitsky, and Dr. Landa had investigated Citizen Orlov's living conditions and passed along their findings. But first the building committee wanted to know what the other residents thought.

Iona Ovseich paused again, looking directly at each person, so they could feel that the responsibility now rested with them.

Dina Vargaftik took the floor. "Klava Ivanovna is right here and can witness that on the day of Kiselis' funeral I, Dina Vargaftik, said that Orlov should be given his room. Of course, it is a separate room with its own entrance and its own tap, and at one time Lyalya Orlov lived a life that couldn't be mentioned in front of children, so where is the guarantee that it won't happen again?"

"Where's the guarantee?" repeated Klava Ivanovna. "I'll tell you where it is—in trusting a person. Not only that, we demanded that Lyalya Orlov sign a pledge, and she did."

Dina Vargaftik grinned crookedly because a written pledge could be added to someone's file and kept in an office, but a living person with all his habits and ways could not be filed away so nicely.

"Vargaftik," said Joseph Kotlyar, "The first day we began living in this building, I discovered that you like things to be in good order and that you're the first to run and report if something's not the way it's supposed to be. But how can you bring yourself to demand that we not trust a person, as if the Soviet Union weren't already almost twenty years old and the elections to the Supreme Soviet of the U.S.S.R. just around the corner."

"Fancy talk is just fancy talk!" cried Vargaftik. "And two can play that game!"

Kotlyar pushed himself forcibly away from the table with both his hands. His prosthesis caught on the bottom part of the table—he had placed his good leg too far in front of him—and he fell down. People tried to help him but Joseph flatly refused their help and was the first to laugh at his own clumsiness.

"Comrade Vargaftik," he said, rising, "in 1919 outside Sandomer, we let a White Pole go on his word of honor. On his word of honor!"

"Ya, ya, ya," said Dina, shaking her head. "The question is did he keep his word of honor. No one's saying anything against Orlov, but children live here, and that cannot be forgotten."

When the room was quiet again, Iona Ovseich summed things up, saying that there was something to both points of view but the overall mood was in favor of Citizen Orlov moving to the late Kiselis' room and to make such application to the Stalin District Soviet of Workers' Deputies.

Everyone agreed with that formulation but Efim Granik did not like the second part, about applying to the District Soviet.

"Ovseich," he said in a loud voice, "there are workers on the District Soviet, and workers live here in this building, but how is it that they have a better idea what Orlov and other people in our building need."

"Efim Lazarevich," said Degtyar with a smile, "do you know

what name should be given to your theory? In party language your theory is called anarcho-syndicalism."

"What theory!" said Efim, tilting his head a little to one side. "A person just had an idea, that's all."

"No," said Degtyar, "it is a theory, a spontaneous theory, one which inevitably arises in the minds of people who are not rooted deeply enough in the working class. You're proposing that we give Orlov the room without any discussion, without looking into the matter at all, but perhaps there's someone in the district who has more need of that room. And maybe there's someone in the city who needs it even more and may also be a person of special merit!"

"Degtyar is right," interjected Joseph Kotlyar. "It's not enough to know how a person stands in a building, you also have to know how that person stands in Odessa, from Peresyp to Tovarny."

"Let's sum up again," said Iona Ovseich. "The activists and the building's residents are in favor of Citizen Orlov moving to the late Kiselis' apartment and will resolve this matter before the twelfth of December, that is, before the elections."

Though no one had authorized her to do so, Dina Vargaftik proposed that it be put to a vote. Degtyar immediately replied that that would be formalism in the case at hand, and formalism was for formalists and bureaucrats, in other words, it played into the hands of the enemies of the Soviet system.

While Iona Ovseich was explaining this point, Madame Malaya walked over to the children, hugged several of them while whispering something to them, and then announced for all to hear that Osya Granik would now recite Dzhambul's poem "The Law."

Osya walked to the center of the room and repeated the author's name and the title of the poem: " 'The Law,' a poem by Dzhambul Dzhabaev," then gasping for breath as after a long run, he declaimed:

"I have known many laws in my life:
Those laws have bent my back,
Those laws have made me weep,
And left deep furrows on my brow!"

Then, while reciting, Osya grew somewhat calmer, and though he began shouting again at the end, he was not gasping for breath as he had been before, declaiming the verses very loudly as if he were at a gathering of young Pioneers:

"I praise the great Soviet law,
A law that brings us joy,
A law that makes the steppe flower,
A law that makes us all equal
In the constellation of fraternal republics!"

The children were the first to applaud but the grown-ups were quick to follow with Joseph Kotlyar shouting "Encore!" in his cavalryman's voice. Klava Ivanovna put her hand over his mouth and gave the floor to Adya Lapidis, who read the poem "On Maidana Near the Church the Revolution Roars" by Pavlo Tychin.

Osya Granik recited again after Adya Lapidis; this time he read a poem he had written himself—about Comrade Stalin and Spain. The lines about Spain told of the fascist bandits murdering children, old people, and women, dropping bombs on peaceful cities and fields where the peasants and farmhands were gathering the bits of grain so as not to die of hunger. Klava Ivanovna nodded her head the whole time; tears streamed down her cheeks and she forgot to wipe them away even though she had her handkerchief in her hand.

When Osya was through, she walked over to him, and kissed him on the forehead. Iona Ovseich gave Osya a firm handshake and asked what marks he was getting in Russian, math, and natural history, and ordered him to get nothing less than A's. Osya replied with a Pioneer salute, turned around, and returned to his place in line.

"Efim," said Klava Ivanovna to Osya's father, "where did you ever get a son like that? Comrade voters, I ask you, where did he ever get a son like that!"

Everyone laughed but Granik scratched his bald spot with his finger and replied they'd better put that question to his wife Sonya, she'd know more about that. But if the truth be told, then he, Efim Granik, had also written some poems in his day, but times were different back then. The children who had already heard about those times a great deal and seen movies about them stood in silence while the grown-ups sighed deeply as if those memories oppressed them to this day.

"All right," said Iona Ovseich, bringing the moment to a close, "what's past is past, you can't live long on memories alone. Does anyone have any questions, comrades? If there are no questions, people can go home. Next week we'll check up on how well people have understood the election regulations, to see if everyone has them down or if some people need a little nudge."

The following week it turned out that the check was going to have to be postponed for another six days since there had been an interruption of the production schedule at the factory where Degtyar worked—the chief engineer, Dronis, a follower of an enemy of the people who had the same last name as he did, had been arrested, and now Iona Ovseich had to be at the factory day and night. There had also been a little snag in Lyalya Orlov's moving into her new room: the Stalin District Soviet had its own candidate for the late Kiselis' quarters and was fighting for the room as well.

"You should have slammed your fist on the table," said Iona Ovseich. "Then they would have understood."

Klava Ivanovna replied that she had done precisely that and her hand was still giving her pain, but nothing could be done without the chairman of the District Soviet.

Degtyar agreed and said that he would call the chairman direct from the factory. And, for her part, Klava Ivanovna should barge into his office and inform him of the way his housing department was behaving, that it was being arbitrary and politically shortsighted.

They put their plan into operation immediately. Klava Ivanovna had just begun a conversation on shortsightedness and arbitrariness in the chairman of the District Soviet's office when the phone rang. The chairman recognized Degtyar's voice immediately.

"Listen, Iona," he said, "let's get right down to brass tacks, I don't have a minute today. One of your activists is here demanding the room for Lyalya Orlov from the tobacco factory. My housing department is very upset. Give me the straight story, is there a rush on this or can it wait? Personally, I'm in favor of waiting."

"He's in favor of waiting!" said Klava Ivanovna indignantly. "He's been told in plain Russian that a ceiling is leaking on a person's head and he's in favor of waiting!"

"Degtyar," said the chairman, laughing into the phone, "she's making mincemeat out of me. I could use a woman like her working for me. All right, we won't settle it your way or mine, I'll send a commission. No, no, they'll be completely objective, there won't be a word to them, no pressure."

The people on the commission proved quite decent and though Klava Ivanovna had been angry at the chairman at first, now she was more than happy because the whole thing was being treated as a serious state matter. The commission found in favor of Lyalya Orlov that very day, and ordered that she be issued an authorization. When Lyalya returned from her shift and found out, she went running to Madame Malaya, threw her arms around her, and burst into tears.

"Stop crying," said Klava Ivanovna, "and you don't have to thank me either. Some people in the courtyard doubt that you've become entirely respectable, but I have no doubts on that score. I trust you like I trust myself."

"Lord," said Lyalya in horror, "they should be ashamed of themselves! Klavochka Ivanovna, I'll be so good, so good!"

"Stop it," said Madame Malaya, "get ahold of yourself, and let's hope nobody points a finger at you. And now I have a question for you: how's your attendance at the political classes at the factory?"

"What do you mean, how is it?" said Lyalya, a bit embarrassed. "If there's a class, I go, and, if there isn't, I don't."

Klava Ivanovna said she disliked that answer. A person who lived a straight life could give a straight answer. Besides, whether there were lessons at the factory or not, she had to come for a consultation at the outpost because the factory was the factory but home was home.

"Lord," said Lyalya, hands pressed to her breast, "who could be against that? It's the other way around, I couldn't be more interested in hearing what Iona Ovseich, Dr. Landa, and Lapidis have to say. Klava Ivanovna, is it true that Lapidis' father came here directly from Greece? And is it true that Lapidis is fond of Anya Kotlyar, or did people just make that up?"

"Do you want me to answer all your questions at once or can you wait a little? In the first place, I don't poke my nose in other people's business. And in the second place, if you're in such a hurry to know, why not go straight to Lapidis and ask him, 'Are you fond of Anya Kotlyar or is that just idle talk?' "

"Oh, he'd kick me right out!" said Lyalya in fear.

"Don't worry," said Klava Ivanovna, "Lapidis is not that much of a fool."

"Everyone says that I'm as light-headed as a young girl," said Lyalya, turning suddenly shy. "Klava Ivanovna, I feel like your daughter, I feel like you're my own mother."

Lyalya laughed, then she and Klava Ivanovna entwined their pinkies and whispered in a loud voice:

"Friends, friends, true and tight, we'll keep the peace and never fight!"

The situation at Degtyar's factory had been turned around considerably during the past week and now he could afford to run the check on the voters as he had intended. "But first," said Iona Ovseich, "I want to report to the voters and to all the building's residents that the question of Idaliya Orlov's moving to new quarters has been resolved in her favor on every level and the keys and the authorization will now be presented to her. We ask that Comrade Orlov approach the table. Everyone must be a witness, or later she'll lose the keys and say we never gave them to her in the first place."

"So let her lose them!" shouted Efim Granik. "A room can't be orphaned, we'll find a father and a mother for it."

Klava Ivanovna ordered Efim to stop the wisecracks and be quiet, today wasn't his day, and it was Lyalya Orlov people wanted to hear.

"I'm no speaker," said Lyalya. "But may you all be as happy as I am. I love you all."

Iona Ovseich was not very pleased by Lyalya's speech: no one expected her to be a Cicero, but a few words could be found when a person was receiving her keys and authorization. He waited another minute—maybe she'd find something to say—but Orlov just stood there and smiled. Stepa suggested they finish it up, give her the room, and that would be that.

"Khomitsky," said Iona Ovseich glowering, "you're the last person we would have expected that from. You were in the Civil War for three years, and you didn't spare anything, even your own blood, for what you have today, including your room, but Soviet society just handed this woman her keys without demanding that she expose herself to gunfire. She didn't even have to set foot inside the District Soviet, it was all just served up to her on a platter."

Stepa waved his hand dismissively. Iona Ovseich turned to Madame Malaya and said that Khomitsky was right about one thing—we should do a little work with people beforehand, help prepare them to speak, and not let things just slide.

"Why are you putting words in my mouth?" said Stepa in surprise. "That's not what I said."

"There's no need to deny it," said Degtyar with a wink. "I could tell by your face what you were thinking."

Stepa replied that if Degtyar could tell by his face, that was another story entirely, and promised to bring a mirror with him to the next meeting; he'd be interested too in comparing his face and his thoughts.

"Ovseich," said Joseph Kotlyar, throwing back his head as he laughed, "Stepa is not as big a fool as you think!"

Everyone laughed. Iona Ovseich waited a few seconds, raised a finger, and stated in a loud voice:

"Enough joking around. Now, comrade voters, let's move on from jokes to business. I have a question for you: why does the Supreme Soviet of the U.S.S.R. consist of two houses? What's the reason for that? Or, is there no reason for it, and one house would have been enough?"

"Ovseich," said Efim Granik with a laugh, "you're always doing that—you turn the question upside down, and then other people must turn it right side up."

Degtyar had every right to be offended by that remark but he did not take offense and confined his reply to the point: "Politics and government are so complicated that it's not always clear right off where the head is, where the feet are, and where the tail is. And that's why we have the saying: put the tail where the head can't get at it."

"That's true," agreed Efim, "that's very true."

"All right," interjected Klava Ivanovna, "your question's been answered, now answer the other one—why are there two houses, not one?"

"Why two and not one?" repeated Efim. "Personally, I would have made only one: there's workers and peasants there, and there's workers and peasants here. There's working people there and working people here. What's there they wouldn't share between them?"

"I see," said Iona Ovseich, drumming his fingers on the table, "I see. Who else wants to answer? Dina Vargaftik does."

Dina Vargaftik said that she didn't raise her hand and didn't want to answer, but, since Degtyar had called on her, she'd answer: "The U.S.S.R. contains many different nationalities, peoples, and minorities, especially in Central Asia and in the Caucasus. On the one hand, they all have common interests, on the other hand, they each have their own interests too. So that means that one, the House of the Union, is for the general interests of the whole U.S.S.R. and the other, the House of Nationalities, is where each group can pursue its own interest."

"Let's say that's so," said Iona Ovseich. "How are the two to be united?"

"Oh," said Granik, jumping up, "and I said two houses were a lot."

"All the same there are two houses," said Iona Ovseich, squinting. "What should we do about them? Shall we dissolve one, comrade voters?"

The voters agreed that since the government and Comrade Stalin had set up two houses, that meant two were needed.

"All right," said Iona Ovseich, "let's not waste time on gab. I'll answer the question: since disagreements will arise between the two houses, mixed commissions have been appointed to deal with them, number one, and, number two, there will be joint sessions. It's theoretically possible they might not come to terms but, in practice, that will be out of the question. Is that clear to you, Vargaftik? And to you, Granik?"

Dina said that personally it had been clear to her before, but Efim replied that he could not answer questions like that on the fly and he needed to think some more.

How are electoral districts shaped? Why in one case does a deputy represent a population of three hundred thousand, and, in another case, a republic, or an ethnic province? Which is more important, the Council of People's Commissars or the Supreme Soviet? And will the deputies receive a salary or not? All these questions were given exhaustive answers. In conclusion, Iona Ovseich said straight out that he was satisfied with how things had gone today but that the main thing was intense activity, so that on December 12, when the Soviet people went to the ballot box, no one in this courtyard would let them down. There was, however, one disappointment: Comrade Stalin had agreed to vote in the Stalin electoral district of the city of Moscow, though the Stalin electoral district of Odessa had kept hoping right up to the last moment.

The doors of the outpost opened on December 12, at 6 A.M. on the dot, just as the Comintern radio station began playing the "Internationale." Degtyar and Klava Ivanovna stood on either side of the door so that people could have free access to the booths and ballot box. The booths were curtained off with thick calico and the voter had every opportunity to cross out one candidate or write in another he liked more, but most people dispensed with the booths and went straight to the ballot box.

The first to use a booth was Stepa Khomitsky and he was immediately joined by Granik, who squeezed into the same booth. Iona Ovseich demanded that Efim get out of there at once: two people in a booth was categorically forbidden—no one should know who someone else was voting for.

"What do you mean someone else!" said Granik with indignation. "He's my closest friend, I don't hide anything from him."

"Even your brother, your own brother," said Iona Ovseich, "doesn't have that right. The Constitution guarantees everyone a secret ballot."

"All right, I'll talk it over with him and then go to another booth."

Iona Ovseich began his statement about the secret ballot again but wasn't able to finish this time: Klava Ivanovna went into the booth, kicked Efim out, and demanded that he go into the the next booth where he could stay until twelve o'clock when the polling place closed. Even after that Efim continued to put up some resistance but by then Stepa was hinting that he wanted to be alone.

When he was inside the next booth, Efim knocked on the partition and asked Stepa if he was done or still thinking.

"No talking allowed, Voter Granik," said Iona Ovseich. "Just use your pencil."

Efim spent fifteen minutes in the booth. His chair could be heard squeaking as if he were undergoing some tremendous anxiety. Twice Klava Ivanovna asked through the curtain if he was feeling all right, and what would he like for dessert: castor oil or a laxative.

In both cases Granik replied he absolutely demanded not to be bothered and in both cases Degtyar took his side.

By the ballot box, Efim unrolled his ballot, examined it thoroughly, folded it into fours, and jammed it through the slot. Then he shook Degtyar's hand, holding it in his while asking loudly: "Ovseich, if the whole courtyard and the whole street writes you in, will there be something about that in the newspaper?"

"Of course," said Iona Ovseich, "and on the radio, too."

"One more question then: what if there's only one vote for you?"

"In that case," said Iona Ovseich, pausing for a second's thought, "the only person to know will be the voter himself, if, of course, he's not a big mouth and knows how to button his lip."

"He's not a big mouth," said Granik. "You can take my word on that."

The district food store had set up a buffet in the small outpost on election day so that the voters could economize on time and not have to run to the store. On sale were bologna sausage, fresh potato salad, beets in sunflower oil, a pig's foot aspic, and spice cake. There were also Greek olives, half a kilo to a customer, and Kirsch herring. At first they were selling the herring by the kilo but people were trying to take more than they should, forgetting about others. And even though some people might not like herring, Klava Ivanovna ordered that each customer be given two pieces and no more. The woman running the buffet said she had no such orders from her boss but Klava Ivanovna pointed to the voters standing in line and replied: "There's your real boss!"

She gave Klava Ivanovna a look of surprise and asked where that boss's seal was for stamping the paperwork.

"And where was the seal in 1917?" asked Klava Ivanovna. The woman at the buffet said all right, all right, she wasn't going to argue. People laughed and said that if everyone could talk like Madame Malaya, then everything would go right all the time.

While Efim was sitting in the booth thinking about his ballot, Stepa had time to go to the grocery store on Tiraspolsky Square and come back. Two bottles were sticking out of his jacket pocket, one for himself and the other for Efim. After they knocked off a drink, Stepa said they should treat Degtyar and Klava Ivanovna to some, after all they'd been there since early morning and hadn't had a bite to eat.

Iona Ovseich flatly refused, saying it was a holiday for some people but he was in harness. Klava Ivanovna refused too but finally agreed to take a thimble's worth, her toast that their people would always live this well and that their children would never know war.

Stepa said that a person shouldn't drink to all that at the same time but for Madame Malaya an exception could be made.

"No exceptions are needed," objected Klava Ivanovna. "We can drink separately to our children never knowing war."

When they were drinking a second time, Klava Ivanovna remembered the gramophone and handed Efim the keys to her apartment: he'd have no trouble finding the gramophone and the records were in a fiber suitcase on a shelf. He should be careful about carrying the suitcase, otherwise there'd be nothing but bits and pieces left of the records.

Efim dashed off but on the way back ran into Iona Cheperukha near the outpost, who demanded to be allowed to wind the gramophone.

"No," Klava Ivanovna answered. "First sober up, then we'll see."

"Malaya," said Cheperukha in a tone of offense, "I was sober enough to vote but now I'm too drunk to wind the gramophone. Does that mean your gramophone is more important than the elections? Efim, you're my witness here."

"You bum," said Klava Ivanovna, clenching her teeth, "go home and sleep it off before your mouth lands you in trouble."

They set the gramophone on a pedestal after removing the ficus plant and placed the records on a shelf. First they played *"La Cucaracha,"* then "Vast Is My Native Land," and then "It's Good When There's Work."

"Ovseich," asked Klava Ivanovna, "do you like Francheska Gaal?"

Iona Ovseich replied that he did like her music, but right now he had something else on his mind: the incident with Cheperukha should not be overlooked. Many people had seen it and could draw the wrong conclusions. "What conclusions?" objected Klava Ivanovna. "That was just drunken talk from a drunk!" Degtyar shook his head: "What you think when you're sober you say when you're drunk."

At nine o'clock the District Committee asked for a report on the voting at their polling place. Iona Ovseich rounded off the total to ninety-five percent, they were only two tenths of a percent short of that. Laughter came through the phone and the person on the other end said that at that rate Degtyar had a chance of taking first place at the end of the line.

"Malaya," said Iona Ovseich, "congratulations, we're in last place."

Things had quieted down somewhat at the buffet: all the herring had been sold, but there was almost half a barrel of olives and no reason to worry they'd run short. Iona Cheperukha asked for a kilo. The saleswoman said that she couldn't weigh out a kilo at once, she'd weigh out half a kilo twice. Klava Ivanovna tried a few olives from the sack and Cheperukha offered her a few more but she refused: the olives could wait but she had a civic task for him—to go to Lapidis' rightaway and drag him back there. If he was so sick that he'd lost all shame and conscience, they'd bring the ballot box to his bed, and that'd be the last ballot box he'd ever see. Cheperukha said that he was willing but on one condition—there was no reason to call him down there, better to bring the ballot box right to him in bed.

Iona Ovseich thought for a moment: it wouldn't be bad to teach Lapidis a lesson, and Cheperukha's idea was a good one, but the rules were the rules, and the ballot box could only be brought to the sick who were bedridden.

Cheperukha was back five minutes later and cried from the doorway that they could cut him up into little pieces, but he was never going to accept another civic task again. This was what happened: first he rang the bell, then he rang it again, but no one came to the door. Then he pounded on the door and shouted for Lapidis to go vote and not keep people waiting for no reason. Then that Greek came running out and slammed the door and now he was saying that Cheperukha broke a pane of glass in the door.

"That's all I need, a civic task!" said Iona, spitting. "I'm a carter, a drayman, and now they want to turn me into an activist!"

Madame Malaya asked if Cheperukha might have accidentally cracked the glass, but Cheperukha swore by his wheelbarrow: "May its wheels fall off if I so much as touched the glass."

Lapidis came crashing into the outpost as if he'd been hurled from behind by a rogue elephant's trunk.

"I know," shouted Lapidis, "that you're setting people on me to break the glass in my door like a bunch of hoodlums! I'm going to inform the Province Committee of this immediately. Let them send a commission here to check on the way you're observing the election regulations."

"Hold on," said Madame Malaya, halting him, "you broke the glass yourself when you slammed the door on Cheperukha."

"I did it?" said Lapidis dumbfounded. "I went to visit myself, I wouldn't let myself into my own home, and then to get even with myself I broke the glass in my own door! Either I've gone out of my mind or—"

Chuckling, Lapidis grasped his stomach with both hands, and began running around Klava Ivanovna. After he had dashed around her once, she tried to grab him by the sleeve and stop him, but she only came up with a handful of air.

When Lapidis had made his last circle, Degtyar, who had been checking the lists to see how many people had voted, said that things were so merry in here you'd have thought they were all done voting and had taken first place in Odessa.

"Think big!" said Klava Ivanovna. "With voters like Lapidis we're lucky if wc hold on to last place."

"What does that mean?" asked Degtyar.

"Ovseich!" said Cheperukha in surprise. "It was you who sent me to go get Lapidis to vote!"

"In the first place," said Degtyar, "you're mixed up. It was Malaya who sent you. And in the second place, a person could have already voted a hundred times since then. And if that person hasn't, he must have a valid reason."

"Lapidis has a valid reason," said Madame Malaya. "He doesn't want to lose a minute's sleep."

"On a day like today?" said Iona Ovseich, shaking his head. "On a day like today a person can't wait for it to be six o'clock. Your lights were on at four o'clock, Malaya. I saw you turn them on and then start pacing the floor."

"That," said Lapidis, "I didn't see. I'm not in the habit of looking into people's windows."

"Let's get to the point," said Iona Ovseich. "They're saying you haven't voted yet, Lapidis. Is that a fact or just idle talk?"

"Not in the least!" said Klava Ivanovna in exasperation. "It's a job to get that one to agree to anything."

"Ovseich," said Lapidis with a foolish giggle, "you just checked the lists and have seen for yourself that there was no check mark by the name of Lapidis, Ivan Anempodistovich, year of birth 1901."

"It's not the check mark that matters," Degtyar calmly replied, "but the man."

"Ovseich," said Lapidis with a wink, "you can tell a man by his check mark."

"What's that supposed to mean?" said Degtyar, inserting his thumb behind his lapel. "Be more exact."

"The law gives me the right to vote between 6 A.M. and 12 P.M.," said Lapidis in an insolent tone, "so please don't hurry me."

"And doesn't it mean anything to you that people have been working here since five o'clock and would like a little rest too?" asked Degtyar in surprise.

"No," said Lapidis, "it doesn't. It's not my responsibility to organize people's time so they have a chance to rest."

"I understand," retorted Degtyar. "I understand you very well. But since you're here, why not vote?"

Lapidis paused for a moment's thought while the others waited for his answer. Once again he broke into a foolish giggle and said that he wouldn't answer Ovseich's question out of respect for the law, since the very question itself was a violation of the law.

"Ovseich," cried Cheperukha, "he's handing you a line of crap!"

The others chuckled but Degtyar let the remark go right past him and continued his conversation with Lapidis:

"And so, Ivan Anempodistovich, that means the letter of the law is more important to you than the spirit, than live people?"

"That's right," said Lapidis. "The law is the law, and if everyone starts poking around with their own interpretation of the spirit, there'll be nothing left of the law."

Lapidis spat on the floor and rubbed it with his shoe.

"Aha!" said Iona Ovseich, "that means that Cheperukha, Khomitsky, Malaya, and Degtyar are fiddling around with the law while Citizen Lapidis is on guard and won't let them get away with it. Is that what you're saying?"

"Ovseich," said Lapidis, taking him by the arm, "you're trying to put unpleasant words in my mouth."

"All right, go vote. Enough cock and bull."

The people in the polling station began grumbling, clearly fed up. Lapidis looked intently about him, then suddenly, when no one was expecting it marched past the table where the ballots were handed out and went straight to the exit, slamming the door behind him.

"Well, Malaya," said Cheperukha, rubbing his hands, "now do you see who broke the glass in his door? He needs his teeth broken."

"There's a bad apple in every bunch," said Klava Ivanovna with a sigh. "On the other hand, we all went after him and a person has his pride. It's understandable."

"Malaya," said Iona Ovseich, stamping his foot, "why are you trying to confuse people when they have the right idea?"

Ninety-seven and four tenths of the building's residents had voted by eleven o'clock. Not bad, said the District Committee, but it could be better.

Dr. Landa came to vote. No one had been concerned about him because he had notified them the day before that he had night duty. Degtyar greeted him and brought him right to the table.

"You don't have to show your passport. This is Landa, Semyon Alexandrovich. I know him personally. Give him a ballot."

Folding the ballot as he went, the doctor headed toward the ballot box with the state seal of the U.S.S.R. on it, stopped, as if he were presenting arms, placed the ballot in the slot, and jammed it in with the palm of his hand.

Iona Ovseich shook his hand and asked him how things had gone on night duty. The doctor said things should always be that good. You could feel a special enthusiasm and awareness with people.

"As a whole that's true," said Iona Ovseich, "but that doesn't rule out isolated excesses."

The doctor shrugged his shoulders to indicate that he personally had seen none.

"Lapidis was here ten minutes ago," said Iona Ovseich, "and he refused to vote. I can't be a hundred percent sure but I have the impression he planned his demonstration in advance. Of course, there's still time before twelve o'clock, and that's his right, but people can see where rights end and sabotage begins."

"Impossible!" exclaimed the doctor. "I can't believe it!"

Degtyar's lips twisted bitterly. "It's hard to believe but facts are facts, and we have to look them in the eye."

Instead of going straight home Dr. Landa first went up to see Lapidis, who was shooting a game of toy billiards with his son Adya. The younger Lapidis was winning, and the older Lapidis explained that his citizen's honor would not allow him to stop playing until he had won a game or at least reached a draw. Dr. Landa said the game could continue for a very long while whereas other things were under a strict time limit. Lapidis objected that a very long while was not the same as forever and that sooner or later he had to be on the winning side.

Dr. Landa just shrugged his shoulders and told Adya that if he really loved his father he would hurry up and lose. Adya answered that his losing meant his father winning, but how could he, Adya, lose, when his father never won? Dr. Landa marveled and said to Lapidis that his son was a real Odysseus, but that ancient Greece was a thing of the past, these were different times now, and that shouldn't be forgotten. "Thank you for the lecture," Lapidis said, pulling back the spring all the way and letting it fly. The little ball darted pointlessly about the board, hitting the posts, and then fell into the hole marked "fire."

"Fire!" said Adya happily, because all of his father's shots fell into the fire.

"Adya," sighed Dr. Landa, "you've got a very good father. I would be ashamed to beat such a good father all the time."

"So he shouldn't lose then!" cried Adya, and then his own ball rolled into the fire.

"Aha!" said Dr. Landa with pleasure, but Adya announced that that one didn't count. They were standing too close to him and trying to make him miss. "Yes," agreed his father, "that shot doesn't count. Take it over."

The younger Lapidis scored a hundred points on his next shot and Dr. Landa waved his hand in dismissal and wished them both victory. "That can't happen!" shouted Adya. The doctor turned around and said, "Adya, you should explain that to your father." Lapidis laughed, "Out of the mouths of babes gems oftimes come, but the question is this Doctor: my son has already been a Pioneer for six months, and so is he still a babe or not?"

At eight o'clock in the evening, Lapidis arrived at the polls, took a ballot, folded it in half, then in half again, and dropped it in the ballot box.

Iona Ovseich was surprised: "What's your hurry? You still have four whole hours."

That's just how it happened, said Lapidis in self-justification: he and his son had been out at Slobodka from five to seven visiting the boy's mother—today was a visiting day—then they waited for the number 15 trolley for half an hour and the ride back took another half an hour, and that's why he was there at eight.

At midnight, when the chimes of the Spassky bell tower had rung twelve times and the radio had played the "Internationale," Iona Ovseich closed the door. In fact he could have closed it at eight o'clock because Lapidis had been the last voter, but the voting regulations had set strict time limits and there could be no exceptions to that rule.

A week later the newspapers printed the complete election statistics. Before the election the Communist Party Central Committee had appealed to all Communists and sympathizers to vote for the nonparty candidates with the same unanimity they should display in voting for Communist candidates, and it had called on all nonparty members to vote for Communists with the same unanimity they would display in voting for nonparty candidates. That appeal had received a historically unprecedented response from the people. More than ninety-one million voters had participated in the election, that is, ninety-six and eight tenths percent. Of them, eighty-nine million eight hundred and forty-three thousand had voted for the Communist and nonparty candidates.

On the twenty-first of December, which happened to be Comrade Stalin's birthday, Iona Ovseich called a meeting of the building's residents and officially informed them that one hundred percent of the voters in their precinct had voted and that the Communist and nonparty candidates had won a clean sweep.

Dr. Landa had been at a medical convention in Moscow and had brought back a record of "Tiritomba." It was sung by an Italian male singer whom people found no worse than Lemeshev, some people even preferred him to Lemeshev. Anya Kotlyar was sitting on a windowsill in the hallway when the record was first played and looked as if she might burst into tears any second.

Klava Ivanovna also liked the record very much but it did not at all make her feel like crying; on the contrary, she felt like whirling and dancing as she had in her youth. Dr. Landa and his wife Gizella had gone to Bolshoi Fontan on their day off and Klava Ivanovna played the record from morning till night. Anya sat with her half the day until Joseph came shouting for her to go home at once: the bread in the oven was the color of a baby's diaper, the towels were blacker than soot, and all she did was sit there listening to that bleating record! Anya got up at once, if only to stop his shouting, but by the doorway found a second to say to Madame Malaya that Vanya Lapidis would never act that way with his wife. There was nothing humorous in what she said; on the contrary, it could have offended Joseph, but he began laughing like a fool.

"When you end up where she is, I'll treat you like Lapidis."

"Go there yourself!" answered Anya.

"You're like a couple of kids," said Klava Ivanovna, spreading her hands.

An hour later Radio Moscow reported that imperialist Japan had attacked Mongolia, with which the U.S.S.R. had a mutual aid agreement. The Japanese had attacked Mongolian border positions and had driven them back toward the Khalkhin-Gol River.

Anya went running in tears to Madame Malaya and begged her to tell the truth—would there be war with Japan?

"Get ahold of yourself!" commanded Klava Ivanovna. "Do you remember what we did to them on Lake Khasan during the last war? I'll promise you one thing—this time there'll be nothing left of them."

"You think I don't know that?" said Anya, regaining her composure somewhat, "but if there's a war, they'll take Sasha and Petya in the army, and they're still children."

"Everyone has children," said Klava Ivanovna in a loud voice. "And there's no reason to raise a panic beforehand."

That evening Degtyar called a meeting in the outpost and said that there was every indication that a new provocation had been launched in the Khalkhin-Gol River area by the Japanese militarists whose memories were all too short. It would seem that they wanted a repeat of Lake Khasan and the Zaozerny Hills. Well, then, they'd get it, if they needed to be taught a lesson.

"I have a suggestion," said Efim Granik. "Issue each of them a samurai sword so they can slit their own bellies and not waste people's time."

Dina Vargaftik was indignant; "Now look what he's making jokes about!"

"What savages they are!" cried Olya Cheperukha. "We should send Budyonny's cavalry and a hundred airplanes there and let them have a taste of that."

A week later the Stalin District Draft Board sent notices to Granik, Lapidis, and Khomitsky on which the following had been underlined in red pencil: bring a knapsack and a two-day supply of food. Stepa and Efim left first, ordering their wives to stay at home, but when they turned onto Lenin Street, they saw their wives, Tosya and Sonya, trying to hide behind trees. And even though both husbands gave their wives a good whacking, they had the nerve to pretend it was mere coincidence and that they were on their way to the bread store. Stepa only said bah and blew his nose onto the sidewalk whereas Efim categorically warned Sonya that he was no samurai but her tricks were going to drive him to commit hari-kari. Sonya began crying and honestly admitted that she had two loaves of bread at home, but why couldn't she walk with her husband who was being called up to the army for war!

"Foolish talk!" said Efim, outraged. "Better to die once and for all than to see those tears of yours every day."

Sonya cried all the more. Tosya took her by the arm and said, "Let those slobs do what they want; young women can always find themselves something better."

"That's something else again!" retorted Efim, adding that soldiers too could find what they needed.

"You should be ashamed of yourself!" said Sonya indignantly. "You're a Red Army soldier, and she was just joking."

On the way back home, Tosya and Sonya agreed that their husbands could have as many women as they wanted as long as they came home alive.

The next day, all three—Lapidis, Granik, and Khomitsky—came back to the courtyard with their knapsacks and their two days' worth of provisions; they'd been fed three hot meals a day in the Kakhovsky Barracks where they'd been quartered. Klava Ivanovna said that Lapidis looked like he'd been stuffing his face at some resort.

There were several more pitched battles in the Khalkhin-Gol River and Lake Buir-Nur region beginning in midsummer. The crack troops of the Kvantunsky army had suffered heavy losses from Soviet tanks and planes and the Mongolian cavalry, and had quickly been rolled back to the east of the Khalkhin-Gol River, which was the border between the Mongolian People's Republic and Manchuria.

In August, before the first class on the Short History of the Communist Party, Iona Ovseich reported that there was information to the effect that the Japanese ambassador to the U.S.S.R., Togo Sigenori, had proposed peace talks. The Soviet Union would be represented by the People's Commissar of Foreign Affairs, Comrade Molotov.

Though no one had asked his opinion, Iona Cheperukha declared himself against the talks—he had his own plan. This caused an outburst of noise and indignation. Comrade Degtyar ordered the room to be quiet, then asked politely: "And what is your plan?"

"The Japanese are very poor people," said Cheperukha. "They can only grow a little rice, beans, and millet on their islands, and they only see meat once every ten years. And so what conclusion do I draw? There is only one conclusion: the lion's share of the Japanese, especially the proletariat, hate the landowners and the capitalists, and so a revolution has to be launched there. But a revolution needs arms to succeed. And that means we should supply the Japanese workers and peasants with bullets, rifles, and machine guns."

"I think that would be interference in other people's affairs," said Degtyar.

"What does that mean—other people's?" said Cheperukha in surprise. "We want to help our own, the workers and peasants, otherwise those samurais will never let up on them. There's a good reason why Leonid Utesov sings: 'I'll gobble half of China and then I'll be stuffed to the throat!' "

"That's not quite what Leonid Utesov says," corrected Degtyar, "but, that aside, your plan does not take the actual situation into account, Cheperukha, and so we'll have to shelve it for a while. And just why it fails to take the actual situation into account—that you'll learn from the Short History of the Communist Party, which we're going to begin studying today." Iona Ovseich paused. "Comrades! Tsarist Russia entered the road of capitalist development later than other countries."

Cheperukha rose from his seat and said that he wanted to add two words but Iona Ovseich paid him no attention and repeated:

"Tsarist Russia entered the road of capitalist development later than other countries. There were very few factories and plants in Russia before the sixties of the last century. The entire thrust of economic development was toward the abolition of serfdom."

"Ovseich," said Cheperukha, rising and speaking without permission again. "You're telling us about the old days! I'm interested in the present and the future, and I don't want to hear about the past."

"He doesn't want to hear about the past!" said Klava Ivanovna, jumping in. "And who do you think you are that what you want or don't want matters! Who do you think you are?"

"Hold on, Malaya," said Degtyar. "I understand your indignation; the other comrades are indignant too even though they haven't said anything about it yet. But you're not right in asking Cheperukha who he thinks he is to speak and ask questions. He has every right to speak and to ask questions, and we should answer them. Citizen Cheperukha, the history of the Communist Party is the history of three revolutions: the bourgeois democratic revolution of 1905, the bourgeois democratic revolution in February 1917, and the socialist revolution in October 1917. Now I want to ask you a question: did Russia and the working class exist before 1905, or did they just suddenly appear out of nowhere?"

"What does that mean—out of nowhere?" said Cheperukha in surprise. "I saw the battleship *Potemkin* with my own eyes when it was standing in the breakwater. And then we ran to Platonovsky pier where they were burying the sailor Vakulenchuk."

"In other words," interrupted Degtyar, "Russia existed back then and so did the working class, and so we have to take a look at the past to understand things."

"I beg your pardon," said Cheperukha. "If anyone has forgotten the past they should take a look back at it. But, personally, I'm more interested in life in the present and the future, than in thinking of life under the tsarist regime all the time. Yes, things were bad then, things were bad, but why keep reminding people when they remember well enough anyway?"

"You say people remember!" said Joseph Kotlyar, slapping his knee. "But I'm sure that everyone doesn't remember. And a person who thinks like you doesn't remember and doesn't want to!"

Cheperukha turned red and jumped to his feet a third time, but Olya grabbed his jacket and pulled him back down.

Iona Ovseich made a sign for the room to come to order so that he could continue the lesson.

"One moment," interrupted Cheperukha, "I'm leaving. Call me when you start talking about the present."

"Go on, you drunk, go sober up!" Klava Ivanovna shouted after him.

Iona Ovseich ordered Malaya to calm down and in passing reminded all those present that attending the classes on the Short History of the Communist Party was entirely voluntary, and, if anyone felt like leaving, the door was always wide open.

That caused a stir because no one wanted to be bracketed or even compared with Iona Cheperukha. Only Olya sat inertly, her eyes blank, but it would have been foolish to expect any other attitude from a woman with a husband like that.

By the next morning the entire courtyard had heard about Iona Cheperukha's defiant behavior, and everyone was of the same opinion: that his employer should be informed and take the necessary action. Only Lapidis was against this idea and kept mechanically repeating that Iona Cheperukha had every right, guaranteed him by the Constitution of the U.S.S.R., to do as he saw fit, and there was no reason to grab him by the scruff of the neck and drag him to the study group.

"Don't you be waving our Constitution around like that!" said Klava Ivanovna indignantly. "Everyone should attend the study group and everyone will, if it kills me. It's voluntary for those who don't need to be told what to do. You attend but then you egg on other people not to. Why? I worry about you, Lapidis!"

Lapidis said that she didn't have to worry about him and, as far as study groups went, he attended them at his factory and even had been assigned to conduct certain classes, but you couldn't compare an engineer and a carter: an engineer had to be outdoing himself constantly or else he'd be in danger of standing still, but a carter didn't have to worry about standing still, he was always on the move. "It's just surprising," said Lapidis with an insolent smile, "that Cheperukha's so cheerful when everyone else is in such a rage."

Two days later an official from the Stalin District police station came to the courtyard, rang for the Concierge, and ordered her to bring him to Cheperukha's. Then Klava Ivanovna was summoned and, in her presence, the official stated that fourteen-year-old Zinovy Cheperukha had been detained that morning on a trolley car where he had been found with a woman's watch and twenty-five rubles in cash.

"One moment," said Klava Ivanovna to the official. "How do you know that he stole them on the trolley car? Couldn't he have taken them from his own mother?"

"That's just what I tried to tell him!" said Olya, in tears. "But he wants me to describe the watch in detail."

"In a state like hers," said Klava Ivanovna, "a person could forget his own name. I couldn't for the life of me describe the grandfather clock that's been ticking away in my apartment day and night for ten years."

Olya burst into tears again and covered her face with her hands. Klava Ivanovna sighed deeply in what could have even seemed a moan. Then for the official from the Stalin District police station she briefly described the kind of life Olya Cheperukha led with her son Zyunchik, whose father was a drunkard from the market. A few days before, said Klava Ivanovna, when all the building's residents were studying the history of the party with enormous interest, Iona Cheperukha was the one and only person in the entire courtyard who stood up in front of everyone and slammed the door as he left.

The comrade from the police station nodded, and you could tell by his eyes that he understood and was sympathetic, but then suddenly he asked about the outpost and the building's activists: "The courtyard has an outpost and activists, and so are you telling me that a drunken father is more powerful than the outpost and public opinion?" he asked.

"Comrade," said Klava Ivanovna with indignation, "I'm surprised that you're being so superficial here. If it weren't for the outpost and the activists, the situation would be entirely different. Zyunchik's mother would have been going to see her son at the children's labor colony on Lustdorf Road a long time ago."

All right, said the policeman, they would release Zinovy Cheperukha and, for the time being, this would just be noted in his file, but Comrade Malaya and the other people responsible should notify the District Committee in writing that they were assuming supervision of the boy.

When the policeman had gone, Klava Ivanovna informed Olya that she could fall to her knees and beg but the courtyard would bring them to a Comrades' Court that all Odessa would come running to see! Olya was not offended and only wiped away her tears, repeating that they had it coming. She thanked Madame Malaya for standing up for her like her own mother and saving Zyunchik from jail.

That evening Iona Cheperukha came into the courtyard pushing his wheelbarrow; he commanded himself to stop, saying, "Whoa!" He left the handles pointing upward, kicked the wheel, and began loudly singing the song about the three tank men: " 'Roaring with fire and flashing with steel, the tanks roll furiously on, when Comrade Stalin sends us into battle, and the marshal leads us into the fray!' " The bulb at the entrance had burned out and the courtyard was dark. Cheperukha had to grope his way along the wall. Near the front door he collided with a metal pedestal left over from the old days and his song was interrupted. Iona cursed the name of Colonel Kotlyarevsky, the former owner of the building, and all the other exploiters who had drunk and still drank the blood of the working class.

A short while later the sound of doors slamming followed by a racket like that of furniture being tipped over came from the Cheperukhas' apartment. Then Zyunchik went running down the hallway with Olya right behind him. Zyunchik didn't say anything as he ran, but Olya was screaming wildly that Iona was coming after them with an ax and that the neighbors should come to their rescue, otherwise there'd be a blood bath.

Nastya, who could see it all through her window, closed both her shutters, but not before yelling "Help!" Iona stopped in the middle of the courtyard and warned everyone to stay out of it if they didn't want to be hacked to pieces. Stepa and Efim pushed Cheperukha's wheelbarrow in front of them and turned it as if they were heading straight for Iona. They ordered him to throw down his ax like a good man before it was too late.

"My wheelbarrow!" said Iona, suddenly bursting into tears. "I was never a thief. I worked, I've worked my whole life like a dog and now my son, my son is a thief! Stepa, Efim, take this ax, kill me dead, I'm asking you, hack me to bits!"

Olya and Zyunchik spent the night at Madame Malaya's. When the lights were off and Zyunchik had fallen asleep, Klava Ivanovna said to Olya: "You have only yourself to blame. It should have waited for morning. I could have had a talk with him myself."

Olya agreed with every word Madame Malaya said and cried into her pillow so that she wouldn't be heard.

The Comrades' Court was scheduled for the eighteenth of September but had to be postponed the day before. On the seventeenth of September units of the Red Army, commanded by Comrade General Timoshenko, had crossed the Polish border to protect the life and property of the people of the western Ukraine and western Belorussia. The Polish-German war, which had erupted at the beginning of September, had revealed the inner bankruptcy of gentry-bourgeois Poland, artificially created with the aid of England and France. In the first ten days of the war Poland had lost all its industrial and cultural centers; the feckless Polish leaders had involved their nation in war and then abandoned it to the mercy of fate. The working people of the western Ukraine and western Belorussia had welcomed their liberators with boundless enthusiasm and were helping the Red Army units purge their land of the Polish lords.

Though there had been no announcement, people gathered in the outpost that evening.

"Comrades," said Iona Ovseich, "a dream which a people have been dreaming for ages has now come true. We can rejoice with our blood brothers of the western Ukraine and Belorussia, who will no longer be ground under the heels of Polish lords. From this day on they will be Soviet people just like you and me."

When Iona Ovseich was through, Lapidis inquired as to the source of that information.

"Which information do you mean?" asked Degtyar. "That the Red Army has taken the western Ukrainians and Belorussians under its protection?"

Lapidis said he was interested in how Degtyar knew that those lands would become part of the U.S.S.R.?

"What else would they become a part of?" said Degtyar with a smile. Everyone turned his eyes on Lapidis to see who could ask such stupid questions.

At the end of October, in a theater in the city of Lvov, the Ukrainian National Assembly, elected by 90.93 percent of the voters, requested of the Supreme Soviet of the U.S.S.R. that the western Ukraine be incorporated as the Ukrainian Soviet Socialist Republic.

"Well," said Klava Ivanovna to Degtyar and the others who were there at the moment, "what's Lapidis going to say to us now!"

Lapidis was not able to say anything because three days later he returned from the city of Drogobych, whose oil refineries he had been sent to inspect as an expert, and Madame Malaya made a point of visiting him to find out how people were doing there. He replied with his usual foolish laughter and showed her two Gutsul rugs which he had bought from peasants. She told him straight out not to try to fool her, only the bourgeois could have rugs like that.

International events pushed Cheperukha into the background. Many people had even forgotten about him but Degtyar said that there was no reason for postponing the Comrades' Court any further and that Madame Malaya should make the announcement. Klava Ivanovna had some doubts on that score: shouldn't they hold off in honor of recent Soviet successes?

"Malaya," said Iona Ovseich with a frown, "I'll answer you with the words of Comrade Stalin: people who aren't experienced in politics allow success to make them careless and rest on their laurels. It's not good humor that we need now, but vigilance, real Bolshevik revolutionary vigilance!"

The Comrades' Court was held in the outpost and the residents of the neighboring courtyards were also invited to attend. Degtyar, Klava Ivanovna, and Dr. Landa sat together, with Iona Cheperukha a little off to one side. To make things clear to all those present, Comrade Degtyar provided a short description of the case, then turned the floor over to Citizen Cheperukha.

"My dear neighbors," said Cheperukha, "I've been living in this building since my father, Avrum Cheperukha, and my mother Rivka Cheperukha, née Kogan, brought me into this world. My whole life has been lived out in plain view of you. I've done physical labor all my adult life and never shirked from hard work. On the contrary, an engineer only has to use his brains and for a man who operates a machine the most important thing is his hands, but a carter needs brains to figure out how to make a few kopecks, and he needs good hands and good legs to boot. An engineer can sit in a chair and think, and a machine operator can sit at his machine too because it's motor driven, but where did you ever see a carter without legs? A carter without legs is like an airplane without wings or a locomotive without wheels."

Granik, Dr. Landa, and many of the others began applauding but Degtyar ordered them to stop and on behalf of all present requested that Citizen Cheperukha get down to the case at hand and not go back to Adam and Eve. Cheperukha replied that he wasn't starting with Adam and Eve because they lived in Paradise while he had been born under the tsars, and the Russia of Nicholas II was a prison of nations, especially for Jews and other minorities. Only the rich had the right to education and medical treatment and a poor man was happy if he could bring home a morsel of bread to his hungry children and wife. And the wife wouldn't know which to do first—give her breast to the youngest or a crust of bread to the hungriest.

"Citizen Cheperukha," interrupted Degtyar, "as the chairman, I'm telling you again—get down to the point and stop lecturing us."

Cheperukha objected that he wasn't lecturing but speaking of his own life when he was still a boy, of his father who was a poor carter, and his family, which constantly went hungry. Then when he was grown up a little, he began earning a little money at the Old Horse Market, guarding sacks for one person, watering the horses for another. And it was that way from dawn to dusk. The working people who had no life apart from the hard labor they performed for a few kopecks would immediately spend that money on drink. They could forget it all as long as they were blind drunk. Working alongside those people he had also gotten the habit of drinking a little—wine, home brew, state-produced vodka, in a word, whatever he could get his hands on. A bad habit is like a typhus louse: you crush it with your fingernail but it's already had time to inject its foul poison into your blood. Now, of course, life was quite different, and there was no reason to drink, but the poison was still in his bloodstream from those days and medicine was still powerless against it.

"Comrades," said Iona Ovseich, rising, "I think that where medicine is powerless, public opinion has power to spare. Instead of honestly and openly admitting his criminal behavior, Citizen Cheperukha has been telling us history from Adam and Eve on, but, no matter how much he was told, or how often he was warned, he can't be found at the classes on the short course even with a flashlight in the daytime. A drunk, a rowdy, and a troublemaker—that's a person who takes an ax in hand and attacks his own son, his wife, and his neighbors!"

"Ovseich," said Cheperukha, extending his hands forward, a pitiful smile on his face, "but I was drunk, I had no idea what I was doing. I give you my word of honor—"

"Cheperukha," said Comrade Degtyar, raising his voice, "you're out of order; no one gave you the floor. The court wants to hear from the witnesses: Anastasya Arkhipovna Sereda."

Nastya said that she had nothing to say except that Cheperukha ran out with his ax and stood in the middle of the courtyard near the drain. She closed her window from fear but she saw Stepa and Efim pushing the wheelbarrow at him and Cheperukha waving his ax around, shouting he'd chop them into little pieces.

Iona Ovseich approved her testimony and asked if she had seen anything similiar in Cheperukha's behavior earlier, before the incident:

for example, had he come home drunk, attacked his wife or son, or cursed loudly?

Nastya answered that she had noticed such things before.

"Comrade Sereda," said Iona Ovseich, "can you remember exactly what Cheperukha said?"

Yes, said Nastya, she could; one time, it was in the month of August, Iona came home drunk, his breath was blue it was so foul, and shouted that parasites were living off the Soviet system; all they did was shoot off their mouths and kiss the bosses' ass and lick it, and there was no one to work.

Iona Ovseich said that there was no need to repeat everything word for word and was about to ask another question when Lapidis said from his seat that it was beyond the Comrades' Court competency to examine such trivialities and he lodged a categorical objection.

"Lapidis," said Iona Ovseich, rapping his pencil against the rim of the water pitcher, "you should be aware that what happens in the courtyard and concerns all the building's residents is within the competency of a Comrades' Court. And if this is not to your liking, you may leave."

"Whether I leave or remain here," cried Lapidis, "is my own affair!"

"Whether you drink a glass of water or not is your own affair," replied Iona Ovseich, "but the way you behave in a public place affects everyone and I advise you not to show any defiance here."

People began applauding, but Lapidis again came out with his own opinion, no longer addressing the chairman but the audience: they shouldn't forget that the Comrades' Court was not just for Iona Cheperukha alone; if need be, other defendants would be found.

That sounded like an open threat and people didn't like that. Kotlyar rose and demanded that the chairman restore order even if that meant removing Lapidis from the hall.

Khomitsky was the next to testify as a witness. Iona Ovseich asked him how long he had been living in the building. Stepa answered that everyone knew that he'd been living there since 1920 when he arrived with Kotovsky's brigade, and then he began speaking of Cheperukha. Cheperukha had been hitting the bottle for as long as he'd known him but lately he'd been drinking a little more. Or maybe he hadn't. Maybe it was just the years taking their toll, and now a half a glass did what it used to take half a litre to do. And as far as the ax went, he personally thought Iona was just trying to frighten them and no one was in any real danger.

"In other words, he was joking," said Iona Ovseich, elaborating on the point.

Tosya, Stepa's wife, shouted from her seat that it was better to visit a husband like that in prison or bring flowers to him across the way than put up with jokes like that. People laughed because Odessa's two main cemeteries, one Christian, the other Jewish, were right across from the prison on Lustdorf Road.

Efim Granik testified after Khomitsky. Unlike the previous witness, he had thought that Cheperukha had posed a danger with his ax though initially Iona had just wanted to put a scare into them and on that point he was in full agreement with Khomitsky. "On the other hand, as the saying goes, all's well that ends well," said Granik.

"Witness Granik," interrupted Degtyar, "we're not interested in hearing what you think. The court only wants to know the facts, only the bare facts."

Granik replied that bare facts were bare facts but in addition everybody had a head of his own, and whether it was forbidden or not, it was still going to think. "For example," said Efim, "you're lying in bed at night, trying not to think, but the thoughts come anyway, because that's how a person's head is."

Dr. Landa laughed, and used some medical expression. The chairman announced that there was nothing humorous here, and sternly warned Efim:

"Witness Granik, you can inform the doctors in Sverdlovka, the lunatic asylum on Kanatnaya Street, about your head, but this is a court, not doctors, and we're issuing you a categorical warning!"

"Ovseich," cried Lapidis in a menacing tone, "science has not yet invented a sword that doesn't cut both ways!"

Dr. Landa frowned while the others, with the exception of Iona Ovseich, simply let the remark pass. Degtyar at once and very aptly replied that a skillful hand could make two swords out of one and use all four edges to strike whomever necessary, wherever necessary, and whenever necessary. And the court was entirely clear as to Witness Granik's testimony, which indicated that he had seen the ax with his own eyes and assumed that it could have posed a danger to life and limb.

"Next witness," announced Iona Ovseich, "Gizella Landa."

When Dr. Landa heard that his wife was being summoned, he glanced with surprise at Degtyar but Gizella had already approached the table and it was too late to do anything about it.

The witness stated that she had heard the defendant's threats and seen the ax in his hand, but did not know whether or not he had intended to attack his wife and son with it.

"Tell us," said Iona Ovseich, "in the past, have you ever had occasion to hear Citizen Cheperukha make threats to other people for other reasons?"

The witness thought for a moment, then recalled that when the outpost had been opened, Cheperukha had helped carry her piano and on the second floor, or between the second and third, she didn't remember exactly, he gave her to understand that he could smash her piano to smithereens.

"My God!" said Dr. Landa, jumping to his feet, "but that was a joke!"

"A joke?" said Gizella with surprise. "Then as usual I failed to get it."

"All right," said Iona Ovseich, "but do you think he was capable of carrying out that threat?"

"I don't know," said Gizella with a shrug of her shoulders, "but if a person has no bad intentions then why should he make threats?"

"Witness Landa," said Lapidis, suddenly rising from his seat, "do you fear for your life when your husband, Dr. Landa, picks up a knife and fork?"

"Ask your own wife that sort of question," said Gizella, curling her lips.

"Citizen Lapidis," said Degtyar, rapping his pencil three times against the water pitcher, "let's dispense with these altercations from the floor, stop trying our patience! The next witness is Vargaftik, Dina Savelevna."

"Friends and neighbors," said Dina, putting both her hands around her throat, "if someone told me that something like what Cheperukha did could possibly happen in our courtyard, I would have strangled that person with my own two hands. But still it's a fact, the truth is the truth: Cheperukha went after his wife and son with an ax in his hands. On that same day his son had stolen a watch and twenty-five rubles and a policeman had come to the courtyard. That your own born son is a thief is enough to drive a person crazy but we have to ask who's the guilty one here: a father who gets up drunk and goes to bed drunk or a boy who's been seeing that since he was a baby? And when Comrade Degtyar had personally told Cheperukha that he had to attend the classes on party history that everyone was supposed to attend, no exceptions, Cheperukha showed him his backside, you'll pardon the expression, and slammed the door so loud they could hear it in Moscow. And that we all saw with our own eyes. What I want to know is where is Cheperukha going to stop, should we give him some more time or take steps now so that we won't have to kick ourselves later!"

While Dina Vargaftik was speaking, Iona could not take his eyes off her; his Adam's apple kept bobbing up and down as if it were on a rubber band. When she turned to go back to her seat, Cheperukha suddenly threw back his head and spat at her. The spit landed on her skirt. Dina showed it to the court and declared that, as a matter of principle, she was not going to wipe it off and would let it remain there as yet another item of evidence.

"Enter that in the minutes," ordered the chairman.

"Listen, everyone," said Iona, raising both fists, "it hurts me that there are pigs like Vargaftik among us Jews!"

"Cheperukha," shouted Klava Ivanovna, "enough of your anti-Semitic hooligan outbursts. Otherwise you're going to end up where you belong so fast it'll make your head spin!"

"Dr. Landa," said the defendant, wiping his eyes with his fists, "you at least should stand up for me, you're an educated man, you're an intelligent person."

People laughed to hear the carter Iona Cheperukha, the son of a carter, certifying someone's intelligence.

"The next witness is Lapidis, Ivan Anempodistovich," said Degtyar. "Remind the court that on the day in question, December 12, when the Soviet people were electing their Supreme Soviet for the first time in history, Cheperukha broke the glass in your door in hooligan fashion."

Lapidis turned pale and appeared on the verge of being ill. Anya

Kotlyar handed him a glass of water. He refused it but she brought the glass up to his lips and whispered: "Drink it, please." Lapidis took a sip. Joseph Kotlyar said "Thank you" in a loud voice. People smiled but Anya Kotlyar blushed.

"Lapidis," said Degtyar in a cheerful tone of voice, "when a man receives support like that, he can find the strength to function day and night like the Turkish Parliament."

"Ovseich," Lapidis finally replied, "this isn't the Turkish Parliament, and we're not Turks. We're Soviet people and we have a Constitution, the basic law of the U.S.S.R. And so, let's respect our Constitution. No one gave us the right to turn a Comrades' Court into a lynch mob. And whether or not Cheperukha broke the glass is a personal matter, one we can resolve without any intermediaries."

"A lynch mob!" exclaimed Iona Ovseich. "What a word to use—lynch mob! No, Citizen Lapidis, your glass is a personal matter but how Cheperukha conducts himself is a matter of general concern. The day before yesterday he broke the glass in your door, yesterday, he didn't want to attend our study group, today he attacked his wife and neighbors with an ax, and tomorrow . . ."

Iona Ovseich suddenly paused, his face turning white as chalk, stunning everyone, but a moment later people were able to sigh with relief as some color returned to his face. Iona Ovseich wiped the sweat off his forehead with his handkerchief and then concluded his thought about what might happen tomorrow, when it would definitely be too late, if steps were not taken today.

"Comrades, neighbors," said Cheperukha, striking his chest with his fist, "I swear by my life, I swear on my mother's grave and my own son's health—this was the last time. If it happens again, then it's straight to Solovki for me."

"Yah, yah, yah," interrupted Klava Ivanovna. "You were making the same promise three years ago and people believed you. People have put up with you for another three years but now the end has come. The building committee makes a motion that Iona Cheperukha be expelled from Odessa."

"Let's see the building committee's motion in writing," shouted Lapidis from his seat.

Klava Ivanovna waved him away and repeated that there was a motion to expell Iona Avrumovich Cheperukha from Odessa. His wife and son could decide for themselves—if they wanted to go too, they could go, and if they wanted to stay, they could stay.

"Comrades," said Iona Ovseich, "who is in favor of this motion? Only residents of this building may vote on it. Those not wishing to vote for or against may abstain."

"Being neither for it nor against it," said Granik, jumping to his feet, "is the same as Trotsky at Brest—neither war nor peace."

"This is not the time to be showing how smart you are," said Degtyar, calling Granik to order.

Stepa Khomitsky motioned that it be a secret ballot and was seconded by Dr. Landa. Joseph Kotlyar, however, was absolutely opposed, saying that such matters should be decided openly, so that the teeth weren't saying one thing and the tail wagging another.

"Kotlyar's motion is accepted," announced the chairman. "I'll say it again: no one has to vote for or against, but everyone should voice his opinion openly, let's not play hide and seek here."

Olya Cheperukha, whose cheeks were burning with shame and anguish so much they looked suntanned, asked if she also had to vote. For the third time Iona Ovseich repeated that everyone had the right to use his own discretion, no one was obligated to vote, but the community also had the right to evaluate the behavior of each of its members. Especially in the case of Olya Cheperukha since the collective had come to her defense.

The majority was in complete agreement with the chairman and the issue could have been put to a vote but once again Stepa Khomitsky, supported this time by Dr. Landa, raised another question: was the verdict of the Comrades' Court final or did it need to be approved by the City Soviet?

"Khomitsky," said Iona Ovseich, genuinely angered, "you're trying to stump me with your questions. People could think that you're purposely creating an obstruction and that Dr. Landa is in collusion with you."

Dr. Landa's face expressed heightened surprise—what collusion? He motioned that they move on to the vote.

The voting proceeded in orderly fashion. Since the overwhelming majority was in favor, only those who voted against or abstained were individually counted. Three people were against—Lapidis, Granik, and Khomitsky, and three people also abstained—Dr. Landa, Anya

Kotlyar, and Olya Cheperukha. Joseph looked at his wife as if seeing her for the first time.

When the chairman announced the result of the voting on the expulsion of Citizen Cheperukha from the city of Odessa, Iona suddenly dashed over to the table and showered them with curses. Then, becoming even more incensed, he called them all sons of whores, grabbed the water pitcher, wound up, and aimed it at the chairman of the court, Comrade Degtyar. Taken by surprise, people were stunned, and only Dr. Landa jumped up, grabbed Cheperukha's arm, and demanded that he immediately put the pitcher back or he would smash it over his head.

Such rough talk from Dr. Landa came as a complete surprise to everyone, but, most surprisingly, Cheperukha obeyed and put the pitcher back. Then he fell to his knees, banging his forehead against the floor like an epileptic, once, twice, three times, and began lamenting in a thin voice like the hired mourners at a Jewish funeral.

By then Degtyar had his wits back about him and ordered Stepa and Efim to pick Cheperukha from the floor and remove him from the room, saying that his presence was no longer required. Cheperukha resisted, reviling himself in the foulest terms, and shouting that he wanted to apologize to his neighbors, but Iona Ovseich only repeated his order.

Olya was still sitting, her gaze vacant. People tried not to look at her because feeling other people's eyes on her would only make it worse.

Klava Ivanovna said that you could only wish a husband and father like that on your worst enemy but, on the other hand, an immediate note should be made in the decision that the residents of the building, and, first and foremost, the activists, had, by their indifference and carelessness, allowed Cheperukha to reach the state of becoming an antisocial element. Landa, Khomitsky, and a few others supported Klava Ivanovna in this while the rest remained silent.

"Comrades," said Iona Ovseich, "I do not agree with the formulation made by court member Malaya, either in relation to the facts or as a matter of principle. As for the facts, you're all well aware of how much we've been through with Cheperukha and we won't go over that again, but as to the principle involved, the political side of the matter, no one has given us the right to cast wholesale disparagement on an entire community because of one lousy black sheep. Moreover, it is our duty to take care that this dangerous infection does not spread to others. When Joseph Kotlyar suffered gangrene in his left leg because of the wound he received during the Civil War, he said to the doctors, 'Cut off the leg.' And, if he hadn't, he wouldn't be here with us today."

People turned toward Kotlyar, who nodded slowly, such anguish in his eyes that no further explanations were required—it was clear that Degtyar had taken his example from life and not just plucked it out of the air.

"Ovseich," said Lapidis without permission, rising from his seat and heading straight for the door, "allow me to bid you and this high assembly adieu: I'm in the habit of drinking kefir every day at nine o'clock. I recommend it to everyone. Adieu!"

"Lapidis," Efim Granik shouted after him, "and where do you find kefir every day?"

Efim had no real reason for asking that question: it was no secret that the Marti ship repair works and the port had their own in-house cafeterias, which were supplied by Torgmotrans, which also supplied the seagoing vessels.

The next morning Kolka Khomitsky told Zyunchik that his father was being sent out of the city to work on a kolkhoz somewhere in the district and that if he showed himself capable of honest labor he could return to Odessa in three years.

"But how are we going to live?" asked Zyunchik.

"Idiot!" said Kolka with a laugh. "They'll take his whole salary so his family can eat."

"And so then how's he going to live?" said Zyunchik in surprise.

"Idiot!" said Kolka, laughing again. "The country's not like the city, you can buy supplies, material and bicycles in the stores there, and everyone has eggs and lard in his hut."

Zyunchik said that he might like to live for a while in the country too but his mother was against it: she said if you lose your apartment in Odessa, you have to wait twenty-five years for another one. His father was grabbing his fly and saying he'd find himself another woman. "And you my little son of a bitch, Zyunya, I'll drag you out of your grave, I'll find you in hell, but I'll make a man out of you yet."

"He's nuts!" said Kolka with a laugh. "The U.S.S.R. goes from the Black Sea to the Pacific Ocean—just let him try and find you!"

"Naw," said Zyunchik, "I'm going to Spain."

"To Spain?" said Kolka in surprise. "You can't go to Spain. There's only the rebels and General Franco there now."

Zyunchik chuckled: "The workers are only waiting for the right moment to spit on Franco!"

Kolka didn't make any objection about the workers who were just waiting for the right moment, that wasn't the hitch: ships used to sail with arms and food from Odessa to Spain during the Civil War but now they'd stopped.

No, said Zyunchik. He'd spoken with a guy from a military ship who'd seen it with his own eyes—the ships were sailing there, but on the sly now.

The decision of the Comrades' Court concerning the expulsion of Iona Cheperukha from Odessa was passed on to the Executive Committee of the City Soviet, and a copy was sent to the Stalin District Soviet. The District Soviet approved the decision two weeks later; there was no reply from the Municipal Soviet.

Now Iona was coming home sober every evening and even Klava Ivanovna admitted that he was as peaceful as could be and God grant that everyone should show as much self-discipline. An independent study class for the short course was scheduled for Saturday. Having changed into a new wool suit, Cheperukha politely greeted his neighbors and took a seat in the back row.

Degtyar stopped for a second when he opened the door and saw Cheperukha, then walked quickly to the table, set down his notebook, announced the subject for the day, and while people were writing it down in their notebooks he turned to Malaya, the leader of the study group, and asked on what basis she had allowed Citizen Cheperukha to participate after he had been expelled from the building and the city of Odessa by a decision of a Comrades' Court? "If he had been sentenced to death that would be another matter," she replied, "but, as it is, the class can only do him good."

"So the right hand doesn't know what the left is doing," said Iona Ovseich. "Where is that going to get us, Malaya?"

The class, including Cheperukha, said nothing, everyone was well aware that Degtyar was right. Only Klava Ivanovna held out and stuck to her own opinion.

"That's enough," interrupted Degtyar. "The discussion is closed. Citizen Cheperukha, please leave the room and do not return here in future."

Iona rose, looked around as if seeking support, then said plaintively: "Comrade Degtyar, I swear on my life, I give you my word of honor—"

"Comrade Cheperukha," repeated Iona Ovseich, "we're asking you for a second time to leave the room and not return here in future!"

Cheperukha groaned like a sick man and left, not quite closing the door behind him.

Iona Ovseich repeated that the subject of today's class was Lenin's work "One Step Forward, Two Steps Back" and said that he would allow himself to begin by quoting directly from a statement by Lenin in which he unmasked Martov.

"I'll quote it verbatum: 'The psychology of the bourgeois intellectual who numbers himself among the "chosen few" who stand above mass organization, emerges with remarkable clarity here . . . Intellectual individualism thinks every proletarian organization a form of serfdom.' Lenin, Volume Six, page 282. Comrades, no doubt you have already drawn the parallel yourselves between Lenin's words and what we still sometimes observe even today when one person comes out openly and directly against the will of the collective while another, for all practical purposes his accomplice, abstains solely out of tactical considerations. I want you to understand once and for all that Marxism is not a dogma but a guide to action and that there is not a single fact or a single phenomenon in life that does not have class and political content and meaning. We must not look away, must not touch things up, but should always remember, every day, every hour, every second, that unconsidered criticism and self-criticism can provide our enemies with an additional weapon, and for that reason we have to make a strict distinction between criticism and carping, between self-criticism and intellectual self-flagellation and all the other aberrations described by Dostoevsky. Tosya Khomitsky, are you making notes on this or just pretending to?"

Tosya said that she wasn't pretending and showed him her notebook. Iona Ovseich pointed out that many of them were using pencils even though notes made in pencil fade quickly. Lyalya Orlov held up her fountain pen. Iona Ovseich nodded approvingly but added that not everyone could get hold of a foreign-made pen but everyone could use an ordinary Russian-made pen with a number eighty-six nib, or, best of all, a lozhechka, the best Russian pen; they didn't tear paper so badly and squeaked less. Sonya Granik asked where she could get a lozhechka if the Two Elephants store on Lenin Street, corner of Zhukovsky, had only rondos, and were out of number eighty-six nibs, and didn't expect more before next month.

"All right," said Iona Ovseich, "then we'll find another solution. The study group leader, Comrade Malaya, will be given a memorandum which she will take to the stationery depot. And there she'll receive a consignment of pens, nibs, erasers, notebooks, and good porcelain inkwells. She can get a little extra too so there'll be enough for our children too."

"Oy, Ovseich," cried Dina Vargaftik, "may you live two hundred years!"

When Klava Ivanovna went to the depot with her memorandum, the manager gave her a very warm welcome. It turned out that he had known Comrade Degtyar personally since February 1917, from the first Soviet revolution. As for the matter at hand, he requested a little patience: they were expecting a shipment of stationery by train from Leningrad any day now.

The manager had told the truth. The goods arrived two weeks later and would have been there even earlier but events in the Karelian Isthmus had forced the rail lines near Leningrad to carry other cargo. Iona Ovseich had foreseen the delay; even before it had been reported on the radio, he had been informed that the Finnish government had insolently turned up its nose at all Soviet offers to extend the Soviet border away from Leningrad and to lease to the Soviet government the Khanko Peninsula in exchange for real compensation in any other border region. On the thirtieth of November, Finnish troops based on the Mannerheim Line, which had been constructed by German, French, and British military engineers, had committed a series of provocations on the Soviet border. The Red Army had now assumed the offensive.

As soon as Anya Kotlyar heard about the war with Finland, her first reaction was fear for her sons, Sasha and Petya. She was certain that Hitler too was going to attack the U.S.S.R. but, speaking with his full authority, Iona Ovseich warned her not to spread panic and desist from provocative conversation because the U.S.S.R. had a ten-year nonaggression pact with Germany signed by Comrade Molotov and Ribbentrop.

At the next class Iona Ovseich gave notice that the Finnish war might be protracted somewhat: despite the freezing weather, there were swamps at the Finnish border which did not freeze over, making progress difficult for Soviet cavalry, tanks, and armored cars.

At the beginning of December, a large mass of arctic air reached Odessa; a thick layer of ice and snow formed on the streets, causing vehicles to skid badly. So that long lines would not be formed at the stores, the Municipal Soviet issued orders that every person be allocated four hundred grams of bread per day. All housewives were instructed to make bags and on the front to indicate their address, last name, and number of people in the family. The bread would be delivered by wheelbarrow straight to each courtyard and someone from each family had to remain home during the day since the stores were unable to predict exactly when the bread would arrive from the bakeries.

At the same time, every citizen, including those who were not working and children, were to be issued four hundred grams of sunflower oil and a half kilo of sugar per month, obtainable at their convenience from the store where they were listed. Many people said that this was a much better arrangement than before—you didn't have to stand in line worrying whether or not your turn would come. Only Lapidis as usual kept grimacing and quite stupidly joked that Finland was the foreskin left from Russia's circumcision twenty years ago and now it had one sixth of the earth's surface in a fever.

When the white bread was delivered at two rubles seventy kopecks a loaf, Granik proposed that his neighbors take half his loaf, first because his family loved the ninety-kopeck bread, second, for two rubles seventy he could buy three loaves of the other bread, and, third, his children ate the bread so fast he could spend a hundred and fifty rubles a month on bread alone.

"It's straight communism with home delivery!" laughed Lapidis, and advised Granik to dry out his extra bread because if they sat around long enough, they were bound to come in handy.

Klava Ivanovna laughed along with everyone else the first time but a joke is only a joke once and the next time she warned Lapidis: "You're lucky that Degtyar can't hear you."

Iona Ovseich invited Klava Ivanovna to come see him. "Malaya," he said, "why is it that I have to find out what Lapidis has been saying through roundabout means?"

"Degtyar!" said Klava Ivanovna, "you've got enough on your mind as it is, all you need is Lapidis. We can shut him up ourselves."

"No," said Iona Ovseich, placing his left hand behind his back and grasping his lapel with his right, "you can't shut him up yourselves. On the contrary, you are all standing around waiting to hear what he has to say next!"

On the evening before their day off, Lapidis, Khomitsky, and Cheperukha received call-up notices from the Stalin District Draft Board. They packed their things that night so as not to have to rush in the morning. They agreed to leave together. Zoya, Lapidis' wife, wept softly in the front hall. Adya spent most of the evening practicing his scales, then played billiards for a while with his father, and went to bed.

The lights went on in Lapidis' place at three o'clock in the morning. Shadows scurried back and forth across the cream-colored curtains, sometimes large with only torsos visible, sometimes small and black as if projected against photography paper. Then the shadows moved off to the right in single file, a door slammed, and men's feet rang out on the iron staircase.

Four people, three wearing topcoats and jodhpurs, moved quickly through the entry hall to the gateway. Around the corner, a motor started up with a rattle, its sound high-pitched at first, like tin rubbing on tin, misfiring, then all of a sudden the motor caught with a powerful roar, and the vehicle drove away.

"Oy!" moaned Klava Ivanovna. She covered her head against the cold air blowing in from the window and told herself to go back to sleep.

About three minutes later the door to Lapidis' apartment slammed again, followed by the sound of another door closing downstairs in the entry hall. The sound of the little bell on the door meant that the concierge, Nastya, had gone back in.

The next morning before dawn, Anya Kotlyar went to Madame Malaya's and asked if it was true that Lapidis had been arrested that night. Klava Ivanovna became angry and called Anya a fool but then at once burst into tears herself and said: "It must be some kind of a mistake, sure Lapidis has a big mouth, but that doesn't make him an enemy of the people or a saboteur!" Anya reminded Madame Malaya that she had warned him a hundred times that Soviet society was all alone in the world, with a capitalist encirclement on every side, and spies seizing on every word, but it was like talking to a brick wall.

Anya began crying too. She'd been talking to Lapidis just two days ago. She'd read in the newspaper about the appeal from the women of Magnitogorsk to all the women of the country to go to the factories and Lapidis had promised to help find her a job at his factory.

"That doesn't matter," said Klava Ivanovna, "we can help you too, and even better."

"Oh, thank you," said Anya, "but I thought that people who lived in the same courtyard and worked in the same factory could get together for lunch and a little talk every so often."

Klava Ivanovna smiled: "You foolish Anya, you thought that a ship-repair plant was like a store where all the salespeople go to the same place for lunch together."

"No," said Anya, starting to cry again, "that's not what I thought, but it's too late to talk about that now, Lapidis has been arrested."

"Button your lip," ordered Klava Ivanovna. "If Lapidis isn't guilty, he'll be back home in a week, and if he is guilty, then things will take their proper course."

"Yes, yes," said Anya, nodding her head and reminding herself that she had not been arrested, Klava Ivanovna had not been arrested, Dr. Landa had not been arrested, but for some reason only Lapidis had been taken; God forbid it was anything but a simple mistake.

Stepa and Iona met by the gateway. Tosya and Olya had announced that their husbands would leave without them only over their dead bodies. In the courtyard of the draft board building, Tosya thought she saw her son Kolka run into the men's room even though just a half an hour ago she had wrapped up his breakfast, which he'd put in his school case, and then she'd sent him on his way to school.

Olya said that if it weren't a men's room, she'd go right in and see for herself, but God knew what people would think if she went in there. Tosya replied that she didn't give a damn what people thought and went into the men's room. The men roared with laughter and began singing in bawdy voices: "Who's afraid of the big gray wolf, our mama's here to protect us." Then they began shouting: "Mama, don't hit me with a wet towel!" Tosya called them a bunch of louts and then emerged from the men's room dragging the two boys, Zyunchik and her son Kolka, by the ears.

"You bastards, you little bastards!" Olya pounded her head with her fists. "Other people have normal children but you two are real bastards. Your fathers' are being taken off to war and all you can think about is getting out of school!"

Zyunchik said that he wasn't a bastard and that he had done all his homework for that day but that he and Kolka had decided to go to the front. Even though her Kolka had not said a word, Tosya had grabbed him by his forelock and the sound of her fist striking his forehead rang out three times. Kolka laughed and asked for more, saying it didn't hurt, just the other way around, but just then Iona and Stepa walked over and said they were being shipped out in twenty minutes. The women should kiss them now if they wanted and then go home. Tosya and Olya wept while Kolka and Zyunchik kept saying that they were going to the front too.

Stepa told the women to cut the dramatics, saying they should think about the children and not worry about them—by the time they were given uniforms and shipped to Leningrad, the White Finns would be fleeing in retreat. Iona added that there wouldn't be enough left of them even to retreat.

Though they were supposed to ship out twenty minutes later, the process dragged on till evening—the province motor pool had provided thirty percent fewer trucks than requested; rubber was in shorter supply than ever. The military authorities promised the heads of the motor pool that they would have a few things to say about the rubber supply to the Province Committee, after which the motor pool people would be pulling the trucks themselves.

A week later a letter written both by Iona and Stepa arrived from Belostok. Two days before this, the Municipal Soviet had finally sent its reply approving the decision of the Comrades' Court to expel

Citizen Cheperukha from the city of Odessa. Olya laughed openly about this, saying they knew what they could do with that decision now. Klava Ivanovna told her not to let her tongue get the better of her and, on behalf of Degtyar, asked what the building committee could do to be of assistance to her. Suddenly brazen, Olya demanded twenty liters of kerosene, as if kerosene were water, a full delivery of firewood, and a half delivery of coal.

"Cheperukha," said Klava Ivanovna, astounded, "are you kidding or are you serious? Twenty for you, twenty for Khomitsky's wife, but every courtyard has its Khomitskys and Cheperukhas, so are we supposed to collect kerosene, coal, and firewood from the whole U.S.S.R. and give it to you?"

Somewhat embarrassed, Olya explained that what she was requesting was for the rest of the winter, up to the spring, and she wouldn't ask for any more. When Iona was home, he'd bring fuel once a week but now there was no one to do that. Now she had to go to the market every day to buy a pail of coal and a bundle of firewood from the goddamned speculators.

"That's true," agreed Klava Ivanovna, "now you go yourself. But don't forget that the Comrades' Court decided to expel your husband from Odessa. You should be grateful that the state still trusts him and took him into the Red Army. You have to live a nice, quiet life with that troublemaker Zyunchik for the next three years—may it only be three."

"Klava Ivanovna," said Olya, clasping her hands as if about to pray, "you asked how the building committee could help me, and I told you. If that can't be, no one's insisting. If you give me what I need, well and good, and, if not, that's well and good too."

"Don't be a fool," said Klava Ivanovna indignantly. "We'll help you but don't be shameless either and try to get a free ride when people are concerned about you."

Through the good offices of the building committee and of Comrade Degtyar personally, Olya Cheperukha, as the wife of a Red Army soldier, was allocated ten liters of kerosene, half a cubic meter of firewood, and fifteen buckets of coal from the fuel warehouse at the fixed state price. The same was given to the family of the Red Army soldier Khomitsky. Nastya helped carry the fuel down to the cellar, and for her help the two women left nearly a full sack of firewood and a good bucket and a half of coal for Nastya in the front hall. Everyone said that the coal was a real treasure, better than anthracite: you could take that kind of coal out of the stove and use it a second time and it would give more heat than new coal.

The weather was even more frigid in January than in December but the Red Army, under the command of Comrade Timoshenko, dealt the White Finns one blow after another in Karelia. Iona Ovseich reported that there was information to the effect that the Mannerheim Line had been breached. He personally was of the opinion that Khomitsky and Cheperukha would hardly be needed to kill the Finns' appetite for Leningrad and the useful minerals of the Kola Peninsula. Nevertheless, Olya and Tosya inquired of Degtyar every day when the war would be over, swearing by their children's lives to keep the information totally secret. In reply Degtyar would close his eyes and earnestly request they ask him no unnecessary questions.

In mid-February a letter arrived from Stepa in which he said he was now in the far north, past the White Sea, and that a month ago Iona had been made a driver and was transferred to another unit; he didn't know where Iona was now and asked for his address.

When Tosya showed her the letter, Olya Cheperukha began tearing her hair and shouting that her husband had been killed, that Zyunchik was now an orphan and would never see his father again. Klava Ivanovna demanded that she put an immediate halt to those hysterics but Olya became even more emotional and shouted for all the courtyard to hear that they had all hated her husband. They had expelled him from Odessa where he had been born and where his father and grandfather had been born, and where they had been tormented under the tsars and where they were tormented nowadays too.

Anya attempted to calm Olya down but Olya replied with a stream of curses, telling Anya to go to her stinking Red partisan Joseph, who had shouted louder than anyone that Iona be expelled from Odessa. Anya said that she wasn't responsible for her husband and that she, like Olya, had abstained during the voting and, deep down, had been against it.

"You bitch," shrieked Olya, "you wanted to steal Vanechka Lapidis away from his poor sick wife! Get out of my sight, you slut!"

Anya turned pale and leaned back against a wall.

Three days later a letter arrived from the military hospital in Petrozavodsk: Iona Cheperukha wrote that while in the battlefield he had suffered frostbite on his left foot, but Major Krishtal—what a doctor, what a specialist, the world needed more like him—had said that the main danger had passed and it would not be necessary to amputate his foot. On the contrary, it would remain just as it was, in one piece, and he'd be able to run even faster than before with his wheelbarrow. In addition, Major Krishtal sent Olya and Zyunchik his warmest Red Army regards. Iona promised to come to Odessa for the summer.

Olya went running with that letter to Madame Malaya and begged her to apologize to Anya Kotlyar for her, otherwise she'd kill herself and her son out of shame.

"Olya," said Klava Ivanovna, sadly, "you give me more trouble than a little child, and your own children will soon have children of their own."

Olya burst into tears of sweet suffering and said who else could she turn to but Madame Malaya, who, apart from her husband and son, was the person she felt closest to.

"Oh, Cheperukha," said Klava Ivanovna, pinching Olya hard beneath the waist, "flattery will get you nowhere!"

On February 29—it was a leap year—the stores gave notice that home deliveries would cease as of March 1, bread would be back on regular sale, and quotas no longer would apply. The quotas for oil, groats, and sugar would remain in place but people should be prepared for the situation to revert to what it had been before the war with Finland.

The entire Mannerheim Line was reeling from the blows of the Red Army and there was a real danger that Soviet troops might push all the way to the capital city of Helsinki. Given that situation, the Finns were urgently seeking a peace treaty. The U.S.S.R., which had proposed a diplomatic solution to the problem three and a half months before, responded immediately, and a peace treaty was signed on March 12. The new Soviet borders included the entire Isthmus of Karelia along with the city of Vyborg—formerly known as Vipuri—the entire northern and western shore of Lake Ladoga as well as certain border regions of Finland west of the Murmansk rail line, and a portion of the Rybachi Peninsula. For the purpose of defending passage into the Gulf of Finland, the Soviet Union was also able to lease the Hanko Peninsula. At the same time the U.S.S.R. once again gave Finland the province of Petsamo and the all-weather port of Petsamo, which had been voluntarily ceded to Soviet Russia by Finland in 1918 and had now been occupied by the Red Army.

When Iona Ovseich described the current situation at the next class on the short course of the party's history, Klava Ivanovna, Efim Granik, Tosya Khomitsky, Anya Kotlyar, and all the others could not agree with the decision to leave the Finns all power in Finland and also to return the all-weather port of Petsamo to them. Why, they asked, had so many of our people laid down their lives? So that with help from England, France, and America, the lousy Finns could build another Mannerheim Line and attack us again? When we had asked them nicely for a little piece of territory beyond Leningrad, they had insolently told us to kiss their ass and wouldn't even hear of our request until they'd been given a good drubbing and then, instead of taking all of Finland, we went and gave them Petsamo back to boot! No two ways about it, the Soviet system was the most honorable and noblest in the world, but this was too much: too much goodness could be a bad thing.

"Stop!" said Iona Ovseich. "From what you're saying it sounds like we Soviet people are against a peace policy without annexation and indemnities. Moreover, it sounds like our government and Comrade Stalin personally do not know what lies in the U.S.S.R.'s interest and what does not."

All right, said Olya Cheperukha, the first to reply, our leaders know better than we do what must be done. Even though her Iona had almost lost his foot because of the Finns, she was willing to agree; since our government had signed that peace treaty, that meant it was necessary. But how come when we could have made mincemeat out of Finland, power had remained in the hands of the landowners and the capitalists?

"A valid question," said Iona Ovseich. "And so, the first point is entirely clear: as the song goes, we don't want an inch of foreign land and will not surrender an inch of our own. As for the question of exporting revolution, which is the proper term in historical materialism for your question, Comrade Cheperukha, the answer is as follows: a child can't skip from the first grade to the tenth, or even less to college, and similarly the working class and productive peasants of a given country have to mature first. It's a different story if they have already matured: then we can help them, then we are obliged to help them."

"And so that means," said Olya with a look of disgust, "that the workers and peasants are still so backward and ignorant that they don't know what's good for them and what's bad for them."

"Considering the rout of the White Finns' army and the success of the Red Army, which the Finnish proletariat could have put to good use but did not, your conclusion is entirely valid," said Iona Ovseich.

When the class had been dismissed, Degtyar asked Olya Cheperukha to remain for a moment. Her first thought was that something bad had happened to her husband again and she clutched at her heart. This time her fears proved groundless—the subject of their talk was indeed her husband but this time in a positive light. Degtyar spoke of the incident from December '37 when Cheperukha had gone to bring Lapidis to vote. Lapidis had treated him so badly that Iona, deeply indignant at such insolence, had broken the glass in Lapidis' door.

"My Iona is so strong," said Olya with a laugh, "that he could have taken the door off its hinges if he'd wanted to."

Degtyar said there was nothing surprising in that, the man had done heavy manual labor all his life, but that wasn't the point here: like every considerate and devoted husband, Iona had of course shared his feelings openly with his wife, hadn't he?

"Did he ever!" said Olya. "He has his faults, everyone has his faults, but in twenty years we never once hid anything from each other. Most of the time, not all of the time, but most of the time we lived like two turtle doves. I wish I had a ruble for every day we spent like that."

Yes, said Iona Ovseich, the whole courtyard knew that, and he could imagine how furious Iona Avrumovich was that day when he had been sent to Lapidis' by the electoral commission.

"Furious isn't the word for it!" exclaimed Olya. "Lapidis told him to go to hell and not to stick his nose into other people's business but Iona cut him off right on the spot: 'Why are you kicking up such a fuss, people might think you're printing counterfeit money in there!' "

"He's a good man!" praised Degtyar. "Then what happened?"

" 'It's none of your goddamned business what's being printed in here!' shouted Lapidis. But when Iona answered him with a few good unprintable expressions, that took the wind right out of Lapidis' sails."

"Wait a minute," interrupted Iona Ovseich. "Is that what Lapidis said—'It's none of your goddamned business what's being printed in here!' "

"That's not all," said Olya with a grimace. "That prim and proper intellectual with his two degrees cursed him like the crudest drayman at the Old Horse Market!"

Olya was about to tell Degtyar that her husband had almost punched Lapidis for those curses and he was lucky to have gotten off with a broken window, but Degtyar was already putting on his coat. His face and eyes looked tired, like those of a man who hadn't slept for days and was suffering pain.

Two days later Olya was summoned to the provincial headquarters of the NKVD, a large gray building with red windows across from the Shevchenko Park of Culture and Rest. There too she was asked about Lapidis and Olya repeated what she knew, adding that she and her husband, who was now in the Red Army and had almost lost a foot in the war with Finland, had never liked Lapidis for as long as they'd been living in that building. The official who was speaking with Olya reminded her of the Comrades' Court in which Lapidis had supported Iona Cheperukha entirely and had been absolutely opposed to his expulsion.

"So what!" retorted Olya. "Everyone in the courtyard knew that if you said something was white, Lapidis would of course say it was black. That's the sort of person he is."

The next week a rumor was afoot in the building that the provincial NKVD would summon Madame Malaya, Joseph Kotlyar, Tosya Khomitsky, Nastya, Dr. Landa, and Dina Vargaftik but there was no question about Olya Cheperukha, who told everyone what a nice young man had spoken with her. Tosya even threatened that if Olya didn't shut her mouth, she'd have to write Iona in the hospital to throw away his crutches and come home to deal with her.

"Tosya, my dear," said Olya, "let me hug you and give you a good kiss. After all, we're the only two women whose husbands are serving in the Red Army."

On March 31, in a decision signed by Comrade Kalinin, the Supreme Soviet resolved to form a new Soviet republic, the twelfth—

the Karelian-Finnish Republic. The population there was not very dense, less than a quarter of Leningrad's, but, in terms of territory, it was easily comparable with such highly developed European countries as Belgium, Holland, Denmark, and Switzerland combined. According to the statistics, reported Iona Ovseich, the Karelians accounted for more than twenty-three percent of the total population; as for the Finns, the Central Statistical Board had received additional information on them but had not completed processing it yet. It was possible that the figures would have to be revised because in the far north it was day half the year and night the other half, making a census a demanding and difficult task.

Efim Granik had a question in connection with the incorporation of the new territory into the U.S.S.R.: could he exchange his apartment in Odessa for one in Vyborg?

"Now where did that whim come from?" asked Degtyar in surprise.

Efim said that it wasn't a whim, just a question, but Iona Ovseich replied that questions didn't fall from the sky, they arose in a person's head out of the thoughts that buzzed around in there. His own personal suspicion was that Efim had once again quit his job and was looking for a place where he'd be able to engage in cottage industry work.

Efim confirmed that he had indeed left his job temporarily but had no intention of doing any cottage industry work. Of course, he might have to for a short while to earn his daily bread, after all, he wasn't a thief or a counterfeiter.

"In other words," interrupted Iona Ovseich, "you're getting your license again?"

"A license!" exclaimed Efim. "How can I get a license if the Revenue Department demands a certificate of health showing that I'm an invalid?"

"Efim," said Iona Ovseich softly, "I'm not your enemy, but you're heading for trouble. The Sovnarkom of the U.S.S.R. and the VTsSPS have condemned the pernicious practice of drifters but all the same you're still chasing after the easy ruble. Soviet society has great patience but there are limits to everything. Do you understand me?"

"I understand, Ovseich, but what harm can it do to the state if I do a little work at home for a week or a month, or two?"

"When a person works at home," replied Degtyar, "he works at home and not at a factory, a plant, a state farm, or a kolkhoz. Just imagine for a minute the U.S.S.R. without plants, factories, kolkhozes, and state farms."

"Naw," said Granik, throwing up his hands, "that's unimaginable."

"Is it then?" said Degtyar in surprise. "But you're trying to grab us by the throat when you say, 'I don't want to work in a factory, I want to work at home!' You're like that old woman who wanted to be the tsarina and was given her leaky washtub back."

Efim said that the comparison missed the point here: he wouldn't agree to be tsar for all the gold in the world. And, as for a job, he promised to drop by the painting department of a local factory.

"I think that's an artel, not a state factory," said Degtyar. "Efim Granik, the small businessman in you has to be burned out with red-hot steel."

That evening Degtyar had intended to drop by Madame Malaya's and tell her to take Granik under her personal supervision, but Polina Isaevna felt poorly and he had to run to the drugstore for oxygen, boil water for her hot-water bottle, then cook her kasha for dinner. He had to refill the hot-water bottle in the middle of the night. Polina Isaevna was moaning softly and wanted to get up herself but Iona Ovseich would not allow her to: when he was home, she shouldn't waste her energy on trifles. And in general she had to watch herself—spring was spring, and it was hard on all people with tuberculosis, not just her.

Toward morning Polina Isaevna began to suffer from arrhythmia and Iona Ovseich suggested he call an ambulance. She, however, flatly refused and reproached him, saying that if he was so fed up with her health problems that he always wanted to confine her in a hospital, he should say so openly now and, no matter how bad she felt, she would get up and go immediately, and he could make himself a new life, with another woman, one who was young and healthy.

"Polya," he said softly, "stop trying to provoke me. No one's sending you to the hospital. And besides, a hospital means good doctors, care, proper nursing, and so there's no reason to make a bugaboo out of it. In other countries people pay through the nose to get into a hospital and poor people can't get through the front door, and here you are putting on airs like some old aristocrat."

Polina Isaevna began crying. He wiped her tears with the edge of the sheet. Somewhat calmer now, she told him to go to work, otherwise, God forbid, he'd be late, and people would point the finger at him.

Polina Isaevna had a very mild heart attack during the day and Klava Ivanovna called an ambulance. The doctor examined the patient thoroughly, gave her an injection of camphor and promised she'd live another forty years if she watched her diet, followed her doctor's orders, and didn't worry herself sick over trifles. The best thing of all, of course, would be the tuberculosis hospital on Belinsky Street with its view of the sea, its garden, chestnut trees, oaks, acacias, birds chirping, and roosters crowing. In a word, it was paradise.

Polina Isaevna said that she didn't want to go to paradise, she wanted what everyone else wanted, to live at home.

Degtyar went right from the factory to Madame Malaya's. She told him that she had called an ambulance but he already knew, having called home earlier. Polina was feeling considerably better and there was no special cause for alarm at the moment. The main thing now was Granik: he had quit his job again and was apparently hoping this would slip by without being noticed. He had to be placed under strict supervision and they had to be on his back every day, otherwise he'd start sliding and there was no telling what the consequences of that might be. Or, to be more precise, those would be most deplorable consequences.

Klava Ivanovna said that things were clear as far as Granik was concerned, they'd be on his back. But what about Orlov? There was information that she was receiving clients again.

"Malaya," said Iona Ovseich, wagging a threatening finger, "you have to back up that statement. Where is your information from?"

"From Dina Vargaftik. She's already seen it a few times from her window."

"Can anyone else confirm that?"

"Nastya. And, if need be, Tosya Khomitsky can say a few words too."

"But how do they know those are customers? A woman of Orlov's age can invite a man to her home, that's no crime."

"Degtyar," said Klava Ivanovna, tightly compressing her lips, "do you want to hear the details of what Dina Vargaftik saw through her window?"

Iona Ovseich squinted until his eyes were narrow slits and blue veins bulged on his temples, then all of a sudden he whacked the palm of his hand: "So, the fish has been stinking for a long time and we've only smelled it today!"

"There's no pleasing you," said Klava Ivanovna with a sigh. "Either we're in too much of a rush, or we're scatterbrained bunglers."

Iona Ovseich paused for a moment's thought, the veins on his temples swelling all the more, turning greenish yellow; he hung his head, his fingers scraping mechanically along the tablecloth, then finally he snapped to, jabbing at his heart with one finger, and said: "My heart bleeds for all of you, Malaya. But that doesn't mean that anyone can spit on me and get away with it. Go to Dina Vargaftik's and sit with her by the window, and gather the necessary information so that we can smash this thing once and for all."

Iona Ovseich found things peaceful at home. Polina Isaevna was standing by the coal stove talking with Anya Kotlyar about Lapidis' wife, Zoya. They were surprised that Adya was still studying music and wondered where his mother was getting the money to pay the teacher. And no less surprising was the fact that Zoya, who had spent more time in the hospital than at home in recent years, had now found the strength to spend the entire day working with blueprints in an office. She even brought home extra work to do in the evening.

Iona Ovseich joked that if Polina were on that schedule, she'd regain her health like Zoya Lapidis.

This angered his wife, who said that such idiotic jokes could come back to haunt him. Anya said that she didn't believe in slandering people and that they'd be better off choosing another subject. Then she burst out laughing as if having recalled something funny and pressed both her hands to her mouth. Exercising her rights as a sick person, Polina Isaevna demanded that she not be subjected to excitement and tormented with guessing games. What guessing games, said Anya with a dismissive gesture, it was just that she'd heard rumors that Lyalya Orlov was seeing customers again.

"Anya," said Iona Ovseich reprovingly, "if I were you, I wouldn't repeat that. If you're sure of what you're saying, that's another story, but it's not good to repeat secondhand gossip. It's unworthy."

They sat together until eleven o'clock drinking tea with cherry jam, which lent the tea such a beautiful color no further tea leaves had to be added to darken it. They dipped "Mariya" biscuits in their tea. Anya kept trying to restrain herself but the biscuits just melted in her mouth. A few times Iona Ovseich joked that a woman with such a healthy appetite should earn good money herself, otherwise her husband would have to work three shifts. Twice Polina Isaevna reproached her husband for meddling in other people's affairs, but Anya agreed with Iona Ovseich and daydreamed aloud about her future job. Most of all she would like to be a nurse or a telephone operator but she had only a seventh-grade education, and not quite even that. The only math she remembered was the multiplication tables and she'd forgotten X plus Y as if she'd learned all that a thousand years ago. That wasn't so bad if it only seemed like a thousand, said Polina Isaevna: she'd tutor Anya and before long she'd be able to pass the courses on nursing.

"Polina Isaevna," said Anya, blushing, "either you're joking or—"

No, interrupted Polina Isaevna, she wasn't joking. On the contrary, she had a vested interest in Anya's becoming a nurse: if she needed an injection, cupping glasses, medicine, enemas, leeches, she'd have her own person right at hand.

"Yes," agreed Iona Ovseich, "it's something to think about."

Joseph Kotlyar came by and was scarcely through the door when he began lodging complaints—they were keeping his wife there all night.

"And do you think you're the one and only?" said Iona Ovseich.

"Well," bellowed Joseph, "how do you like that old ladies' man! Degtyar, I envy you; your bald spot is bigger than my head but you're a great specialist on the women of the courtyard; you know how to worm confidences out of them."

Anya blushed deeply but Polina Isaevna began pestering her husband to tell the story of the thirteenth feat of the famous ancient Greek hero Heracles.

That surprised Iona Ovseich—the thirteenth? There were only twelve feats. Every fifth-grader knows the twelve, said Polina Isaevna, but there's also a thirteenth. One time Heracles spent the night with a beautiful young woman by the name of Penelope. At first she liked him because he was so strong and never tired but finally she got so tired herself that she wasn't up for anymore. The next day when she told people that they had done it thirty-two times, no one believed her, but later they figured out that her lover could only have been Zeus or his son Heracles.

Joseph laughed so hard he almost fell off his chair and demanded that Polina Isaevna say how many times they made love again. Anya tugged her husband by the sleeve and said that she felt so ashamed she wished she could just disappear.

"There's no harm in it," said Degtyar, reassuringly, "a joke is a joke. People can allow themselves a little something extra every so often."

"A little something extra like Heracles or his daddy Zeus!" said Joseph, choking with laughter.

The subject of Lyalya Orlov came up again as the Kotlyars were leaving, and Joseph said that she'd have trouble finding herself a Heracles these days, but this time the joke fell flat.

Iona Ovseich saw his guests to the stairs, wished them a good night, and asked Anya to give serious consideration to Polina Isaevna's offer. Anya called back that her husband would be against it. In a voice that was purposely loud, as if in a threat, Iona Ovseich replied—just let him try!

At the end of the work week, before class, Klava Ivanovna and Dina Vargaftik waited for Degtyar by the outpost. After the three days they had spent in conscientious observation, there wasn't a shadow of a doubt left about Lyalya Orlov. Not only that, the day before yesterday, when it had still been light out, some suspicious type had asked Zyunchik where Orlov's apartment was. Zyunchik had answered: "What do you want to see Orlov for?" First the man called him a snot-nose, then he said that Orlov was a laundress and that he was bringing his laundry to her. The same thing happened again yesterday when Kolka, Oska, and Adya Lapidis were out in the courtyard. Oska and Adya had replied that Orlov wasn't a laundress, but Kolka, who already knew more about life than his school principal, brought the man straight to Orlov's door.

Iona Ovseich listened in silence with his eyes closed, picking at his buttons with his thumb. Klava Ivanovna demanded that he open his eyes and say something.

"What do you want me to say, Malaya? That we're all a bunch of helpless nitwits? If I say that, it's as if I've said nothing."

"We should have seen it coming," interjected Dina, "when she got that room with its own entrance and tap. I kept saying this was going to happen."

"Vargaftik," said Iona Ovseich with a frown, "you're profoundly mistaken. It's our duty to try to improve people's lives all the time, but no one has given us the right to rest on our laurels and put our vigilance on hold."

"Ovseich," said Dina, waving her short arms, "I'm no philosopher like you, but I'll say it again: when conditions are right, a person will stop hiding his real ways. And Lyalya Orlov is the best example."

"All right," said Klava Ivanovna, "let's tear out our hair and shout for help."

"Malaya is right," said Iona Ovseich, taking the text for the short course from the table and sticking it under his arm. "Concrete measures must be taken, we've played enough blindman's buff."

The lesson of the day was entirely devoted to the subject of "The Bund and the Bundists' Opposition Line." The class had done its homework. Lyalya Orlov spoke three times: on the Bundists walking out of the Second Congress; on the alliance between the Mensheviks and the Bundists and "economists"; and on Plekhanov, how the weight of his previous opportunistic mistakes had drawn him to the Mensheviks.

Iona Ovseich praised them all and singled out Lyalya Orlov in particular for not only reading the basic literature, but the background works as well. The only thing which she had failed to make perfectly clear was that Plekhanov went from being a conciliator of the Menshevik opportunists to being an out-and-out Menshevik, and ended up sinking into that swamp.

"And hence," said Iona Ovseich, raising his index finger, "one other very important conclusion follows: every last person is pulled down by the weight of his past mistakes and you have to keep a sharp eye out to keep from getting your feet stuck in the mud. It's easier to prevent a forest fire than to extinguish one, and it's simpler to walk around a bog then get out of it when you're up to your neck in the mud."

While Iona Ovseich was adding these remarks, he looked Orlov straight in the eye. She nodded her head gravely. Anya Kotlyar looked around, then coughed into her fist. Tosya Khomitsky nudged her in the side as if Anya were allowing herself to be indecent.

Immediately after class, Klava Ivanovna informed Lyalya that she and Degtyar and Dina Vargaftik wanted to come see her. Lyalya turned red as a beet and said she couldn't have them come by today for anything, the place was a horrible mess, bedlam!

"You should be ashamed of yourself," interrupted Klava Ivanovna. "We're not strangers! Thank God we're all friends here and didn't just meet yesterday."

When they entered Orlov's room, Klava Ivanovna was surprised by how neat and gleaming it was. Only the robe and corset, tossed over the back of a chair, spoiled the image somewhat. On the other hand, said Dina Vargaftik, these things only showed you how clean and tidy the woman was.

"Lyalya," said Madame Malaya, "I'm starting to think you're a very conceited woman. To say that a room like this looked like bedlam!"

"Oh, Klava Ivanovna," protested Lyalya, "look at that floor, it's black as dirt, it'll need six months of scraping."

"All right," said Madame Malaya with a dismissive wave of the hand, "put out some tea, pie, and cherry brandy, your guests want a little civilized relaxation."

Iona Ovseich sat down in an armchair, rocked back and forth a few times, praising the springs and remarking on how soft the chair was. Dina took a seat on the couch and she too praised the springs, which didn't squeak in the least.

"Comrades," said Orlov, "I'm very sorry but I have to go."

"Stop," said Klava Ivanovna indignantly, "otherwise your guests might think that you come from someplace like Moldavanka or Bugaevka. Where's your Primus?"

The Primus was in the pantry. There was a little shelf for salt, pepper, tea and bay leaves above the stove. Klava Ivanovna lit the Primus herself and a minute later it had begun humming like a good worker's acetylene torch.

"You can see right away that the Primus has a real draw," said Iona Ovseich.

Lyalya explained that the top was almost new, she had gotten it from a stove man she knew and so she shouldn't be praised for how well it worked. Iona Ovseich replied that self-criticism was a good thing but there were limits to modesty too.

Klava Ivanovna set the teapot on the table and reprimanded Lyalya for keeping her pepper, bay leaves, and boxes of tea above the Primus, which gave off strong fumes.

While slicing the pie, Lyalya looked over at the door and said again that she had promised to be somewhere and didn't want people wasting their time on account of her. Klava Ivanovna took her by the waist with both hands, sat her down on the couch, and told her to forget everything in the whole world apart from her guests.

The conversation began on the subject of how people spent their evenings after work.

"I propose," said Iona Ovseich, "that the lady of the house speak on that subject first."

Instead of responding, Lyalya suddenly rose, walked to the door and opened it, as if checking it or about to leave. Klava Ivanovna had risen to go after her but the lock had already clicked shut and Lyalya was on her way back.

Dina Vargaftik laughed: you might think Orlov was expecting a cat burglar. No, said Orlov, she wasn't expecting anyone, it was just that when you lived alone, you got in the habit of checking your door before you went to bed.

"Wait a minute," said Klava Ivanovna, "you've got time before going to bed, you've got guests."

"That's true," said Lyalya, blushing, "but I usually go to bed around this time if there's nothing that needs doing around the house."

"But, Lyalya," said Dina Vargaftik in surprise, "your lights are often on until after midnight, I've seen that myself."

"When she turns off her lights is her own business," said Iona Ovseich in Lyalya's defense. "There are people who can't sleep in a dark room."

That was true, admitted Lyalya. She'd been afraid of the dark since she was a child, and her late mother had been afraid of it too.

"I don't know why you're afraid," said Dina with a shrug, "you're never alone in the evening."

Lyalya's hands trembled, her spoon clicking in her glass. Just then someone inserted a key into the outside lock on her door. They could hear the sound of a key trying to turn but being prevented by the safety. Then he knocked two times and then two times again. Lyalya wanted to get up but her legs had turned to jelly. Klava Ivanovna ordered her to stay where she was, and went to open the door herself.

When the man saw Klava Ivanovna in the doorway, he automatically glanced into the room and apologized at once—he was on the wrong floor. Lyalya was white as a sheet and had not turned around once. Madame Malaya invited the man in, saying it was awkward talking in the doorway. When the man refused politely, Klava Ivanovna took him by the sleeve and rebuked Orlov for being so inhospitable to her guest. This wasn't a kindergarten; they didn't have to play cat and mouse. The man tried to tear his hand free but Klava Ivanovna had a firm grip on it and in a silken voice asked him how his wife and children were. They must, of course, be waiting for their daddy to come home, but daddy, that old dog, was out sniffing around.

"Stop that!" shouted the man. "I'll call the police!"

"He'll call the police!" said Dina Vargaftik with a laugh. "We're the ones who'll call the police."

"Citizen!" said Iona Ovseich, walking in brisk military fashion to the door. "Let's not waste words here. You've been invited in, so come in."

The man smiled, shook his head, as if involved in a stupid misunderstanding, and came in.

"Your name? Place of work?"

The man smiled again as if whether he answered the questions or not was entirely his own choice, but Degtyar said in a voice loud enough for all to hear: "We're not asking you to answer, we're demanding it!"

The man looked intently at them, thought for a moment, and then suddenly, to everyone's surprise since he was so respectable in appearance, he reeled off a stream of the foulest curses. Klava Ivanovna automatically released his arm. The man spoke as loudly and as coarsely to Lyalya as if she were a streetwalker, then turned his back on them and slammed the door behind him.

Dina darted out after him and shouted to him from the landing: "Hey, lady-killer, come back, the brothel's open!"

"All right, Orlov," said Klava Ivanovna, "now you can't deny it!"

Lyalya held her head in both hands, hiccuping and shuddering. Klava Ivanovna brought her a glass of water. Lyalya reached out as if about to take it but then she struck the bottom of the glass with her fist. The water splashed Madame Malaya's face. Lyalya laughed like a mad woman, and shouted for them all to get the hell out of her apartment. Iona Ovseich calmly and politely replied that the courtyard had gone to some trouble to get her that room and could take it back from her. Lyalya crumpled up one corner of the tablecloth and pulled it toward her, sending the cups and saucers to the floor, three or four of them smashing to pieces. Lyalya told them all to go to hell again and then ran out to the stairs. Klava Ivanovna was afraid that she would jump over the banister headfirst and was about to run after her but Iona Ovseich stopped her: "That prostitute loves herself too much to jump headfirst out of shame!" he said.

He was right; Lyalya had simply run outside and would probably return in an hour or two when her need to make scenes had passed.

Lyalya did not spend that night at home. The radio had already played the "Internationale" and Moscow had gone off the air, when Klava Ivanovna and Dina abandoned their observation post by the window. Degtyar had visited them once, before midnight, and informed them there was no reason to sit there and wait—the woman would come home sooner or later—she wasn't a wolf to run off to the forest. Klava Ivanovna was well aware of that, but her heart was so heavy that she was ready to go to the ends of the earth to find Orlov and let her have it for all her dirty tricks and all the excitement she had caused.

The next morning when the radio had once again played the "Internationale" and Radio Moscow had announced the beginning of its broadcast day, Madame Malaya was rinsing her mouth with water. There was always a very bitter taste in her mouth in the morning. She threw on her robe and ran across the courtyard, her rubbers flapping on the granite slabs. She leaned against Orlov's door and listened intently, promising herself that she'd go away after hearing the first stir from inside which would mean that Lyalya was home.

Fifteen minutes passed with Klava Ivanovna continually giving herself one more minute but she had not heard a single sound that a person might make moving around or simply turning over in bed. Then she rapped softly at the door with her fist so as not to startle anyone out of sleep. There was no answer. Klava Ivanovna knocked louder, waited, then knocked twice, then twice again, just as the lady-killer had the night before. A sound came from the room as if someone were turning the pages of a book. Klava Ivanovna was breathless with delight. Forgetting that she had promised herself to leave without saying a word, Klava Ivanovna told Lyalya she'd better open the door or else she'd be in serious trouble. There was no answer, and the rustling sound from within, instead of stopping as Klava Ivanovna had expected, only grew louder; something sharp scratched on the door, and a cat gave a plaintive, early morning meow.

"You poor thing," whispered Klava Ivanovna, "in there all alone, and your master left you and ran away. The bad stupid woman."

The next time the cat meowed, Klava Ivanovna did not respond but only shook her head and began plodding down the iron staircase. There was a beautiful, genuine marble staircase in the main entrance where Kotlyarevsky himself had once lived, but all the rest of the staircases were made of iron, their banisters rusty now. The bastards, the bloodsuckers, Klava Ivanovna cursed aloud, they always made everything just a little bit worse for the working people.

The light was on by the concierge's door. Klava Ivanovna opened a small ventilation window and shouted: "Nastya, come here. Tell me exactly what time you came out today and when Orlov left for work."

Nastya swore to God that she had been out since four-thirty, she'd swept the courtyard and watered it down. The hose was full of holes; it shot water in every direction like a fountain, and every time she asked for a new hose they promised her one for May Day, then for the October holidays. All right, said Klava Ivanovna, she'd see what she could do about the hose, but what she needed to know now was when Lyalya Orlov left for work. Nastya replied that she hadn't seen Orlov today, but she'd seen her yesterday when she ran through the courtyard to the street.

"Which way did she go?"

Nastya said that she didn't know, the gate was iron, and you couldn't see through iron. Klava Ivanovna asked angrily: "What do we need a concierge for then? To catch mice?" She ordered Nastya to go out to the street immediately and keep a sharp lookout all day. Now Nastya took offense: she should have been informed yesterday, and now it was drop everything for an emergency.

"Don't get smart," interrupted Klava Ivanovna, but inwardly she knew that the concierge was right in this case and should have been notified ahead of time.

Even though Iona Ovseich had categorically forbidden any panic or stir, that afternoon Klava Ivanovna phoned the factory where Lyalya Orlov worked and asked to speak to her, saying that her aunt had arrived from Kherson. Aunt or uncle, made no difference, she was told, Orlov hadn't shown up for her shift.

At eleven o'clock that night Nastya locked the gate. The people who came back later—from the theater, the movies, or just from a stroll—were upset because the gate wasn't supposed to be locked before midnight, and they promised to lodge a complaint with Comrade Degtyar himself. At first Nastya argued with them, telling each of them to mind his own business and not to stick his nose where it didn't belong, but later she decided to be the first to suggest they complain to Degtyar and then people wouldn't say a word.

Efim Granik arrived at twelve o'clock and began an absurd conversation with Nastya through the gate. He was holding a large six-liter jar in his hands, which she guessed right away held paint, and, though no one had asked for an explanation, Efim began justifying himself by saying that he was bringing home some benzine and then immediately switched the subject to the gate: a lock on a chain should be hung on the gate and should be reachable from the outside and every family should be issued a key.

Nastya replied that Efim thought he was so smart—if you gave everyone a key and then something happened, everyone would start blaming everyone else.

Efim flared up at these words and shouted that she had no reason to cast those lousy aspersions, he, Granik, was a Soviet to his marrow and he was going to complain to the Municipal Soviet, the Province Party Committee, and higher. Nastya said he could complain wherever he pleased, but if he was going to be that impertinent, he could stay outside there all night, and Comrade Degtyar was going to hear about this conversation tomorrow.

"Nastya," said Efim, losing all self-control, "open the gate, or I'll stick you in this jar until you're as gold as a statue!"

"Benzine wouldn't turn me gold as a statue," said Nastya with a snide laugh, "and we'll see what color you turn tomorrow when you have to face Comrade Degtyar!"

"All right," said Efim, finally reining himself in, "let's stop arguing and ask the real question, which is who gave the concierge the right to insult the older people in the building."

She reluctantly unlocked the gate and let him pass.

"Hurry up and carry your benzine," Nastya cried after him, "before it goes flat!"

Efim stopped for a moment in the main entry hall and whispered his reply so as not to wake anyone up: "You bitch! I'll make you dance the fox-trot on your knees!"

The last to come home was Dr. Landa, who slipped forty kopecks into Nastya's pocket and remarked that he had had a tough shift that night. Nastya fingered the coins in her pocket and sighed: they could cut her up into little pieces but she'd never want to be a doctor, she said.

Dr. Landa said that he understood that, especially since both their jobs had a lot in common—you worked day and night, with constant anxiety, and everyone had complaints.

Nastya cited Granik as an example of people with complaints, telling how he had come back home with a can of yellow paint and yelled loud enough for all Odessa to hear for her to open the gate.

Yes, agreed Dr. Landa, Granik had his odd side. He wished Nastya a good night, wondering how good her nights could be with that kind of job.

A young moon shone in through Nastya's window and for a long time she was unable to fall asleep, thinking first of Lyalya Orlov running across the courtyard, then of Efim Granik with his "benzene," and of Dr. Landa, who was on duty around the clock. You might think he was the only doctor in Odessa. He used to give her a ruble, then it was down to half a ruble, and now it was forty kopeks. There was a reason people said kikes watched their kopecks.

The next day the whole courtyard knew that Lyalya Orlov had not spent the night at home and had not gone to work. Iona Ovseich was profoundly indignant and demanded that Klava Ivanovna give him a satisfactory explanation as to how word had gotten around. Klava Ivanovna shrugged her shoulders and counted on her fingers the people who knew—herself, Degtyar, Dina Vargaftik, the concierge, and that was it.

"It's a miracle!" Degtyar laughed loudly as if very amused. "But this isn't a church and miracles don't happen. The person with the big mouth only has himself to blame!"

No matter how hard Klava Ivanovna tried to get the truth from Dina Vargaftik and Nastya, she received a flat "no" to all her questions.

"That means," said Degtyar, on the offensive again, "that miracles don't happen except when they do? Is that right?"

Klava Ivanovna endured these reproaches for an entire day and then, no longer able to restrain herself, she said to Degtyar that you couldn't hide an awl in a sack and that if he wanted something kept secret, then only the two of them should know about it.

"No," fumed Iona Ovseich, "because then it'll be clear that Madame Malaya was the one who blurted it out! I forbade you to phone the factory, but you disobeyed. I said that no signs of anxiety or unnecessary alarm were to be shown, and you stood outside Orlov's door listening. Malaya, as one comrade to another, I'm advising you to give up this partisan warfare!"

Klava Ivanovna was not surprised that Iona Ovseich knew about her phone call to the factory—he must have called himself and been told about the aunt from Kherson—but it was a perfect mystery how he knew about the door; Nastya might have seen her leaving the main hall but there hadn't been a soul around when she was standing listening by the door. On the other hand, whether anyone had seen her not, the fact remained that Degtyar had known everything but hadn't said a word until the subject came up.

Olya Cheperukha brought back frightening news that evening: a nicely dressed woman around thirty-five had hung herself on a tree over by the trolley depot. People said she was beautiful.

No one had ever considered Lyalya Orlov beautiful but people always spoke well of the dead. The information about her age and clothes seemed completely right.

Klava Ivanovna was heart-stricken when she heard the news. Though Degtyar pretended that, given the locale and Lyalya's character, it could not have been her, he did agree to one emergency measure: Malaya should go to the morgue for a look. If they asked her for her name and address, she should say her last name was Ambramovich or Ivanov, whatever seemed right on the spot. She was to give any address.

"What about Orlov?"

"As for Orlov," said Iona Ovseich angrily, "say her name is Khaya Srulena Zhopasruchenko!"

A little old man was on duty in the morgue. He politely asked for the deceased's name and age. Though she had prepared for this, Klava Ivanovna now became somewhat confused and the old man suggested she make a visual identification. Klava Ivanovna sighed with relief and laughed in spite of herself, having just realized that he had not been asking for her name. The old man said nothing and Klava Ivanovna herself told him of her mistake. No, explained the old man, they were interested only in the names of their clients, meaning the people who were brought in there; anyone who came on his own two feet wasn't a client. In the end, he advised her to look in the morgues of the city hospitals. Though a weight had fallen from her a moment before, Klava Ivanovna became afraid again, for she had thought all corpses were brought straight there from the street. That was true, confirmed the old man, corpses were, but sometimes the person was still breathing and had a slim chance—then they took him to the hospital and every decent hospital had its own morgue.

Klava Ivanovna began to hurry out but the old man advised her to postpone it until tomorrow: what was the sense of rushing when there was a tragedy. Especially since she wasn't looking for her daughter, her sister, or a sister-in-law.

"How do you know that?" asked Klava Ivanovna, stunned.

"How do I know? If you'd been working here since 1895, you'd know too."

"I wonder who you think she is to me then," said Klava Ivanovna.

The old man said that he didn't know, but you didn't go looking in the morgue unless you were afraid something had happened. He told her he could tell the ones who were looking for a loved one.

No, said Klava Ivanovna with indignation, he was off the mark this time: pity was tearing her heart apart and she'd give half the life she had left to live if no tragedy had happened.

"Half your life," said the old man, shrugging his shoulders. "Yesterday a man came here and said he'd give his whole life. And the whole world on top of that. By the way he looked you could tell he was a party man."

"What did he look like?" said Klava Ivanovna, dry in the mouth. "Was he old? Young?"

The old man shrugged his shoulders again: "As you well know, madame, they don't hold auctions here, and the lowliest beggar can bid a billion and be none the poorer for it. The party man was older, and looking for a man. But people sometimes pretend to be looking for a man when it's a woman they're looking for. And vice versa. But still you shouldn't lose heart, all isn't lost yet."

"No," said Klava Ivanovna, suddenly bursting into tears, "you shouldn't even try to console me—what do all our tears and emotions matter when a human life is at stake!"

Degtyar was in complete agreement with the man at the morgue: better to sleep on it. And though he made no claims to being able to tell the future, he was a hundred and one percent certain there was no reason to go to the morgues in the first place.

"Ovseich," said Klava Ivanovna, wiping her tears with a handkerchief, "you have nerves of steel, you can sleep soundly with cannons firing over your head."

Degtyar said that he could not sleep soundly with cannons firing over his head, but people often made mountains out of molehills.

The next morning Klava Ivanovna had just dragged herself from bed after a terrible night when a woman from the municipal hospital clinic, formerly the Jewish hospital, brought a note: the doctor requests you come by the hospital at your convenience. Klava Ivanovna grew dizzy and weak-kneed. The woman said that Madame Malaya had turned pale as a corpse and that she should calm herself down, otherwise excitement would put an end to both her worries and her joys.

"Watch your mouth," replied Klava Ivanovna.

"Oh, it's always getting me in trouble," said the woman with a laugh.

"Hold on," said Klava Ivanovna, withdrawing a ruble from her purse and handing it to her. "Here."

At first the woman refused since she could see that Madame Malaya was clearly not Mrs. Rockefeller but in the end she yielded: people might think you were too proud if you refused overmuch.

Since it was not visiting hours at the hospital, Klava Ivanovna needed to register and obtain a pass, and though this took no more than a half hour of her time, she declared that the only way to deal with such bureaucrats and formalists was by reporting them to the People's Comissariat of Health.

The doctor was in the duty room filling in patients' files. When Klava Ivanovna knocked, he continued working as if he hadn't heard or seen her. All of a sudden her heart skipped a beat unpleasantly. Standing by the door, she was surprised at her own fear of this ordinary person, but she patiently waited until the doctor noticed her. For a few seconds he looked at her without saying a word, then immediately and without preamble informed her that everything was all right, the danger had passed but there was still the psychological trauma.

Klava Ivanovna twirled a finger at the side of her head to indicate craziness and asked: "This?"

The doctor replied that wasn't the case, thank God, but when a woman opened her veins to punish a man, it wasn't something she forgot for quite some time. Klava Ivanovna bit her lip, but a moan escaped her anyway. She told the doctor that she had warned Lyalya a hundred times, but she went her own way and now she was paying for it.

Unfortunately, sighed the doctor, a person had to do that to learn for himself, to see that he didn't have to.

No, said Klava Ivanovna, if people tried to stop you from doing something, you didn't have to try it for yourself, you could trust other people. But everyone wanted his own way, and there was the result.

Yes, agreed the doctor, people should be improved so that everyone didn't want his own way, then everything would be in its proper place.

It was a spacious ward, with room for about twenty people. There was a stool by every bed, and beside those of the seriously ill there were bedpans, some of which had not been emptied and still contained urine; the windowsills were lined with pans, jars of food, bras and panties.

Lyalya hid under the sheet when she saw Klava Ivanovna coming.

"Uncover your face," commanded Klava Ivanovna, "and look me in the eye."

Lyalya did not respond but only pulled the sheet further over her. The other patients signaled Madame Malaya not to press the point but to make small talk instead.

"Lyalya," said Klava Ivanovna, "the people at the factory want to know when you'll be coming back and send you their regards. Iona Ovseich sends you his regards too, and says you shouldn't let your nerves get the better of you and should keep yourself in hand. When a person believes that things are going to be all right, that's ninety percent of the job."

Klava Ivanovna carefully pulled the corner of the sheet aside. Lyalya made no more attempts to hide and now they could talk in peace.

"Orlov," said Madame Malaya, bending close to Lyalya's ear, "this isn't the place for a discussion, but I would have never believed you could be such an idiot!"

Lyalya admitted that she would never have believed it either but when the three of them had come to see her and then that man had started knocking at her door, her brain had gone completely out of commission.

"I haven't had a moment's sleep because of you," said Klava Ivanovna. "And yesterday I went to the morgue."

"And so," said Lyalya with a laugh, "did you find me there?"

"An idiotic joke," said Klava Ivanovna with a wry expression. "If it happens again, it'll be your turn to look for me. Degtyar couldn't be more right: the more you get, the less grateful you are."

Lyalya brought her hands out from under the sheet. Her bandages had wet through with blood. Madame Malaya sighed deeply, telling Lyalya she had to eat the right foods now, more carrots, carrots would restore her blood quicker. If need be, Degtyar could find a way of helping her through the building committee. That offended Lyalya—she wasn't destitute! She turned over onto her right side, her back to Madame Malaya, and asked her to leave for a minute, she had something to take care of.

"You suddenly become bashful at all the wrong times," said Klava Ivanovna angrily. "Stay where you are, I'll get you the bedpan."

The woman in the bed beside Lyalya's told Madame Malaya to get a half-liter jar from the bathroom: Lyalya had to be tested for sugar.

"Sugar?" said Klava Ivanovna, alarmed. "Did they find diabetes in her?"

Lyalya said that tests showed that the sugar level in her blood was high and now the doctor wanted to check her urine.

"Oh, if it's not one thing it's another," said Klava Ivanovna, spreading her hands.

While Lyalya was busy with the bedpan, Klava Ivanovna reminisced about old man Kiselis, who had desperately desired to go on living, if just for another year, six months, to be able to vote along with everyone else, and help people to appreciate the wonderful times they lived in.

"Oh, Lyalya," said Klava Ivanovna, shaking her head, "who could have suspected this would happen when we decided to grant you the authorization to move into Kiselis' room!"

"Mother Malaya," said Lyalya, blinking rapidly, "I give you my Pioneer word of honor I'll be good."

Lyalya was in a nice mood until Klava Ivanovna got up to leave. "I'm never coming back to the courtyard, I've been too disgraced. I can't."

"Orlov," said Madame Malaya affectionately, "don't make demands when people meet you half way. You should be happy with what you get. People can be patient but that patience has limits."

Madame Malaya went straight from the hospital to Degtyar's factory. Iona Ovseich was in the party office discussing production problems with other party members: there were ten days left until the end of the month and they were sixty percent behind schedule; it was entirely the fault of the suppliers, the rubber and leather factories which continued to hamper the shipments of raw materials.

Klava Ivanovna opened the door and stood in the doorway. Iona Ovseich looked at her blankly and said: "Citizen, please close the door."

Madame Malaya took a step forward so she could be seen more clearly and not taken for a stranger, but Degtyar repeated himself, and louder this time: "Citizen, close the door!"

About five minutes later a man came into the corridor, suggested Madame Malaya have a seat on the bench, and handed her a fresh newspaper. He took a pack of Avto cigarettes from his breast pocket and lit one.

"Wait a second," said Klava Ivanovna, "I know you from somewhere."

The man smiled and reminded her that they had met at the Stalin District Committee. That's right, said Klava Ivanovna, now she remembered too. The comrade from the District Committee finished his cigarette, begged her pardon, and returned to the office where the production problems were still under discussion.

Klava Ivanovna sat for an hour or more, reading everything of interest in the newspaper. She had begun dozing off when Degtyar's office grew noisy and the door opened. People began to leave but Degtyar was the last to appear. Klava Ivanovna marveled that a comrade from the Stalin District Committee who'd seen her once in his life had recognized her, while a person who'd been living in her building for twenty years pretended in front of other people that she was some kind of stranger and should shut the door behind her.

Iona Ovseich listened closely, then invited her into his office where he replied with utter frankness that it was time to drop the provincial ways she'd picked up in Moldavanka, where everyone was free and easy with everyone else. She should have a clear idea of what could be done, and where, and when. "Listen," he said, "time doesn't stand still, life keeps moving ahead."

Klava Ivanovna cited the example of the comrade from the District Committee again, but Iona Ovseich would hear none of it: he wouldn't keep his door half open in the District Committee either. "No," said Klava Ivanovna, holding her ground, "no matter how important someone is, he should stay simple and always be accessible to people. Like Lenin. Like Stalin."

"Malaya," said Iona Ovseich heatedly, "take Comrade Stalin, take his speech at the Central Committee Plenum in March '37, and there'll you find complete answers to your questions: our party has its generals, its party officers, and its party noncoms. Not in the old sense, of course, the way it was before the Revolution, but everyone should know his place. So, let's not waste time on meaningless talk. Tell me —why are you here?"

"I came here so you wouldn't worry for no reason. Orlov's been found."

"I see," interrupted Iona Ovseich, "it turned out the way I predicted. The slut's in the hospital where they gave her an enema while you were running around to morgues like an old fool."

"She slit her wrists," said Klava Ivanovna. "She's lucky to be alive."

"Let's be frank," said Iona Ovseich. "People don't fail when they're serious."

"She swears it'll never happen again," said Klava Ivanovna, shaking her head. "It's the first time, and the last."

"Time will tell," said Comrade Degtyar. "When does she plan to go home?"

"She says she won't go back to the courtyard, she's been too disgraced there."

"Oh!" said Iona Ovseich with a grin. "Here comes the blackmail and the extortion. She shouldn't count on us asking her forgiveness and going down on our knees. On the contrary, we can see this for what it's worth."

"And what about the psychological trauma?" said Klava Ivanovna, frowning.

"It's a surgical question," said Iona Ovseich. "They sew up the veins. We're doctors here too in our own way."

Klava Ivanovna sighed deeply. "Ovseich, please let Dr. Landa go see Lyalya in the hospital, she'd like that."

"Malaya," said Iona Ovseich, raising his voice, "stop bringing me charity cases! People are always ready to make hay with their troubles, especially if they're imaginary."

Degtyar's prophecy literally proved true the following day when Lyalya bluntly demanded that she be given living space in a different building.

"Hold on," said Klava Ivanovna, "yesterday you promised that was the last time but now I'm starting to think you're playing games with us here. You need a new address so you can go back to your old ways. Lyalya, I'm telling you nicely, people's patience has a limit."

Orlov lay in bed, her eyes looking up at the ceiling, as if Madame Malaya had not spoken to her. Then she repeated what she had just said, now adding a threat that the next time she wouldn't fail.

When Degtyar learned of this conversation, he grew genuinely furious and ordered information assembled to bring Orlov to trial for prostitution. Malaya resisted even though deep down she knew he was right, and asked for another week, even a few more days.

"You're too indulgent!" Iona Ovseich shouted. "Malaya, you're a typical overindulgent person, and I'm telling you you're going to come to a bad end!"

Klava Ivanovna visited the hospital three days later. Lyalya greeted her like her own mother, and then launched into a tirade of curses against herself as if she'd overheard everything Degtyar had said about her. Madame Malaya ordered her to act like a normal person to which Lyalya responded by rubbing her cheek like a silly kitten, and purring: "Mama Klavockha, I'm just an ungrateful little girl and I should be beaten with a strap. The doctor's releasing me tomorrow and I'm going home."

"Oh, Lyalya," said Madame Malaya, shaking her head, "a person should try to balance their emotions, but you're always at one extreme or another."

Lyalya told Klava Ivanovna to bend down and she gave her a resounding kiss. Then, with her mouth half covered by her hands, she began singing:

"I'm not Daddy's girl,
I'm not Mummy's girl,
I grew up on the street,
I was laid by a hen."

After leaving the hospital, Lyalya had two more days of sick leave, which she spent at home. She was visited by Anya Kotlyar, Dina Vargaftik, and Tosya Khomitsky. They talked about the spring, which was warm that year, you could go out without a coat, and they all envied Lyalya for living alone and being her own boss.

Nastya visited her twice and she too was envious: everybody worked one shift every twenty-four hours, but a concierge worked three and had to get up in the middle of the night and open the gate for whoever was there. And if there was something they didn't like, they ran straight to Degtyar, Jews or Christians, it didn't matter, and then you had to give an account of yourself.

Lyalya gave Nastya a teapot and a kerchief as presents. The top to the teapot had gotten lost but you could cover it with a saucer. Nastya didn't have a saucer the right size and Lyalya gave her the one she'd been using.

"You're young," said Nastya when leaving, "there's no reason for you to sit home. When you ring for me, pull twice, once hard, then softer the second time."

At the end of the work week Iona Ovseich also intended to pay a visit to Lyalya and had notified Malaya that she should accompany him, but his conversation with Granik had run way over time. At first they spoke in Degtyar's room but then Polina Isaevna arrived and told them to move to Granik's because Anya Kotlyar was coming to be coached in math.

"Go take a little walk with your mother in the park, kids," Efim said to his children.

Sonya said that Osya hadn't done his homework yet, and she was going out with Khilka.

"All right," said Iona Ovseich, "but Oska should stay here and move over to the window."

Sonya shrugged her shoulders: she had nothing against the idea but the child wouldn't be comfortable using the windowsill for a desk, his knees would be up against the wall.

"That doesn't matter," said Iona Ovseich. "Let him get used to discomfort, we don't need any spoiled babies."

"I'd think the two of you could sit by the window," said Sonya, sticking to her guns.

"And I'd think," said Efim, fuming, "that my guest and I could sit at the table and my son could use the windowsill for a desk! Maxim Gorky used to save his money for candle stubs and would read under the table at night so his landlord couldn't see him. And so what? He became Maxim Gorky!"

Osya moved his notebooks, books, and inkwell to the windowsill. Though the forty-watt light hung from the middle of the ceiling, it lit the room well and he wouldn't have to strain his eyes. Iona Ovseich checked for himself and asked Sonya to double-check.

"Comrade Degtyar," said Sonya with utter sincerity, "we trust you more than we trust ourselves."

Without any prompting, Osya confirmed that there was plenty of light. It was much darker during second session in school, and still he could see fine there too.

Sonya left with her daughter. For a while the two men sat in silence, enjoying the peace. They could hear Osya's pen squeaking as he wrote the number eighty-six.

"Efim," said Iona Ovseich, "you should be proud of your son. He has an important quality—he can concentrate quickly."

Granik smiled and stroked his chin. Then he suddenly remembered that he had not offered his guest any refreshments. He ran to put a pan of water on the stove. The Primus was faster and gave off no soot but the stove made no noise.

"You're doing pretty well," said Iona Ovseich approvingly, "you've got a Primus and a stove; all you need is an electric hot plate and you'll have a full set."

Efim set a large plate of biscuits on the table, as well as some lump sugar and two jam dishes, but they proved unnecessary because Sonya had forgotten to buy jam that day.

"What do we need jam for?" said Degtyar, spreading his hands. "There's tea and biscuits and lump sugar. All we need is some tongs."

"Let Dr. Landa use tongs," said Efim, "but I'm in the habit of using a knife." Iona Ovseich replied that using a knife was dangerous, you could cut yourself. "A horse has four legs and it can still stumble," objected Efim, "but I, and my father, and his father, who knew the Torah and Talmud almost by heart—what a smart Jew the man was—we all always used a knife and never cut ourselves."

Efim struck the lump of sugar and split it in two; then he struck the two halves, splitting them into nearly equal pieces.

"What a marksman!" said Iona Ovseich in wholehearted praise. "Bull's-eye! You've got a good eye."

"A real expert doesn't need a good eye," said Efim. "His hand knows what to do."

Osya forgot about his homework and began listening intently to the two men talking. Iona Ovseich noticed and told the boy to show him his notebook.

Osya brought it over. It turned out that he had already finished his arithmetic and was now doing his drawings for botany class. Iona Ovseich praised him, stroked his head, and reminded him of the German proverb: *Morgen! Morgen! Nur nicht heute! sagen alle faulen Leute!"* which he then translated as: "Tomorrow! Tomorrow! Not today! That's what all lazybones say!" Then Degtyar asked what days the young authors' club met in the Pioneer outpost, and gave Osya a severe warning not to be tempted by easy, flash-in-the-pan writers but to keep the example of Pushkin, Lermontov, and Nekrasov always before him.

"Ovseich," protested Efim, "you'll make the boy dizzy by comparing him to those writers."

"No," replied Iona Ovseich, "compliments only make fools dizzy, but intelligent people understand them correctly. Osya, go back where you were and keep working, and now, Efim, I have a question for you: how many door plates can you make out of a six-liter can of brown paint? Let's say six liters, no more."

The question had caught Efim off guard, his ears ringing from the rush of blood as if someone had pressed an electric buzzer and forgotten to take his finger off. Iona Ovseich waited patiently but time was awasting and he expressed his apprehension that Granik had gone deaf.

No, Efim finally replied, he had not gone deaf, he wanted to figure it out first so he could give an exact answer. But he couldn't give an exact answer because every painter had his own sense of measure. It was like a person's appetite: one man ate a loaf of bread and a slab of butter for breakfast and it was not enough, another man had half a roll and a glass of tea, and that was plenty for him.

"Stop talking nonsense and answer the question," said Iona Ovseich. "Let's say we're talking about Efim Granik, a person we both know well."

Efim thought for a moment, then explained that he still couldn't give him an exact answer. "Let's take the breakfast example again: one morning you have a good appetite and eat a loaf of bread and a pound of butter, another time you have no appetite or you're in a bad mood or you're coming down with a cold, and you have half a roll and a glass of tea."

"So," said Iona Ovseich, "I see that you want to be Vanka the Fool and Hershel Ostropoler all at the same time."

"I beg your pardon," said Efim, raising his voice. "Don't insult the head of a household and the father of a family!"

Iona Ovseich let that remark pass and said that in future he would not allow Granik to cheat the state and the Soviet system: the Revenue Department could tax Granik at the highest possible rate.

"Comrade Degtyar," said Granik in alarm, "you can see for yourself that the Graniks don't drink beer and fruit-flavored mineral water but plain tap water. The children need shoes, coats, notebooks, briefcases, at least one for the two of them to share. I'm no crook—I earn my crust of bread with my own two hands."

"Stop it!" ordered Iona Ovseich. "You're whining like a beggar with your own son sitting and watching you. When a man drags home a can of gold paint in the middle of the night, that's a crime against Soviet society and the Soviet people. And we're not going to remain just passive witnesses to it. Now you draw the proper conclusions."

On his way out, Degtyar shouted that Granik could turn off the stove: the tea had already started boiling. Efim sat motionlessly at the table, clutching his head with both hands. Osya too said that the tea was ready. Suddenly Granik jumped to his feet, grabbed his chair, lifted it in the air, and slammed the back of the chair against the floor. The seat and hoop went flying and the second blow smashed both front legs and the top half of the back.

"I'll kill him!" shouted Efim. "He'd better never come to my house again or I'll kill him like a dog!"

"Daddy, Daddy!" Osya's whole body was trembling and he was gasping for breath.

"My son, you still don't know me!" shouted Efim in a frightening voice. "There'll be nothing left of him when I get through with him!"

Osya wept and pleaded with his father not to kill Iona Ovseich, otherwise the police would come and arrest him, and they'd be left without a father.

"Don't say that!" roared Efim. "I should kill him, otherwise I'll lose my own son's respect."

Osya swore that he would respect his father all the more for not killing Degtyar.

"You coward!" laughed Efim. "You pitiful coward!"

Osya stared at his feet. Efim wiped the tears from the bridge of his son's nose, using his middle finger on which he always squirted paint from a tube when he needed a close look at it. He told his son to go sit at the table, his tea had already gone cold.

Three days later, on Monday evening, Granik put on the suit he'd been given as a prize for his work on the outpost, told his son to iron his Pioneer scarf so it wouldn't hang down like a turkey's throat, and then the two of them set off to Degtyar's. At first Iona Ovseich squinted automatically on opening the door and seeing his guests. Efim and Osya said a polite hello, then Degtyar raised both his hands aloft and bowed in traditional old Russian style.

Osya laughed and said that the Old Russian heroic epics they were reading in school about Dobryna Nikitich sounded like that.

"That's right, Joseph, son of Efim," said Iona Ovseich with praise. "Learning helps us with the lessons of fleeting life. Who said that?"

Osya honestly admitted right off that he didn't know, while his father furrowed his brow and asked God to help him remember.

"Don't do that," said Degtyar, grinning. "God only helps those who help themselves. You have to reread your Pushkin, my dear Efim Lazarevich. Can't hurt."

Iona Ovseich removed a dress from the couch, which he handed through a door to Polina Isaevna, who began throwing it on. Meanwhile the three of them sat down at the table.

"Comrade Degtyar," said Efim, "allow me to inform you that, as of today, Efim Lazarevich Granik will be employed as a master craftsman in the painting department of the October Revolution factory, formerly known as the Gena. Do you have any complaints on that score?"

He did have one complaint on that score, replied Iona Ovseich—against himself, for not immediately thinking to put a bottle of wine on the table!

By the time Polina Isaevna came out, they were already drinking a bottle of 05 and munching on salted rolls.

"What's this!" said the indignant hostess. "Isn't there any butter in the house, or white bread, or herring?"

Efim objected that you could be served butter, herring, and white bread in other homes, but salted bagels were a special delicacy.

"He's right," seconded Iona Ovseich. "I remember like it was yesterday the crawfish they used to sell on Greek Street, corner of Rishelevsky, before the Revolution. They didn't taste too bad either. The people of Odessa always had a good appetite."

Then Iona Ovseich reminisced about a small market in Peresyp, not far from the Gena factory where he'd begun working for the underground. They sold crayfish from a cart which they'd brought in from the Zaplaza settlement. He had made efforts to find out why he had never seen the likes of those crayfish again. Compared with them, the ones they brought in now from the Dniester flats outside Belyaevka looked like blue chicks beside a hen.

Efim made a hand signal to Osya meaning it was time for him to go, but Osya was very curious about Iona Ovseich's struggle against tsarism and wanted to hear how the gendarmes beat him with their whips. In reply Iona Ovseich inquired what marks Osya was receiving in history. In 1905 boys Osya's age were already making history themselves. In mid-June the battleship *Potemkin* had cast anchor and hoisted a red flag. Then the other warships raised a red flag as a sign they were preparing to shoot, but in this case it could also have been interpreted as a signal for a revolutionary uprising. The boys of Peresyp built barricades along with their fathers and older brothers. Later on, the tsarist authorities brought them to trial; included were a hundred and forty children between the ages of eleven and fourteen.

Osya guessed that this was after the slaughter on the Potemkin Stairs, which he'd seen in the movies. Iona Ovseich said that was right but added that there had been no shooting on the stairs, that was something dreamed up by the director of *The Battleship Potemkin,* Sergei Eisenstein; the shooting had taken place at Kanava, especially near Peresyp Bridge. A great many people were killed who had little political awareness and were not organized. They had broken into warehouses, rolled out barrels of wine, smashed the bottoms, and plunged their heads right in. Dozens, hundreds of drunken people passed out and drowned in those barrels, and the Cossacks and police not only did not try to help them but, on the contrary, shot them in the back. This was the most convincing proof that it was in the interest of the tsar and the bourgeois to induce the people to drink so they'd be easier to deal with. There was a sea of fire everywhere, and the famous pier that ran the length of the entire port burned down then.

"Now, my son, you have a clear picture of what Uncle Degtyar is like!" said Efim grandly.

"That's right," said Iona Ovseich, squinting merrily. "Uncle Degtyar is very special: he has five fingers on each hand and five toes on each foot; he has two ears, two eyes, and a total of one nose, unlike anybody else in the world."

Osya laughed. Iona Ovseich patted his cheek and sighed deeply.

He and Polina Isaevna had had two boys in 1921, twins; they both had died of hunger.

Efim left at five-thirty so as not to be late for work. The gate was still locked and he banged on the concierge's window three times with his fist. Nastya came running out barefoot in only her nightshirt, called him a lousy kike, but not loud enough for Granik to hear, and then wished him the shakes for the rest of his life, whatever he had left to live.

"You slut," replied Efim evenly. "Look, my pockets are full of gold paint. Do a weight check on me."

Nastya went to open the gate, saying he should choke on his paint, and that she wanted nothing to do with him.

"You bitch," he said, wagging a finger at her, "you talk like that to me, you'll be on your way out of Odessa on a prison train in twenty-four hours!"

Nastya clutched her stomach to contain her laughter and promised to inform Comrade Degtyar: he should have himself a laugh too.

"Stool pigeon!" said Efim, chuckling. "I don't give a flying fuck about you. I've got the whole working collective of the October Revolution factory behind me!"

The conversation with Orlov which Iona Ovseich had postponed had to be postponed yet again because of the Kotlyars. Though Joseph had at first taken a calm view of Anya being tutored in math by Polina Isaevna, he now suddenly grew bristly: it turned out that once or twice his wife had failed to make him lunch and had given him a piece of sausage and yesterday's bread for dinner. Anya came running to Degtyar's all in tears, saying her husband had said things to her she could never bring herself to repeat, and asked for protection.

"Joseph," said Iona Ovseich in surprise, "a person could think you were from Central Asia and your father was a rich landowner."

Joseph replied that he was not a landowner's son, and had only seen Central Asia in the movies but he didn't need his wife studying arithmetic instead of making dinner for her husband.

"Aha," said Iona Ovseich, "you have remnants of feudalism in your mentality: if a husband doesn't want something that means his wife doesn't need it either!"

"No," said Joseph, slamming his fist on the table, "only one person can be the boss! Let her go work ten hours a day at a punch press at the Lenin factory and I'll cook the meat and the borscht."

Let him cook his own slop, cried Anya, she wouldn't even touch it with a finger.

"Go home," ordered Joseph, "or this is going to get worse. I'm telling you it'll get worse."

"Kotlyar," said Iona Ovseich with a smile, "this isn't going to get any worse, and don't try to scare her. In the U.S.S.R. women have the right to economic and mental freedom, a right guaranteed them by the Stalin Constitution."

"Ovseich," said Joseph Kotlyar, raising his tone of voice, "I'm no Efim Granik. I'm not like that slut Orlov. You got off easy with her, but with someone else you might end up spitting blood."

"Joseph Kotlyar," replied Degtyar politely, "to a person who threatens me in my own home, what I say is—there's the door, please use it."

"Are you kicking me out?" said Joseph, turning pale.

"Citizen Kotlyar," said Iona Ovseich, moving forward, "I'm not kicking anyone out. I'm asking you to leave."

"And I'm asking you not to interfere in my family life!" said Joseph, slamming the table again.

Iona Ovseich asked him to leave a third time but, before doing so, clearly emphasized the fact that the right of every Soviet citizen to an education was not interfering in someone's family life but one of socialism's more important achievements.

"Ovseich," said Joseph, clenching his hairy fist and bringing it right up to Degtyar's nose, "it's not your goddamned business to be instructing me. If you want my wife to go to technical school, then you cook me my dinner. The law gives me the right to a hot meal every day."

"And the law gives me the right," said Iona Ovseich, rising and picking up his telephone, "to call the police to help restrain a petit bourgeois who's out of bounds!"

Anya sat as still as a doll. Polina Isaevna walked over to her husband and tried to snatch the phone from his hand but Joseph stopped her.

"Don't bother. Thank God, I have one leg left, I can leave on my own."

Iona Ovseich hung up the phone, opened the door, and reminded Anya that she had a lesson that day at nine-thirty and please not to be late for it.

Polina Isaevna gestured to her husband as if to say: why aggravate a person when you don't have to!

"Polina," said Iona Ovseich, stamping his foot, "don't tell me what I already know."

It was announced that the requirements for the medical courses in which Anya planned to enroll had been changed. In addition to the tests already scheduled, there would also be examinations on the Constitution of the U.S.S.R. and zoology. That came as a complete surprise. Anya was seized by panic and said now she had to fail and there was no way out.

"Don't get confused," said Iona Ovseich. "It's one thing when there really is no way out, and another when you have yet to find a way out."

In the case at hand, the latter, fortunately, proved true: Like a domestic servant who had so identified herself with the kitchen that she could imagine no other way of living, Anya had simply not seen the solution.

"Are you saying I should stop keeping house altogether?" said Anya fearfully.

"Let's pose the question another way," said Iona Ovseich. "What's more important to you right now: to cook and clean for your husband or to get a medical education? If it's the former, then keep on living as you have been, but if it's the latter, then throw down your pots and pans and devote all your time to school."

"Oy," said Anya, clutching her temples, "Joseph will file for divorce!"

"You little fool," said Polina Isaevna with a laugh, "he'll love you all the more. When a wife spends all day in the kitchen, her husband takes it for granted, but when she tears herself away from her studies to cook, he'll be grateful for half a bowl of soup."

Joseph was more indignant than anyone about the additional examinations on the Constitution of the U.S.S.R. and zoology and asked his wife where she would find the time to prepare properly for them. Anya said that she had been racking her brains over that problem, and that she'd have to cut down on her sleep.

No, said Joseph categorically, she could cut down on whatever else she wanted but not her sleep; when a person didn't get enough sleep, it ruined the nervous system, and, thanks to Degtyar, they were having enough scenes at home as it was.

On Saturday, though Polina Isaevna had planned an outing to the movies to see *If War Comes Tomorrow,* Iona Ovseich called it off: it was time to visit Orlov, it had been put off long enough already. At the outset Lyalya was somewhat embarrassed, but Iona Ovseich immediately began speaking about the tobacco factory, which was experiencing difficulties with raw material, cigarette papers, and packing materials; then they moved on to Lyalya's relationship with the factory collective and it turned out that it couldn't have been better.

"All right then," said Iona Ovseich, looking her straight in the eye, "but does that give a person the right to stage an attempt on his own life?"

Lyalya covered her face in her hands and asked Iona Ovseich not to return to that subject, so painful and shameful for her. No, insisted Iona Ovseich, to act like an ostrich was a lousy policy, all the shame must be brought out into the light of day.

"It'll never happen again," swore Lyalya, "once I get my health back."

"What you did was pathetic theatrics," said Degtyar. "During the Civil War we used to face death consciously for the good of the people, we accepted death with our heads held high, but the bourgeois always tried to intimidate the Bolsheviks with some hoaxes of suicide. I'll tell you something else; if a person wants to kill himself—ninety times out of a hundred we should write that person off!"

Lyalya replied that she hadn't wished to frighten anybody: it was just that she was in total despair and couldn't go on living.

"Yes," said Iona Ovseich, "but until you got caught at it, you were perfectly able to sleep with strangers for money!"

Lyalya burst into tears. Iona Ovseich drew his chair right beside hers, took her hand, and suggested that she feel how his heart was missing beats. Lyalya touched his heart through his shirt but Iona Ovseich said she couldn't feel anything like that and, opening his collar, he thrust her fingers inside. Then, for the sake of comparison, he placed his own hand under Lyalya's breast, pressing it firmly, and said that she could run marathons with a heart like hers. That was true, agreed Lyalya, breaking into giggles.

"You silly little fool," said Iona Ovseich, brushing his cheek against her head. Her hair smelled pleasantly of soap, "you still don't know anything about life."

Lyalya could not say a word, she was in such a fit of giggles. Her fingers jumped inside Iona Ovseich's shirt, catching on his chest hair. He ordered her to calm herself at once and gave her a few light spanks.

Oy, cried Lyalya, jumping to her feet, she hadn't pulled the curtains, and when the light was on in her room, you could see everything from the courtyard, like a movie. Iona Ovseich replied with a joke: when the films breaks, there's nothing to see.

Lyalya went back to the couch. Iona Ovseich placed both his hands under her arms and asked her to sit quietly and not fidget as if she were waiting for a train. Lyalya agreed but immediately began fidgeting because it tickled too much. Now she moved onto his knees, saying it took a strong man to support her weight.

"Orlov, Orlov," said Iona Ovseich, trying to call her to order, "you're not paying attention to what I say."

"Don't say anymore then!" she said in a suddenly saucy voice, sealing his lips with the palm of her hand. She told him that if he couldn't keep quiet, then he should make a sound like a steer—moo, moo! Iona Ovseich shook his head in various directions but, having lost all sense of measure, Lyalya threw her arms around his neck and pressed herself to him with all her might.

The tension made her feel faint. Iona Ovseich tried to keep her from falling but they both tumbled to the floor. The guest ended up on top of the hostess whose legs were spread. Her eyes glittered as if she were running a high temperature. He tried to get up, his hand accidentally lifting her dress, his fingers brushing something warm and wet. Lyalya shrieked, her legs convulsing and her lips trembling like an epileptic's. Iona Ovseich began making lowing sounds, he ground his teeth; inwardly everything fell away as if he had gone flying into an abyss where there was nothing to catch hold of. He thrashed a few times, wriggled free, and, resting his palms on the floor, pushed himself back up onto his knees and stood up.

"Foolish jokes have foolish endings," said Iona Ovseich.

"You're wet," said Lyalya, pointing. "It should be washed out with water or else it'll leave a mark."

Iona Ovseich drew his hand across his pants: there was a large wet spot near his fly.

"Give me your hand," said Lyalya. "Help me get up."

"You're not a child," replied Iona Ovseich. "You can get up yourself."

"What, do you leave your own wife lying on the floor like this?"

"Orlov," said Comrade Degtyar, stamping his foot, "now you're going too far!"

"Why too far?" asked Lyalya in surprise. "I just want to picture how Polina would react to this scene."

"What scene?" asked Iona Ovseich. "Say what you mean."

Lyalya stood up, straightened her dress, and quoted the well-known folk saying, "You live and learn, but you still die a fool."

"Orlov," said Iona Ovseich, threatening her with a finger, "I can see that you've got a fine mess in that head of yours. You'd better do some real thinking, otherwise you and I won't be friends."

At the end of May, Khomitsky and Cheperukha sent postcards saying that they would be demobilized any time soon. Iona Ovseich ordered Klava Ivanovna to work with the other activists to prepare a reception worthy of their Red Army men.

Though the children were in the thick of exams at school, Gizella Landa assembled them in the outpost and taught them new songs—"Moscow in May," "My Beloved City Can Sleep in Peace," and "Katyusha." The children quickly memorized the words but did not work well together as a chorus. Regular practice sessions were required, causing some parents to grumble. Klava Ivanovna told Gizella to turn a deaf ear to all that talk; people had big mouths; let them blab all they wanted, and, if need be, ways could be found to quiet them down.

The courtyard was entirely ready to welcome the two soldiers by mid-June as Madame Malaya reported to Degtyar but he unexpectedly voiced another idea—maybe it should be postponed for a while.

"What's the problem?" said Klava Ivanovna, taking fright. "You shouldn't keep anything from me."

Iona Ovseich said there was no cause for alarm, on the contrary;

she should ask him easier questions, ones about personal not public life.

The very next day the radio and newspapers reported that the revolutionary efforts by the workers of the Baltic countries, led by Communists, had been crowned with victory. The workers and peasants had taken power. A people's government, headed by Comrade Paletskis, had been formed in Lithuania, in Latvia, headed by Comrade Kirchenstein, and in Estonia, headed by Comrade Vares.

Klava Ivanovna was profoundly indignant: Degtyar had known all that before, how could he have kept such events secret from her!

Tosya Khomitsky and Olya Cheperukha had the strongest emotional reaction: on the one hand, they could be proud that at this historic moment their husbands were serving in the ranks of the Red Army right there, in the north. But, on the other hand, they had had valid cause for anxiety: fascist gangs, followers of Ulmanis and Smetona, were firing on Red Army soldiers at every corner—from windows, gateways, and attics. Comrade Degtyar gave the two women a one hundred percent guarantee that nothing bad was going to happen to guys from Odessa over there. The women regained their composure for half a day, then started running out every two minutes to see if the mail had come and would then go back home with long faces.

Finally, on June 27, both wives received complete information about their husbands, not by mail but from someone who had seen them. That day Dr. Landa had gone to the Razdelnaya settlement as part of his medical duties. It was getting late in the afternoon and he was already preparing to leave for Odessa when all of a sudden there was Iona Cheperukha right before his very eyes. Dr. Landa was dumbstruck in surprise. Cheperukha swore by the life of his son Zyunchik that he had been certain he was going to run into someone from the courtyard, not necessarily Dr. Landa, but definitely someone. He said that Stepa Khomitsky wasn't far from there, at the Kuchurgan settlement. They could hop a ride over there on a freight train, but Dr. Landa had only ten minutes before his own train arrived. So, he and Iona drank a small bottle of wine and kissed each other soundly when saying good-bye.

"All right," said Degtyar, putting his arms around Tosya's and Olya's shoulders like the three comrades in the movie *Maxim's Youth,* "so who was raising a stir and sounding the alarm for all Odessa to hear! Answer me, or we'll put the panic mongers up against the wall and shoot them with red tomatoes."

Both women admitted their guilt without a murmur, but immediately found something new to weep and wail about: it was just a stone's throw from Razdelnaya and Kuchurgan to the border, and Rumanian aristocrats and fascist gangs were operating there.

"You're panicking again!" said Iona Ovseich, with jolly indignation. "It's not like it was twenty years ago when they could grab Bessarabia from us. Soviet military weakness is a thing of the past."

In large red letters that covered one wall, Efim Granik wrote out the slogan: "Not one inch of foreign land, nor will we surrender an inch of our own!"

On June 28, regular units of the Red Army crossed the Dniester River in a line extending from the Black Sea to the foothills of the Carpathians. Exactly two days later they were in Northern Bukovina and in the Akkerman, Izmail, and Khitin districts as well as in that part of Bessarabia where the Moldavians lived. The twenty years of oppression by the Rumanian aristocrats was now only a memory.

Efim Granik proposed a bet to Joseph Kotlyar—five rubles to one—that Tiraspol was finished as the capital and the Moldavians would now make Kishinev their capital city. Kotlyar replied that he was no fool; Efim might just as well hand him the money because not only Bessarabia, but all Rumania, Bucharest included, would soon be in the Soviet pocket.

A day later Efim said to Joseph: "Though this has not been confirmed by the Supreme Soviet of the U.S.S.R., I'm willing to bet there are now sixteen union republics as opposed to the eleven we had last year." Joseph again refused to bet. Efim calculated that if things kept going at the rate of five new republics a year, then a world victory for the Soviet system was not so far off in the future, especially since whole districts of China were already under the control of the national liberation army and the Chinese Communist authorities.

Olya Cheperukha finally received a letter from her husband. The letter was from the city of Bendery, which was on the other side of the Dniester and directly across from Tiraspol. In the opening lines Iona reported that he was alive and well, then went on to describe the city; the population included many Jews, Moldavians, and poor people, but the most surprising thing was the low prices at the markets: he personally had bought twenty rolls for twenty kopecks, and one soldier in his company, Ata Durdyev, who couldn't speak two words of Russian, bought a Swiss watch and wristband for a ninety-ruble bond. Fool's luck! He could have done the same thing if he'd had a bond with him, but who could have known? Now the populace would accept only cash. Olya laughed and said that as usual Iona was pulling her leg and trying to get her upset, but a day later a letter arrived from Stepa Khomitsky from the town of Kalarasha, and he wrote the same thing though he couldn't have known what Iona had said in his letter from Bendera.

Efim calculated that twenty rolls would be enough for one day for himself, his wife, Oska, and Khilka, and if you figured a ruble for all the rest—herring, onions, sugar—that came to a ruble twenty a day, or thirty-six rubles a month, and he had a salary of three hundred and seventy-five. To the cost of food you had to add rent, water, electricity, kerosene, matches, and soap, but you'd still be left with almost half your pay.

Joseph Kotlyar said that really wasn't bad at all, but there was one little inconvenience: you had to get paid in Odessa and go shopping in Bendery or Kalarash. Efim answered that shopping once a week wasn't so terrible, the English imported meat from Australia, which was in the other hemisphere. Joseph thought of another objection: the Bessarabians weren't such fools that they would keep things at the old prices, and Efim would waste money on traveling. And for ten rubles you could buy a kilo of good herring in Odessa.

From Khomitsky and Cheperukha's next letters it was clear that prices were indeed changing but, according to Granik's calculations, a round-trip ticket would still more than pay for itself.

"So hop the next train," said Kotlyar.

"What about the pass!" said Efim with a laugh. "Who's going to issue me a pass? I'm no big shot who can skim the cream off the milk."

"So you have to become a big shot then," advised Joseph.

No, said Efim, waving his arms about, he didn't want to be a big shot; administrators had to worry about other people. And for a person to like worrying about other people, he must be born with such a desire.

"Efim," said Joseph, curling his lips, "Degtyar is right—you can't get anywhere with you. You're a brake on the locomotive of our Revolution."

For three days Olya and Tosya had been working side by side in the middle of the courtyard with their copper bowls making apricot jam. Klava Ivanovna and Dina Vargaftik had lent them their Primuses and so they each could make two batches at a time. When they had to go to the Market or the store, the other women were glad to take their place and warned them not to rush, especially when crossing the trolley tracks, anything could happen when you were in a rush, God forbid.

"Don't predict bad things!" the soldiers' wives replied merrily, and calmly left to go shopping.

Zyunchik and Kolka had spent an entire day hanging around Lanzheron and were tanned black as devils. Zyunchik had to retake his algebra exam for the fall but all a boy of his abilities had to do was study hard for three days and he'd receive an A. Olya confided to Tosya that his father had better pay some attention to him before the child went to total ruin!

Iona and Stepa were demobilized at the end of July but gave no advance notice of their arrival. They appeared in the courtyard in broad daylight and Olya began shouting hysterically: "Everybody, come see who's here!"

Iona shouted that Santa Claus had come, so come get your presents.

"My little fool," said Olya, weeping, her tears dampening her husband's shirt, "it's July, Santa Claus isn't coming!"

Iona placed a new silk kerchief on his wife's head. The kerchief had foreign letters along its edges surrounding jolly monkeys leaping from palm tree to palm tree. Olya said that the palm trees were exactly like those in Arcadia, but wear a kerchief with monkeys on it so everyone would laugh at her—not for anything in the world!

Stepa had also brought a kerchief with monkeys on it and Tosya said straight out, "You bought it, you wear it." Anya Kotlyar immediately tried it on, and the dark brown monkeys went very well with her green eyes, but Tosya had already changed her mind and besides you didn't sell the presents people gave you.

That evening Tosya and Olya put on their dresses and flat-heeled chamois sandals and went with their husbands to the Twentieth RKKA Theater, formerly the Postyshev. They were showing *City Lights,* which they had already seen two or three times but you could see Charlie Chaplin a hundred times and still want more.

The date for welcoming the demobilized Red Army soldiers Khomitsky and Cheperukha, which had originally been scheduled for mid-June, had to be switched and restructured somewhat because of changes in the international arena; on the one hand, the U.S.S.R.'s new borders were a significant factor for peace, and, on the other hand, Hitler's victory in France was fraught with danger. The children's concert was ready in two days' time: Gizella had already put a lot of work in with the children, and not much practice was required now to prepare them.

There were six people at the presidium for the welcoming reception: Comrade Degtyar, the demobilized Red Army soldiers and their wives, and Klava Ivanovna. The official opening of the evening was held up for fifteen minutes due to a shortage of chairs, and for all that time Efim stood by the presidium with his arm around the shoulder of his friend Stepa Khomitsky. Klava Ivanovna even needled him that Efim would only be friends with celebrities now.

"Malaya," said Comrade Degtyar, "new relationships between people are forming right before your eyes. Keep an eye on them. Tide and time wait for no man. If you don't pay attention, the millstones of history will crush you and leave you behind."

Olya Cheperukha seemed on pins and needles and kept asking what time it was. Iona Ovseich notified the audience that the presidium members were beginning to worry about the delay; things couldn't be dragged out any further, and he declared the ceremonies open.

In a brief opening address he sketched out the political map of Europe today. Countries that had been independent a short while ago, like Denmark and Norway, had now lost their independence. In May the German Army had also taken control of Holland, Belgium, and Luxembourg, thereby circumventing the famous Maginot Line. As for France, its fate had been decided long before the outbreak of hostilities, because a fifth column, which had penetrated sections of the government and military by frightening people with the bugaboo of communism, had systematically prepared the country for the inevitable treachery. Though Paul Reynaud had had certain noble intentions, he was unable to do anything at all in practice. Between the twenty-seventh of May and the fourth of June—in other words, at the most critical period—England and its Prime Minister, the unbridled anti-Soviet Winston Churchill, who had replaced the well-known appeaser Neville Chamberlain, abandoned France to her fate while they themselves were busy evacuating their own troops from Dunkirk. According to a Reuters report, an army of three hundred thousand was pulled out, and Allied France became the next victim of betrayal. Paris fell on June 14, exactly one month before Bastille Day, and eleven days later, on June 25, in the Compiègne woods, in the same railroad car where twenty-two years earlier Marshal Foch had dictated terms of surrender to a defeated Germany, France now acknowledged its own defeat. The peace of Versailles, whose imperialist nature the Soviet Republic had stressed from the very outset of its own existence, had collapsed like a house of cards.

The weakening of the imperialist camp had been paralleled by the growth of the U.S.S.R., both in terms of territory and size of population. The U.S.S.R.'s border with Europe had been shifted significantly westward and was now stronger than ever. The introduction of communism in other countries, a possibility fully demonstrated at the historic Eighteenth Party Congress, was acquiring new momentum with each passing day, and it would not be long before the age-old dream of the workers, peasants, and all the working people of the world would be realized: from each according to his abilities—to each according to his needs.

"But," said Degtyar, "outside the cordon of our motherland, we still observe extreme opposites: wealth and poverty, luxury and squalor, the gluttony of the sated and the howls of the hungry.

"Our blood brothers, the Moldavians and Ukrainians, groaned for twenty-two years under the yoke of aristocratic Rumania. On one shore of the Dniester there were joy and happiness, and on the other—the tears of mothers and the sobs of children; on one shore there were laughter and mirth, and on the other—suffering and unemployment. The famous Ukrainian writer Mikhailo Kotsyubinsky vividly described how plant lice had attacked the Bessarabian peasants' vineyards, but the Rumanian lords were a hundred times more horrible than plant lice or locusts. Under the guise of agrarian reform they took away as much as three quarters of the land belonging to the peasants. The number of illiterate people in rural Bessarabia was approaching eighty percent.

"Comrades," said the chairman solemnly, "today we have here with us two soldiers demobilized from the Red Army, Stepa Khomitsky and Iona Cheperukha, who participated directly in the liberation of the peoples of Bessarabia. They were able to see the traces of that capitalist paradise with their own eyes, and wish to share what they saw with us today. Please welcome them!"

The applause might have been three times longer and louder if Cheperukha had not stopped it himself. First he expressed his gratitude to the party, the government, and to Comrade Stalin for their trust in him, and to his neighbors and fellow residents for their welcome. As for the capitalist paradise of which Comrade Degtyar had just spoken in detail, there was only one thing that could be said: that it was all the truth, the bitter truth, and there were no words, no colors, no expressions to describe it. He took an example from life. One time in the middle of June, the commanding officer of his unit had sent him, Cheperukha, to the settlement of Chadyr-Lunga on a secret mission. It was scorching hot, there was a drought, and the dust on the leaves was as thick as your finger. He went to one house for something to drink. The Moldavian he met could still speak a little Russian from the old days when Bessarabia was ruled by Nicholas II. Little by little they made themselves understood. The Moldavian brought him a pitcher of wine, sheep's milk cheese, a copper dish full of polenta, half a dozen cucumbers, and a little butter to put on the polenta while it was still hot. The wine was good, straight from their cellar, and the two men spoke their minds. It turned out that this Moldavian had never seen a tractor and had never even heard of combines! With his own eyes he, Iona Cheperukha, had seen a wooden hoe. The old man was very surprised to learn that on the other side of the Dniester, in Tiraspol, Kotovsk, or Balta, you couldn't buy something like that for any amount of money, and to see one you had to go to the historical museum in Odessa on Feldman Boulevard. Then he had asked the old man about his voting rights. The old man had laughed bitterly and had begun to weep: a blow in the face from the landowner's stick—that was all the rights he had!

"Cheperukha," shouted Granik from his seat, "did you help the old man work his fields with that hoe? Or did you drink the wine, eat the cheese, and keep going?"

Iona honestly admitted that he had not helped the Moldavian with his hoeing, but after June 27, 1940, the Red Army of workers and peasants had thrown that hoe on the scrap heap along with the Rumanian aristocrats.

People applauded loudly. Degtyar shook Cheperukha's hand, thanked him on behalf of the entire audience for serving the U.S.S.R. well on its borders, then gave the floor to Stepa Khomitsky, who was also a participant and eyewitness and wished to share his impressions.

Stepa said that his unit had first been stationed in the town of Kalarasha, then had been transferred to the south, to Tatarbunary, where he too had chanced to meet an elderly Bessarabian, a small businessman who clearly remembered the uprising in Tatarbunary in 1924. When he spoke of the reprisals against the working class and the peasants, this Bessarabian, who had seen a lot in his time, began to cry and said he hoped Stepa and those near and dear to him never saw anything of the sort even in a dream. Some of the braver souls had swum the Dniester to the Soviet side under a hail of bullets but many were cut down by machine gun fire.

When Stepa told him about the elections to the Supreme Soviet, the right to education, to work, and to rest, and that he too would have all those rights, the Bessarabian had sighed deeply and bitterly reproached him: "Young man, it's a sin to laugh at an old person."

"Stepa," said Granik, jumping to his feet, "send him my address or let him come here and see for himself!"

No, said Stepa, shaking his head, he wouldn't send him Granik's address and there was no reason for him to come there either: after June 27, the Bessarabians had all that for themselves, in their own country.

Comrade Degtyar shook Khomitsky's hand firmly, warmly thanked him for his interesting story, and opened the floor for questions. Klava Ivanovna spoke for everyone, saying that it was all as clear as day, but Joseph Kotlyar proved to have a question: his wife wanted a kerchief with monkeys on it, like Tosya's and Olya's. Where could you get one?

The outpost exploded with deafening laughter. Anya hid behind Lyalya Orlov's chair. Lyalya signaled people to take pity, otherwise the poor woman would die of shame. But no one, including Joseph Kotlyar, felt like taking pity. Dina Vargaftik said that she didn't envy him for what would happen to him later at home, but meanwhile people were laughing and the chairman had to use his power to bring the room back to order. Quiet finally returned but then the chairman committed a serious blunder: he proposed that all questions concerning Olya's and Tosya's toilet be addressed privately to them by the men. A new storm of laughter arose. Tosya and Olya covered their cheeks with their hands. Efim, of course, tried to outshout everyone else, asking when Madame Khomitsky and Madame Cheperukha could see him concerning their toilets. Sonya, who was in her ninth month, tugged at her husband's sleeve and asked him to stop making a spectacle of himself but Efim didn't stop until Iona Cheperukha brandished his fists and said that Efim would have to see him first.

When the storm had subsided, the children's chorus, accompanied by Adya Lapidis on the accordion, sang Khomitsky's and Cheperukha's favorite song, "The Red Army," with lyrics by the poet Surkov and music by the Pokrass brothers. Then they sang "If War Comes Tomorrow, If Tomorrow We March," "Unharness the Horses, Peasants," and "Field, Little Field." Unable to restrain herself, Klava Ivanovna joined in the singing, followed by Iona, Stepa, Degtyar, and everyone else. The chorus concluded with the song about the two falcons, Lenin and Stalin. This time people just listened, automatically humming to themselves—two bright falcons sat on a tall oak tree, one falcon was Lenin, and the other falcon was Stalin.

Then Comrade Degtyar announced that adults and people over sixteen years of age could now dance till they dropped. Anyone not wishing to dance could sit on a bench and watch. Iona Cheperukha danced every dance, one after the other: the tango, the waltz, the fox-trot. At a special request from Iona, Adya played *Freilichs* and Iona danced, making such pretzels of his legs, that people gasped, marveling at the strength of a man his age. Though no one had asked for his opinion, Efim Granik kept repeating like a parrot that Iona had eaten enough of that poor Bessarabian's cheese, butter, and polenta to feed the whole courtyard for the rest of their lives.

Anya Kotlyar was the first to leave: her examinations began the next day and it was her last night before the battle. Iona Ovseich told her to grasp the reins firmly with both hands and not to relax her grip no matter what ups and downs might occur.

The first examination was on alegbra and was the most difficult. Anya did extremely well: she received a strong B and the commission said she almost received an A. Klava Ivanovna and Polina Isaevna said in unison that Anya should continue her studies when the courses were over and become a doctor and that if Joseph wanted to stay in step with his wife, he had better begin to educate himself.

When Anya had passed all the examinations and had been enrolled, Iona Ovseich repeated that remark to Joseph. In reply Joseph lit a thick hand-rolled cigarette and said that he could already feel his wife's education in his pocket: she needed new shoes, a new dress, a new jacket, in other words, it was spend, spend, spend. And where was he going to get the money?

"Kotlyar," said Iona Ovseich, "I don't think you're taking the right attitude."

A few days later Dina Vargaftik went to Degtyar to complain that Kotlyar's nail-making machine was again pounding away over her head until twelve o'clock at night. The first time Iona Ovseich did not respond, wishing to believe this was an isolated incident; however, after a week the machine was still banging out nails and it was absolutely clear that this was not an isolated incident but genuine recidivism.

Comrade Degtyar took Madame Malaya with him to pay a call on Joseph, who was operating his machine and not in the least ashamed of it. On the contrary, he volunteered an explanation of its various parts and let Malaya turn the handle. Anya was in the kitchen preparing for tomorrow's classes. Klava Ivanovna called her in and asked her to sit with them. Anya agreed but kept saying again and again what difficult homework she had for the next day and how much work they were assigning her now.

"Let's take the bull by the horns," said Iona Ovseich, and he asked Joseph Kotlyar straight out whether or not he accepted the decisions of the Eighteenth Party Congress on the building of communism in the U.S.S.R., and how he interpreted them in his own day-to-day life. Kotlyar did not make him wait for an answer and said that he was a Stakhanovite at his factory and overfulfilled the plan every month even though the quota was regularly increased, but now his wife was studying to be a nurse and his expenses at home had increased one and a half to two times. Besides, as a medical worker, his wife wanted to dress better and better, since she was now surrounded by doctors and professors, and she was ashamed of having a husband who was so old and poor. Well, he couldn't do anything about his age, that was God's doing, as they said, but he still had the strength to earn a little extra money.

Comrade Degtyar shifted his gaze to Anya, asking her what she could add. Anya said that she had nothing to add but that her husband could go anywhere he wanted to, she wasn't holding him back. If he wanted, they could divide their room and live together like roommates, strangers.

"Calm down," said Joseph, "you're not a doctor yet. I'm the one feeding you, not the other way around."

"That's right," said Anya with a bitter laugh, "and the authorization's in your name, and the furniture's yours, and the couch is yours. And my entire somatic structure is fed on glucose at your expense!"

Klava Ivanovna said that she and Ovseich hadn't come to be part of a lovers' tiff, but to ask Joseph Kotlyar how long he would continue to perform cottage industry work and laugh right in the face of all his neighbors and the whole courtyard.

Joseph, who had conducted himself politely until that moment, suddenly began shouting as he had twenty years before when he was a partisan: it wasn't enough that these so-and-sos had turned his wife against him and put him on a powder keg, now they were demanding that he live as if full communism had already been built and feed two families on one lousy paycheck! His rudeness mortified Anya to her depths, and she cried that they should divide the apartment or she'd do something terrible to herself. She began running toward an open window. Klava Ivanovna was stunned but Iona Ovseich rose and calmly warned Anya that if she and Joseph didn't want to handle this nicely, other ways could be found.

A week later, like a bolt from the blue, a telegram arrived from Anya's mother in Nikolaev: Petya and Sasha had applied to aviation school, been accepted, and had already left. Joseph grasped his head with both hands and sat swaying back and forth for a long time. Still in her shoes, Anya threw herself on the couch and covered her head with a pillow. Joseph unstrapped his prothesis, tossed it in the corner, and lay down beside his wife.

"What's happening in the world?" he asked. "Who can tell me what's happening in the world? Why should I be making sure there's food to eat and clothes to wear when everybody's doing just what they feel like, my wife, my sons. Where's people's gratitude, where's their conscience, if they don't even ask. They don't have to, but they could just ask for advice."

"My God," whispered Anya, "what an egotist, what a callous egotist you are! At a time like this all you think of is yourself. Why wasn't I struck blind the first time I laid eyes on you! Why couldn't my legs have become paralyzed on the way to get married!"

"Anya," said Joseph, "I love you. I love our sons. I want us all to be happy, but nobody listens to me and everybody does what he wants to."

Joseph kissed his wife on the cheek. She automatically rubbed the kiss away with her hand and asked him to breathe in the other direction because the smell of cheap tobacco on him was too strong.

Joseph sighed, hopped one-leggedly over to his machine, and stamped out a few nails. He began reminiscing aloud about Fedka Dykhan, who in 1919 had been tried for cutting three fingers off his left hand because he so strongly desired to go home to his new wife. "You bastard," said his commander, Yukhim Zhuravel, to him, "you cut off the fingers you didn't need, but you left the big ones. But we don't need your head or your whole lousy life."

Fedka was executed on the bank of the Kodyma River by a firing squad composed of Ivan Panchin, Mikola Pustovoit, and a third man, Joseph Kotlyar.

"And so" Joseph said, "there it is: a person cuts off a part of his own body, but somebody else comes along and says: 'might as well get rid of the rest of him.' "

"All right, all right," said Anya dismissively. She'd heard enough of those partisan stories, she was not the same stupid girl she was twenty years ago. Yesterday a man in an MK came to see Lyalya Orlov but Joseph Kotlyar would go on reminiscing for the rest of his days about how he waved his sword and put Whites up against the wall.

"Anya," said Joseph, "I still have a few bullets left in my gun."

Anya had heard the line about the bullets before and let it go right past her. Then she began figuring aloud when she would have some free time and be able to go see Sasha and Petya. She couldn't go before the winter when she had her own vacation from school. "We're bastards," moaned Anya, "we're bastards to have left our sons in Nikolaev. We need this lousy room like a dead man needs a poultice. *Oy, vay iz mir!*"

The nail machine was pounding like a hammer. Joseph threw the nails in a bin and kept turning the handle until the radio played the "Internationale" and the day's broadcasts were over.

Anya made up a bed for herself on the couch and warned Joseph not to touch her: she had three two-hour classes tomorrow and a difficult practical in Professor Geshelin's clinic.

Anya had to get up in the middle of the night: Efim Granik had come running and urgently demanded that Anya go see Sonya, who was feeling very ill. He had already been to Dr. Landa's but, as bad luck would have it, he was on duty at the hospital. Examining Sonya's stomach, Anya marveled aloud at why a venereologist and dermatologist would be given night duty so often.

The pain was greatest on the upper right side, indicating a gall bladder problem but, given the term of Sonya's pregnancy, no time should be wasted on further diagnosis, and Efim ran to call an ambulance. While they were waiting for the ambulance to arrive, Anya placed fresh mustard poultices on Sonya's calves and gave her a belladonna tablet and aspirin. After taking the aspirin, Sonya's perspiration increased and they wrapped her up snugly in a winter blanket. At first she felt a little worse, her heart was racing and she was short of breath, but then she took a turn for the better.

When the ambulance arrived, Anya told the doctor that the patient was evidently suffering labor contractions, complicated by a dyskinesia of the bile ducts. The doctor did not respond affirmatively or negatively to this information but gave Sonya an injection and told them to get her dressed. Efim asked where they were taking her—if it was to a maternity clinic, he'd go along, but if it was to the hospital, he wouldn't.

Sonya was taken to Maternity Clinic Number 5 on Old Portofrankovskt Street, now known as Komsomol Street. Anya rode in the ambulance but Efim was not allowed to.

Anya returned in tears the next morning; they had performed an emergency Caesarian section on Sonya, otherwise she might have died giving birth. One baby was dead, the other alive, but no prognosis could be made yet. Efim began shouting that he would hold them accountable for the death of his child and that he would take it to the government. An outsider might have thought this was Crazy Mishka, a famous Odessa idiot, shouting and not a normal person.

Efim spent the entire day on a bench outside the maternity home, keeping Oska and Khilka by his side. Klava Ivanovna came at three o'clock to bring the children back for supper but Efim would not hear of it. Klava Ivanovna returned home for a pot of soup, thick with meat and garnished with braised green beans, and brought it to them.

"Eat, children," said Efim, weeping, "eat. One of your little sisters has already eaten her fill, she doesn't need anymore."

Klava Ivanovna shook her head and demanded, in the name of Sonya and his three other children, that Efim not allow himself to fall to pieces.

Oska was carefully chewing a piece of meat but coming upon a tough sinew, he stood up and went around the corner to spit it out. When he was around the corner, he pressed his cheek against the wall and rubbed it hard several times until it gave him pain.

For the next three days the doctors feared for the life of the mother and child. Efim didn't go to work at the factory even though it was the end of the month and every man was worth his weight in gold. The factory had the right to bring him to court in accordance with the new law on drifters and absentees passed by the Supreme Soviet of the U.S.S.R. on June 26, 1940. He could have faced four months in jail, but since there was no malicious intent in this case, they took pity on him and limited themselves to a final warning.

Iona Ovseich drew two conclusions from the story of Sonya's childbirth and they both supported each other: firstly, the courtyard now had a decent medic in the person of Anya Kotlyar, and, secondly, Efim Granik had once again demonstrated his utter inability and lack of desire to observe labor discipline.

Efim took offense at that and said it would be interesting to see how Degtyar would have acted in his place. Iona Ovseich replied that, whether he liked to or not, he had to remind Granik that in 1921 when the entire country was suffering from famine, he also had two sons. Granik could hear the remaining details from Polina Isaevna but it was appropriate to communicate one of them here and now: there hadn't even been time to stand by their little graves and properly weep for them.

Three weeks later Sonya was released from the hospital and came home. Comrade Degtyar picked up her baby and said that it was the spitting image of its father but hoped it had a better character. Klava Ivanovna had laid out a pile of diapers on Sonya's table, a half dozen of which were flannel. Sonya was horrified when she saw them: who needed such extravagance! But it turned out there was more to come: Tosya Khomitsky and Olya Cheperukha brought over a white enamel basin, a zinc washtub, and a pail for boiling the diapers.

White as a sheet, Sonya was sitting in a chair while Efim set a three-liter teapot in the center of the table along with glasses and cups, then invited them all for tea. Klava Ivanovna was the first to voice a suspicion that the tea might be too strong and she was not mistaken; the teapot contained some port from the Agricultural Institute's wine cellar. Cheperukha praised Efim for his good idea, poured a glass for himself and for Stepa, and then a second. He told the young father that they should go to Pushkin Street.

Comrade Degtyar said that it wouldn't be very nice for the host to leave at such a moment but Sonya sprang to her husband's defense: after all the anxiety and worry he'd been through, he fully deserved to go out and enjoy himself with his neighbors, who were almost like family.

"Ovseich," cried Cheperukha from the doorway, "have you read the book about the three musketeers? That's us."

Madame Malaya shouted her advice after them: the young people should put their address in their pockets so people would know where they lived.

Though their legs obeyed them poorly the entire way back, the young people found their way home without any outside help but they became somewhat confused when they reached the gate where a brand-new ZIS-101 was parked.

"Stepa," said Cheperukha, "I've got night blindness: take a look at the number and the name of the street."

Stepa took a look, read it aloud, and it was right. Efim whacked the fender of the car, shook his hand, and said, "It's a good automobile, so shiny it hurts your eyes."

Orlov came out of the front door of the building, dressed to kill from head to toe, followed by two men. One ran ahead, got into the car, and opened the rear door from inside. Iona doffed his cap but Orlov did not even have time to notice; she was already in the back seat, laughing and hitting the man beside her on the arms.

The car sped away like a racehorse and a second later was already around the corner. Iona and Stepa blew kisses after it and Efim began singing loudly enough for the whole street to hear. It was a song he had heard in the old days from a high school boy:

"When the king offered me
Paris, his capital,
If I would abandon and forget
My beautiful girl,
I answered the king:
'Keep your Paris,
I love my beauty more,
She's more beautiful to me!' "

The next day Iona Ovseich had a talk with all three musketeers and asked them to describe the men who had come out of the building with Orlov and to make every effort to recall the car's license plate and any distinguishing features about the automobile. As bad luck would have it, they had all been so spellbound by the car that it had never entered their minds to look at the plate and memorize it.

Iona Ovseich learned even less from Nastya: she was unable to say what kind of car it had been but was sure it was foreign because it was so shiny and beautiful.

Klava Ivanovna was furious: where did people work who had a ZIS-101 at their disposal for going around whoring at night! And that bitch was up to her old tricks again; as the saying went: no matter how much you fed a wolf, he always had one eye on the forest.

"Calm down, Malaya," said Comrade Degtyar. "There's nothing easier than indignation."

"Nothing easier?" said Malaya, becoming even more worked up.

"I'm going to the NKVD this very second and I'll come back with a Black Maria to rid our courtyard of that slut once and for all!"

"Malaya," said Comrade Degtyar, stamping his foot, "you're not going anywhere. We got ourselves into this mess and we'll get out of it ourselves!"

The ZIS arrived for Lyalya again at the end of the work week. Zyunchik and Kolka ran to call Madame Malaya but something had possessed her to go to the movies to see a Charlie Chaplin film she had already seen a hundred times. Klava Ivanovna was ready to tear her hair out when she found out: she somehow had the feeling that she had been set up. Though Comrade Degtyar had absolutely forbidden it, Klava Ivanovna dramatically dashed over to Lyalya's apartment the next morning, pounded on the door with her fist, and warned Orlov for the last time to shut down her bordello, otherwise what would happen would make all Odessa gasp. In response Lyalya looked blankly at Madame Malaya and played dumb. She even told Malaya to go ahead and do something that would make all Odessa gasp, that might be quite interesting.

"Malaya," said Iona Ovseich angrily, "you're ruining my game with your independent partisan attacks. Now she's laughing in your face because Soviet law says a thief has to be caught red-handed."

"Red-handed!" said Klava Ivanovna, stunned. "According to you I'm supposed to grab his dick when he's screwing Orlov and hold it till the policeman arrives!"

"Malaya," said Comrade Degtyar, blushing scarlet, "you're forgetting your place! Do as you're told and don't get any clever ideas or they might boomerang on you!"

They decided to go back to the old method: Nastya would keep a round-the-clock lookout for Orlov's visitors and make a record of them. Klava Ivanovna and Dina Vargaftik were to keep a sharp eye out from their window.

On the third day Dina said it was a stupid idea, they should inform the proper authorities. They could bring Orlov in and give her a good talking to.

"Vargaftik," said Madame Malaya in a silencing tone, "if we want your advice we'll ask for it, meantime button your lip."

The ZIS stopped coming and Orlov had no visitors. They had the feeling that Orlov was lying low and waiting for the right moment, when their vigilance had lulled. Iona Ovseich alerted Malaya to the fact that in such periods of transition a very sharp eye had to be kept, but then other events forced their concern over Lyalya into the background.

Zoya Lapidis suddenly began suffering from her attacks again, and what to do about Adya was now in urgent need of discussion. At his mother's first attack, the boy, trembling all over in fear, had gone running to Anya Kotlyar. Anya herself was so frightened that a bottle of iodine fell from her hands and smashed, filling the room with a hospital smell. Anya sent Adya to get Madame Malaya while she went to see his mother.

The Primus was on and the air was thick with blue fumes which burned the eyes and made breathing difficult. Zoya was throwing Gobius fish from the frying pan to the floor, pouring sunflower oil on them, and demanding that they dance the fox-trot with her. Catching sight of Anya, she splashed oil on her too and ordered her to dance a fox-trot also. Anya slipped and it was a miracle she stayed on her feet. She grabbed Zoya by the arm and brought her out to the hallway. Zoya began crying; she called Anya a fat bitch, then suddenly struck Anya's cheek. Anya was rooted to the spot in utter surprise.

"Lapidis," shouted Klava Ivanovna from the stairs, "stop your tricks!"

Zoya struck Anya a second time but now she wasn't weeping; on the contrary, she laughed and said that her Vanechka had liked fat bitches. Though it was stupid to be offended by a sick person, Anya still felt so insulted and so anguished that she wanted to run away to the ends of the world.

"Zoya," commanded Madame Malaya, "march into your room and act decently or else who the hell knows what people are going to think!"

Zoya took Klava Ivanovna's hand and asked her to wipe away her tears and smooth the wrinkles under her eyes. Vanechka might come home and see her looking old and fall out of love with her forever. Klava Ivanovna replied that Lapidis wasn't fickle but a good family man who loved his wife. Zoya frowned and said, "he's been hiding long enough, he should come home now."

Madame Malaya spent the night at Lapidises' and the next few days were calm. Then the whole thing happened again and they had to call an ambulance. Zoya kicked and fought with all she had, bit one orderly's nose, and demanded that Vanechka come to her, she didn't want to go to him. Klava Ivanovna gave the orderlies two towels to tie Zoya's hands and feet. After tying her, they lifted her up and, one in front, one in back, they carried her out to the gateway where the ambulance waited. Madame Malaya and everyone else were upset that the ambulance had not pulled into the courtyard but instead had parked a mile away. The doctor responded: "It's none of your business!" Madame Malaya shouted after him that she was going to have a little talk with the proper authorities and we'd see how fresh his mouth was then!

The Lapidises had no close relatives who could take Adya in. At first Klava Ivanovna looked after him, but her duty to the community and social commitments also required her attention and she had her own housekeeping to do. She didn't have the strength for it all. It was true that Anya, Sonya Granik, Dina, and Tosya also put in a little time caring for Adya but each of them had more than enough problems of her own.

Comrade Degtyar proposed placing the child in the orphanage on Bolshoi Fontan. Klava Ivanovna began to cry and said that Adya was an exceptionally obedient child; in his place, without a mother or father, another boy would have long since ended up in a street gang.

"Malaya," said Iona Ovseich angrily, "your tears are of no use to anyone. Either take responsibility for the boy or let him go to the orphanage."

When Adya found out that they were planning to send him to the orphanage he did not come home to spend the night. Klava Ivanovna and Anya found him at the train station; he was sleeping on a bench, his cap under his head, hiding under his coat.

"Adya," said Klava Ivanovna in a firm tone of voice, "I tell everyone that there's no boy better than you and now it turns out I wasn't telling the truth."

Anya Kotlyar turned away, her shoulders shaking as if she had a bad case of hiccups. Adya looked up with his big blue eyes, like his mother's, and a lock of hair fell onto his forehead. Klava Ivanovna took out a comb and combed Adya's hair, then pulled his head to her. After a moment of silence they set off on their way.

The boy could not be placed in an orphanage immediately; two or three days were needed to process the necessary papers at the Stalin District Executive Committee. During that time Zyunchik talked Adya into running away with him to the Caucasus and they were only caught at the Znamenka Junction. Olya Cheperukha was hysterical. She heaped the foulest curses on Lapidis, Zoya, and that stinking Trotskyite, that traitor, who had abandoned their own son to the mercy of fate, and she demanded that Adya be taken to the orphanage at once or to a labor colony, whatever, but otherwise he would lead all the other children astray.

When the boys were returned to Odessa, Iona Ovseich notified them with the utmost severity that they would be fully accountable to the law for their actions: enough of that, they were grown-up now.

Zyunchik received a good beating from his father and his whole body was covered with bruises. The next day the Cheperukhas, father and son, went with Adya Lapidis to the Kotovsky Theater to see the movie *Fighter Planes.* Mark Bernes, who played the role of a pilot, sat down at a piano and sang: "My beloved city can sleep in peace tonight, and dream, while turning green with spring."

On Monday Adya did not have to go to school Number 92 which he had been attending since first grade: in the early morning Klava Ivanovna and Anya had taken him to the orphanage and handed him over. While the admission papers were filled out, the principal told them what a healthy community they were. They held first place for amateur theatricals in the entire district, and their former wards included engineers, doctors, and one airplane designer.

"Adya," said Klava Ivanovna, buoyed by this, "study your math hard. You might be a designer as well as a musician."

The principal looked at Adya's fingers and said they were long as Paganini's. Adya would have every opportunity to continue studying music in the orphanage, there was a piano and wind instruments in the "Red Corner". They showed movies there regularly, twice a month, or organized a group outing to a movie theater; they didn't let anyone be bored there. That day Adya would be given a new suit, dark blue or gray, whichever color looked better on him, he would have a bed of his own, and would make fast friends with the other children.

Klava Ivanovna kissed both of Adya's cheeks, categorically forbade him to be lonely or withdraw, and gave her word to visit him every Sunday. Anya shook Adya's hand like a grown-up and, for her part, promised to bring him interesting books and sheet music.

That evening Comrade Degtyar said: "Mark my words, Malaya, he'll like it so much there he won't want to come back home."

At first, Iona Ovseich seemed to have been right: three days passed without incident but on the fourth a man from the orphanage came looking for Adya. Looking as if she had been struck on the head with a hammer, Klava Ivanovna grabbed the man by the collar and it cost her great effort not to spit in his face. Infuriated, he called Klava Ivanovna a deranged woman but the remark had no effect on her and she ran through the front door of the Lapidises' part of the building. On the way in, she vowed that she'd make mincemeat of Adya if she found him in his house.

Adya was at the piano, his head on the keyboard, asleep and dreaming sweet dreams. He did not hear Klava Ivanovna tiptoe toward him and stand over him. She kissed the top of his head gently, then picked up a pillow from the couch which Zoya had embroidered with a picture of three silly kittens that looked right out at you. She held it in her hands for a moment, then put it back. She took the key from the door, slipped it into her pocket, and went back to see the man from the orphanage. She apologized for her rudeness and told him that he should go, and she'd bring the child back herself.

All the way back on the trolley, Klava Ivanovna kept explaining to Adya that she was old and sick and couldn't look after everyone, but that he'd be going right home as soon as his mother was better.

"Did you understand everything I said?" she asked again before leaving him.

Adya answered that he had understood and would later prove that he had: Klava Ivanovna visited him on Sunday, and on the following Sunday, and both times heard only good reports on Adya.

This cheered Iona Ovseich as much as if he had won ten thousand rubles and he merrily teased Madame Malaya, who had been ready to sing a requiem at a christening.

The Orlov business had not budged a millimeter in all that time. Not only that, everything had taken shape exactly as Comrade Degtyar had foreseen: taking advantage of the courtyard's having other concerns and being unable to devote sufficient attention to her, Lyalya had come out of hiding entirely. Again visitors in MKs paid her calls every evening. Zyunchik and Kolka climbed up the fire escape and looked into Lyalya's room over the curtain tops and made such faces that a person could die of shame.

Madame Malaya was beside herself with indignation and anger and demanded that Comrade Degtyar immediately take drastic measures, but she got the usual song and dance in reply: they shouldn't force the issue, the primary task was to collect the information properly. One time Klava Ivanovna was simply unable to restrain herself and she said: "Ovseich, if there was anybody else in your place, I'd think he had his finger in the pie."

Comrade Degtyar stared at her and said: "And if there was anybody else in your place but you, I'd send her flying out of Odessa like a bullet."

Klava Ivanovna took offense. When they had both cooled down, Comrade Degtyar said: "Malaya, are you certain that all those fancy cars, those ZISs and MKs that come for Orlov are bringing only business executives and managers? What if they contain people of even greater stature?"

Klava Ivanovna reeled as if from a blow to the face.

"I'm not so sure, Malaya," said Comrade Degtyar, shaking his head. "Until we have all the facts on what's going on and who with, we should make every effort to use the forces of the courtyard to restrain Orlov."

The next class on the short course was scheduled for Sunday. Principal attention was focused on materials from the Eighteenth Party Congress, which had taken place in March. Iona Ovseich dwelled on that portion of the conference's decisions which directly indicated that the city committees, the province committees, the district committees, and the Party Central Committee, along with the People's Commissariats, bore the responsibility for all the industrial and transportation enterprises of the city and province, and demanded that constant attention be devoted to industry and transportation.

It was a lively class. Many people raised their hands and wished to speak, including Lyalya Orlov. Iona Ovseich gave the floor to them all with the exception of Orlov, whom he made a point of ignoring. In the end, Lyalya got the point and in an insolent tone of voice announced that somehow she would manage without the classes and slammed the door behind her as she left.

Iona Ovseich asked Malaya, Dina Vargaftik, and Anya Kotlyar to remain after class.

"Comrades," he said, "let's get down to cases with Orlov. We've waited a long time, and we've been more than patient, but now the end's come. Anyone who spits on the opinion of the collective spits on the collective itself—no proof is demanded, it's obvious. In that connection I propose that Orlov be subjected to a total boycott. The courtyard wishes you three to take the initiative in carrying out the boycott."

Dina Vargaftik was the first to respond, saying that Degtyar had taken the words right out of her mouth. But it was another matter to put it into practice.

Klava Ivanovna said, "Let's start with us three, as Degtyar proposes, and tomorrow, or, at worst, the day after tomorrow, the whole courtyard can be included."

Anya shrugged her shoulders: in her mind she understood that it was necessary, but what if Orlov started speaking with her, how could you not reply to a person?

"Comrade Kotlyar," said Iona Ovseich with a smile, "trust my experience: no one has ever succeeded in running with the hare and hunting with the hounds. It's one or the other."

It would have been utopian to count on the boycott producing immediate results. "If we take a comparison from warfare," said Comrade Degtyar, "this is closest to a siege: sooner or later the enemy will not be able to stand any more and will surrender—then you can dictate terms. However, in the initial stage the most important thing is to put all the measures from start to finish clearly into practice."

Madame Malaya took half the building, and Dina Vargaftik and Anya Kotlyar together took the other half. Comrade Degtyar proposed a secret competition to see who worked faster, Malaya alone or the other two together.

When they began putting the boycott into operation it proved much more difficult than in theory, as Iona Ovseich had warned. Some people said that as it was they hadn't exchanged two words with Orlov in ten years while others agreed but immediately added the reservation that they were unable to run into Orlov and then pretend not to have noticed her: you had to be a good actor to do that and they hadn't been to the theater even once in three years.

"You don't have to pretend anything," Klava Ivanovna would reply, "this is for real."

Lyalya continued acting as she had before, as if nothing had changed. It could even have seemed that she was smiling more brazenly and wiggling her butt more shamelessly. Degtyar had assumed that there would be a period of exaggeration like this when a person had lost all sense of moral vulnerability but did not wish to acknowledge it, and primarily to himself. Klava Ivanovna insisted that an additional lightning blow be struck—a caricature of Orlov to be posted in the entry hall. Iona Ovseich was categorically opposed—there was no reason to hang out their dirty laundry for others to see.

Taking advantage of the fact that Degtyar and Malaya had more important concerns at the moment, Joseph Kotlyar continued to make his nails. It was no longer as possible to influence him through Anya as it once had been. According to her, they were now just living under the same roof, and she was not responsible for him.

Degtyar was terribly busy during the entire ten-day period preceeding the May holidays and could not find a second to contact the Revenue Department with regard to Kotlyar and had to entrust the task to Malaya. Klava Ivanovna informed the Revenue Department that Kotlyar's sons were no longer dependents because they were now studying in a military school. In point of fact, his wife should no longer be viewed as a dependent either because she could be earning her own living but officially, in terms of her social position, she would be considered a student until she completed her courses. Joseph's taxes were doubled but he still had a few kopecks left in his pocket.

Iona Ovseich said that in this case the law lagged behind life but since it was still on the books another means had to be found. In a word, Anya herself should report to the Revenue Department and describe her actual situation, specifically, that she was not a dependent since she could earn her own living. When Joseph learned of Degtyar's plans, he became foolishly cheerful—to be able to earn money is one thing but to bring home real rubles was another matter entirely—the little student should tell the great economist Degtyar that.

Anya repeated that conversation verbatim to Comrade Degtyar, who listened calmly and intently, then said: "Time doesn't stand still. Kotlyar, you have to make a choice—either or."

Anya suddenly burst into tears: for nearly all last year she had been so heartsick that it had pained her to enter her own home. Though he was not a medical man, Iona Ovseich explained that this was the normal course of events: when a person went into the fresh air after a long illness, it always made him dizzy and his heart raced at first.

Anya had not had time to go see Sasha and Petya during the past few months but now she had the opportunity to take two days of holiday and request a few extra days but money proved the sticking point. Joseph offered her the money, but it would have been humiliating to accept it after all the words that had passed between them. She could start earning her own money in a few months and she would visit them then. The children wrote regularly, jokingly referring to each other as Junior Lieutenant Kotlyar and Senior Lieutenant Kotlyar, so Anya felt she knew enough about their lives to wait.

When the problem of Sasha and Petya was under discussion, Iona Ovseich came up with a new idea: to write to the aviation school about Joseph's nail machine and let his sons, who were an inch away from becoming Red Army commanding officers, be apprised of their father the cottage industry worker.

Anya's heart sank: no, that would disgrace the Kotlyar family throughout the Soviet Union! It took some effort to persuade Iona Ovseich to postpone it and she promised to discuss it herself with her sons when she saw them next.

Klava Ivanovna did not approve of that compromise: a bad example was like cholera, if it was not contained it could do untold damage. Granik was watching Kotlyar and slipping back into his old ways a little too. That came as a complete surprise to Iona Ovseich: what kind of example could a healthy horse like Efim Granik take from Joseph Kotlyar, a disabled Civil War veteran!

"At one time Efim had an ulcer removed from his stomach," said Klava Ivanovna, "and he has a new baby at home. Sonya has to buy mother's milk, she doesn't have enough of her own."

"The stomach ulcer is his own business," said Iona Ovseich, slapping the table. "And everybody has children. The Soviet system cares for people like a mother and a person has to be utterly shameless to complain here."

Klava Ivanovna was silent. Though it was not like him at all, Iona Ovseich lost his temper entirely and began shouting that with this kind of mentality and these kinds of people, another twenty years would pass and we still wouldn't have built communism. There were all sorts of people like Lapidis who put sticks in our wheels, mocked us, and went all the way to outright treason, but the Soviet system had polished them off once and for all. There were a great many people who had a little bourgeois hiding in their souls, and Lenin could not have been more right when he warned of the danger posed by the petit bourgeois element.

"Ovseich," said Klava Ivanovna, "I'm almost sixty years old. I suffer from gout in the legs. Every night I drink fifteen valerian drops in a quarter glass of water and put a hot-water bottle on my heart. I'm not asking for gratitude but tell me where my work has fallen short."

There were tears in Klava Ivanovna's eyes. Iona Ovseich took her hand, placed it on the palm of his, and stroked it a few times as if it were that of a little child.

"Malaya, if I were Mikhail Ivanovich Kalinin, I'd give you a medal. But the main thing for me is that I'd like to live a few years under real communism. And believe me, Malaya, there's a chance of that."

No, said Klava Ivanovna, shaking her head; it was enough for her that their children and grandchildren would live under communism. Yes, said Degtyar, that was true, that was the way the world was, you gave your life for the future and your descendants reaped the fruits. The first two generations of Russian revolutionaries knew only hard labor and the gallows, but they paved the way for the third generation: before rising to the stars, people have to fall back to earth and be smashed to bits.

"What do I need all that clever philosophizing for, I'm not planning on flying to the stars, I just want people to have it good on earth *and* I want your answer on what should be done about Kotlyar and Granik." When Klava Ivanovna finished speaking, Iona Ovseich massaged the bags under his eyes and said, "So it all falls on me, does it, the philosophizing and the action? All right, May Day is coming right up, people should relax and enjoy themselves, but on the fourth or fifth of May we'll summon Kotlyar and Granik in for a confrontation with the activists."

"What good will that do?" asked Klava Ivanovna in surprise.

"Kotlyar and Granik will start fighting, each one trying to prove he's right and the other one's a bastard," said Iona Ovseich, tilting his head to one side. His bald spot, handsome in its form like Lenin's, had an unhealthy sallow tinge. "I think that the activists will find the right solution."

Degtyar proved to be two hundred percent correct: Kotlyar and Granik almost came to blows in the front hall even before the meeting with the activists could begin. At the confrontation, Joseph called Efim a criminal who bought up stolen paint from shady types. He could only marvel at the Soviet system's patience in forgiving such people. "You grass widow!" Efim laughed in reply, and promised to tear off Kotlyar's other leg so that lousy man could no longer walk the earth and soil it. Joseph flushed darkly, and grabbed Efim by the lapel, shouting:

"You're not a Jew, you're a kike! Russian people are right when they say there are Jews and there are kikes. And you're a dirty kike!"

Comrade Degtyar demanded that Kotlyar cease his anti-Semitic propaganda but Joseph seemed to be suffering from malaria, he was trembling all over and gagging.

"Comrades," Kotlyar said, "Comrade Degtyar, Madame Malaya, Stepa Khomitsky, Nastya, Tosya, you all know I'm a Jew, but I'm asking you all to testify in court that this lousy private trader and cottage industry worker has insulted a Red partisan who lost a leg in the battle for Soviet power, and threatened to tear off my other leg so that I wouldn't be able to walk on Soviet ground for which I spilled my own blood! It's doubly painful to see and hear such things today when the entire nation is so earnestly working to build communism, and no Graniks are going to get in our way and stop us!"

Efim appealed to his comrades and neighbors to testify in court too because, right before everyone's eyes, the community had seen a rank and file worker insulted, a worker from the October Revolution factory, which had a glorious tradition of class struggle against tsarism, the bourgeoisie, and autocracy. If they looked more closely, they'd see that, by insulting Granik, Joseph Kotlyar had inflicted an insult on the entire working class, and it would be a fatal error to view Efim Granik's request as if it were coming from him alone. No, the honor of the entire collective was at stake here, and no shopkeeper who was a Red twenty years ago but today was a typical double-dealing degenerate from head to toe was going to be allowed to spit in our faces and jeer openly at us!

During both harangues, Comrade Degtyar sat with his eyes closed, listening closely. When they both finished, he rose and took a few steps in front of the rest of the activists and said: "Before the Revolution, the circuit court was to the right of the train station if you were facing it. Lawyers and judges you bought, sold, and resold for a ruble used to make their speeches there. Those speeches always had a single goal: to prove that crows were white and snow was black. Now, as if in some absurd dream, I have just heard the same sort of empty verbiage from that court which we buried almost a quarter of a century ago.

"Who gave you the right," said Degtyar, turning back toward the table, and striking it with his fist, "to waste people's precious time! Who gave you the right to juggle the most holy of words like a clown at a fair, to mask your own true face! We have gathered today to hear sincere confessions and like good comrades we wanted to help you correct your mistakes. And what we've come up against is phrase-mongering, deliberate demagogy, and low, cowardly attempts to wriggle out. There is one single question I want to ask: when will Kotlyar and Granik finally quit private enterprise and stop casting a shameful shadow on our entire courtyard?"

Joseph Kotlyar and Efim Granik both looked to either side as if seeking supporters, though it would have been obvious to the worst fool that it was ridiculous to seek the support of the people you were shaming with your behavior. People were sitting with their heads lowered and did not even want to look in their direction.

"Comrade Degtyar," said Joseph, "give me the floor."

Iona Ovseich gave him the floor. Kotlyar thanked him, smiled, and opened with a question: is it permissible from the medical point of view to separate a child from the breast when summer is just around the corner?

"What does that have to do with anything?" interrupted Iona Ovseich. People laughed, pointing to Joseph's thick hairy chest. Tosya Khomitsky replied that it was a bad mother who breast-fed her child right up to the summer and then suddenly stopped when the weather was at its hottest.

Iona Ovseich peered at Joseph. Klava Ivanovna also confirmed that a child must not be weaned in the summertime. Kotlyar then posed another question: all his life he had been used to working in the evenings after coming home from the job; how could they expect him to break himself of that habit one, two, three, especially in the summertime, when there might be light until nine o'clock or later.

People laughed again. Olya Cheperukha made a suggestion: Kotlyar should bring a certificate from a postnatal clinic and then he wouldn't have to be weaned until he was buried.

"Comrades," said Iona Ovseich, tapping his finger, "this is not a joking matter. Though Joseph Kotlyar seems to agree in principle, the postponement he's referring to here does not suit us."

"Degtyar," said Joseph with a smile, "you're talking to me like you were dealing with a speculator and not a person who was given his license by the Stalin District Revenue Department. To take your point of view, it means that the Soviet system makes bad laws and you're the only one who knows what kind of laws it should have."

"Stop!" said Iona Ovseich. "Now even a blind man can see what the goal of all your maneuvering is."

"Swindler!" cried Efim. "People can see right through you."

"As far as the laws are concerned," said Degtyar, taking a step forward and placing his fist on the rostrum, "our answer is that the practice of the Soviet system has far outstripped the laws because it is no secret that jurisprudence is still functioning in the old way. And as for the daily life of our working class and kolkhoz peasants, new norms of relationship, new morality, and new ideology are being born here every hour, and Maxim Gorky was a million times right when he said: 'Whoever's not with us is against us.' And that, Citizen Kotylar, was, is, and will be our revolutionary socialist legality. And anyone who doesn't like it—out of the way!"

At first Joseph sat as if spellbound; then he jumped to his feet, pulled up his pant leg, tore off his shoe, and struck his chair with his prothesis, breaking the plywood. To keep from falling, Joseph grabbed the rostrum that was next to the presidium table and demanded that Degtyar show the legs that he lost fighting for Soviet power.

"Kotlyar," said Klava Ivanovna, slamming her fist against the table, "you've been profiteering on your lost leg for twenty years now. Enough! My husband, Boris Davidovich, gave his life. My heart is still bleeding over that, but he's moldering in his grave and can't say a word about what he gave!"

Excitement caused the blood to rush to her head and she took a sip of water straight from the pitcher, holding it with both hands.

"Malaya," said Iona Ovseich calmly, "you're getting upset for nothing. I'm submitting the following proposal for review by the activists: to inform the administration of the school where Alexander and Piotr Kotlyar are studying of their father's behavior, which they can then look into at a Komsomol meeting."

"What do my children have to do with it!" shouted Joseph.

"Cottage industry worker, lousy private businessman," said Anya, weeping. "Because of him our children are being disgraced in front of the whole Soviet Union. I'm asking you, Comrade Degtyar, I'm begging you, as a mother, the children must not know anything about this."

Joseph was about to sit down but his prothesis had lodged in the plywood, the paint on the foot had been scratched, making for an unpleasant sight, like that of skin torn from a living body. Stepa Khomitsky bent down and helped dislodge the remnants of the chair which he then pushed out of view.

Degtyar joked that Stepa would have to pay for repairing the chair. And now a small question for Joseph Kotlyar: why should he be so afraid of a letter to his sons' school if he was living and working in strict accordance with Soviet law?

"Why?" said Joseph, taking out his handkerchief and wiping the sweat from his forehead and neck. "My late mother Sura-Beila used to say that when you sling mud at a person, even if he's pure as the snow, some of it will stick to him."

"Citizen Kotlyar," said Iona Ovseich, bending forward as if to see better, "I don't understand the parallel: who's slinging mud here? Be precise."

Joseph did not reply, his fingers automatically crumpling his handkerchief. Degtyar again demanded he be precise since the impression had been given that it was the activists and the courtyard who were slinging the mud.

"Ovseich," said Stepa with a laugh, "that stone was thrown at me. Joseph always has complaints about my plumbing."

Iona Cheperukha suddenly recalled that he too had his own complaints about Khomitsky's plumbing. Degtyar looked at him with fond and understanding eyes. When Stepa and Iona had finished settling their accounts, Degtyar requested for a third time that Joseph Kotlyar be precise and specific: who were these vile Soviet people who were slinging mud at him when he didn't deserve that at all?

"All right," sighed Joseph loudly, "let's make an agreement. My license is valid for six months, until July. And I'll make a promise here before the activists and the entire courtyard that when it expires that'll be the end of that."

Degtyar proposed that a document fixing those terms be drawn up and be signed by three people in addition to Kotlyar himself. Though it wasn't necessary to include this in the document, he added, it was, however, necessary to be utterly frank in admitting that, in agreeing to a postponement until July, the courtyard collective was permitting a certain inconsistency and liberalism.

Since they had concluded their business with Kotlyar, they could now move on to the next point, Efim Granik's behavior.

"Efim Granik," said Comrade Degtyar, "how long are you going to try our patience and make us accomplices in your machinations against the state and the people!"

"Ovseich," said Granik indignantly, "please find other words for speaking to me or there'll be trouble!"

"Efim Granik," said Degtyar even more loudly, "how long are you going to try our patience and make us accomplices in your filthy machinations against the state and the people!"

Efim leaped to his feet as if he had been scalded and demanded that they clear a way for him at once: he was going directly from there to the Province Party Committee and in fifteen minutes he'd be talking to Kolybanov himself. He'd get them to take some action; the party would look into this to see who gave people the right to insult a skilled worker from the October Revolution factory!

"Comrade Concierge Sereda," said Iona Ovseich, "please inform us when, how many times, and at what hour Granik brought paint home, and how many times you personally, with your eyes, saw that he had a receipt for it."

Nastya recalled three occasions when Efim had brought a bucket home in the middle of the night and had insulted her with the foulest language, and as for receipts, she never saw one.

"Listen," said Efim, losing the last of his self-control, "I've already warned you and I'll warn you again, Nastya, you're only going to have yourself to blame!"

Sonya's baby, which she was holding in her arms, pressing its face to her cheek, was awakened by the shouting and started crying. Sonya turned her back to the activists and gave the child her breast but the child did not want to feed. Degtyar requested that the nursing mother be excused from obligatory attendance. Everyone voted in favor, with the exception of one person, Efim Granik.

"You Freemason!" Joseph Kotlyar shouted from his chair. "You lousy Freemason, you're capable of making your wife and children suffer so people will feel sorry for you."

"Comrade Chairman," said Granik, "if that nail merchant doesn't stop the provocation and slander, I'm leaving the room!"

"No," said Joseph with a laugh, "you won't leave the room, they'll come get you and take you where you belong!"

"Informer!" shouted Efim in response. "To hell with your fucking denunciations."

"Citizens Granik and Kotlyar," said Comrade Degtyar in a tone of severe warning, "cut out the street talk and let the activists do their work."

Efim folded his hands across his chest and looked with a mocking gaze at Kotlyar, who demanded that the chairman immediately give him the floor on a point of principle. Since the activists had no objection, the chairman granted Kotlyar's request and gave him the floor.

"Comrades," said Joseph, "how can I find the words for a proper answer to that shabby Freemason! Our laws may allow an invalid to earn a little extra money at home, but they do not grant that right to healthy people who have both arms and both legs. And that's how it should be. There's a shortage of manpower at the plants and factories, anyone who wants to can work two jobs, or three. The question is how long is our courtyard going to tolerate this shady dealer who's ready to rip off something for himself wherever he finds a weak spot!"

Before giving Granik the floor to reply, Iona Ovseich remarked that the law granted every citizen the right to work more than one job, which meant to obtain *additional* earnings from a state enterprise. The activists demanded that Efim Granik explain why he was setting up his own little shop and why Soviet enterprises didn't suit him.

"My dear neighbors," said Efim, pressing his hand to his heart, "ever since I was little I've gotten into hot water thousands of times because I like to tell the truth to people's faces. In the U.S.S.R. we have the shortest workday in the world—eight hours, while in America and other countries people work twelve and fifteen hours. The proletariat there can only dream about what we have. But, on the other hand, I have to take two trolleys to the factory and two trolleys back. Not only that, the car usually goes off the track over by Peresyp Bridge, and then you have to wait. The question is who will give me an extra job that I can be a couple of hours late for if I have to?"

"There is a job like that!" shouted Klava Ivanovna. "And you don't have to be late for it either. They're looking for a night watchman at the city industrial warehouse and that's right near here."

"Put in a full day at the factory, then put in the whole night at a warehouse?" said Efim with a smile. "I'm not against it, but what does Sonya have to say?"

Klava Ivanovna said that she'd take care of Sonya.

"It looks like they're marrying me off without asking me first," said Efim.

Degtyar clicked his pencil against the pitcher and ordered an end to be put to that unnecessary polemic. Then, on behalf of the activists, he submitted a proposition: to draw up a document on Efim Granik's voluntary decision to fully relinquish his license, within one week's time.

Efim was upset: why did he get a week when Kotlyar got until the end of July? Either they should both get to the end of July, or Kotlyar should get one week too.

"You troublemaker!" shouted Joseph. "You lousy tradesman!"

Iona Ovseich slammed his hand down on the table: all right, they both could have till the first of July, and not one second longer.

The dangerous abscess Kotlyar and Granik represented had been rendered harmless for a time, and now the question of Orlov came to the forefront again. The information collected by Nastya, Madame Malaya, and Dina Vargaftik might have seemed sufficient but it had, said Comrade Degtyar, one critical flaw: Orlov, as a single woman, could explain her behavior by saying that she wished to start a family, which was why she had various admirers calling on her.

“A fine thing!” said Klava Ivanovna indignantly. “That way, any prostitute can prove that she’s still purer than the Virgin Mary!”

“Malaya,” said Iona Ovseich with a frown, “you’re getting overheated again. Listen to me: you have to contact Dr. Landa.”

Madame Malaya spread her hands: “What does Dr. Landa have to do with anything?”

“I’ll tell you what,” said Comrade Degtyar, whacking his knee. “When a woman has that many men chasing her, any disease is possible. And so why not call in a dermatologist, they are the specialists on venereal diseases?”

Madame Malaya asked a question in reply: “But what if it turns out that there’s nothing wrong?”

“Nothing wrong?” said Iona Ovseich in surprise. “There’s no chance of that being the case. Send Landa to see me.”

Dr. Landa balked at first when asked for a consultation: violating a patient’s right to privacy was punishable by law. And a compulsory examination was absolutely out of the question.

“Semyon Alexandrovich,” said Degtyar, “clients you had never seen before used to come to you off the street, and, according to our information, they still sometimes do. I want to ask you a question: how do those people know your address when you don’t have a plaque saying that Dr. Landa lives here and receives patients with venereal diseases at his home? In other words, it’s not your concern how Orlov ends up seeing you. You only have one concern as a doctor: to establish the fact that Orlov is a carrier of venereal disease.”

Dr. Landa grew pensive, pressing his eyes hard with two fingers as if wishing to force them inside his head, and then he offered a counterproposal: first wait for the results of the boycott—such a forceful measure would surely cause Orlov to think twice and own up.

“Landa,” said Iona Ovseich, placing his hand on the doctor’s shoulder, “you’re a specialist when it comes to gonorrhea and syphilis, but you’re no specialist when it comes to tactics and strategy with people. So, enough of this idle talk: do what you do best.”

That year Olya Cheperukha was the first to open the season for cherry jam. She stood in a line at the GUM at the corner of Lenin and Karl Leibknecht streets from six in the morning until eight o’clock in the evening and bought a Leningrad Primus. Now she owned two

Primuses and could be entirely independent. When Klava Ivanovna saw the Leningrad Primus operate, she said that she would like to borrow it just for the pleasure of using it. Tosya, Dina, and Sonya followed suit: Olya held both her hands in front of her as if restraining a surging crowd and cried in a policeman's voice: "Ladies, form an orderly line!"

The jam turned out exceptionally well: its color was as translucent as honey with a reddish tinge, and, once a person tasted it, there was no stopping him. Iona Ovseich made a point of bringing his wife Polina Isaevna to the jam making and said in front of everyone that it was no sin for her to pick up a few tips from Olya. Olya shrugged her shoulders and argued that no special skill was required and there was no reason to praise her. Then she sent Zyunchik to fetch some saucers, each of which she filled to the brim so that the jam overflowed onto people's fingers and had to be licked off. Her neighbors took their jam home, then returned the saucers to her.

On the occasion of the opening of the jam season, Iona Cheperukha took Stepa and Efim to the Agricultural Institute's wine cellar. Olya was not as worried when Stepa and Efim were with Iona. He had settled down considerably after the Finnish war and no longer drank like the draymen from Kostetskaya, but there was no guarantee it wouldn't crop up again.

Iona, Stepa, and Efim returned a short while after sunset. Olya was waiting in the gateway on pins and needles, and kept saying that she would have been better off being blinded when she first met that carter and gave him the most precious thing a young girl had to give. Iona walked into the middle of the courtyard, to the spot where Olya had spent the whole day on her feet working with her Primus stoves, and there began a drunken dance, promising to spit in the face of anyone who said that he didn't have the best wife in the world.

Olya called her husband a cheap bootlicker and attempted to drag him home. At one point they were almost to the front door when Iona grabbed his wife around the waist and began dancing a tango to his own accompaniment:

"The weary sun
had bid the sea fond farewell.

In that hour you confessed,
you confessed your love!"

Stepa and Efim clapped their hands and sang a wordless refrain: tara-ra-tara-ra-ra! Then Klava Ivanovna came out and weighed in against the merrymakers—here was a woman right before their eyes and they were acting like the Persian shah's eunuchs. She swept them both into a tango, one against each cheek. They stumbled, which irritated her, but then she narrowed her eyes sweetly and allowed herself to be transported to another place, as if she had gone back thirty years in time. She threw back her head and continued to dance.

The next day Zyunchik came home with good news: he had passed all his tests for the eighth grade and now wanted to study in an artillery school. A senior lieutenant came to see him and said that there could be some problems for a person with grades like Zinovei's, but there were positive factors as well: first, he had finished eighth grade, and, second, he had a strong desire.

Olya burst into tears when she learned of this: she should have only rejoiced in the fact that her son would become an officer in the Red Army but her heart was heavy and there was nothing she could do about it.

But Iona's heart was not heavy and he explained to his wife that the Mannerheim Line, which they had made a mishmash of when his unit had been stationed in Karelia, was considered the strongest in the world—who was going to attack the U.S.S.R. just to get their heads smashed! They had a nonaggression pact with Hitler and she should be happy about that, America and Japan were at the other end of the world, England was barely able to stand on its feet, and there was no one else to worry about.

Exactly one day later the newspaper *The Bolshevik Banner* supported in full everything Cheperukha had said concerning Germany. The Ukrainian newspaper *The Black Sea Commune* printed the same material, which, in addition, many people had heard on the radio.

To accommodate the wishes of the courtyard's residents, Iona Ovseich set up an evening of questions and answers on international topics. His first duty, he informed them, was to cut off all gossip and imaginary fears and to do so by rereading them the report published by TASS, that is, the Telegraph Agency of the Soviet Union, on June 14 of this year. Though there was no difference, he would read from the text as published in the newspaper *Pravda,* the organ of the Central Committee and the MK VKP/b/.

"I quote," said Comrade Degtyar; " 'Even before the arrival of the English ambassador, Mr. Cripps, and especially after his arrival, the English press and the foreign press in general began to whip up rumors about an "impending war between the U.S.S.R. and Germany." According to those rumors: (1) Germany had allegedly presented the U.S.S.R. with claims of a territorial nature and now Germany and the U.S.S.R. were negotiating a new and closer agreement between them; (2) the U.S.S.R. had allegedly rejected those claims and in that connection Germany had begun concentrating troops at the borders of the U.S.S.R. with the aim of attacking the U.S.S.R.; (3) The Soviet Union in turn had allegedly begun intensely preparing for war and was concentrating its troops along the German border. Despite the obvious absurdity of those rumors, authoritative circles in Moscow have nonetheless considered it necessary, in view of the persistent dissemination of those rumors, to authorize TASS to state that these rumors are propaganda clumsily concocted by the forces hostile to the U.S.S.R. and Germany and which have a vested interest in the widening and unleashing of war.

" 'TASS announces that: (1) Germany has not presented the U.S.S.R. with any claims whatsoever and is not proposing a new, closer agreement, and, in view of that, no negotiations on the subject could have taken place; (2) according to Soviet information, Germany has been observing the conditions of the Soviet-German pact just as undeviatingly as the U.S.S.R. has been, and, in view of this, the opinion in Soviet circles is that the rumors about Germany's intention of breaking the pact and launching an attack against the U.S.S.R. are utterly groundless, and the recent transferral of German troops, released from operations in the Balkans, to the eastern and northeastern districts of Germany must be assumed to have been motivated by considerations which have no bearing on Soviet-German relations; (3) as the result of its peace policy, the U.S.S.R. has been observing and intends to continue observing the conditions of the Soviet-German nonaggression pact, in view of which the rumors that the U.S.S.R. is preparing for war with Germany are false and provocational; (4) the summer training of Red Army reserves now in progress and the forthcoming maneuvers have no other purpose but the training of reserves and checking the functioning of the rail system which, as is well known, is performed each year and, in view of that, to depict these Red Army measures as hostile to Germany is, at the very least, absurd.' Close quotes. Comrades, could there still be anyone who fails to understand after what we've read publicly here? Especially since, judging by the style, Comrade Stalin had a hand in writing this."

Granik was the first to respond. He said that in light of the TASS report, it was plain to even the worst fool that there would be no war with Germany, the pact with the U.S.S.R. had Hitler bound hand and foot, and now he would like to ask a question of substance: how was the railroad system functioning in Central Asia where the cadres of specialists were still young and the anti-Soviet Basmaches had been active at one time, and what lessons had been learned on this subject from last year's maneuvers? He also requested information about the Transcaucasus where there were tall mountains and the possibility of avalanches.

Iona Ovseich thought for a moment, then replied that he did not have that specific information at his disposal right now; however, considering the overall good job done by the railroad workers in both Central Asia and the Transcaucasus, Comrade Granik's question could be given a positive answer, for otherwise the railroad system would have been operating poorly, which was not in fact the case.

Last Sunday, said Dina Vargaftik, she'd gone to Vesyoly Kut station, a little past Razdelanaya, and had bought a ticket an hour before departure with no trouble at all: there had been no line, no crush, even though traveling was always harder in the summer. And the station was so neat and clean that it was a pleasure just to sit there and relax awhile.

Joseph Kotlyar objected that the example cited by Dina Vargaftik proved nothing. Efim replied quite reasonably that when things were a mess, you felt it everywhere, and the same was true when things were in order.

Stepa Khomitsky had a question about the freezing of American funds by the German government. Iona Ovseich provided an exhaustive answer to that question: the point there was that the day before, as the Soviet press had reported, the American President Roosevelt had frozen German funds in America—in other words, had placed them under something like temporary arrest, and for that reason the German government had imposed a freeze on American funds. It was perfectly obvious that Hitler had no other choice in the situation.

"Comrades," said Iona Ovseich, peering at his listeners, "do you understand now what a freeze means?"

Klava Ivanovna nodded her head and added that all capitalists, whether or not the U.S.S.R. had a treaty with them, should bash each other's heads.

Iona Ovseich pressed a finger to his lips: "Malaya, your thinking is correct from the political point of view but diplomatically it leaves something to be desired."

While they were on the subject of news, said Iona Cheperukha, he was wondering what had happened to the calf that had been born on the Spartacus Kolkhoz in the Ovidopolsky district with two heads, four eyes, two noses, and three tongues. The newspaper *The Bolshevik Banner* said that it was completely healthy but could not lift its heads because they were so heavy.

"Cheperukha," said Iona Ovseich, narrowing his right eye, "as a Red Army soldier, you can draw the right conclusion here yourself: if the newspaper hasn't reported any additional news on the subject, it means one of two things: either it wasn't necessary or it wasn't allowed."

People laughed because Degtyar had wriggled out of a ticklish spot so nimbly, but Cheperukha said that he had another question: yesterday *The Bolshevik Banner* had printed an announcement that the clinic of the Odessa Medical Institute was buying a one-horse wagon along with a horse and harness.

"Hold on," said Iona Ovseich, "you're reporting a fact, not asking a question."

"No," said Cheperukha, sticking to his guns, "I am asking a question. My wife is fed up with having a carter for a husband, she wants a husband who works in a scientific institution, and so what I'm asking, Comrade Degtyar, is can you make an effort to get me a permanent position at the Odessa Medical Institute where they are buying a one-horse wagon with a horse and reins?"

People laughed again. Iona Ovseich shook his head and admitted that he hadn't been right: "What Cheperukha said was not a fact, and not even a question, but a demand, and a demand we are going to satisfy!"

Klava Ivanovna was the first to shake Cheperukha's hand, while Iona Ovseich said, "Cheperukha will yet be the head of a horse-transport brigade."

Olya's eyes were gleaming. Anya Kotlyar and Tosya Khomitsky leaned over to her and they looked like the leads from the famous movie *The Three Friends*.

Just as the evening was concluding, Sonya Granik rose, holding her child in her arms, and, with a somewhat sad expression, said: "I must be a fool, Comrade Degtyar, but I didn't get it—is there going to be a war or isn't there?"

Iona Ovseich looked directly at the audience and smiled: "Comrades, it seems to me we spent a good two hours on that question. I will read the TASS communiqué once more, part two, point two, where it says in black and white that: 'Germany has been observing the conditions of the Soviet-German pact just as undeviatingly as the U.S.S.R. has been.' Sonya Granik, repeat after me: 'Germany has been observing . . .' "

Sonya repeated the words and many others automatically whispered the words too. In conclusion Comrade Degtyar gave Efim Granik a personal assignment: to work on an individual basis with his wife on the subject in question. Efim expressed his confidence in coping with the assignment and at the same time made a counterproposition: that his workload should also include an additional housewife needing to be worked with on an individual basis.

"Watch out," said Madame Malaya, "you can get a hernia that way!"

Efim had no time to reply because just then the loudspeaker at the corner of Evreiskoi and Lieutenant Schmidt Avenue boomed out: "Attention! Attention! As of seven o'clock we are in a state of alert!"

Fifteen seconds later, though the words were still reverberating in people's ears, the loudspeaker repeated the message: "Attention! Attention! As of seven o'clock we are in a state of alert!"

Sirens began wailing from two directions, the knitwear factory and the brush factory, and then the steamboats and locomotives blew their whistles. The radio announced that enemy aircraft had dropped incendiary bombs on factories in Peresyp and Zastava. People were standing, their faces pale, and Klava Ivanovna shook her head and kept saying that she didn't envy the people in the Ilichevsky, Vodnotransportny, and Lenin districts—the main commotion was there.

The all-clear was sounded throughout the city at eleven twenty-five. Even though the center of the city had not been affected, Olya Cheperukha confessed that a weight had fallen from her heart. Anya Kotlyar and Sonya Granik wiped away their tears while the children ran around as if it were a holiday.

A day later, summing up, *The Bolshevik Banner* said that the practice alert had once again demonstrated the complete military readiness of the city's people, even though in certain districts, sand had not been delivered in time, and the fire-fighting equipment—axes, hooks, shovels—had not been hung on the special boards for them. However, when the alarm was sounded, Osoviakhim detachments eliminated these errors.

When they were reviewing the alarm drill in the outpost, Iona Ovseich notified all building residents that they should check their preparedness on a daily basis: there could be another drill in three days, a week, two weeks. The responsibility for the execution and supervision of this program rested entirely with Comrade Malaya. Degtyar, by party decision, was being dispatched to take part in the state vegetable procurement campaign, there having been an unprecedented harvest that year. In 1938 Odessa province had delivered twenty-six thousand tons, and twenty-nine thousand five hundred in 1939, but in 1940 the yield had come to sixty-two thousand seven hundred and thirty tons and this year upward of seventy-five thousand tons of vegetables were expected. Degtyar could report extremely good news from the kolkhoz fields of the Soviet Baltic states: Latvia had completely finished all its sowing in considerably less time than ever before.

"Ovseich," said Cheperukha, "what's the story on mackerel?"

Comrade Degtyar squinted and said that although this question had nothing to do with either antiaircraft defense or agriculture, he would still cite a few statistics: fifteen hundred to two thousand had been caught by net fishing, seine nets were bringing up to a centner and more a day, and yesterday, in the Budakov district alone, a ton and a half of first-class mackerel were caught, each one as long as from the tip of your finger to your elbow. They'd be available in the stores today or tomorrow.

"A ton and a half," cried Efim from his seat, "is nowhere near enough for all Odessa."

Mackerel wasn't bread, Olya Cheperukha said quickly, it was not something everyone had to eat.

The days became hot and dry but there was no longer any need to worry about the grain: the entire province, both the northern and the southern districts, was preparing for the harvest drive. Neighboring Moldavia had set Odessa a good example by lowering market prices: prices had nearly doubled in Bendery and Tiraspol, and in Kishinev had risen thirty to forty percent for poultry, vegetable oil, and eggs.

Before his departure, Degtyar dropped by to see Dr. Landa and reminded him that all the time limits concerning Orlov had already passed and nothing had moved an inch. Dr. Landa did not attempt to justify himself: he honestly admitted that he had let it drag on unforgivably long but when Comrade Degtyar returned he would be given a complete picture of this interesting problem.

"Landa," said Iona Ovseich, shaking his head, "I can't be everywhere at once, as a medical man you should know that. It's in your own best interest that I don't have to remind you of this again. I'll be back in Odessa on Sunday."

As promised, Degtyar returned to Odessa on Sunday. He intended to take the evening train back out into the countryside. This time Dr. Landa demonstrated his thoroughness—he had the information on Orlov in hand: five years ago she had been treated for a fungus in the venereal dispensary and, according to their records, was now completely healthy.

"Landa," said Iona Ovseich, tilting his head to one side and peering in Landa's eyes, "a fungus or gonorrhea, it doesn't make any difference. Diseases don't disappear, they only camouflage themselves. And Orlov was working and is still working at a tobacco factory with an infection like that!"

Dr. Landa spread his hands: the specialist had concluded that she was completely healthy.

"We'll deal separately with the person who kept the file on her illness," said Degtyar. "But what were we doing, what was the medical supervisor and the tobacco factory administration doing when they hired Orlov! Now you don't have anything to say, like a typical intellectual—let there be a flood as long as I'm not affected. I'm enraged by this gullibleness and carelessness!"

Once again Dr. Landa spread his hands. Iona Ovseich said that tomorrow at eight, the venereal clinic would summon Orlov right from her shift for a reexamination, and she would be subject to prosecution for the premeditated concealment of her disease. That was one thing. At the same time they'd spur the Province Health Ministry into action and they could take a good hard look at the tobacco factory—millions of people smoked cigarettes, and the infection could pass from one mouth to another! That was two. And the third thing was that the courtyard should have its say too and have it in such a way that all the Orlovs heard it, however many there were between Odessa and Chukotka.

At eleven o'clock Comrade Degtyar was telephoned by the Stalin District Committee and ordered to appear at once, without wasting a second. Iona Ovseich had begun issuing Madame Malaya instructions concerning Lyalya but had to break them off immediately. Iona Ovseich had just hung up the phone when a messenger arrived with the same message: report to the District Committee immediately.

"What's the rush, comrade?" Madame Malaya asked the messenger.

The messenger did not answer her question but only hurried Iona Ovseich again though he couldn't have been moving any faster.

Zyunchik and Kolka came running in half an hour later: they had been swimming at Lanzheron Beach when some character wearing a straw hat and glasses told another guy that Hitler had crossed the Soviet border, saying that he heard it himself on an English-language radio broadcast. From London. Kolka stayed near that suspicious character to trail him while Zyunchik ran for a policeman but, wouldn't you know, you could never find one when you needed one.

"You dope," said Cheperukha to his son, "you should have found one instead of running home!"

Fifteen minutes later Radio Moscow announced that Comrade Molotov would address the nation.

A hush fell over the courtyard as if everyone had lost the power of speech; the only sound was the crackle of static in Dr. Landa's radio, which he had placed on his windowsill. A loud click was heard, followed by a rustling sound, that of papers being shuffled, then the voice of Comrade Molotov came on. Stammering, taking long pauses between words, he said that the Soviet government and its head, Comrade Stalin, had charged him to report that Nazi Germany, in an unprecedented act of treachery, had violated the nonaggression pact, committed a criminal attack on the U.S.S.R., and was bombing our cities.

People expected Molotov to go on to speak of the Red Army's counterattack, of battles on German territory itself and in East Prussia where Germany bordered the U.S.S.R. They expected him to say that Soviet planes had bombed the German capital Berlin to ruins, but he said nothing at all about any of that. His next words were: "Our cause is just. The enemy will be smashed. Victory will be ours!"

Efim Granik said that Comrade Stalin himself could be expected to speak next. Personally, he thought that would be this evening or tomorrow when it would be possible to report on the Red Army's offensive and victories. Although no one voiced that opinion, nearly everyone shared it, because the very fact that Comrade Molotov had spoken first on the radio indicated there was even more important news, which could only be about Soviet victories and the complete rout of Hitler's army. Only Joseph Kotlyar, when he was alone with Cheperukha and Khomitsky, said that the situation looked lousy: Molotov had said that it was a surprise attack but how could it have been a surprise if a week ago TASS itself had reported that the Germans were transferring their troops to the Soviet border. Stepa said that he had no interest in that, Joseph should share his thoughts with his wife. Cheperukha brought up the Mannerheim Line again, pointing out how in the severe conditions of the Karelian-Finnish winter the Soviet air force and artillery had smashed that line to bits even though it hadn't been built only by the Finns but by Hitler along with the French and English. And the Americans had to be added to that list too.

"Boys," sighed Joseph, "I'm telling you, it's bad, it's bad."

Madame Malaya walked over, looked at them, and asked why they had such long faces. Cheperukha replied that she should look in the mirror, she'd see her face looked the same.

Tosya Khomitsky called from the third floor for Joseph to run home, Anya was sick.

When Joseph came in, Anya was lying on the couch and kept

opening her mouth every few seconds as if she weren't getting enough air and was on the verge of suffocating. Tosya was slapping Anya's cheeks while Sonya Granik stood by holding little Lizochka in her arms, saying slapping wouldn't help, her calves should be pricked with pins. At first Tosya disregarded that advice but then she picked up a pin and jabbed it a few times in Anya's calves and thighs.

The pain brought Anya around somewhat and she asked: is it true that there's war with Germany or had she had a bad dream?

"Anya," said Joseph, bending over her, "do you feel better or should I call a doctor?"

Anya looked at her husband as if he were a stranger and repeated her question: is it truc that therc's war with Germany or did she only have a bad dream she couldn't wake up from?

Yes, said Joseph, it was true. Anya clenched her teeth and began gasping for breath again. Klava Ivanovna arrived, ordered everyone to move aside so as not to deprive Anya of oxygen, and told Anya to get ahold of herself immediately. At first Anya did not react, then she suddenly burst into tears, began shaking her head, and said in Yiddish that God should send her death to her; she deserved it and she had had a premonition that she would never see her sons again.

"Stop panicking!" said Klava Ivanovna. "Sasha and Petya only entered flying school a year ago and it's a three-year program. By the time they graduate people will have already forgotten about the war."

No, groaned Anya, she had a horrible premonition in her heart that she would never see her sons again.

"Joseph," said Klava Ivanovna in a tone of command, "go to the railroad station this minute and buy her a ticket for Kharkov. Let her go see her Sasha and her Pinya, and when she comes back, we'll have a different sort of conversation."

"Anya," said Joseph, "do you want to?"

Yes, said Anya, she did want to. He should buy her a ticket for the day after tomorrow: she had to arrange it at work and bake a pie for the children so that she would not arrive empty-handed.

Down below, on the first floor, Olya Cheperukha was stamping her foot, banging a pot cover like an epileptic and demanding that, at a time like this, Zyunchik withdraw his application from artillery school, while Iona was trying to convince his son of the opposite—that now was just the time to enroll.

"Zyunya, do what your mother tells you," said Olya, tearing at her hair. "Or today is the last day you'll ever see her alive!"

Iona grabbed a pail of water, raised it over his head, then hurled it to the floor, demanding there be no hysterical scenes in his house and no threats made: the Red Army needed good men and he was going to give them one!

"You idiot," said Olya, in tears, "he's still just a child, he hasn't seen anything of life yet."

Zyunchik said that he had already seen everything and understood everything and they shouldn't worry about him.

Olya wept all the louder. She tried to put her arms around her son but he turned on his heel like a soldier and left the room.

"Bastards." Olya pressed her fingers to her temples and rocked back and forth on her chair. "For you I was always just a cook and cleaning woman, but nobody wanted to know what I was feeling in my heart. Bastards."

Iona Ovseich returned from the District Committee at three o'clock. All the building's residents who were home at the time assembled in the outpost within ten minutes.

"Comrades," said Iona Ovseich, "you all heard Vyacheslav Mikhailovich Molotov's speech on the radio. The Nazi cutthroats, armed to the teeth with the latest in technology, have attacked the border regions of our motherland. At the same time, German planes bombed border towns, airfields, railroad stations, and large cities in an area extending from the Black Sea to the Arctic Ocean."

Iona Ovseich paused for a moment and reported that they had information concerning successes in several sectors where regular units of the Red Army had entered the battle. However, it must be clearly understood that they were dealing with a treacherous and dangerous enemy. At the same time, all panic and confusion must be nipped in the bud, and anyone guilty of these offenses would be punished with all the severity of wartime law. Since it was not far from the border, Odessa was in the war zone and full power was being transferred to the command of the Red Army.

"What about the Province Committee and the Province Executive Committee?" asked Granik.

"The leaders of the Province Party Committee," said Iona Ovseich, "as well as of the Province Executive Committee, will be cooperating with military organizations." Personally, he, Degtyar, had received instructions to return to the countryside and proceed with the state vegetable procurement campaign for the fall and winter periods.

Iona Ovseich paused again. Cheperukha took advantage of the moment to voice what was the general opinion: it was a good sign if the highest leaders could be sent from the city to procure vegetables at a time like this. Degtyar neither agreed nor disagreed but made special mention of the fact that at the bread stores and grocery shops lines were forming for baked goods and soap though there were no grounds for this. Who this served required no explanation. And the conclusion here was that anyone who indulged himself like that, whether consciously or unconsciously made no difference, would be treated in the appropriate manner.

Joseph Kotlyar said he knew from experience that during the Civil War, Odessa, as a seaport close to the border, had teemed with spies. There was a building on what was called Catherine Square then and was Karl Marx Square now, across from the monument to Catherine the Great, and spies had been interrogated in the courtyard of that building. Anyone deserving it was done away with right on the spot. So as not to alarm the populace with shooting, they placed an ancient Ford tractor in the front gateway. It clattered and wheezed so loudly that it muffled all other sounds and was all you could hear from one end of Odessa to the other.

"That tractor is of no interest to us today," said Degtyar, "but vigilance must be increased a hundred, a thousand times: there cannot be too much of it—better to be mistaken ten times than to slip up once."

Degtyar was scheduled to return to the countryside on the evening train. Granik advised him to take along a hundred-and-fifty-pound sack so that Comrade Degtyar could bring his wife and neighbors some nice potatoes, saffron straight from the bush, and a couple of fat hens if there was room for them.

A blackout was announced for the city that night: only blue light bulbs could be left on, blue not being visible from the sky. Those who had no blue bulbs were to cover their windows with shutters and thick curtains, and plug up the chinks with cotton batting.

Madame Malaya, Stepa Khomitsky, Iona Cheperukha, and Dina Vargaftik checked the building from the street and the courtyard. A strip of light was clearly visible under Granik's shutters: none could be seen in Dr. Landa's but his curtains were themselves too light in color.

When he was notified of this, Dr. Landa took measures without saying a word whereas Efim went out into the street, spent a long while examining his window from one position, then a second, then a third, and finally announced that if it was observed from below, that is, from the ground, something could be seen, but if viewed from above, the sky, nothing could be seen.

At first Madame Malaya listened calmly and waited for Granik's conclusion but then she said now was not the time for disputes. She was going straight up to the Graniks' apartment, smash the bulb, and cut the cord. Efim answered that she should go ahead, smash and cut all she wanted, but he wouldn't be wasting his time in the meanwhile: the Soviets were still in power, the police and the NKVD still existed.

Klava Ivanovna spat and said: "The man's a Jew, a Jew, but you won't find a worse fool even among the *goyim.*"

"Panic-monger!" shouted Efim in reply. "I'll teach you to spread panic!"

Madame Malaya started for the courtyard. Efim stayed with her for a few steps, then dashed ahead and raced to his apartment on the third floor. The strip of light grew shorter and shorter as if it were being cut into pieces until it finally disappeared entirely.

To the right of the gate, which had been given a coat of black lacquer for May Day, there was a gleaming new galvanized tin drain. Klava Ivanovna shook her head: it absolutely had to be painted, otherwise it would be as bright as a mirror. Stepa said that her glasses ought to be painted too, because they gleamed in the moonlight. That angered Klava Ivanovna: what a time to act smart!

A drone could be heard from the sea, from the direction of Lustdorf, past which lay the Dniester estuary and Rumania. Madame Malaya stopped and cupped her hand to her ear. The drone had grown considerably louder and was approaching.

"Madame Malaya," whispered Dina, "are those ours or theirs?"

Stepa said that they were Soviet seaplanes, you could tell by the sound. Half a minute later Iona agreed: "Yes, they are ours, seaplanes or biplanes, they're flying so low."

The searchlights, which until then had probed only the sky over the port, now swept toward Lustdorf. Madame Malaya said that German people lived in Lustdorf and began listening intently again. The tops of two searchlights met and shaking slightly began creeping toward the city.

"Malaya," said Cheperukha, "I don't like this."

Iona had finished his sentence when the antiaircraft guns began firing, the searchlights found the place in the sky where the shells burst and illuminated ten or twelve white puffs of smoke. Then, one after the other, the antiaircraft guns fired five more shots, the searchlights immediately found the new puffs, which were all in a row.

"Good job," praised Madame Malaya. "Good grouping."

The next morning everyone in the city was saying that two German planes had been shot down between Lustdorf and Akkarzha the previous night. The newspapers carried nothing on the subject but many people heard reports on the radio and spoke with people who had seen it with their own eyes.

That afternoon Stepa Khomitsky received a notice from the draft board. He was supposed to sign a receipt and return the counterfoil but Stepa flatly refused: the summons instructed him to appear at twelve o'clock and it was already well after three. At the District Draft Board Stepa tried to explain why he was late but no one was interested; he was immediately handed about thirty notices and ordered to deliver them. There were notices for Granik, Cheperukha, Grisha Vargaftik, and Dr. Landa.

Since the men had not yet returned home from work, Stepa delivered the notices to the wives and told them to sign for their husbands. Sonya Granik's hands were shaking so badly that she wrote her own first name by mistake and forgot to put in her last name entirely. Stepa said that she was worrying for nothing: Efim would be sent to a unit in the rear for retraining which would take no less than six months, time enough for three wars to be fought and won.

Degtyar's notice came that evening after the sun had set. That day Polina Isaevna had gone out to the country to be with her husband and relax a little in the fresh country air. Klava Ivanovna accepted the notice on her own responsibility, then ran to the Stalin District Committee, which was in direct communication with Degtyar. The people at the District Committee read the notice and said that it was premature to summon Comrade Degtyar back from something as essential as the state vegetable procurement campaign: they would speak with the heads of the draft board tomorrow.

The next day the draft board, taking into account the primary importance of the state procurement of farm products, agreed to grant a postponement until July 1; three days later, however, another notice arrived for Degtyar and this time Iona Ovseich was summoned back immediately by a telephoned telegram.

Iona Ovseich found all the courtyard residents still at home with the exception of Dr. Landa. Khomitsky, Granik, Cheperukha, and Grisha Vargaftik had received their notices four days before and had gone every morning with their knapsacks to the draft board, where they had been kept until twelve o'clock and then, after a roll call, allowed to return home for lunch. In the evening they would be instructed to report again the next day.

Madame Malaya and the other women and children were digging slit trenches in the Alexandrovsky Gardens, as a refuge from machine gun fire from the sky and from the shrapnel of exploding bombs in the event German planes broke through over the city. Before going home, the men would stop by the gardens, the women and children would run to meet them, leaving their shovels and pick axes in the trenches. Indignant, Madame Malaya demanded that people show some sense of duty and called what they were doing by its rightful name—sabotage.

Comrade Degtyar's notice was for five o'clock and on the way to the draft board he paid a visit to the gardens to say hello. Greeting everyone with a general wave of the hand, Iona Ovseich took Klava Ivanovna's shovel and showed her the proper way to hold it, press it with the foot, and lift the dirt.

"Now there's a difference for you," said Klava Ivanovna loudly. "When the men stop by, the women want to run home with them. But it's just the other way around when Degtyar stops by. Tomorrow we'll set up a different system."

Madame Malaya was a bit late in putting her new plan into operation: at nine o'clock that evening Iona Cheperukha ran home for a minute to inform the courtyard when they would be shipped out. There was no exact information but most likely the train would leave from Tovarny station—they should all hop on a number 12 trolley and look for them out past the January factory, or, at worst, by the Second Gate.

Klava Ivanovna went with Dina, Tosya, and Olya. Sonya said that she was feeding her baby and would catch up with them on the next trolley. Klava Ivanovna was against that: she could skip one feeding, it wouldn't kill anyone, Sonya wouldn't be able to find the train herself. No, insisted Sonya, the baby had to be fed first.

As Klava Ivanovna had warned, Sonya spent the whole night wandering the city as far as the First Gate and then turned back. She stopped by the January factory to rest a little and rub her legs. While there she was overcome with emotion and suddenly grabbed her hair as if she wanted to tear it out. She began striking the back of her head against the wall. A lone locomotive pulled in from the direction of Odessa-Malaya. The driver was looking straight ahead, the switchman's horn sounded, the locomotive stopped for a second, then began backing up. Sonya covered her mouth with both hands, and, keeping them there, set off for the Alexandrovsky Market where the number 12 trolley swung around and returned to the city.

Madame Malaya was in Sonya's house holding her child. Osya had run out for bread and Khilka was drying diapers on the Primus because every last one of them was wet.

"Well," asked Klava Ivanovna, "did you see him?"

Sonya shook her head. Klava Ivanovna said that she hadn't seen them either, no one had: the train hadn't been at Tovarny station but at the other end of town, at the Sortirovochny station.

That day Zyunchik brought home news from the barbershop on Tiraspolsky Square: Yudka the Cracked, the city's beloved madman, was a spy. Some people were saying that he was working for the Japanese, others that he was in the Germans' employ. Many people remembered him from 1926 when he was known as Yudka the Variety Show and everyone was stunned: for fifteen years people had seen him hanging around every day, for fifteen years people had loved him like a member of the family, and then he turned out to be a spy!

"Comrades," said Iona Ovseich, "if anyone still needs an example of what laxity and carelessness can lead to, here's one for them in spades."

Degtyar met with the same situation at the draft board as Khomitsky, Granik, Vargaftik and Cheperukha had: the date he was to be shipped out kept being postponed. Tosya and Olya drew their own conclusions from this: if the draft board could allow itself such delays, that meant that the situation itself permitted it, because, in the end, what could be simpler than giving a man a field shirt and boots and putting him on a train. Hearing this one time, Joseph Kotlyar was unable to restrain himself and said: "Girls, did you ever hear of what they call a fucking mess?" Anya immediately slapped him on the mouth and called him an old idiot.

Every morning the radio broadcast the Soviet Information Bureau report: the Germans were suffering enormous losses, especially of their planes, tanks, and troops.

The women kept asking Comrade Degtyar the same question over and over, or rather, the same two questions: when will our men go on the offensive, and will the war be over by the fall or could it stretch to the end of September? Iona Ovseich answered the first question directly, saying that if any high command announced the date of its counteroffensive beforehand, that command and its army would end up less than a memory. As for the second question, whether they'd succeed in finishing Hitler before the end of summer, the answer depended a great deal on how the people acted in occupied Europe and in Germany itself.

Madame Malaya personally had no doubt that the peoples of Europe and the German working class would be taking a strong say in things, in a week or a month, even though the Communist Party was deeply underground and Comrade Telman was in prison, Sonya Granik would say—God willing, then unfailingly ask why the German working class hadn't overthrown Hitler already.

"Sonya," said Madame Malaya, shaking her head, "I just told you: Ernst Telman is in prison and there's nobody who can take Telman's place in Germany right now. And so that means first Telman has to be freed."

Yes, agreed Sonya, first Telman had to be freed, but who was going to free him if all the Germans were Nazis? Olya Cheperukha admitted that she also thought all Germans were Nazis. Klava Ivanovna clasped her hands and marveled that she had two such fools for neighbors living in the same courtyard.

Battles were taking place in regions that just one year before had been incorporated into the U.S.S.R., and to avoid unnecessary casualties, the Red Army had withdrawn to the old borders where there were fortifications made of reinforced concrete and armor plating that had been built before 1939, before the wars with Finland and Poland.

The Bolshevik Banner reported that the Agricultural Institute had trained a contingent of machine operators and was dispatching them for the harvest campaign. Every day the Odessa Dairy Combine printed an announcement: unlimited quantities of whey available at the price of twenty rubles a ton. The people of Moldavanka, Peresyp, and Fontana who were keeping house bought the whey by the barrelful.

Sasha and Petya Kotlyar sent a postcard home: for outstanding achievement in their military and political subjects, they would be given ten days' leave in July, and they said their parents should give them a suitable welcome. The card was postmarked June 21.

"That's it," said Anya. She wasn't putting it off anymore, the hospital would have to manage without her for the three days she was off visiting her sons. It was too late for the Kharkov train today, she'd buy a ticket for tomorrow.

Anya packed her suitcase in plenty of time so there'd be no need to rush the next day. She stood in line two hours for the ticket but there were no reserved seats left, and she had to take general seating. When she came home from the station, a man with a summons to the draft board was waiting. Good timing, said the man, please sign this.

Anya held the paper in her hands. Joseph stood behind her pale as death.

"Comrade," said Anya, "there's no mistake here?"

The man replied that he was not a part of the draft board but just delivered the notices to the names and address indicated, in this case, to Anna Moiseevna Kotlyar.

"And are you Anna Moiseevna Kotlyar?"

"Anya," said Joseph, "there's no mistake."

Anya also knew there was no mistake: back when she was about to graduate from her course, she had been taken for military evaluation. All medical personnel were liable to a call-up, but none of them had any worries at the time, they were all much too proud of themselves.

When the man had left, Joseph picked up the notice again and said: "I didn't tell you to take those courses, you wanted to be completely independent, and here's the results. But Tosya, Olya, and Sonya will be staying home."

"You old fool," said Anya weeping, "do you really think it bothers me that other women will be staying home and I won't?" It was something else that bothered her: how could she have kept postponing taking a train to the children at a time like this!

Anya laid her head on the table and began figuring a way she could be with her sons for even a day.

"Joseph," she said, "take off your prothesis and go on crutches to the draft board and say I'm not home and I'll be back in three days."

"Anya," said Joseph with a groan, "don't lose your head: you can end up in front of a firing squad for pulling tricks like that in wartime."

All right, said Anya, she'd face a firing squad, but she wanted to see her children first. Then she thought of another idea: Joseph should have a talk with Degtyar and then the two of them should appeal to the draft board and ask them nice and proper. The draft board wouldn't refuse Degtyar.

"Anya," said Joseph, scratching his head, "you're naïve."

A minute later Klava Ivanovna came running over. "Quick, come say good-bye, Degtyar is leaving."

People were gathering in the courtyard. Iona Ovseich shook hands with everyone, commanded people to keep their heads high, and promised to return soon. Nastya brought out a cottage loaf, which she then placed in a coarse calico bag. She tied it with a string, tossed the loop over Iona Ovseich's shoulder, and then suddenly burst into tears: "Oh, Ovseich, why are you leaving us all alone! Oh, Father, now there's no one to talk to and share our troubles with."

Polina Isaevna, who had been keeping herself well in hand till that moment, now broke into tears as well. Klava Ivanovna gave Polina her kerchief to wipe her tears, then put her arms around Degtyar, and they kissed three times. Then she told everyone to hurry up and say good-bye, the trenches in the Alexandrovsky gardens weren't getting any deeper while they were standing around there.

The next morning the courtyard saw Medical Nurse Anya Kotlyar off to the army. Everyone said it was a rare thing for a wife to be taken to the front while her husband stayed at home.

Joseph was working a double shift at the factory and coming home only to sleep.

The Soviet Information Bureau reported that in the last twenty-four hours the Germans had lost one hundred and seventy-three planes in air battles and to antiaircraft fire.

In some sectors German tanks had succeeded in penetrating deeper. Sergeant Ivan Bondar alone had set fire to four Nazi tanks with Molotov cocktails. Ivan Bondar was awarded the rank of Hero of the Soviet Union (posthumously).

Klava Ivanovna would read the newspapers aloud and point out that Hitler couldn't take losses like that very long. Everyone would be home for the October holidays.

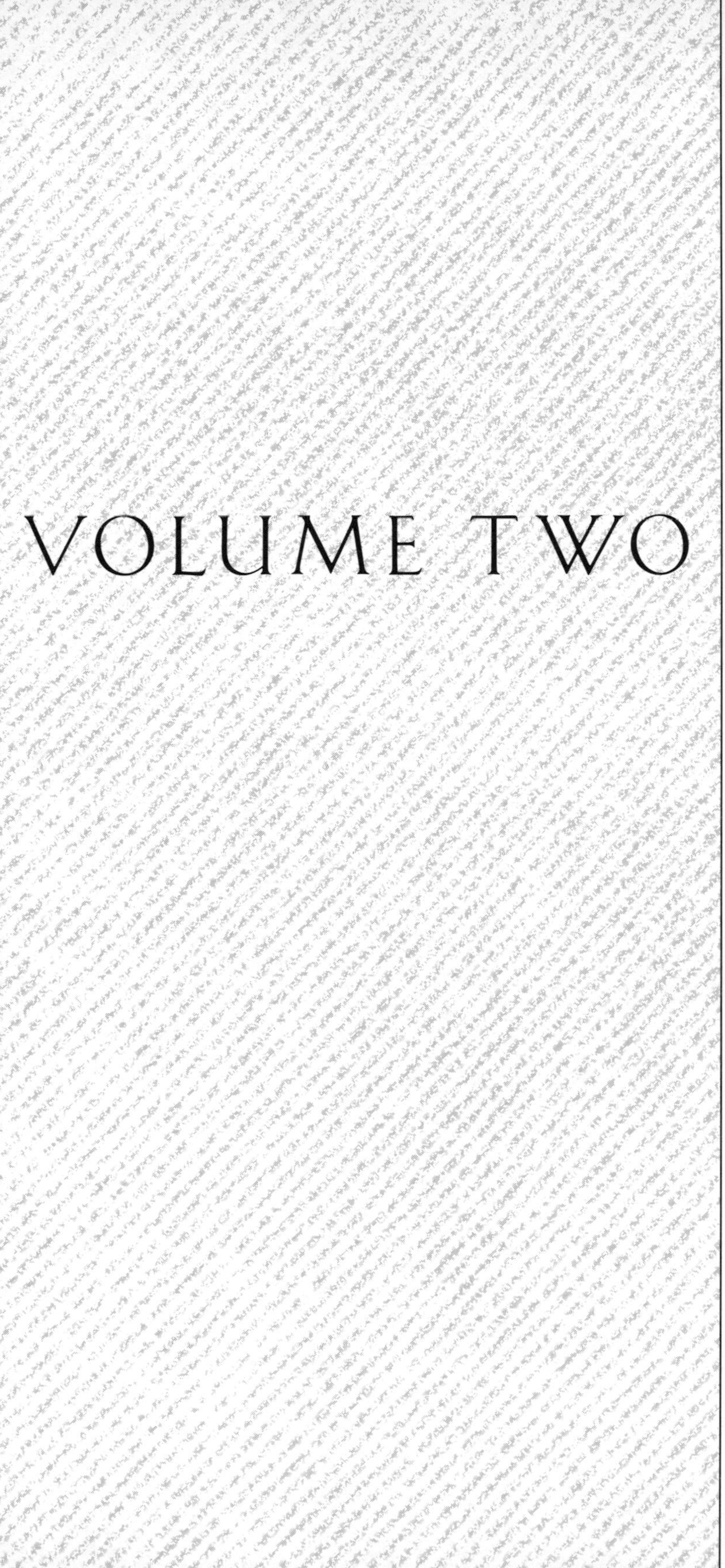

VOLUME TWO

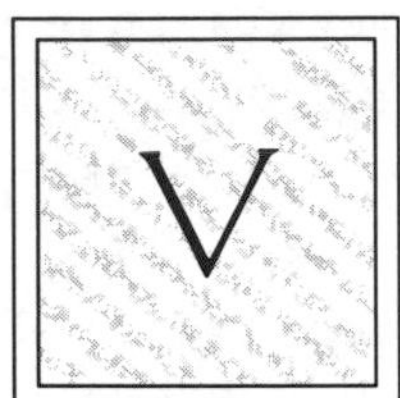

On October 16, 1941, on orders from Moscow, the Odessa defense district was evacuated. Units of the Rumanian army entered the city. Marshal Antonescu declared Odessa the capital of the new Rumanian province of Transistria.

The Soviets resumed control of Odessa two and a half years later, on April 10, 1944. Two weeks before, on March 26, troops of the Second Ukrainian Front under the command of Marshal Ivan Stepanovich Konev reached the Prut River, the official border of the U.S.S.R. and Rumania. In July a new Soviet offensive was expected any day because Bessarabia and Kishinev remained under occupation, and German airplanes, which had their own airfields and bases in Rumania, were bombing Odessa nearly every day. At the beginning of August, the German planes attacked at night, between nine and ten o'clock; dropping incendiary bombs which made Deribasovskaya Street bright as day. The sudden shadows of trees and buildings would spread with theatrical speed. They would drop a dozen bombs and then fly toward the sea.

In mid-August Captain Iona Ovseich Degtyar was detached to Odessa to perform party and economic duties. Two weeks later the divisions with which he had reached the Prut, forced the Prut, approached the rear of the Rumanian city of Yassy, then crossed the Prut again, this time from west to east, and, joining the troops of the Second Ukrainian Front, encircled the German forces in the Yassy-Kishinev area. The operation was completed on the third of September: the German "South Ukraine" armies were smashed, and the enemy lost two hundred and fifty thousand soldiers and officers as casualties and prisoners.

Iona Ovseich found his wife, Polina Isaevna, Tosya Khomitsky, Olya Cheperukha, and Dina Vargaftik back in the courtyard. Olya and Dina had returned from evacuation in May and now even felt that they had not been anywhere at all. Klava Ivanovna had been the very first to return, having arrived with the troops. She had left Baku in the summer of the previous year and, gradually moving from one city to another, had made her way back to Odessa. Now the Province Executive Committee had sent her to the Shiryaevsky district to help harvest the tomatoes and grapes.

Nastya was rooted to the spot when she saw Comrade Degtyar, then she rushed to kiss his hand, which Iona Ovseich had difficulty tearing free. Nastya wept as she told him of her sufferings under the Rumanians, how she had been dragged day and night to their headquarters and ordered to name names; she was questioned about Degtyar and what members of his family were still in Odessa; they wanted to know about Klava Ivanovna and Dr. Landa and what had happened to the belongings in his apartment. She had not said a word and that Rumanian fascist bastard had beaten her with his whip and kicked her in the teeth with his boots.

Nastya opened her mouth: three front teeth were missing, and two or three on the side.

There had also been trouble with Degtyar's apartment until Polina Isaevna had returned: Nastya had had to run to the police to fetch an inspector; people had come with an authorization for the apartment but she had padlocked the door and wouldn't give them the keys.

"Good," said Iona Ovseich. "I understand, Anastasya."

For the entire rest of the week Iona Ovseich spent twenty-four hours a day at his factory even though he had not yet been officially ordered back to work: first he had to wind things up on the military end. Polina Isaevna would leave for school in the early morning, because there were only a few days left until classes started and during the occupation the school building had been turned into a rat's nest and had not been repaired at all, not even given a coat of whitewash.

Nastya was indignant at the way the Degtyars were neglecting their own health. She demanded that Polina Isaevna give her the keys to their apartment so that she could clean it up and also that Polina surrender her bread cards and money so Nastya could buy her potatoes, onions, and tomatoes. Despite Polina's resistance, Nastya had her way. Late that evening when the Degtyars returned home, their place gleamed, and a rich aroma of fried onions and bacon fat wafted from a pot.

On Saturday evening Dina and Olya came by to see Degtyar, both with the same request: that Comrade Degtyar help them find the furniture and things which they had left behind in their apartments when they had been evacuated from Odessa. Iona Ovseich said that they should draw up a list, which he would personally check and present to the Province Executive Committee's Department of Internal Affairs. It turned out that Dina had already been to the police where she had been told that first she should find out who the suspects were and then report their names to them.

"Who do you suspect?" asked Iona Ovseich.

Dina shook her head—if she only knew who to suspect!

Iona Ovseich joined his hands and placed them on the table. "What did Nastya have to say on that score?"

"Nastya says nobody told her to stand watch and I should have taken my stuff with me to Tashkent, and not expect people to take care of my things when they were suffering under the Rumanians for two and a half years."

Iona Ovseich thought for a moment, opened his mouth part way, tapped his fingernails against his teeth, and said: "I see. Call the concierge, we'll straighten it out."

"Anastasya," said Iona Ovseich, "Olya Cheperukha, Dina Vargaftik, and other people from the building were evacuated from Odessa in 1941 and couldn't take all their belongings with them, especially their furniture, and they left most of it in their apartments. What happened to those belongings and that furniture?"

Nastya signified her ignorance with a gesture: a woman kept chickens near her hut and then one time she couldn't find where the chickens had laid their eggs, but Vargaftik and Cheperukha wanted her to look all over Odessa and even outside the city for their eggs.

"Anastasya," said Iona Ovseich, "you don't understand. It's me who wants to know, not Vargaftik and Cheperukha."

Nastya again cited the example of the hens who lay their eggs in places no one knows about but then Iona Ovseich stopped her and asked why she had mentioned Tashkent when she was well aware that Dina had spent those two and a half years living and working in the town of Sol-Iletsk, not far from the Urals, while Olya Cheperukha had been in the town of Krasnovodsk, near the Caspian Sea.

Nastya said that she hadn't meant anything by that and it was Dina and Olya who had thought up that one: she herself still didn't know where that Tashkent was and what peoples lived there.

Iona Ovseich drummed his fingers on the table as if tapping out a message in Morse code, then requested that Tosya Khomitsky be called in. Nastya said that she couldn't wait around just to shoot the breeze: she had to go sweep the sidewalk on Troitskaya Street or else the police would fine her.

"That doesn't matter," said Dina, "you'll come up with the money to pay."

Nastya was offended: she'd take Dina to court for an insult like that. The Rumanians were gone now, and you didn't have to bribe the police to investigate who could pay and who couldn't.

Tosya arrived. Iona Ovseich invited her to sit down and not stand in the doorway like a beggar waiting for a handout. Tosya answered that, thank God, she was no beggar, she received money from the military because her husband had been at the front almost since the first day of the war, and she earned a few kopecks herself. Things were quite easy for her now, it had already been a month since Kolka had been called up and she didn't have anyone to take care of. Tosya ran a finger under her eyes, sighed, and asked why she had been called in.

"Why have you been called in?" said Iona Ovseich. "I've been talking with the concierge Sereda about the furniture the people evacuated in '41 left in their apartments. According to Sereda, she didn't see anything, didn't hear anything, and doesn't know anything. I would think you'd be able to tell us a little something since you were here throughout the entire occupation."

Tosya said that she had nothing to add, and that Nastya should sit down and think until she remembered who came to see her and who she took around to people's apartments.

"Do you mean the people who came from the police?" asked Iona Ovseich.

Tosya answered that she didn't know who they were, maybe they were police, but they were not in uniform. Nastya burst into tears and shouted at Tosya: "Oh, you Rumanian whore! And who was selling milk at a stand in the market!"

Yes, confirmed Tosya, she had had a milk stand at the market but Sereda would answer to the NKVD for calling her a Rumanian whore and all the rest of it.

"Hold on, Khomitsky," said Iona Ovseich, "why go straight to the NKVD?"

Dina volunteered that if Tosya said the NKVD, she must have good reason for it.

Iona Ovseich shifted his eyes to Nastya. She stopped crying, wiped her tears with her fist, and began speaking about the shady deals Tosya was involved in. Tosya's only response was to twist her face and grimace foolishly.

"Khomitsky," said Iona Ovseich, "we don't like your silence. We want to hear a clear yes or no from you."

Tosya repeated that she had kept a milk stall at the market and had no intention of hiding the fact.

"Comrade Degtyar," interjected Olya Cheperukha, "when the Rumanians were here, Tosya couldn't receive any money from Stepa, who was in the Red Army. She went into business so she could have money to live."

"When the Rumanians were here," answered Iona Ovseich, "the underground blew up German headquarters, and in revenge they shot poison gas into the catacombs and blocked up all the ways out."

Tosya said that not everyone was capable of blowing up headquarters and generals but her Kolka had built a radio receiver to pick up broadcasts from Moscow, and on November 7 he had scattered leaflets around the city. And he could have paid with his life for that too.

Iona Ovseich inquired where he had gotten those leaflets. Tosya replied that she didn't know, they could ask Kolka when the war was over and he came home.

"Khomitsky," said Iona Ovseich, peering into her eyes, "let's suppose that something of the sort did take place. Can anyone confirm it?"

Tosya thought for a moment and nodded at Nastya, who replied by shaking a finger and laughing bitterly: "No! Comrade Degtyar is not a fool to believe all that nonsense! Now everyone's going to have been a partisan or in the underground but under the Rumanians they were at the market speculating and making money off other people's misery!"

Tosya said nothing, then walked right over to Nastya, ripped the kerchief off her head, and shouted: "You scum! You forgot about Sonechka Granik and her children, and you forgot about little Liza when they were rounding up the Jews! You scum, you think the walls don't have ears!"

Nastya turned white as chalk, requested Comrade Degtyar and everyone else there to testify in court how she had been reviled by that Rumanian speculator.

Iona Ovseich attempted to calm the two women down but Tosya Khomitsky was so out of control that there was no stopping her.

"Scum!" cried Tosya again. "Who brought the police a lantern to help them look through the cellar where Sonya was hiding with her children! And when they didn't find little Liza, who said that they should keep looking, the third kike had to be there somewhere!"

"Lies! countered Nastya, "nothing but lies. They took Sonya along with Osya, Khilka, and Liza right from their apartment to the station, and from there to Domanevka. They took all the Jews to Domanevka."

Tosya shook her head and stared darkly at Nastya, who brandished a fist and said that that Rumanian speculator better not stare at her, there was no reason to, her conscience was clean before Soviet society.

"Clean is it!" mimicked Tosya. "The outhouse in the courtyard is cleaner than your conscience. I'll get even with you yet for sending the police to search for the Red Army soldier Kolka Khomitsky—"

"Hold on, Khomitsky," interrupted Iona Ovseich. "All these indirect accusations are no good. When was your apartment searched under the occupation, and for what reason?"

Tosya did not answer. Nastya took a step closer to Comrade Degtyar. She said there were plenty of searches, once every blue moon and every time hell froze over.

"Anastasya Sereda," said Iona Ovseich angrily, "that kind of talk is out of place here."

Tosya remained silent. Olya Cheperukha took advantage of the moment to inform Comrade Degtyar that Lyalya Orlov and Madame Aga, the Karaite who lived in number 45, had also seen Sonya Granik with her two children, Osya and Khilka, walking beside her, and she had not been holding her baby.

"Sereda," said Iona Ovseich loudly, "now there's three people saying one thing while you're saying another."

"Comrade Degtyar," said Nastya, pressing both her hands to her chest, "may I choke if any single word I'm saying isn't true."

Iona Ovseich shifted his gaze from one woman to the other. Suddenly Nastya covered her face with her apron and cried in a nasty voice that that was a concierge's fate—nobody believed you, nobody considered you a human being, and all you did was follow other people around with a dustpan.

"Cut the hysterics!" said Iona Ovseich, calling her to order. "I've heard nothing but words so far, and the Soviet system doesn't allow people to be slandered. If a person's innocent, he's innocent."

Iona Ovseich gave them all permission to leave; Dina and Olya remembered their furniture only when they were in the courtyard and it was too late to go back.

Klava Ivanovna arrived the next day. She had received the news that Degtyar was back in Odessa but had not been able to tear herself away before Sunday.

Klava Ivanovna brought with her two bags of tomatoes, a wicker basket of grapes, and a pound of cow's butter especially for Polina Isaevna, who had been having problems with her lungs again.

"Malaya," said Iona Ovseich after they had kissed and had a good look at each other, "so, it's not difficult to become a dependent and live off someone else."

That upset Klava Ivanovna, who said that he and Polina should have as many years of happiness as she had kilograms of grapes, potatoes, and onions which she had left behind in the countryside. She hadn't wanted to lug them all in and look like she was a speculator. And anyway, people who were on their toes, not to mention the speculators, went outside Odessa to get their food, to Balta, Ananev, Shiryaevo, Tsebrikovo.

Iona Ovseich said that speculators were characteristic of wartime and it didn't take a prophet to foresee it would happen in Odessa, which had been ruled by the Rumanians for two and a half years. The surprising thing was that to this day people were still running private stalls at the market and the New Bazaar and selling food, clothes, tools, and even books. On Torgovaya Street, between Podbelsky and Franz Mering, there was a hunchback, who looked like a Greek, who had as many books in his stall as a good public library and quite an enviable assortment too. The question was, how did one man amass those thousands of books!

"How!" said Klava Ivanovna, shaking her head. "There's a bloodstain on every one, and all that's left of the owners are bones and ashes. . . . Ask the man selling them, he'll tell you about his father and his grandfather, who were secondhand book dealers and spent their last kopeck on books."

Iona Ovseich suddenly turned pale and grasped his left side as if his heart were giving him pain. The suddenness of it all made Klava Ivanovna turn pale too and, instead of helping him immediately and giving him valerian drops, she began tugging at his hand and asking how he was feeling. Iona Ovseich wanted to answer but could not, the pain was so fierce near his diaphragm where he had had a resection on two ribs in 1942, after Mozdok.

When large beads of sweat appeared on his forehead, Iona Ovseich felt that the attack had receded somewhat and told Klava Ivanovna not to pay any heed to such trifles: "We're not dead as long as we're alive, and when we're dead, they'll bury us."

"My God," whispered Klava Ivanovna, "where does he get the strength? Prison, the Revolution, the war, work, work, work, and then war again. If he was made of pure steel, he would have rusted to bits a long time ago."

"That's just the reason I didn't," joked Iona Ovseich. "God made man of clay. You lose a piece, they add back a piece and you're good as new."

Madame Malaya switched the subject to the medals Captain Degtyar had been awarded—the Order of the War for the Fatherland, the Red Banner, and Red Star—but Iona Ovseich did not respond to that and said they would speak about it some other time. Right now there were more important matters, and one of them was particularly important.

Klava Ivanovna guessed that he meant the way Nastya Sereda had acted under the Rumanians. Iona Ovseich agreed that Nastya was important too but first and foremost he wanted to find out what was known about Sonya Granik and her three children.

Klava Ivanovna said that it was known that Sonya had been taken to Domanevka with Osya and Khilka, and that little Liza had not been with them.

What basis was there for accepting that information as valid, asked Iona Ovseich, if Anastasya Sereda had with her own eyes seen Sonya taken from her apartment with her three children.

"Nastya couldn't have seen that," said Klava Ivanovna.

"How do you know that she couldn't have?" asked Iona Ovseich.

Klava Ivanovna paused for thought, her lips moving as if she were doing mental addition and subtraction. Iona Ovseich looked to the side and began waiting for her to finish but, at that rate, they could be there till morning.

"Malaya," said Iona Ovseich, "you've changed a lot in the three years since we last saw each other."

Klava Ivanovna stopped moving her lips, sighed deeply, and said that Degtyar was wrong on that point: it was just that she had given a certain person her word not to say anything for the time being in order to help a child who had been left without a mother, sisters or brothers, and whose father was at the front.

"All right," said Iona Ovseich, yielding, "I won't ask you who that person is, I'll tell you—it's Tosya Khomitsky. She knows that little Liza is alive and she knows where Liza is."

Now Klava Ivanovna's conscience could be clean because Iona Ovseich had guessed it by himself, and it would be unseemly for her to keep mum. She repeated the same explanation Tosya had given her: if Efim returned from the front alive—there hadn't been a word from him yet—then he could take Liza, but if, God forbid, something happened to him, the child could think her new parents were her real parents. The fewer people who knew about all this the better, because you could always count on one person acting like a bastard. Tosya's sister, who was keeping the child for now, had sold her house in Krasnye Okna and had moved to Gradenitsy, not far from Belyaevka.

"Malaya, have you seen the child with your own eyes?" asked Iona Ovseich.

Yes, said Klava Ivanovna, she had seen the child with her very own eyes, she was the spitting image of Sonya, except that the eyes were a little slanted, like Efim's.

Iona Ovseich placed a finger inside the collar of his field suit and pulled it to loosen it, then walked over to the window where he opened the shutter. The acacias were in reach. He said no other place had a summer like Odessa's and that our people had been risking their necks at the front for three years now but it wouldn't be much longer. "Yes," sighed Klava Ivanovna, "Hitler's neck will be broken before the winter, and if Churchill and the Americans hadn't played games and had opened a second front a year earlier, the war would be over and won by now."

"Malaya," said Iona Ovseich, reaching through the window and breaking off an acacia branch, "tell me how it happened that little Liza's life was saved."

"Kolka Khomitsky saved little Liza," said Klava Ivanovna. "He found out that there was going to be a roundup of Jews late that night and he warned Sonya but it was too late. She ran to hide in the cellar with the children but Kolka saw the Rumanians going to Nastya's and so he ran down to the cellar too. Sonya didn't want to give him her baby for anything in the world. Osya, with tears in his eyes, tried to talk her into it but nothing happened until Kolka grabbed the child away from her. Then Nastya brought the police down into the cellar and they found Sonya with her two children; the third one was gone. They slammed Sonya's head against the wall but she kept saying that her little girl had died two days before and that she had buried her at the cemetery herself. Nastya hit Sonya in the face with her lantern and shouted that she was lying through her teeth, that she had seen her yesterday holding her little Jew baby in the hall by the window. Sonya replied that she had indeed been standing with Liza by the window but the child was already dead by then and she had been looking out the window, waiting for the right moment when no one was in the courtyard and she could leave to go bury the child.

"Kolka didn't know what happened after that: Liza began to whine and he was afraid someone would hear. He left the cellar through Cheperukha's shed which had a door that led out to Troitskaya Street. Then the police went to Tosya's apartment. Nastya was with them and she said that Tosya and her little bastard could be hiding the Jew baby but the police could see that there was no one there. They warned Tosya that if she was hiding anything they'd put her and her son up against a wall."

"Malaya," said Iona Ovseich, "we must find some other witnesses besides Tosya Khomitsky."

Klava Ivanovna was surprised—why were witnesses needed if the living child they had saved could serve as proof.

"No," Iona Ovseich observed, "Tosya was up to no good too, she was running a stall at the market, selling milk."

"Hold on, Ovseich," said Madame Malaya, "a person has to make a living somehow. So why is it all right to work in a factory or a workshop but not to do business?"

Iona Ovseich thought for a moment, then replied: "You surprise me, Malaya. When capitalist ways are restored for a short time and a person immediately becomes a private businessman, we don't have the right to close our eyes to the truth. The question is, did that person want that under Soviet rule as well and just hid that desire deep in his heart?"

Yes, agreed Klava Ivanovna, there are quite a few people who say one thing but think something else entirely in their heart of hearts, and the war allowed them to tear off their mask, but if we take Tosya, during the NEP years, she was allowed to engage in private trade but she didn't, and the most important thing is that in saving little Liza she and Kolka had risked their own lives.

"Malaya," said Iona Ovseich, shaking his head, "you're mixing up apples and oranges: what's good is good and no one's arguing that, but when something is dubious, there's no reason to hide your head under your wing and lull yourself with beautiful fairy tales and legends. Not only that, according to Khomitsky, her son Kolka regularly listened to radio broadcasts from Moscow and scattered leaflets and proclamations on November 7, but once again there's no one to confirm it. I'll tell you something else, she doesn't even know where he got those leaflets. In one sense Sereda is right: now there are a lot of people trying to make you believe that they were partisans or served in the underground during the occupation."

"But what will happen," asked Klava Ivanovna, "if we don't find any other witnesses—will Tosya remain under suspicion while Nastya can walk around free as a bird like everyone else?"

"That shouldn't be the case," said Iona Ovseich. "We'll be able to find other witnesses. And, as far as Anastasya is concerned, I'll choose a way of making it plain to her that a voluntary confession is better than one made under pressure."

That evening Klava Ivanovna returned to the Stalin kolkhoz in the Shiryaevo district while Iona Ovseich sent Olya Cheperukha to fetch Nastya. Though she had not been invited to, Olya sat down at the table, propped her head on one hand, and began speaking about her furniture: the end of the war was almost in sight, her husband would be coming home from the front, her son would be arriving soon, and all she had in the entire apartment were two chairs and one couch. Iona Ovseich said there was nothing so terrible about that, a few days on a wood floor was not like being up to your waist in water in a trench.

"Comrade Degtyar," interjected Nastya, "let Olya come with me and I'll give her two of my chairs and a wardrobe; they only crowd up my place, you can't even turn around there."

Degtyar said that she and Olya should come to terms about the chairs and the wardrobe themselves, but right now Cheperukha should go home and do her housework.

"Comrade Degtyar," said Olya, squinting her eyes, "you're just as strict as you were before the war."

"Cheperukha," said Iona Ovseich, "turn out the light in the front hall when you leave; there's no reason for it to be on."

Olya turned out the light, slammed the door, and then waited a moment before pressing her ear to the panel of the door, but she could not hear anything being said inside; all was still except for an occasional squeak as if the shutters were opening and closing in the breeze. She was just about to leave when suddenly a woman's voice began howling, hitting the highest note, like a person in utter despair. Then in a flash the voice grew still and when it resumed it was normal and even, like a person keening over a corpse when it was still at home and you could sit beside it.

Late in the evening of the next day, just as the radio was broadcasting a communiqué from the Soviet Information Bureau that Soviet troops had taken Bucharest, the capital of Rumania, Nastya was standing by the gate waiting for Iona Ovseich to return from the factory. Coming home from the second shift, Lyalya Orlov arrived right after Comrade Degtyar and accidentally witnessed the whole scene: first Nastya tried to grab Degtyar's arm, then she ran ahead of him, fell to her knees, and began striking her forehead against the ground. Iona Ovseich tried to sidestep her but Nastya threw her arms around his legs, struck her forehead against the ground again, and wailed loudly: "Oh, Comrade Degtyarchik, oh, my darling, don't, don't!"

Iona Ovseich braced himself against the wall with his right hand to keep from falling, then yanked his left leg and then his right leg free. Nastya thrashed as if struck twice in the stomach from below and cried out: "Oh, for the love of God, don't do it, Comrade Degtyarchik!"

"You bitch!" said Lyalya Orlov. "Now you're calling on God. Why didn't you remember God before! Bitch!"

Iona Ovseich climbed the iron stairs, the taps on his shoes tapping on each step: tap, tap, tap . . .

On Saturday Nastya was summoned to the police station at 12 Babel Street. Tosya Khomitsky, Lyalya Orlov, and Madame Aga, the Karaite from number 45, had been called in the day before. The women did not say a word to anyone, but Dina Vargaftik was saying that plenty could be learned by putting your ear to the ground.

There were interruptions in the water supply every day and people had to go to Pushkin Street, corner of Troitskaya, about half a mile, for fresh water, though salt water was available quite close by, on Preobrazhenskaya Street, in the courtyard of the Isakovich baths, a quick five-minute walk. That evening Nastya began readying a large can and an iron barrel which together could hold about a hundred liters, placed them on a cart whose wheels were from a child's bicycle, and set out for water early the next morning when people were still asleep. By eight o'clock, when it was time for her to go to the police station, she had already managed to wash both courtyards, the front and the back, the sidewalk by the gate, and a portion of the pavement. Steam rose imperceptibly from the warm stone and asphalt and passed over her hands, face, and ears, like the moisture from a vaporizer.

Nastya was wearing a white sailcloth pinafore, as she had on the eve of important holidays before the war, and on its right side, she had pinned a tin, numbered badge, brand new, issued a week before by the police; and she wore a blue sailcloth kerchief over her head. She had put on a pair of men's rubber overshoes to water down the courtyard, then she changed into a pair of low boots with laces and polished hooks. She took her passport, her union card, and a certificate, issued her by Comrade Degtyar personally before the war, in May '41, stating that she conscientiously fulfilled her duties in keeping the courtyard neat and clean. She set off for the police station at 12 Bebel Street. Near the Alexandrovsky Gardens she remembered her antiaircraft brigade badge, which was in her wardrobe; it wasn't good to turn back when you were halfway there but she did anyway. Next to the tin badge she had been wearing, the brass chain on which the antiaircraft badge hung gleamed like gold.

Nastya spent the entire day in the police station. It was said that Iona Ovseich went there as well, at least Dina Vargaftik, on her way to the Vorovsky garment factory where she worked, had seen him at the corner of Babel and Kangun, a hundred feet from the station.

Around ten o'clock, when it had already grown dark and it was time to turn on the lights, though they were trying to economize on electricity, Nastya arrived with her water wagon. Tosya Khomitsky said there wasn't enough water in the ocean to wash the blood off that dirty bitch.

Nastya watered the grass in the courtyard and the grapevines by the gate: she put what was left of the water on the stove and sat down waiting for it to heat up. Lost in thought, she forgot about the water until it had boiled over onto the stove. Now she had to wait for it to cool because you couldn't wash with boiling water.

It was still cooling at midnight when Nastya went out to lock the gate. Everyone, including Lyalya Orlov, was already home. Nastya washed her face, then washed her hands, feet, and the rest of her in the same water. So her hair would dry faster, she tossed a few wood chips in the firebox, placed her chair beside it, and sat fluffing up her hair with her hands and bending a bit closer to the stove to keep the heat from going to waste.

The lack of air made Nastya tired and there was a ringing in her ears. The ringing was stifling and she closed her eyes only to see the color red, like blood from a wound before it's been darkened by the air. Nastya wanted to get up and drink a glass of cold water but her legs wouldn't obey her and her stomach felt as heavy as if it had been packed with sand. Then her mouth felt heavy too; her tongue swelled and she couldn't catch her breath. She was very frightened now but still her legs would not obey her.

At around four o'clock in the morning someone tugged on the bell by the gate and raised a racket. Dogs began barking on Pokrovsky Lane where the military command was located; the bell on the gate rang again and someone knocked seven or eight times; the dogs started up once more and barked and howled until dawn for no reason, a bad omen.

Nastya usually opened the gate at six o'clock. Lyalya Orlov purposely left five minutes later so as not to have to ask Nastya to open it.

From the main hall Lyalya had noticed that the gate was locked, but, just to make sure, she had walked over to the lock and tugged it hard enough for the concierge to hear it, then walked off to one side. Nastya didn't come out. Lyalya knocked the lock against the gate again, pulled the cord on the concierge's bell, waited thirty seconds, then pounded her fist on the door with such force that the panes almost went flying.

It was around a quarter past six. Losing all patience, and now late for her shift, Lyalya shouted to Nastya to stop her Rumanian tricks or else she would get a lifetime's worth of steam baths at Solovki.

Dina, Tosya, and Olya came to the gate. They had nearly an hour left before their shifts began and could have waited but this was a matter of principle. Dina said that they should break the window and crawl into Nastya's room if nothing happened soon. The women listened for a minute, then Lyalya struck the window frame with both her hands, the upper panes cracked, and all four shutters, the ones outside and those inside, opened wide. Lyalya began climbing up onto the windowsill with Olya and Tosya supporting her from the back. Now Lyalya could see Nastya sitting calmly by her stove and shouted for her to open the gate or give them the keys, but Nastya paid no attention and did not even turn her head. Lyalya climbed over the sill and walked closer, stopping by the bed. The women outside asked why it was taking her so long but Lyalya was unable to answer, unable to move. She was holding onto the bedstead with all of her might and staring as if hypnotized at Nastya. Nastya's elbow, which had been leaning against the stove, suddenly slipped off and Nastya swayed forward as if she were falling. Lyalya screamed wildly, dashed to the windowsill, and jumped back into the hallway.

"Girls," said Lyalya in tears, "I shouted at her, but she was sitting by the stove—dead."

Outside someone rang the concierge's bell and, without waiting for a response, began hammering at the gate. Tosya said they could put her in jail for it, but she was going to look for the keys. The person outside began pounding on the gate; this time he must have used a piece of metal, the noise was so loud.

When they found the keys and opened the gate, there stood Joseph Kotlyar. Dina rushed toward him and shouted that a person could think it was the police pounding on the gate with a revolver. No, said Joseph with a laugh, it was somebody more important than the police, it was Joseph Kotlyar pounding on the door with his wooden leg.

"He chose the right moment," said Dina, after Joseph had kissed and hugged Olya, Tosya, and Lyalya in turn. When he was done embracing them, Joseph was about to go into Nastya's and greet her as well. "You chose the right moment," repeated Dina Vargaftik, "but for saying good-bye to her. Nastya's in her room dead."

The police arrived an hour later. Iona Ovseich had notified the building residents not to go into the concierge's or touch anything: that could impede the investigation and cause unnecessary complications.

"What complications?" said Tosya Khomitsky with a grimace. "A dog's death to a dog."

"On the contrary," said Olya Cheperukha, "she lucked out again. Another person might do good all his life and suffer terrible pain when dying but she not only escaped God's judgment but people's too."

Iona Ovseich was staring hard at Tosya Khomitsky, but she did not notice or pretended that she didn't.

The police took Nastya's body to the forensic morgue at 2 Valikhovsky Lane, where an autopsy was performed. They concluded that death had been the result of natural causes—a myocardial infarct and a thrombosis of the cerebral vessels.

Since Anastasya Sereda had no relatives in Odessa and the courtyard had refused her body, it was loaded into a vehicle and taken directly from the morgue to the Slobodka cemetery, which was near the province mental hospital.

Joseph Kotlyar stayed with Tosya the first day; the apartment in which he had lived until his wife had left for the front and he himself had been evacuated was now occupied by Madame Lebedev and her daughter Nina, both from Bugaevka where they had had a house, but it had been hit by a bomb in '41 and burned to the ground. When Joseph Kotlyar tried to enter his own apartment, a moment he had been awaiting for three years, Madame Lebedev slammed the door in his face and shouted that he should go back to Tashkent, there was no reason for him to be there. Joseph calmly explained that he had been evacuated to the town of Lower Tagil, in the Urals, and had never been in Tashkent, and that if she didn't allow him into his apartment nicely, he'd enter by force and smack her in the mouth.

Madame Lebedev replied the only thing he could do by force was kiss her you know what. She had paid rent to the Rumanians for two and a half years, and was paying the Soviets now, and Kotlyar would only get in over her dead body, and she had already outlived ten men like him, and would bury him with the rabbis across the road from the Second Christian Cemetery.

"You Rumanian bitch!" shouted Kotlyar, pounding his fist on the door and warning her that he was going straight to the police and she'd better be ready.

He was just trying to frighten her by saying that. First, it was necessary to discuss this with Comrade Degtyar, of course, and seek his advice.

Iona Ovseich listened closely and said that the case at hand was a variation on situations that were happening by the dozen now in every Odessa courtyard: on the one hand, he, Joseph Kotlyar, was one hundred percent in the right, and, on the other, Madame Lebedev, also had the right to a roof over her head.

What did that mean—on the other hand, said Joseph, seething, if the City Soviet had given him the authorization for the apartment and not taken it away, whereas Lebedev had seized it on her own?

"Hold on there," said Iona Ovseich. "According to preliminary statistics, more than two thousand buildings have been destroyed in the city, and you can figure how many apartments that means."

Joseph replied that he didn't know how many apartments that might mean, but, on the other hand, he did know that more than two hundred thousand people had been deported from Odessa and killed, and each of them had had a roof over his head. So Degtyar should calculate how many apartments that meant if there were six hundred thousand people living in Odessa before the war.

Iona Ovseich sighed deeply, scratched his chin with a fingernail, and advised Kotlyar to act in the following manner: for the interim he should settle in the concierge's place since it was free, while at the same time petitioning the District Executive Committee for the return of his own apartment, and he would have Degtyar's complete support in that.

When Klava Ivanovna returned and learned of the situation, she said straight out that it was a shame and a disgrace that a disabled Civil War veteran, a Red partisan who had been evacuated and whose wife and two sons were at the front, should have to take refuge in the concierge's apartment while some Madame Lebedev and her daughter Nina, a couple of Rumanian whores, were living in his apartment. It was as if the Soviet system had blindfolded itself and plugged its ears.

"Malaya," said Iona Ovseich, slamming a finger against the table, "stop talking, hold your tongue! The Soviet gave you no mandate to speak on its behalf, and arbitrary actions are not allowed."

Klava Ivanovna replied that she was not calling for arbitrary actions, on the contrary; still, justice had to be done so that everyone could see it clearly with his own eyes.

"If a person had a chance to leave during the occupation and stayed on, that's his fault," said Iona Ovseich. "And if he had no chance to leave that's his hard luck. What we have to do here is make clear distinctions and not raise a ruckus. Personally, I'm entirely on Kotlyar's side, but that's beside the point. What matters here is the law."

When Madame Lebedev was called in to the Stalin District Executive Committee and asked to relinquish the apartment, she shouted that she had been without a husband since the first days of the war, she had suffered for two and a half years under the Rumanians, and now the Soviets had returned and were throwing her out on the street. Her daughter Nina had a fit of nerves during this conversation; she began frothing at the mouth, her hands twisted like ropes, and her mother began shouting that the girl was dying.

Every day Joseph went to the Stalin District Executive Committee, which was entirely on his side, and there he would be told to continue living in the concierge's apartment. They weren't kicking anyone out today and tomorrow they would have another look at the matter.

A letter arrived from Anya, who was working in a field hospital: she was happy that Joseph was back in Odessa, and it wouldn't be long before they all would be home and having dinner together. She had not had any letters from Sasha and Petya for a long time and was very worried: Joseph should forward to her the letters he received from them. Joseph replied that he had not had any letters for a long time either, but that was understandable because they were still writing to his old address in the Urals and he was already back in Odessa. The city had changed somewhat, though much more change might have been expected: vegetables and grapes were on sale at the market; Klava Ivanovna had just returned from a kolkhoz and given him eighteen pounds of potatoes, a kilo of sunflower seeds, and a bottle of oil as a present, and, in return, he had given her a teapot and kettle, which he had made when he was still in the Urals; it could boil two liters of water in five minutes. He had kept another one like it for himself.

Madame Lebedev finally regained her composure because one day after another passed and nothing changed. Sometimes Kotlyar lost his self-control, banged his wooden leg against the door, and shouted that Lebedev and her daughter, that Rumanian slut, should count the minutes of life they still had left. Madame Lebedev laughed in response behind the door and told Joseph to go back to where he had lost his leg, not to mention whatever else he was missing.

Twice Klava Ivanovna warned Madame Lebedev that she would answer in a court of law for these remarks but this produced no visible results and Degtyar himself was forced to intervene.

"Lebedev," said Iona Ovseich, "we don't approve of Joseph Kotlyar's behavior, but no one is going to be allowed to mock a former Red partisan and insult him with anti-Semitic remarks. During the first days of Soviet power, Vladimir Ilich Lenin gave notice that any sort of pogroms were outside the law."

Madame Lebedev replied that Kotlyar was creating a tempest in a teapot, she didn't even think such things, and who did they think they were anyway, Degtyar and Malaya, to be questioning people all the time and trying to confuse them.

"Who is Degtyar!" said Klava Ivanovna, stunned.

Lebedev looked Degtyar insolently in the eye. Iona Ovseich fingered one button of his field shirt and smiled with only his lips. He said her question was entirely appropriate and needed to be answered, but just how was another matter entirely.

A week later Madame Lebedev was again summoned to the District Executive Committee and informed that, on the basis of their information, she had not lived in Bugaevka, and, as for her husband, whom she said had been killed during the first days of the war, she was to bring them a notice or certificate from the military board. As she had the last time, Madame Lebedev struck her head with her fists but no one stopped her. They asked only that she leave the premises.

The next morning, before leaving for work, Joseph knocked politely and asked how Madame Lebedev and Nina were feeling: did they need anything from the drugstore or a doctor, he had a little free time at the moment. No one answered; a cat was meowing by the door. Joseph rang the doorbell loudly and promised the cat a piece of fish because it was dying of hunger with those people. The cat began scratching at the door. Joseph pulled at the doorknob and the door opened. This came as such a complete surprise that Joseph was somewhat confused and instead of entering at once, he only opened the door partway, then went to call Madame Malaya.

There was no one in the front hall but from the doorway to the bedroom Klava Ivanovna could see Madame Lebedev and her daughter lying side by side on the bed, their heads toward the window. The worst could be thought from the expression on their faces. Joseph said at once that they had committed suicide. Klava Ivanovna picked up Lebedev's hand to feel her pulse but could not find it; she then picked up Nina's hand with the same lack of success. Joseph was pale as a ghost. Klava Ivanovna ordered him to fetch a mirror; she wanted to check to see if they were still breathing. Joseph went into the front hall where the bureau had been before the war. Now there was a lustrous oak wardrobe in that corner with cut glass, copper, and a full-length mirror. He shuffled his feet as if he were in someone else's home and was just about to open the wardrobe door when Klava Ivanovna called out to him.

"Kotlyar, there's no need for a mirror. I can feel Lebedev's pulse. Go call an ambulance."

Before Joseph had returned, Klava Ivanovna had also found Nina's pulse, and when the doctor and ambulance arrived, she immediately told the doctor where to feel for it. Saying that he had been taking pulses for forty years, the doctor unbuttoned Madame Lebedev's jacket and Nina's, and signaled Klava Ivanovna to be quiet. Then he listened through a stethoscope and told the orderlies to go downstairs and get stretchers.

Joseph was so pale that the doctor asked: "Relatives of yours?" and assured him that they were in no danger. They had swallowed a large quantity of Luminal. They'd be given a couple of good irrigations in the hospital, and they'd return home to the bosom of their family in a day or two.

Klava Ivanovna laughed and said thank God it had turned out all right. Then she informed the doctor that Joseph Kotlyar had his own family and that his wife had been at the front since the onset of the war. The doctor looked intently at Joseph and said, "Try to take it easy, you're a man with his whole life ahead of him."

As the doctor had promised, Madame Lebedev and Nina returned home two days later. The District Executive Committee granted them an extension, and Klava Ivanovna told them they had Comrade Degtyar to thank for that.

That evening, though they still had an entire week left, Madame Lebedev went to see Iona Ovseich and honestly admitted that they had formerly lived in the Ovidopolsky region, in the village of Akkarzha, and that her husband had abandoned her and her daughter before the war, started a new family, and had given her no help at all.

"And can one assume that your marriage was not registered?" interrupted Iona Ovseich.

Madame Lebedev replied that she wouldn't have gone to register her marriage with a son of a bitch like that, might he rot wherever he was now. They had almost died of hunger under the Rumanians and Nina had said, "Let's move to Odessa, Mama, you can earn a little money doing laundry there." And so for two and a half years they had been suffering agony waiting for the Soviets to come back. They no longer even felt like human beings.

"Lebedev we have information that you and your daughter did day labor for Rumanian officers, businessmen, and administrators, and worked side by side with them for days on end, and not only as laundresses," Iona Ovseich announced.

Madame Lebedev burst into tears and said that was all a pack of lies, Nina had never gone out with officers, but only with a corporal who had promised to marry her and who had said that the Bolsheviks would win and return.

"Well, and how about you?" asked Iona Ovseich. "Did you believe that? Were you waiting for the Soviets to return or were there lapses?"

Madame Lebedev said that she had believed the Soviets would return and had waited for them from beginning to end. When the Soviets had retreated and the Germans had advanced all the way to the Volga, she told Nina they should all drown there.

"Hold on," said Iona Ovseich, "if your belief was so strong, how come your daughter went out with the Rumanian occupier?"

Madame Lebedev repeated that he was different from the others; he was always polite, brought them food, had his own farm near the town of Moineshti, but still he turned out to be a bastard: in '43, when they were sent to the Don, he didn't send them a single letter. Nina was in a family way because of him, and she was so full of hatred that she went to a midwife and had the child destroyed even though she was already in her sixth month and could have suffered serious consequences. And she hadn't betrayed any Jews like that bastard, Nastya Sereda: if people were hiding that was their own business, and if someone had something to atone for, that was their problem. All the furniture she had found in the apartment was still in place, except for the wardrobe which they had dragged over from the doctor's apartment in the other wing. Right from the start Nina had said, "When the doctor comes back, we'll tell him right away so he doesn't waste time chasing around the city."

"Lebedev," said Iona Ovseich, "as I understand it, you have no great desire to leave Odessa, is that right?"

"Comrade Degtyar," she said, "why do you take such an official tone with me and call me by my last name? I have a first name—Fenya."

"So," repeated Iona Ovseich, "you don't want to leave Odessa. But what's the solution, my dear Fenya? Kotlyar is moving back into his own apartment and we're going to lock up the concierge's place and hand the keys over to the authorities."

"Comrade Degtyar," said Madame Lebedev, flushing and covering her cheeks with her hands, "if you wish, I could stay on as the concierge."

Iona Ovseich smiled. "My dear Fenya, I can see that you think I'm so all-powerful that I can just wave my wand and make any wish come true."

Madame Lebedev did not make a direct reply but swore on her own life that she would never again act like the fool she'd been that time when the devil had possessed her to yell at Degtyar.

"All right," said Iona Ovseich, summing up, "for the time being there's one thing I can tell you: you were quite right to openly describe the real situation to me and not get on your high horse."

The next Monday Fenya Lebedev was hired as the new concierge. Kotlyar moved back into his own apartment, and Fenya moved into Nastya's. Klava Ivanovna said they shouldn't have been in such a hurry to take Fenya on and should have taken a closer look at who she was; a person who was able to come to terms so quickly with the Rumanians during the occupation needed to be checked out thoroughly. Iona Ovseich replied that he hadn't acted impulsively and people could be checked out by the way they acted. Fenya could always be fired.

The results weren't bad the first month. Even Klava Ivanovna admitted it, but there was still an unpleasant residue in her soul and she held to her initial opinion: if a person had come to terms with the occupier, that must never be forgotten.

On October 18, when the troops of the Third Belorussian Front, under the command of General Chernyakhovsky, moved onto the offensive and invaded East Prussia, meaning the actual territory of Hitler's Germany, a notice arrived from the army that Senior Lieutenant Pinchas Josephovich Kotlyar had died heroically in an air battle while fighting for his motherland.

Joseph smoked all night, at least two packs. Klava Ivanovna sat beside him, wondering aloud as to whether Anya should be notified at once or whether it would be better to wait awhile. Joseph felt sick the next morning: first he had a splitting headache, then his jaw began trembling and he lost the power of speech. A doctor was summoned at once from the polyclinic. He examined Joseph and said he had suffered a minor stroke; the main thing was that the symptoms were not increasing. If there was no one to look after him, he could be hospitalized.

Joseph spent the first day home in bed. The next day a cab was called and Degtyar and Malaya helped Joseph down the stairs. He was taken to the city hospital's neurological department. As soon as the cab had pulled away, Fenya Lebedev said, "The kikes are clever, clever, but God sees the truth."

When Klava Ivanovna learned of Fenya's remark, she said that she should be put up against the wall for that alone, and wagged a threatening finger at Iona Ovseich. "Oh, Degtyar, Degtyar, we'll have our hands full with that one."

"Malaya," said Iona Ovseich, calling her to order, "don't exaggerate: when a person is moved out of an apartment, he's not obliged to like you for it and be grateful to you."

"Oh, Degtyar, Degtyar," repeated Klava Ivanovna. "I'm telling you we're going to have our hands full with that one."

Two letters arrived from Anya Kotlyar at the same time: her hospital was in Yugoslavia, a very beautiful country, where the populace greeted the Red Army like its own, with hugs and kisses. Everyone invited you to his home and the people were overjoyed. But she was beside herself with worry—she had received only one letter from Sasha in a month and there hadn't been a word from Petya.

Joseph had regained the power of speech but was still too weak to write. Klava Ivanovna wrote for him, sending the warmest greetings from all the people in the building to Anya and her hospital, and their wish for a swift victory over Hitler: she informed Anya that Joseph was suffering from some swelling in his fingers, it would pass in a few days, and then he would write to her at once.

Klava Ivanovna had exaggerated slightly about it passing in a few days but after a week and a half Joseph felt considerably better and was able to write himself, though his handwriting was now somewhat worse than it had been. He wrote that he too had not heard from Petya in a long while and enclosed a letter from Sasha which the mailman had delivered literally half an hour before.

The ward physician had promised to release Kotlyar in about three days. On her own initiative, Fenya Lebedev had brought a few pails of water to the sick man's apartment with the intention of cleaning it for him, but Klava Ivanovna would not allow her to, and did the job herself, helped by Tosya Khomitsky. When they had finished cleaning, the apartment shone like a dance studio. In an apartment like this you could live till you were a hundred, said Klava Ivanovna, if you managed to escape grief, of course.

The next day Klava Ivanovna received notification that Senior Lieutenant Alexander Josephovich Kotlyar had died heroically in an air battle while fighting for his motherland.

"No!" Klava Ivanovna cried to the whole courtyard. "No!"

Then she threw herself on the couch and dug her fingernails into the wood. Dina and Tosya tried to lift her up but she dug her fingernails in deeper and shouted that they should all go to hell and leave her alone.

Iona Ovseich said that he'd inform Joseph, he'd just wait until his health was entirely back.

Fenya Lebedev shook her head and said that apartment brought everyone suffering, she and Nina had been lucky to get out of there in time.

Just before the October holidays, a tall young man, almost a boy, bearing a strong resemblance to Adya Lapidis, came walking into the courtyard. Olya Cheperukha was the first to spot him and asked who he was looking for. The boy said that he wasn't looking for anyone, he had just dropped by his own courtyard for a look. It was then that Olya was certain it was Adya and not just someone who looked like him. She wept and laughed from joy all at once.

That evening at Klava Ivanovna's, Adya told how he had run away from the children's home when the fascists surrounded Odessa; he had been evacuated on the ship *Georgia* and put in the hold along with some horses. The ship had been hit by a bomb when still in port, a fire had broken out, and an explosion had destroyed the steering mechanism; they had been towed by the destroyer *Shaumyan;* then, in the open sea, the tow cables had snapped, German airplanes had attacked, and the *Georgia* made it on its own all the way to the Crimea. Word reached them that the Germans had sunk one ship, the *Bolshevik;* many people had managed to jump overboard but the fascists strafed them from their planes.

"Adya," said Dina Vargaftik, wiping her tears with her kerchief, "do you remember my Grisha? He was killed back in '41."

From the Crimea Adya had moved on to the Caucasus, then to Astrakhan, Aktyubinsk, Kzyl-Orda, Tashkent, Samarkand, Chardzhou, Ashkhabad, Krasnovodsk, then the Caucasus again, and now he was back in Odessa.

"Wait a minute," said Klava Ivanovna, "when did you have time for school if you were moving around so much?"

Adya said that he had finished seventh grade and had been given his diploma. He had worked for a while on a cotton kolkhoz, as an apprentice lathe operator, and also on the railroad and in the oil industry. He had been arrested by the police one time, they had thought he was a pickpocket, but they had released him quickly and found him a place in a boarding school.

Tosya and Olya wept. Klava Ivanovna said none of it mattered; what counted was that he had remained a good person and not taken the wrong road.

"Aunt Malaya," said Adya, lowering his head, "do you know where my mother is?"

Klava Ivanovna sighed deeply: she had tried to learn of Zoya Lapidis' whereabouts as soon as she had returned to Odessa but no one had any information: many of the patients in the mental hospital had disappeared but no one knew where.

"Aunt Malaya," said Adya softly, "what do you think, is she alive?"

Klava Ivanovna shrugged her shoulders: why shouldn't she be alive! Dina and Tosya shared that opinion and told Adya that this was the worst war in human history but that miracles of all sorts happened during a war: one person might have been in a deep bomb shelter and five minutes later it got a direct hit and there was nothing left of him; another person was under fire day and night at the front, and came home healthy and without a scratch.

Adya said that he had read in the paper that the Germans were killing mentally ill people and performing experiments on them. Yes, confirmed Klava Ivanovna, she had read that too, but, in the first place, it was only now and again that Adya's mother was not herself, and, in the second place, the Rumanians were not as brutal as the Germans.

Adya was about to ask about his father as well, but Klava Ivanovna interrupted and changed the subject to Adya's future: since '42 the Lapidises' apartment had been occupied by the Panasyuk family from the village of Chervony Kut; the father and son had both been killed at the front and so the rest of the family could not be moved out; besides, the District Soviet would not grant a minor an authorization for the apartment. And so that meant one of two things: either Adya should stay with someone in the courtyard for a while, or, better still, enroll in a trade school to learn lathe work, metalwork, or plastering, and find a space in a dormitory. And he could attend the music school for young workers in the evening if he desired; in other words, it was all up to him. All doors were open. Olya Cheperukha began crying: if her Zyunchik were a few years younger, he'd be there with Adya and not freezing in some barracks in Siberia.

Adya expressed a desire to enroll in a trade school, to study lathe operation, especially since he had a little training in it already. Iona Ovseich wrote a recommendation that Adya be accepted for the dormitory as he had nowhere to live in Odessa.

Klava Ivanovna made Adya promise that he would come visit every Sunday. Adya gave his word and kept it for three Sundays in a row, then began skipping.

Right after New Year's Tosya Khomitsky received a photograph of Stepa and Kolka from Poland and a letter which the two of them had written together—half by the father, the other half by the son. Kolka had grown a mustache and it was difficult to recognize him right off. Everyone in the courtyard was astonished and said that it was a rare thing and a good sign for a father and son to meet like that: God was one thing but fate was another.

A week and a half later, Moscow saluted the troops of the First Belorussian Front who had liberated Warsaw, the capital of Poland. Two days later a notice arrived saying that Nikolai Stepanovich Khomitsky had died a hero's death fighting for the motherland. The mailman brought a letter from Kolka the next day but could not deliver it to Tosya: she had locked herself in her room, did not want to see anyone, and would not answer the door. Klava Ivanovna was afraid that Tosya would harm herself and suggested breaking down the door, but Iona Ovseich was categorically opposed: some people need total solitude in their grief.

Three days later Tosya opened her door and went to work, but she locked it again when she returned, and kept this up every day for a month.

Fenya Lebedev sympathized deeply with Tosya and couldn't get over it—the father was at the front for three and half years and he was still alive, while the son barely had time to button his uniform before he was in the next world. Hearing this, Madame Malaya asked Fenya to shut her mouth: people's hearts bled for the dead but they should rejoice for the living, and not contrast them one to the other.

On Red Army Day, February 23, Joseph Kotlyar stopped by Tosya's and gave her a present of two bars of scented soap from an American ship and a jar of stewed meat he had bought at Customs Square. Tosya embraced Joseph, they kissed, and they both wept loudly. Tosya swayed on her chair, striking her head against the wall. Joseph put his hand in the way to soften the blow.

There had been no letters from Anya for a long time. Her medical unit was now in Hungary, which already had its own provisional government and had declared war on Hitler, but suddenly, when it was least expected, there were reports of heavy fighting in the Lake Balaton region. A few days later Joseph learned that the Germans had apparently surrounded the Soviet troops near the city of Székesfehérvár, and though he had no grounds for this, he got it into his head that Anya had either already been killed or was being killed right at that very moment. Degtyar shamed him in front of others and asked how a cavalryman, who had personally known the legendary brigadier Grigory Ivanovich Kotovsky, could fall victim to such weakness and cowardice.

After the death of his second son, Joseph's left shoulder had begun twitching badly. Iona Ovseich said a person could live with a twitch like that for two hundred years, it wasn't a genuine ailment, just nerves. Joseph did not respond to that remark. Degtyar warned Klava Ivanovna that he didn't like Kotlyar's mental state and asked her to keep an eye on him.

Without letting Joseph know, Madame Malaya began checking with the military about Anya, but they had no information. She wrote a letter to the front commander, Marshal Malinovsky, and received a reply: Medical Lieutenant Anya Moiseevna Kotlyar had successfully undergone an operation for wounds to her jaw and face, and was making a rapid recovery at present.

"Oy, oy," said Klava Ivanovna, feeling weak in the knees, "but still it means you're alive, Annushka."

A reply came from the military office a week later. Madame

Malaya took the letter from front headquarters, which had been lying on her table for quite some time, and showed it to the military commissar of the Stalin District so that he could see what good work he and his office were doing.

Dr. Landa arrived out of the blue in mid-March, a colonel's three large stars on his epaulets. Olya Cheperukha said: "Wait and see, our Landa will make general yet."

People in the courtyard thought that Landa had been demobilized and had come home for good, but it turned out that he had been given ten days' leave to deal with his apartment in Odessa.

Landa and Iona Ovseich threw their arms around each other and kissed soldier-style, then Landa was given a well-deserved reproach: if he had only come to deal with his apartment, he shouldn't have bothered. It would have been enough to write to Degtyar, who would have taken care of everything, and just as well as Landa could have.

Semyon Alexandrovich laughed: why should Degtyar do it, if Landa could!

"That's true too," said Iona Ovseich, "especially since an artillery captain is obliged to obey a colonel, even if he is in the medical service."

"Degtyar," said Dr. Landa with a merry wink of the eye, "I'll tell you a secret: there are no stripes on the underpants we hand out in the hospital, not even for a field marshal of the artillery."

A smile playing on his lips, Iona Ovseich asked if Dr. Landa was still working in dermatology and related diseases?

No, said the doctor, with a chortle, he was a urologist now, but he still dealt with the "related diseases." Europe was Europe after all.

In Odessa, said Iona Ovseich, the Rumanians had also left a very painful legacy of that sort, and even though his factory did not produce food, he had still succeeded in organizing a medical checkup for the workers.

"Ovseich," said the colonel, "I can see that you still take everything onto yourself. That's bad for your health."

Iona Ovseich rubbed a button on his field shirt thoughtfully: if a person could ensure the health of the collective at the cost of his own, that was simple enough arithmetic, you'd think.

The colonel replied that he was with him two hundred percent but the difficulty lay in that simple arithmetic: it was not always clear if good would come of it or the other way around.

The colonel laughed and whacked Iona Ovseich on the back as if Degtyar had been caught in a trap.

"Dr. Landa," said Iona Ovseich, bending slightly forward, "when a squad is being sent out to do reconaissance, the commander plans the operation using simple arithmetic, so that it's clear that good will come of it and not the other way around, to use your expression. Of course, some casualties are inevitable, but we take those casualties deliberately and aren't afraid of them because we're well aware that good will come of them, and not the other way around."

The colonel thought for a moment, squinting as if from bright sunlight. Iona Ovseich was just about to smile at having gotten the last word when suddenly he met with a reply:

"Comrade Captain, allow me to point out that when a person works his whole life in medicine, he becomes used to thinking like a doctor. And in our work you can only hope that good will comes of what you do, because sometimes it's just the other way around."

Iona Ovseich spread his hands, sighed deeply, and said with a cunning look in his eye: "Landa, in '37 Lapidis was still living in this courtyard, and back then you cited the same sort of reasons. All those years have passed, you've been through the war with Hitler, do you mean to say the facts of history and life have produced no correction in your thinking?"

"Correction," said Colonel Landa, "isn't the right word. We've lost fifteen to twenty million people. When you deal with those who have remained alive, you have to keep that figure constantly in mind."

Iona Ovseich frowned. "I don't know where you got those figures. Comrade Stalin, the Supreme Commander in Chief, has not provided us with any such information. But, that aside, I'll say those figures must be kept in mind, but viewed from what angle, that's the real question."

"We're all Soviet people," replied Colonel Landa, "and we share a single ideology. My late father was a private businessman and in 1942, when Leningrad was freezing and dying from hunger in the blockade, his son was accepted in the party as a candidate member. I'm not alone in that—people like me number in the thousands, the millions."

Iona Ovseich kept striking his middle finger against the table after identical intervals. He threw his head back slightly to try to relieve the tension in his neck and said that he remembered old Landa well, there was no need to remind him. And he was well aware of how intent people were on joining the party before a battle because everyone wanted to die a Communist, but wartime is wartime and peacetime is peacetime, the two are not the same. After the Revolution and the Civil War, there were similar attempts by people, but life shows conclusively where such romanticism can lead in practice.

"Captain Degtyar," said Dr. Landa with a laugh, "you were a combat soldier at the front and that of course was a mistake on the part of our command: I would have put you at headquarters where they worked out strategy and left battlefield tactics to others."

Three days later Madame Era, who had taken over Colonel Landa's apartment on her own accord during the occupation, was moved out and the rightful tenant returned to his home. Gizella arrived from the city of Chimkent, which made Dina Vargaftik think of her own Grisha and she wept bitterly. Gizella, feeling a twinge of guilt despite herself justified her existence by saying that war didn't differentiate between a Semyon Landa and a Grisha Vargaftik, but Dina replied that whether it did or not, it still had taken her Grisha, who had been under fire while other people were working in hospitals.

"Some people are luckier than others," said Olya Cheperukha. "It's always like that. The rich only get richer."

These conversations made Klava Ivanovna profoundly indignant: you didn't have to like Gizella, and you could be envious of her, but it was wrong to be spiteful toward a person only because she had better luck than you did.

A day before his departure, Colonel Landa had a truck deliver two wooden beds, a good oak table, half a dozen chairs, and a large mirror; he took the wardrobe back from the concierge's apartment after Fenya Lebedev had informed him where it was. Three soldiers helped him carry the furniture.

Though not present himself, Iona Ovseich counted on his fingers the number of items Landa had had delivered and said straight out to Klava Ivanovna that, formally, Landa had the legal right to do so, but, from the moral point of view, he had to remember that there were people around who would see all this with their own eyes.

Two packages arrived from Stepa Khomitsky in Germany, both containing buttons, safety pins, and thread. There were various types of buttons—some for underwear, some for women's dresses, for jackets, overcoats, and many other items, some so fancy they could only be used by the circus. Tosya looked at those goods and said that you'd have to search long and hard to find another fool like her Stepa.

When Joseph Kotlyar saw the haberdashery shop that Khomitsky had sent home, he said: "Tosya, your Stepa's not such a fool. The war will be over in a little while, women will start sewing clothes for themselves, and those buttons will sell like hotcakes. And those pins and thread are worth their weight in gold today. If you don't feel like standing in Shchepny Row or the New Bazaar, find someone to take them off your hands. But, if you want my opinion, do it yourself—we're not rich enough to be feeding the speculators."

Joseph proved right. On her first Sunday off, Tosya went to the market and Shchepny Row and disposed of a hundred spools of thread in half a day. On the way home she bought some cow's butter, a pound of peasant sausage, a loaf of bread, and a quart of wine.

"Tosya," said Kotlyar with a wink, "all you're lacking now is a sexton in the storeroom."

Tosya drank a glass of wine and burst into laughter; she drank another glass and suddenly burst into tears: how could she eat that sausage, that butter, that bread, when her Kolka was rotting in the ground and would never sit at that table again, never lie on his bed facing the window, never kick the door when he came into the room? And how many times had they talked about that door—there was no one to paint it or fix it, but there were two good strong legs to break it!

Joseph began reminiscing about Pinya and Sasha and his shoulder began twitching badly. Tosya took his hand, stroked it, and asked what the doctors said. Then she poured the rest of the wine into their glasses, and said she hoped that those who were still alive today had seen the end of their grief.

During the week Tosya alternated trips to the market, the New Bazaar, and to the Old Horse Market, so that she would be less conspicuous and not give the police any reason to find fault with her. In the evening she would invite Joseph over. After the fourth or fifth time, Joseph was about to refuse, the wine was making him feel worse, but Tosya was offended and said she'd bought for two and now she would have to drink alone. Joseph gave in but on condition this was the last time.

A little after twelve o'clock Joseph got up to go home. Tosya stopped him, seated him on her bed, unstrapped his prothesis, but then said he should take off his pants himself. They both nearly overslept that morning. Joseph went out and knocked loudly at her door as if he had just arrived that minute. Tosya shouted she had no time now, he should drop by after work.

Joseph dropped by again on Saturday evening and spent a long time trying to convince Tosya not to drink but the evening proved a repeat of the previous one. The next morning they did not have to rush to work and slept for as long as they could keep their eyes closed. When they woke up, they didn't say anything for a while, just played with each other. Tosya laughed and said that Joseph must have cut quite a dashing figure in his youth, then added a bawdy remark. She said the same of her husband Stepa, who was now with all those German women in that lousy Germany but it wasn't as funny this time. Joseph pulled on his pants, hopped on one leg to the sink, picked up the soap, and shook his head: his poor Anya was killing herself in the hospital and didn't suspect a thing.

On Sunday Tosya sold five hundred safety pins; people were buying them by the dozen and some took two or three.

"Malaya," said Iona Ovseich, "remember what I told you about Tosya Khomitsky's merchant ways. Now you see it wasn't a chance remark."

Klava Ivanovna shrugged her shoulders: what was Tosya supposed to do with all that thread and pins—make a hair shirt or a shirt of mail out of them!

Iona Ovseich frowned. "A joke is a good thing in the right place but when it's out of place, it's not even a joke anymore."

It wasn't clear who started the gossip but soon the courtyard was buzzing about the ardent friendship that had suddenly sprung up between Khomitsky and Kotlyar. Dina Vargaftik make an apt remark about Joseph and many people repeated it: she said you might think he'd grown a new leg, he was prancing around like a rooster.

Klava Ivanovna invited Tosya to visit her and informed her of the talk that was going around. Tosya burst into tears and said, "Let them say whatever they will. I have nothing to feel guilty about."

"I believe you," said Madame Malaya, "but you should take some steps to keep from fueling that kind of talk."

Late that evening, Tosya had already closed the shutters when someone began knocking loudly at her door. Taken by surprise, Tosya began trembling and instead of opening the door right away, she stayed by the window. A minute later there was another knock at her door, this time with a hand and a foot. Tosya turned pale and ran to open the door but the key, as if on purpose, stuck in the lock.

"One minute!" cried Tosya, sticking a knife handle into the key ring. The key now made a turn and a half but the ring was bent out of shape.

"What's going on here?" said Klava Ivanovna with indignation in the doorway. "Why are you barricading yourself in here?"

Tosya showed her how badly bent the key ring was but Klava Ivanovna did not even look at it and began quickly pacing the room as if she were in a hurry and afraid of missing something.

"What are you looking for?" asked Tosya.

Klava Ivanovna did not answer the question but inquired why Tosya had closed her shutters when everyone else kept theirs open. Tosya explained that everything that went on in her apartment was clearly visible from the building across the way.

Klava Ivanovna grimaced. "And what goes on in your apartment that you have to hide?"

"What could go on here?" asked Tosya in reply.

"No," said Klava Ivanovna sternly, "answer me. What could be going on here? First there's talk in the courtyard about hanky-panky with Kotlyar, then your shutters are closed, then your door won't open. Too many things, Tosya. Until now I've been defending you to Degtyar, but now I'll have to take a closer look."

"You don't have to defend me," said Tosya. "Some defender! You spent almost three years in hiding after you were evacuated when you could have stayed here. There was no reason for you to return, we won't go under without you."

Klava Ivanovna was stunned for a moment and though she stood facing Tosya it seemed that she did not see her, or that she saw her but did not recognize her. Tosya's lips were curling as if she were on the verge of tears. Klava Ivanovna walked over to the window and opened the shutters. Pale moonlight fell onto the windowsill. She looked out—the buildings seemed under a spell, the last clumps of snow around the trees. She said in a soft voice: "God, what beautiful nights we have in Odessa." Feeling weak, Tosya lay down. Klava Ivanovna stood by the bed, touched Tosya's forehead, wished her good night, and walked away. She stopped again by the door where she stood in silence for a moment, then sighed deeply.

"You silly woman, I'm old and I understand everything. I'm not thinking about myself, what counts is that you're all right."

A day later when she came home from her shift, Tosya found a letter awaiting her: her husband's fellow patients in the hospital informed her that Stepa had stepped on a mine which the Krauts had set in the town of Shpremberg. He had been wounded and suffered a concussion but was out of danger now.

On Sunday Tosya put on her silk dress—almost brand new, she had bought it in '40 when Stepa had come home from the war in Finland and Bessarabia—white sandals, her watch, and went to the Church of the Assumption. The church was crowded, the air dim and stuffy; a cripple lay on a folding bed by the columns—only his head and eyes were visible and this she found disturbing. She moved to another place but still could feel those eyes on the back of her head. She rubbed her head a few times but the feeling did not go away.

Far in front, past the candelabras and the small candles, the iconostasis, a series of gilded rectangular frames containing images of Christ, his apostles, and the saints, loomed high above people's heads. The old man at the pulpit was replaced by a young man who in a bell-like bass voice wished long life to the leader of the people, the author of all our victories, Marshal Joseph Stalin, and to his Red Army, which had smashed the mortal enemy of the Russian land, the bloody Adolf Hitler. The choir picked up the refrain, their voices reverberating against the walls, rising to the cupola, and escaping through the open windows to Kirov and Red Army streets.

An old woman was selling candles by the church door, small ones for ten rubles apiece and large ones for twenty-five. Tosya bought two large candles, one in memory of her son Nikolai and the other for the safe recovery of her husband Stepa. Then in the church porch she recounted her money, turned around and bought two small candles—

for all those she did not know by sight or by name but who had been alongside her son and her husband. She gave her remaining rubles and change to beggars; some thanked her, others took the money without saying a word and then extended their hand again.

In the bread store, the salesgirl had already punched Tosya's ration coupon and weighed her bread when Tosya remembered that she didn't have a kopeck in her pocket. The salesgirl became angry, took back the bread, and threw the bread-card coupon back at Tosya.

Meeting Tosya in the courtyard, Klava Ivanovna inquired if there had been many people in church today. Tosya was surprised that Madame Malaya knew where she had been, but Madame Malaya said that one look at her face had been enough to know where she was going and what she was doing. Though there had been no reproach in Klava Ivanovna's words, Tosya said in her own defense that she had gone for no special reason, her heart had just been heavy, that was all.

"No atheists in foxholes," said Klava Ivanovna with a sigh. "The priests know the right time to catch people and bring them back into the church."

Tosya replied that no one had caught her or brought her back but Klava Ivanovna just shook her head and smiled bitterly: the priests didn't have to go to each person individually, the very fact that churches and monasteries existed was enough. "During the years of Soviet power, people had forgot how the priests had robbed the people and drunk their blood along with the tsars and the landowners, and now we have to start all over from Adam and Eve."

Olya Cheperukha received a telegram at around ten o'clock in the evening. She almost fainted when she opened it and saw that it was from her son. Zyunchik informed her of his new address, which was only a series of numbers. Olya ran upstairs to Degtyar's to get some idea where her son had been sent. Iona Ovseich made it quite clear that since Zyunchik himself had not indicated the address that meant he was not allowed to, but he personally was of the opinion that the Soviets had entirely enough troops in Germany and there was no sense in sending young officers fresh out of school there.

A letter arrived from Zyunchik a few days later. He did not say where he was but he asked if Olya remembered how much he had wanted a pet tiger of his own when he was a boy. He had wanted everybody in Odessa to be afraid of him and run when they saw him coming with his tiger. And now, just yesterday, he had met a man who had caught three tigers singlehandedly and sold them to a zoo.

"My God," exclaimed Olya, turning hot then cold, "Zyunchik's somewhere in India!"

Iona Ovseich read the letter closely twice even though he had understood Zyunchik's allusion as to his whereabouts after the first reading, since, beside the tigers, there was also mention of the surprisingly beautiful vegetation which was southern, like that of the Caucasus, and also northern, like that in the tundra, near the Arctic Circle.

"Cheperukha," said Iona Ovseich, "I can't be certain that your Zinovy is in India specifically, but at least Germany is in the exact opposite direction."

Olya was carefree and lighthearted for an entire week but then something possessed her to brag to Gizella Landa that her son Zyunchik was already an officer and had been transferred to India on special assignment.

Gizella was very surprised. "How do you know about it if he's on special assignment?"

Olya smiled, reached into the front of her dress, and pulled out the letter. While Gizella was reading the letter, Olya explained that Zyunchik was no fool and had managed to say everything and nothing all at the same time.

It truly was very delicately written, agreed Gizella. Personally, she had never suspected Zinovy of any such diplomatic talent, but all the signs seemed to point not to India but to the Soviet Far East, somewhere near Korea or Manchuria, which were now under Japanese rule.

"The Japanese!" said Olya with indignation. "What do the Japanese have to do with anything!"

Gizella shrugged her shoulders: every schoolchild knew that India was subtropical, even tropical, while the only place whose flora was both southern and northern, and, in addition, had tigers, was the Ussuri region of the U.S.S.R.

"And even you must know where the Ussuri region is," added Gizella.

Olya replied that she was not as educated as certain other ladies and had the right not to know such things because she had been working from dawn to dusk her entire life, and had not had any spare time for reading books.

"Olechka, why are you getting angry?" said Gizella. "Maybe I'm wrong and you're right."

No, said Olya, suddenly beginning to weep, now she realized that she had been deceiving herself and inventing stories about India. Of course, Zyunchik was in the Far East, the Japanese were there, and they were capable of the lowest tricks.

"What are you talking about!" said Gizella with a laugh. "If the Japanese were afraid of us in '42, and '43, fighting us now would be suicidal for them. We're not like the Americans. We'll smash them to bits in ten days."

Gizella's argument was correct and Olya would have said the same thing in her place but a lot could happen in the ten days they were smashing the Japanese to bits and no one could see even one second into the future and guarantee that Zyunchik would come out of it safe and sound. Iona Cheperukha had been at the front from the very first day of the war and had been wounded five times. Now he was taking part in the offensive in Czechoslovakia and death was on every side, but she had never worried like that about him. And those Americans and English, those bastards, were used to having other people doing their dirty work for them. They'd be messing around with the Japanese for another ten years until our Soviet men took over the job and did to the Japanese what they'd done to Hitler.

Olya kept saying this over and over again everywhere she went until finally Iona Ovseich had to issue her a serious warning to curtail her provocative remarks about the war with Japan, otherwise she would be held accountable under the laws of wartime.

With a crazed look in her eyes, Olya asked in a very thin voice: "Comrade Degtyar, you tell me, a mother, the truth: will the Japanese surrender soon or are those rotten Americans just waiting for us to sacrifice our own children?"

"Cheperukha," said Iona Ovseich, "I'll say it again: stop this talk about the war with Japan. Our chief task right now is to trap Hitler in his own lair, and everything else is secondary."

Olya burst into tears. "If you had a son of your own, Comrade Degtyar, you wouldn't treat this so lightly."

Iona Ovseich reminded her that he had had two sons, and that he had lost them both during the most critical period for Soviet power when hunger and typhus reigned throughout the country.

Yes, said Olya, she knew that, but could you really compare what happened almost twenty-five years ago with what was happening today. Iona Ovseich gazed pensively off in the distance, lost in thought. He sighed deeply and cited the example of his own wife, Polina Isaevna, who had almost lost her mind back then and had come down with active tuberculosis; it was a miracle she survived but she had never lost her humanity.

"Comrade Degtyar," said Olya, "I know all that, but that was twenty-four years ago and there's been a lot of water under the bridge since then, and we're talking about today, this minute."

"Cheperukha," replied Iona Ovseich, "a mother's love is a sacred thing but there is something even more sacred, love for the motherland, for the Soviet state, and a mother's love cannot be allowed to turn into a mother's blindness. That can lead you very far astray."

Olya listened attentively to every word Comrade Degtyar spoke, tension causing deep creases to form in her forehead; all the same, it was difficult to understand, which she admitted, then said for a third time that it was impossible to compare what happened then with what was happening today—that had come and gone but this was here and now.

"The weather makes old scars ache," said Iona Ovseich. "Believe me, Cheperukha, the weather makes old scars ache."

Soviet troops took Berlin on May 2. Olya told everyone there would be complete peace in a day or two. She was certain that, now that they had inflicted a crushing defeat on Hitler, there was no reason for the Japanese to continue the war; they would have to agree to an unconditional surrender. So not to miss any news, Olya never turned the radio off and would often wake up in the middle of the night, having heard call signals indicating that important announcements would be broadcast from Moscow.

On May 8, the Germans capitulated. The terms of the surrender were ratified by the German High Command and signed by Field Marshal General von Keitel, Admiral General von Friedeburg, and Colonel General Paul Stumpf, in the presence of the commander in chief of the Red Army, Marshal of the Soviet Union Zhukov, a representative of the Allied Expeditionary Forces, Air Marshal Tedder, commander of the Strategic Air Force of the United States, General

Spaatz, and the commander in chief of the French Army, General De Lattre de Tassigny.

May 9 was designated Victory Day and Comrade Stalin addressed the nation. In the evening, after the guns were fired in salute, Iona Ovseich assembled all the courtyard's residents in the open air and read Stalin's speech a second time so that not only the grown-ups, and not only their children, but their grand children and great-grandchildren would never forget the words spoken by the leader of all peoples and the military commander of genius, Comrade Stalin:

" 'The great day of victory over Germany has come . . . The great sacrifices borne by us in the name of our motherland's freedom and independence, the innumerable hardships and suffering which our people have undergone during the course of the war, the intense efforts that were made in the rear and at the front and offered up on the altar of the fatherland, have not been in vain. The Slavic people's age-old struggle for their existence and their independence has concluded in victory over the German invaders and over German tyranny. From now on, the great banner of the freedom of nations and peace between nations will wave over Europe.' "

People congratulated each other again, they hugged and kissed as passionately as if they had not seen each other for a thousand years. Tosya Khomitsky went back to her apartment; Kotlyar stayed on for a while then he too left. Suddenly Dina Vargaftik became hysterical, raising her hands over her head and asking her Grisha to look down from heaven to see people rejoicing.

After the salute was fired, Olya Cheperukha walked over to Iona Ovseich and asked him to explain something: Comrade Stalin had said that the war in Europe was over and there would be peace there now, but he had not said anything about the Far East; so that must mean that the Germans had surrendered but the Japanese hadn't.

Iona Ovseich placed his hand on her shoulder and pulled her close to him. Yes, he said, the Germans had surrendered and the Japanese hadn't, but that was only a matter of time now, not a question of who would win. Olya said that we shouldn't worry about it then, let Churchill and the Americans fight the Japanese by themselves and we would open a second front for them like the one they opened for us.

Comrade Degtyar smiled: in her own way Olya Cheperukha was right—we were different from the Americans and Churchill.

VI

On August 23, the Kwantung Army, composed of thirty-one infantry divisions, and eleven brigades, two of which were tank brigades, surrendered. Five hundred and ninety-four thousand soldiers and officers were taken prisoner. The Japanese had suffered thirty thousand casualties. The Red Army occupied Manchuria and the major cities of Mukden, Changchun, Port Arthur, Girin, Kharbin, and also North Korea, with the cities of Yuki, Rashin, Seishin, and Genzan.

On September 2, as a speaker read Comrade Stalin's address to the nation in connection with the victory over imperialist Japan, a day the peoples of Russia had been awaiting for forty years, since 1905, Iona Ovseich, Klava Ivanovna, and many other of the building's residents dropped by to see Olya Cheperukha to congratulate her personally: Zinovy Cheperukha was the only one in the entire courtyard who had participated in the war against the Japanese.

Olya exchanged kisses with each person, wiped her lips, and kissed them again. Then everyone left except Iona Ovseich and Klava Ivanovna. Olya brewed strong tea and set out six lumps of sugar and a kilo of good apples on the table. Klava Ivanovna gave Olya a present of two bottles of fruit liqueur, apricot and cherry. Iona Ovseich spread his hands: no one knew if the war was really over yet and people were already feasting as they had before the war. They each drank a small glassful, Iona Ovseich diluting his with a little water. Olya Cheperukha said that on an occasion like this he should drink it straight, then she suddenly burst into tears.

"All right then, Cheperukha," said Iona Ovseich, merrily smacking the table, "who was right about Japan—you or me! If we had done things your way, the Americans would control Manchuria and Korea today. They would have restored the capitalist system, and have placed the Red Chinese Army in a terribly difficult position."

Olya continued crying, confessing that her heart was heavy as if something had just that moment happened to Zyunchik.

"Don't be so superstitious!" said Klava Ivanovna. "A person should always keep hoping and believe things will turn out all right. Especially since the war is behind us now."

Once again Olya said that her heart was heavy and that she felt like screaming.

"Cheperukha," said Iona Ovseich, "you haven't answered my question yet—who was right?"

Olya wiped away her tears and Madame Malaya answered for her that Comrade Degtyar had been entirely right; otherwise the Soviets wouldn't have such strong positions in the Far East today, not to mention the Red Chinese Army, which, in the course of one month, had found itself in a better position than it had held in ten years; the day was not far off when we would see Soviet power throughout all of China.

"Cheperukha," said Iona Ovseich, "you should be proud of having a person like our Madame Malaya in your home and to be drinking tea with her at the same table."

In mid-September Olya received word from Zyunchik that, in the battle for the city of Dairen, he had lost his right leg, a little below the knee, actually not in the battle itself but later on in the hospital when gangrene had set in as a result of a wound from a dumdum bullet. Olya's voice sounded like a man's as she shouted from unbearable emotion. She tore at her hair and kept saying that her hair had gone as gray as a hundred-year-old woman's. Tosya Khomitsky sat beside Olya and said that she wished her Kolka had lost both his legs, if only he could have come home. Olya did not respond to that but demanded to see Degtyar and Klava Ivanovna so that she could hear them say one more time that a mother's premonitions were only foolish superstition.

Iona Ovseich visited Olya that evening to try to lift her spirits a little but she began tearing her hair again, shouting that she didn't care about Japan or Manchuria, she wanted her son to have two arms and two legs, as he had when she gave birth to him and not to be a cripple on crutches.

"Cheperukha," said Iona Ovseich tenderly, "a mother's heart is a mother's heart and we understand. But sometimes, in his grief, a person can say more than he should."

In reply Olya told Iona Ovseich that he should find a woman like that, and go to hell with her. And there was no need to threaten her: as long as a person was alive and intended to live a long time he could be scared, but when death came scratching at his door every night, he didn't have any reason to be afraid anymore.

Iona Ovseich shook his head: there was no reason for fear here; she should just think about what she was saying.

Cheperukha lay down on the couch, closed her eyes, and in a soft voice asked Iona Ovseich to leave; she was in no mood for listening to his political lectures today, her heart was in too much pain. Iona Ovseich rose and, when leaving, said that he bore Olya no grudge, on the contrary, he had nothing but compassion for her; they'd return to that conversation sometime later on.

A week later another letter arrived from Zyunchik: for a few days the doctors had feared it would be necessary to cut off a little more of his leg above the knee, there had been symptoms of necrosis, but all the danger had now passed and he was healing quickly. He had been shown special care by Katya Tukaev, a laboratory assistant from the town of Ulan-Ude, who had sat by his bedside for days on end.

"My God," said Olya, bracing herself against the wall, "now I'm supposed to be happy that my son didn't lose even more of his leg."

"No," said Klava Ivanovna, "now you should be happy that your son is returning home with the woman he's going to marry."

Madame Malaya proved a good prophet: three days later Zyunchik wrote to his mother that his wife Katerina was proposing that he take up permanent residence in Ulan-Ude in the Buryat-Mongolian A.S.S.R., but all he wanted to do was return to Odessa. Katya said that they could have a whole house to themselves in Ulan-Ude, but in Odessa they'd have to live with his parents, two families to one room.

That same evening Olya wrote back to Zyunchik saying that his father, mother, and he himself had all been born in Odessa, had lived their whole lives in Odessa, and would die there when the time came, but if someone preferred Ulan-Ude, he should go live there, she wasn't opposed.

"Olya," said Klava Ivanovna, "I swear on my life that no one but us two will ever read this letter. At a hard time in his life the boy found a friend and now you want to destroy all that in one second. If I hadn't seen you go off to the maternity clinic and come home with a son, I'd have thought you were the boy's stepmother, and not his own natural mother."

It's a stepmother who would let them both go off to the ends of the earth, answered Olya, but she wanted Zyunchik to return to Odessa and find himself a good wife with respectable parents here.

"Hold on," said Klava Ivanovna, "what gives you the right to speak that way? Zyunchik is already a family man."

"What do you mean, a family man?" said Olya with indignation. "They couldn't have gotten married during the five days he was in the hospital. She was only his mistress during the war."

For a moment Klava Ivanovna was speechless. Olya took advantage of her silence to cite the example of her own Iona, who could also have found himself a woman and then thought he should bring her to Odessa and kick out his wife with whom he'd lived for twenty years.

"Cheperukha," said Klava Ivanovna, entwining her fingers and squeezing them tightly together, "you're surprising me more than I've ever been surprised. Your son lost a leg in the war and at that terrible time a wonderful girl from the town of Ulan-Ude fell in love with him and they got married, and now all of a sudden his own mother is barring his way, acting worse than a witch."

"That's right," agreed Olya, "I'm worse than a witch, but I want my son to chose a wife for himself in Odessa so we'll know what kind of family she comes from, and the fact that he lost a leg doesn't concern anyone, the only one that hurts is him—and his mother."

Klava Ivanovna sighed, read the letter again, crossed out the line about Ulan-Ude—then sealed the letter saying she was going right by a mailbox and would mail it herself.

Olya put a hand across her face and began crying: why did everyone do what he wanted, why wasn't anyone willing to give in to her, while she had to spend her whole life giving in to other people—her son, some girl named Katya from Ulan-Ude, Madame Malaya, and everyone else who crossed her path.

On her way back, by the gate, Klava Ivanovna met a woman from the post office delivering an express telegram for Kotlyar but the woman didn't know the apartment number.

Klava Ivanovna read the telegram and handed the woman a ruble. "You don't need the number. Anya is coming back after four years at the front."

Klava Ivanovna ran up the spiral staircase to the third floor where she shouted: "Dance, Kotlyar, dance!" But when she opened the door, she froze in the doorway—there was Anya right before her very eyes.

"Annushka!" said Klava Ivanovna, feeling weak in the knees. "Annushka!"

Anya took a step toward her, extending her hand to greet her. There was a noticeable cavity on the left side of her jaw. Without meaning to, Klava Ivanovna let her eyes linger there a moment, then rushed to throw her arms around Anya and clasp her tightly. Anya stood there for a moment, then carefully removed herself from the embrace. Klava Ivanovna took half a step back, looked closely at Anya again, then said: "Anya, I swear by my life, you're just as beautiful as ever. Even more beautiful."

Joseph was standing beside Anya and asked her to tell Madame Malaya what he had said, which was word for the word the same as Malaya.

"Joseph," said Anya, rudely interrupting him, "decency demands that an outsider lie about such things, but it's disgusting when your own husband does it. I'm tired, I want to sleep. Madame Malaya, you should drop by another time."

"Anya," said Klava Ivanovna, extending her hands as if requesting something, "it's been so many years since I've seen you. This is a very special day for me!"

Anya repeated that she was tired and badly wanted to sleep. Madame Malaya should drop by another time.

Klava Ivanovna said good-bye, closed the door tightly, and had only managed to take two or three steps when she heard Anya's voice plaintively calling for her sons Sasha and Petya. When they didn't respond she threatened that they would regret it.

"Annushka," moaned Joseph loudly, "please, don't. There's no help for us. When a person's dead, he's dead forever."

Anya called out to Sasha and Petya again. Klava Ivanovna felt that she was going out of her mind and waited with horror for Anya to call out for her sons a third time. A minute passed, then another. Anya cursed herself vilely for what she had done in the summer of '40—a person had to have the heart of a wild beast to have postponed going to see her own children at a time like that! But she did not call out to her sons again.

Iona Ovseich said that they should arrange a meeting between the women of the building and the front-line soldier Anya Kotlyar: that would be helpful to Anya's own morale and to the other women as well.

When she was informed of this, Anya flatly refused: first, hundreds of thousands, millions of Soviet women had been at the front, second, she didn't want to hear what other people had to say and she didn't want to say anything herself.

"Lieutenant Kotlyar," said Iona Ovseich, closing his eyes, "you think that now, since we've achieved victory, everyone can just let his nerves go. That's an unforgivable mistake on your part. Peacetime has its own problems, and no less than there were at the front."

Anya replied that she could see a clear difference between the two and asked that she be left alone. Comrade Degtyar would be better off looking for propagandists and activists among other people, those who still had their health and strength.

"All right," said Iona Ovseich, "you can follow the dictates of your conscience but for our part we're going to announce a meeting between the women of our building and the front-line soldier, Anya Kotlyar."

It turned out as Iona Ovseich had said it would. Advance notice was given about the meeting, which was to be held on Sunday in the premises of the former outpost. The day before, through Joseph, Anya informed Comrade Degtyar and Madame Malaya that not only would she not attend the meeting in the outpost but would not be home at all. Iona Ovseich said that he would take that into consideration, but added, for anyone who might have forgotten, that there was an old proverb which said that if the mountain would not go to Muhammed, then Muhammed would go to the mountain.

On Sunday, at first light, Anya dressed and quietly left her apartment. His face in the pillow, Joseph was sleeping like the dead. Klava Ivanovna dropped by a little later to wish the Kotlyars a good morning but the words never left her mouth; she could sense with her entire body that Joseph was home alone with no idea where his wife had gone and when she would return. To be entirely sure, Madame Malaya demanded that Joseph swear on his life that he really did not have any idea where she was. Instead of swearing, Joseph clutched his head and a tear rolled from his right eye as he shouted that Anya had gone to Lanzheron to drown herself: for three days straight all she had been thinking about and talking about was death.

"You old idiot," cried Klava Ivanovna, "how could you keep silent about that and not inform anyone!"

Klava Ivanovna's legs turned cold from horror: she had a sudden vision of all the building's tenants festively dressed on their way to meet with the front-line soldier Anya Kotlyar, who was lying in the outpost dead, her face blue and her stomach swollen like any drowned person.

When Madame Malaya brought this shocking news to Iona Ovseich, he was sitting at the table and enjoying a hot breakfast which Polina Isaevna had made for him on his day off and which consisted of potatoes cooked in their skins with onions and herring, and barley fritters with jam on top. Only the heads of the herrings were left, lying on a pile of potato skins. Iona Ovseich had just started on the fritters.

"Malaya," said Iona Ovseich, "stop panicking and try the fritters."

Klava Ivanovna replied that she did not have nerves of steel like him, and the first bite she took would stick in her throat.

"Malaya," repeated Iona Ovseich, "stop panicking and try the fritters: they're good for calming the nerves."

Polina Isaevna, who had not interfered until then, groaned softly and shed a few tears: in 1921 when both their sons had died of dystrophia, Degtyar had also sat there with a stony face and God only knew what people thought of him; then he spent the whole night walking the city alone, and she gave up hope of ever seeing him alive again.

"Malaya," said Iona Ovseich, "stop panicking, and sit down with us at the table. Sweets are good for the nerves."

Klava Ivanovna picked up a fritter with her bare hands, and took a sip of tea. Iona Ovseich compressed his lips, his eyes moving from his guest to his wife. Polina Isaevna instinctively lowered her head and said that if her husband was so calm, that meant everything would turn out all right.

Madame Malaya finished her fritter. Iona Ovseich closed his eyes for a few seconds, then asked, seeming to be addressing himself, how a person who had been through all the trials of war and the front line could suddenly lose heart and commit suicide.

Klava Ivanovna sighed deeply: "Every person experiences moments when he forgets who he is."

"But, Malaya, do many people put an end to their lives? Don't use the example of Orlov. I haven't forgotten how you ran around to all the morgues."

Klava Ivanovna honestly admitted that, as far as she could remember, she knew no one who had committed suicide though they might have threatened to more than once, but, on the other hand, once a person had laid hands on himself, it was too late to shout for help.

All right, said Iona Ovseich, hitting his knee, let's stop arguing the point. He asked both Madame Malaya and Polina Isaevna to find the patience to wait until six o'clock, when the meeting was scheduled.

"Oh, Degtyar," moaned Klava Ivanovna, "where can I find nerves and a head like yours?"

"Malaya," said Iona Ovseich, wagging a finger threateningly, "everyone has nerves, and everyone has a head, the point is not to lose it."

Somehow or other Klava Ivanovna held out until four o'clock but then was unable to sit still for another second: first she stood either by the window or the gate, and then she ran to Kotlyar, Dina Vergaftik, Cheperukha, or Tosya Khomitsky. Klava Ivanovna shared what she knew with Dina but the others could only guess what the trouble was. It was not yet six o'clock when people began gathering in the outpost and a rumor began spreading: early that morning, when it was still dark, Anya Kotlyar had gone off somewhere and had not yet returned.

Klava Ivanovna attacked Dina Vargaftik, calling her a blabbermouth and a gossip monger. Dina's feelings were hurt so badly that she wept and said that if her Grisha were still alive no one would dare insult her like that, but since Grisha was only dust now, people could do whatever they wanted to her.

Iona Ovseich arrived at six o'clock, ordered that the audience be silent, and then solemnly announced: "The meeting between the women and other residents of our building and Anya Kotlyar, who served at the front as a lieutenant in the medical corps, is now declared open."

People shrugged but Iona Ovseich had foreseen that reaction and, in order not to waste time, he proposed that all those participating in the meeting recall the general outline of Lieutenant Anya Kotlyar's life—an ordinary Soviet woman, homemaker, mother, and wife, until the war, which was how many of those there today knew her. Then he moved on to the turning point in her remarkable life story when she liberated herself entirely from her husband, whose views of women had retained certain medieval qualities. Here Iona Ovseich was compelled to pause because loud whispers had erupted in the audience.

"Comrades," said Iona Ovseich in calm warning, "anyone who doesn't like this can leave or, if need be, can be shown the door."

Olya Cheperukha laughed and asked why the woman of the day had not appeared or at least sent her husband in her place.

"What makes Degtyar any worse than her husband?" said Dina loudly and with indignation.

"Dina," said Klava Ivanovna, calling her to order, "stop your foolish jokes!"

Dina shrugged her shoulders and looked embarrassed. Iona Ovseich raised one hand calling on people to act in an orderly and civilized manner because it had been fifteen years since the Old Bazaar had closed. Just then a miracle occurred; as if it had been arranged beforehand, the woman of the day, Lieutenant Anya Kotlyar, walked into the outpost.

Klava Ivanovna felt as if she had been struck in the back of the head by a rock, her legs turned to jelly, and it was a good thing that Fenya Lebedev was there to lend her a hand. Olya brought over a little bottle of ammonia, which she held to Klava Ivanovna's nose. She opened her eyes and her first words were to Anya Kotlyar: "You bastard, how could you allow yourself to make people worry so much!"

Anya gazed at Madame Malaya for a second, then walked to the table where Comrade Degtyar was sitting and sat down beside him without saying a word, as if she were a stranger there.

"Dear neighbors," said Iona Ovseich, "the short break is over, now let's get on with the job. I'll go back to where we stopped: having freed herself from the influence of her husband whose views on women were somewhat medieval, Anya Kotlyar enrolled in medical courses, was trained as a nurse, and applied the knowledge given her by the state directly at the front lines during the war against the Nazis. Her spirit was not broken by losing two sons and she continued to fight the enemy until the very end when Soviet soldiers planted the banner of victory on top of the Reichstag and Hitler's generals had accepted and signed a complete and unconditional surrender. Now, some people in the West are trying to rewrite history, saying it wasn't the Red Army, but the Allied Expeditionary Forces in North Africa, at Tobruk, who created the real turning point in the war, but the people have long since replied to those pseudohistorians, or, to be more precise, those falsifiers, with a proverb: the hen sleeps and dreams of millet."

"But Anya Kotlyar and I," interrupted Klava Ivanovna, "would put it another way—their bark is worse than their bite!"

Iona Ovseich had no objection to that but lay special stress on the fact that words were not what mattered here, and time would soon make everything abundantly clear.

When she was given the floor, Anya Kotlyar flatly refused to give a speech, saying that she was in complete agreement with Comrade Degtyar, who himself had been at the front where he had been wounded twice. And, as people knew, she had spent Victory Day in the hospital. She was certain that everyone would understand her as a mother when she said that she had no desire to go on living and wanted to die so she could be with her sons.

Klava Ivanovna quickly pushed the water pitcher and a black glass made from the lower half of a bottle over to Anya but there was no need for that: Anya sat down in her chair, pushed the glass aside, and placed her hands palms down on the table. The women in the audience wept softly, wiping their tears away with their fingers.

"Comrades," said Iona Ovseich, his voice heavy, "we came here today to meet with a soldier who had been at the front and what we have seen is a mother's terrible grief which leaves scars that will never heal. And this is no accident. We know of millions of examples in which mother and soldier, mother and warrior, were united in one person. On behalf of the building's activists, I make a motion that we elect a women's soviet and that its first chairperson be the former Soviet Army lieutenant Anya Kotlyar."

Iona Ovseich's motion met with unanimous applause. Klava Ivanovna congratulated the new chairperson of the women's soviet, kissed her, and pressed her cheek to Anya's. Then the other women came up to Anya, congratulated her, and pressed their cheeks to hers. Anya held on for the entire time and only at the end, when no one any longer expected it, did she suddenly cover her face with her hands.

Dina Vargaftik once again mentioned her own Grisha, who had long since turned to dust, and said, "Time will pass, little by little you'll forget, life goes on. The most important thing is that a person doesn't feel all alone in the world."

The next day Joseph Kotlyar made a point of seeing Comrade Degtyar and shaking his hand: Anya had not let him fall asleep until the middle of the night discussing her plans for the women's soviet.

The following day Anya took a job at city hospital. A few days later Adya Lapidis returned to take up permanent residence in the courtyard: the Kotlyars had allocated him one of their two rooms and had taken full responsibility for his care. For his part, Iona Ovseich promised to intercede with the Stalin District Executive Committee to make the adoption legal.

Polina Isaevna, who was suffering from her tuberculosis again, wiped her tears on her pillow and said what wonderful people we live among without even noticing it. Joseph Kotlyar brought her a dozen eggs: friends of his from the country, not far from Varvarovka, on the other side of the Nikolaev Bridge, had brought him four dozen, and so why not figure that they'd only brought three dozen.

"Joseph, forget it. We're not beggars," said Polina Isaevna indignantly.

"Eat the eggs and get better to spite your enemies," said Joseph.

"Enemies," said Polina Isaevna with a bitter smile, "I have no enemies. My greatest enemy is the Bacillus Kochii. But if you have so many friends around you what's a puny bacterial infection?"

When Iona Ovseich learned about the eggs, he warned Joseph that he had no need of presents, he was paid a salary, not at market but at state prices. Polina Isaevna told her husband that eggs were fifteen to twenty times higher than state prices, which made the whole thing a ridiculous comedy.

"Polina," said Iona Ovseich, smacking his hand against the table, "I will not allow anyone to say in my presence that state prices are a ridiculous comedy!"

Polina Isaevna shrugged her shoulders: Degtyar hadn't understood what she meant.

"No, my dear Polina Isaevna," said Iona Ovseich, whacking the table a second time, "I understand you. It's you who doesn't understand me."

Advances were paid on the fifth of the month and the first thing Iona Ovseich did was to repay his debt to the Kotlyars.

"With that money," said Polina Isaevna, sticking to her guns, "plus a little of his own, he could buy half an egg."

Iona Ovseich restrained himself this time, saying only that a teacher of arithmetic, especially one sick in bed, should do her division and multiplication in her head, otherwise she'd lose her qualifications.

Polina Isaevna began weeping and said that she understood—who would want to look after a sick wife all the time, she'd be better off dead.

"You don't need to die," said Iona Ovseich. "What you need is a pneumothorax, not to abandon yourself to the mercy of fate."

Polina Isaevna sighed: her devoted husband had forgotten that she had had one done before the war.

"Arithmetic again!" said Iona Ovseich with a laugh. "Polina, you've got to take care of yourself."

In the middle of the month, Joseph's friends from outside Nikolaev came to see him again and he bought a kilo of cow's butter from them. Anya cut off a good-sized piece of it and brought it herself to Polina Isaevna.

"If Iona finds out," said Polina Isaevna, pressing her hands to her heart, "he'll kill me on the spot."

Anya said she shouldn't worry about that. She should eat the butter and improve her health. Talking about it wasn't going to put any meat on her bones.

A week and a half later Adya brought Polina Isaevna a huge piece of a puff-pastry pie covered with thick cream. Polina Isaevna tried to refuse it but Adya said that he had just been accepted into the evening music school for working youth and his Aunt Anya was in seventh heaven. All right, said Polina Isaevna, giving in, then they should share the pie together, half the piece for her and half for him. She told him to get the bottle of cherry brandy and two glasses from the chest of drawers. Adya brought only one glass, saying that he didn't like cherry brandy, it was too sweet and tickled his throat.

"You don't like cherry brandy?" said Polina Isaevna in surprise. "So then take some apricot or plum liqueur."

Adya sat without budging, his eyes lowered. Polina Isaevna peered intently at him for a moment, then suddenly burst into tears: she understood, he was afraid that her disease was infectious. He just shouldn't lie and try to make her feel better.

Adya did not try to console her. He said that it was time for him to leave or else he might be late for music school.

Now Anya Kotlyar had a new worry: Adya needed a piano and she asked her neighbors to find out if anyone had one for sale. Price was no obstacle, she'd use her last kopeck to pay for it. Iona Ovseich found a short-term solution: there was a piano in the "Red Corner" of his factory and Adya was given special permission to use it twice a week when there were no meetings there. Anya thanked him for this but kept asking how a David Oistrakh or an Emil Gilels was supposed to come out of conditions like that. Iona Ovseich disliked that rhetorical question and urged Anya Kotlyar to pay close attention to what she was saying.

It was getting on toward winter, and one day when a fine drizzle-like snow had begun falling, a flat cart pulled up to the gate carrying an upright piano, its top and sides covered with a horse cloth. The driver and his helper, both of whom had canvas harnesses slung over their shoulders, picked up the piano from either side, swaying a little like longshoremen on gangplanks. They walked up to the entrance, both moving carefully so as not to lose their footing, and began carrying the piano up to the third floor. While they were carrying it, Olya Cheperukha stood down below and Dina Vargaftik up above, both of them helping the two men keep in the right direction. Anya ran on ahead to open the door.

As they were rolling the piano down the corridor, the old casters, which hadn't had to move once in the last fifty years, squealed something terrible; it sounded like every woman in the building was giving birth at the same time. Dina spoke up, "These days anyone can give birth but not everyone can get ahold of a piano. For that you need a husband like Joseph."

"Dina," said Anya Kotlyar, "I don't look into your pot to see what's cooking."

"Take a look if you want," answered Dina. "You won't find a piano in there."

That evening Degtyar had a conversation with Klava Ivanovna about the new purchase: how did Joseph come up with that amount of money, enough to pay for a piano? They should find out exactly how much he earned at the Lenin factory, even though you could be certain in advance that the piano cost at least three or four thousand rubles more.

"How did he come up with the money?" Klava Ivanovna repeated the question. "I'll tell you. In the first place, Anya brought some back with her from Hungary. In the second place, Joseph does a little cobbling at home at night."

Iona Ovseich thought for a moment, then said that the two items should have been reversed—in the first place, Joseph does a little moonlighting at home, and all the rest should be in the second place. That brings up another question: where does he get the leather and other raw material?

Klava Ivanovna said that Joseph did not get any leather or other raw materials from anywhere, he cut strips from torn footwear that an old man brought him.

"But what about the soles, the vamps, the counters, and insteps?" asked Iona Ovseich with a laugh.

"Degtyar," said Klava Ivanovna, "I've seen the old man who brings Joseph the bags of old torn shoes and slippers."

"Malaya," said Iona Ovseich, grasping his nose with two fingers as if he were preparing to blow his nose, "at the front we used all sorts of camouflage uniforms, white in the winter and yellow with green spots in the summer. And we decorated the tanks and artillery with branches from trees but those decorations weren't to make them beautiful."

"Do you think I'm a fool!" said Klava Ivanovna indignantly. "You mean to say that the old man with the sacks is just for decoration while in fact Joseph has other sources. I'll tell you my answer to that —no, no, no!"

Polina Isaevna, who had been sleeping or just pretending to, now demanded that her husband and Madame Malaya stop their stupid arguing: those people had adopted an orphan, clothed and fed him, bought him an expensive instrument so the boy could develop his talent, and, instead of respecting them for that, the two of them sat there quibbling about where the money came from. He didn't steal it and he didn't kill for it, so what business was it of theirs!

Iona Ovseich paused to prolong the silence, then said calmly, as if speaking to himself: when a person's been sick for a long time he looks at life differently—the merest details become the most important thing, and the most important things are just details. When Maxim Gorky was critically ill on the island of Capri, he didn't allow himself to write, to keep from producing distorted images of life. But Polina Isaevna Degtyar, née Kisyuk, wanted to impose her ideas on the whole world and wanted people to live by her rules and her schedule.

Polina Isaevna covered her eyes; a tear emerged at the far end of one eyelid, clung there for a second, then ran into her ear.

"Degtyar," sighed Klava Ivanovna, "I'll tell you something. Sometimes sick people see things more clearly than we healthy ones do."

"Don't confuse the issue," said Iona Ovseich, striking his knee with his fist. "For Christ's sake, please don't confuse the issue!"

Just before New Year's the courtyard was given triple cause for celebration: the demobilized Sergeant-Major Stepa Khomitsky came home, followed two days later by Sergeant Iona Cheperukha, and, on December 31, the very last day of the year, Lieutenant Zinovy Cheperukha arrived with his wife Katya, a native of the town of Ulan-Ude. Though Katya still had more than five months to go, many people guessed that she was already in the family way. On January 1, Iona Ovseich dropped by the Cheperukhas' to wish them a happy new year and, while he was there, to pass on personal instructions to Anya Kotlyar, as leader of the women's soviet, for her to take the female half of the family—the mother-to-be and the grandmother-to-be—under her personal supervision.

"And what about the grandfather?" said the elder Cheperukha with alarm. "Degtyar, you forgot about the grandfather."

Zinovy Cheperukha, who was sitting on the bed and holding his prothesis in his hands, also lodged a complaint with Comrade Degtyar, not about the way he was doing his job, but about his, Zinovy's, living conditions: two families, not to mention the current addition, were living in one room, ten meters square.

"My dear Zyunchik," said Iona Ovseich with a smile, "you're barely off the train and you're already demanding living quarters of your own. But two thousand two hundred buildings were destroyed in Odessa. If it hadn't been for the war—"

Zyunchik interrupted Iona Ovseich to say that if it hadn't been for the war, he'd have two legs like everybody else.

"All right," replied Degtyar. "What are you specifically proposing—that somebody be kicked out of his apartment and it be turned over to you?"

"Zyunya," interjected Iona Cheperukha, "let your old man say something here. You and your bride live with me as long as you have to, and when something opens up, you'll be first in line for it."

"Well said, Iona," praised Comrade Degtyar. "Hurray for the old guard!"

"For the old guard and the new, both of them," answered Iona, pointing a finger to his guard's insignia.

"You should put that away in your pocket," said Olya, "and stop driving people crazy with it. What we want to know from you, Comrade Degtyar, is if there's a chance that my son, who left a leg and half his life at the front, will get an apartment this year so he can live like a human being, or isn't there?"

"There's a chance," said Degtyar," and a very good one. We're giving high priority to the question of residential construction, but right now no one can give you an exact scientific answer that it will take one year, or two."

Zinovy Cheperukha laughed. "And how about life on Mars, Comrade Degtyar, is there life there or not?"

Iona Ovseich replied that some jokes were better than others, but some jokes fell flat. Zyunchik retorted that some ears were better than others; some ears heard things one way and some heard them another.

"Stop this nonsense," said Olya. "I want a clear answer from Comrade Degtyar: when can my son count on having a place of his own to live in?"

Degtyar spread his hands. Zinovy rudely remarked that Degtyar should put his hands in his pockets and stop waving them around, there was no reason for him to make himself out to be an important official who spoke for the whole Soviet Union.

Not for the whole Soviet Union, no, calmly replied Comrade Degtyar, but, for his little corner of it, yes, and no one was going to get in his way, nothing could stop him, not even death.

Katya Cheperukha was surprised that they were spending so much time talking with a person who was not in a position to help them; she put her arms around her husband and said: "Why the hell should we stay in Odessa where you can't make a move without bribing someone? We'd be better off to go back to Ulan-Ude where we could have our own house, our own farm, our own everything."

"Katya," said Olya with a grimace, "no one's keeping you here if you don't like it, and as far as bribes go, I'll tell you one thing—that if everyone was like our Degtyar, people would have forgotten that word a long time ago."

Zinovy jumped up from the couch and hopped on one leg over to the table. "No one's saying that Degtyar takes bribes, but I'd bet my life that a few empty apartments could be found in Odessa if you paid the right price. And if Degtyar doesn't know about them or doesn't want to help, then he shouldn't speak for other people. This is a priority for us too! Us, us! How about us!"

Iona Ovseich asked that the ventilation window be opened, it was getting hot and smoky in the room. He rested his hand on Zyunchik's shoulder and said: "My dear Zyunchik, when you were born in this building and, pardon me, ran around outside with your bottom bare, when you didn't want to do your schoolwork and skipped school for weeks on end, when there wasn't enough fuel in the Cheperukha house, when bread was in short supply, when your exhausted father had to push his cart and wanted instead to drive a horse cart at the Odessa Medical Institute, which is one of the best in the Soviet Union, you always came to Comrade Degtyar. And just let anyone try to remember a single case when I sent you packing and said it's not my affair, take care of it yourself the best you can."

Olya shook her head and wiped a tear from the corner of her eye with her kerchief. His hand trembling, Iona Cheperukha filled people's glasses from a bottle of wine and then proposed a toast to their dear guest with whom they had spent the years of their youth, their family years, and who they were now seeing again, thank God, after the bloodiest war in history, the likes of which they'd never see again, God willing.

After downing her second drink, Katya turned a little red in the face, pointed both hands at her mother-in-law, who was sitting with her arms around Comrade Degtyar, and asked if they were related by blood or marriage.

"Katyusha, my dear girl," said Olya loudly, "we're more than relatives. Around here people say your mother's not the one who gave birth to you but the one who brought you up."

Iona Ovseich thanked her for the warm words, shook everyone's hand, and hurried off saying the courtyard was big and he had to wish everyone a happy new year.

Iona Ovseich returned home a little after twelve, and started making the bed, first turning off the light; the moon was so bright that no other light was needed.

Iona Ovseich lay down on his couch, and then, after a moment of silence, said to his wife: "Polina, I have the feeling that I spent the day in some other courtyard with people I don't even know."

Polina Isaevna did not reply, apparently already asleep. Iona Ovseich turned onto his other side and had just begun dozing off himself when she answered him: twenty-five years ago, during the NEP period, he also had that same feeling, and he had it during the dispossession of the kulaks and collectivization, and now he had it again.

No, said Iona Ovseich, that was one thing back then, but this was something else again: back then it was enough to explain things to people; they would listen closely and try to understand, but now everyone's just waiting for the chance to spring his own theory.

Polina Isaevna yawned loudly, tapped her lips with her fingers, and said: "Maybe it's not a question of other people, maybe you yourself have changed. You used to be able to listen to people, and now you can't, or maybe you don't want to."

Iona Ovseich became angry: how do you like that, another theoretician has popped up.

The moonlight fell right onto her eyes and Polina Isaevna felt an unpleasant anxiety near her heart and asked her husband to close the shutters. Iona Ovseich got out of bed and held his pants against his stomach: he had grown very thin lately and all his clothes were too big for him. He closed one shutter but left the other one open. Polina

Isaevna complained that the light was still too bright, and said he should close it at least halfway, but Iona Ovseich said, no, a person shouldn't indulge his every whim.

Before going back to his couch, Iona Ovseich walked over to his wife's bed and kissed her on the forehead. She groaned softly and once again he said no attention should be paid to whims, adding they were all a result of letting your nerves get the better of you.

There was a cry outside followed by the sound of fast footsteps, as if someone were being chased. A second cry was followed by a woman's laughter, rising and falling.

"Polina," said Iona Ovseich, "today when I dropped by to wish the Biryuks a happy new year, they were sitting at the table and didn't ask me to join them. I told them that before the war the Granik family had lived there, and the woman of the house, Sonya Granik, had been so hospitable that it would have been hard to find her equal even in Odessa. In reply Marina Biryuk giggled and asked who lived there before the Graniks, in other words, who had the Graniks driven out of the apartment after the Revolution when the Soviets came to power."

"Marina is a beautiful woman in excellent health," said Polina Isaevna with a sigh. "They say she didn't waste her time while her husband was away at the front."

Just before dawn when the first trolley had passed down Soviet Army Street, Polina Isaevna began coughing badly and brought up a good deal of blood along with the phlegm. Iona Ovseich said an ambulance should be called, but Polina Isaevna asked him to wait awhile: it might just be an isolated incident and pass by itself.

The coughing attack recurred that evening and the next night as well, and once again she brought up a good deal of blood. Iona Ovseich called an ambulance and helped the orderly with the stretcher so that Polina Isaevna would not waste any of her strength unnecessarily. He wrapped her up in a blanket and then he and the orderly carried her down to the ambulance.

The doctor said that only medical personnel were allowed in the ambulance. Iona Ovseich told his wife that he would take a number 4 trolley to Shevchenko Park and hitch a ride from there to the tuberculosis hospital. "There's no need for you to go anywhere," replied Polina Isaevna. It was a waste of time for him to stand by the fence, and an icy wind always blew in from the sea there.

Polina's Isaevna's prediction proved correct: first Iona Ovseich waited half an hour for the trolley, then he stood outside the entrance; the porter wouldn't allow him in and kept the door locked. Iona Ovseich explained that he needed to say a few words to the doctor but the porter had ceased replying and then, as if purposely wishing to mock a person standing out in the freezing cold, he began poking about in his little cast-iron stove.

Suddenly Iona Ovseich lost his patience and shouted: "You want three rubles! But you don't want three years, you Rumanian bribe-taker!"

The porter stopped poking about at his stove, told Iona Ovseich to go to hell, and said he'd call the police. Iona Ovseich answered that he was going to bring the police there himself right away but the porter wasn't listening now and had gone back to poking at his stove.

At home, having recovered a little from the freezing cold, Iona Ovseich admitted to himself that he should have listened to his wife and stayed in the apartment but still that porter was a real bastard and needed a good tongue-lashing from his superiors.

The bed, which always squeaked when Polina Isaevna turned over or even just put her hand behind her head, was now completely silent. The squeaking had irritated Iona Ovseich a great deal, especially at first, and Polina Isaevna had tried to move as little as possible.

Iona Ovseich made the bed and placed the pillow at an angle as they did in the hospital, but that didn't look good, somehow it was too official. He removed the bedspread, fluffed up the pillow, and turned down one corner of the blanket, as if his wife were just away for a few minutes and would be coming right back. Then, after pacing back and forth between the door and window for a short while, he lay down again, picking up a copy of *The Bolshevik Banner.* Certain kolkhozes were experiencing serious shortages in connection with repairing farm machinery for spring fieldwork, the first postwar spring, and, as usual, the leadership was heaping all the blame on objective factors. Then his thoughts returned to Polina Isaevna. Her illness required that she eat more butter, eggs, cream, meat, steamed milk, in a word what was needed was that the country should not have spent the last four years waging the bloodiest war in history, but should have been living in peace, constantly raising its economic level, and laying a firm foundation for communism.

Iona Ovseich took off his shirt and pants, laying them neatly on a chair. His long johns were a bit frayed at the bottom, and the laces were so short that it was hard to tie them in a bow. Iona Ovseich picked up a sewing kit, and a piece of string which could be wrapped twice around his legs, leaving plenty extra. He added them on to the laces, then tested them, not to check if they held, but simply for the pleasure of tying a bow without twisting his fingers into a knot.

His thoughts and the little tailoring job which had produced immediate and tangible results made the time fly—he did not even have to get up to turn off the light, it went off by itself. First thing tomorrow morning he should go see Anya Kotlyar to borrow some butter and a few eggs for Polina. Some people thought eggs were more beneficial when soft-boiled, but he wouldn't cook them before he went, the doctor could decide on the spot.

Things couldn't have worked out any better: Anya Kotlyar had the second shift and she was able to relieve Iona Ovseich of the task of going because she wanted to see the doctors herself and speak with them about Polina Isaevna. On the way she stopped by the market and bought a dozen eggs so that the sick woman would have a week's worth: you could never tell about the market, it was either a feast or a famine there.

Iona Ovseich had also planned to visit his wife around midday but he couldn't get away because of a serious breakdown in a machine in the cutting section; he had to organize a repair crew immediately and mobilize them to work at top speed, otherwise the problem could drag on till Saturday, and might be put off again until Monday. It was late in the day before he was able to tear himself away for a minute and make a phone call. There was only one physician on duty who advised Iona Ovseich to call in the morning when the full staff would be on. Iona Ovseich answered that he was quite familiar with hospital procedure and insisted that he be given a five-minute meeting tomorrow before the beginning of his shift and that the head physician be informed that he had called to check on his wife's condition. On his part, he would speak with the people in charge by midday tomorrow or the first chance he got. The physician on duty agreed and asked for Comrade Degtyar's phone number just in case.

"Doctor," said Iona Ovseich, "if the head physician needs me, he can always find me in the factory party office or at the District Committee."

The duty physician apologized for his blunder, which made it appear that he didn't trust Comrade Degtyar.

There was no urgent need for Iona Ovseich to call the hospital the next day; Anya Kotlyar had already managed to run by before work to bring Polina Isaevna some warm milk, then called the factory party office from her own hospital. Iona Ovseich had just dropped by the office for a minute from the cutting section. Anya informed him that Polina Isaevna had not had a good night, the excretions had increased.

"But her morale, how's her morale?" asked Iona Ovseich. "Morale is what counts."

Anya had no information about the patient's morale because she hadn't been allowed into the ward. The doctor had only informed her of the objective aspects: temperature thirty-eight, a serious shortage of breath, blood being spat up. "That's curious," said Iona Ovseich. "Even good morale is not considered an objective factor. Very curious."

Though he had only two fingers on his right hand, Stepa Khomitsky had assumed the post of plumber and handyman in the building whose population had increased three times in comparison with the prewar times.

When the Rumanians had been in power, the plumbing had deteriorated badly and now a day didn't pass without Khomitsky's services being needed.

Iona Ovseich arranged for Stepa to be given some of the factory's obsolete vises and one-hundred-and-fifty millimeter pincers, and he knocked together a decent workbench out of scraps so he could work at home in the evening. Tosya was upset because their room was now half filled with piles of scrap metal and looked like a village blacksmith's shop. Stepa said nothing and went on with his work: you couldn't find new faucets for love or money and the only solution was to rebuild the old ones, otherwise people would be without water.

In one respect, however, Stepa's approach was foolish: he charged his neighbors for his work at prewar prices and meanwhile the cost of a loaf of bread at the market had now risen to a price that was fifteen times higher. Tosya would say that he was born a fool and would die a fool, but Stepa's response was that people were still being paid the same salaries.

"Our Stepa," shouted Cheperukha drunkenly, "wants to turn back the clock to the way things were before the war! But time races like my horses when they're well watered and well fed."

On February 9 Comrade Stalin delivered a historic speech to the voters at an election meeting of the Stalin District of the city of Moscow. Along with the tasks of the first postwar Five-Year Plan, which was to fully restore the prewar level of production by 1948, Comrade Stalin also presented grandiose prospects for a new and mighty increase in the U.S.S.R.'s national economy during the next three Five-Year Plans or perhaps in a somewhat longer period of time. The smelting of cast iron would increase to fifty million tons a year, steel to sixty million tons, coal mining would produce five hundred million tons, oil would rise to sixty million tons, and the production of electrical energy would increase to two hundred and fifty billion kilowatt-hours. In that manner we would create the material and technical basis for communism while at the same time safeguarding ourselves from any fluctuations in the international situation. The building of a communist society, which was interrupted by Nazi Germany's treacherous attack in 1941, would now assume a tempo unheard of before even in this country, and communism would go from being humanity's bright dream to becoming a fact of daily life.

On election day, Iona Ovseich gathered a few people around him and in strict confidence informed them he personally thought that Comrade Stalin seriously intended to be alive for a while under communism and that, by the way, wasn't a bad guarantee itself.

Right after the elections the courtyard set to work studying Comrade Stalin's historic speech. The meetings were held in Iona Ovseich's apartment since he was living alone now. Klava Ivanovna, Tosya Khomitsky, and Dina Vargaftik would come early and stoke the stove so people would arrive in a warm apartment where they would feel comfortable.

The first class was devoted mainly to the U.S.S.R.'s economic situation at the end of the war when Hitler had been wiped out in his lair. Comrade Degtyar presented a clear picture of the unparalleled destruction and plunder carried out by the occupiers during the years in which they held sway. The total number of factories destroyed or rendered useless came to thirty-one thousand eight hundred and fifty. Those factories had employed around four million workers. In the coal-mining industry the Donbass and the Moscow coal fields had been destroyed, and one hundred and thirty-five thousand mines, which had formerly yielded more than a hundred million tons of coal per year, had been plundered; in the field of energy, the occupying forces had burned or blown up sixty-one major power plants and a large number of smaller ones. In ferrous metallurgy, sixty-two blast furnaces had been destroyed, two hundred and thirteen open-hearth furnaces, two hundred and forty-eight rolling mills, and the number of coke furnaces destroyed had assumed monstrous proportions—four thousand seven hundred, in other words, almost five thousand! Seven hundred and forty-nine heavy and medium machine building plants employing nine hundred and nineteen thousand workers were also destroyed, as were sixty-four machine-tool plants, and forty-one electrotechnical enterprises. The Nazi invaders also destroyed thousands of plants in light industry, textiles, and food production.

As far as Odessa was concerned, no figures were needed, for everyone had had the opportunity to see for himself. It was enough to mention that the October Revolution and Dzerzhinsky plants, the Bolshevik ship repair yard, the bread-baking plant, the meat packing plant, the confectionary and jute plants were razed to the ground. When the men of the January Uprising plant returned with their party organizer Savitsky to rebuild their factory, they found piles of broken brick and kilometers of twisted steel. The department head Khizhnyakov, the mechanic Bobrovsky, the electrician Medynsky, and the machinist Gorelick began literally creating a new power plant, the heart of the factory, out of nothing. In 1941, Konstantin Simonov, who was in Odessa at the time as a military correspondent, wrote as follows about the heroes of the January Uprising plant: "Here people worked around the clock because work time was not measured in hours or in sleepless nights, but only by the time it took to produce a tank: "When we finish the tank, I'll go get some sleep, that was the only measure of time at the factory."

Two and a half years later, in 1944, the people who had returned to their factory, which was then in total ruin, made their own system and rules, as in the unforgettable year of 1941 when the very life of Odessa was at stake. The results were known to all and there was no reason to mention them again: the people at the January factory overfulfilled the plan for 1944 by a factor of two.

The temporary loss of a series of highly important industrial and agricultural regions in the initial period of the war, the colossal damage wrought on the Soviet economy by the enemy, the diversion of millions of workers from production, all this caused the U.S.S.R.'s national economy to fall to a level lower than that of 1940 despite the exceptional achievements made in the eastern regions of the Urals, Siberia, and Central Asia.

Iona Ovseich paused briefly. Dina Vargaftik shook her head and wept softly into her handkerchief: the factories, mines, kolkhozes, state farms, the sowing machines and harvesters could all be rebuilt, but there was no force on earth able to raise those who had fallen. Her Grisha had been the number-one lathe operator in the Red Trade Union factory and now would have been willing to work day and night to fill and overfulfill the plan. Often he would come from the third shift when it had already grown light, and never once did she hear a word of complaint from him that he was tired or not feeling well, or just wanted to rest after working all night. On the contrary, he was always full of laughter and jokes, his eyes were always merry.

Klava Ivanovna told Dina to stop crying: enough tears had been shed, the dead were gone, and we had a duty to our children and grandchildren; you couldn't make any headway if you were always looking behind you.

"You're right, Malaya," seconded Iona Ovseich, "and it should be added that the work we do is not only for our children and grandchildren but is also the best monument to the dead because we're putting their dreams, which they clung to till their final breath, into practice."

At the next class Iona Ovseich had good news to report: two thirds of the country's workers had already entered the socialist competition and new groups were joining all the time. Innovative lathe operators—Dina Vargaftik would be particularly glad to hear this—had increased their speed from seventy to eighty meters a minute to one thousand to fifteen hundred meters. The people who worked at such rates were now popularly known as "speeders," or those who outrun time. Since special significance was being attached to increasing the activity and initiative of the masses, production conferences at plants and factories had become incredibly animated, numbering, according to early figures, no less than three and possibly even four million participants in the current year.

Dina mentioned that her Grisha had been a member of his section committee and twice had received free trips to a vacation spa; once he had the trip transferred to his wife's name and the chairman of the factory committee had not objected, saying that our wives deserved to rest even more than we did.

"Well, but not everyone was so lucky in finding a wife as your Grisha," said Anya Kotlyar.

Dina's entire body shuddered as if she had been whacked on the back unexpectedly and a second later she replied that she didn't know about anybody else, but Joseph Kotlyar could have envied her Grisha.

Let's say that's so, said Anya, but why turn the dead into angels when we should care about people when they're alive.

Olya Cheperukha was indignant—who said anything about angels! Dina had had her problems with Grisha but everyone remembered quite clearly how much they loved each other, and that he was always her defender. And if anybody didn't like that, he should keep his thoughts to himself, other people weren't interested.

"Let's put a finer point on this," said Iona Ovseich. "Grigory Vargaftik did not only defend his wife, he gave his life for the motherland. The fact that he wasn't alone and millions of others did the same is another matter. Today we should not mourn but we should roll up our sleeves and find a practical solution to the problem posed to the party and people by Comrade Stalin: to create the material and technological base for communism during the upcoming three Five-Year Plans, that is, by 1960. We have all the necessary conditions and the most reliable guarantee of all, comrades, you and me."

The shift toward the tasks facing the nation which Iona Ovseich had executed had a calming effect on the audience, and that included Dina Vargaftik; dredging up the past only brought bitterness and pain.

On the eighteenth of March, a resolution passed by the Supreme Soviet gave the force of law to the new Five-Year Plan but, in point of fact, the nation had already begun work according to that plan and many quotas had already been successfully overfulfilled. The Donbass miners had pumped out six hundred and fifty million cubic tons of water from flooded mines. In terms of volume, this was tantamount to draining a lake with a surface of seventy square kilometers and a depth of ten meters. Also in the Donbass approximately two and a half thousand kilometers of collapsed mines had been cleared, roughly the equivalent of digging a tunnel from Moscow to Paris at a depth between two and seven hundred meters.

After Comrade Degtyar had cited that last figure, Iona Cheperukha laughed and said that of course we needed mines like we needed air to breathe, but still a tunnel from Moscow to Paris might come in handy too. It would be interesting to ask Maurice Thores a few questions.

"Iona," said Degtyar, wagging a finger, "it's a good thing they can't hear us overseas, otherwise they'd already be worried."

"I don't give a damn about them!" shouted Iona. "Where were they hiding when it was time to open a second front and our people were shedding their blood!"

Iona Ovseich spread his hands: "Everybody knows where they were, and, if events had taken another form, Grisha Vargaftik, Kolya Khomitsky, the Kotlyar brothers, and millions of other people might be with us today."

Since the talk had taken a personal turn again and now many of the women, not just Dina Vargaftik, had begun wiping their eyes, Klava Ivanovna asked Comrade Degtyar to be specific about the level of the gross national product that would be reached by the end of the Five-Year Plan in 1950.

Iona Ovseich answered that by the end of the Five-Year Plan the gross national product would be two hundred and fifty billion rubles but stressed the point that this was in terms of 1926–27 prices when NEP was still in practice and prices were relatively low; for example, in Odessa you could buy a dozen eggs then for twenty kopecks.

"Eggs!" cried Iona Cheperukha. "And wine, good Moldavian wine from Tiraspol cost five kopecks a glass during NEP, and the wine from Balta and Ananev was three kopecks a glass."

"One moment," said Iona Ovseich. "Speaking of NEP, we should introduce a corrective at once: in the first place, there was still unemployment back then, and, in the second place, it was harder to earn fifty rubles a month then than it is to earn five hundred now. Most important of all, we would not have had the socialist industry and the kolkhoz system without which we could not have withstood the four years of war against Hitler and achieved our historic victory."

"Oh, you can always go back to the beginning," said Klava Ivanovna, slapping her knee, "otherwise someone will remember that a glass of wine cost three rubles but will forget that you could count the number of collective farms in the country on your fingers and that the kulaks were getting rich and the people were looking around and asking where's the Soviet system they had risked their necks for. Marina Biryuk, you lived in the countryside during those years, give us an example from your own experience."

Marina said that she had still been a girl back then and so had no experience, but she had kept her eyes open. In the next village over, Chobruchi, people lived like human beings because the head of the village council was an intelligent man, but in Vapnyarka, the head of the village council was a fool. Along with the kulaks he also resettled Piotr Goncharenko, Vasilya Goncharenko, and Yukhim Panasovich Bondar, who were hard-working people and kept their hut, livestock, and land in good condition.

"Hold on!" interrupted Klava Ivanovna. "What kind of example is that? Are you saying that the Soviet system made mistakes when it dispossessed the kulaks and sent innocent people off to do hard labor?"

Marina shrugged her shoulders; she wasn't talking about the whole Soviet system, she was just talking about what she had seen with her own eyes in her own village.

Klava Ivanovna jumped up from her chair. Iona Ovseich ordered her to be seated, then said in a loud voice: "Sometimes two-headed babies are born, or calves with two bodies and the tail where the head should be. Anyone interested in such things should go to the museum. Citizen Biryuk, we're not asking you what kind of family you come from or what kind of farm you kept. We're aware that your husband, Major Andrei Petrovich Biryuk, who was awarded many combat medals, including the Gold Star, currently holds an important position in the Soviet sector of Berlin, near the border of the American sector. And it's too great an honor for a fool from the Vapnyarka village council to be mentioned again here and used as an example."

Marina said that she didn't give a good goddamn about that fool from the village council and she hadn't thought of him in a dog's age, but then she'd been forced to remember him here and now people were angry and saying that she was defending the kulaks. This talk pained her heart and as soon as the class was over she was going home to write to her husband in Berlin and tell him to have his general inform the military authorities that mud was being slung at the wife of a Soviet officer.

"My dear Marina Biryuk," said Iona Ovseich with a smile, "I don't think anyone here is trying to threaten you. On the contrary, you were given the floor so you could speak your mind. Some people liked your example about the people in your village and some didn't. Everyone has the right to his own opinion. But there's no reason to try to intimidate us by saying you'll write to Major Biryuk. We don't scare easily. I'll tell you a secret: we can also write to his unit if need be, and our word will be as good as yours."

"As good?" cried Klava Ivanovna, "it's a hundred times better!"

"So that means," said Marina, beside herself now, "that Degtyar and Malaya speak the truth but I'm a liar, and my husband won't believe me, the general won't believe me, and the military authorities won't believe me! So then why did you call on me? To run me down in front of everyone? I'll never set foot in here again and don't you people be coming by my door either!"

Marina threw on her kerchief, tied it around her head, and started for the door. Though everyone had heard what she said, no one had expected her to act on it so quickly. Dina Vargaftik, Tosya Khomitsky, and even Klava Ivanovna automatically moved their chairs back to let Marina get by. Anya Kotlyar alone laughed out loud, took Marina by the shoulders, and forced her to sit back down. Marina made an effort to rise but Anya, who had the hands of a surgical nurse, pinned her in place and would not allow her to move.

Anya laughed again. "You can't say anything to a person."

"You can say what you want, people can't shut up," said Marina, panting with excitement, "but I don't want to hear it. Degtyar and Malaya can try to intimidate other people but they shouldn't waste their energy on me."

Klava Ivanovna was white as a sheet, her blue eyes having turned a deep black. Iona Ovseich said she should have a drink of water, the argument didn't amount to a hill of beans. No one was interested in anyone but himself, no one had the patience to listen to anyone else. He had nothing against Marina Biryuk leaving, she could go if she wanted to; the classes on Comrade Stalin's speech and the materials from the Supreme Soviet were strictly voluntary, no one was obliged to attend; on the contrary, people were very interested in the subject and requested such classes more than once. And good riddance to anyone who didn't want to be here.

Lyalya Orlov was upset: "How could you say such a thing! It's very interesting at our factory too but how can there be any comparison. And a woman, especially one who isn't working, should be grateful to people who come to her house and share their thoughts."

Marina wagged a finger at Lyalya Orlov and asked loudly: "Who are you to be lecturing anyone? Do you think people have short memories? Well, they don't, and word gets around."

Lyalya narrowed her eyes, plugged her ears with her fingers, and quickly turned aside.

"Marina," said Anya Kotlyar, "aren't you ashamed of yourself! I never expected that of you."

Marina looked at everyone as if seeing them for the first time and said that her mother-in-law's right arm was paralyzed, she had two children at home, Lesik was going to school, the third session, they didn't have enough room, and she had to look after Zinochka all day long. The military authorities had promised to help her find a kindergarten, and promises were all she'd gotten so far. You worked like crazy at home from morning till night and then here people stuck it to you that you didn't work! A job was like going to a health resort—you left in the morning and you had no idea what went on at home.

Klava Ivanovna shrugged her shoulders: if anyone really wanted a job they were looking for nurses at the kindergarten. Nurses were needed everywhere. And you could find a place for your child at the same time.

No, said Marina, she didn't want to be a nurse: the state had spent good money training her to be an accountant; any common woman could be a nursery maid, you didn't need an education for that.

As she listened, Klava Ivanovna promised herself not to respond and interrupt the class any longer, but Marina's last remark exceeded all bounds.

"What do you mean—any common woman! And what do you think you are then? Do you have some special sort of blood in your veins, did your father own his own farm, with its own farmhands! Marina, your husband is an officer in the Red Army, but your mentality, I'm afraid to say what it is."

"Don't be afraid," said Marina with a foolish laugh, "I'm not afraid and there's no reason for you to be either. We're all friends here."

"Malaya," said Iona Ovseich in a tone of command, "sit down and don't get us off the track. Comrade Biryuk wants to work in her field, the one the state trained her for, and that's an entirely legitimate desire, and she needs to be given help finding a kindergarten for her child. I'll deal with that myself, and I request the chairperson of our women's soviet, Anya Kotlyar, not to sit idly by but to put everyone to work on this."

Anya shrugged her shoulders: she was ready to help. But what was the point of it, if the kindergarten situation was no better than the housing situation.

"Comrade Kotlyar," said Iona Ovseich, grasping the table with both hands, "keep your comparisons and conclusions to yourself. We're better off giving some thought to how the women's soviet can aid Marina Biryuk, so that she can leave her children and ailing mother-in-law home without having to worry."

Anya Kotlyar smiled: it was easy for men to give advice.

"Men don't have anything to do with this," said Iona Ovseich. "I'm not giving advice as a man. Every woman here would gladly agree to give an hour or two a day to a help a neighbor who was busy at work. Colonel Landa's wife wouldn't refuse the courtyard children a few classes. She has her certificate and earns a decent living in the music school."

Dina Vargaftik was the first to say that she was in full agreement with Comrade Degtyar's idea but how could it be put into practice if everyone was working the same shift.

"My dear women comrades," said Iona Ovseich, "we withstood a most bloody war and emerged the victors. And while restoring the country, we have already begun building the material and technological base for communism, and so the question is—can we do all that and still be unable to give some help to the wife of a Soviet officer!"

"Degtyar," said Klava Ivanovna, "enough explanations. The chairperson of the women's soviet should be given the task of coming up with specific measures to help the family of Major Andrei Petrovich Biryuk, who has been entrusted with a very important position in Berlin by the high command."

Iona Ovseich put the question to a vote: "Comrades, who is in favor of the motion?"

Everyone was in favor of it; Iona Cheperukha added something on his own behalf: "Marina, if there's anything I can do for you, come see me any time, day or night."

Marina laughed out loud and said that she liked Iona Cheperukha the best of them all: he was always in a good mood and made other people laugh.

"Marina my dear," said Iona in delight, "then what are you waiting for!"

It was late that evening, past eleven, when a ruckus took place in the Cheperukhas' that the whole courtyard could hear. It had started over a trifle. Zyunchik and Katya had come back from the last show of the movie *The Girl of My Dreams* and Olya immediately began attacking her daughter-in-law: why did she eat her dinner and then leave her dirty dishes on the table? Did she think other people were servants to pick up after her? All right, she was willing to clean up after her own son, but why should she do it for his wife, who was a hundred times healthier and stronger than she was!

Zyunchik sat down on the couch and unfastened his prothesis. As Katerina helped him, she replied to her mother-in-law: they had had to hurry to catch the last show and she hadn't had time for the dishes.

"No," said Olya, holding a finger to her daughter-in-law's face, "that wasn't the first time. It's the hundred and first." And instead of standing up for his own mother, her son wasn't saying a word like his wife had cut off his tongue!

"Stop it, Mama," said Zyunchik.

Olya wrung her hands: her son was telling his own mother to keep her mouth shut, his mother who had fed him with her own milk, and for what!

"Stop it!" repeated Zyunchik, and threw his prothesis on the floor. "I didn't come back to my hometown, I didn't come home to be criticized at every step of the way. I have as much right to be here as you."

"That's right," agreed Katerina, "he was born here, and he was taken off to the front from here, and we have as much right to be here as you do."

"Iona!" cried Olya. "Iona, this woman wants to drive us out of our own home! Who is this person you've brought here, my son!"

Zyunchik said that it was she who had insisted that he return to Odessa, to this madhouse.

"You know what, son," said Iona, grasping the back of a chair firmly with both hands and slamming it against the floor, "if this is a madhouse, no one's keeping you here, no one's forcing you to stay."

Katerina wept bitterly: they were driving a pregnant woman out into the street and all her husband did was just sit there and take it.

"My God," said Olya, clutching her head, "we never spoke to each other like this before in our home, never! What a disgrace, what shame has come on us!"

Zinovy grabbed a plate from the table, threw it on the floor, and, hopping on one leg, began trampling the broken pieces.

"Zyunya, you're lucky you're an invalid," said Iona, trembling and shaking, "otherwise I'd make mincemeat out of you!"

"Don't lay a hand on him," insisted Olya, "don't you dare lay a hand on him!"

Iona did not reply but turned toward the door, tore his coat from a nail on the wall, and ran out.

He came home the next morning without his coat and the wine on his breath could be smelled a mile away.

"You drunk," said Olya, weeping into her pillow. "What are people going to say, what are our children going to think?"

"You felt crowded, ten meters wasn't enough for you, you want ten meters for everyone," muttered Iona. "That's why I spent the night at the railroad station, so you could have plenty of room."

The next day Marina Biryuk expressed her sympathy to Iona and then immediately switched the subject to herself: if people in a family couldn't see eye to eye, how could she agree to have people she barely knew in her home while she was away all day at work.

Iona shook his head: what did that mean—people she barely knew? The people here had been living in this building as long as there'd been a Soviet government, and some had even been here before, and so what basis was there for not trusting them?

"Iona," said Marina with a laugh, "but you fight with your own son and your own daughter-in-law."

"Not with my son," said Cheperukha, taking offense. "It's all because of my daughter-in-law. She's from Ulan-Ude, which is farther from Odessa than Siberia. And now she wants things done her way here."

"I'm a newcomer too," said Marina as if she were a schoolgirl in first grade.

"Marina," said Iona in a warm and neighborly tone of voice, putting his arm around her waist, "if you need a cart to transport wood, coal, or furniture, you don't have to look for some stranger to pay more than you should: there's an old drayman by the name of Cheperukha. The city he lives in, that we'll keep a secret. He'll deliver the goods to your house and even help you unload them."

Olya had a talk that evening with her husband, calling him an old fogey who would be a grandfather in a couple of months and who was acting like a shameless womanizer.

"Olya," said Iona, placing his hand over his heart, "I have nothing but sympathy for the woman, that's all there is to it."

"And Joseph Kotlyar had nothing but sympathy for Tosya while his wife and her husband were shedding their blood at the front. And the whole courtyard knows about that."

"Joseph Kotlyar has been an invalid since the Civil War," said Iona, "and shouldn't be criticized for being home while his wife was at the front."

"Don't be a fool," said Olya angrily, "I'm talking about hanky-panky, not about catching saboteurs."

"And I'll tell you something about Stepa when he was in Germany," said Iona. "Some of those German women are so shameless that there are no words for it."

"You womanizers," said Olya, crying, "you rotten womanizers. We spend our whole lives killing ourselves for you, cooking and cleaning, without a moment for ourselves, and even when you become grandparents, the husband still wants to act like a little boy."

Iona bent his right arm at the elbow and giggled. Olya gave him a good slap in the face but he didn't take offense: when you deserved it, you deserved it.

There was peace in the Cheperukha home for three days but on the fourth day Olya and Katerina had another misunderstanding. Olya was cooking borscht and asked Katerina to keep an eye on it while she ran to the store for a minute, but Katerina was so engrossed in her reading that she forgot all about the soup. Olya could smell the borscht burning in the hallway and there was her daughter-in-law sitting right there and she couldn't smell it.

"Such a fine young lady you are," said Olya indignantly, "the money you brought into this family could almost pay for two carrots."

"Back home in Ulan-Ude," answered Katerina, "a pregnant woman could even let a house burn down and people wouldn't yell at her. But in Odessa all people do is yell at each other."

"My God," said Olya, clutching her head, "where I am supposed to get the strength to listen to all this without losing my temper."

As a disabled war veteran, Zinovy badgered the military authorities twice a week for an apartment. In addition, the Kirov factory, where Zinovy had been training as a milling-machine operator for three months, also interceded on his behalf; he was now producing a hundred and forty to one hundred and fifty percent of the daily quota. His co-workers said that Zinovy Cheperukha was something like the pilot Meresev: to stand on one leg by your machine for a whole shift was no easier than pushing pedals in an airplane, especially since the pilot had a comfortable seat to sit on.

Still, Zyunchik had made no real progress in finding an apartment and Olya told him he should go see Comrade Degtyar and ask him nicely. Degtyar would apply pressure in the right place. Zyunchik laughed in reply like a foolish child and said: Degtyar was good at doing little tricks and explaining how simple they were, but finding an apartment was no little trick.

Iona supported his wife insisting that Zinovy personally request Comrade Degtyar's help; he did not hesitate to remind his son that he wasn't the only thing Degtyar had to think about. Even better, Zinovy should go there with Katya, the two of them, so Iona Ovseich could see her pregnant again; his conscience would prompt him, tell him it was time to act and that it couldn't be put off any longer.

This time Katerina took her in-laws' side. The three of them pressured Zinovy together and forced him to give in.

Iona Ovseich welcomed them warmly, shook Zinovy's hand, and put his arm around his shoulder. He brought up a chair for Katya so that she could sit away from the draft and asked them to feel at home.

Before any conversation began, the host categorically insisted that his guests try the coffee which he had brewed himself from barley; he had ground the barley, then added a little red pepper, salt, and fried bread crust. Not a single crumb had gotten into the glass, he had already strained them all out, but, just to be on the safe side, he wanted to pour the coffee through a piece of cheesecloth one more time.

The guests said that wasn't necessary. Katerina finished her cup and asked for another. As he poured the coffee, Iona Ovseich remarked that his house was like Georgia where a guest's wish was the law. Katerina grew indignant: a fine thing, Comrade Degtyar was alone but he had a dozen guests a day.

"To get to the point," interrupted Zinovy, "we've come about finding a place to live."

Iona Ovseich smiled. "I know, you don't have to tell me. And I can see that you're almost a family of three now."

"That's right," said Zinovy nodding, "and so here's the question: what should we do now? Ten meters for four grown people is one thing, but ten meters for four grown people and a new baby is something else."

"Hold on!" said Iona Ovseich. "Until the child is born, we have to deal with the situation as it exists here and now."

All right, agreed Katya, but then Comrade Degtyar should move in with them today and stay between the two families so that people kept their distance and didn't nag her no end, or else anything could happen, she couldn't be responsible for herself.

"I heard that Siberians were even-tempered people with strong nerves," said Iona Ovseich, "but it looks like it's just the other way around."

Katya burst into tears: nobody's nerves could stand what went on here, they criticized you and lectured you at every turn.

"My dear girl," said Comrade Degtyar with a smile, "a person has to keep learning his whole life and it's never too late to start."

Katerina felt the blood rush to her head and was about to start shouting but Comrade Degtyar had already switched the subject to the most important issue—housing. The first order of business, he said, was to form a commission to investigate the housing conditions of the young Cheperukha and of his father, especially since both of them had taken part in the war and received combat decorations. Second, a certificate should be obtained from a medical institution attesting to the fact that Katerina was pregnant. Third—and Degtyar would assume full responsibility for this—the community would plead their case and provide a recommendation for the Cheperukhas as among the building's longest tenants who had a moral and legal right to a better situation. It was likely that the District Executive Committee would appoint Comrade Degtyar to the commission; then, as the investigation began, all the documentation would be in the right hands, and, consequently, opinion would be inclined in their favor right from the very start.

"Do you have anything against it?" asked Iona Ovseich in conclusion.

Zinovy Cheperukha had nothing against the idea but he wasn't clear on one point: why was there any need for the District Executive Committee to appoint a commission if there already was an authorization for the apartment and the tenants were registered and had a receipt which expressly stated that the apartment was ten square meters.

"You're quick on your toes," said Iona Ovseich, narrowing his eyes. "But I see things a bit differently. Let's start from the beginning, with the authorization. Who has it? The tenant, Iona Cheperukha. Where's the registry of tenants? In the building administration office. Where's the receipt? The original is in the office safe and a copy was given to the tenant, meaning once again, Iona Cheperukha. So then the question is what do Zinovy Cheperukha and his wife Katerina have to do with any of this?"

Though the last question flowed directly out of the preceding one, Zinovy exploded: "A person decorated with the Red Star and the medal for victory over imperialist Japan and who has one leg made out of papier-mâché doesn't have to prove who he is!"

"Calm down, boy," said Iona Ovseich. "This isn't something I'm just making up myself. No matter what approach you take for getting a place to live—the military authorities, the factory, VTEK—no one's going to examine your case without appointing a commission, so don't make me say the whole thing all over again. When tens of thousands of people are demanding a place to live, every case should not just be looked into by one commission, but a commission on top of that one and another one on top of that. And still that wouldn't be enough."

Zinovy lowered his head like a young bull. When he was in the army, everything was clearer and simpler at the front.

No, said Iona Ovseich, the problems the nation were facing today were the direct result of the war, there was no arguing that; otherwise something very much amiss might be said.

It was plain from Zinovy's face that he was prepared to start arguing again but now Katerina entered the conversation, saying that everyone in the courtyard knew that Degtyar had as much power in the city as the chairman of the District Soviet, and, not only that, he was the chairman's buddy.

Iona Ovseich's right eye squinted: if he'd understood her correctly, Katerina was making a gentle hint about his being close with the chairman. Yes, it was true, he did know the chairman of the District Executive Committee a little, they'd worked together in the political department of a machine and tractor station back in '33.

Katerina tried to sit closer to the table to be close to Comrade Degtyar but her stomach prevented this.

"Katya, Katya, Katerina," said Iona Ovseich with a smile, "it's like the song says—she combed out her hair pretty and waited for an officer to come by. You're from Siberia but you're more cunning than a woman from Odessa."

Katya flushed and said you learned from those around you. Zinovy was listening and looking at them like a stranger; there was something chilling in his eyes.

"Zinovy, wake up!" ordered Comrade Degtyar in a loud voice.

"Good lord," said Katya with a laugh, "now he can sleep till the roosters start crowing without even turning over."

Jokingly, Iona Ovseich said that not everyone is like Benya Krik, who drove off with the love of his life to the vineyards of Bessarabia. That was the first Katya had heard of Benya Krik but said that he sounded like a good guy who was probably tops in what he did.

Sullen and glum, Zinovy explained to his wife that Benya Krik, was the famous Odessa bandit, Mishka Yaponchik, who was executed by the Soviets.

Katerina gaped at Comrade Degtyar.

"Zinovy's right," said Comrade Degtyar with a grimace. "But in this case we weren't using Benya Krik as a political example."

The room grew still for a minute. The communal electric meter could be heard humming loudly, someone must be using an iron or an electric hot plate. Iona Ovseich listened intently, then shook his head in reproach: people had been warned a hundred times, people had been told a hundred times not to use appliances but apparently until you gave them a good shaking up and brought them to court, it didn't mean anything to them.

Katerina laughed, saying they had the same problem in Ulan-Ude with moonshine. "The city Soviet and the police say you're not supposed to make it or you'll be tried for it, but people just lock their doors and do what they want."

This surprised Iona Ovseich: what raw material did they have for making moonshine in Ulan-Udc?

"Oooo," cooed Katerina. "From potatoes, that's one, from sugar, that's two, and from different kinds of berries, that's three. And they also imported sugar beets by the sackload from the warmer regions. We send them forest berries and mushrooms, and they send us beets in return. So it pays for itself. And the moonshine costs next to nothing."

"And do you know the technique for making it?" asked Comrade Degtyar.

Of course she knew, said Katerina with a shrug; they'd make their own for the holidays. Her father would go out hunting for game, so they'd have appetizers to take with their drinks. She used to go with him and she had her own rifle, and so, when she wasn't in school, she'd tend the cows at home and feed the piglets if her mother didn't have the time. But usually her mother wouldn't let her. She'd tell her to go study, she had to take care of her hands, so they didn't get all calloused.

"All right, let's see your hands," ordered Iona Ovseich.

Katya laid her hands palms up on the table, then turned them over. Iona Ovseich stroked them, and then concluded that if those hands ever had anything to do with cows, it was only to wash them in milk when there wasn't enough water in the house.

"Oh, go on, you!" said Katerina, narrowing her eyes.

Iona Ovseich began fidgeting in his chair and raised the subject of moonshine again, saying he had a very plain method of his own for making it at home. Suddenly, Zinovy rose to his feet, took his wife to the door, and only when he was at the door did he ask: "Will you keep us informed about the commission or do we have to remind you?"

"You don't have to remind me," said Iona Ovseich. "We'll remember it ourselves."

As soon as they had set foot inside their apartment, Zinovy attacked his wife: why had she spoken with Degtyar as if she wanted to play up to him! Katya retorted that she hadn't been playing up to him, just talking politely. You could make scenes at home, you didn't have to go visiting to do that.

No, insisted Zinovy, the entire way she'd acted from start to finish reeked of bootlicking, and what she had said about herself and her family was bootlicking too: people were always frank when they wanted to play up to the people in charge.

Her husband's reproaches and insults made Katya burst into tears. Her in-laws were entirely on her side: Zinovy shouldn't be so smart and independent; talk was cheap, but a person could end up in real life all alone with his conceit and a bare ass.

"You idiots!" shouted Zinovy, grabbing a crutch and slamming it against the floor, "you perfect idiots!"

Olya waved her hands, saying, "My God, just let things be quiet, just let there be a little peace in the house." Iona took a pitcher from the table and drank half its contents, his Adam's apple bobbing like a horse's. Then he threw himself on the bed without getting undressed and covered his head with a newspaper. Ten minutes later when everyone had cooled down, Iona jumped up, pulled on his cap, and went out, slamming the door behind him.

Around midnight, when the radio news was just ending, another row broke out in the Cheperukhas' apartment and lasted until one o'clock when Klava Ivanovna knocked at the door, taking a personal hand in the matter.

Marina Biryuk left a little early the next morning, on her way to the market for a few pounds of potatoes. She ran into Iona in the front hall and asked if there really had been a row in the courtyard all night that sounded like people were being robbed and murdered or did she just imagine it?

"My dear Marina," answered Iona Cheperukha politely, "it's a bad habit to use other people's troubles as your entertainment!"

"Iona, my dear," said Marina with a laugh, "if everyone were entertained by other people's troubles, what would become of those troubles!"

"Marinochka, my darling!" Like a cavalryman, Iona took her hand, pressed his lips to it, and stood motionless for ten or fifteen seconds as if he were on guard.

The next Monday Marina Biryuk found work in her field, as a bookkeeper in the cafeteria of the ORS state university, on Pasteur Street, corner of Red Army. Klava Ivanovna was the first to congratulate her, saying that was a job worth looking for!

Comrade Degtyar asked Klava Ivanovna personally to make sure that the chairperson of the women's soviet, Anya Kotlyar, did not let things slide in the matter of helping the wife of Officer Biryuk's family, especially since Marina was starting a full-time job on Monday and had two children and an elderly, invalid mother-in-law at home.

Anya Kotlyar found a good initial solution: she spent the first half of the day in the Biryuk apartment. Like all old women, Marina's mother-in-law was a little capricious—bring me this, take this away, pick up your feet when you walk, don't pound—but Zinochka was an angel of a girl.

Dina Vargaftik kept an eye on things for a few hours in the afternoon. Klava Ivanovna had to take over the next day because all the other women were on their shift. Anya Kotlyar, Dina Vargaftik, Tosya Khomitsky, and Olya Cheperukha all took turns for the rest of the week, and Gizella Landa took Zinochka to her place twice and gave her music lessons.

To avoid confusion, a strict schedule was set up for the following week but first thing Monday morning, Olya Cheperukha's turn, the schedule was interrupted by unforeseen circumstances: Katya's contractions began and she had to be taken to the maternity clinic at once.

Tosya was only able to spare twenty minutes in the morning and Zinochka was left with no one to watch her. She ran outside and her old grandmother was frightened half to death until Marina came home from work and went out looking for the girl.

The same thing happened again on Friday. Marina's mother-in-law insisted that Marina complain to Degtyar, who was in charge there, and, if he didn't take measures, she should lodge a written complaint against Degtyar.

"Mama, why should I do anything so foolish?" said Marina. "Be quiet if you don't know what you're talking about. People are just doing all this for a thank-you."

By the third week the schedule was no more than a piece of paper. When Marina informed Klava Ivanovna, instead of expressing sympathy and promising to correct the situation, she spoke of how children had grown up during the first years of Soviet power when their parents spent the whole day at the factory. Marina was furious: a mother's child was running around the streets like a homeless waif and Malaya was handing her an empty line of talk like that!

"Shut your dirty mouth!" commanded Klava Ivanovna.

"I will not!" replied Marina, and said it again: she'd had enough stupid red flags waved in her face.

When Iona Ovseich found out that the schedule had been disrupted and the entire effort was in jeopardy, he first condemned Madame Malaya, who had nothing more intelligent to do than to compare the Soviet system as it was today, with its concrete plan for building communism, with the way it was thirty years ago.

On Comrade Degtyar's suggestion, the activists decided to hear the women's soviet's account of its accomplishments, especially the help given to the family of Soviet Army Major Biryuk.

Predictably the chairperson of the women's soviet, Comrade Kotlyar, had not analayzed the reasons for the disruption, had made no further plans and had not come up with measures to solve the problem. Her pitiful attempts at an explanation—the women were too busy at the factory and with their own housework—could have served as some slight justification if it had been a question of one woman in particular and not of the collective as a whole, which was healthy and able-bodied. After hearing the women's soviet's account, the activists made the following resolutions: to issue Comrade Kotlyar a strict warning and to require a radical restructuring of all the women's activities. Comrade Malaya was to provide the necessary cooperation while, at the same time, stepping up her supervision.

Marina Biryuk asked what specifically Malaya's necessary cooperation would entail since all that woman did was wiggle her butt like a woman trying to catch a husband and didn't get a kopeck's worth of work done.

Klava Ivanovna was indignant: "What's going on here, why isn't anyone telling her to shut up? She hasn't been living in our building long enough to be one of us."

"Don't shout, you don't scare anybody," replied Marina crudely. "If you can help, help, and, if you can't, then stay home and keep your mouth shut."

The concierge, Fenya Lebedev, shook her head and shushed Biryuk. Iona Ovseich observed it all in silence, as if studying what he saw and the more people said the better.

"Comrades," said Lyalya Orlov, raising her hand and receiving permission to speak, "it hurts me to hear the tone of voice Citizen Biryuk uses when addressing our own Klava Ivanovna. In the end, nobody owes Marina anything, and she should thank people for whatever they did do for her."

"No, Orlov!" said Comrade Degtyar, finally ready to speak his mind. "No! Once we had made the decision, we must carry it out as responsibly as we can and in accordance with our laws of morality. Major Biryuk's wife, who wants to help out directly in production and not just sit home, is right on all counts, and Comrade Malaya has no reason for playing any games with her. How long the Biryuk family has been living in our building is of no importance, because no one has given us the right to set up any residence requirements, directly, indirectly, or in any form or guise."

After the meeting, Comrade Degtyar spoke privately with Malaya; he said that for the second time in the last few days she had behaved as if she were living in a vacuum where time played no role.

"Degtyar," said Klava Ivanovna, her voice trembling with offense and anger, "I don't recognize you. You're conducting a very cunning policy and people might not understand it; they've gotten used to thinking that black is black and white is white."

Iona Ovseich smiled slyly, then cited a well-known fact of physics: "When a wheel made of many different colors is spun rapidly, it all turns white, and it's no longer possible to see the colors separately with the naked eye."

"What do you mean by that?" said Klava Ivanovna with a start.

"What I mean by that, Comrade Malaya, is that in practice, when life moves faster and faster every day, a very experienced eye is needed to tell the colors apart."

"And so," said Klava Ivanovna, "there's only one conclusion then: I'm too old and my eyes are no good."

"Don't exaggerate, Malaya," said Iona Ovseich angrily, "and try to improve your approach, or else you might slip behind. And laggards get it in the neck. People should keep the main goal in front of them at all times—they're building communism, and we have to instill communism into daily life, not tomorrow but today, right now, this very minute, because it's a long process and years will be needed. Personal likes and dislikes have to take second place."

Marina Biryuk had no reason to complain the next week; on the contrary, she thanked Klava Ivanovna and exclaimed what wonderful people lived in their courtyard. But after another week, gaps began appearing in the schedule again. Zinochka and Lesik ran around the city; one time they climbed up to the roof of the building and stood together by the edge, causing people in the courtyard and the street to gasp. That evening Marina gave them both a good beating. Her mother-in-law cried that they were shoving her alive into her grave. For an entire week Marina brought her youngest child, Zinochka, to work with her. For the first two or three days her superiors looked the other way but then informed her this wasn't a nursery.

Marina appealed to Comrade Degtyar and reminded him about his promise to help her find a kindergarten for Zinochka. She'd already spoken about it at work ten times but the trade union committee said that it could give her an application or even two but it couldn't find her a place in a kindergarten.

All right, said Iona Ovseich, Marina should write a statement to the chairman of the District Executive Committee with a copy to the director of the Board of Education—the kindergartens were under his direct control—and leave it at that. She would receive an official answer in a week or two. For his part, he would make regular inquiries to keep the pressure on.

On Saturday Iona Ovseich had been extremely busy at the factory and could not devote any attention to Marina's problem the next day, and so Klava Ivanovna and the chairperson of the women's soviet, Anya Kotlyar, made the report on the temporary help being afforded Officer Biryuk's family. This wasn't so much a report as a series of feeble excuses. It was the same story as last time; neither of them found anything more solid to say than that the other women were burdened with their own chores.

Iona Ovseich pounded the table with his fist: "What does that mean, burdened! When the women go from the factory to the kolkhoz to help the kolkhozniks bring in the harvest, nobody talks about burdens! And when the factories were evacuated and rebuilt in the bare steppe, nobody talked about burdens! And in '41 when people dug trenches day and night, there was no talk of burdens!"

As if they had rehearsed it, Klava Ivanovna and Anya Kotlyar replied at the same moment that there was no comparison between front-line Odessa and the Odessa of today.

No, said Iona Ovseich, pounding his fist again, we're always at the front line: either at the front where people give their lives or at the front of peacetime labor and construction! Find me even one newspaper where the party and government don't speak every day about the front!

At the next meeting of the building committee and activists, the chairperson of the women's soviet, Anya Kotlyar, asked to be relieved of her duties.

"We will relieve you of them," said Iona Ovseich, "but not when you want it, but when we find it necessary to."

On behalf of, and on assignment from the initiative group, party member Stepa Khomitsky made a motion to restore and reopen the outpost so that the children of the courtyard would have a place to relax and enjoy themselves, and to make it better than it had been before the war.

Iona Cheperukha was the first to speak on the issue: he personally was entirely for the motion, they even had a cart for hauling the building materials; there was just one little detail missing—the building materials.

Yes, agreed Degtyar, building materials were a problem today, not because there were less, on the contrary, there were more, but the demand for them had grown immeasurably. That had to be taken into account and until they could fix a specific time frame, there was no sense in trying to read tea leaves.

Katerina Cheperukha had given birth to twins—Grisha and Misha. Grisha was half an hour older than Misha. A week later Katya was released from the maternity clinic. Iona Cheperukha, the grandfather, got hold of a droshky with a lantern on it, harnessed his horse Boy, gave him a good brushing, oiled the gear until it gleamed, then seated the new grandmother and the new father and drove to the hospital. Zinovy was against this small-town ostentation—better to be modern about it, either go by car or by trolley. That offended Iona to his depths: if his son didn't like his father's profession, he should find himself another father. And Zinovy was very much mistaken about small-town ostentation: in small towns people hired cabriolets or gigs.

Katya laughed when she saw the lantern on the droshky: "Oh, it's right out of the movies!" Though it was warm and there wasn't a cloud in the sky, the new grandmother insisted that the hood be raised: a wind could spring up at any moment and blow dust on the babies. Katya said weather like that never turned windy. But Olya recalled the time when she had returned home with Zinovy; the weather had been good then too when all of a sudden the wind started blowing, raising clouds of dust like you see in open fields.

The droshky was a success with the people of the courtyard. Marina said that if she ever happened to marry again, she was going to insist her husband hire a carriage like that.

"Marinochka," said Iona, pressing his hand to his heart, "my horse Boy and I are always at your service."

Olya took her husband by the elbow, pinched him hard, and warned him that that was only an advance, full payment would come later.

That evening Klava Ivanovna and the chairperson of the women's soviet, Anya Kotlyar, brought the new mother a set of cotton diapers and three pairs of rompers made from women's stockings but so well done you could hardly tell. A few minutes late Comrade Degtyar arrived straight from the factory; he gave three kisses each to the grandfather, the grandmother, and the principal culprits—the father and mother. Then he took a bottle of eighteen-proof port from the side pocket of his coat and placed it on the table, asking that glasses be brought.

"My dear Zinovy!" said Iona Ovseich, raising his glass and holding it in front of him. "It wasn't that long ago that you were running around the courtyard in your birthday suit, playing with a wooden sword, pretending you were Chapaev. You went to school like all Soviet children, boys and girls. I'm getting old now but thank God I still have my memory, but I don't remember you bringing home great grades every year."

Iona Cheperukha, Olya, and Zinovy himself agreed that his grades had not been the best.

"My dear Zinovy," continued Iona Ovseich, "I can still hear you singing loud enough for the whole courtyard to hear that song about the doctor, which was not part of the children's repertoire: 'Mama, I love a doctor, Mama, I want to marry him!' And now you're a father yourself, or, to be more precise, twice a father. Your sons were born at an important time: the Soviet people are directly involved in creating the material and technological basis for communism, and, to look ahead a little, when your sons are the same age as their parents are now, we can imagine their voices ringing out as they sing the praises of the Soviet Communist republics! Meanwhile, at present, we have decided to restore the outpost, so your children can enjoy it as you did before them, not a bad present, I'd say. May you live to a hundred without growing old, and may our children flourish!"

Tears were gleaming in Iona Cheperukha's eyes when he set down his empty glass. His family and the guests laughed at him a little but Iona himself stubbornly denied those tears and argued that they were just seeing things.

"My dear fellow Iona," said Comrade Degtyar, "a person, and especially a soldier, must never be ashamed of the right sort of tears and try to hide them. There was a French writer by the name of Stendhal. He knew Napoleon personally, and disliked him. But one time he saw Napoleon in the theater, crying at a play about the hard life of a poor young girl. From then on, Stendhal said, his attitude toward Napoleon changed, and he had much more respect for him."

Iona was very moved and openly admitted that Comrade Degtyar was closer to him than his own brother. He went out to the hall and returned with his canvas pants, stuck his hand into one leg from below and pulled out a beautiful flat bottle on which there was a picture of a pretty girl wearing nothing but stockings. Comrade Degtyar took the bottle in his hand, showed it to Katerina, then turned it over as if wanting to examine the back of it. Handing it back to Iona, he said jokingly: "I think you might have made a pretty good lover in the old days."

Iona filled their glasses, tapped the picture of the girl in stockings, and said: "Ovseich, now's your chance to see what she tastes like."

"You old wolf," interjected Olya, "you're a disgrace to your children and your grandchildren."

The host and Ovseich drained their glasses, the others lagged behind them. There was a smell of fusel oil in the room. Iona tapped his foot and started to sing in a drunken voice.

Comrade Degtyar signaled Cheperukha to stop singing and said that he had good news for his generous hosts: he had spoken with the comrades at the Stalin District Executive Committee today and they had made a firm promise to send a commission there in a day or two.

"Dear Degtyar," said Iona, unbuttoning his shirt, "thank you so much for all the good things you've done for us, and what you're doing for us now!"

"Zinovy," said Klava Ivanovna, "do you remember how you laid into Comrade Degtyar? Aren't you ashamed of yourself now?"

The commission was delayed by a week because the District Soviet had dozens of other pressing matters whose number only increased by the day. And it would have been delayed even longer, if Comrade Degtyar had not reminded them of their promise and kept the pressure on.

In addition to Iona Ovseich, the commission was composed of a woman worker from his factory, a deputy from the District Soviet, and a man from the Stalin District Housing Office, a soldier who had lost an arm at the front. The woman proved very likable; she had lost her husband during the war and now lived alone with her son. She was openly sympathetic to the Cheperukhas but, on the other hand, as the saying goes, the more the merrier. The Cheperukhas' place was dry and bright, the little hallway counted for something too, and most important they were all family. She lived in a new development on the outskirts of the city and people there had apartments where strangers lived in adjoining rooms and you wouldn't believe the scenes that led to.

The deputy chatted with the Cheperukhas while helping the official from the housing office measure the length of the walls three times with a tape measure. He also measured the size of the doorways: one was functional and gave entrance to the room, and the other one, which had formerly led to the next apartment, was covered over with wallpaper. The width and depth of the two were identical and taken together totaled one and two-tenths square meters. The total area of the room was twelve and a half square meters. In combination with the hallway, which was not figured in the rental cost, it came to around twenty meters.

"Hold on," said Iona Ovseich. "For all these years the room was ten meters, now it's twelve and a half. What, did it grow in the meantime?"

The official from the Stalin District Housing Office shrugged his shoulders: there was nothing surprising about that—at some point someone must have taken an approximate measure or just didn't include the fractions when multiplying, and the mistake was passed on from one document to the next. Now this new information had to be communicated to the building administration, the bookkeeper should record the extra two and a half meters and enter it on the apartment authorization.

Zinovy, who up till that moment had been standing to one side as if none of this concerned him, now exploded: he had thought Degtyar was going to head a commission of human beings but these people were nothing but inspectors general and horses asses.

The shouting had awakened Grisha and Misha and they began crying in unison. In half a second, Katya had her blouse off and was giving a breast to each of the babies. She raised a fist to Zinovy warning him to keep himself in hand, then began singing softly:

"Lullaby and good night,
Everything is all right.
Lullaby and good night,
Sleep, little boy, sleep tight."

The babies quieted down, suckled a little longer, then fell asleep. The comrade from the housing office marveled that the children were so little but still recognized their mother at once and understood what she wanted.

Katya placed Grisha and Misha back side by side in the washtub where they slept but the deputy advised her to place them head to toe so they'd have more room, and both the mother and the grandmother agreed they'd be more comfortable like that. Zinovy spat on the floor, then began berating the official from the Stalin District Housing Office again: was his principal aim in coming there really to find out if the Cheperukhas were paying the correct rent on their room, especially when the difference was a matter of kopecks!

The official calmly explained that was not his chief aim and if the Cheperukhas themselves hadn't called for a commission, everything would still be the same as it had been before. As far as providing living space was concerned, the commission had no apartments at its disposal; all it did was report its conclusions to the District Executive Committee.

"In other words," said Zinovy, "you can advise the District Executive Committee, but it's up to the committee to take that advice or not."

The official from the housing office scratched the inside of his ear with his little finger and said that was correct, adding that Zinovy Cheperukha should accompany him as he made his rounds and provide him solutions for satisfying everyone.

"Zinovy," said Iona Ovseich, "I think you should have a better idea than most people about the sort of war we've just been through."

"In other words," concluded Zinovy, "first I have to suffer in wartime, then suffer again in peacetime. But the people who stayed here under the occupation are now all calmly living in their own apartments. And some of them even took over places from people who were evacuated, and Jews killed by the Germans."

"Hold on, son," interrupted Iona Cheperukha, "you're not right about that. Your mother was given our apartment back right away."

"Our apartment?" interjected Olya. "But now there's twice as many of us."

"But, after all, everybody was not obliged to return to Odessa," said the official from the Stalin District Housing Office. "Novosibirsk, Chimkent, and Tashkent aren't bad cities either."

"Listen," said Zinovy, turning chalky white, his voice becoming suddenly hoarse, "who do you think you are? Just who the hell are you? And how did you end up in Odessa?"

The official from the housing office did not answer the question but informed the deputy and Degtyar that, as far as this situation was concerned, he had a clear picture of it. The deputy wished the tenants good-bye and advised the new mother to take special care of the babies' ears: "They're still not old enough to tell you if their ears hurt, but ears can cause temperatures and diarrhea, and they'll stop eating, and get painfully thin."

That evening Iona Ovseich made a point of dropping by to see Cheperukha again to say that Zinovy had not chosen the right strategy: he should have watched and listened quietly, and not come charging out of the gate.

"Watch and listen quietly!" said Zinovy, beginning to lose his temper. "That guy came to Odessa from the taiga and now he's telling me I'm supposed to live in Chimkent or Tashkent!"

"By the way, your Katerina is from the taiga too," Iona Ovseich reminded Zinovy.

"But my grandfather, my father, my mother, my children, and me, we're all from Odessa," said Zinovy, becoming very worked up. "And I won't let anyone speak to me like that!"

"Zinovy," said Iona Ovseich, shaking his head, "keep the steam down, the boiler might blow. You fought at the front and you lost a leg, but you're still a child. Take old Degtyar's word for it, you're still a child when it comes to life."

The next week, two commissions came a day apart to visit Zinovy: one was from his factory, and the other from the military authorities. Though their members were different, civilians and military, they came to the identical conclusion: Zinovy Cheperukha was in need of living space and in that connection would now be officially placed on the waiting list. They didn't specify when he would be given space, roughly a year or two.

Iona Cheperukha shrugged his shoulders: so what was two years? Two years was nothing. The war had lasted four years and they got through that, and this was only half of that.

"You old donkey!" said Olya, furious. "You can go live in a barn, but what about the children! If only Degtyar would get the outpost ready, but what do we do till then?"

Suddenly Katerina came up with an idea: the outpost could be used even before it was renovated, it wasn't doing anyone any good as it was now. All it needed was some good repairs. And in Ulan-Ude they had built their own house themselves.

"Katerina," said Iona, completely delighted, "you're a Siberian, you are, but your mind is clear as a diamond, just like Grandpa Cheperukha's!"

At the Kirov factory Zinovy was promised that a little building material would be thrown his way: boards, lime, cement, paint. On his side, Iona had a talk with the managing director of the medical institute's supply department and he too was promised a little something, although it wouldn't come out of their current but out of their used supplies.

Only one detail required attention at that point: to inform Comrade Degtyar of the idea and request him to organize the courtyard to lend support to the house builders.

Iona Ovseich listened to it all intently from beginning to end and made a point of dwelling on the building materials Cheperukha had been promised by the medical institute because institutes of higher learning were not self-supporting and were funded entirely by budget. Zinovy repeated this was only a matter of used supplies, but Iona Ovseich quite reasonably replied that these were not times in which a state institution could just throw things out, because people who did private business could gather that stuff until they had enough to build a whole manor house with a mezzanine.

Zinovy didn't understand—what did manor houses with mezzanines have to do with anything?

"With the fact," explained Iona Ovseich, "that we will be categorically opposed to allowing the premises of the outpost to be turned into a private dwelling."

"It's not going to be a private dwelling," objected Zinovy. "On the contrary, it is a way to increase state living space because the building belongs to the state." The Cheperukha family wanted to use its energy and its own means to help restore the building.

Comrade Degtyar whacked Zinovy on the shoulder: if the Cheperukha family wanted to use its own energy and its own means to restore the outpost to what it was before the war, so it could be used by all the children, no one here would be against that, and they'd even be thanked for what they did.

That was perfectly true, agreed Zinovy. And the outpost, which would not be a private dwelling, would be placed at the disposal of the children as a place for civilized rest and relaxation as soon as he and his family were given an apartment.

"My dear Zinovy Ionovich," said Comrade Degtyar with a smile, "I've been around too long, it's been a long time since I was a child. Many years before the Revolution, my late father used to say to me: it's easier not to give somebody something, than to give it and then get it back. And I'll say it again: it's not a question of my property or yours or anybody else's, it's a question of the outpost, which is community property. And it's something that we, the community, using its own resources, built out of the old laundry room. And I'll remind you of something—when you were still a boy you proved you had political awareness by actively helping the grown-ups work. And now, after all these years and after all you've been through, you want to take a step back."

Zinovy expelled his breath loudly as if he had just drunk a good glass of vodka, and asked: when was the community planning on restoring the outpost?

"Since the decision has already essentially been made," said Iona Ovseich, "the next stage will begin as soon as we get hold of the building materials."

"But what if that's in three years?" asked Zinovy.

"Cheperukha," said Degtyar, squinting with one eye, "don't try to trap me, I'm not a mouse."

"All the same," said Zinovy, developing his idea, "if it really takes three years, and the factory and military authorities are promising me a place much earlier, then why not take up the Cheperukha family proposition?"

Comrade Degtyar shook his head: Zyunchik was still trying to trap him. Once again he said—one year or three, that didn't matter at all, but he would never allow the children's outpost to be turned into an apartment just for Cheperukha. Besides, another factor had to be taken into account; if Zinovy Cheperukha made the outpost into an apartment, then the factory which gave him the building materials, and the military authorities, and everybody else could consider him taken care of and take him off the waiting list, and that way the children would end up with nothing. In the end, this wasn't an individual case but a question of principle.

"Hold on," said Zinovy. "And what if a disabled war veteran with a wife and two children has nowhere to live, is that an individual case or a question of principle?"

"That's untrue and malicious slander!" said Iona Ovseich, whacking the palm of his hand. "You've got four walls and a roof over your head!"

Zinovy moved quite close to Comrade Degtyar and began rubbing his hands rapidly as if he were about to attack. Iona Ovseich opened his mouth as if gasping for breath, his head recoiled and he began shaking. Zinovy filled a glass with water from the pitcher and placed it in front of Iona Ovseich. "Here, Degtyar, drink it."

For a second or two Iona Ovseich looked at him glassy-eyed as if not understanding what he meant, then he picked up the glass and took a swallow. His lips twisted in mockery, Zinovy said that when he was in Mukden, a Chinese man had taught him the proper way to drink water—before it was swallowed, it should be held in the mouth so that the tongue and the roof of the mouth could absorb the necessary particles from the water. Those particles went along the nerves straight to the brain; otherwise it all went down to the stomach and the most precious part of the water left the body with the urine.

It was impossible to tell whether or not Iona Ovseich was taking the advice the Chinese man from Mukden had given Zinovy, but the last sips he took were slow, and he kept the water in his mouth for two or three seconds. When there were only a few drops at the bottom of the glass, Iona Ovseich placed it back by the pitcher, wiped his lips with the palm of his hand, and addressed a question to Zinovy: was the courtyard's position concerning the outpost clear, or was further explanation required?

Zinovy suddenly burst out laughing: he'd thought that Comrade Degtyar would have yielded a little after being given the Chinese man's recipe, which could come in handy for the rest of his life. No, said Iona Ovseich, drawing a line in the air, not for the advice of one Chinaman, not for the advice of six hundred million.

Zinovy went to the District Housing Office the next day. He was seen by an official named Ivan Nefedych Parfentev, who had also been a part of the commission. He listened to Zinovy without speaking, then inquired as to Comrade Degtyar's opinion of the matter. Zinovy was on the verge of pretending that he didn't know because there had been no specific discussion of the issue, but Ivan Nefedych had already guessed how things really stood.

"Listen, Cheperukha," said Ivan Nefedych, "I'll have a little chat with your Degtyar, and, just to be on the safe side, I'll put you in for an appointment with the chairman."

Three days later Ivan Nefedych telephoned Cheperukha at the Kirov factory to inform him that he was to come meet with the chairman; he shouldn't come alone but with his wife and children.

Zinovy objected obstinately, he wasn't bringing any wife or children, he wasn't a beggar asking for charity.

"Listen, Cheperukha," said Comrade Parfentev, becoming angry, "do as you're told, and save your tricks for the circus."

When the chairman received Zinovy, Ivan Nefedych presented the case himself, reporting on the commission and its findings, and, concerning the outpost, said outright that it was in a state of severe neglect, and that repairs done solely on community initiative would not be enough.

"So, Parfentev," said the chairman, drawing his conclusion, "you're in favor of putting the contract into private hands and the community is against it."

The babies began crying, Katya rocked back and forth on her chair to quiet them. The chairman asked how old they were, then addressed Parfentev again: "Here's the thing, Parfentev, you have a little talk with the community, and have Degtyar come by and see me. Just don't put it off. Cheperukha has to have an answer in hand within five days."

"And so that means there was no reason for us to have come today?" said Zinovy, looking from the chairman to Parfentev.

"What do you mean for no reason?" said the chairman in surprise. "You'll be given a final decision in a week."

"But today was just to chat and go home?" said Zinovy, pressing his point.

"No, to get to know one another," corrected the chairman. "Put yourself in my position and tell me if I have the moral right to grant your wish without consulting with the community. That's one side of the question. And the other side is this: do you think the community won't say a word to us if we stand in its way?"

"What does the community have to do with it!" interjected Katerina. "What counts is that Degtyar is your friend, and we're nobody, outsiders, and you don't give a damn about us. But Comrade

Parfentev saw everything with his own eyes and told you what has to be done."

The chairman leaned back in his chair, placed his hands on the arms of the chair, its black lion heads visible under his fingers, and said that Degtyar was no more his friend than Cheperukha was. As for the commission, it was its job to investigate and report, but the executive committee used its own discretion when implementing a practical solution.

The Cheperukha family left. The chairman told Parfentev to stay. Zinovy wanted to wait in the reception room but the secretary told him that was not allowed and that they should wait in the corridor. Still angry after the exchange in the office, Katerina cursed the secretary. Offended, the secretary replied by calling her a slob and then threatening to call the police, but the Cheperukhas were already in the corridor.

Comrade Parfentev came out about ten minutes later, red in in the face, his forehead beaded with large drops of sweat. His empty sleeve spilled out of his pocket.

"Are you out of your mind, woman!" said Parfentev, attacking Katerina. "That's no way to do things. You've got to use a little strategy. All right then. As of now the situation is like this: Degtyar is completely opposed and is collecting signatures from the tenants. I think this is going to have to go to the City Soviet. But that's no disaster, the main thing is will Degtyar collect enough signatures or not."

"Zinovy!" cried Katerina, losing her temper again, though not waking the children this time, "I swear we've got to get the hell out of Odessa. I never want to see this place again!"

Odessa had nothing to do with it, said Zinovy, and she should hold her tongue or else he wouldn't be responsible for what he did. Comrade Parfentev laughed and told Katerina that was good advice because all Odessites were a little nuts and could not bear to hear a bad word said about their city.

On Saturday evening Iona Ovseich called a meeting of the activists in his home and officially informed them that the Cheperukhas were attempting to seize control of the outpost. He said that while this was all still in the planning stage the community should write a letter to the chairman of the Stalin District Soviet.

Dina Vargaftik was the first to take the floor: "No one's denying that Zinovy and his family have a right to living space, but it has to be understood that Comrade Degtyar can't produce a room for them just like that." She herself would be more than willing to be in the Cheperukhas' position—so what if they were a little crowded and didn't have all the conveniences, the family was all together after the war while her Grisha was moldering in his grave, and she couldn't even go to visit that grave.

"And to make up for it," said Dina, beginning to weep loudly, "I have a room of my own, plenty of space, no one bothers me, no one—"

"Hold on, Vargaftik," interrupted Klava Ivanovna, "you're mixing up two different things. Iona Cheperukha and his son Zinovy, who lost a leg at the front, aren't to blame that they're still alive and that your Grisha was killed. War isn't choosy. My son was at the front for a year, then he was transferred back to Moscow to work on designing airplanes. The way you see it, he's guilty before those people who continued to fight and die at the front. But the way I see it is that the party and government know best what has to be done, and no one has the right to be angry at someone just because he's still alive and your husband was killed. My husband Boris Davidovich was killed by kulaks in 1930. And so what was I supposed to do—get enraged and hate the people who weren't killed and are still alive today? And my solution to the Cheperukha problem is this: let them repair the outpost, and, for our part, we should help them do it. Then in a year or two when they're given an apartment, out they go. Whatever expenses they incur in repairing the outpost will end up being used by our children."

"Malaya," said Iona Ovseich, placing his clenched fists in front of him, "I've already explained all this to you: we've had NEP once and we won't have it again. Not one ruble, not even one kopeck of one ruble that belongs to the people will ever go back into a private pocket, and your double-entry bookkeeping doesn't fool anyone here. And I'm giving you all notice that no one is leaving here to go home until we have reached a concrete decision on how to restore the outpost with the community's own energies and means, work that must begin immediately, literally tomorrow."

"Degtyar," said Stepa Khomitsky with a laugh, "but what if tomorrow we put it off until the day after tomorrow? And then to the day after the day after tomorrow?"

"Khomitsky, your sarcasm is out of place here," said Iona Ovseich. "You were the one who made the motion on behalf of the initiative group to restore the outpost for our children."

"That's true, I did," said Stepa, "but then life came up with a little surprise. A disabled veteran, an officer, is in bad need of a place and he's assuming all the expenses, and in the end he'll give the outpost back to the children."

"And then we'll have cat soup, as the children say," said Iona Ovseich.

"Comrade Degtyar," said Anya Kotlyar, the chairperson of the women's soviet, "Zinovy Cheperukha has children too."

Iona Ovseich grinned: "It looks like there's a conspiracy here—Malaya, Khomitsky, and Kotlyar! Nevertheless, a letter from our community demanding that the outpost be returned to the children is going to be sent, and anyone who takes issue with it can write a letter of his own. However, before that happens it would seem proper to inform everyone here that the opinion expressed in our letter is shared fully by the leadership of the Stalin District Soviet."

"Why didn't you say so right away?" said Klava Ivanovna in surprise.

"You know, Malaya," said Iona Ovseich, narrowing one eye and placing his thumb under a button on his shirt, "it somehow never occurred to me that people I've known so well and so long could have allowed such a mess to occur in the first place."

A week later Zinovy received a written reply from the District Soviet: in so far as the community wished to restore the outpost by its own efforts and for the general use of all the children, broadly understood to include the children of neighboring buildings, we do not consider it possible to satisfy the request to use the former Pioneer outpost as an apartment.

After reading the letter, Zinovy began running around the room like a madman, shouting threats about Degtyar which included bringing him to court for falsification. Then, despite the efforts made by his wife, mother, and father to restrain him, he went up to Degtyar's place on the third floor, where he repeated those threats.

"You're still wet behind the ears," shouted Iona Ovseich in reply.

"And even though you're a disabled war veteran, you'll be held fully accountable under the law for slander!"

No, said Zinovy, stomping his prothesis, he was going to go around to all the apartments and collect signatures and bring them to the Province Party Committee himself, then they could figure out who was the slanderer and falsifier here!

All of the neighbors Zinovy visited expressed no objection to seeing the outpost temporarily used as lodgings, but since no one had officially and formally asked their opinion, they refused to sign. Tosya Khomitsky was the only one who signed without any discussion. Iona Cheperukha took the sheet of paper from his son, spat on it, crumpled it into a ball, and tossed it into the wastebasket.

As Parfentev had predicted, it proved necessary to appeal to the City Soviet. Zinovy wanted to go with his family but Parfentev stopped him—he wouldn't be let in to see the mayor with a brood like that! Zinovy made an appointment but it turned out that he could not see the chairman right away and had to speak with his deputy first. Their conversation was short: Zinovy placed all his papers on the table—the documents from the factory, the military authorities, the District Social Security Department, and the District Housing Office. He also informed the deputy that the former Pioneer outpost had been vacant since 1941, and that major repairs and expenses were needed to restore it.

Two weeks later a City Soviet commission arrived, headed by a deputy, Comrade Rakhuba, a lathe operator from the January Uprising factory. Since he was already familiar with the case, Comrade Parfentev accompanied the commission. They went from one apartment to another, and to their question was there any objection to granting the disabled war veteran Zinovy Cheperukha temporary use of the vacant Pioneer outpost, everyone answered that personally he had nothing against it, let the Cheperukhas fix it up. Klava Ivanovna also gave her consent but insisted that Zinovy Cheperukha state in writing his obligation to vacate the outpost and turn it over to the children immediately upon his being given an apartment. Deputy Rakhuba replied that that went without saying, because the law stated that not only could a person not have two dwellings in the same city, he could not have two dwellings even in two different cities. Still, Klava Ivanovna stuck to her guns: the law is the law but a statement in writing is a statement in writing, and it was no great burden to assume.

August came, and the sun shone from morning till night. The Cheperukhas complained that they were losing a golden opportunity to begin construction. There still had been no answer from the City Soviet. Fuming, Zinovy swore he would write to the Supreme Soviet of the U.S.S.R.

On August 14 the Central Committee passed a resolution concerning the magazines *Zvezda* and *Leningrad.* Iona Ovseich immediately organized a tenants' meeting to discuss the resolution. He devoted special attention to the so-called creative work of the notorious poet Anna Akhmatova, who, even in the grim war years, when people were sacrificing their lives without a thought to themselves, was singing the praises of cats and dogs in her poems, if they could be called that. "As for the not unknown writer, Mikhail Zoshchenko, this slanderer and mud-slinger," said Iona Ovseich, "has found an imitator in our own courtyard but our courtyard author's slanders lack Zoshchenko's literary form; our man has neither Zoshchenko's experience or talent."

People laughed because everyone knew to whom Comrade Degtyar was referring, though he did not mention any names. At home Zinovy had been threatening to make a life-size cutlet out of Iona Ovseich. Olya would clutch her head and tell her son to shut his mouth but Katerina would calm her down: you couldn't make a cutlet out of someone like Degtyar, who was all skin and bones.

At the beginning of September a letter addressed to Zinovy Cheperukha arrived from the City Soviet, informing him that he had permission to proceed with repairs on the former outpost and use it as a dwelling until such time as he was given living space of his own. Permission had been granted in view of two circumstances: firstly, the premises were currently vacant and did not appear on the approved list of major repair projects; secondly, the declarant, Zinovy Ionovich Cheperukha was an officer who had served at the front, a category 2 disabled veteran who had been decorated by the government.

Olya Cheperukha was not at home. She had gone with Klava Ivanovna, Dina, Tosya, and Lyalya to a kolkhoz for a week, and so Iona Cheperukha had to mark the occasion alone.

He dropped by the District Housing Office and insisted that Comrade Parfentev be his guest at his home. Comrade Parfentev was very busy and said that he needed this like a hole in the head but he gathered his papers, put them in a drawer, and left with Cheperukha.

The next day Marina Biryuk caught sight of Iona Cheperukha through her window as he was hauling medical equipment with his horse Boy. She shouted for him to stop for a second and ran outside.

"Marinochka," said Iona, twirling his walking stick over his head, "leave your dirty kitchen and come sit here beside me and we'll take a drive to paradise!"

Marina replied that everybody wanted to go to paradise but there was one part of them that kept them out, but now wasn't the time for jokes: people in the courtyard saw Cheperukha bringing Parfentev home yesterday, and this morning Degtyar had come by and demanded that she, Marina, stand as a witness to that. The concierge had come with Degtyar. She had seen Cheperukha and Parfentev through the window drinking and slapping each other's hands as if they were coming to terms on a bribe.

"What kind of bribe!" shouted Iona. Out of fright Boy began to stir. "With what money!"

All right, all right, said Marina with a wave of her hand, she wasn't from the police.

That evening Iona warned his son that every tack and every hair on every brush and every can of paint had to have a circular seal on it.

"And what if the seal's square?" asked Zinovy with a laugh.

"If it's square," said Iona angrily, "it won't be a seal! This is nothing to joke about, you can joke with your Katerina when the power company turns off the lights."

Zinovy shook his head and sighed deeply: he had always respected his father and bragged that his father was a proud man and not afraid of anyone in the world.

"Son," said Iona, drawing a line in the air, "don't be obstinate. If you want, I'll tell you a secret: even though Degtyar is trying to put a stick in our spokes, he's not doing it for his own benefit, and, personally, I respect him for that."

"But spreading gossip that you bribed an official from the District Housing Office, who does that serve, him or other people?"

Iona waved his hand dismissively and said he still wasn't sure how much truth there was in all that, not to mention the fact that it might have been a tactical move, to put a little fear into him.

Zinovy held his head and howled as if from a sudden pain but Katerina laughed and said to her father-in-law: "All you people here in Odessa live by your wits and everybody's pretty good at outsmarting themselves too."

"Bite your tongue, you Siberian," said Iona, raising his voice a little. "I'm going to go to that Siberia of yours and check up on how good people are there, either that or my Katerina reformed real quick here in Odessa."

Instead of a week as they'd planned, the women spent two weeks on the kolkhoz. Aside from grapes, tomatoes, and potatoes, Olya brought back five kilos of flour but she'd had great trouble in getting that much because it had been sweltering all summer, including May; the ears of corn were empty and any that had seed were burned by the sun. The feed for the livestock had also burned and the peasants whose huts were thatched with reeds, went looking for some other form of covering—tile, tar paper, tarpaulin—to have on hand when winter came. For roofing, you could get whatever your heart desired, said Tosya Khomitsky, even a pail of butter.

Comrade Degtyar said that this was all idle talk and gossip, especially because they didn't understand the science of economics and were allowing themselves to draw general conclusions on the basis of limited observations which also needed to be thoroughly filtered first. When her husband Stepa spoke out in support of Degtyar, Tosya told them both to go to the devil and stop trying to confuse her. Then she left for the Church of the Assumption to pray that God would let the famine spare them and that people would make it through the winter to the spring and that the vegetables would come up and they would have food.

"Stepa," said Degtyar, in a tone of very serious warning, "your wife Tosya's conversations with God are her own personal business, but the conversations she has with people in the courtyard are a primary concern of ours."

Stepa ordered his wife to stop spreading negative propaganda. Tosya answered that she didn't give a damn for his orders, but she stopped making prophecies until one day on the porch of the Church of the Assumption she met a nun who had traveled all the way from

Tatishchev, outside Saratov, to Odessa, on charity alone. On her own initiative, and without an invitation from Degtyar, Tosya brought the nun to see him and had her repeat everything she had seen.

Taken by complete surprise, Iona Ovseich was caught off guard and instead of kicking the both of them out, he listened to what the nun had to say—that the harvest was bad everywhere and they were facing a famine even worse than that of '21.

"Listen," said Iona Ovseich, finally getting ahold of himself and addressing the nun, "you're going to be in big trouble if I ever catch you around here again. I see right through you. You're not an Orthodox nun, you're from one of the sects, and you're going around trying to recruit people to your way of thinking."

The nun did not confirm or deny this but thanked him for his hospitality, hastily collected herself, and left the room. Tosya caught up to her by the gate, at the same time almost colliding with Klava Ivanovna.

"Aha," said Klava Ivanovna with pleasure, "that's all that was missing! You're seeing nuns now, are you. I just heard one of them shouting by the railroad station that the Jews have brought down a wave of deaths on all of Russia."

"But your Jews, they crucified Christ," said the nun.

"I'm calling a policeman right now," said Klava Ivanovna, immediately incensed. "We'll look into this at the NKVD and find out where this fascist is from! Tosya, take her by the arms and don't let go of her."

Tosya grabbed the nun by the arm and pressed it hard under the elbow causing the woman pain. The nun began crying and swore to God she'd never come there again, just let her go in any direction out of Odessa.

"No, only in one direction!" shouted Klava Ivanovna, and pointed to the end of the street where the buildings abutted a steep cliff that led to the sea.

Tosya spat in the nun's face, called her a filthy bastard, and let go of her arm. The nun did not wipe her face but, sensing she was free to go, ran quickly down the street as she'd been told to.

"All right," said Klava Ivanovna, "now you've seen the sort of people who say they talk with God. Tosya, I'm telling you this like your own mother: if you go looking for something in an empty place you won't find anything but emptiness."

Tosya was about to mention Academician Filatov, whom she had seen in church, but changed her mind because Klava Ivanovna always had an answer and an explanation for everything, and you had to be in the mood to argue with her.

It was warm all of September, right to the end, and even through the first ten days of October. The Cheperukhas would get up at six o'clock in the morning and work on the outpost until eight, and when they came back from their shifts they'd put in another three or four hours until midnight. They would bring Grisha and Misha out into the courtyard. The children would lie quietly in their washtub causing the neighbors to become openly envious: such quiet children, that's a rare stroke of luck! On some evenings a raw wind would blow in off the sea and they would have to leave the children inside where their grandmother Olya would look after them but then Zinovy would say there was no reason to waste time, Olya should come out and work too.

Of all the neighbors, Tosya helped the most on the outpost. She was quite skillful at scraping walls and Iona Cheperukha announced that she was the only one he'd entrust that job to. Tosya laughed, called him a sly dog, and demanded that she be given Degtyar as her pupil.

"Tosya, he's like you, he'll never learn," said Iona.

While scraping the wall, Tosya reached the place where many years before Efim Granik had painted the words: WE WERE BORN TO MAKE DREAMS COME TRUE! The sky blue paint had faded somewhat but if it were just touched up a little, it would be good as new. Katerina said there was no reason to touch it up, this wasn't a Pioneer outpost or a propaganda center, but Zinovy and his father were in favor of leaving it. Tosya wiped away her tears as she remembered as if it were yesterday her son Kolka singing at the opening of the outpost. Olya also wept and said it should stay where it was, it wasn't bothering anybody.

No, insisted Katerina, it has to be painted over, otherwise it'd look ridiculous: an apartment with a family living in it with a slogan on the wall!

"What do you mean, a slogan?" asked Iona in surprise. "What do slogans have to do with anything. That's a line from a famous song, all the children know it by heart."

"Papa, Mama," said Katerina, beginning to lose patience, "this isn't an outpost anymore. A lot of years have passed since then, do you understand, a lot of years! Zinovy, are you going to say anything to them or are you going to keep mum like your tongue was cut off by an ax!"

"My God," said Olya, wringing her hands, "listen to the way she talks to my son—has your tongue been cut off with an ax! It's enough to send you to any early grave."

Zinovy asked his mother not to make a scene and ordered the writing be left on the wall.

Degtyar came to the outpost on Sunday to check on their progress. Anya Kotlyar and Adya were lending a hand that day. Iona Ovseich praised them for offering their friendship and assistance, and wished them success. Then he asked the Cheperukhas, father and son, to spare him a few moments, in private, so as not to disturb or distract the others.

Though she had no grounds for it, Olya grew anxious. Five minutes later Iona returned to the outpost while Zinovy went with Comrade Degtyar to have a look-see at the invoices and other vouchers because, as Comrade Degtyar had learned, the District Executive Committee might spring a surprise inspection and catch them napping. Zinovy assured him that they couldn't be caught napping because all the paperwork was in perfect order; Degtyar objected that law-breakers and criminals, present company excluded, always thought their affairs were in perfect order but audits and the OBKHSS found the infringements all the same.

Irritatingly, Degtyar proved right: in the outpost there was a still unsealed can of white lead whitewash weighing eight kilos and two hundred grams for which there was no bill or receipt of any sort. Zinovy explained that there was no document because the Kirov factory had been unable to allot him any from its own supply and so he had to buy it from a secondhand dealer at the Old Horse Market.

"And of course the secondhand dealer didn't provide you with a copy of his receipt," said Iona Ovseich with a grimace. "The upshot of it all is that the state has to take Zinovy Cheperukha on his word."

"And why shouldn't it take me on my word?" objected Zinovy.

And if Degtyar was really so worried, wouldn't it be simpler just to pour it into a pail or hide it?

In reply to that line of reasoning Comrade Degtyar made an analaogy with hunting: certain predators, the fox in particular, were in the habit of covering their trail, but as soon as a hunter was on that trail, it was rare that the fox escaped retribution.

"What do foxes and retribution have to do with anything?" asked Zinovy indignantly. He hadn't stolen anything and just the thought of having to hide it made him sick. They were just talking about one lousy can of whitewash.

"Cheperukha," said Comrade Degtyar, "the law doesn't deal in that sort of arithematic, one jar, three jars, ten. It only makes distinctions between petty larceny and felony. If each family in our courtyard acquired one such can of paint by stealing it, you'd need a truck to transport them all. That's one thing. Another thing is that, all right, let's suppose you did in fact buy it from a speculator at the Old Horse Market, but do you mean to say you didn't know it was stolen? Or did you just decide, who gives a damn that he stole it from the state, what counts is that I need it. In other words, you became an accomplice to the crime."

Zinovy was silent, his gray eyes darkening and becoming the color of the sea when the sun goes behind a cloud. Bracing himself with both hands on the table, he rose, walked over to the door, inserted the key, and said: "Leave, Degtyar, I have to do some work."

Comrade Degtyar did not move from his seat and replied: "Let's not get our hackles up."

Zinovy warned him that he was locking the door, Iona Ovseich might have a sudden need to take a leak and wouldn't be able to get out.

"Call your father in here," said Comrade Degtyar.

Zinovy warned him again that he'd be locking the door in a second. Iona Ovseich rose with military speed, passed Zinovy sideways so not to brush up against him, then, after taking a few steps, he turned around.

"Zinovy, I watched you grow up. We both fought at the front and yet for some reason we can't communicate."

Zinovy locked the door and then like a man with two good legs walked quickly across the room and sat by a window.

Klava Ivanovna appeared on the scene three minutes later. Everyone thought that she was there to spend a little time with the children but this time they were mistaken: the first thing that drew her attention was the can with the white lead whitewash that was worth its weight in gold these days.

"Cheperukha," said Klava Ivanovna, "where did you get that paint?"

Zinovy repeated the explanation he had given Comrade Degtyar. Klava Ivanovna listened intently, nodding her head, and then at the end expressed her surprise: if everything really was the way Cheperukha said it was, why keep the can in plain view of everyone where it could turn into a headache for other people!

"Klava Ivanovna," said Zinovy, pressing both hands, one on top of the other, to his heart, a gesture his father always made, "why should I hide it if I haven't stolen anything?"

"My dear Zinovy," said Madame Malaya, pursing her lips, which made it plain how old she'd grown, "in times like these you have to be on guard every minute. One person is a crook and he steals something, another person is honest and pays for it with his own hard-earned money, but both of them turn out to be connected. If the crook couldn't have sold it, he wouldn't have stolen it in the first place."

"Hold on," said Zinovy, "what makes you so sure he's a crook?"

"What makes me so sure," said Klava Ivanovna, stressing the word "me," "doesn't matter, but if the police find out, there could be serious trouble."

"She's right, son," interjected Iona Cheperukha. "We shouldn't be angry at Degtyar. Not at all. We should be good to him like old neighbors who never deceive one another and have nothing to hide. Get rid of that can like it never existed and no one ever saw it."

"It's too late," said Klava Ivanovna. "There's no turning back the clock. That'll only cause more trouble."

Dina Vargaftik was the next to drop by. She wanted to see how the work was going and her eye too was caught by the can. She tried to move the can with her foot but could not. She stopped by the windowsill on which there was a box of nails and said: "Some people have all the luck. Some people have to kill themselves to find a dozen nails, and here's a whole fortune of them."

Zinovy walked over to the box, grabbed a handful, and gave them to her, saying there was no need for her to kill herself over nails. Madame Vargaftik explained that she hadn't been hinting and had no ulterior motive for her remark. Her Grisha had been a jack of all trades, she said with an audible groan, and if he were alive today, they would have made their room beautiful, but now all she had left to do was watch other people fix up their places.

That evening Iona and Olya took a bottle of cherry brandy and went to visit Comrade Degtyar. Katerina was also prepared to go but her husband stomped his prothesis and said: "Two bootlickers are enough."

They returned about an hour later. Iona was not in a good mood and Olya was completely out of sorts. Zinovy asked why and they said it was all because of Polina Isaevna. She had been released from the hospital two days ago, and people in their coffins looked better than she did. It was a good thing Anya Kotlyar had brought her some butter and a few eggs, otherwise she would have had nothing to eat because her husband was so pure when it came to such things.

All right, said Zinovy, let's get to the point: what grievances does he have against us? "He doesn't have any," answered Iona. "He just gave you a neighborly warning so it doesn't happen again. But there's a danger the Stalin District Executive Committee might find out and then they'll have to send a review commission over."

Zinovy laughed out loud but his laughter was mirthless: "Why should the Stalin District Executive Committee send someone to inspect us if everything is on the up and up? It's something else again if someone informs."

Iona sighed: Degtyar had the same idea. There were plenty of envious people in the world and they were always glad to see their neighbor's hut burn down.

The children woke. Katerina sang a soft lullaby to them about two great heroes who would soon grow up and triumph over all the terrible beasts in the forest. When those heroes were still little, they ate so well and so much that everyone marveled. One time, the older boy, Grisha, sneezed and his sneeze knocked a tree over, and the younger one, Misha, laughed and his laughter knocked down another tree.

"All right," said Zinovy, slapping his knee, "either a commission will come or it won't—it doesn't matter either way."

"No," said Olya, crying, "commissions don't waste their time. There's always something that can be found with anybody."

"But listen," said Zinovy angrily, "commissions don't come to break the law! It's just the other way around."

Iona shrugged his shoulders: "It costs time and wear and tear on your nerves to prove that everything's legal."

Iona Cheperukha proved closer to the truth: a week later a commission arrived from the Stalin District Soviet and ordered that the repairs be brought temporarily to a halt. They selected Stepa Khomitsky to help calculate the amount expended on materials. A good deal of work had already been completed and only approximate judgments could be made—a kilogram one way or the other. The commission's impression was that more money had been expended on materials than was covered by the receipts. Zinovy was furious and, like a broken record, kept repeating the same thing again and again: except for the can of whitewash, nothing else had been bought under the counter, not one gram of paint, not a single nail.

Ivan Nefedych Parfentev visited the scene.

"Listen, Cheperukha," he said, "stop harping about the can."

Like a fool, Zinovy again said that it was the God's honest truth, one can of whitewash and that was it!

"You're soft in the head," said Ivan Nefedych. "You're from Odessa but you're still soft in the head!"

Though he was not a member of the commission, Parfentev had brought a building engineer from the District Housing Office and whispered to Zinovy that the engineer had also brought a specialist from the Kirov factory. At first, the commission balked and said they wouldn't allow the specialist to take part. Comrade Degtyar was also indignant at this invasion of uninvited guests but the man from the Kirov factory quite reasonably replied that since the factory was helping one of its own workers by giving him supplies, it had the right to supervise the use of that aid and to make sure it was not being abused.

The conclusions reached by the building engineer and the specialist from the factory did not confirm the commission's suspicions that more had been spent on building supplies than could be accounted for by the receipts. Iona Ovseich insisted that in the interests of truth two other specialists be called in, chosen by the commission this time. The results could be compared.

"Comrades," said Zinovy, on the verge of tears from his vexation at seeing all this time going to waste, "call in a hundred and twenty inspectors and the OBKHSS, just let us get some work done around here!"

Iona Ovseich smiled: to permit the repairs to continue under such circumstances was tantamount to sanctioning it.

Klava Ivanovna was of a different opinion and made a counter-proposal: if some infraction was in fact discovered, the outpost could immediately be placed in the hands of the community, which would conclude the repairs.

After some vacillation, the commission agreed and two weeks after the check had begun, the Cheperukhas were once again rising at six in the morning to work a few hours before their shifts began.

Marina Biryuk took open delight in the whole thing and told anyone she ran into that this time Degtyar had bitten off more than he could chew. A few days later Marina's problems in finding a kindergarten for Zinochka were successfully resolved. Someone launched a rumor that Marina had taken advantage of her job in the cafeteria to grease the right palms, but Marina replied with her usual nerve that they could lick the grease off her ass if they wanted.

On November 7 Zinovy received a good present from the state: a motorized wheelchair with three large bicycle-like wheels built especially for invalids. The little motor clanged and clattered and clouds of light blue smoke poured from the exhaust pipe but somehow in the cool weather the noise and smoke made Zinovy feel warmer and even gave him pleasure of a sort. When he saw the vehicle for the first time, Iona Ovseich said to Zinovy that life in the U.S.S.R. was getting better all the time.

One morning, a few days later, Iona Ovseich had problems at home. Polina Isaevna was feeling poorly and he had to make breakfast for her but just as he was leaving for work Zinovy and his wheelchair pulled up at the gate. There was room enough for another person.

"There's a reason they say that God allows miracles," said Iona Ovseich happily. "I've never been late to work once in my life but today there was a real danger of that happening. Thanks, neighbor."

On the way, Iona Ovseich asked if the commission had sent Zinovy their written conclusion. Zinovy shrugged his shoulders: he hadn't received any conclusion, written or oral, but that didn't bother him much.

"Carefree is one thing, careless is another," said Comrade Degtyar with indignation. "All right, I'll give them a little reminder."

Zinovy thanked Comrade Degtyar but asked him not to trouble himself again: "It'll come when it comes." Iona Ovseich did not reply but when saying good-bye at the factory gate, he said:

"Sometimes people think that if they don't pay any attention to a disease, it won't pay any attention to them. But the disease does pay attention to them and then a day comes when they have to pay attention to it, but by then it's too late."

A large crowd was entering the factory. Comrade Degtyar nodded to the left and the right, shaking people's hands or simply waving in greeting. Zinovy watched for a minute as the people crowded by the gate, marking time with their feet. Iona Ovseich shouted for the people in front to get a move on and the line picked up its pace.

An answer arrived from the Stalin District Executive Committee on the evening of December 4, the day before Constitution Day. The answer was positive: the District Executive Committee permitted repairs to continue though they also issued a strict warning that in the event of any violation, that permission would be annulled and the case turned over to the competent authorities.

One thing led to another: now that all the problems had passed and they could finally breathe easy, Katerina suddenly took it into her head that she absolutely could not live without a toilet of her own. Her in-laws and husband explained that the courtyard bathroom was quite nearby, no more than thirty or forty paces. She should just imagine that she lived in a large apartment and had to go the length of the corridor. But the Siberian wouldn't budge: she wanted a toilet of her own and that was that!

They called in Stepa Khomitsky. He said that the plumbing was already in place but all the same nobody would take on the job without the District Executive Committee's permission.

"What's the solution then?" asked Iona.

Stepa thought for a moment, scratching the back of his head, and suggested that the young bride could always run to the District Executive Committee where there were plenty of bathrooms.

"Don't be so smart," said Katerina, taking offense.

"He's not," said Iona, sticking up for Stepa, "he's just making a joke: He thinks you need a bathroom of your own."

When Klava Ivanovna was told, she stated flatly that she was absolutely against the idea because then Degtyar's predictions would start coming true: the Cheperukhas weren't occupying the outpost temporarily but wanted all the conveniences there, and soon the place would be another Vorontsov Palace.

Katerina argued that by today's standards an indoor toilet was normal and that people shouldn't have to run the length of the courtyard in freezing cold weather.

"So don't run, no one's forcing you to," replied Klava Ivanovna. "You can keep on living with your in-laws, they've had a bathroom put in. And, by the way, there are ten apartments in this courtyard that could make the same complaint you are. And so what do you think we should do, raze this old building and put a new one in its place? But where the state is supposed to get the money and building material for all this is of course no concern of yours. What matters is that Katerina Cheperukha be well off, nobody else counts."

Comrade Degtyar observed all this in silence and did not intervene. On the contrary, he said to Malaya that the Cheperukhas should apply to the District Executive Committee so that finally everyone could see with his own eyes what a blunder had been made. Klava Ivanovna objected that the Cheperukhas had nothing to do with this, Katerina was the only one involved. Iona Ovseich replied that when one member of a group launches a project, the other members can always pretend that they're not involved. That makes for a good trial balloon.

Klava Ivanovna invited Zinovy to her apartment and warned him not to apply to the District Executive Committee under any circumstances, otherwise they'd lose everything they already had; Degtyar wouldn't yield this time. Stepa Khomitsky, who was quite familiar with this type of problem, also advised Zinovy to exercise restraint for now, but later on, after the Cheperukhas had made the outpost habitable and everyone was used to them living there, they could try again.

Katerina kept up the fuss for a while longer, saying winter was just around the corner, she had little children and piles of diapers, but, in the end, she understood: better to have some inconveniences in your own apartment, than to live in someone else's with all the conveniences.

Just before New Year's people came from the Stalin District Executive Committee to check for violations in the approved repair plan. They made a thorough check of the corner where the tap and drain pipe were located. They warned Zinovy Cheperukha not to do anything foolish or he'd bear the responsibility for it personally and then wished him good luck in his new home.

The walls were still unfinished. Iona recalled that ten years before when they were redoing the laundry room, they had heated and dried various parts of the wall with Primus stoves but that method wasn't suitable now given the shortage of kerosene; the only possibility was to use a potbellied stove. This they did, extending the flue through the window and directly into the courtyard. Two days later they had to remove it because the concierge, Fenya Lebedev, threatened to call the fire department. Iona crudely replied that he didn't gave a damn about her threats. Fenya complained to Comrade Degtyar, then went to the fire department and brought a fire inspector back. The upshot was that the Cheperukhas paid a twenty-five ruble fine, money that could have paid for a few extra loaves of wheat bread at the market.

Polina Isaevna reproached her husband for not stopping the concierge: the Cheperukhas weren't causing anyone any harm, and what they'd been doing was out of necessity, not malice. Iona Ovseich asked his wife to lie still and not interfere; to stop a person from doing his real duty was the greatest crime of all.

Iona Cheperukha proposed they have a traditional housewarming. He'd go to Peresyp, over by the Baltsky Highway where he knew someone with first-class stuff, better than any whiskey.

Both the women were for Iona's idea but Zinovy was definitely against it: you couldn't have a party when people were walking around hungry and worried.

"Hungry, cold, and worried!" said Iona with a broad gesture. "Next you'll be saying that people are dropping on their feet and there are corpses all over the sidewalks—1921, 1930, back then people really were swollen up from hunger. And, it was all right, thank God, they survived."

They held the housewarming on New Year's by the old calendar, the thirteenth of January. Adya Lapidis played the accordion. Stepa and Iona danced a cossack dance. Comrade Degtyar dropped by for five minutes while Polina Isaevna stayed home alone. He drank a glass with the hosts, then he took Olya's scarf, lifted it over his head, and swung it around in a circle twice.

People clapped and shouted: "Encore!" Wiping her tears, Klava Ivanovna kept saying: "God, it feels like before the war again."

Tosya Khomitsky put her arms around Zinovy, who had been her Kolka's best friend. She too broke into tears, then she threw a plate to the floor so there would be nothing but goodness and happiness in that home. The plate didn't break and she had to throw it a second time.

Joseph Kotlyar and Anya were a little late but redeemed their guilt at once: they had brought the Cheperukhas a baby carriage for two. The carriage was so wide that it got stuck in the door and had to be brought in the window.

"Kotlyar," said Iona Ovseich in a tone of praise, "you give presents like the Demidov, the merchant from the Urals who had his own mint and made Catherine the Great look like a beggar woman!"

At the table Iona Ovseich said a few nice things to Joseph Kotlyar, this time concerning his relationship to Adya; in a short time they had bought the boy a piano, an accordion, a desk with two pedestals, and a gabardine suit; you don't see that every day, even with a child's own real mother and father.

Joseph sighed deeply: "Degtyar, I lost two sons. What else do I have now in the world? But I can take a hint: you want to know where I got the money to buy presents like that. I think you already know: besides running the punch press at the Bolshevik factory, I do another shift at home as a shoemaker."

"Joseph," said Degtyar, bending slightly closer to him so as not to have to speak too loudly, "people in the courtyard are saying that they've seen you at the secondhand market with new pairs of shoes that look like factory work. Be honest, tell me, as one shoeman to another, where can you get that kind of high quality material these days, especially leather and box calf?"

"Degtyar," said Joseph, taking offense, "I can see you don't trust me much. I tell you that I'm doing a little shoe repair and you answer that I've been seen selling fashionable shoes in the secondhand market."

"That wasn't my answer to anything," said Iona Ovseich. "I just told you what people are saying about you."

"That's what they say!" said Joseph angrily. "They say they milk hens in Moscow, but you have to look high and low for a quart of milk at the market!"

Iona Ovseich sat straighter, gave Kotlyar a cold look, then rose from the table. Joseph tried to stop him, saying it didn't feel like they were done talking, but Iona Ovseich said an all-inclusive good-bye and explained that he had to rush back to his sick wife, who had been alone all day now as it was.

The guests stayed another half an hour, then went home. Tosya Khomitsky had had too much to drink, and, not only that, she had not been eating appetizers as she drank; on the staircase she started trying to prove to Stepa that famines come every thirteen years: 1908, 1921, 1933, and now again. Stepa also had had a little too much to drink but had retained full clarity of mind and quoted different figures: the last famine under Nicholas II had been in 1912, and it was nine years to 1921, and from 1921 to 1933 was twelve years, where was she getting the thirteens?

Though Tosya had nodded her head as Stepa had figured aloud, she began harping on thirteen again: every thirteen years, thirty-three plus thirteen was forty-six.

"Don't predict bad things," said Stepa, "or they might come down on you."

Then, out of the blue, Stepa suddenly remembered the hanky-panky between Tosya and Kotlyar and struck her a hard blow. Tosya began crying and said it was all a pack of lies, and nothing had happened. Stepa hit her again, then walked on ahead to open the door.

When they were home and in bed, Tosya began speaking in a mournful tone about little Liza Granik, who was now in the countryside and nobody knew whether her father was dead or alive. She was quiet for a time, then started in with her thirteens again, predicting bad luck for the Cheperukhas: they'd held their housewarming on the thirteenth and the dish hadn't broken the first time.

"You fool," said Stepa, "it's a little of everything with you tonight."

Astonishingly, something bad did happen to Iona Cheperukha the very next day: when he was driving his horse Boy up Kherson Slope, going up from Peresyp, the axle on a three-ton truck coming the other way suddenly broke, the horse took fright, and bolted to the side. The barrel of cottage cheese Cheperukha was hauling to the patients at the therapeutic clinic fell off the back of his cart and onto the pavement. More than half spilled out, and in a very inconvenient spot as well, one where there was horse manure on top of the snow. Iona gathered up as much as he could. Passersby helped a little. They picked up what was left behind as unfit for the hospital and cleaned it off. Anyone who had a newspaper or any sort of paper made a container of it and filled it to the top, and those without paper gathered it in their hands and ate it on the spot.

Two people who had been present from start to finish got on the cart to go with Iona as witnesses. On the way, Iona allowed each of them to take another handful, especially since the cottage cheese on top wasn't perfectly clean.

Despite the witnesses, Iona still got a good tongue-lashing at the hospital. They threatened to fire him. And no one believed that Boy, who had been born in Odessa and spent his whole life around cars, would shy to the side, just from fear, as his master would have it.

The hospital administrators ordered a report written up, obliged the driver Cheperukha to make good the loss, and appointed a commission to check on Boy's condition: was he properly shod and receiving all the food allotted him?

When the steward and an assistant from the commission examined Boy, Iona was so agitated by this insult that he came close to hitting the assistant. He wanted to walk away from those stupid people who didn't understand a single thing and only knew how to cut up corpses and make their diagnosis after the death.

Cheperukha's neighbors in the courtyard were very sympathetic. Iona Ovseich said to Polina Isaevna that of course the housewarming being on the thirteenth and the plate not breaking were stupid superstitions but there absolutely was some sort of symbolic coincidence there—the son had just held his housewarming and literally the next day look what happened to the father!

"Degtyar," sighed Polina Isaevna, "a person could think you were glad."

"Polina," replied Iona Ovseich, "I can't be glad about that, especially since many patients had to do without food that day."

Anya Kotlyar arrived, bringing a dozen fritters fried in butter and a piece of sheep's milk cheese that couldn't have weighed less than half a pound.

"Anya," said Polina Isaevna indignantly, "if you don't stop bringing me presents like these, I'll never be able to pay you back."

"Polina Isaevna," said Anya, holding her hands palms up in front of her, "my Joseph might have ten thousand faults but no one could ever deny that when he shares with a person, it's from the heart, and he'd curse you out if he ever heard any talk of being paid back."

Iona Ovseich was sitting by the window with a copy of *Pravda* in hand and took no part in the women's chat until Anya Kotlyar repeated what she'd heard from Tosya Khomitsky, a horrible story about an old woman in an out of the way village over by Lake Kunduk, sixty miles outside of Akkerman, who had eaten her two grandchildren. Polina Isaevna had just managed to ask where the children's father and mother were, when Iona Ovseich came swooping down on Anya like a golden eagle and categorically forbade her to set foot in his house again if she was going to be the bearer of such rotten lies and provocation.

Anya shrugged her shoulders and again said that she hadn't made it up but was just repeating what Tosya had told her, and Tosya hadn't made it up either.

"All right," said Iona Ovseich, throwing his newspaper onto the table, "but just look around at your own life, and tell me what your own family had to eat today. Then give me a straight answer to this—do you really suppose that people would be eating like that if there really was a famine in this country?"

"Why are you using me as an example?" said Anya in surprise.

"Why am I taking you as an example?" repeated Iona Ovseich. "I'll tell you why. If you're able to bring my sick wife food as a present, that means it's something you're able to do, and I have to assume you didn't take the last of your family's food for it."

Anya drew her hand across the scar on her cheek and said, "No one's saying that there's a famine in Odessa and that people are dying here, but they are in Moldavia; Khomitsky wasn't the only one she'd heard that from, and there were cases of people dying from dystrophia. And, as far as Polina Isaevna was concerned, she had to eat well, otherwise where was her organism going to get the strength to fight from?

"Comrade Medical Corps Lieutenant," said Iona Ovseich, whacking the table, "that's not your problem! And let me ask you this: and where did wounded partisans get their strength from when they hid in the forest for ten days, bleeding, without a drop of water or a crust of bread, and not only that they had to keep a sharp lookout because death could be waiting for them behind any bush! And, thank God, they survived."

As a military nurse, Anya Kotlyar too was able to cite many striking examples of people literally coming back to life before your eyes; when Leningrad was under siege and people were only getting an eighth of a pound of bread, if you could've even called it that, people with ulcers were cured of them even though no diet had done them any good in peacetime.

"And so what conclusion should we draw?" asked Iona Ovseich.

"War is war," replied Anya, "and what a person can survive in wartime, he can't necessarily survive in peacetime."

"That means," said Iona Ovseich, "it's not a question of what someone eats but of his mental attitude."

"That's right," agreed Anya, "the mental attitude is the main thing." But then she added at once: "For everyone to be in a wartime state of mind, there has to be a front and bombs falling. People have to be wounded and killed."

"Let's say that's so," said Iona Ovseich. "But then how are you going to explain the Kuzbass where people lived in tents and were lucky to get hot food once a week. What about the White Sea-Baltic Sea, what about Magnitogorsk, when people were up to their waists in icy water when the temperature was twenty below!"

Anya honestly admitted she couldn't answer that: you needed a higher education for that and she was only a middle-level medical worker, but the people on the construction sites in the Kuzbass, the White Sea-Baltic Sea, and Magnitogorsk might have felt that they were at the front.

"Aha," said Iona Ovseich, raising a finger, "so that means bombs don't have to be falling on people's heads, that it isn't necessary to have casualties for people to perform miracles of determination and heroism."

Anya motioned with her hands: "So then what's the point, why don't things always turn out well?"

"Why not!" Iona Ovseich inserted his thumb under his lapel and began pacing the room. "You do some serious thinking about the arguments and propaganda you've been spreading all evening, and then you tell me."

Anya replied that she wasn't spreading any arguments or propaganda, especially since she had had one peculiarity ever since she was a child—she couldn't put her feelings into words.

"That's all right," said Iona Ovseich assuringly, "you expressed yourself well. A person doesn't do that well without practice."

Anya shrugged her shoulders: what kind of practice? Where was she supposed to practice? She didn't have time to look up at work and at home Joseph was pounding away with his hammer until midnight. She had no one with whom to speak.

Iona Ovseich smiled: in Odessa even little children knew that nobody liked to talk like shoemakers and barbers, who get information and news from all their different customers. And, of course, they tried to repay the favor.

On February 23, when everyone was celebrating Red Army Day, also known as Soviet Army and Navy Day, a rumor spread through the courtyard that at the market and New Bazaar the police had caught a gang that was selling piroshki whose filling was made of human flesh. The rumor was a hair-raising one and Comrade Degtyar requested Stepa Khomitsky, Klava Ivanovna, and Dina Vargaftik to determine its source immediately.

When they went to see Joseph Kotlyar, he said straight out that Degtyar's orders were unsuitable because the rumor was everywhere and could be heard in various parts of the city: Moldavanka, Slobodka, Vorontsovka, Peresyp, Bugaevka, Dalnye Melnitsy, and, if you want, even in Akkurazha. There was a guy from Akkurazha who worked in his factory and who went home for Sundays and he heard it first there, not in the city.

"Tell Joseph Kotlyar," said Iona Ovseich, "that every chain has its beginning, and they might just begin in negative attitudes like that."

"What I think," said Joseph in reply, "is that when people have as much bread to eat as they want, those rumors will all fizzle out."

Zinovy Cheperukha, who spent every free minute he had studying for the entrance exams to the polytechnical institute, said almost the exact same thing.

"A strange coincidence," said Iona Ovseich with a laugh. "It looks like Kotlyar and Cheperukha form a single bloc. Instead of condemning the gossip-mongers, they're showing what approval and sympathy amounts to."

Stepa Khomitsky said he didn't see any approval or sympathy in that, but to blame everything on the bread shortages would be wrong from the political point of view. Anyone who spread panic at the front was shot on the spot.

People's spirits were lifted when the warm breezes began blowing in March and the snow began melting from the fields, revealing the black, glossy earth that looked as if it had been smeared with grease. So evident was the change in morale that Klava Ivanovna compared it with a thermometer which had been hung in direct sunlight.

In one morning the market, the New Bazaar, the Alekseevsky and Old Horse Markets now sold more meat than they had in the three days before, including beef and pork, not to mention mutton and veal, and the prices were four or five times lower than that of bread. It was a cause for rejoicing, even though, looking ahead a little, you could predict that the animal stock would have to be replenished, which would take no little time. But, on the other hand, if things were easier today than they were yesterday, why spoil the mood for yourself and for others by thinking about what tomorrow might bring, especially since the situation might suddenly take a turn for the better and tomorrow prove even better than today.

Joseph Kotlyar told a foolish joke. "If you have a place to make love and someone with whom to make love and you have nothing with which to make love, it is a comedy." People laughed, but no one laughed louder than Joseph, who translated the joke into today's terms: if you have meat and teeth with which to chew that meat you should eat at once, otherwise your teeth might fall out and then you'd have nothing to do it with, meaning enjoy today.

Anya dropped by to see Polina Isaevna to see how she was doing and treat her to some broth made of first-rate ingredients with lots of fat in it, such a broth was a sight for sore eyes. They began speaking of Joseph and Iona Ovseich said that the old gray horse was acting pretty frisky these days.

"Oh," sighed Anya, "he's still as stupid as a boy, and at his age too. Before the war I thought he was an old man but it turned out the other way around. I got old before he did."

"And just look at my Degtyar," said Polina Isaevna with a sigh. "I look like his grandmother when we're side by side."

"The American writer Mark Twain wrote a story about a man who figured out that he was his own grandfather. That could happen. All the same, Joseph Kotlyar shouldn't forget how old he really is because people around him still remember," Iona Ovseich said.

Anya told her husband of the entire conversation, which he disliked hearing intensely. He rolled himself a thick cigarette, took a few puffs, and said that first Degtyar should make sure his own wife ate well and then try to scare people with his advice and his threats.

Though there was no cause for alarm, Anya and Adya began sealing the bags containing leather scraps. You could never tell what would happen and sometimes such little things could make for big trouble. As Adya worked his face was sad and pensive, like a person remembering the distant past. Anya tugged him by the arm so he would shake off his bad thoughts and cheer up. "It's all right," said Adya, "it's nothing." The boy had tears in his eyes but he was smiling. At that moment he looked so much like his father, Vanechka Lapidis, that Anya could not restrain herself and began crying.

"Oh, you are two of a kind," said Joseph.

Anya wept all the harder and told her husband not to make crude jokes. Joseph became angry and said that anyone who didn't like his jokes could move in with Degtyar. Adya responded that Degtyar wouldn't have room for all those people.

"Don't worry," said Joseph, "Degtyar will find room for everyone, there's no limit!"

The Revenue Department checked on Kotlyar twice during April, the second time a day after the first, when no one would be expecting it. The day before the second visit Joseph had brought home a sack of scrap leather. Out of compassion for the poor invalid, the concierge, Fenya Lebedev had grabbed the sack from him to carry it up to the third floor. Taken by complete surprise, Joseph cursed her vilely instead of thanking her.

"Good lord," said Lebedev, throwing up her hands, "who cares what you've got in that sack, even if it isn't just leather but gold and diamonds."

"You're a fool, a total fool," said Joseph. "They need someone smart for your job."

"Somebody like you, huh?" Fenya snapped back.

In response Joseph threatened her with a finger and said that she better not get too big for her britches, there were plenty of people in Odessa who'd like her job and, if need be, they'd go find one.

During the Revenue Department's second visit, the official was accompanied by Dina Vargaftik because Klava Ivanovna was in bed with a temperature. He carefully emptied all four sacks containing shoes and scrap leather. Joseph stood by and observed with a smile as if he were not involved. The official said he saw nothing to smile about, on the contrary; then he demanded to be shown the sack from the day before. Joseph picked up the empty sack, which was lying by the revenue agent's feet, shook it out again, and handed it to him.

"Don't pretend to be more than you are," said the official angrily, "and don't try to make fools of people either. We have information that you've been receiving goods illegally direct from the factory."

"Then why did you come here?" said Joseph in surprise. "You should go to the factory."

The official lost all patience then and said that he would send the OBKHSS here and then we'd see if Joseph changed his tune.

"Comrade," said Joseph with a smile, "there's a folk saying—better to lose with the wise than find with a fool. Why should I be afraid of the OBKHSS? The OBKHSS is the guardian of the law, not some old witch carrying a bag full of children. Comrade, I didn't lose my leg in the last war, I lost it in the Civil War when you were still tied to your mother's apron strings."

That same evening Iona Ovseich was given a complete report on the visit of the official from the Revenue Department. Dina had been deeply ashamed for Joseph Kotlyar, who had allowed himself to speak with a grown man as if he were an idiot who didn't understand anything at all. All in all, people didn't change much: Kotlyar was still the same as he was before the war, when she and Grisha brought him up in front of the building committee for destroying the building, and he'd stay like that till the day he died.

"Is that it?" asked Iona Ovseich. "You're free then, you can go home."

In the end Dina said once again how ashamed she had been because of Joseph's gibes, especially the ones at the OBKHSS, but Comrade Degtyar only saw her to the door, whacked her on the back, and wished her a good night.

Polina Isaevna had heart problems during the night. At first she fought against the pain silently, enduring it, but soon it became unbearable and they called Anya Kotlyar. Anya gave her two injections, one after the other, put mustard plasters on her back, and sat with her until daybreak when Polina Isaevna began to feel considerably better. Iona Ovseich spent the entire time lying quietly on his couch, a heavy sigh escaping him two or three times. Anya said that she could give him an injection too, it couldn't do any harm, but he refused it.

When Anya returned to her apartment, Joseph had already made himself breakfast and was strapping on his prothesis; time was short and he was in danger of being late for his shift. The Bolshevik factory was far away, out past the Peresyp Bridge, you had to take two trolleys and still walk a good stretch on foot.

Anya was on evening duty that day in the hospital. She had time to drop by Polina Isaevna's again and prepare some lunch for her. Iona Ovseich called home from the factory. Polina Isaevna told him not to worry and was about to hand the phone to Anya to confirm that she was all right but he said not to, it wasn't necessary.

Adya also stopped by to see Polina Isaevna on his way home from music school, spending about five minutes with her. Polina Isaevna asked how his preparations for final exams were going and what the conservatory was putting on this year, then she burst into tears: if his father and mother could only see their son, how proud they'd be! Then she added that God should give everyone a second father and mother like Joseph and Anya, telling Adya to go home and practice. When saying good-bye she took his hand and asked him to play some Chopin a little louder than usual so she could hear it there in her apartment.

Adya did as she asked, and she could hear him playing particularly well that day. Polina Isaevna's tears flowed ceaselessly and a bittersweet feeling arose in her soul; she wished that the past would return for a moment, those years when they were still young and healthy and had all of life before them.

Iona Ovseich came home from the factory early—the radio had just announced that it was eight o'clock Moscow time. Polina Isaevna was still under the spell of the music which Adya had played especially for her, and she said how lucky they were to have such decent people as the Kotlyars for neighbors. Degtyar registered no expression. Polina Isaevna repeated her testimonial but apparently her husband's thoughts were so far away that he simply didn't hear her.

"Polina," said Iona Ovseich, "I'm going to tell you a piece of news that will stun you."

Polina Isaevna grew extremely tense even though she knew full well that people did not start like that when they had bad news.

"Literally a half an hour ago," said Iona Ovseich, "I was informed by telephone that Efim Granik is alive."

"Unbelievable!" cried Polina Isaevna, turning pale.

"I'll tell you something else. He's not only alive, he's in Odessa even as we speak."

Polina Isaevna was so stunned that she forgot to ask who had been the first to find out and to call Degtyar.

"And I'll tell you another thing," continued Iona Ovseich; "he's wandering the city, afraid to come to the courtyard."

"My God," said Polina Isaevna, "he must have gone out of his mind when he found out that Sonya and the children had been killed!"

"No, he didn't go out of his mind," said Iona Ovseich. "But you have to think that a man who didn't show his face for so many years after the war had to have some good reason for that."

The next day, just as the sun had begun setting, all the people of the courtyard saw Efim Granik with their own eyes. He was standing by the tap in the courtyard where the children liked to play before the war. Craning his neck as he looked around, he appeared to be gazing up at the sky but the sky couldn't have been more ordinary that day: no rain clouds, no clouds at all, no flocks of birds, not even a single bird, just a sky the same dark blue that a spirit lamp's flame sometimes acquired when it was burning soundlessly.

"Fima!" screeched Dina Vargaftik. "Fimochka!"

Efim continued looking up at the sky as if his name hadn't been called. First, the stretch of sky above the courtyard would darken, becoming almost black, then would grow light once more. Dina called out to him again and this time he turned his head. His eyebrows rose very high, he bit his lower lip and smiled.

"Who could ever have expected it, who could have thought it!" said Dina, pressing her hand to her heart with such force that her fingernails dug into her chest. As if deranged, she could not help thinking again and again of her Grisha, who would come back home one fine day just like Efim, and stop by the tap where the children liked to play before the war, and the death certificate she had received from the military would turn out to have been just a mistake.

Dina wanted to invite Efim to her place but though her health was not back completely yet, Klava Ivanovna had already managed to dash out into the courtyard, grab Efim by the arm, and start dragging him away. When they were on the stairs, Efim said he wanted to go to his own place, his own apartment, but Klava Ivanovna pretended not to have heard him. At her doorway Efim repeated that he wanted to go to his own place, his own apartment. Klava Ivanovna came to a sudden stop as if staggered, and clasped her hands.

"Fima, are you that out of it! People have been living in your place for a long time now."

"You mean my room isn't mine anymore?" asked Efim. "Where am I going to live now?"

"At the Isakovich bathhouse!" answered Klava Ivanovna, the way people used to do in Odessa before the war when asked a stupid question.

Efim suddenly rose to his feet and said it was time for him to leave, and started for the door. Klava Ivanovna was so caught by surprise that she remained sitting on her chair and only caught up with Efim on the stairs. He insisted that he had to be going.

"Where do you have to go?" Klava Ivanovna finally asked.

Fima thought for a moment, ceased insisting, and they both went back to Klava Ivanovna's.

An hour later after Madame Malaya had given her guest a piece of soap and a towel and sent him off for a bath—you need a good washing after a long trip—the courtyard already knew that Efim Granik had come back to Odessa from a camp somewhere far past the Volga. He had spent two years in the camp, ending up there right after the war, along with other soldiers who had been prisoners of war, and who had been liberated by the Americans and then turned over to the Soviet command.

In many ways it was Efim's own fault that he had spent two full years in a camp. When questioned by a commission as to why he, a Jew by nationality, had remained alive when in the Nazis' clutches, Efim had replied that good luck had played a part in all that. Even some of the soldiers in his own company thought he was a Tartar, and one of those soldiers was a real Tartar, by the name of Gabitov from the town of Syzran. When the Germans took them prisoner in '42 outside of Malgobek, in the Caucasus, they lined them up and ordered all commissars, communists, and Jews to step forward. He already had one foot in the air when Gabitov grabbed his shirt from behind and restrained him. He didn't know where Gabitov was now, and whether he was dead or alive, but Gabitov could back him up on that.

The commission had listened closely, but, as for the sole witness who could corroborate the story, if he could be found, the commission only smiled. The commission had already encountered dozens upon dozens of such stories of good luck. And, as far as Efim's looking like a Tartar was concerned, that resemblance was confined to the fly, since the Tartars also practiced circumcision. "How can I prove it to you if you won't believe me?" asked Efim. One member of the commission, with a major's insignia, looked Efim straight in the eye, then bent to the man beside him and whispered something in his ear, but that man waved his hand in dismissal and ordered that the guard be called.

After Efim's bath, Madame Malaya brought him to see Degtyar. Iona Ovseich and Polina Isaevna were surprised at how well he looked, the years didn't seem to have affected him. Efim said that was because of the long steam bath he had just taken. He'd poured a hundred basins of hot water over him.

"You counted?" said Polina Isaevna with a laugh.

That's right, answered Efim, his face twisted by a cunning grimace. Then he began telling them how the Germans had disinfected him and the other prisoners of war: the Krauts brought them to a hut where there was another Kraut sitting by a barrel of tar. He'd dip in his scoop and whack you with it on your back, your legs, your face. Then they were taken to a bathhouse, lined up backs to the wall, and the Krauts started spraying them with burning hot water from a hose. Anyone who tried to dodge the water was beaten with a hose and got a double dose of hot water. Then they were taken out naked into the freezing cold and they had to run around in the snow, and that went on for three days in a row. He'd felt cold ever since then and so he loved to douse himself with hot water. And he had seen Hitler in the flesh one time, just like he was seeing them now, only even closer up.

"Did he talk to you?" asked Klava Ivanovna, stunned.

No, said Efim, shaking his head. He just pointed his finger at me and said: *russisches Schwein, russische Dreckscheisse, russisch Vanka.*

"And where was your camp?" asked Iona Ovseich.

Efim thought for a moment, moving his lips, then said the camp was in France, the city of Metz, not in the city itself, a little off to one side of it.

"And the French Resistance didn't make a single attempt to free the prisoners?" asked Iona Ovseich in surprise.

Efim thought for another moment and it was clear by his face that he was recalling images from the past, then he suddenly turned toward Polina Isaevna and asked: where could his Sonya and the children have gone, and why hadn't they come back after all that time?

Polina Isaevna was not able to utter a single word because of the sudden lump in her throat. Klava Ivanovna answered for her, saying that ten million people must have lost their lives in the war, if not more, and what was done was done and not even God himself could do anything about it. Efim should rejoice that his little daughter Liza was alive and being cared for by good people.

Efim said that he had a son, Osya, who wrote poetry, and a daughter Khilka, and their mother's name was Sonya, but he didn't recall any Liza—was she their little sister?

So as not to upset the others, Polina Isaevna turned toward the wall, her shoulders twitching as if she were suffering from a bad case of hiccups. Iona Ovseich peered at Efim and drummed his fingers on the table.

"Stop that," said Klava Ivanovna. "I've got a headache as it is."

Iona Ovseich stopped for a second, then resumed drumming his fingers because his nerves required some release of their tension.

Suddenly Efim rose, said it was time for him to go, and began heading for the door. This time Klava Ivanovna was able to stop him before he left.

"Where do you have to go?"

Iona Ovseich was displeased by Klava Ivanovna's action: Efim should have been allowed to leave, but he shouldn't be left alone, an eye should be kept on Efim.

Five minutes later Efim rose again and declared that he wanted to go home and asked to be given his keys back. No, Iona Ovseich answered very clearly, he wouldn't be given the keys back: the apartment that had once belonged to him, Efim Granik, was not his anymore but belonged to Major Biryuk, who was presently with his unit in Berlin while his family was living here.

All right, said Efim, since people had thought he was dead, he didn't have any objection to Major Biryuk being given his apartment, but now that he'd come back, the Biryuks had to leave, he wanted to go home.

"Efim," said Iona Ovseich, rising from his chair, "no matter how often you keep saying that, the real situation is not going to change. You were released from the camp on the amnesty for the thirtieth anniversary of the Revolution. That's number one. And number two is that it's irrelevant to argue that something should be a certain way because it has been that way before. And number three, one can only admire how well your memory starts working when the subject is your apartment."

Efim squinted his right eye and bit his lip, a smile freezing on his face.

"Cut the grimacing," said Iona Ovseich in anger, "you were always a past master at that."

From behind Efim, Polina Isaevna signaled her husband not to badger a person in Efim's condition but Iona Ovseich asked her to lie quietly and not interfere in other people's business.

"Degtyar, I think that's enough for today," said Klava Ivanovna. "Poor Efim is overwhelmed as it is. He should rest up for a while."

Klava Ivanovna's remark was something that Polina Isaevna could also have said but Iona Ovseich limited himself to a frown this time: Madame Malaya had already stood up, taken Efim's arm, and was on her way to her apartment.

Foreseeably, the question of housing for Granik was a mess from the very start. His behavior remained within bounds during his first few days of staying with Klava Ivanovna, but then he began getting up in the middle of the night, fumbling around with the chairs and under the bed, and saying he was going out for a walk about the city. Klava Ivanovna's heart would leap with fear when Efim returned from those absurd night walks, and it didn't take much to frighten a person her age.

Degtyar did not approve in the least of all the bother being made over Granik, then said straight out that he'd been nursemaided long enough, it was time for him to find a job at a factory and a place in a workers' hostel. And if he didn't like postwar Odessa, there was plenty to chose from between the Black Sea and the White Sea and the Sea of Okhotsk.

Iona Ovseich transmitted this message to Granik through Madame Malaya but, not certain that she would pass it on, he repeated it himself to Efim. Efim listened quietly, a masklike smile frozen on his face, then once again demanded the keys to his own apartment, saying he couldn't open the door without them and didn't want to smash it in with an ax.

Iona Ovseich requested Efim to cease making threats. All of a sudden Klava Ivanovna began to laugh, depriving the moment of all its seriousness.

"Malaya," said Iona Ovseich, pale with fury, "Malaya, I'm giving you a very serious warning! And if you find all this so humorous and amusing, deal with it yourself, I have no time for trifles."

Klava Ivanovna and Efim went back to her apartment. He got up in the middle of the night for his usual walk. She didn't close her eyes for a second, listening intently for every sound from outside, promising herself that this was the last time, she couldn't stand it anymore, he had to find a place of his own. It was then that she thought of the outpost: Efim had put so much work into the outpost that he had every bit as much right as the Cheperukhas to use it as a temporary residence. In the darkness of her room, Klava Ivanovna could distinctly see the words written on the sky blue paint: WE WERE BORN TO MAKE DREAMS COME TRUE! That memory pained her heart for a moment, but, all in all, she felt happy now because a solution to the problem had finally occurred to her.

Klava Ivanovna spoke first with Iona Cheperukha. He was of two minds about her suggestion of allocating a little space to Efim: on the one hand, a person should have a roof over his head, especially a person who had lived in their building and had taken an active role in building the outpost; on the other hand, there was a family living there now with two little children; they had just cleaned out all the rubbish and put the place in order, and now they would have to start looking for another place all over. It was Zinovy's decision.

Zinovy literally thought it over for a minute and then replied—yes, the man had to be allocated a little space, and he proposed a plan to do a little remodeling—one of the windows could be made into a door whose upper panels could be replaced with glass to allow in some light.

Klava Ivanovna was happy that everything had moved so quickly and so well but then she encountered resistance from both the women, Olya and Katerina. Olya was opposed to the very idea of Granik living with her son's family: Granik was unpredictable now, doctors would have to be consulted. Katerina threatened to appeal to the District Executive Committee, for if they violated the terms approved for the project, they could all be kicked out.

Zinovy told Katerina that she wouldn't dare take that step and her reply was to call him a fool who didn't know his ass from his elbow.

Though she was not involved, apart from having settled in Granik's empty apartment a long time ago, Marina Biryuk began egging on Iona Cheperukha, saying she used to think he was a man, but now that had all proved to be a front, and it was his daughter-in-law who wore the pants in the family. Iona replied jokingly that it was better to borrow ten thousand rubles and lose them at gambling than to have one Efim Granik as your neighbor, but there was a certain truth to what Marina said: he had lived cheek by jowl with the man half his life and now that Siberian Katerina was setting the tone, wanting everything done her way. True, she wasn't alone in that, but arm in arm with Olya, but that didn't change the picture.

A week later Zinovy won over Katerina, but she set one condition: Granik should petition the Stalin District Soviet, the way they had, and obtain permission to replace the window with a door; they'd figure out what to do about the door frame later on. Zinovy accepted that condition and, in turn, proposed an additional idea: for the time being, he and Granik could set up a screen that would divide the entire width of the room in two, and while the weather was still warm Granik could use the window to enter and leave; that way, they wouldn't have to bother anybody about anything. Katerina imagined the scrawny Granik jumping through the window and once again she protested. Zinovy explained that Granik wouldn't have to jump: they'd build two or three stairs on the inside and on the outside.

"Listen, Zinovy," said Katerina, grimacing, "you Odessa people are very tricky, you think you're smarter than anybody."

"What do you mean by that?" said Zinovy, a fire in his angry gray eyes.

"Nothing," said Katerina, "except that you're all of one stripe and you certainly stick together, that's all."

Comrade Degtyar, who like Granik and Cheperukha, was also an Odessite, did not support the new plan, and made it perfectly clear that he would not permit any redivision of the outpost. If Zinovy Cheperukha simply wanted to allot Granik a little space, that was his business, but any other option would require paperwork.

At first, Klava Ivanovna argued the point with Degtyar but later on saw it his way: a new wall and a new door in the outpost would mean that two families would be living there, and, consequently, the City Soviet would have to find apartments for two families before the outpost could be returned to the children.

Zinovy bought four sheets of plywood and a dozen rods at the market on Shchepny Row. The goods could not be kept in plain sight, the police were keeping a close eye on everything, and he had to go with the owner to Vodoprovodny Street, not far from Chumka.

Zinovy stayed down in the courtyard with his motorized wheelchair while Efim went up to the third floor. The woman there brought out the key to the attic. She did not hand it over at once but first looked down and saw the wheelchair. The owner called her a fool and tapped a finger to his temple. She issued a lowing sound in response which made it clear that she was a deaf mute. She leaned out the window for a better view of the courtyard.

The plywood and the rods were under a pile of rags on top of which was a cage of rabbits. When the cage was placed to one side, Efim sat down by the cage and took out one of the rabbits. Half closing his eyes, he began rubbing the rabbit against his cheek, forehead, and chin. The owner removed the goods, then told Efim to put the rabbit back, it was bad for him to keep rubbing it like that.

Efim smiled and said: "I'm not worried."

"I meant bad for the rabbit, not for you," said the owner. "Let's get out of here, we're wasting time."

They wired the rods to the wheelchair to avoid attracting the attention of the police. Efim carried the plywood by hand but it made for an awkward load and he had to stop every twenty paces until he realized he could carry it on his head. The sun was bright, said Efim, and now he had an umbrella bigger than the Chinese emperor's; he'd be the envy of everybody. Zinovy laughed—when things went too smooth and easy for a person, he always let it go to his head.

Back home, however, things did not go so smooth and easy: Katerina and Olya began posing obstacles again, united in saying that plywood and rods were more than a screen but a whole wall. They also presented a new objection: if all the people in the courtyard were so kindhearted, why was it that the Cheperukhas had to give up a part of their apartment for Granik! Zinovy tried to turn the whole thing into a joke, reminding Katerina that she herself had said that Odessites were very tricky and stuck together. So then where was her logic?

Iona Cheperukha took Olya home and Katerina was left alone and without support. Suddenly she began weeping bitterly: "Well, tell me why I don't have the right to live like a human being like everybody else does, instead of being a nervous wreck!"

"Katya," said Zinovy, putting his arms around her and kissing her, "is our life really any worse or any harder than other people's? Look at Efim Granik, look at Tosya Khomitsky, look at Dina, look at Adya Lapidis, and then tell me who's got it harder!"

"That doesn't prove anything," said Katerina. "You were in the war, and so was your father, and so was I. That's it, I don't want to hear any more about it. Otherwise, there won't be any end to it."

That evening when the whole family had sat down at the table for dinner, Olya said that while Efim Granik was hiding as a prisoner of war, the Germans had shot his wife and children. Then the Soviet government had been in a hurry to release him before his term was up and send him to Odessa, so he could live off them.

"Shut your mouth!" exploded Iona. "You're in no position to judge!"

The partition was constructed with hinges so that, as soon as need be—if a commission came or some other sort of check was run—it could be folded up in a jiffy and put away.

Dina Vargaftik gave Efim an iron bed as a present. It was the perfect width, allowing just enough room for a person to pass. First, a neatly sewn coarse-cloth sack filled with old quilted jackets and rags was placed on the bed, it was in no way worse than a spring mattress stuffed with seaweed. Efim himself said it was soft as a featherbed, you didn't feel like getting out of it in the morning. By his window was a stool with a bucket of water on it, in case he wanted a drink of water during the night: he could wash up and do his clothes at the tap in the courtyard, ten steps away. Some of the neighbors didn't even try to hide their envy: the man has a whole ocean of water right at his fingertips all the time.

Stepa cut a section of rubber hose for Efim to attach to the tap. The water streamed out at great pressure producing a procedure like that once used in the Sharko shower baths at Dr. Yasinovsky's famous hydrotherapy institute on Sverdlov Street. Sometimes Stepa would also come out early, just as the courtyard was waking up, and douse himself along with Efim, like a couple of little boys.

Efim's food situation was not the best: a bread-ration card could be obtained only from a factory, or if permitted, through one's place of residence, but he had not managed to place himself in either category. True, the situation wasn't catastrophic, because the Kotlyars, Tosya Khomitsky, the Cheperukhas, and Klava Ivanovna herself invited Granik for dinner at least once a week. Not only that, if any of his neighbors in the courtyard asked him for help on their places, Efim wouldn't refuse, and they would be quick to repay the favor.

Iona Ovseich patiently waited for the philanthropy to end. One day the police swooped in out of nowhere to check people's internal passports, and it was a good thing they had time to warn Efim, who slipped out the gate without being noticed. But this matter was not limited to words alone.

"Malaya," said Iona Ovseich, furious, "now you see what your liberalism leads to! I'm giving you three days to get Granik registered as a resident of the city and to get him employment, otherwise I'm going to call the police and people will get what they've got coming."

At the Stalin District police station Klava Ivanovna and Efim were told that they needed certification of living space from the District Executive Committee.

"Comrades," said Klava Ivanovna with a smile, "you must be new here. My name is Malaya, and I can take full responsibility for this. You can call Degtyar in person at the party office, he'll confirm it."

The official answered that he wasn't going to be making any calls, not to Ivanov, not to Petrov, and not to Degtyar either. They should bring documentation from the District Executive Committee, otherwise, they'd speak again in forty-eight hours, and that would be a different sort of conversation then.

Though the square footage of the former outpost would have permitted it, the Stalin District Executive Committee refused to issue a certificate because the right to live there had been granted as an exception to the officer and disabled war veteran Zinovy Cheperukha and his wife, who had also served at the front. And as for Granik, who had been released under the amnesty, he should go get a job in a factory and a place in a workers' hostel.

Klava Ivanovna replied by recounting the tragic facts of Efim Granik's life. His entire family had been killed, he had been in a Nazi concentration camp, but the response was still the same: he should go get a job at a factory, and, in the future, if his behavior was good, he might be put on the waiting list for housing, but meanwhile he should look for a hostel.

"What do hostels have to do with anything?" said Klava Ivanovna, losing patience. "The man has a little place to live, and he doesn't need anything from you but your permission."

Klava Ivanovna was told that she was keeping them from their work, there were people waiting outside who had taken time off from their jobs. She should go to the City Soviet and write a complaint that the Stalin District Executive Committee refused a passport to her Fima Granik.

In a fit of temper, Klava Ivanovna promised that she would write a complaint not only to the City Soviet and the Supreme Soviet, but one straight to the Kremlin, to Comrade Stalin. But on the way home her thoughts took a different turn, toward Dina Vargaftik, who was living alone and, considering the amount of square footage she had, had every right to register a person with her. Efim was lagging a little behind, his usual smile on his pale face. Klava Ivanovna told him to shake a leg and wipe that stupid smile off his face, otherwise who knew what the hell people might think.

Dina said that she'd like to help Efim but was afraid to: first, because people would say there was some intrigue going on here, and, second, if Efim got a pass, that meant he'd been given a place to live and when the Cheperukhas moved out of the outpost, he'd settle in there for good.

"First," replied Klava Ivanovna jestingly, "you still have to ask if Efim would want it, he's already looking around, and, second, a person can be issued a temporary pass which does not grant him the right to any living space. And in a year or two the housing situation will be easier anyway."

Dina agreed to have Efim registered temporarily with her. She did this in memory of her Grisha, who had always been ready to give you the shirt off his back.

"Efim," said Klava Ivanovna, "why are you sitting there like a lump. Thank the woman. You should fall to her feet."

Three days later the police stamped Efim's new passport for a six-month residence.

Now Klava Ivanovna was able to report to Degtyar with a clean conscience that Efim Granik was again, as he had been before the war, a full-fledged resident of their courtyard.

"Good," said Iona Ovseich in praise, "you completed part one. And what about employment?"

As far as employment was concerned, replied Klava Ivanovna, people were needed everywhere, but Efim mustn't be pushed too fast. He should rest a little longer in familiar surroundings, with people he'd known all his life.

"Oh, Malaya," said Iona Ovseich in reproach, "you refuse to understand that only work gives a man dignity, and without work a person isn't a human being."

Polina Isaevna was also of the opinion that in the case at hand Malaya was making a mistake: if she could get even just half her health back, she'd be in her school day and night.

"No," said Klava Ivanovna, refusing to yield, "there's no comparison here; Efim is a special case and needs special treatment, especially since he has such a mental burden to bear."

Degtyar smiled: "So, let's send him to a health resort and then, if he's in the mood, we can ask him to do a little work."

"Ovseich," sighed Klava Ivanovna, "everybody's character is different. I feel like crying when I look at Efim."

"That's old age," said Iona Ovseich. "That's old age, Malaya."

About a week later Efim began speaking of Liza for the first time. Klava Ivanovna had brought him to the Khomitskys so they could all decide on the next step together: should the girl be left in the countryside for a certain period of time, until she'd grown up a little—that would make it easier to prepare the child to understand her real situation—or should she be brought to live with her father as soon as that could be arranged? Tears appeared in Efim's eyes, and he asked about Osya and Khilka again. When would they be given back to him? Klava Ivanovna only shook her head and continued discussing the question of little Liza.

Stepa suggested that Efim and Tosya go see the girl and talk with her, maybe she didn't want to go anywhere. Besides, where were they going to live, and who would look after the child?

"Stepa is right," said Klava Ivanovna.

Tosya said they shouldn't invent problems, she'd look after the child herself; the main problem was the abrupt change in the little girl's life. If Tosya had known that Efim was still alive, she would have brought the girl back to Odessa, and there'd be nothing to think about now.

"Tosya," said Klava Ivanovna, "life goes on and there's no turning back the clock. As the saying goes, if ifs and ands were pots and pans."

For a moment the room grew still and Adya could be heard playing the piano and down in the courtyard Lesik and Zinochka were singing a two-part harmony of the song that was the favorite of disabled war veterans who begged on the trolleys: "At the bottom of the letter, written in a different hand, it was his own daughter writing, calling her father to come home!"

Efim listened intently, a smile frozen on his lips. Tosya was the first to break the silence, saying she would go see her sister tomorrow and didn't need anyone to go with her.

Little Liza was brought back to Odessa late Saturday night. She was given a glass of milk and some fruit drops and slept in the same bed with Tosya. When her father came by in the morning and wanted to give her a kiss, she turned away from him and said to Tosya that she didn't like this man and wanted him to go away.

For a moment Efim was at a loss, then he extended his arms and said: "Liza, I'm your father and you're my own born daughter."

The girl did not respond. Pressing close to Tosya, she repeated that she didn't like this man and wanted to go back home to her mother and father.

"Lizochka," said Efim, pressing his fists to his chin with such force that his knuckles went white, "if you want to be with your father, come here to me. Tosya, Stepa, explain it to her!"

Efim bit his lower lip, his eyes blank with pain. The little girl burst into tears and tried to hide behind Tosya, who kept moving to the side.

Klava Ivanovna arrived. In her outstretched hand was a candy rooster on a stick and, before giving it to Liza, she asked if she recognized Grandma Klava. Liza stared at Klava Ivanovna and it was clear that she did remember her. Stepa laughed and answered for her: "She recognizes you. You see a grandma like that once and you remember her your whole life."

"Stepa," said Klava Ivanovna, waving the candy rooster threateningly at him, "don't spoil things for us here."

While Lizochka was eating her candy rooster, Efim stood by the door, afraid to go any closer to her and frighten her again.

"Lizochka," said Klava Ivanovna, "that man is your papa. When you were still very little, your papa went off to war, and so you can't remember him. Now, go over to him, put your arms around him, and give him a big kiss."

Efim took a step forward but Klava Ivanovna told him to stay where he was. Then she took the child by the hand, but Liza grabbed hold of Tosya's skirt and nothing could tear her away. Tosya made a little gesture meaning they should stop pestering the child and then in a loud voice asked Lizochka to get dressed: the two of them were going to the market and then to the zoo. Klava Ivanovna asked if she could come. Tosya said it was up to Lizochka. Lizochka shook her head and said no.

"I thought you were a good girl," said Klava Ivanovna, genuinely offended, "but you're as pouty as your late mother."

The remark about Liza's late mother had flown out of Klava

Ivanovna's mouth, but it was too late now, for the girl was weeping bitterly. All of a sudden Efim ran over to Liza, took her in his arms, pressed her head to his cheek, and began weeping himself. Taken by surprise, Lizochka forgot that she didn't know this man and put her arms around him. Efim's eyes were nearly closed as he swayed from side to side, groaning loudly.

Tosya turned away toward the window, her shoulders trembling. Klava Ivanovna covered her face in her hands. Stepa too was caught in the mood, and two or three times began pacing the room, then would knock at the window as if requesting permission to enter. Then he said it was time to stop crying, otherwise they'd all drown in tears.

Lizochka calmed down and asked Efim to let her go. She walked over to Tosya and reminded her about the zoo: they should get going, otherwise they'd be too late and the zoo would be closed. Klava Ivanovna wiped away her tears and she too said they should hurry, the animals liked to go to sleep early, when it was still light out. This time Lizochka did not protest.

The women left and the two men remained alone in the apartment. Stepa put a bottle out on the table and told Efim to run downstairs and get Cheperukha. The two men returned three minutes later, Cheperukha's pants' pockets bulging so much they looked like jodhpurs.

Stepa filled their glasses to the rim, gave the command—to horse—then said they should all be happy and never know grief, and their enemies should die like dogs. Then they drank to Efim, who was just starting to rebuild his family, then to being together again, and after that they drank without making toasts, just polishing off their drinks and chasing them with pickles and bacon fat. Iona had gotten the bacon fat from the therapeutic clinic for people with serious liver problems and kidney stones who were forbidden to eat fats.

The dishes on the table were now empty and Iona suggested they go for a walk to the New Bazaar. There was good wine from Moldavia on sale in the meat section. On the way, Efim told the story about Hitler and Ribbentrop coming to his concentration camp. They were as close to him as Stepa and Iona were now. They chose a few people and took them off to cut oak trees. Both Hitler and Ribbentrop had daggers with swastika-shaped handles at their sides. They used those daggers to cut off people's skin and were especially fond of tattoos, which were then used on briefcases, handbags, purses.

They each drank a glass of wine in the meat section, and it went down easy. Then, at a kolkhoz stall in Baranov Street near a blacksmith's, Iona ordered another round. All of a sudden Efim began creating a scene; he threw himself to the ground, grabbed people's legs, and hollered that his throat should be cut then and there, he wasn't going to get up again. People tried to help but Stepa and Iona picked Efim up themselves, brought him over to a wooden bench, and stuck two fingers down his throat, turning his head to one side so that nothing would get on their clothes.

When Efim had come back around and was able to stand on his own two feet, they went back to the meat section. Iona reminisced about the wine you could get before the war in the cellar on Pushkinskaya Street, today's couldn't compare. Stepa said that by and large food had changed a lot, some of it was quite tasteless now: before the war you could buy white bread for two rubles seventy kopecks a kilo, you could sit on it and it would rise back up again. Kolka liked to do experiments with bread and Tosya would whack him on the neck with a towel and Kolka would laugh.

"He's gone now, my Kolka!" Stepa stopped and began crying, then he wiped away his tears and they continued on their way.

As for the changes in food and in the climate as well, Iona voiced the opinion that a lot of gases had accumulated in the air from all the shells, bombs, and fires, and they were invisibly seeping into the earth, buildings, and everything else.

"My Kolka's gone," said Stepa, stopping again and covering his face in his hands. Efim stood beside him, shuffling his feet unconsciously.

When they returned home, Iona and Stepa were both given a good scolding, especially because of Efim, who looked perfectly awful. Katerina helped him up the steps, opened the window for him, and put him to bed. She took off his army boots, which were a few sizes too big, and which Efim wore on his bare feet. Katerina placed the boots by the bed and slammed the window so hard behind her when she left that it was surprising the glass didn't break.

The next day Iona Ovseich had a frank and practical talk with Stepa Khomitsky. Iona Ovseich did not go into details since no excesses had been committed yesterday but focused primarily on Efim Granik, whose behavior and way of life were, whether he intended this or not, creating an unhealthy atmosphere. People were people: some people thought conscience demanded that Granik be helped, some people looked back on the years they had spent with him, and others simply felt sorry for the man. But what did it all come down to in practice? In practice it all came down to this: the man was not working, in other words, he was a parasite, but he could drink and carry on in grand style, like a merchant. On other people's money, of course.

Stepa said that they had not been carrying on in grand style like merchants and that it shouldn't be forgotten that Efim was very weak. The blame should fall mainly on him, Stepa, and Cheperukha.

"You must not assume more blame than is actually warranted," objected Iona Ovseich. "I'll be frank with you about something: to this day I can't fathom what price a Jew had to pay to stay alive in a Nazi concentration camp."

Stepa reminded him of the story about Efim's being taken for a Tartar. Iona Ovseich made a dismissive gesture, saying he'd already heard all that and found something strange about the psychology of that former camp inmate: on the one hand, it was useful for him to pretend that something was wrong with his mind, on the other hand, he had his wits about him enough to exploit people's compassion.

Stepa said that he didn't see it that way at all, it was simply that the man was a little cracked from all that he'd been through.

"It's simple but it's not so simple either!" said Iona Ovseich, drawing a line in the air. "When a person has something on his conscience and wants to forget a part of the past, it's very convenient to act the way Efim Granik is acting."

"Ovseich," said Stepa, placing his hands, which were covered with red and black callouses, on the table, "would you act any differently in his place?"

Slightly offended, Iona Ovseich said that the comparison was highly inappropriate, but then requested Stepa to keep a close eye on Granik: a chance remark, a look, mimicry, could sometimes tell you more about a person than a whole page of autobiography. No extra time or effort would be needed for this because Tosya would be taking care of little Liza and Efim would be coming by regularly. Then he and Stepa could compare their findings and see who was right.

"Ovseich," said Stepa, frowning, "you're not going to make a detective out of me. I'm a plumber not a detective."

"A detective?" said Iona Ovseich, narrowing his eyes. "I'm very surprised the word even occurred to you."

The next Sunday, Tosya, Efim, and Lizochka went to see a movie about Tarzan at the Utochkin Theater. Lizochka laughed so loudly that the people sitting near them asked them a few times to keep the girl quiet but Efim rebuffed them, promising to call the manager if they didn't shut their mouths. Tosya whispered a secret to Lizochka: her father was as strong as Tarzan, so there was nothing to worry about. Lizochka held on to Tosya with one hand and to her father's sleeve with the other, and didn't let go until the movie was over.

They went for a walk in the municipal park after the movie. They bought Lizochka two glasses of flavored water for four rubles forty kopecks, then walked to Primorsky Boulevard. They bought a bag of sunflower seeds from an old woman in Vorontsov Lane and shucked and ate them as they went.

The entire port from Lanzheron to Luzanovka could be seen from the Potemkin stairs. There were many ships in the water and cranes were lifting crates into the air where they would pause for a few seconds before turning and depositing them on the dock. Though they appeared small from a distance, the crates were in fact very large, twice as large as the trucks that pulled up beside them.

"Tosya," said Efim, "you couldn't imagine how much paint you need to paint all that!"

A man on a scaffold was painting a mast. A light breeze was blowing, sometimes from in front of them, sometimes from in back. Efim said he'd be glad to have a job like that, working out in the fresh air all day. Then for God's sake, replied Tosya, he should go to the shipyard or the port. He could always find work there.

"Lizochka," said Efim with a smile, "would you be proud of your papa if he painted ships?"

Lizochka turned her face toward Lanzheron, the sun shining directly in her eyes, and said that she wanted to go for a ride on a ship. Tosya said that she could have as many rides as she wanted when her father had a job painting the ships. No, replied Lizochka, she wanted one now, not later.

The little girl was squinting from the sunlight, her Tartar-like eyes gleaming. Tosya gave her hug, sighed, and said, "Your eyes are just like your father's."

Efim began singing in a quiet voice: "I'm not my father's child, not my mother's child, I grew up on the streets, I was hatched by a hen."

"Lizochka," said Tosya with a smile, "were you hatched by a hen too?"

When they returned home, Efim asked Tosya for the best photograph she had of Kolka so that he could paint a large portrait of him in oils.

Anya Kotlyar gave Lizochka a birthday present—a fustian dress, wool tights, and a little red cap. She looked like something from a fairy tale. Efim made a wolf mask from cardboard and put it on; Grandma Malaya sat down beside him with her knitting, and the picture was complete. Tosya had invited Lesik and Zinochka Biryuk; Marina had lent them her phonograph and collection of prewar records for the entire evening: "The roses are blooming in Chair Park, the almond trees are in flower, blizzards dance in the frozen north, and people dream of happy faraway lands."

Olya Cheperukha had brought her grandsons Grisha and Misha up to Tosya's third-floor apartment to hear the music that made your heart thrill as if you were twenty years old again. Zinochka and Lizochka couldn't leave the little boys' side and kept saying "goo goo" to them, marveling at how small they were, they didn't seem real. The girls asked if they could hold them for a little while.

"Children," said Klava Ivanovna, "my dear children and grandchildren, your grandmother Malaya wants you to be happy all the time, she wants more for you than she wants for herself. Lizochka, Zina, come over here and sit on your grandmother's lap and give her a hug."

The girls did as they were asked. Klava Ivanovna closed her eyes, tears streaming down the bridge of her nose.

"Lizochka," said Olya, "tell me the truth, isn't it more interesting here in Odessa? You don't ever want to go back to Gradenitsy, do you?"

Everyone waited for the answer. Lizochka walked over to Tosya and asked why her papa and mama hadn't come for her after so much time. Efim shifted his gaze from Tosya to the child, a smile frozen on his face. Klava Ivanovna sighed loudly and told Efim to wake up and not sleep on his feet with his eyes open, night was still a long way off.

They played a record of songs from the movie *The Bright Path.* The men and women sang with such harmony and feeling that it made you want to go outside, line up, and march, march, march. Klava Ivanovna was the first to give in to that feeling; she began marking time with her feet as she picked up the refrain:

"There are no obstacles for us on land or sea,
We fear neither the ice nor the clouds!
The flame of our soul, the banner of our country,
We shall carry through worlds and ages!"

The record was cracked and skipped but that didn't bother anyone. They played it three times so the children could memorize the words.

When Grandma Malaya began singing, Lesik and Lizochka began laughing so hard they couldn't get a word out. Zinochka grew angry with them and in a loud voice told them it was naughty to laugh at old people. Then all the children promised Klava Ivanovna they would learn the words to the song, but not right now, some other time, right now they wanted to be out playing in the courtyard.

"You children should be ashamed of yourselves!" said Malaya, covering her face in horror.

When she removed her hands, the children were gone. Tosya Khomitsky laughed and apologized saying they were out before she'd even noticed.

Olya Cheperukha shook her head: "You're laughing, Tosya, but the children here used to be different—for your Kolka and our Zyunchik, Klava Ivanovna's word was law."

Madame Malaya shook her head too, a great weariness in her eyes. She asked that the song, "There are no obstacles for us on land or sea" be played again because she wanted to learn all the words to it, but when it was over she waved her hand and smiled bitterly: the years took their toll and nobody could give you back what they took.

The next Monday Efim started work as a painter at the ship repair yard. When his passport was being examined in the personnel department, they saw that his registration was temporary, but they said it didn't matter; when the time came, they'd extend it. His papers were accepted without any red tape, all he had to do was rewrite his autobiography in as much detail as possible in a page, a page and a half, paying special attention to the last five years. Efim was well aware that this was necessary since the shipyard was part of the port. There were foreigners all over the place, all sorts of people, and you couldn't tell who they really were straight off.

That evening Klava Ivanovna went to see Degtyar twice but he wasn't home either time, and she had to try him a third time, getting out of bed when it was almost eleven o'clock. Iona Ovseich was weary, it was the end of the quarter. The supply department had messed up and failed to obtain the raw materials in time. The party bureau had been in session from early that morning; the head of the department had been issued a strict warning, the cutting department had been idle all day, and tomorrow fixers would have to be sent to Kirov and Ostashkovo.

"On the other hand, I've brought you some good news today, Degtyar," said Klava Ivanovna. "Guess what it is."

Iona Ovseich was not in the mood for guessing: if he guessed that would be nice, but if he guessed wrong, all the pleasure would go out of it. Too big a risk.

"All right, I'll tell you then," yielded Klava Ivanovna. "Efim Granik has taken a job as a painter at the ship repair yard without anyone pressuring him to. So who was right, you or me?"

Iona Ovseich replied that in the case at hand it didn't matter who was right, it was something else that mattered: what kind of information did Efim Granik provide about himself to the personnel department.

"What does that mean, what kind?" said Klava Ivanovna in surprise. "Efim's not the sort to invent a new autobiography for himself."

Iona Ovseich squinted an eye slyly: "Malaya, are you so sure you know the story of his life for the last five years, starting from 1942? For a Jew in danger of being taken prisoner by the Nazis, there was only one solution—to blow his brains out. And if he didn't blow his brains out and survived a Nazi concentration camp, that has to mean one of two things: he either has supernatural luck—and none of us believes in the supernatural—or it's the enemy's way of repaying some special services."

What kind of services did Efim have the brains to provide them with, said Klava Ivanovna, shrugging her shoulders. He was an oddball even before the war, the whole court loved to laugh at him.

"That's true," agreed Iona Ovseich, "but still, tell me how a simpleton like that can pass himself off as a Tartar for three years in a row, and fool a treacherous and ferocious enemy. Where's the logic? Can you help me see the logic here, Madame Malaya?"

Klava Ivanovna answered that she couldn't help him see it, but said her heart could feel it was the truth. Not only that, there was other proof: they released Efim from the camp, they issued him a passport, and permitted him to return to Odessa.

"Malaya," said Iona Ovseich, "we're still too trusting and humane. Still too much."

Efim gave half of his first paycheck to Tosya to pay for Lizochka. Tosya said it was too much, the girl ate like a bird, but Efim had reasons of his own: he would have to work for more than a year to compensate them for taking care of the child all those times.

"Fima," said Tosya, genuinely offended, "if I hear that kind of talk again, you and I are going to be bitter enemies."

On the evening before the Feast of the Protection, Tosya dressed Lizochka in her best dress and a light coat with a hood, took her by the hand, and set off with her for the Church of the Assumption. Thousands of people had gathered by the main entrance on Soviet Army Street and for Tosya and Lizochka to elbow their way through them was out of the question, and so they had to go around by Kirov Street to Assumption Lane. Tosya stopped Lizochka and pulled a copper cross on a chain from inside her dress. Tosya walked up to the stairs to a side door and pressed herself against the wall; there was less of a crowd there and you could breathe the fresh air. Candles were burning in a large chandelier, the little flames were pulled in various directions, no two going the same way. Lizochka watched them closely, trying to guess which way one or another of them would blow. Sometimes she was right, and sometimes she wasn't. Lizochka asked Auntie Tosya why the flames were always moving and didn't burn evenly like they did in a lantern. Tosya said it was because of the draft. "No," said Lizochka, shaking her head, "a draft blows candles out, but these are still burning. And they burn like that in the church in Belyaevka too, but at home if you open the door and the window, the candles go right out." Lizochka thought for a minute before figuring it out herself: "Angels fly around in churches and when they move their wings it makes the candles move." The old woman beside them heard what Lizochka said, patted her on the head, and called her a smart girl. Tosya repeated that the church was drafty and angels didn't have anything to do with it.

The next day Lizochka told Grandma Malaya that they had gone to church yesterday, and there were angels flying around the ceiling, and she'd been the only one to spot them.

"Don't talk nonsense," said Grandma Malaya angrily, "there's no such thing as angels."

Klava Ivanovna and Tosya had a long and unpleasant conversation on the subject. Number one, who gave her permission to take the child to church, if her father was living right there and didn't know anything about it? Number two, to take a more formal approach, why did she put a cross on the child and take her to a church and not to a synagogue, even though she shouldn't take her either place?

As far as the cross was concerned, Tosya informed Malaya that they had put a cross on her back in '42 and nothing but good came of it, the girl survived, safe and sound. And there was no big difference between a church and a synagogue, it was the same God for everybody.

"You fool," said Klava Ivanovna, brandishing a fist in Tosya's face, "the Nazis did everything in the name of God. They killed in the name of God, they burned in the name of God, and they killed infants in gas chambers, and that was in the name of God too! And which way was God looking when your son, who risked his own life to save another child, was out facing German bullets!"

Tosya lowered her head without answering. Klava Ivanovna demanded that Tosya look her in the eye and not hide from her.

"Look me in the eye!" Klava Ivanovna demanded a second time.

"What do you want?" Tosya raised her head, her eyes yellow as sand. "What do you want from my soul! I don't know anything, I don't understand anything, I don't need anything, leave me alone, for God's sake, leave me alone!"

Efim displayed complete indifference when he found out that Lizochka had been to church with Tosya and said only that the cross should be taken off. Lizochka dug in her heels and wouldn't agree to removing the cross for anything in the world. Tosya asked her nicely, commanded her, threatened her, but all to no avail.

That night, when Lizochka was sound asleep, Tosya carefully lifted the child's head, removed the cross, and hid it. Nothing happened the next day but the day after Lizochka went up to Tosya and burst into tears, confessing she had lost her cross.

"Think where you were playing and go look for it there," said Tosya.

Lizochka spent the whole morning searching for the cross in her room, in the hallway, in the courtyard, and by the gate, but it was nowhere to be found. Tosya went out twice to help her look and said that was enough, it would turn up by itself. Lizochka asked Tosya to buy a new one for her; if the old one turned up, they could sell it. Tosya promised to buy her one but then explained that there was only one master craftsman in all Odessa who made them and they'd have to wait. That was all right, said Lizochka, they could wait awhile.

By the end of the week Tosya's heart was heavy, as if it were weighed down from every side. Klava Ivanovna reproached her for making so much of so little, but her reproaches only made Tosya feel worse.

When Tosya was in a more cheerful mood and began talking again, Klava Ivanovna herself was relieved and she took Lizochka for a whole day and went walking near the sea with her. They ate two meat-filled piroshki in Arcadia Park and each drank a glass of cherry juice, which all together came to ten rubles. Klava Ivanovna also bought a children's book for Lizochka; the girl would be starting school next year, it was time to get her ready.

They dropped by to visit the Kotlyars that evening. Klava Ivanovna asked Adya, who by then was studying at the conservatory, to show Lizochka how to play the piano.

"Adya," said Joseph, who was sitting on a stool with sawed-off legs and making heels for a pair of women's shoes, "show her how to play, then let her try her own hand at it. But first check what kind of pitch she has."

Joseph explained to Klava Ivanovna that there were two completely different kinds of pitch—perfect and musical—but people always mixed the two of them up. For example, you could have ordinary musical pitch and be a first-class pianist, and it could also be the other way around, you could have perfect pitch and not be able to play the simplest scale.

"What's the difference?" asked Klava Ivanovna.

"It's all in the fingers," said Joseph, "what counts is the fingers. Adya, show Grandma Malaya. You have to be born with the right sort of fingers, you can't buy them. Malaya, I'm telling you he's going to make our courtyard world famous."

Adya told Joseph to calm down, saying that he was talking too much; in reply, Kotlyar twisted his lips bitterly and sighed: "All right, I'm a fool, you teach her. I don't need anything, it's all for you."

Adya tapped out a few beats and Lizochka repeated them after him; then they tried the fourth and first octave and a subcounteroctave on the piano. Lizochka laughed while they were trying the subcounteroctave because the notes sounded like a cow mooing or a huge bear stomping through the forest.

Anya arrived from the hospital half an hour later. She had had an especially good day: a patient from Zastava had been released and promised her a kilo and a half of goat fat that was supposed to be very good for people with lung problems. She said she was going to run over to Polina Isaevna's for a minute to tell her the news and would be right back.

Adya played "Christmas Tree" and *"Chizhik-Pyzhik."* Joseph sang along and Klava Ivanovna waved her arms like a conductor. Lizochka laughed out loud and wanted more.

Anya was clearly out of sorts when she returned. Joseph asked her what the matter was, saying it must be problems with Polina Isaevna's health again. Klava Ivanovna sighed bitterly, told Lizochka to thank Adya, and then said good-bye.

Joseph had accepted a good many orders and would sit up until two o'clock in the morning, having to finish his work by the light of a kerosene lamp. After twelve he used only a needle, waxed thread, and rubber glue, so as not to disturb his neighbors. The seams on patches required great accuracy, especially on women's shoes. Joseph had to strain his eyes, which gave him pain; there was a weight at the back of his neck and his neck felt like it was made of wood.

Joseph set the alarm for five o'clock; he had to leave for the factory by six. He prepared his prosthesis so as not to waste time in the morning, and smoked a hand-rolled cigarette—a little pleasure, though it might stimulate his nerves for the night—and went to bed.

"Joseph, are you asleep?" said Anya after a minute.

Joseph laughed and said that he didn't sleep like a man someone wanted to give a hundred rubles to, he slept like a man someone wanted to take a hundred from.

"This evening," whispered Anya, "when I stopped by to see Polina Isaevna and promised to bring her a kilo of goat fat, Degtyar looked daggers at me."

"Then what?" said Joseph.

"Then he turned sideways to me and said, there was a limit to the Soviet authorities' patience, or did Kotlyar think there wasn't?"

"What did you say back to him?"

"I said that we weren't doing anything that needed any thinking about or any discussion."

"That was good."

"Then he said, thank you for your hospitality to Polina Isaevna, and a separate thank you to Joseph Kotlyar for the jokes he's been spreading around."

"What jokes?" Joseph turned his head, the moonlight now shining directly in his eyes. Clouds of smoke were rising from a roof chimney on a house across the way, round and puffy at first, then elongating as they went off into the sky. "What jokes!"

"My God, you're asking me!" groaned Anya. "How many times have I told you, you don't know how to button your lip. You're always shooting off your mouth and telling jokes like you were all alone on a desert island."

"Hold on," said Joseph. "Give me an example of where I shot off my mouth."

"Poor Adya," said Anya in tears, "his father couldn't keep his mouth shut either, and now this. To hell with you if you don't have any feeling for the child, we can live without you."

"They're not burying me yet," said Joseph, "so don't start measuring me for a coffin, all right? And as for that Ovseich of yours, fuck him. Fuck him ten times over. I'm not afraid of him."

"You donkey," said Anya with a bitter laugh, "you old donkey, bragging in front of your own wife."

Joseph became angry: "I understand. What you want is a husband like Ovseich, who lectures his tubercular wife day and night, but a piece of meat or an egg, that's something the neighbors can bring over."

"That's right," said Anya happily, "say it again, and louder this time, so all of Odessa can hear, and then later on you'll ask me for a specific example of you shooting your mouth off."

"You're a fool," said Joseph, angry again. "Nobody's forbidding people to tell jokes and laugh at his neighbor, jokes won't kill you."

"Good God," groaned Anya, "forbidden or not, what does it matter! You've got to remember what the times are like and who you're joking with!"

"Anya, I'll tell you an interesting story," said Joseph with a laugh. "Two guys, Franz and Schwanz, are in prison. Franz asks: 'What are you in for?' Schwanz says: 'For being a bad runner.' That's surprises Franz, who says: 'They're even putting people in for that?' Then Schwanz tells him what happened: the wall between him and his neighbor was so thin, you could hear every word, and his neighbor had been the first to run to the proper authorities. 'You idiot,' says Franz, 'you sat there eating peas and waiting.' Schwanz took offense at this and said that he wasn't an idiot, just the other way around. He was the first one to start running, but his neighbor was a better runner and outran him."

The bed in Adya's room began squeaking as if he were tossing and turning or shaking with laughter. "Look at that," whispered Anya, "the boy heard every sound from in here, even though the wall is solid and the door is shut tight, and the neighbors must have heard it too then." Joseph said that he didn't give a damn about the neighbors, the people who stuck in the craw of Soviet power should be worried, but he had given everything he loved most for the Soviet Union.

"Joseph," said Anya, joining her husband on the couch, "swear by my life that you won't go shooting off your mouth wherever you happen to be."

No, Joseph flatly refused, saying that if you swore an oath like that it would have to be for a reason, because you really were a big mouth. Anya pressed herself up against him, put her arms around his neck, and kept insisting, but once again Joseph refused, saying he knew his rights and no one could scare him. And the example she'd used of Vanya Lapidis wasn't a good one; number one, that was several years ago, in '39, and number two, there's no smoke without fire, they don't arrest a person for no reason.

After the October holidays, Iona Ovseich, in conversations with Malaya, Stepa Khomitsky, and other neighbors, let it slip unintentionally that he would not be greatly surprised if the party and government passed a decision to abolish the ration-card system before New Year's, in other words, bread and the other food products would be sold freely to the whole population.

Discussing that piece of news with Anya, Joseph remarked in passing that making a decision was easy, but a strong economic base was needed to carry it out and agriculture's wounds from the war hadn't healed yet, it was limping on both feet. Not only that, Churchill's speech in the American city of Fulton showed that we had to strengthen our defenses and always be on guard but that ate up so much money, enough for two agricultures.

Anya shook her head: if the Americans had been through even a quarter of what we'd been through, they'd have kicked out that Churchill before he even had a chance to open his mouth.

"As if Churchill is the only snag!" said Joseph indignantly. "There's the Truman Doctrine, and the Marshall Plan, and Wall Street!"

On Saturday Anya brought Polina Isaevna a peasant loaf and a glass of sour cream. While Polina Isaevna broke off pieces of bread and dipped them in the sour cream, Anya started a conversation about the economy. Iona Ovseich came home from work and heard the second half of that conversation. He asked Anya Kotlyar for the source of her information that all the U.S.S.R.'s money was going to the military budget if Gosplan statistics showed that approximately one fifth was budgeted for defense, while the lion's share was slated for industry and agriculture, and if the current Five-Year Plan projected an annual increase of no less than seventeen percent for agriculture.

Anya admitted that she had no idea how much money was being spent for agriculture and the rate of increase projected by the Five-Year Plan, and said she would like to know the latest details. Iona

Ovseich said they would save the economics lesson for another time. "Right now let's go back to the question—what is the filthy source of her information about the allocation of capital investment in the national economy?"

"What does that mean, filthy?" said Anya indignantly, her face turning very pale and her lips blue as if from the cold.

Polina Isaevna spoke for her husband and said that he was speaking openly with her, as someone he felt close to, and meant her no harm; Anya was getting upset over nothing. Iona Ovseich told his wife he could speak for himself and repeated his question about the filthy source of Anya's information. "Not only that," added Iona Ovseich, "one can only marvel at the Kotlyars' suspicious unity with the lackeys of plutocracy like the Laborite Clement Attlee; Attlee says that the Soviet Union is using all its money for military purposes and that's why, he says, so little's being allocated for the peacetime economy and the people. And here our courtyard economists are saying the same thing, literally word for word! And that at a time when Comrade Stalin has already personally replied to Clement Attlee—Mr. Attlee doesn't know the first thing about the science of economics but he's a practiced hand at anti-Soviet propaganda."

When Anya reported this conversation and the comparisons Degtyar had made to her husband, Joseph slammed his cobbler's hammer against the iron anvil with such force the chandelier tinkled. Adya was in the next room, outlining his notes on the fundamentals of Marxism-Leninism, and the sound made his entire body twitch as if from an electric shock.

Then Joseph began shouting, demanding that his wife go immediately and inform Ovseich that Kotlyar was no Lapidis. He had lost a leg in the Civil War when Soviet power was hanging by a thread. And in 1944 he had lost his sons at the front and he had nothing left to lose, and so Degtyar better shut his dirty mouth if he wanted to go on living!

Adya came into the room, put his arms around Joseph, and asked him to calm down. But that only made Joseph yell all the louder; his cavalryman's voice traveled through the walls and could probably be heard in the courtyard.

"Joseph," said Anya, pressing the palms of her hands to her cheeks with all her strength as she implored him to control himself. "Joseph, don't fuel the fire."

"I spit on that fire," roared Joseph in reply, "and your Ovseich better take back what he said or there's going to be trouble like you never saw before!"

"Oh, what a stupid man," said Anya, sitting down on a chair and rocking back and forth. "There's a good reason they say a person's tongue is his own worst enemy."

"Look," said Joseph, finally calming down a little, "you were at the front for four years, you received a lifelong disability, so then explain to me how come you're so careful and cautious all of a sudden. Why are you always looking back over your shoulder at Degtyar?"

"I'm not looking back over my shoulder at him!" said Anya in a loud voice. "I just have great respect for a person who has devoted his whole life to other people and demanded nothing in return."

"Nothing?" said Joseph with surprise in his voice.

"Nothing," said Anya.

"In other words," said Joseph, grimacing, "your respect for him and the fact that you listen to Ovseich more than you do to your own husband, and the fact that his opinion means more to you than mine, you consider all that nothing."

Adya laughed and said Joseph could make as good a Sophist as Socrates himself, who stood up for the truth with such courage that he ended up having to drink poison of his own free will.

"Button your lip!" barked Anya. "Go to your room and do your homework."

Adya replied that this would help him prepare for the practical exams on the short course; there was a seminar tomorrow, and the teacher had assigned the students to find examples of antagonistic and nonantagonistic contradictions in daily life.

"Don't be so smart," said Anya angrily, "they gave you textbooks for that. You can use examples from your own life when you're earning your own living and have a family of your own."

No, said Adya, shaking his head, the teacher required they bring in examples from concrete reality to every seminar, and so there was no putting it off.

Joseph supported Adya completely and said that he was a thousand percent right: people should use their own brains and not wait for their parents to predigest everything for them.

"That's right, that's right," said Anya, "mislead the boy. It's not enough for you that the child's been orphaned once already."

If Anya could have recalled her words, she would have but it was too late. Adya had lowered his head like a young bull and was glowering at her with angry eyes.

"He's no child!" said Joseph with a wink. "He's a young bull, it's high time he started having children of his own. Come a little closer, boy."

Adya walked over to Joseph, who hugged him, tousled his hair, and said that there was a man who lived on Bolshoi Arnautsky Street, corner of Lenin, who had a German motorcycle for sale, a "Zundap." Did Adya have a little spare time today so they could take a look at it together?

"Listen to you!" said Anya indignantly. "You ask him but did you ever ask me?"

"What, you want a motorcycle too?" said Joseph in surprise. "All right, we'll buy two of them and hitch them together like a team of mares."

Everything worked out so smoothly with the motorcycle that it seemed to have been God's will: on the day before Stalin Constitution Day, Joseph brought the man the money, and exactly one week later the government issued a decree repealing the ration-card system and reforming the currency—one new ruble was now worth ten old ones. The man who had sold Joseph the motorcycle came running to the courtyard and kicked up a row demanding his motorcycle back. Many of Joseph's neighbors took the man's side and demanded that Kotlyar give back the motorcycle, otherwise it would be outright robbery. Joseph suggested that anyone dissatisfied with what he was doing should address himself to the central laundry where complaints were accepted twenty-four hours a day. Dina Vargaftik was the most furious of all, calling Joseph a swindler and a low bastard, but then she herself said that there was nothing surprising in any of this: money always went to money, it was always like that and always would be.

A meeting was held on Sunday in the large hallway on the second floor. Iona Ovseich warmly congratulated all the building's residents on the currency reform and the repeal of the ration-card system, a major new step toward increased prosperity and further development. Despite the fact that during the war the enemy used every means in its attempt to undermine the Soviet economy, counterfeiting enormous quantities of Soviet currency, thereby causing a temporary resurgence of the black market and speculation in occupied territory, the party and the government, acting in the interests of the working class, the kolkhoz peasants, and all other workers, had done everything possible to maintain salaries and prices for consumer goods at their old prewar level, and, at the same time, had deemed it possible to reform the currency at a rate of ten old rubles for one new ruble. You didn't have to be a great mathematician to figure this out: people who earned their living by working would lose practically nothing in the reform, whereas the more the speculators and operators acquired illegally, the more they now stood to lose.

"The Soviet people have responded with profound gratitude to this latest manifestation of the party and government's concern. However, there are those, and some in our courtyard as well, who have gone all out to rip off as much as they could, not only from private citizens but also from the state; in the last few days before the currency reform these people struck on the clever idea of depositing all their capital in savings banks where they could exchange their first three hundred old rubles for the same number of new ones, and the next three thousand on preferential terms.

"Anya Kotlyar," said Iona Ovseich, making a point of turning away, "you can lift your head, we're not looking at you."

People laughed because it was just the other way around: until that moment Anya had been holding her head steady but when Iona Ovseich turned away, she in fact had lowered it.

"Comrades," said Iona Ovseich, crossing his hands on his stomach and fiddling a bit with his fingers, "I think we should give the floor to Anya Kotlyar so we can hear what she wants to tell us."

Finally Anya raised her head and said that she had not deposited any money in a savings bank on the eve of the reform because they couldn't know beforehand whether the terms would be preferential or not. Her last deposit was no secret, and had been entered in her savings book: anyone who wished to see it was welcome to look.

Iona Ovseich thanked her for her complete openness and trust but also emphasized that the privacy of a person's deposits were protected by law and no one would be allowed to violate it. Still, if one recalled the fact that there existed a type of deposit in which the depositor's name remained secret from the bank and even from the state, then a person could have two, three, or even five such accounts, and one could only marvel at the Kotlyars considering them such simpletons by voluntarily offering their passbook for inspection.

Anya said that she swore by her life that she was telling the whole truth; they had in fact gone to their savings bank but to withdraw money not to deposit it; they had just bought Adya a motorcycle and needed money to pay for it.

Iona Ovseich smiled: "It only takes one time to withdraw money but if a person goes three or four times, and to different banks on top of that, that's a different story."

"A different story, that's putting it mildly!" cried Dina Vargaftik.

Many people agreed with Dina and supported her but then Zinovy Cheperukha, though his father and wife tried to restrain him, suddenly attacked Dina like a street hoodlum, cursing her left and right and demanding that she cite concrete facts, otherwise Kotlyar had the legal right to bring her to court for slander and blackmail.

"Young man," said Iona Ovseich politely, "I think you're addressing the wrong person here. I'm the one who has to be brought to court because I was the first one to raise the issue."

"That's right," Zinovy replied insolently, "the two of you together, to teach you not to sling mud at a person and blacken his name!"

"But if we can find witnesses and proof," said Iona Ovseich, striking the back of his chair with his fist, "will you change your tune then or won't you!"

"First find the witnesses!" retorted Zinovy in a tone of utter disrespect.

"No," said Iona Ovseich, pressing his point, "give me a straight answer: what tune will you sing if the proper authorities uncover the person Zinovy Cheperukha was standing up for, and determine the reason behind that mysterious unity?"

"Why are you trying to scare him, Comrade Degtyar?" said Marina Biryuk, rising from her seat. Her chestnut hair was down like that of the German actress Marika Rokk in the film *The Girl of My Dreams*. "Everyone in the courtyard can see the sort of life the

Cheperukhas lead and so there's no reason to try to scare him. As for Kotlyar, I personally don't know whether he was involved in any speculation or shady deals. The man works eighteen hours a day and earns a good living."

The hallway grew still. Only Efim Granik stifled a chuckle in his fist. People gazed at him in surprise and shrugged their shoulders. All of a sudden he became quite cheerful and asked a favor of all those who were present or absent for that matter—to answer a simple question: how many legs does a centipede have?

"Efim Granik," said Iona Ovseich, stamping his foot, "save your demented jokes for some other place, people can see right through you here!"

"Don't you insult me," shouted Efim. "I'm not afraid, I'm not afraid of anybody in the world. And don't snarl at me like an angry wolf! I'm pretty good at snarling too."

"Fima, sit down and be quiet," said Klava Ivanovna, "otherwise people might get the wrong idea."

Iona Ovseich called Comrade Malaya to order and suggested she not intervene unless asked to. As for Efim Granik's reply, he promised to return to that subject at a more appropriate time and in a more appropriate place.

Efim stared at Comrade Degtyar, shaking his head and moving his lips as if talking to himself, but in such a way that other people could guess what he was saying. Stepa Khomitsky was the first to figure it out and merrily waved a threatening finger at Efim, while reminding him of the children's saying: step on a line, break your mother's spine. People laughed, then out of the blue, Iona Cheperukha offered Comrade Degtyar and all his other neighbors anodized napkin rings and buttons for long johns, no limit on quantity. Klava Ivanovna said that napkin rings were no longer in fashion and he should sell them for recycling at five rubles a ton.

All right, answered Iona, napkin rings were out of style but buttons for long johns weren't: on the last day before the currency reform he had bought three hundred rubles' worth, and was willing to let them go for half price.

"Iona," responded Marina Biryuk, "even if you pay full price where are you going to find that many men!"

"That's disgusting," said Lyalya Orlov with a grimace.

Cheperukha held his head, having just realized that he'd be going broke on this venture. The people around him sighed with sympathy but they could not be of any help to him: buttons for long johns were not the sort of thing you stocked up on for twenty years in advance.

"Iona Cheperukha," said Iona Ovseich, calling him to order, "stop clowning around and interfering with our work."

Even though she had been sitting quietly until that moment, Katerina unexpectedly stood up for her father-in-law, who was being insulted in front of his own son, a disabled war veteran, and all their neighbors.

"Sit down in your seat, Katerina Cheperukha," ordered Iona Ovseich. "I didn't give you the floor."

"He didn't give me the floor!" said Katerina with a foolish laugh. "Oh, then I'll plead for him to let me speak."

Iona Ovseich turned pale and his fingers trembled. Klava Ivanovna shouted at Katerina, then said to Zinovy that he should tell his wife to apologize at once, and, if she had no shame, then he should apologize for her.

"No need to," said Iona Ovseich, "let her finish speaking. Everyone has the right to say what he thinks, irrespective of persons."

Efim Granik, who had been forgotten in all this, now rose to his feet without asking permission, walked out to the center of the floor, and began shaking his head back and forth like a horse while moving his lips rapidly. People were caught completely off guard and were dumbfounded and, by the time they had their wits back about them, Efim had already sat down again. Stepa Khomitsky was the first to offer an explanation:

"One person said his piece. And that was the next one."

Many people expected Iona Ovseich to become truly angry now and take definite measures, but it all passed quite peaceably.

"Not bad pantomime," said Iona Ovseich. "The actor clearly had rehearsed it thoroughly and was just waiting for the right moment."

Efim raised his head and looked at Comrade Degtyar for a second, then took everyone else in, with eyes that were so tired and so sad it made people's hearts bleed with pity. Klava Ivanovna said Efim should go outside and get a breath of fresh air but Iona Ovseich forbade this, demanding that Malaya not turn the meeting into a charitable institution.

An ambulance arrived at Iona Ovseich's at three o'clock in the morning: the physician determined that Degtyar had suffered a heart attack and suggested he be hospitalized. He refused outright. "Be careful," said the physician, making a note. He then asked Iona Ovseich to sign a release saying he had refused his suggestion that he be hospitalized.

Iona Ovseich spent half a day in bed, drank a glass of sweet tea, and ate a piece of bread and margarine; he waited until Polina Isaevna had left for her job at the school, then, dressing a little warmer than usual, he headed out for the factory.

Polina Isaevna returned a little after nine. The apartment was dark and silent as a cellar. She turned on the light and ran to the telephone, almost dying of fright until she reached the party bureau and heard the voice of her own husband.

Klava Ivanovna came by about ten minutes later, bringing Anya Kotlyar with her to give the heart-attack victim a shot for the night. Polina Isaevna poured her guests tea from a thermos bottle and asked them to a wait awhile. As far as her Degtyar went, only the grave could straighten that hunchback.

"It's enviable," sighed Anya, "the man's not afraid of death."

"He just doesn't have the time to think about it!" said Klava Ivanovna.

Polina Isaevna telephoned again and received firm assurance that he was just putting on his coat. Anya placed a little canister containing the syringe on the Primus stove, set the flame as low as possible, but she had to add water twice before the sick man was finally there in the flesh.

"You criminal!" said Polina Isaevna, launching an attack. "You think your life and health belong just to you alone! They don't, you're lawfully married. Do you remember that you have a lawfully wedded wife!"

Iona Ovseich spread his hands wide apart and said that King Solomon had seven hundred wives he could forget, but poor men like Degtyar couldn't forget.

"You criminal," said Polina Isaevna. "Sit down on the couch and roll up your sleeve so she can give you the injection."

Iona Ovseich replied that, personally, he didn't want the injection but since the majority was for it, he would submit to their will.

Anya lightly massaged the arm, which was all skin and bones, dabbed it with iodine, and injected the needle in a flash.

"Not too painful?" she asked.

"It's over!" marveled Iona Ovseich. Anya smiled and said that if all patients were like him, she'd like to run a twenty-four hour sanatorium not a hospital.

"My dear nurse," replied Iona Ovseich jestingly, "I should make special mention of the wonderful care you have provided to my whole family, but that would make for something of a mutual admiration society, and so then I won't say a word."

Klava Ivanovna clapped her hands without quite meaning to and said you had to be fast on your feet like Degtyar to have it both ways at the same time.

Early the next morning when it was still dark and people had just woken up and were getting ready to go to work, the police arrived to check passports. The first person the concierge, Lebedev, brought them to was Zinovy Cheperukha. Efim Granik had just opened his window and was preparing to climb out. The policeman ordered him to go back in and then to present his papers. Efim answered that he was late for work, they should check his papers without him, but the policeman took him firmly by the arm and again told him to go back down.

Leafing through Granik's passport, the policeman examined the pages empty of notation, and shook his head in reproach. Zinovy and Katerina were standing nearby waiting.

"And so, Efim Lazarevich Granik," said the policeman with a sigh, "this means you're living in one place and registerd in another. Is that right?"

"Comrade Inspector," said Efim with a shy smile, "I just dropped by here for a visit, but I always stay where I'm registered."

The policeman looked from Zinovy and Katerina to Lebedev, and then a cunning gleam flashed in his eye. He suggested that they all go upstairs to where Efim Lazarevich was not a chance guest but a legal resident.

"Comrade Officer," said Efim, smiling again but without the shyness of before, since the policeman had proved such a nice guy, "Private Granik requesting permission to depart for factory!"

The inspector did not reply one way or the other. He sat down on a stool, took a fresh sheet of paper from his map case, and said to Lebedev: "We'll write this up."

"Listen, Sergeant," said Zinovy, "this man came back to Odessa, his family had been killed, his room was taken over. I served at the front and so did my wife. We gave the man a little temporary place to live, he's registered in another apartment, that's the way it worked out."

The inspector nodded, covering half a sheet of paper as he wrote. He read it to himself then aloud so that they would not have to waste time reading it individually. Then he asked them to sign it. He placed Granik's passport in his map case, rose, and told the concierge to take him to the next apartment.

On the way Fenya Lebedev swore by her own life and her daughter's health that this was the first she had heard of these dirty dealings, it had never even crossed her mind. "But you know how people are."

Klava Ivanovna made everyone swear not to inform Iona Ovseich of all this, the man was having heart spasms as it was. She went to the passport department, the chief of police, the Stalin District Executive Committee. It dragged on for three days until Efim was fined one hundred rubles for violating the passport system; it could have been worse. Efim put half the money on the table and the rest was chipped in by Zinovy, Tosya Khomitsky, Anya Kotlyar, and Klava Ivanovna herself. Without being asked, Marina Biryuk donated five rubles of her own accord.

During the three days the case dragged on, Dina Vargaftik had sworn a thousand times on the memory of her Grisha that no matter how much money they gave her she'd never be fool enough again to risk her neck to make someone else happy.

On Sunday evening Polina Isaevna was home baking piroshki with jam for New Year's. Iona Ovseich had invited Klava Ivanovna over and said to her: "Malaya, that was the first time since 1924 that you deceived me."

"What do you mean deceived you?" said Klava Ivanovna, whacking her knee. It was just that he had plenty to do without having to worry about that.

"Malaya," repeated Iona Ovseich, "that's the first time you deceived me since '24 when you were nominated to be an activist. Who can I trust now, Malaya?"

Klava Ivanovna hit her knee again but did not have time to reply because the concierge, Lebedev, had rung the bell and was now standing in the doorway, her face blank as a wall, her head shaking as she said in a whisper: "They're taking Kotlyar. A Black Maria came. They're taking Kotlyar."

Klava Ivanovna and Polina Isaevna stayed in their chairs, too stunned to move. Iona Ovseich walked over to the window and looked down: there was a dark blue van by the gate; the driver was tightening the radiator cap so the engine wouldn't freeze up in the cold.

On Soviet Army Square where three streets begin—Gorky, Tolstoy, and Podbelsky—the city had received a lovely present: a glass map of such enormous proportions that it seemed straight out of a fairy tale. The map showed the main construction sites of communism, which, in addition to the planting of forests, comprised the grandiose and historically unprecedented plan for the "transformation of nature." The principal rivers, canals, and reservoirs were drawn in a blue that was so bright that even the real sea couldn't begin to compare with it. In the evening when it grew dark, the red stars—future hydroelectric stations with an annual production of billions of kilowatt-hours of electricity—would blaze with light. About six feet behind the map, seated in a wicker chair made of reinforced concrete, his arms resting on the arms of the chair, Comrade Stalin gazed pensively into the distance.

All day long, from morning till night, children raced their bicycles around the map. To introduce some order, the young mothers arranged competitions. Those who circled the map first were taken from their bicycles and held high in the air, the victors. For a few minutes, the bike traffic would stop, the children's ardor would cool as people applauded the winners, and then it would all start over again from the beginning.

A few days later a children's road station was set up next to the map and serviced by a van harnessed to two ponies. The van was yellow with large red suns on its sides.

When Klava Ivanovna saw this beautiful sight for the first time, she said that an excursion must absolutely be organized for the entire courtyard; people wasted their time on trifles of all sorts and had no time for what was truly important. Iona Ovseich smiled and said that Malaya wanted people to see the world through her eyes. Klava Ivanovna replied that she didn't want anything but for people to be happy and to see with their own eyes how plans were made a reality.

Iona Ovseich smiled again and said: all right, Malaya should try to organize an excursion and bring the entire courtyard to Sobornaya Square, that is, Soviet Army Square. He'd take on the role of excursion leader. He had only one request—that he be notified at least one day in advance.

A week later Klava Ivanovna went to see Degtyar and admitted that he had been right: when she had proposed the excursion to Soviet Army Square, all the neighbors had laughed like Vankirutyutyu, saying a person could go for a stroll to that square but an excursion, that meant a trip to the Crimea, the Caucasus, or Leningrad, where the cruiser *Aurora* was docked.

"Malaya," said Iona Ovseich, shaking his head, "they're right in their own way, and if we couldn't convince them it's our own fault."

"Mine, you mean," replied Klava Ivanovna. "But I say there's no reason to have to convince them: we should just go around to all the apartments with a list of names, tell people what day and what time the excursion is, and have them sign beside their name."

"And then what," said Iona Ovseich, squinting, "call in the police, line up people by twos, have them hold hands, and march them off to the square?"

Klava Ivanovna remained silent for half a minute, sighed deeply, then said: "All right, I am an old fool, I don't know anything anymore, but I do know that you have to work with people. Or isn't that true anymore either?"

"Malaya," said Iona Ovseich, staring at her with sad eyes, "three years ago when it was a question of whether or not the outpost should be turned into an apartment for the Cheperukhas, we acted like unforgivable cowards, and today we have no place to meet with people and discuss things openly, heart to heart. And that was predictable too."

Yes, said Klava Ivanovna, shrugging her shoulders, Degtyar had predicted it, but who would have ever thought it would drag out three years?

"Malaya," whispered Iona Ovseich, "it's dragged out more than three years."

"Three years," said Klava Ivanovna with a soft groan. "Efim Granik is still living in his little cubbyhole and his daughter Lizochka is still staying with people who aren't family."

"What does Efim have to do with it, what does Lizochka have to do with this!" said Iona Ovseich angrily. "We have to work with people ten times harder than we did yesterday, a hundred times harder. No one's going to create the right conditions for us, we have to create those conditions ourselves."

Iona Ovseich rose to his feet, grasped his lapel, and began pacing the room.

"Malaya," said Iona Ovseich, "pay close attention. Go see Efim right now and stay there while he paints an announcement that next Sunday will be a voluntary workday for the improvement of the courtyard. We'll deal with the details later, but I don't want this put off for another moment. The announcement should be beautiful, a chestnut tree in one corner, an acacia in another, and a spruce tree on top like the ones near the Kremlin wall. Anyone who has a shovel or a hatchet should bring it and those who don't should borrow one."

The announcement was posted in the entry hall the next day. Early Sunday morning the concierge, Lebedev, went around to everyone individually reminding them one more time. Iona Cheperukha took the number 12 trolley to Valikhovsky Lane where Boy was stabled, saddled him, then drove to the plant nursery to pick up the saplings. Iona Ovseich had made all the arrangements well ahead of time, working through the Stalin District Executive Committee, and now they only had to be picked up.

People gathered in the courtyard between nine and nine-thirty. Iona Ovseich greeted them and asked if they'd all had a good night's sleep and guaranteed those who had not, that, after a day out working in the fresh air, they'd make up for it with interest. Katerina laughed, saying she hoped the men would have a little energy left for the women. Marina Biryuk laughed too but everyone else listened in silence and waited.

"Comrades," said Iona Ovseich, "all of us read the newspapers and so there's no need to explain again that the transformation of nature which has seized our country from one end to the other does not only concern those who live in rural locales but directly concerns you and me, meaning the city. Take a walk through the Alexandrovsky Gardens on Stalin Avenue—you'll be horrified by how many chestnuts are scattered all over the ground. Those precious seeds are not becoming new young trees that could help protect us from the steppe's hot dry winds, provide fresh oxygen for our lungs, and shade us from the scorching heat."

"And people with high blood pressure shouldn't be out in the sun at all!" cried Klava Ivanovna.

Iona Ovseich nodded in agreement and signaled not to be interrupted again.

"Take a walk in Shevchenko Park," said Iona Ovseich, wagging a finger threateningly, "and you'll see with your own eyes the mighty oaks, the tsars of the steppe, drop their acorns on the grass. In Odessa those acorns are worth more than gold and yet many children don't even know what they look like!"

Stepa Khomitsky laughed and said: "You should ask how many of us know what they look like."

"You're right, Stepa," said Comrade Degtyar with a bitter smile, "but, as they say, the past and the future are two different things. Now the people are the master in their own house and our patience has come to an end. We're gathered here today to perform voluntary Sunday labor but we are only a small part, a cog in the all-union plan to transform nature. One hundred and twenty thousand hectares of state forest plus six million hectares of state and collective farm forest plus much, much more and that's the situation nationwide!"

Klava Ivanovna and Stepa Khomitsky clapped their hands and were followed in this by Comrade Degtyar and everyone else. Lizochka Granik, Lesik Biryuk, and his sister Zina shouted a loud Pioneer hurrah. Little Grisha and Misha, who until then had been clinging to the skirts of their mother Katya and grandmother Olya, now cheered too and suddenly began chasing after each other around the courtyard.

For a minute people forgot why they had gathered there and were caught up in the children's game, urging them on. Lesik, Zina, and Lizochka pretended that they were trying to stop Grisha and Misha but in fact they all ran around the courtyard three times before the grown-ups could stop them.

"I wish to thank all the dear mothers of the courtyard for having such fine children," said Iona Ovseich with a deep bow. "And now, comrades, to work!"

The concierge, Lebedev, had brought a bucket of lime and a new shovel, which she handed over directly to Comrade Degtyar. Iona Ovseich himself drew the first circle where a tree was to be planted but it was immediately clear that he lacked the artistic touch and Efim Granik was asked to do the job.

"Efim Lazarevich," said Comrade Degtyar, "the people want to return its trust to you. Can you handle that? If you're not up to it, we can lend a hand."

People realized that Comrade Degtyar was joking, but his face was so serious that Efim himself was a little confused and asked if he could make one or two test circles. He had no cause to doubt himself and his circles proved better and more precise than if they had been made with a compass.

Iona Ovseich laughed and said: "I was testing you on purpose because I knew you'd do well. You're hard on yourself and you let yourself be discouraged. You have to have more confidence in your artistic abilities, especially when you're surrounded by friends."

Granik replied that he had complete confidence in his own artistic abilities as long as he was working alone with no one to disturb him, but always got a little shaky when people were looking over his shoulder.

"Comrades," said Iona Ovseich with a cheerful frown, "so now we see that our artist is afraid of the collective and criticism, while we view this just the other way around—the collective and criticism help the artist. Which of us is right?"

Stepa Khomitsky was the first to speak up: people shouldn't be asked questions that have been answered a long time ago, otherwise they might start changing their mind.

"Stepa," said Iona Ovseich, gesturing threateningly with a finger, "with ideas like that you'll end up alone, in complete isolation."

When they finished choosing the sites for the saplings and began prying up the slabs of granite with crowbars, Iona Cheperukha drove into the courtyard with a tremendous clamor, as if he were pulling a thousand carts behind him. He had brought a dozen saplings, including two apricot trees. In addition he brought regards from Anya

Kotlyar, who was standing by the prison on the Lustdorf Road bringing a package for her husband Joseph. She said she would be back home as soon as the prison authorities had accepted the package and she requested that they not start work without her.

Efim Granik giggled and dropped the shovel into the bucket, splashing lime on everyone in the vicinity.

"Cheperukha," said Iona Ovseich angrily, "you've already found the time for an early morning drink while people have been waiting here wasting their precious time!"

"An early morning drink!" said Cheperukha indignantly. "By the time I stopped by the market, the sun was already up over the Ovidiopolsky Highway and some kolkhoz workers tried to talk me into helping them carry their baskets in from the station. But I told them, 'My dear children,' I said, 'my dear little sons of bitches, today's an important day in my life, it's a voluntary work Sunday to improve my own courtyard and the person in charge of it is Comrade Degtyar.' And those ignorant people had never even heard of Comrade Degtyar."

"Cheperukha," said Iona Ovseich, turning visibly pale, "stop your blabbing!"

"Ovseich," shouted old Cheperukha, "do you think I kept my mouth shut with them? No! I told them, 'Go to Solovki, you sons of bitches, go find the bastards that drank your father's blood and they'll tell you who Comrade Degtyar is!' "

People gazed curiously at the elder Cheperukha, who had lost all sense of measure. Marina Biryuk was still purposely egging him on while laughing like a madwoman herself.

"Comrade Biryuk," said Iona Ovseich, finally forced to call her to order, "tell us what's so funny so we can laugh along with you!"

Marina Biryuk shrugged her shoulders and replied that she didn't even know why she was laughing, and then began laughing all the harder. The others, Klava Ivanovna included, began shaking like puppets when all their strings are pulled at the same time. Only Dina Vargaftik stood off to one side and said of Marina that she neighed like a foolish mare neighed for a stallion.

Marina let the remark pass but Cheperukha took offense, demanding that Dina make it clear what stallion she was referring to because

Boy had been a gelding for quite some time, or, to put it in medical terms, had been castrated.

"Cheperukha," said Iona Ovseich, narrowing one eye, "I can see that you're back to your old ways."

"Ovseich," said Cheperukha, squinting with pleasure, "when people remember the best years of their lives, why not enjoy their memories too and laugh along with everyone else, even if there is something foolish about it."

Comrade Degtyar paused for a moment or two, then replied: "There's a grain of truth in what you say but it's the grain of truth that the lie is ready to use so it can look like the truth; in other words, it is barefaced demagogy, and that's worth some special attention here and now."

People were a little confused—things had started well but were ending badly. Stepa stepped forward and made a counterproposal: Cheperukha should receive some individual counseling but right now the command was—attack!

"No," said Comrade Degtyar, "I think we should finish this conversation first!"

"And what I think," interjected Katerina, "is there's been enough tongue wagging already. If we're here to make some improvements, then let's make some improvements."

Adya Lapidis, who was standing off to one side with a crowbar in his hands, now raised it high and brought it down with all his might. The crowbar struck a glancing blow to one corner of a slab of granite and sparks flew. The children cheered and asked to see it again.

"Get the children out of here," ordered Iona Ovseich, "it's too dangerous for them."

The mothers brought the children home but they were back five minutes later. Klava Ivanovna organized a special team for collecting chestnuts in the park on Stalin Avenue and was putting everyone to work, including Grisha and Misha. She gave the command "Forward, march!" and began singing:

"All right, my girls, all right, my beauties,
Let the country sing songs of us,
Let it praise our names in song,
Like it praises other heroes!"

The children began swinging their arms and stamping their feet in rhythm to the song but their voices could not be heard even though they were moving their lips like good little soldiers.

"Hey, team," said Klava Ivanovna indignantly, "why aren't you singing! Come on, join in!"

"All the world's roads are open to us,
And the earth sends us its regards,
The flowers grow and the children are happy,
And the fields are rich with grain!

Klava Ivanovna gave the command "Join in!" again but no one joined in. She brought the work team to a halt and let them know they were not going a single step further until they started singing along with her.

"Grandma Malaya," said Lesik Biryuk, "we don't know that song."

"You don't know that song?" said Klava Ivanovna, stunned. "Who's your singing teacher? Who's your principal?"

While Lesik was trying to remember what the principal's name was, little Grisha stepped out of line and recited a poem he had learned by heart in kindergarten:

"I'm sitting on a cherry tree
Eating one cherry after the other.
Then Uncle Stalin comes and says:
You must obey your mother!"

"Well done!" said Klava Ivanovna in praise. "You're little but you've got pluck. And, as for the rest of you boys and girls, you're going to gather chestnuts and sing along with me until you know the song backward and frontward."

The children sang as they picked the chestnuts from the ground. Then Lesik shimmied up a tree and gave it a good shaking until the ground was covered with green needles like an enormous sea urchin. Klava Ivanovna organized a competition among the older children and a separate one for Grisha and Misha. As long as there were plenty of chestnuts the children competed peacefully, but then they began arguing over each chestnut and ended up really fighting over them. Misha tried to hit Grisha in the eye and Grisha grabbed his brother's collar with both hands and began pulling him down to the ground with all his might.

"Bad kids!" cried Klava Ivanovna. "That's not the way people compete, that's the way aggressors act!"

The two brothers continued fighting, as if they had gone deaf, and Klava Ivanovna was forced to take decisive action: she put Lesik in charge of Misha and took control of Grisha herself and told them they were not to go anywhere near each other. Three or four times the brothers tried to start fighting again but Lesik and Malaya were keeping a sharp lookout and nipped it in the bud.

By lunchtime they had collected two pails full, not counting what they had in their pockets, which were all stuffed to bursting. Lesik picked up the pail to carry it to the courtyard and empty it there but just then the children's mothers arrived and said it was time to go home, it was way past noon.

While Katya was holding Grisha and Misha by the hand and crossing the street with them, they suddenly tore free and began running back toward the park. A truck was just turning the corner of Roza Luxembourg Street but fortunately the driver was able to put on his brakes in time. For a second Katerina was stupefied, then she grabbed both boys by the ears, promising to tear them off if they ever did that again. Klava Ivanovna sided with the children entirely, saying they had a hundred times more political consciousness than their mother and didn't count every minute of work they did on a volunteer Sunday.

"You old bag," shouted Katerina, loudly enough for the whole street to hear, "don't you turn these children against their father and mother. Two can play that game!"

Klava Ivanovna turned white as a sheet, shaking her head vigorously. Marina Biryuk shrugged her shoulders and said it was nothing to get upset over.

"That's right, that's right," said Klava Ivanovna, tears streaming down her cheeks, "nothing to get upset over. I'm just a stupid old woman."

Lesik, who had been appointed team leader, lined up the work brigade and singing, "All right, my girls, all right my beauties," they set off for home.

The work in the courtyard was half done. Iona Ovseich was trying to convince people to work another couple of hours but the women answered that the cooking and cleaning wouldn't get done all by themselves and Sunday only came once a week.

"Comrades," said Iona Ovseich, finally losing patience, "I'm ordering you to stay here and finish the job. We're not doing it for someone else, we're doing this for ourselves!"

The women left, the men stayed. Cheperukha harnessed up Boy because he had to return him to the stable to groom and feed while it was still light.

"Ovseich," said Stepa Khomitsky, "how can you complain? People came and did as much work as they could. You want everybody to be like you."

"Stepa," said Iona Ovseich, an expression of suffering on his face as if he were experiencing a sharp pain under his breastbone or in his heart, "I don't want anything, but just remember how it was back in '37 when we built the outpost for the children."

Zinovy Cheperukha came into the courtyard: he had been in the library since early morning working on a course project in electrical engineering. The deadline had passed two weeks ago but the Kirov factory had been so overloaded that he hadn't even had time to open a book.

Iona Ovseich called out to Zinovy, asking him to give the old folks a hand. Cheperukha looked around and asked where the old folks were, he didn't see any.

"Zinovy," said Iona Ovseich, walking over to him and placing his hand on Zyunchik's shoulder, "do you remember when the boys of the courtyard—you, Kolka and Osya, may they rest in peace—helped your fathers and mothers build the outpost?"

Zinovy said that he remembered it well, but was now also on his guard a little.

"Don't worry," said Iona Ovseich reassuringly, "no one's referring to your living there now. It just came up, that's all."

"Now I understand," said Zinovy, "the people from our courtyard left halfway through today. Good lord, so then let's roll up our sleeves and finish it ourselves!"

"Zinovy," said Comrade Degtyar with a bitter grin, "do you really think that's what I was driving at?"

"Stop the nonsense!" Zinovy extended his hands forward, palms out. "Somebody coming by might think there was a death in the family when everybody's alive and well."

Zinovy picked up a shovel, drove it into the ground, and brought up a huge chunk of earth.

Klava Ivanovna was in ecstasy: "You're as strong as your father was twenty years ago!"

Zinovy said that he was probably even stronger because he was compensating for the leg he'd lost, and when he used to play soccer that leg had been as powerful as that of the famous Zlochevsky, who played for the Odessa Dynamo team and who once almost killed a Turkish goalkeeper.

Hearing her husband's voice, Katerina shouted through the window for him to come and have lunch right away, otherwise it'd get cold and she wasn't going to heat it up a third time. Then Grisha and Misha came to get their father, but they both stayed out in the courtyard and helped with the work. Now Katerina lost her temper completely, came for her children, and said she wished her husband would come down with the cold he deserved.

"You Siberian pain in the ass!" Zinovy shouted after her. "Another five minutes, you can time it."

But it didn't take five, it took him ten times that. Anya Kotlyar had delivered the package for Joseph in prison and returned to the courtyard just as they had begun digging a hole for the last sapling and were choosing the stones to place in the bed around it. Efim Granik and Adya poured the dirt into the hole from pails to make a nice little hill shape, so that the mound would not have the same shape as a grave. Anya picked up a pail and needed no prompting to join in the work.

Zinovy asked how her husband was feeling. Anya made a dismissive gesture and bent over further to pick up more soil.

"Annushka," whispered Klava Ivanovna, "it's been three years, almost half, and the second half always goes quicker."

Iona Ovseich walked off to one side when the conversation turned to Joseph Kotlyar, then began to examine the saplings closely, even shaking them a little to check that they were firmly in the ground.

The saplings held so firmly that they seemed already to have sent their roots down deep. Iona Ovseich smiled, clapped his hands loudly, and said: "In three years our courtyard will be so beautiful a garden people will come here from the Bolshoi Fontan to learn from us."

Anya emptied her pail, tamped the earth with her foot, then suddenly burst into tears.

"Quiet, quiet," said Klava Ivanovna, putting her arm around Anya, "people can see."

"Let them see," whispered Anya, "I don't care anymore. Joseph's being transferred somewhere near the Volga or maybe even further away. I could bring him some packages here, fruit, vegetables, a little bar of soap, but there he'll be all alone surrounded by crooks, thieves, and criminals."

Adya used his shovel to even off the edges of the bed. Iona Ovseich observed it all in silence, then suddenly turned and said in a loud voice: "Kotlyar, we're asking you nicely to stop that talk. Everyone's in the place he deserves to be. Your husband was warned in plenty of time, and he was warned more than once."

"What," said Anya, shaking her head, "what did you warn him about, Comrade Degtyar?"

"Do you want us to make it perfectly clear? That can be done," said Iona Ovseich.

"Yes," Adya said, suddenly, "we want you to, because before, when food was scarce, they brought something to Polina Isaevna every day, and you closed your eyes and stopped up your ears but when the need passed, suddenly you could see again, and hear that Joseph Kotlyar was telling all kinds of jokes!"

"You little snot-nose!" said Iona Ovseich, his whole body trembling. "I knew Ivan Lapidis all too well, and you're of the same breed he was. I'm going to call the dean at your conservatory tomorrow. You're not a little boy anymore, and you bear full responsibility for what you say. Zinovy is a little older than you are but he had time enough to lose a leg at the front, but the people pay for your food with their hard-earned money so you can receive a higher education and so you can also spread your filthy cosmopolitan propaganda."

"You have no right to criticize me!" said Adya, flushing deep red. "It's not my fault that I don't have a father or a mother! During the war, I worked in a munitions factory, everybody knows that. And don't think I'm afraid of your labels either: you're a dirty cosmopolitan yourself!"

"Adya," said Klava Ivanovna, waving her arms, "be quiet, I'm asking you, shut your mouth!"

"Don't get mixed up in this, Malaya," said Iona Ovseich. "Let this bum show us what else he's got inside!"

The neighbors opened their windows and looked down into the courtyard. Iona Ovseich made an a gesture of invitation and said: "Very good, let the whole courtyard hear."

"Adya!" said Zinovy, grabbing Adya in his iron grip. "Go home!"

"Let me go!" Adya tried to jerk free, then suddenly burst into tears like a little boy. "I'll kill him right now!"

"Some killer!" said Zinovy with a terrible look in his eyes. "Kill me first, I can't stand the sight of other people's blood."

Perfect silence reigned for a moment. Efim Granik was the first to break it. "An actor! Zinovy should have studied acting instead of electrical engineering."

Then everyone else began buzzing. Adya made a pitiful figure, his head lowered. Iona Ovseich looked around and Madame Malaya announced that the voluntary Sunday work was over, people could go home.

"Yes, comrades," said Iona Ovseich in confirmation, "you worked well today and deserve your legal right to relax."

Efim pretended not to understand: "What do you mean—relax? Tomorrow's Monday for me, personally speaking."

Late that evening Anya went to Degtyar's to ask about Polina Isaevna's health, saying that now she was working one and a half shifts at the hospital and didn't even have the time to call on her ailing neighbor, who at one time had helped her find herself and her profession. Where would she be today without her profession? Nowhere, like so many women who stay home and cook dinner for their husbands.

Polina Isaevna wasn't feeling well: God should make our enemies that weak. In past years she used to complain about her husband, that he devoted too little attention to her, but now she could say with him right there in the room that he was a wonderful person and a wonderful husband if he had all that much patience for her.

"Polina," said Iona Ovseich with a frown, "please, that sort of talk is out of place."

"Comrade Degtyar," said Anya in a polite tone, "I'll take the liberty of intervening here: if a wife wants to thank her husband, who can deprive her of that right? That seems better than quarreling to me. Joseph and I used to fight too but I can promise you that will never happen again."

"My dear woman," interrupted Iona Ovseich, "please leave me out of any conversations you might wish to have about your husband."

Anya lowered her head and her lips trembled. She seemed on the verge of tears but it was actually her jaw wound acting up.

"And besides, I'm well aware of the purpose of your visit," continued Iona Ovseich. "You're here to convince me that Adya is still a foolish boy who doesn't realize what he's saying. Or am I mistaken?"

"That's right, that's right, you're mistaken, comrade," said Anya with a joyfulness that was out of place. "If Adya finds out that I was here, in your home, he'll never want to talk to me again! That boy has lost too much already, he's not afraid of losing anything anymore!"

"Leave!" said Iona Ovseich, rising and pointing to the door. "Leave while you still can."

"My God," said Polina Isaevna, wringing her hands, "what's going on here! Iona, Anya, please don't do this! Don't!"

"Oh yes I will!" replied Anya rudely. "You thank him for everything he's done to cause you your condition!"

"You fool," shouted Iona Ovseich, "you're a total fool! The woman's had tuberculosis for fifteen years and now you're blaming me for it!"

That night Iona Ovseich had heart trouble. Usually he would feel a pain first—under his shoulder blade, in his elbow, his little finger—but this time he was caught completely by surprise. He took validol all night and placed mustard plasters on his chest. Polina Isaevna pleaded with him to spend a day in bed, half a day, but as soon as the radio announced it was seven o'clock, he brewed himself some tea for the tannin, which stimulates the nervous system greatly, ate a piece of bread and sausage, wrapped another in a sheet of newspaper, and left for work.

As soon as he arrived at the factory, he phoned his wife to tell her that he'd be running around all day and there would be no point in her calling him at the party office.

Iona Ovseich was a wreck when he returned home that evening. There were huge dark circles under his eyes and the veins on his forehead were distended, as if there were a tourniquet on him.

"It's suicide, that's what it is," said Polina Isaevna. "I don't want my husband's death on my conscience. I'm going to write to the District Committee and ask them to appoint a medical commission and hospitalize you by force."

"Polina," said Iona Ovseich, barely able to smile, "a person can only be forcibly hospitalized in an insane asylum."

It was past ten, an hour at which no one expected guests, when Adya Lapidis knocked at the door.

"Comrade Degtyar," said Adya, "may I come in for a minute please? I need to talk to you."

"You need to talk?" said Iona Ovseich, automatically taking a step back toward the light. "We'll talk here."

Adya thought for a second, took a step toward the table, then said softly: "The dean called me today and gave me a warning: I'll be expelled from the conservatory if they receive another report on me that's confirmed."

"That's interesting!" said Iona Ovseich, narrowing his right cyc. "And just why are you telling me all this? Did the dean mention me by name? Or are you looking for me to support you?"

"No," said Adya, placing his hands on the back of a chair, his long thin fingers trembling. "I don't expect any support from you. I just want you to tell him the truth."

"Adya," said Polina Isaevna, becoming upset, "you don't realize what you're saying!"

"I want you," said Adya with difficulty, as if short of breath, "I want you to tell him the truth."

"Easy does it," said Iona Ovseich. "Easy does it. You've come to see me at home in the middle of the night. I don't know what you have concealed in your pocket, but you're threatening me in the presence of my wife of thirty years. Get out, you son of a bitch, get out of here!"

Iona Ovseich grabbed a stool and raised it high above his head.

Adya ducked instinctively and struck his chin on the back of the chair; a thin stream of blood trickled from either corner of his mouth.

Polina Isaevna covered her face with her hands, then jumped up, moistened a towel, and was about to press it to Adya's mouth but he had already wiped it with his hand, which was now smeared with blood. He looked daggers at Iona Ovseich and walked out.

"My God," said Polina Isaevna, running around the table, pressing her fingers to her temples, "what's going to happen now, what's going to happen now!"

"Nothing's going to happen. Stop panicking," ordered Iona Ovseich.

"He knocked out all his teeth and he'll say that he was defending himself against you!" said Polina Isaevna, unable to get ahold of herself. "And I'll have to appear as a witness. Anya Kotlyar gives us injections and her Adya leaves here covered in blood. What's going to happen now!"

"Stop panicking!" repeated Iona Ovseich. "I've been taking care of you all my life. I've been dealing with doctors and hospitals all my life because my wife has diseases of the lungs, the heart, the head, and who the hell knows what else! And it's all from laxness and indulgence when you should be trying to take yourself in hand!"

Polina Isaevna sat down on the bed and cried. Iona Ovseich sat down beside her, stroked her back, and said that he had gotten too worked up. It happened to everyone, he wasn't as young as he used to be either and didn't have the strength he once had. And there was no reason for her to worry about Lapidis: Adya wasn't the kind of person to run to the authorities and lie for his own benefit. He could guarantee her that even Anya would never hear about any of this.

Iona Ovseich proved absolutely right. Not only that, a day or two later, Adya provided additional material against himself out of his own foolishness: the Komsomol committee and the dean learned that he had been speaking with a number of students in defense of Professor Rabinovich, who, at meetings and in the newspaper *The Bolshevik Banner,* had been criticized for being a "rootless cosmopolitan" and who now had been removed from his post upon the demand of the other professors and teachers.

A boy from the conservatory came to the courtyard and informed Anya Kotlyar that Adya's fate was hanging by a thread: the order had been written and needed only to be signed—Adya would be expelled for a year and sent to do hard physical labor. But the dean wanted to give him a year's suspended expulsion since Lapidis was an orphan and had worked as a lathe operator in a munitions factory during the war. However the school had no documentation from the factory and they told Adya to have confirmation sent, but he said he wouldn't. If they didn't want to believe him, he said, they didn't have to. He knew what was true and what was not.

Anya ran right to Madame Malaya, who then went to Degtyar and told him the whole story. "Well, how do you like that idiot!" she said, spreading her hands.

"Idiot?" said Iona Ovseich in surprise. "No, Malaya, you're wrong there. He's taking a definite position and line."

Klava Ivanovna brushed that idea aside, saying: "What kind of line can a twenty-year-old who's still a child be taking? Degtyar, you must help him."

"Malaya," said Iona Ovseich angrily, "either you're faking or your brain really has got soft from old age!"

Keeping it a secret from Adya, Klava Ivanovna wrote to the factory where he worked as a lathe operator during the war asking them to provide documentation on their letterhead and to have it certified. But, by the time the letter had arrived in the Urals and the answer been sent back to Odessa, Adya's stubbornness had turned everyone against him, including the dean, who now shared the opinion that Lapidis should spend at least a year in the factory as part of a regular workers' collective and then, depending on the results, the question of his returning to the conservatory could be raised again.

Zinovy found Adya a job at the Kirov factory, first as an apprentice but after a month and a half he was promoted to a regular worker. No one was surprised by his rapid progress because a lathe operator and a pianist have much in common—they both need especially sensitive fingers.

"Yes," said Klava Ivanovna, "it's fashionable to be a lathe operator or a baker now but what's it going to do to Adya's hands?"

Iona Ovseich was very much disturbed by what he called the attitude prevalent in Odessa on the part of every fat mother taking her little fat children by the hand to the Stolyarsky Music School. "What do fat mothers have to do with it?" asked Klava Ivanovna indignantly.

"Adya grew up without a mother or a father. It's a miracle he didn't become a street kid or a crook!"

"Malaya," said Iona Ovseich, losing his patience, "you and I have been living in the same courtyard for more years than I need to mention but I'm starting to think that you can never really know another person!"

Klava Ivanovna was insulted: the folk saying was right—too much cleverness and you were a fool!

"Malaya," said Iona Ovseich, wagging a finger threateningly, "all of us still have some bourgeois roots in us and all they need is some good fertilizer to start blossoming so fast it'll make you dizzy."

"To listen to you," said Klava Ivanovna, refusing to yield, "we're farther from communism today than we were fifteen years ago when no one was even thinking about the plan to transform nature or the great engineering feats of communism."

"Malaya," said Iona Ovseich, glowering coldly at her, "great success can make us complacent and good natured, but complacency and vigilance can never go together—it's one or the other!"

Klava Ivanovna yielded on that point, but then another question arose: "We defeated Hitler and we really did it alone. America and England are far away, so who do we have to fear now?" Degtyar should answer that for her, and without any philosophizing.

"All right," said Iona Ovseich, "I'll answer that question, and without any philosophizing, as you asked. During the four years of World War I, England, France, Russia, and America suffered three million casualties, but in a period of two years in Europe alone more than three million people died from Spanish influenza, a microbe too small to be seen with the naked eye."

"What of it!" said Klava Ivanovna. "That's no example."

"Yes it is," said Iona Ovseich, pounding his fist on the table. "It's a classic example of how an invisible enemy is ten times, a hundred times more dangerous than one you can see!"

"Hold on," said Klava Ivanovna. "What does that have to do with Adya Lapidis?"

"I'll tell you," said Iona Ovseich angrily. "The straight path isn't to his liking. He may not have a stone hidden in his hand yet but he could at any time. Go ask Khomitsky, go ask Zinovy, ask Dina Vargaftik if they're prepared to vouch for Adya in writing, today, right now. And how about you?"

Klava Ivanovna shrugged her shoulders: "What's the need of that? Adya's not a criminal."

"Malaya," said Iona Ovseich, grimacing, "don't play the fool with me. I can tell by your eyes that you know what I mean."

Degtyar was right: Klava Ivanovna did indeed know what Degtyar meant, especially since the entire courtyard to a man had been expressing surprise that Adya Lapidis, who was grown now and had a good head, had messed up his life so badly. You told him in plain Russian that white was white but he had to go against everyone and insist that white was black.

When the first pain had passed, Anya Kotlyar also grew furious with Adya and every day she reminded him of the old saying: you've made your bed, now lie in it.

Only Efim Granik took the whole affair in good spirits, explaining to all the neighbors that this turn of events could only work to Adya's benefit since the deeper an artist or musician experienced the life of the people the better it was for his art.

Making some free time on Saturday evening, Iona Ovseich visited Zinovy. Following the old Russian custom, Katerina bowed deeply to welcome her guest, then set the table, placing a small carafe in the center.

"Katerina," said Iona Ovseich, smacking his lips, "I can see that you have a pretty good idea of how to treat people in authority."

"Oh, don't say that," said Katerina with a dismissive wave of her hand. "I'm as far from you Odessites as our Lake Baikal is from your Black Sea."

"A very apt comparison," said Iona Ovseich approvingly, "but with today's technology that's only a day's travel."

Zinovy filled their glasses to the brim but Iona Ovseich poured half of his back into the carafe. Katerina said indignantly that her guest did not wish their home full happiness, but Iona Ovseich replied that certain allowances had to be made for him.

"All right," said Zinovy, raising his glass, "may our children never be afraid of locomotives."

"Hold on," said Iona Ovseich, "I want to add something to that toast: may this house, the parents and the children, have all the comforts that modern science and technology can provide!"

Instead of tossing back his drink, Zinovy passed his hand in front of his eyes as if driving away a hallucination. Katerina emptied her glass and quickly poured herself another. Then they all drank together. Iona Ovseich cut himself a slice of cucumber, placed it on top of a piece of bread, took a bite, chewed it thoroughly, and wiped his lips with the palm of his hand. Then he asked Zinovy if he would show him around the old outpost if that wasn't a problem; it had been so long since he'd been there, he'd forgotten what it looked like. Zinovy remained in his seat and replied that Comrade Degtyar was free to do as he pleased: he could tap the walls and look into every cupboard and corner.

Iona Ovseich frowned but accepted the offer and rose from the table. After examining both rooms, he stopped by the tap and used his foot to check the cement floor under the sink and then turned on the water for a minute. He asked how the inspection had gone and then addressed a question to Katerina: would she object greatly if he interceded with the housing department of the Stalin District Soviet to seek permission for them to have a toilet installed there?

"Comrade Degtyar," said Katerina, clasping her hands, "may you live a thousand years in good health, and when your last day comes the Cheperukha grandchildren will be in the front row of the mourners."

"Katerina," said Iona Ovseich sadly, "the places in the front row are already taken but if you act as the funeral director, I think you might prove more useful at my death than I have been during my life."

Katerina replied that that was impossible because Comrade Degtyar was a hundred times more useful to people than she was and anyway modern medicine would find a way to prolong his life. Iona Ovseich thanked her for her kind words while Zinovy looked on in silence, his brow furrowed, as if he didn't understand what was going on in his own home.

"Zinovy," said Iona Ovseich, "you look like the sexton who has to read the psalter to laymen but then sees he can't tell one letter from the other."

Katerina winked and said she knew the reason. Comrade Degtyar cupped a hand to his ear and asked her to tell him the secret. Zinovy gave his wife an angry glance; she sealed her mouth with her hand and began making sounds like a deaf and dumb person.

"All right," said Iona Ovseich, his tone sad again, "I'll say it myself. Zinovy, you think I came here with some ulterior motive, some intrigue to get you evicted from the outpost. I'm not saying this to insult you, but people have the habit of judging other people by themselves, even if they don't realize it."

Zinovy replied that Degtyar could not consider himself an exception to that rule either.

Referring to Zinovy, Katerina said in a loud voice that fools make foolish jokes. Iona Ovseich shook his head: Katerina was wrong to attack her husband, especially since there was a grain of truth in what Zinovy said. All the same, it was surprising: a guest came to their house and brought them good news but they tested the coin with their teeth to see if it was counterfeit or not. Zinovy had allowed himself to be tactless again but sometimes coins were in fact false.

"But I trust you, Comrade Degtyar, like I trust myself," said Katerina. "Even more."

"All right," said Iona Ovseich, summing up, "let's not count our chickens before they're hatched. We'll meet again in a week. But there should be somebody here at home during that time, someone from the housing department may drop by."

Olya was alone with the grandchildren on Thursday when a deputy from the Stalin District Soviet dropped by accompanied by a plumber from the building administration. The plumber explained that problems might be encountered in laying a sewer line because goods were stored in the basement of a neighboring building. Without a pause, the deputy replied that people's health was more important to them than a thousand bales of cotton and gabardine, especially when there were children in the house. Olya brought both of her grandchildren over to the deputy and told them to thank her like good little junior Pioneers. Misha did as he was told but Grisha wouldn't, saying that he wasn't a junior Pioneer yet and not even all the children in the older group were junior Pioneers yet.

"Good boy!" said the deputy, stroking Grisha and tugging his ear affectionately. "People should always act on their principles."

The plumber said that he needed to go down into the basement to be able to come to a more definite conclusion but it was too late to do it today.

"Comrade Deputy," said Olya indignantly, "who's he trying to kid? We had a courtyard laundry right here under Nicholas II and during the first years of Soviet power we built an outpost for our children—the plumbing couldn't have disappeared in the meantime."

The plumber replied that ancient Rome also had a sewer system.

"He's looking for a bribe!" cried Olya. "He wants his palm greased but I'll give him the finger instead!"

She gave the plumber the finger right to his face. The deputy laughed and asked Olya to keep calm. The plumber told the deputy that this was the last time he would go around with her on business like this. She could write up her own conclusion, he wasn't taking any responsibility for it.

"Listen here," said the deputy angrily, "don't you take that tone with me!"

The plumber replied that he wouldn't take any other tone with her and that he was going to write a report to the chairman of the District Executive Committee.

"What kind of report?" asked the deputy, dumbfounded.

"A report saying that you're sticking your nose in where it doesn't belong and showing favoritism to some people," the plumber replied in an insolent tone.

"You bribe-taker," said Olya Cheperukha, paling from excitement. "How dare you speak to a deputy like that? She's not someone you know from your days as a swineherd."

The plumber let the insult pass and informed the deputy that, without the consent of the city industrial department, no sewer line would be laid there, and that department only gave its consent once in a blue moon.

"Don't listen to him," said Olya, wringing her hands, "I've been living here thirty years. This building used to belong to Colonel Kotlyarevsky, you can ask Madame Malaya, and there used to be a laundry room here and then it was turned into an outpost so the children could have a place to play. After the war the outpost was turned into an apartment and now my son is living here. He lost a leg at the front, his wife was at the front too, and they also have two children now. Comrade Deputy, you can't imagine what wonderful children they are!"

The deputy said that every parent and grandparent thought their children were the best in the world but there was no cause for hysterics here, that would only make matters worse.

"What's your decision then?" asked Olya, clutching her grandsons to her and unintentionally halting by the door as if barring the way.

"There's been no decision yet," said the deputy calmly, "and I'm not the one who decides things, I only report to the executive committee, but first they'll need a specialist's conclusions."

"Meaning him again?" said Olya, pointing at the plumber. "The Soviet system can't take a step without him?"

"Don't worry," said the deputy. "There are laws in the Soviet Union and everything will be done according to the law."

As soon as Zinovy learned of what had taken place during the inspection visit, he ran straight to Iona Ovseich and said that this was not a matter of self-interest but of principle and that he would write directly to the first secretary of the Province Committee.

"Go ahead, write to him," replied Iona Ovseich. "But first you should ask yourself whether the plumber's got the trump card here or whether he's just looking for a few rubles like certain other members of his profession do."

Zinovy was indignant: what kind of trump card could he be holding if they already had running water in the apartment and it was plain as day that if the place was once a laundry room, it had to have had plumbing!

"You're an odd bird, Zinovy," said Comrade Degtyar with a smile. "But where's your proof that all the plumbing had been properly installed, especially since it was put in nearly a hundred years ago? Second, where's the proof that it's still in good condition after all those years and still serviceable today?"

"Hold on," said Zinovy, "I have running water, don't I?"

"Yes, that's a fact, you do," said Iona Ovseich, smiling again. "But that's still no proof that everything's up to code."

Zinovy thought for a moment, sighed bitterly, then asked what Comrade Degtyar recommended.

"Now, finally, you're talking like a man," said Iona Ovseich, whacking the palm of his hand against the table. "First and foremost, you have to hold your horses. We'll make sure that the housing department sends over a qualified specialist who has full authority to reach a final conclusion. Do you follow me?"

Zinovy was silent for a moment, then extended his hand to Iona Ovseich and said that in the past he had not always been entirely fair to Comrade Degtyar but that would never happen again.

"You're a hotheaded person," said Iona Ovseich, shaking his head in reproach. "I don't want to hear any more remarks like that from you: you always followed the dictates of your conscience. And when you helped Adya Lapidis find a job at the Kirov factory so an eye could be kept on him, it was your conscience as a worker that prompted you."

Iona Ovseich looked intently at Zinovy as if they had not seen each other for a long time. Then, since they were on the subject, he asked how Adya was doing at the factory—with the collective, the other workers; what did they talk about, what did they say about management, movies, books? Zinovy replied that he and Adya worked in different departments and practically never saw each other, but if Iona Ovseich wanted to learn the details, he should contact the Komsomol committee and the department committee.

Iona Ovseich took Zinovy by the arm above the elbow and said that Zinovy should be explicit about who he meant should do the contacting, him or Zinovy?

Zinovy said he had no reason to be in contact with those committees because they already knew him well there and, if need be could find him right away, and if Comrade Degtyar were needed all they had to do was pick up the phone and call his factory.

Iona Ovseich grasped his lapel, tilted his head to the side, and requested Zinovy's permission to ask him another question: why was it that when it was a question of installing a lavatory in the former outpost, which was now Zinovy Cheperukha's apartment, Degtyar hadn't given the difficulties involved a moment's thought and had taken the whole problem onto himself, whereas Zinovy Cheperukha, who was young and bursting with strength and energy, responded to Degtyar's request by saying he didn't want to help and put himself to any trouble over the fate of his younger comrade Adya Lapidis.

Zinovy adjusted his prothesis, loosening the straps a little, then made a move as if about to rise from the table, but stayed where he was and said that openness should be met with openness: for all the time he'd been living in the outpost, he'd run out to the courtyard to use the lavatory, and it was no problem; his health hadn't suffered because of it, and his own sons could have done the same thing. But, and Degtyar should mark this well, for a toilet of his own, even a bathroom, he, Zinovy Cheperukha, would never become an informer.

Iona Ovseich paled, then turned red as a boiled crab. Clearly having difficulty in breathing, he unbuttoned his collar and then went for Zinovy: "You hothead, you've simply gone out of your mind now, you should be sent right to Slobodka! Where did you ever get that idea? Where! You'll never hear another word from me on this subject. And as for the lavatory, and even the bathroom as you put it, you didn't have to worry about that and you won't have to in the future because that old fool Degtyar is your neighbor and twenty-five years ago he used to hold you in his arms, and, in gratitude, that little boy pissed on my new cheviot suit."

Zinovy remained silent, a confused look in his eye. Iona Ovseich extended his hand and said: "All right, let's shake hands! But if I ever hear you say anything like that again, I don't want to know you."

On Saturday an engineer from the housing department came to the outpost, this time alone, without the deputy, and spent ten minutes inspecting the premises. Then he said that on Monday afternoon one member of the family should drop by the executive committee; work could start right away. Zinovy opened a sideboard and pulled out a decanter in which orange and lemon peels were floating but the engineer flatly refused to drink, explaining that his ulcers had been acting up.

"All right," agreed Katerina, "but one little glass won't hurt. I guarantee it."

Early on the morning of the next day, Cheperukha was in Shchepny Row with his horse, Boy. All sorts of people came up to him asking what he was in the market for. For a long time he could not find anything suitable but finally two men appeared who told him to come with them to Vatmansky Lane. They brought out a toilet tank that was nearly perfect and a complete kit for a shower but said that he'd have to wait a couple of days for the toilet bowl.

When Iona returned home, Stepa Khomitsky and Zinovy had finished the measurements and were gouging a hole in the floor with a crowbar so that a pipe could be run into the basement and connected with the sewer system. In the afternoon Stepa warned Lyalya Orlov, Dina Vargaftik, and everyone else who lived in that wing not to flush their toilets until the next morning because a new T-pipe had to be laid and the sewer system would be temporarily open. People were very upset by this and went running to Comrade Degtyar to complain: it wasn't enough that Zinovy and Katerina had taken away the children's outpost; it wasn't enough that this son of a carter was installing a bathroom for himself as if he were the famous Filatov or some general; now people were supposed to suffer so he could have all the conveniences!

"My dear comrades," said Iona Ovseich in surprise, "why are you coming to me? I can intervene if something's being done illegally but that doesn't apply in the case at hand. But if the technical side of the problem is not to your liking, you can demand that Cheperukha halt working and find a way of continuing it without bothering other people."

Dina Vargaftik and Lyalya followed Comrade Degtyar's advice and warned Zinovy that if he didn't stop doing just as he damn pleased the entire police force would be there in a minute. Though she had not been spoken to, Katerina laughed right in Dina's face and called her a busybody, reserving much viler remarks for Lyalya Orlov. Dina put a hand to either side of her head and demanded that Lyalya immediately bring Katerina to court for those slanderous insults, she'd stand as her witness. Lyalya burst into tears and said that was the first time in her life she'd heard expressions like that, as if this were a red-light district and not a civilized courtyard.

Zinovy took Katerina by the shoulders, pushed her inside, and slammed the door behind her. He stayed outside and apologized for his wife. Lyalya wiped her tears and said she wasn't the sort to hold a grudge. Dina began chewing her fingernails and talking about her Grisha, who had once protected her like a brick wall, but now just anybody could insult her and ridicule her. Zinovy replied that no one was ridiculing her, it was just that everyone's nerves had a limit, that was all.

"So that's it, is it?" said Dina, immediately regaining her composure and ceasing to bite her nails. "In other words, Katerina wasn't ridiculing us, but you apologized to us just because we're a couple of little fools. Yes, you're right, we really are fools if we could believe you for a moment and take you at face value! Lyalya, you stay here, I'm going for the police."

Dina turned and had taken a few steps toward the front gate when Iona Ovseich and Stepa Khomitsky suddenly came walking out.

"All that noise and no punches being thrown!" said Iona Ovseich good-humoredly.

Dina shouted that nobody better dare put a hand on her and try to stop her: she was going for the police and the police could figure out who had the right in this country to ridicule women who were alone, especially when everybody knew she was alone because her Grisha had given his life at the front!

"Calm down," said Iona Ovseich, taking Dina by the arm, and giving her a slap, "and let me say something."

Dina replied that she wouldn't calm down until she was dead but nobody better lay a hand on her while she was still alive and kicking.

"Calm down," repeated Iona Ovseich, and slapped her again. "Number one, you're not going to the police: we're not going to disgrace our courtyard in front of the whole city. Number two, can't you people really come to terms by yourself without an intermediary, without me having to intervene constantly?"

Dina pointed at Zinovy and asked him in Comrade Degtyar's presence to repeat the filth that his Katerina had spewed all over Lyalya, who had been living in their courtyard since the day she was born, while they'd brought that Katerina here three years ago from the sticks of Siberia where they had never even heard of Odessa.

Iona Ovseich ordered an immediate end to the bedlam, warned them that he would tolerate no nonsense, and demanded that they all should live in peace and friendship as befitted Soviet people and not get each other's hackles up over nothing.

"That's what you call nothing!" said Dina, sharply. "Then why did you send me and Lyalya here to make Cheperukha stop working?"

"I sent you?" said Iona Ovseich in surprise.

"No," said Dina, laughing hysterically, "Duke Richeleaux sent us! Lyalya, tell him what Katerina said to you!"

Lyalya shrugged her shoulders. Comrade Degtyar categorically demanded that Dina Vargaftik not twist his words around because he had made it perfectly clear both to her and to Orlov that he wasn't going to intervene and said that the neighbors should straighten it out themselves.

"I want an answer," said Dina, refusing to yield. "Did you send us to see Zinovy or didn't you?"

"Listen, Vargaftik," said Iona Ovseich, exhaling forcibly, "don't start any provocations here. I advised you on how best to work things among yourselves but you went to see Zinovy to make a scene and you got Orlov on your side on top of it."

Though Comrade Degtyar had not been speaking to Lyalya, she now confirmed that he had in fact only given them advice and had not sent them there in the strict sense of the word.

"In other words," said Iona Ovseich, raising one finger and moving it back and forth in the air like a pendulum, "if you want to go, you go, and if you don't, you don't. And, while we're at it, Vargaftik, we could take a clue from you and bring up the story of your faking the papers so Efim Granik could get a residence pass."

"Faking?" said Dina, flushing a ruddy red. "Yes, it's true, but the whole courtyard knows that I just wanted to help Efim, and I got no benefit from it, only trouble."

"It's not so simple as that," said Iona Ovseich, moving his head forward and a little to the side. "I'll be serving on a jury tomorrow: it's a similar case, faking the papers for profit."

"People, he's gone out of his mind!" cried Dina. "Why are you all being silent as mice? You all know the whole truth about it, so why are you being silent as mice!"

Lyalya Orlov said it was time for her to go home and promised not to flush her toilet until the next morning. Stepa picked up his wrench, T-pipe, and bolts, and went down to the cellar. Iona Ovseich asked Zinovy to take him inside the apartment and show him how the work was going.

In less than a day they had done an amazing amount of work. Comrade Degtyar praised Zinovy while at the same time reminding him that when we're worried about speed, we sometimes forgot about quality. Zinovy replied that at the Kirov factory their motto was quality first, speed second. And it turned out that they got both. And what kind of a person would do worse work at home than he did at the factory?

Zinovy smiled and said that he was only joking, of course. Iona

Ovseich replied that no excuses were needed, he had gotten the joke, and reminded Zinovy of the foolish suspicions that had come into his head when they had last spoken about Adya Lapidis. Even take today, practice had demonstrated how right he had been: Lapidis' mouth had already attracted attention, and not only in his department.

Zinovy replied that half an hour ago Dina Vargaftik had been shooting off her mouth too, but everybody knew that shooting off your mouth was just that, and nothing more.

Iona Ovseich shook his head: "There's mouths and there's mouths, and, that aside, we musn't forget that negative attitudes don't come out of nowhere. They grow in people's souls like in a greenhouse and when it gets too crowded for them there, they start sending out their poison tongues and, bip, bap, before you know it, the infection has spread!

"Cheperukha, my dear man," said Iona Ovseich, looking Zyunchik intently in the eye, "you were at the front and I don't have to tell you what infection is. If circumstances warranted it, people like that were taken out to a field or put up against a wall, and you didn't always have a verdict from a court or a tribunal in your pocket."

No, said Zinovy. Personally, he didn't know of a single case like that.

Iona Ovseich paused to think a moment, automatically turning on the faucet. At first the water gushed out but then gradually slowed until it finally stopped. Iona Ovseich sighed deeply—just like a person's life, but you didn't think about that when you were young, death was so far off that you couldn't imagine that the world could exist without you.

That was true, agreed Zinovy. After all these years he could still feel his amputated leg, and sometimes at night, especially just before dawn, the toes gave him pain, and then he'd dream he was massaging the leg and putting it in hot water.

In the hallway on the second floor Klava Ivanovna was singing her favorite song: "All right, my girls, all right, my beauties!"

"Malaya's really gotten old," said Iona Ovseich, "but still sometimes she's like a little child. I've been able to count on her completely for many years now, since '24."

Zinovy smiled, saying he could remember as if it were yesterday Malaya demanding that Oska Granik salute and give his Pioneer word of honor that he would never again set foot inside a church or a synagogue. And Oska kept his word: nobody could hide from Klava Ivanovna.

"Listen, Zinovy," said Iona Ovseich, his eyes sad and half closed, "the old guard is gradually dying off. That's the law of life, and there's nothing you can do about it. When one soldier falls, another takes his place. Zinovy, there's something wrong about the attitude in our courtyard. I can't sleep at night worrying about the people who live here. We have to create a new group of activists from people who are young, strong, and healthy. I want you to head them up. I'll recommend you for membership in the party."

Water began flowing from the tap again. Down in the basement Stepa struck the pipe three times to signal them to turn off the faucet at once. Zinovy reacted after the first bang but turned the handle with such force that it caused the pipe to make a grinding sound.

"It's my fault," said Iona Ovseich. "I forgot to turn off the faucet. Don't be mad at old Degtyar."

Zinovy shrugged his shoulders, saying it was nothing. As for the activist group, it needed some thinking about, but there was one thing he could say straight off: he wouldn't make a good leader, you needed to be born with a taste for that.

"My dear Zinovy," said Iona Ovseich, wagging a finger, "drop the camouflage. I've been around, and I can smell a leader a mile away."

For a moment they stood in silence, then Zinovy said he had to turn in his course work in three days, barely enough time as it was. Iona Ovseich squinted and said he could take a hint—it was time for him to leave. Zinovy now had an apartment with all the conveniences and that stubborn old Degtyar should be on his way. Right?

Zinovy said not quite. Iona Ovseich gave him a friendly whack on the shoulder and praised his frankness.

Klava Ivanovna opened her window all the way and began singing loudly, like a formation of Pioneers:

"All right, my girls, all right, my beauties,
Let the country sing songs of us.
Let it praise our names in song,
Like it praises other heroes!"

Colonel Landa arrived late that evening with his wife Gizella, who had spent more time traveling with her husband in the last three years than she had in Odessa. Iona Ovseich dropped by to see them for a minute, to shake the colonel's hand and welcome him back on his final return to hearth and home, but, instead of shaking hands, they hugged each other hard like soldiers and kissed each other's cheeks.

"Ovseich," said the colonel in a loud voice, pulling Degtyar into the light, "the years haven't taken their toll on you. On the contrary, you're becoming younger all the time."

Iona Ovseich smiled, saying that a person had better watch out when a colonel started envying a captain.

"Ovseich," said the colonel with a laugh, "I have the feeling that it's 1936 and you've just come by to see me and celebrate the completion of the outpost."

"You're off by one year," said Iona Ovseich. "The outpost was built in '37."

The colonel accepted the correction, voicing surprise that he could have made such a mistake. Iona Ovseich replied that there was no reason for surprise, people's memories often failed them, it happened to everybody, not just Dr. Landa. The colonel was on the verge of saying that it was easier for Degtyar to remember such things since he hadn't left Odessa since '44 but then dismissed the idea, got a bottle from his suitcase, poured three glasses, and said: "To our beautiful native city Odessa!"

"And may our memories stay young until we're a hundred!" added Iona Ovseich.

When their guest had left, Gizella asked her husband what Degtyar had meant by his toast but Colonel Landa dismissed the subject.

"I don't like him," said Gizella, huddling as if from a chill. "I never liked him."

Two days later a truck pulled into the courtyard. Colonel Landa helped the workers unload. The neighbors said that in his place someone else would have just supervised and given orders, but, on the other hand, his wife didn't lift a finger.

"Lyalya, just look at that beauty, will you?" said Dina Vargaftik. "Look at that beauty. Why is it that some people have all the luck!"

"Dina," said Lyalya, narrowing her eyes sweetly, "you can't always judge a book by its cover."

"No," moaned Dina, "some people have all the luck, but my husband died in a foreign country and didn't even leave me the address of his grave."

Even without being asked, Efim Granik carried four chairs up to the Landas' apartment. He stood motionless in the middle of the room holding the chairs until Dr. Landa told him to put them down.

"I haven't been here for maybe nine years," said Efim, closing his eyes, his lips twisting in a grimace. "Dr. Landa, do you remember the time we carried the piano downstairs and your wife was so afraid we'd smash it to bits? But we were just trying to scare her a little, for the sake of a joke."

Colonel Landa walked over to Granik, put his arms around him, and gave him a friendly whack on the back.

"Oh, Dr. Landa," said Efim, beginning to cry, "if you only knew how bitter my heart is."

"Stop it," said Colonel Landa, "stop crying, Granik."

Lizochka was in the courtyard calling for her father. Efim wiped his tears and said that he had promised to take his daughter to an evening show at the movies, she'd never been to an evening show before, but right now he felt as much like going to the movies as Dr. Landa felt like going dancing.

"Efim Lazarevich," said Colonel Landa in a tone of command, "your Liza doesn't need a father who has tears in his heart and whose heart is always bitter."

"Yes," said Efim with a smile, "the country needs builders now, not hired mourners."

Klava Ivanovna arrived, saying she'd come to help straighten out the apartment, Gizella couldn't do it all by herself. But it turned out that extra hands only meant extra hindrance. The colonel thanked Madame Malaya a hundred times for her help, and, though it took some convincing, sat her down on the couch, and gave her some fresh copies of Bulgarian newspapers so she could look at the pictures. Klava Ivanovna sat quietly for five minutes, then said she knew the Bulgarians well enough and didn't need newspapers; at one time there had been entire Bulgarian villages outside Odessa. Then she set to work moving the flower pots from the night table to the windowsill.

"Listen," said Gizella in an offended tone, "I think this is my house and I decide where things go."

"Gizella, be quiet and do as you're told," replied Madame Malaya.

Instead of standing up for his wife, Colonel Landa suddenly began chuckling as if he'd been told a good dirty joke. Now Gizella was utterly insulted and announced that she'd leave if she was in the way there.

"What do you mean—in the way?" said Klava Ivanovna with a shrug. "You can stay, nobody's kicking you out."

Gizella's eyes grew cold and angry but this time she restrained herself, thanked Madame Malaya, and returned the flower pots from the windowsill to the night table.

"Landa," said Klava Ivanovna indignantly, "what's going on in your house? She decides everything and you sit there like a bump on a log!"

The colonel spread his hands apart to signify his helplessness. Madame Malaya suddenly grabbed him and pulled him close to her, ordering Gizella to play "Rio Rita" on the piano so the two of them could dance to it.

Gizella looked like she didn't know whether to laugh or cry. Klava Ivanovna and Colonel Landa had already done a couple of turns, both of them half closing their eyes in pleasure, when Gizella struck her first chord. She began playing better than the best piano players used to when accompanying silent films at the Shock Worker cinema, now the Gorky.

Dina and Lyalya were drawn by the sound of the music and they wanted to dance too but Madame Malaya would not surrender Colonel Landa to anyone.

"Landa," said Klava Ivanovna, who after every three steps would raise her hands in the air and snap her fingers like a young Spanish woman, "I'll live to see you make general yet!"

Dina Vargaftik danced with Lyalya, both of them delighted with Gizella's playing, which had entranced them all. Lyalya tossed her head back abruptly as if someone were trying to give her a kiss she preferred to avoid, the gesture causing nearly all the wrinkles on her neck to smooth out. Dina said that Lyalya's neck could rival the young girls of today, whose skin was like dry bark, they were so scrawny.

Gizella played "The Froth of Champagne," "Favorite Waltz," and

"Carioca." For no apparent reason Dina burst into tears but Lyalya kept smiling all the time, her brows arched high like a schoolgirl's.

When they stopped for a breather, Klava Ivanovna kissed Gizella hard and said to everyone: "My children, if you only knew how dear to my heart you all are!"

Then they danced a few more times to "Rio Rita" and "The Froth of Champagne." As a finale, Gizella played "Chelita" and Klava Ivanovna sang along from beginning to end.

"Klavochka Ivanovna, you're still a girl!" exclaimed Lyalya, clapping her hands in delight.

"That's right," agreed Klava Ivanovna, "and soon I'll be a little girl all in white with my hands folded across my chest."

That remark upset Dina Vargaftik: what foolish talk, Klava Ivanovna would outlive us all! That was not necessary, said Klava Ivanovna with a frown, that was not necessary for anyone, everything should just go the way it was supposed to.

When their guests had left, Gizella said to her husband that she was surprised at how those simple people clung to the past. The colonel disliked his wife's words and remarked that her manners were also an example of clinging to the past. This offended Gizella, who told her husband that he was every bit as much a product of that courtyard as their neighbors.

Zinovy Cheperukha finished work on his apartment in mid-week and sent Grisha and Misha to fetch Comrade Degtyar and Madame Malaya. Klava Ivanovna did not keep Zinovy waiting but Iona Ovseich told the boys to tell their father that he didn't have a free minute right now and that he would come by tomorrow evening if his schedule permitted.

"You shouldn't take it personally," said Klava Ivanovna. "Comrade Degtyar does the work of ten men."

The next day Iona Ovseich telephoned Zinovy at the Kirov factory and asked him to drop by his office on the way home. There was a thick fog from early morning on and the foghorns wailed every five seconds. Zinovy's stump was giving him a lot of pain but since they had an appointment, he got into his motorized wheelchair and drove to Degtyar's shoe factory. There was a pass waiting for him at the gate but he had to leave the wheelchair outside. The watchman promised to keep an eye on it.

When Zinovy entered the party office, Comrade Degtyar was just concluding a meeting and apologized to Zinovy for the delay. They were discussing preparations for the republic's industrial exhibit. With the chief engineer present, Iona Ovseich listed the best modelers and master craftsmen who were to make the samples and then warned the department heads that he would hold them personally responsible for everything on exhibition. They voiced no objection to this; on the contrary, they emphasized that no one was going to make any allowances for the quality of the raw material or the tight deadline. While saying this, they looked at Zinovy, who was following their conversation closely. The modeler who had spoken last now addressed Zinovy directly, promising that the factory's shoe designers would come through and give their all, as if the shoes were for Paris. Iona Ovseich rebuked the modeler because his remark smacked of a nasty cult of the foreign, then cited the well-known fact that Russian shoes competed in the world market even before the Revolution and that women's boots were very popular in Russia long before Europe even thought of the idea. The modeler cringed a little but admitted his blunder and in turn cited the well-known fact that in France the poorer classes had long been in the practice of wearing wooden shoes, called sabots, De Maupassant even described them in his stories, and those sabots were exactly like the bast sandals that were worn in old Russia, except for the backs and sides. Iona Ovseich thought the comparison with bast sandals quite apt and while they were on the subject he mentioned the ancient cities like Ryazan and Kozelsk where the making of bast shoes had reached the level of an art.

"But," said Iona Ovseich in a tone of summation, "the Russia of bast sandals is part of the distant past now and that mustn't be forgotten for a second."

Then, without pausing, Comrade Degtyar addressed Zinovy Cheperukha, referring to him as one of the leading workers at the Kirov factory, and asking how things were going for him in his personal life, had the bathroom been finished or were there still some loose ends requiring further help?

The way the question was worded by Comrade Degtyar caught Zinovy somewhat by surprise since just the previous evening Grisha and Misha had tried to bring Degtyar over to celebrate the end of construction.

"Zinovy," said Iona Ovseich with a cordial smile, "you're not saying a word. Other people might feel out of place here but we're all friends."

Zinovy too smiled in reply and repeated his invitation of yesterday for Degtyar to celebrate the end of construction with them.

"Of course," said Iona Ovseich, "I forgot, we should inform everyone of what's been going on, otherwise we'd be starting at the wrong end. Before the war Zinovy Cheperukha, who is here with us now, lived with his mother and his father, an ordinary Odessa drayman, in a small room. As a boy he became quite accustomed to using the lavatory in the courtyard."

The chief engineer laughed amicably, followed by the department heads and Zinovy himself. Iona Ovseich extended his hand and asked them to quiet down, then continued: "But today, on the eve of the second postwar Five-Year Plan, Zinovy Cheperukha has an apartment of his own with all the conveniences, his own running water, his own toilet, his own shower, in a word, everything people could only dream of before."

One after the other, the department heads rose and shook Zinovy's hand. The designer asked Zinovy to tell him a secret—what part had Comrade Degtyar played in all this? Zinovy answered the question with another question: what part did a designer play in making his designs?

"Stop it!" said Comrade Degtyar. "None of us does more than he should, and let's drop the subject for good."

Despite the injunction, the head of the procurement department asked Comrade Degtyar to explain how he could work round the clock at the factory and still make time to deal with the needs and concerns of his neighbors in the courtyard.

"Comrades," said Iona Ovseich, whacking the table, "I've already asked you once to drop the subject and I won't ask you again."

When the two of them were alone, Iona Ovseich was silent for a moment and walked over to the window, which looked out on the factory yard; a shift had just ended and the workers, among them a great many women, were streaming out the gates. With excitement in his voice he said: "What a marvelous working class we have! What people! No matter how much we give them, we'll still always be in their debt."

Iona Ovseich asked Zinovy to postpone the celebration until Saturday because he had a conference at the District Committee that day and with the agenda they had ahead of them he'd be lucky if he caught the last trolley home. By the way, added Degtyar, Khomitsky, Landa, and Marina Biryuk should also be invited to the dinner along with him and Malaya, five people, that would seem to be enough. It wouldn't be a bad idea to invite a representative from the Stalin District Housing Office but he would leave that up to Zinovy.

Aside from those mentioned by Comrade Degtyar, Zinovy also invited Efim Granik, Lyalya Orlov, Dina Vargaftik, Anya Kotlyar, and Adya Lapidis. Katerina had her doubts about Anya and Adya even though she didn't have anything against them personally. Olya Cheperukha went even farther than that, saying Comrade Degtyar might not like having them there. Zinovy's eyes flashed as he shouted: "That's enough of your women's nonsense!" and that was the end of that.

When Iona Ovseich saw how many guests there were, he said you needed half a day just to say hello to everyone and shake everyone's hand. Iona Cheperukha paid Comrade Degtyar a sincere compliment, saying that his handshake was as firm as it had been twenty-five years ago, as if time had no power over him.

"Flattery will get you nowhere!" said Comrade Degtyar, wagging a finger threateningly before giving Iona Cheperukha a warm hug.

Dr. Landa, who had brought his German Leica and magnesium flash with him, asked Degtyar and Cheperukha to hold that pose for a second, they could move when they heard the camera click. Iona Ovseich requested Colonel Landa not to forget to photograph Iona Cheperukha, the veteran transportation worker, the master workman Stepa Khomitsky, the veteran activist and community leader, Klava Ivanovna Malaya, and Marina Biryuk, the wife of a professional officer and holder of the Gold Star, and to take fewer pictures of him, Degtyar.

"Don't worry, Ovseich," replied Colonel Landa. "You lucked out, that's all; you just happened to be standing next to the veteran transportation worker Iona Cheperukha, but I can cut you out of the picture when it's developed."

Everyone laughed merrily. Iona Ovseich smiled too but said that there was a time and place for jokes.

Iona Cheperukha announced that it was time to sit down at the table before the vodka went flat. People had begun pulling out their chairs when Iona Ovseich raised his hand and said in a loud voice: "Comrades, I don't think any of us has been going hungry, and we're not here to eat and drink but to celebrate a second housewarming for the combat veteran Zinovy Cheperukha, who was born and grew up in this building!"

Iona Ovseich clapped his hands and everyone else followed suit. Then Degtyar asked Zinovy to show them the apartment, which had changed so much that it was now as different from what it had once been as night from day, even though it was still in the same spot.

Zinovy opened the bathroom door, which had an ivory yellow plastic handle, and invited people in three at a time to keep the room from being overcrowded. He turned on the sink and the shower, then pulled the chain on the toilet: the water in the bowl swirled and foamed as if shot from a fire hose. A few minutes later when the last three came in for their look around, the tank had filled again and all it took was one pull of the chain for the water in the bowl to swirl and foam again.

"What lucky people!" said Lyalya, not hiding her envy.

"Why the long face, Orlov," said Iona Ovseich with a wink. "Today Cheperukha, tomorrow Orlov, and Degtyar the day after."

Dr. Landa's camera clicked again and this time the flash was so bright that Dina Vargaftik shut her eyes and couldn't open them again for quite some time.

"Landa, you should make two copies," said Iona Ovseich. "We'll keep one to put in the new outpost we'll build for the children."

Dina Vargaftik finally opened her eyes and asked Dr. Landa to take her picture over because she'd look like a blind woman in the last one, and the children would laugh at her. Landa explained that she had shut her eyes after the flash had gone off, but Dina would hear none of it and the doctor was forced to give in. Everyone crowded into the bathroom for the picture and once again Zinovy turned on the faucet and shower, then pulled the chain. The toilet flushed with a roar and people turned toward the camera, looked right in the lens, and smiled, beaming.

At the table Comrade Degtyar called upon Iona Cheperukha to

speak, as the father of Zinovy, who they were celebrating today, and as an old citizen of Odessa like his grandfather before him who could still remember when Pushkin was living in exile here and used to walk the streets of the city to hear the voice of the people.

"Dear neighbors," said Iona Cheperukha, holding his glass in front of him, emotion making his hand tremble, "Comrade Degtyar has just mentioned my grandfather, who lived here in Odessa in Pushkin's time. But what was so good about his life! Nothing, exactly that, nothing: he left my father a couple of scrawny horses and my father left me a wagon, or to put it in plain Russian, two wheels and a shaft but it was I, his son, who had to fill in for the horse. And today my son Zinovy is close to graduating as an engineer, he has an educated wife, and the state has allotted him an apartment of his own with all the conveniences, meaning water, and its own shower and toilet. I ask you, what more does a man need? When I was a little boy, my mother used to give me five kopecks on the holidays and send me to the Isakovich baths on Preobrazhensky Street, but my son and his children have their own bath at home and they can stay there as long as they like and no one on earth has the right to say to them—that's it, the baths are closing!"

Iona had tears in his eyes but the guests were laughing merrily and insisting that the speaker continue.

"And I hope," said Iona, wiping his tears with his thumb, "that if a father visits his son and feels like taking a shower himself, the son won't say—that's it, the baths are closing!"

Old Cheperukha began crying again. Klava Ivanovna and Olya Cheperukha shook their heads, and little Grisha and Misha ran to their grandfather without being told, pressed up against him from either side, insisting that their grandfather drink his vodka before it went flat. The guests laughed all the louder and all the merrier. Iona Ovseich rose to his feet, followed by everyone else, and he proposed the first toast, to the children.

"To our children," repeated Iona Ovseich, "to our future, and to peace throughout the world!"

After they had chased their drinks with appetizers, Klava Ivanovna began singing and conducting, "All Right, My Girls, All Right, My Beauties," using her hands to signal people to join in:

"Long may you prosper, land where
A single will united peoples into one people,
Long may you blossom, land where
Men and women march together freely!
All right, my girls, all right, my beauties!"

Their voices rang in harmony, as if they had rehearsed it a hundred times the day before. Iona Ovseich half closed his eyes with pleasure, tapped his foot to the music, and sang heartily during the refrain. As usual Adya Lapidis was glowering a little but he too sang heartily. Only Anya Kotlyar was sitting woodenly, with her lips shut tight.

Though his eyes were closed, Iona Ovseich could see the expression on Anya Kotlyar's face and was waiting for that woman with her haughty air to stop spoiling the mood for the others. Olya walked carefully up in back of her and bent over her, but instead of smiling or making a friendly response, Anya grew even haughtier and began shaking her head as if people were clutching at her, bothering her. Olya laid her hand on the back of Anya's head and suddenly Anya put her face in her hands and began trembling as if in hysterics.

"Anya Kotlyar," said Iona Ovseich calmly, "we're guests here, this isn't our home."

Anya kept her face in her hands as if she were not being spoken to. Comrade Degtyar again asked her to calm down and reminded her of the famous folk saying that you didn't bring your own rules to someone else's monastery.

"What do monasteries have to do with anything!" said Klava Ivanovna, joining in. "Her Joseph's very sick, gangrene has started on the other leg."

Comrade Degtyar sat up straight in his chair and said that gangrene didn't kill people in this day and age; there were plenty of qualified doctors and surgeons, as good as Dr. Landa, where Joseph Kotlyar was now.

Dr. Landa smiled and confirmed that fact: not only were they as good, they were ten times better. Iona Ovseich narrowed his right eye as if he were taking aim, stared intently at the colonel for a few seconds, then requested Zinovy, as the host, to put on a lively record because there were certain people here who wanted to turn a wedding into a wake.

While Zinovy was fussing with the record player, Anya took her hands from her face; the right side, where the wound was, had turned very blue. She whispered: "That's all right, Comrade Degtyar, I'm still waiting for a wake in this courtyard where I'll dance like it was a wedding."

"Speak up, Anya Kotlyar," said Iona Ovseich, leaning back hard against his chair, the seat squeaking dryly, "speak up so everyone can hear."

"Good God," said Olya Cheperukha, wringing her hands. "And I kept saying, Zyunya, we shouldn't invite her! But does anybody listen to me!"

Iona Cheperukha slammed his fist on the table and two bottles of vodka fell to the floor, one smashing to pieces. "Don't you start carrying on like that! Anya Kotlyar has heartache and you want to kick her out, like a diseased dog. I'm ashamed, I'm ashamed in front of my children and my neighbors."

"You know what, Dad," said Katerina, sticking up for her mother-in-law, "you should run things your way at home but there's nothing to be ashamed of here. And for a guest to come wanting to make trouble, you tell me, what kind of a person is that!"

"Children, children, stop it, please! I beg you, stop it!" said Klava Ivanovna, waving her arms around.

Olya Cheperukha took Klava Ivanovna by the shoulders and told her to try to relax. Lyalya and Dina handed her a glass of water and a powder to calm her down. The others didn't even budge, as if they hadn't seen or heard anything.

"Zinovy," said Iona Ovseich, "this is turning into a strange spectacle and the host isn't saying a word."

The record was over and Zinovy turned off the record player. He looked around, then took the carafe of vodka from the table and walked over to Anya, his prothesis squeaking as he went. He poured out two glasses and gave one to her. He clinked his glass loudly against hers, raised it, then polished it off in one gulp. All in a flutter, Marina Biryuk demanded the host fill everyone else's glass and anyone who didn't want to drink could just sit there and smack his lips. Iona Cheperukha, Stepa Khomitsky, and Efim Granik didn't have to be asked twice and poured their own vodka. Colonel Landa shared his portion with Comrade Degtyar who was pale, the veins on his temples very distended, and his hand on the table by his glass did not seem alive.

"Degtyar," said Iona Cheperukha, "the ice is getting thicker outside."

"All right," said Iona Ovseich, rising. He picked up the glass and held it in front of him. "I want to propose a toast to Russian cordiality and hospitality!"

Zinovy put another record on while people were finishing their drinks, one he had been saving specially for his guests. He switched the record player back on and people were afforded genuine pleasure when a woman's voice, on a par even with Klavdiya Shulzhenko, began singing:

"Mishka, Mishka, where's your smile
So full of passion and fire!
The dumbest mistake ever
Is that you're leaving me."

When the dancing started, Lyalya and Dina grabbed hold of the colonel, monopolizing him so that the other women could not even approach him until the colonel himself invited Anya Kotlyar to dance.

Lyalya kept saying all evening that Colonel Landa, who was already almost a general, behaved so simply, as if there was no difference between him and the rest of them.

Though her partner spoke to her many times in an effort to strike up a conversation while they were dancing, Anya kept her head lowered from the very start and stared stubbornly down at her feet.

"Mademoiselle," exclaimed Colonel Landa in despair, "stop hypnotizing me. I can barely keep myself from falling at your feet, but there are people around, like Comrade Degtyar."

Anya smiled but did not lift her head; on the contrary, she lowered it even further so that now her hair tickled Colonel Landa's chin and lips.

"Anya, my dear," whispered Dr. Landa softly, "Everything will be all right, believe me, everything will be all right."

It was a long-playing record with short pauses between songs. The colonel was about to ask his partner for the next dance but Zinovy was a step ahead of him. Katerina stared goggled-eyed at her husband and could not contain her surprise.

Anya wanted to go home when the dance was over but Stepa and Efim dogged her heels and blocked her way. Anya was confused. Right there in front of everyone Marina Biryuk admitted that she would die of envy if that arrogant woman didn't give her one or the other, Efim or Stepa.

"Marina," said Iona Cheperukha, running over, "what do you need those broken down old men for? Take me, I'm better!"

No, said Marina, refusing to yield, she wanted only Stepa or Efim.

Closely observing this comical scene which had arisen on its own, Comrade Degtyar said: "A person could think this was some kind of secret Freemason meeting with its own rules, its own purposes, and its own special language."

"What do you mean, a special language?" said Klava Ivanovna in surprise. "It's just that people are feeling good, and each knows what the other means."

Efim stuck out his lip like a black African and shouted in a guttural voice: "Peace! Friendship! Friendship!"

Before the guests could react, Iona Ovseich had grabbed a newspaper out of his pocket, rolled it up, and whacked it against the table with all his might: "Stop clowning around, Granik! We paid for peace with our own blood, and we won't allow anyone to make a joke out of this just to amuse bums who don't even have passports."

Efim was startled. His lips trembled, but remained protruding.

"Take off your stupid mask—you're not in America!" ordered Comrade Degtyar.

The record was over. Zinovy turned off the record player. Silence reigned for a moment. The first to break it was Iona Cheperukha:

"Ovseich," he said, and heaved a deep sigh, "I understand you very well and I sympathize. When a woman like Marina walks by and doesn't even stop, you've got to be made of stone not to get jealous and upset."

"No, my dear Cheperukha," said Iona Ovseich, "right now I'm upset by someone else, and not just one person either, but a lot of people, you included. I want to make myself clear on that."

"Don't be upset," interrupted Colonel Landa. "Everyone understands you very well, but why spoil the party? If you don't like it here, you can do a one-hundred-and-eighty-degree turn and say goot-bai!"

"Goot-bai!" repeated Iona Ovseich in a nasal voice, as if mimicking Landa. "But, please, Dr. Landa, as the saying goes, don't darken our doorstep again!"

Adya Lapidis, who hadn't uttered a word the entire evening, grabbed Anya Kotlyar by the hand and shouted: "Let's get out of here, Aunt Anya, let's go!"

It was all so sudden that no one had time to stop them. Adya literally dragged Anya forcibly behind him. Zinovy ran after them but they had already disappeared out the gate.

When Zinovy returned, Comrade Degtyar stared at him, grinning.

"Well, did you catch them, my host?"

Olya moaned loudly and swore she'd leave that place before she held another party there again. Parties just made enemies!

Iona Ovseich objected; on the contrary everything was now in place, and there was no need for them to be afraid of enemies—their enemies should be afraid of them.

Colonel Landa said a general farewell, politely bowed, and left. The rest of the guests also began to say their good-byes. They thanked the hosts for the company and for the real stuffed fish—soon there wouldn't be anyone left who'd still remember how to make it—and hoped the whole family would be happy with their new shower and toilet.

Iona Ovseich, Malaya, and Stepa Khomitsky left together. In the middle of the courtyard Klava Ivanovna stopped automatically, looked around, and said: "Degtyar, explain to me why people can't be like they were before the war? Why does something bad have to happen every time?"

"Malaya," said Iona Ovseich slowly, raising his head as if counting the stories and windows, "you've just started forgetting, that's all. You forgot how much time we had to spend with Lapidis, with Cheperukha, with Granik, Orlov, and with those same Kotlyars. But you're right about one thing: people were more willing to learn and absorbed things more easily."

Stepa laughed and said they were young back then, and young

people had better memories. Iona Ovseich answered that it didn't matter: as the doctors said, for every poison there was an antidote.

After the guests left, Iona Cheperukha sat down on the chair in the middle of the room. The women complained that he interfered with their cleaning things up, but he continued to sit where he was and talked in a loud voice about Comrade Degtyar.

"Degtyar," he said, "wants everyone to be happy, and that's understandable. Let's take me, Iona Cheperukha, for example, and my wife: our son Zinovy returned from the front alive. He has two children. He'll graduate soon an engineer and he's been given an apartment of his own with all the conveniences you could imagine in this day and age. What's there not to be happy about? Of course you should be happy and be grateful to the Soviet system and thank it. On the other hand, let's take Dina Vargaftik, who lost her husband and is now all alone in the world, or Anya Kotlyar, who lost both her sons at the front, and now her Joseph is hauling stones in some camp. What's there to be happy about in all that? But Degtyar wants everyone to be equally happy and all laugh the same way.

"Son," said Iona Cheperukha, "tell me, am I right or wrong?"

Zinovy said that his father was a hundred percent right about everything but you could see there were some gaps in his education as far as economics and philosophy went. In a socialist society certain differentiations still existed. Everyone could not be satisfied in equal measure. Consequently, not everyone could feel equally good. And as for Degtyar personally, he couldn't wait for everyone to be equally happy. The question was where did his impatience come from and what was it all about?

"Son," smiled the elder Cheperukha, "if you see things clearly, why didn't you ask Degtyar when he was sitting here and drinking with us?"

Olya got angry again and attacked her husband: "Will you finally shut your mouth!"

Zinovy moved from the chair to the couch and now his tired face could be seen. Olya demanded that he go to sleep right away, because every day there was the factory, then the institute, then work on the apartment—you had to be as healthy as a horse to keep going.

Zinovy closed his eyes, leaned his head against the back of the chair, and told his father to sit down next to him.

"You were saying why didn't I ask him?" said Zinovy. "Do you think Degtyar would admit he's impatient? On the contrary, he thinks everything's going too slowly. He started before the Revolution and he measures from there. He thought that the goal was close at hand, that he'd see it with his own eyes any day now, but in fact it turned out that a lot more time was needed than they could have supposed or counted on before the Revolution. And the years go by, the man's in a hurry, he's running out of patience."

"What you're saying then is," said Iona Cheperukha, drawing his own conclusion, "that Degtyar can only get more and more nervous."

"Time will tell," said Zinovy.

Iona pulled his son's head toward him and kissed the top of it while telling him to go to bed. But after Zinovy had unfastened his prothesis, massaged his stump, and rolled up the pillow into a cylinder, Japanese style, Iona Cheperukha returned to the conversation.

"Zinovy, either you didn't finish or I have such sclerosis that I didn't quite understand: on the one hand, we can see that Degtyar does everything for other people, but on the other hand, it turns out that his goal is more important for him than people."

"You've got a loose tongue," shouted Olya. "Leave the child in peace. The factory, the institute, and a little sawing and stuccoing aren't enough—he also needs a philosopher for a father!"

Iona sighed deeply and said that now Degtyar would be on his mind all night. But Olya gave him some advice: it would be better to have Marina Biryuk on his mind instead, there was no need to get so upset over Degtyar.

"You fool," answered Iona, "You cowed, ignorant person!"

"Papa," said Katerina, joining the conversation, "don't go overboard. Go home and go to bed. It'll all pass by tomorrow."

During the night Degtyar called an ambulance for Polina Isaevna. Her asthma attack was so bad that it seemed the end had come. No ambulance came for a long time. Iona Ovseich called again and ran for Anya Kotlyar. Anya injected Polina Isaevna with ephedrine, which brought her considerable relief. She stopped wheezing and thrashing, only moaning softly. Finally the ambulance came. The doctor said she had to be hospitalized, but Polina Isaevna flatly refused. She would have nothing to do with any hospitals.

"Don't talk nonsense," interrupted Iona Ovseich. "If it's necessary, it's necessary."

The doctor thought for a moment, then nodding at Anya Kotlyar, he said that since there was a medical technician on hand, they could wait until morning.

When the ambulance left, Iona Ovseich lay down on the couch without undressing. Anya drew a chair up to Polina Isaevna's bedside, turned off the ceiling light, turned on the table lamp, and opened a book on her lap.

"Annushka," said Polina Isaevna, "turn on the big light. You're ruining your eyes."

Anya took Polina Isaevna by the hand, stroked it, and told her to sleep. "Annushka," whispered Polina Isaevna, "how's Joseph? Is his health all right?"

"Go to sleep," said Anya, waving her hand to dismiss the question, "you need your sleep."

The next morning Radio Moscow broadcast the new resolution by the party and government on the latest reduction in state retail prices for manufactured goods. The population would stand to directly gain about seven and eight-tenths billion rubles from this reduction, not to mention the additional benefit it would derive from the decrease in prices at kolkhoz markets.

There were tears in Polina Isaevna's eyes. She said that financially speaking life was getting better and better for everyone. It was a good time to be alive, if you had your health. "Annushka," said Polina Isaevna with a smile, "do you know anyplace where health is for sale?"

Anya made breakfast for her patient. Iona Ovseich was in a terrible hurry and couldn't even sit down and drink a glass of tea. Polina Isaevna said that he was going to run around like a madman all day on an empty stomach and he wasn't as young as he used to be.

"You should worry about yourself," answered Anya. "Your husband, thank God, is still on his feet."

Polina Isaevna closed her eyes and hid her hands under the blanket. Anya was surprised at how little space Polina Isaevna took up in that bed with the nickel-plated headboard. Anya's heart was seized by a horrible premonition and she lost her breath for a moment.

"Annushka," sighed Polina Isaevna, "I do think about myself

sometimes. But what good did he get out of his life with me? Always sick, always doctors, the ambulances, oxygen tanks, the ephedrine. Anybody else in his place would have quit ten times over and would have been right too."

"Stop it," said Anya indignantly.

"Yes," Polina Isaevna grinned. "It is easy to be indignant when you're not involved."

Anya said that everyone was right in his own way. She was about to bring in Adya, Joseph, and herself as examples, but changed her mind. Poor Polina Isaevna had enough heartache of her own.

At ten o'clock Iona Ovseich called from the factory. Anya picked up the receiver, held it silently for a few seconds, then asked Polina Isaevna if she could get up and come to the phone. With great difficulty Polina Isaevna lowered her legs and put on her slippers; her body lurched forward as if she were drunk, then suddenly she fell back against her pillow.

Iona Ovseich asked why it was taking so long. Anya replied that Polina Isaevna was in the bathroom right now but was feeling fairly well. Iona Ovseich said that he couldn't wait anymore, the Komsomol activists were waiting for him; today they were discussing the progress of the competition, the initiative taken by Lidya Korabelnikova of the Moscow shoe factory "Paris Commune," and the complex economics of raw materials. According to the preliminary data there were fairly good indications, and so the patient should try to equal the efforts made by the Komsomol.

Iona Ovseich laughed and asked Anya to tell his wife that the comrades from the party committee had promised him a couple of kilos of oranges and a half dozen Italian lemons. Anya agreed to tell her and the conversation ended.

Polina Isaevna was breathing heavily. Her cheeks kept falling and swelling. Anya brought over the oxygen tank but her patient waved it away: she didn't need it, she'd manage.

Anya said that it was time for her to go to work and suggested calling Klava Ivanovna. Polina Isaevna shook her head: It was shameful and insulting, Madame Malaya was almost twenty years older. Anya objected, saying that was foolish. Those old women were a hundred times stronger and healthier than Polina Isaevna and Anya. Madame Malaya could sit for a while.

"Don't force me, don't make me!" said Polina Isaevna and began to cry. But she quickly got hold of herself and told Anya to go or Anya would be late for work on account of her.

Iona Ovseich returned home early from the factory. It wasn't even ten o'clock. He went straight from the door to the bed, put his hand on Polina Isaevna's forehead, and said that her temperature was normal, a good sign. Polina Isaevna agreed and told the joke about the old doctor who was called to come see a patient, but who ran around so much that day that the patient was dead by the time he arrived. Of course, the whole family was crying. The doctor asked whether the deceased had sweated before dying. They answered, yes, he had sweated, and the doctor said that was a good sign.

"Polina," said Iona Ovseich with a frown, "I'm not a doctor, and you're not deceased yet!"

Polina Isaevna agreed. However she wanted to stay on the subject of death but Iona Ovseich refused, suggesting he tell her instead what the Komsomol members and young people had said today when discussing the initiative taken by the Moscow Komsomol member Lydia Korabelnikova. Iona Ovseich said it had been a long time since he had been so pleased. The participants had made calculations with the figures in hand. Zina Bondarenko, who worked on the production line, a most ordinary girl to look at, was not afraid to tell the whole truth to her comrades right in the face: "We are calculating the economy here in kilograms and meters, but we should be doing it in grams and millimeters, otherwise we'll start overlooking the details." And what was most important, the young people themselves, without any prompting, came to the conclusion that it was in this way and only in this way that we could achieve communism.

Polina Isaevna said that she agreed in advance with everything the Komsomol members had to say, then asked him to speak more quietly since her head was ringing like a bell tower.

"Polina," said Iona Ovseich angry again, "I don't like your depressing defeatist attitude one bit. Whatever else they've done, the Germans invented one good saying: 'if you lose money—you haven't lost anything, but if you've lost your spirit—you've lost everything.' "

When Iona Ovseich calmed down a little bit, Polina Isaevna asked him where he had eaten lunch today, and whether he had eaten lunch at all.

"Oh," exclaimed Iona Ovseich, "that's what you think's most important: work so you can have a bowl of soup, then eat this soup so you can have the strength to work for the next bowl of soup!"

Polina Isaevna said that any words could be twisted and then it would turn out that it was really not necessary to eat, not necessary to rest, and you didn't need your health, you only needed one thing—to work from morning till night, to drudge away around the clock.

"Drudge away!" repeated Iona Ovseich. "I like that jargon expression, especially on the lips of a teacher: not labor, not work, but drudge away!"

Iona Ovseich lit the Primus to boil water for dinner and to put into the thermos for the night: Polina Isaevna might need a hot-water bottle, a compress, or simply feel like having a glass of tea with lemon. Polina Isaevna asked why he was bothering with the kerosene, the soot, the smell, the noise—the electric hot plate could boil the water in five minutes and do it nicely and cleanly.

Iona Ovseich replied that just the day before yesterday at the District Committee there had been a discussion on that very subject, and today throughout the entire city an announcement had been posted in every front hall to economize on electricity. Polina Isaevna said that she understood, but there were also extreme cases: a wife who was very sick, a man who came home tired from work—

"Polina," Iona Ovseich interrupted, "there's no need for any false demagogy or sympathy here. If the Primus had been too much for me, I wouldn't have used it. But since I did, that means it wasn't too much for me."

"Oh, Degtyar, Degtyar," said Polina Isaevna, sighing deeply.

Iona Ovseich made tea, putting almost an entire spoonful of leaves in each glass—hard work for the heart, but good for the spirit. He threw in a slice of lemon. The tea lost some of its former amber color, and he drank it without sugar in three gulps, as if he'd been lost in the desert for days.

"Ah!" said Degtyar, then clapped and rubbed his hands vigorously. "People drink wine, vodka, alcohol, but there's nothing in the world like strong tea!"

Polina Isaevna wanted to get up to put some cutlets and macaroni on the stove before Degtyar started arguing they would taste good even when cold, but this time she was mistaken: he promised to cook everything normally and asked her to stay in bed and rest.

The cutlets were slightly overcooked and crunchy.

Iona Ovseich ate with a great appetite. He ate a spoonful of sauerkraut, which only added to the crunch. Polina Isaevna asked him to chew his food with his mouth closed and be a little quieter about it.

"Polina," said Iona Ovseich with a frown, "if I'm not mistaken, this is my home."

After dinner, Iona Ovseich put the dishes into a mustard solution to dissolve the grease, rinsed them, wiped them with a towel, and put them away in the pantry. Polina Isaevna begged him to eat an orange for dessert. "I swear by my life that you will," she cried, but Degtyar only grew angry and asked that she stop being so hysterical.

For the entire day at the factory Iona Ovseich had not been able to open a newspaper and he realized that if a party worker began his morning without reading the editorials in *Pravda,* he should be thrown out on his ear.

"Don't torture yourself over it," said Polina Isaevna, "I think you could write articles as well as the editor himself."

Iona Ovseich had turned his back to the bed, absorbed in his reading. For a half hour he studied the information on questions of party life, the economy, and Soviet construction, and then he came to the fourth page. His eyebrows went up, his lips began to move, and his eyes expressed astonishment; laughing loudly, he said: "An amazing incident took place in Kazakhstan! Two master predators met on a forest path, a bear and a tiger. Who do you think won? The tiger, of course? Nothing of the sort! The clumsy bear tossed him about so much that the tiger died on the spot. But the bear had also been fatally wounded. They found him dead one and a half kilometers from the place where the fight had taken place."

Degtyar began to laugh again and openly admitted that he wouldn't have believed it if he'd read it anywhere else: the tiger was almost like a lion, the tsar of beasts!

"There's the tsar for you, Polina!" Degtyar tore himself away from the newspaper and turned his head toward her.

Polina Isaevna lay in bed with her eyes closed, the wrinkles smoothed out on her forehead. Her nose was yellow as wax and blue along its edges. Her lower lip hung down slightly, a darkness gaping over it. Iona Ovseich felt a blow to his heart, and an icy cold shot through his stomach. He tiptoed over to the bed, bent down low, listened, and put his fingers on her forehead, which was firm and round as if his fingers were touching bare bone.

"Polina!" shouted Iona Ovseich, his voice suddenly hoarse. "Polenka, my love! God, what should I do? What should I do?"

Iona Ovseich ran to the telephone, his fingers trembling badly, and he dialed the wrong number a few times until he finally correctly dialed 03.

"Ambulance!" shouted Iona Ovseich into the receiver. "Hurry up, don't delay. A person's dying!"

Iona Ovseich was so excited that he forgot to give his address. A woman's angry voice demanded that he stop his criminal pranks or else she'd trace his telephone number and report it to the police. It was only then that he realized why the stupid misunderstanding had occurred.

Iona Ovseich admitted his blunder. "It's my fault, but for God's sakc, hurry!"

"All right," answered the woman. "We're on our way. Wait by the gate."

On the way downstairs Iona Ovseich remembered that Polina Isaevna was now all alone. He went back upstairs and knocked at Anya Kotlyar's. Without saying a word, Anya grabbed her syringe case and started running to Polina Isaevna. On the way Degtyar explained that she was very sick, he had never seen her like that before, but Anya didn't listen and ran even faster. She froze for a second in the doorway when she saw Polina Isaevna.

"Hurry," Degtyar demanded. "Don't stand there like a piece of wood!"

Anya went up to Polina Isaevna, took her hand, and, closing her eyes, tried to find her pulse. After ten seconds she carefully put Polina's hand back, clutched her face with both hands as she had at the Cheperukhas' party, and began to tremble all over.

Iona Ovseich shook her by the shoulders and said that they had to call Dr. Landa before the ambulance came, but Anya did not reply. She looked at him with eyes so dark they seemed to be only pupil. Quietly she left the room.

Polina Isaevna was buried in the second cemetery on Lustdorf Road, now called the Black Sea Road. The funeral was attended only by her neighbors and two teachers, representing the school where she had worked as a mathematics instructor for many years. Degtyar's factory had offered its brass band for the funeral and his co-workers expressed their desire to be side by side with their comrade as he accompanied his wife and friend on her final journey, but Iona Ovseich refused.

When they returned from the cemetery, Klava Ivanovna, Colonel Landa, Stepa Khomitsky, and both Cheperukhas went to visit Degtyar and, as custom dictated, to sit with him for a while in the house which his wife had now left forever. Madame Malaya looked around at the plywood cupboard, the mirror with black veins, the nickel-plated bed, the leatherette sofa, the old-fashioned sideboard, the couch, the speaker on the wall. Then she shook her head and said:

"Was there anything good about her life? Her children died when they were still little. Then illness, war, illness again. There wasn't always a crust of bread in the house, and she loved people so much, she loved to entertain."

His eyes still swollen and red from tears, Iona Ovseich looked intently at Madame Malaya. She sat on her chair, seeing nothing, hearing nothing, as if she were alone in the room, and quietly moaned.

Efim Granik came by later with a marble slab on which the late woman's name and the dates of her birth and death were painted in beautiful gold letters, and below, after the word "grieving" was the signature "I. Degtyar," as if written in Iona Ovseich's own hand.

Everyone liked the slab, especially Klava Ivanovna. She even asked Efim to make one like it for her, it'd be needed soon enough. Efim smiled sadly. It was possible to get marble and gold paint and to write something, but whose signature would appear on it?

Stepa Khomitsky laughed quietly and said: "Don't worry. If someone dies, we'll find someone to sign."

Colonel Landa lowered his head, bit his lip, and wiped the bridge of his nose with his fingers. Iona Cheperukha said he was going to the store for a bottle. They had to drink to the memory of the dead.

Klava Ivanovna looked angry and drew a line in the air with her finger, saying: "Cheperukha, I don't like this."

Iona Ovseich sat motionless at the table. His eyes opened and then closed as if he were being overcome by drowsiness. Colonel Landa said: "Ovseich, you need some rest," and said good-bye.

The others rose one after another. Klava Ivanovna suggested to Degtyar that someone should spend the first night with him, but he said there was no need for that, and besides, the telephone was in easy reach.

"Comrade Degtyar," said Efim, shaking his head, "telephones can't talk all by themselves."

Iona Ovseich didn't reply. He only whacked Efim on the shoulder, thanked them all for their consideration, and wished them good night.

Around eleven o'clock the telephone rang: since she was going to stop by Gaevsky's drugstore to get something anyway, Lyalya Orlov had decided to find out if Iona Ovseich might need something.

"No, Orlov," said Iona Ovseich, "I don't need anything."

Iona Ovseich spent the whole night sitting at the table by the window: the moon looked like a boat in a fairy tale, its prow rising and frozen on the crest of an invisible wave. The stars shone with such purity that it caused an unearthly cold to penetrate his soul, and keen as the prick of a needle he could feel the limits of human life—from one specific time to another. Iona Ovseich recalled the last evening when he had just begun to read the newspaper, and Polina Isaevna was still alive. No one could have imagined that death was not somewhere far up ahead, but right there, right at his side, another minute, another second, and it would all be over.

Iona Ovseich wiped his eyes: millions of tiny grains of sand burned the corneas. He felt like applying a wet handkerchief to reduce the heat, but he had neither the strength nor the desire to get up—he just wanted to sit and sit, and let the minutes and seconds fall by themselves like pebbles into a boundless, fathomless sea.

Before dawn he dozed off a little, and the moment he opened his eyes, he had the feeling that he had fallen asleep in someone else's house, that the people who lived there had left him there alone while departing, themselves, never to return. For a moment Iona Ovseich felt like a small boy. He remembered his mother and father although he had not thought about them for a long time, then he turned and saw Polina Isaevna's empty bed, and with extreme clarity realized that he was not in someone else's house but in his own, his very own home, except that in the span of a few minutes everything had abruptly changed and would never be the same again.

At seven o'clock Iona Ovseich turned on the radio. They were broadcasting the news: everywhere, in the cities and in the villages, the population was discussing the resolution on the latest reduction in prices. The workers and collective farmers warmly thanked the party and government and in response to their concern for them, promised to work even harder, and to be even more diligent in fulfilling the second postwar, Five-Year Plan (the fifth, all told) ahead of schedule. Nikita Agashkin, a metal worker at the Leningrad factory "Electroenergy," with whom a correspondent had spoken, had cited some very interesting figures: solely because of the decrease in prices for shoes his family could buy two extra pairs of boots or shoes this year.

Iona Ovseich heaved a sigh. Polina Isaevna had heard about the new decrease in prices, but would never benefit from them.

There was no water in the faucet. He would have to get a pail and go down to the courtyard. Iona Ovseich also took his shoes to clean them off while he was down there. The ground in the cemetery was wet after the rain, and a lot of mud had stuck to his shoes. When he returned, Lyalya Orlov was waiting at the door. She had brought him a bottle of hot milk from which steam was rising. She had also brought two eggs—one soft-boiled, the other hard-boiled, because she didn't know which Iona Ovseich preferred.

"Orlov," said Iona Ovseich, looking her straight in the eye. "I'll accept this from you so not to insult you, but this is the first and last time. Wait, I'll pour the milk into a dish and give you back the bottle."

Lyalya remained by the door. He told her to come in and not wait in the corridor like some beggar. Iona Ovseich had to repeat his invitation before Lyalya came in. The first thing she saw as she entered was the chair between the dead woman's bed and the wardrobe. The oxygen bag hung on the back of the chair and various jars, vials, and boxes of powders were neatly arranged on the seat.

"Lord," said Lyalya, beginning to cry. "This is all that's left of a person!"

Iona Ovseich went on foot to the factory to speed up his circulation. The morning was sunny, and sparrows chirped happily in the trees.

Housewives stood in line with their cans at the dairy, chatting loudly with each other. Singing cheerful songs, cadets from the merchant marine school marched to their mess hall for breakfast. Everything was the same as it was yesterday, the day before yesterday, as if the world had remained unchanged.

"Yes," said Iona Ovseich aloud to himself, "a person dies, but life goes on. Polina! Polina!"

At the factory people tried to be sparing of Comrade Degtyar and not bother him with trifles, but in the last three days so many problems had accumulated that, despite all their good intentions, it was impossible to postpone things any longer, and Comrade Degtyar himself would have been the first to agree. Most importantly, there had not yet been any discussion or meetings on the new decrease in prices in the various departments. The factory committee had posed no objection to limiting the discussion to one shift change. Where that idea came from was a separate question, one that needed to be examined on its own, but now it was necessary quickly to bridge the gap so that the people on the assembly line and in the workplace would not feel neglected.

The members of the party bureau and the factory committee who were in the factory at the time were invited to Iona Ovseich's office. First, he gave them a good dressing down; then, since there was not a moment to spare, he moved right on to concrete problems. Having been oppressed by their sense of guilt, the people now took heart again, and fifteen minutes later each one of them was on his way to his allotted section and in the time left before the lunch break they coached the rank and file workers and reported back to the party bureau. Iona Ovseich took the information by telephone and asked specifically which workers would be speaking and what their basic thesis would be.

Late that evening when the third shift came on in the factory, Iona Ovseich could finally allow himself a short rest with a clear conscience. Strictly speaking, this was not a rest but simply a respite, because his mind still swarmed with ideas and calculations, but as the saying goes, where there's a will there's a way. In all the departments, in each section and on every shift, the workers unanimously assumed increased social obligations and promised to review them with an eye to even greater increases. This was a genuine, spontaneous outpouring like those which had occurred during the first Five-Year Plan, and like the Stakhanovite and Busyginite movements, when people outdid themselves and proved to all skeptics and doubting Thomases that nothing was impossible.

Today for the thousandth time Comrade Degtyar confirmed that it was only necessary to organize people at the right time and direct their energy, and then in a few years those figures on the material and technological base of communism, which Comrade Stalin had cited in February of 1946, would become a reality in the next four to five years.

Iona Ovseich sighed, thinking again of Polina Isaevna, who had so hoped to live to see that day.

He was slightly dizzy from all the intensity and excitement. Black dots flashed before his eyes and there was a sudden unpleasant ringing in his ears. Iona Ovseich remembered that besides the glass of milk and the two eggs Orlov had brought him that morning, he had not had a thing in his mouth all day. Mentally he reproached himself for this, but nonetheless there was a good feeling, a respect for the human spirit which holds the reins firmly in its hands and is stronger than doctors and specialists might imagine. Perhaps, if she had thought less about her illnesses, Polina Isaevna would be alive today.

Several times in the middle of the night Iona Ovseich felt weakness and an unpleasant irregularity in his heartbeat, but nothing so bad considering the weight of the past few days. Worse could have been expected.

The next morning Lyalya brought him another present: a vermicelli cake with some raisins inside, and a piece of real Moldavian sheep's cheese. Iona Ovseich was genuinely angry, but it turned out that this time he was not angry at the right person: Lyalya had baked the vermicelli cake with Madame Malaya, and Tosya Khomitsky had supplied the sheep's cheese. All right, said Iona Ovseich, that was enough; he'd rather hear what Orlov had to say about the way her fellow tobacco factory workers had responded to the new decrease in prices.

Lyalya said that the entire collective had responded in a positive and practical way. And her brigade had assumed a supplementary obligation in comparison with others—only to turn out products of good and excellent quality.

"That's the way it should be," said Iona Ovseich, "only high- and first-quality goods. But is that a real obligation or just talk?"

Lyalya's eyes opened wide. What did he mean, just talk? They were already only producing high- and first-quality products.

"Only high and first quality?" said Iona Ovseich in surprise. "Then what kind of increased obligation could you have assumed?"

Lyalya shrugged her shoulders. What kind of a question was that! You had to struggle all the time, and, if you didn't, quality would keep slipping lower and lower, there'd be more rejects, and the brigade would take a nosedive.

In other words, said Iona Ovseich, putting a finer point on it, it was a question of consolidating the gains that had already been achieved. One could only congratulate a brigade which understood that it was one thing to achieve the gains and another to consolidate them.

This was the first time Lyalya had heard any real praise from Comrade Degtyar in the past several years. She blushed deeply and had to catch her breath, but she quickly took herself in hand and calmly answered that in her brigade every worker understood this as well as she did. Then Lyalya began telling him everything in order, beginning with the comrade from the party bureau coming to see them before the meeting, and her co-workers deciding to assume increased obligations, but Iona Ovseich was no longer listening. He switched the subject to the recent past, saying he was surprised by the great leap in consciousness this simple woman had made, she who had caused them so much trouble and who at one time had almost committed a foolish and fatal error.

"Do you remember, Orlov," said Iona Ovseich, smiling warmly.

Lyalya covered her face with both hands. "Don't, don't!"

Iona Ovseich looked at Lyalya and admired her in spite of himself; though she was close to fifty, she still retained the ability to blush as shyly as a girl, and many a woman could envy her figure.

"Orlov," said Iona Ovseich, carefully wiping his eyes as if he had specks of dust in them, "there's some nice guys in the electric department at our factory. When you have some free time, come see me, and I'll introduce you."

Lyalya blushed like a girl again, covered her face with her hands, and said that men disgusted her: all they wanted was a bedmate and a maid, but a man you could talk to heart to heart was hard to find—they were one in a million.

Iona Ovseich placed his hand amicably on her shoulder and told her to open her eyes, but Lyalya stubbornly refused. Then he took her by the elbows and pulled her off to one side:

"Now, Orlov, tell me the truth: will you let me be a matchmaker for you or not?"

Lyalya shook her head. No, not for anything in the world!

"Orlov," said Iona Ovseich with a sly wink, "it won't cost you a lot."

Lyalya stopped shaking her head, gave him a reproachful look, and said softly: "You know I respect you more than anyone in the world. Why are you suggesting such a thing to me?"

Comrade Degtyar sighed, released Lyalya's hands, and said that as far as matchmaking was concerned, he, of course, was only joking, and there was no need to be insulted.

Lyalya replied, "God, these insults." She turned aside and furtively brushed away a tear. For a moment they were silent, each thinking their own thoughts. Then Iona Ovseich took a pan out of the sideboard and placed the cake in it so Lyalya could have her plate back, but she suddenly jumped up without saying a word and ran out of the room.

Iona Ovseich automatically went after her to call her back but quickly changed his mind.

The oxygen bag was still on the back of the chair. Iona Ovseich picked it up, with a deep sigh, folded it in four like a newspaper, and stuck it into the bottom drawer of the wardrobe where old shoes and clothes were kept.

Orlov did not reappear for almost an entire week. During this time Dina Vargaftik came to visit him twice. She brought a meat pie and one filled with jam, saying both times that she had intended to visit him on the day after the funeral but had been afraid that it wasn't proper. Iona Ovseich said the pies were wonderful, especially the one with the jam filling, and asked how things were going at the Vorovsky factory—were there frequent interruptions in the delivery of raw materials? By the way, the factory manager had complained again at a City Soviet meeting but many people had the impression that the problem lay elsewhere. Dina said they were correct, but did not go into details; rather, she tried to change the subject to more personal topics—Iona Ovseich was all alone now and a person, especially one in such a position of authority, needed his shirt washed and pants ironed, and to eat at the proper time, and a man is a man. Iona Ovseich listened closely, nodding his head in agreement. Dina suddenly brought up the subject of how outrageous Anya Kotlyar had been that evening at the Cheperukhas, saying she was surprised that a woman could be so crude, so vulgar. Red splotches appeared on Dina's cheeks from excitement; her lips became dry, and she automatically licked them in order to moisten them.

"Dina," Iona Ovseich asked out of the blue, "why don't you ever visit Efim Granik? Especially since he was registered at one time in your apartment."

Dina waved with her short, fat arms. That was all she needed, that crackpot. Let someone else be the lucky one, thank God, she hadn't sunk that low yet.

Iona Ovseich frowned: you might have found nicer words for a neighbor.

Dina said, for God's sake why should she be the one who should think about Efim? Why her and not Lyalya Orlov, who had so many men when she was young that she could have supplied half of Odessa. Did it do anything for her? No Lyalya was just as old and alone as she was.

Iona Ovseich did not respond. His guest lowered her eyes and held her breath as if waiting for something, but they both remained silent. Only the creaking of chairs could be heard, their glue having cracked from the heat over time and their screws having worked loose. Finally, Dina sighed and her lips trembled noticeably. Her voice was hoarse as she apologized for bothering him and talking nonsense. She made a movement as if intending to get up, but remained in place and sighed again.

"All right," said Comrade Degtyar, rising and extending his hand in a friendly fashion. "Stay well, Dina. I can see that you've gained weight. A good advertisement for Odessa."

Dina walked slowly, carefully, from the door to the corridor, as if afraid to lose her balance. She staggered on the stairs, but managed to grab hold of the banister. Descending the stairs, she looked back despite herself, sensing that Iona Ovseich was standing in his doorway, waiting, but in fact his door was shut tight.

A day later Lyalya Orlov came to see him, this time in the late evening. It turned out that she had come once when it was still light but Comrade Degtyar had not returned yet; now she was here because she urgently needed to consult with him about her brigade. Iona Ovseich said that he had no objections, but the tobacco factory had its own party organization and party secretary, and she should have seen her own people first.

"And you're not one of my own!" said Lyalya, shrugging her shoulders.

"All right," said Iona Ovseich. "Let's get down to brass tacks."

Degtyar sat on the couch by the window and Lyalya took a seat at the opposite end. She thought about how best to start, then began by asking the question the girls in her brigade had been asking themselves. The entire nation, the entire country, was moving toward communism, and shouldn't they be feeling that personally and in their brigade?

Iona Ovseich smiled and said: "What does that mean, feel? You have to be more precise. What does feeling mean?"

Lyalya asked him not to interrupt and answered the question the way her brigade had: of course, they should feel it. If they didn't, how would they know the country was moving toward it.

"And what did you decide?" said Iona Ovseich, unintentionally interrupting again.

As was her habit, Lyalya covered her face with the palms of her hands like a schoolgirl and shook her head. Spreading her fingers apart to see Comrade Degtyar, she said that, first, starting next month, one person would be given the wages for the entire brigade and everyone else would take what they had coming from a common fund. No records would be kept. Second, every week the entire brigade would go to the movies, the theater, or a museum, then discuss it and exchange opinions.

"Good," Iona Ovseich nodded. "Everything's clear on the first point, but, as for the second, what about those who have a family at home, a husband, children?"

Lyalya took her hands from her face, looked at Iona Ovseich in surprise, then asked: "But isn't our brigade a family? And anyway, we have only one married woman."

Iona Ovseich rose from the couch without answering, paced for a short while, then stood at the window looking at the street where children were playing hopscotch under the street lamps. He walked around the room again and said: "How can I answer you, Orlov? Above all, what your brigade is proposing is a very interesting initiative, and as they say, initiative is worth more than money. For my part, I wish you success, but first thing tomorrow, no postponing it, you have to go see the party bureau and coordinate it with them, make sure this isn't suspect spontaneity."

Orlov shrugged her shoulders: why did she have to go to the party bureau? The girls thought this up themselves for their brigade, and Comrade Degtyar, who understood things as well as anybody else, fully approved.

Iona Ovseich sat down on the couch and, without thinking, grabbed Lyalya by the hand, raised it slightly in the air, and then, without releasing it, fell straight to his knees in front of her.

"Orlov, if I thought you hadn't understood me, I would repeat it all from the beginning, but you understand me very well—I can tell by your eyes."

"Let go of my hand," said Lyalya, "you're hurting me."

Iona Ovseich wagged a threatening finger at her: if she was going to act like that he could take off his belt and spank her.

Lyalya stared at him with her sea green eyes. Iona Ovseich suddenly recalled that distant evening before the war when the two of them had sat that same way in her room. For a moment he felt a mysterious lift in his mood. He sighed deeply, let her hand go, and said that tomorrow he had to speak to the regional propagandists—and he would have to stay up late to prepare properly.

After Lyalya left, Iona Ovseich lay down for five minutes to rest and almost fell asleep, but caught himself in time. He jumped to his feet, gathered some cold water in his palms, splashed it on his face, grunted, and sat down to work. The subject of tomorrow's address, the law of quantity and quality in historical materialism, had firmly lodged in his memory over the years and he probably didn't need to look at his notes. But life did not stand still, and each time the general theses had to be illustrated by fresh statistics from the Central Statistical Board and also by examples from everyday life. His figures on the province, the city, and specifically in the Stalin district, were from the *Notepad of an Agitator,* and from his own notes which he had taken at the last City Soviet meeting. The information on the district and city had a great clarity and persuasiveness about it but it was only in combination with a grandiose vision of the entire country that the information created a true image of the actual historical scope and the gigantic transformations that were taking place.

Iona Ovseich drew a graph with a red pencil—figures and diagrams—so that the propagandists could see with their own eyes how quantity turned into quality, and would then be able to convey this to their listeners. Despite the bloodwar, which had set the country back ten to twelve years, the national income, according to totals of the fourth Five-Year Plan, that is, at the end of 1950, had exceeded the level of 1940 by sixty-four percent, instead of the thirty-eight percent called for in the plan. The capacity of the rural power stations alone had doubled. Labor productivity on the Volga-Don was ten times higher than during the construction of the White Sea-Baltic Sea; the collective farm "The Revolutionary Achievement," in the Talnovsky district, Kiev province, whose chairman was Fedor Dubkovetsky, one of the pioneers of the collective movement in the Ukraine, last season collected a harvest on its lands of twenty-one centners per acre. The Kotovsky district of Odessa province was a match for him, having brought in three hundred and eighty-one centners, that is, almost four hundred, of sugar beets per hectare, and Evgeny Vikotorovich Blazhevsky, who had been trained in the collective farm fields, set a record for the entire country—seventy centners of corn per hectare.

During the Five-Year Plan the government's expenditure for satisfying the cultural-domestic needs of the population had come to five hundred and twenty-four point five billion rubles, with special attention given to national health care—around one hundred billion rubles.

A good example of the cultural situation was the summer movie theater Komsomolets, which had more than a thousand seats and was in the very center of the city—on Deibasovskaya Street, and an example of health care was the new outpatient ophthalmology clinic next to the Filatov Clinic on Proletarian Boulevard not far from Maly Fontan, so that from its windows the patients whose sight had been restored could enjoy the Black Sea with their own eyes.

Iona Ovseich sighed instinctively: the tuberculosis clinic on Belinsky where Polina Isaevna spent so many weeks and months of her life was also close to the sea. On the days when she was feeling somewhat better and he had come to visit, Polina Isaevna had sometimes asked him to walk with her along the cliff above the Lanzheron and Otrada beaches, but he had never had a free minute.

"Oh, Polenka, Polenka!" Iona Ovseich sighed again. He gathered up his papers, piled them neatly, then rolled up the graph and tied it with a ribbon to keep it from unrolling.

After getting undressed, he thought one last time about tomorrow's address. The comrades from propaganda would definitely be present at the activists' meeting. Then, his conscience clear, he allowed himself to drift toward sleep.

A full moon was visible above the roof of the neighboring house. The shadow of the window transom fell onto the couch. Iona Ovseich was between two stripes of black. He squeezed his eyes shut like a child to make everything perfectly dark, but the strain made colored circles swim before his eyes. Then he turned to his left side, tried to relax, and soon fell asleep.

This was the first night since the death of Polina Isaevna that he had slept from evening until morning. At short intervals he dreamed of red columns, each with two circles at the base, in which Iona Ovseich immediately recognized his diagrams. Then some woman or girl came—it was hard to tell her age by her figure. She looked at the red columns, with an ambiguous grin. Iona Ovseich wanted to grab her by the hand, but she pressed her elbows firmly to her sides and slipped nimbly away. Despite his failure, Iona Ovseich felt a pleasant languor in his entire body, as if he were sinking into soft, warm soil, and then slowly, smoothly, sometimes shaking from a sudden jolt, he would free himself and soar over melon fields, where melons lay in pairs everywhere, large, juicy, and with golden rinds.

Iona Ovseich woke up the next morning with a pleasant sensation in his mouth, as if he had spent the entire night eating something tasty. Still, fifteen minutes later, he was hungry as a wolf, but the cupboard proved to be bare. Though annoyed, Iona Ovseich unintentionally slammed the door and began to think about Orlov: when you didn't need her she was there, and when you did, she wasn't around, of course.

A moment later, the doorbell rang and it was Orlov. On her way there she had run into Dina Vargaftik, who had been very surprised that Lyalya was going to visit Degtyar at such an early hour, or could she have just been leaving his place? Lyalya had replied that Dina could think whatever she liked, but she was going to see Comrade Degtyar to find out at what time he would be addressing propagandists today.

"Orlov," interrupted Iona Ovseich, "I'm not interested in gossip. As for the lecture, you could have called me at the factory."

Lyalya was a bit taken aback by this unexpected reply. Then she walked over to Degtyar, raised her hands in front of her, palms out as if she wished to pat him but could not bring herself to do it. Then in a soft whisper she said: "Don't get angry at me, it's not my fault. And you have a glow today, you really look quite young."

"Not young," said Iona Ovseich with a sudden laugh, "just hungry as a wolf."

"Oh lord," said Lyalya in despair, "and like a fool, I didn't bring you anything!"

Lyalya was about to run home, but Degtyar stopped her and said that it was one thing if she just happened to stop by and another when it was done specially. To forestall any further conversation, he immediately said good-bye and reminding her that the activists' meeting began at seven o'clock on the dot, he accompanied Lyalya to the door.

It was a sunny morning. Iona Ovseich walked without hurrying, deeply inhaling the spring air. He felt unusually light-hearted, as if, with the wave of a magic wand, all his troubles and worries had been removed, including those at home, where Polina Isaevna had been chained to her bed for so many years. In his youth, before the Revolution, Iona Ovseich had been fond of the poems of Heinrich Heine, the famous German poet. The poet, who at the end of his life was very ill, had written one poem about his mattress as a grave or as a prison, Iona Ovseich could no longer remember exactly, but what was striking about the poem was the poet's courage and his ineradicable faith in life. Crippled by paralysis, the poet still wanted to love and hate until his last breath and to display all his creativity.

Near the factory a line from some poem by the poet came into Iona Ovseich's mind: "Let's run away! You will be my wife!" He tried to remember the next lines, which were about love, a father's house, but he could summon no more no matter how hard he tried. He could remember what the poem was about but the words themselves seemed to have vanished into thin air.

There was a group of high-spirited young people crowded near the front door of the factory, causing him to slow his pace. The young men and women parted to make way for him but Iona Ovseich wouldn't permit this and stood in the line with everyone else. Expressions of approval came from various sides. Iona Ovseich waved in reply; then having come alongside a pretty, though still apparently quite young, girl, he frowned menacingly on purpose, cast a penetrating glance at her, and surprised himself by reciting the lines:

"Let's run away! You will be my wife!
We will rest in another land,
In my love you will find
Your homeland and your father's house."

At first the girl was confused and blushed deeply, then she made a face and started giggling like a silly eighth-grader.

"How old are you?" Comrade Degtyar asked curiously.

"Too old for you!" the girl answered in a sharp tone. The people around them laughed amicably. She raised her head, now looking unconstrainedly at Iona Ovseich and not resembling a silly eighth-grader, at all.

"You're very quick with your tongue," said Iona Ovseich in praise. "But I'd be curious to know how quick you are at work."

"Don't worry," she said without a pause, "you won't have to finish it for me."

They all began laughing again, although there was nothing funny about her last remark. Iona Ovseich paused automatically, then was about to ask which shop this sharp tongue worked in but the line surged from the rear; he had to step aside, and the girl vanished from sight.

He continued to think about her and after a telephone conversation in which he hadn't been able to finish his sentence before the operator disconnected him, a thought flashed into his mind—he should go around to all the departments and look for her, but, as they say, the game was not worth the candle, especially since today they were up to their ears with more important and pressing problems.

During the lunch break Comrade Degtyar invited the department heads, and the trade union and Komsomol activists in to see him to talk about the new initiative taken by the workers Zhandarov and Agafonov at the Lublin smelting-mechanical foundry. The two workers had proposed that every aspect of production be performed with excellence. Before the conversation began, several people unwrapped the newspapers in which they had brought sandwiches from home, a herring tail with onion or a pickle, to whet the appetite, and they bit off as big a piece as possible, quickly chewing and swallowing so as not to delay everyone else. Comrade Degtyar shook his head reproachfully and said that their lunch could have waited; he urged them to hurry since they only had a half hour lunch break, and they would not steal time from work.

But they were unable to confine themselves to the time allotted and needed another fifteen to twenty minutes after the bell. Iona Ovseich assumed full responsibility but, most important, the time had not been spent in vain, and everyone had felt that. In the course of the conversation it became evident that not everyone understood the concept "every aspect of production." Comrade Degtyar asked the specialists, mechanics, and technicians to speak out on the subject, and when they did, it became quite clear: the new initiatives demanded more fundamental training in the field of technology as well as in the field of economics for all those involved in production. In that connection it was proposed that a special school or seminar (whatever it was to be called) be organized for the workers with the task of the factory and Komsomol committees to achieve one hundred percent attendance.

Summarizing this short conversation which occurred between the two lunch bells, Comrade Degtyar asked all present to take special notice of the remarkable fact that the initiative that had arisen right there today was a typical example of initiative from below since, on their way there, no one could have thought or imagined the turn of events that had in fact taken place.

That evening at the meeting of the propagandists of the Stalin district, to illustrate the law of the passage of quantity into quality, Iona Ovseich cited two examples from just one day of contemporary life: a shock worker from the tobacco factory, Idaliya Orlov, had come to see him very early that day to discuss the initiative her brigade had taken, and several hours later the shoe-factory collective had also come up with a new initiative.

"Comrade propagandists," Iona Ovseich said in conclusion, "a specter is haunting Europe, the specter of communism! But today the specter of communism is you and me, incarnated in our magnificent achievements, the thunder of millions, in the roaring turbines of Dneproges, and the majestic flow of the Volga-Don!"

Lyalya Orlov, who was sitting with a pencil and pad in the last row, applauded loudly. Several people automatically turned around. Lyalya became embarrassed and wanted to hide, but as usually happens with shy people, she made even more noise instead of calming down.

"Comrades," said Iona Ovseich cheerfully, "you see here before you that same Idaliya Orlov from the tobacco factory of whom we were just speaking."

Now all the activists turned and gave her a friendly round of applause. Lyalya covered her face out of habit, but they showed her no mercy, demanding that she come forward and tell them about her brigade and the new initiative.

Lyalya protested with all her might, but finally had to yield and tell the whole story from the beginning as she had told it to Comrade Degtyar. Everyone listened with great attention and then immediately proposed that the local press pick up this story of outstanding initiative.

The person sitting next to Iona Ovseich bent close to him and, covering one side of his mouth with his hand, said a few words. Iona Ovseich rose, obviously agitated, and asked for silence: "Comrade propagandists, I can inform you that the Stalin District Committee completely supports your motion and will petition the proper departments."

As soon as the meeting was over, Lyalya was one of the first to leave so it would not appear she was waiting for Iona Ovseich and the District Committee official, and she wandered around the streets of the city for a long time, almost until midnight. She wasn't back when Iona Ovseich returned home. He went to see Malaya in order to tell her the good news which would bring her happiness, after she had spent so much time and energy on Lyalya Orlov. Madame Malaya sat in an armchair, with a scarf thrown over her shoulders, her eyes opening and closing as if she were fighting drowsiness. When Iona Ovseich had finished his story about Lyalya Orlov, she rested her head on the palm of her hand and was silent for a moment, then said quietly, as if talking to herself: "Joseph Kotlyar is dead."

Iona Ovseich thought for a second, then said decisively: "May he rest in peace."

Madame Malaya closed her eyes, only her lips moving as she muttered, "Look what can happen to a human being. He loses one leg in the Civil War, and the other in a camp from gangrene. Then he dies far from home."

"Malaya," said Comrade Degtyar, grasping his lapel and bending forward, "get ahold of yourself and stop your hysterics."

Klava Ivanovna raised her head and smiled like a child, though to whom or at what wasn't clear. She told Degtyar that he should go home, she was an old woman and had the right to a little rest.

At six o'clock in the morning the radio broadcast the good news: the first day of subscriptions to the new government loan for the development of the national economy of the U.S.S.R. was a great success throughout the country. The Leningrad shipbuilders had decided to lend the government their monthly pay, and the high-speed lathe operators, Martynov, Androchnikov, Kislytsya, and Oglymamedov, working for the last year of the Five-Year Plan, wished to loan the government two months of their pay. The noble example was followed by many production workers at the "Electroenergy" factory, the "Skorokhod" factory, and the workers of the Vasily Island district food-supply center.

The initiative taken by the Leningraders was supported by the steel foundry workers of the "Zaporozhstal" plant, Paetrenko, Martynov, and Kobylintsyn, and the Don miners Panteleimon Kontsedalov, Ivan Khizhnyak, and Mitrofan Rakhuba, who yesterday had dug the first few tons of coal for the sixth Five-Year Plan, now signed up to loan the government ten weeks' wages.

That evening Iona Ovseich spoke with Khomitsky and Orlov concerning the subscription campaign in their courtyard. In previous years, the campaign had usually been begun on the third, fourth, and sometimes the fifth day, as if in tacit acknowledgment that the courtyard was less important than the plant or factory. Of course, this was basically a mistaken view, and it was time to be done with it. And so, beginning tomorrow morning, they had to proceed with the subscription before people could leave for work. The goal was one hundred percent, not as in the past when only housewives and the unemployed had subscribed.

"Comrade Khomitsky, Comrade Orlov, is everything clear or not?" asked Iona Ovseich.

Lyalya answered that everything was clear to her, but Stepa had a question about the new aspect this year. Where had it come from: instructions from above or—

"Comrade Khomitsky," interrupted Iona Ovseich, "I repeat: our goal is one hundred percent, not as in past years when only housewives and the unemployed subscribed. What the actual amount will be can be decided on the spot, but of course it shouldn't be less than twenty-five rubles, to be paid immediately, in cash. You know all this, I'm not telling you anything new."

Lyalya had the morning free, because she was on the second shift that day. Lebedev, the concierge, was furious: some bastard had left the courtyard faucet wide open and now it was gushing like a fountain, so Stepa had to fix it at six in the morning.

Lyalya immediately informed Comrade Degtyar about the faucet. He turned pale and shouted that this smelled of outright sabotage, but he quickly regained his self-control and apologized for his inappropriate outburst, then ordered Stepa to stop up the water pipe with a wooden plug and to join in the subscription campaign. Stepa replied that people needed water and many people didn't have a tap in their apartment. So he had to fix this first, then he would go around to people with the subscription list. Although Lyalya had been the first to raise the alarm, she now supported Khomitsky and asked Comrade Degtyar to entrust the subscription to her alone for the next few hours.

"Orlov," said Comrade Degtyar, leaning his head forward and glowering, "you're oversimplifying the picture: it's one thing when you go to people with Stepa Khomitsky, a Communist, a World War II disabled veteran, and it's another when you go alone. But if you wish to take the entire responsibility on yourself, we'll meet you half way. Give it a try and for a start you sign me up for a hundred rubles. Come for the money this evening."

Lyalya laughed happily and said that at that rate she'd have the whole courtyard signed up by lunchtime. Iona Ovseich frowned and asked her to be more serious, advising her to begin her rounds with

Colonel Landa and his wife Gizella who could serve as a good example to the others.

When Lyalya rang Landa's bell, the colonel had already finished breakfast, but said he was prepared to drink another cup of coffee with such a charming guest, although, to believe the famous Soviet poet, the hours flee, and time drags weights on a rusty chain. Lyalya got a little embarrassed and said she had just eaten. The colonel winked playfully and took the subscription list from Lyalya's hands, reading loudly and with expression like a real actor: "Degtyar, Iona Ovseich: one hundred rubles!"

There was a pause in which the colonel stared silently at the list, shrugged his shoulders, and said this time without expression: "A hundred rubles—that's not bad for a housewife," and asked to put him and his wife down for a hundred rubles apiece. Gizella took her purse from the cupboard, took out two hundred rubles, and placed them on the table. Then they both signed the list. The colonel thanked Lyalya Orlov for the great honor of being second in the courtyard right after Comrade Degtyar, and wished her success in her noble work, so important for the people and the country.

Lyalya thanked him in return and admitted that it was not she but Comrade Degtyar himself who had thought of Colonel Landa.

"Thank you," said Colonel Landa, firmly pressing his hand to his heart. "Thank you for your trust. And I wish you every success in your work and your life."

A car honked twice. The colonel grabbed his overcoat, buttoning it on the way, and again asked that his warmest thanks be conveyed to Comrade Degtyar. Gizella slammed the door with all her might and did not even wish Lyalya good-bye.

Lyalya went next to see Zinovy Cheperukha. Olya and Iona were already there and feeding their grandchildren before taking them to kindergarten. Katerina expressed surprise that Madame Orlov was up so early and asked how a woman who looked so healthy could suffer from insomnia? Lyalya said that she didn't suffer from insomnia, it was just that the subscription campaign had begun, and three had already subscribed, each for a hundred rubles, and one of them was a housewife. Olya immediately guessed that it must have been Gizella Landa, whose husband was paid three thousand rubles a month, and all the money went for her alone. Lyalya replied that Colonel Landa had pledged two month's salary at his hospital and, anyway, it was indecent to count other people's money. Of course, Olya agreed, adding that if her husband or son earned even half of that she wouldn't count it either, but, as it was, she had to mind every kopeck.

"Mama," retorted Zinovy, "calm down. No one's forcing you to pledge a hundred rubles."

"And where am I supposed to get the money to lend anyone?" said Olya, losing her temper for no apparent reason. "Do I get paid, receive a pension, or is some millionaire uncle sending me packages from America?"

"Mama, calm down!" said Zinovy.

"My son," interrupted Iona Cheperukha, "don't raise your voice to your mother. She's right: how's a housewife supposed to loan people money?"

Lyalya shifted her glance from one to the other and wanted to put in a word, but they wouldn't let her. Finally, Zinovy pounded his fist on the table: "Enough, we won't go broke over ten rubles!"

"You can't pledge ten rubles," said Lyalya. "The minimum is twenty-five."

"What do you mean you *can't* pledge ten rubles?" said Iona Cheperukha, interrupting again. "In the Soviet Union pledging for a loan is voluntary. That's number one. And number two, just today it turned out that I didn't leave my wife any money even for bread. What should she do: go steal some money so Lyalya Orlov can fulfill her pledge plan?"

"Listen, Dad," interrupted Zinovy, "you clearly have not thought this through. Think about it when you have some time, and meanwhile I'll put in twenty-five rubles for Mama, and that's that."

Lyalya handed Olya the list. Olya signed, took the money from her son's hands, counted it, then handed the money and the list to Lyalya, who slipped the money in her pocket. Iona Cheperukha offered her his hand and wished her success. Lyalya replied with a firm handshake, but continued to stand in place as if the matter was not settled.

"Madame Orlov," said Katerina, "if you stand around here, you might not have time for your next subscription."

Lyalya answered that she had plenty of time. She had the second shift today, but this year there were instructions that everyone was to make a pledge, not just the housewives.

"Instructions?" Iona Cheperukha jumped out of his chair as if he'd been pricked by a needle. "Show me these instructions in writing, otherwise get out of here before I kick you out!"

Tears appeared in Lyalya's eyes. She bit her lower lip and took her handkerchief out of her pocket, but, forgetting why, she simply crumpled it in her hand.

Olya and Katerina suddenly began yelling at Grisha and Misha even though the boys had eaten unusually quickly today. Their grandfather interceded for them, saying that no one should vent their anger on children, even their own mother. Grisha and Misha both clung to their grandfather. Katerina shouted that the old man was turning the children against their parents and grabbed the boys by the hand to tear them away from their grandfather. She tugged hard but to no avail.

Zinovy dressed in silence, as if none of this commotion concerned him in the least. When Lyalya looked at him, he turned his back, said that he was late for work, and slammed the door. Lyalya stayed a couple of minutes longer. The rest of the household went about their business as if no one were there but them. Then, loud enough for all to hear, Lyalya said: "When you needed a bathroom and a toilet, you found the money, but now you turn your back. All right. I'll tell Comrade Degtyar."

"Who does she think she is, trying to scare us like this!" yelled Olya. "Lyalya, we earn our living with our bare hands, not by shady deals. And we've seen dozens of your sort before!"

"Olya," retorted Iona Cheperukha, "leave personalities out of it and don't insult anyone. She's doing what she was told to."

Lyalya had already opened the door but heard what was said and replied that no one had told her to do anything; she'd asked for this community assignment herself. Olya laughed loudly and said that people had a good memory. They had still not forgotten what "community assignments" certain fine ladies from the courtyard took on themselves before the war.

"Stop it I tell you!" said Iona, brandishing his fists.

The Cheperukhas had taken so much time that all the others had already left for work, and now the only people home were housewives. Stepa was tinkering with the water pipe; it turned out that not only was the faucet broken but the thread on the pipe was ruined. Lyalya continued on her rounds alone. Some needed convincing, others did not, but in the end the women would make a pledge and give her whatever money they had on hand. Only Major Biryuk's mother refused point-blank, saying that without her daughter-in-law Marina she wouldn't even buy a box of matches. Lyalya did not insist. On the contrary, she politely inquired as to the old woman's blood pressure, saying she shouldn't let it get too high and promising to drop by another time.

The next morning Lyalya reported to Comrade Degtyar on the events of the previous day and the two of them set out immediately for the Cheperukhas. The scene there was the same as it had been the day before. Iona Ovseich wished them all good appetite and asked Zinovy if he might interrupt the family meal for a moment. Zinovy invited Degtyar and Orlov into the other room. Iona Cheperukha followed them in. Five minutes later when the conversation had become boisterous, Olya and Katerina also peeped in.

"Zinovy," said Comrade Degtyar, "at my factory I gave two months' salary as a loan to the government, and now I've added a hundred rubles. And you, as you know, have pledged a month's salary, although many people at the Kirov factory considered it possible to pledge a month and a half or two months' pay. That's one side of the coin, and the other is that you make a watertight compartment between Zinovy Cheperukha at the factory and Zinovy Cheperukha at home."

Zinovy answered that he could not comply; on the contrary, and that's why there was no reason to make two people out of one and force him to subscribe twice: as worker and as housewife.

"This means," Iona Ovseich said with emphasis, "Khomitsky can do it, Orlov can, Landa can, Degtyar can, but the Cheperukhas can't!"

"That's right," shouted Katerina. "The Cheperukhas can't because they have little children and before you stop up one hole three new ones have opened!"

"Oh, oh, oh! You poor unfortunate people," said Comrade Degtyar, horrified by her remark.

Then, overcoming his emotion, he pointed a finger at Olya and shouted that they should ask her about the life she and her children had led in the same building in 1913!

"What does 1913 have to do with it?" said Olya, spreading her hands. "You mention '13 as if the world had been standing still since then. Next you'll be bringing up Pushkin and other old fogies like him."

"How dare you speak that way about Pushkin!" said Lyalya indignantly.

"That doesn't matter," said Iona Ovseich soothingly to her. "On the other hand, when you wanted to take the outpost from the children and turn it into a private apartment, what unctuous voices we heard! But let there be no mistake about it: the Soviet Government can stroke the wrong way, too."

"Is that a threat?" asked Zinovy, crossing his prosthesis over his good leg.

"No," replied Comrade Degtyar, "it isn't a threat, it is just a curious parallel. Especially since the Stalin District Executive Committee, as I recall, allowed Zinovy Cheperukha and his family temporary residence in the Pioneer outpost."

"And now's the time to remind us?" asked Zinovy in a nasty tone of voice.

"Son," shouted Iona Cheperukha, "don't jump into the fire before your father. No one is threatening you. We lost our temper a little, and Comrade Degtyar lost his a little too. We have to be nice to each other, like old neighbors. Ovseich, I don't want to pledge twenty-five rubles, I want to pledge fifty."

Comrade Degtyar raised his eyebrows: "Why are you addressing me? Orlov is the authorized pledge agent. Speak to her."

"Lyalechka," said Iona, smiling as he had in his distant youth before he had courted Olya, "show me where I'm supposed to sign."

Zinovy observed carefully as his father signed and counted out the money—a ruble, three rubles, five—and stacked the bills on the table. When it was over, Iona Cheperukha shook Comrade Degtyar's hand and repeated that people must be nice to each other.

"All right," said Zinovy, kissing Grisha and Misha. He nodded to everyone else, then slammed the door so hard that it reverberated in Granik's room.

"Iona," said Comrade Degtyar, as Zinovy's shadow flashed by the window, "you've shown me that people should be nice to each other. Say it again."

"Ovseich," said Iona Cheperukha after a short pause, "you know the saying: morning is wiser than evening. But there are exceptions. Let's wait until evening."

The same thing had happened again: they had wasted the whole morning with the Cheperukhas and missed all the rest, including Efim Granik, although he lived right next door, on the other side of the wall. Degtyar said that Granik must have heard the entire conversation from beginning to end. And so he could have dropped in himself and subscribed; but he hadn't. No, objected Lyalya, it was just that Efim was the kind of person who would never drop by another person's house without an invitation.

"Orlov, Orlov," said Comrade Degtyar, wagging a threatening finger, "you remind me of Malaya: she's always ready to think well of a person—it makes less trouble for her."

Late that evening Iona Cheperukha dropped by to see Iona Ovseich. In the doorway, he announced he would only stay a few minutes, but he was there until the Kremlin chimes struck midnight. They spoke of the past. Cheperukha shook his head, his eyes sad; life went by and no one could stop it. Before the war, especially after 1939, and the Eighteenth Party Congress when Comrade Stalin had said that socialism had finally been built and now they would begin to build communism, everyone could hope to live to see communism, but then that bandit Hitler attacked, and millions of people were killed. Everything had to be rebuilt from scratch. Iona Cheperukha said he still counted on living a few years under communism, but time took its toll. Today, coming home from work on the trolley, one passenger had suddenly taken ill. By the time they had gotten people out of the way so the man could breathe, he was dead.

"Cheperukha," said Comrade Degtyar quietly, every once in a while pressing his hand to his heart and massaging it lightly, "your example is just the usual bourgeois view of life. People die, that's not news! Karl Marx was critically ill during the last ten years of his life, but he did not stop working for a single day and died in his chair when he was left alone for two minutes."

"Karl Marx!" exclaimed Cheperukha. "Men like that come along once in a million years, but us, we're simple, ordinary people."

"Cheperukha," said Comrade Degtyar, bowing his head and staring at Iona, "sometimes simple, ordinary people are ready to pretend to be even less than they really are to evade their responsibilities. That's bourgeois thinking too."

"Ovseich," said Iona with a bitter grimace, "you're always insulting me, and I came here with an open heart. Here is seventy-five rubles, from Zinovy and Katerina."

Iona Ovseich thought for a minute, narrowed his eyes, then quickly pushed the money back and said: "Better late than never. But take the money to Orlov. She's in charge of the loan pledges with Khomitsky. That has already been explained to you once. They're the only ones who have the right to put people down for the subscription."

Iona took the money from the table and said good-bye. Comrade Degtyar saw him to the door. In the doorway Degtyar stopped and demanded that Iona be completely frank: was that money from Iona's pocket or had Zinovy really handed it over?

"Ovseich," said Iona Cheperukha, bringing the rubles up to his nose and inhaling deeply, "A smart guy once said money has no smell, but you want to prove the opposite. Adieu, good night."

Early the next morning, no matter how much she felt like sleeping after the second shift, Lyalya was already up and about, calling on Efim Granik. Last year he had cut through the wall and made a door for himself, two folding panels with large pieces of glass painted bright orange. He had also installed an electric buzzer of the sort used on ships. She had to press the buzzer several times before Efim opened the door though the sound could have woken the dead. Lyalya looked around his room, her eyes indicating the floor under the bed, as she said that he must be hiding a woman under there, otherwise he would have answered the door right away. Efim said he wasn't hiding anybody. He had no reason to hide anyone because from the world where his Sonya was now it was hard to see what was going on in this one.

"Hard's not the word," said Lyalya with a sad sigh.

Efim said that could be too, then inquired as to why Madame Orlov was visiting him at such an ungodly hour, when the roosters were still sleeping. Lyalya said that she had meant to call on him yesterday and the day before yesterday, but she'd been detained with her pledge list by the other neighbors.

"Pledge list?" said Efim in surprise. "I subscribed at the shipyard five days ago."

Lyalya shrugged her shoulders and smiled: "Fimochka, you work eight hours a day at the factory, and the rest of the time you live here. Twenty-four minus eight is sixteen."

"So you come here before it's even light out to teach me arithmetic?" frowned Efim. "But I'm too old for the first grade."

"What do you mean, old?" said Lyalya indignantly. "Our Efim Granik—old? Spit in the eye of anyone who says such a thing."

"In short," interrupted Efim, "if you're here to get me to subscribe twice for the same loan, you can leave now and not waste any more of your time."

"Fima," said Lyalya in a loud voice, "calm down and get hold of yourself. I can call Comrade Degtyar down here. He already predicted what your attitude would be."

Efim went up to the door, opened it wide, and pointed to the courtyard: "Leave," he said.

Lyalya stood motionless. Efim repeated: "I'm asking you nicely: leave."

"Fimochka," said Lyalya with sadness in her eyes, "I'm not angry at you. And what I said about Degtyar, that was a stupid joke. I'll come by again tomorrow morning."

"Good," Efim agreed, "but remember, no later than six, or I won't be here."

That evening, a little after ten, Comrade Degtyar, Orlov, and Stepa Khomitsky dropped by for a cup of tea at Efim's. They had brought a bottle of Moldavian wine with them, but Efim refused any because his liver had been acting up.

"Your liver is acting up," said Comrade Degtyar jestingly. "But we should not have to suffer too!"

Efim put the teapot on the electric hot plate. Iona Ovseich asked how he paid the Cheperukhas for electricity, since they were on the same meter and it was easier to pull out a person's wisdom tooth than get a kopeck out of Katerina. Efim replied that he dealt solely with Zinovy, who would rather give away his own money than take someone else's, and his relationship with his wife was their own private business.

"Granik," said Comrade Degtyar, jokingly wagging his finger, "you're in a combative mood today."

Efim sat down at the table and spent a few seconds silently observing the spiral on the electric oven as it became red hot; Comrade Degtyar said that this was the way the old aristocrats had once sat by the fireplace in the rich homes of Odessa and watched the blazing coals, bewitched. The scholars explained this as atavism, that is, a return to the primeval social structure, when people had just learned how to make fire and would sit in a circle around the bonfire to protect themselves from the cruel frost. "But those fireplaces and bonfires don't interest us, we're up to our ears in our problems.

"Efim," said Comrade Degtyar, "I'm thinking of you in particular here: this morning the community pledge agent, Idaliya Orlov, came to see you, but her visit produced no results. She told us that you simply got out of bed on the wrong side. Stepa and I want to think so too, especially because the entire courtyard has subscribed, with the sole exception of you."

Drops of water rolled down the teakettle onto the red-hot spiral and hissed loudly, startling everyone.

Stepa said that you had to wipe things well before putting them on the hot plate: residue could form and damage the coil and right now you couldn't get hot plates at any price.

Lyalya took a cloth from the back of the chair on which the hot plate was sitting, carefully wiped the teapot, then shook the cloth and put it back.

"Well," said Comrade Degtyar, "are we going to play mum or what?"

Efim lowered his head so far that the guests could see his glossy bald spot, which was round as a saucer; then he carefully scratched a green spot on the oilcloth with a finger.

"Efim Granik," said Comrade Degtyar, "your guests might think that you're on a sit-down strike."

Efim raised his head, looked at Degtyar with his Tartar eyes, and pretended to be surprised: if his guests were there to drink tea, there was no hurry, they had the whole night ahead of them; the teapot was finally boiling, but if it was too slow for anyone, they could write a collective complaint to the power plant.

"You're playing the fool again," said Comrade Degtyar, striking the table. "Orlov, hand me the subscription list. Put him down for fifty rubles and just let him try to say no!"

"No!" shouted Efim, shaking his head as if struck by electricity. "And don't you dare call me a fool or I'll kill you!"

Iona Ovseich automatically leaned back, turning very pale. Lyalya covered her cheeks with her hands. Stepa asked everyone to calm down, they were getting themselves worked up over nothing. But Efim was furious and began shouting that for the many years he'd lived there, Degtyar had been threatening people and trying to intimidate them day and night! And on what basis, who had given him the right?

"Listen to this ex-camp prisoner!" cried Iona Ovseich, brandishing a fist. "Did they put you there by mistake? No, they let you out by mistake!"

The Cheperukhas began to knock on their side of the wall as a signal for them to speak more quietly before they woke the children up. Stepa went over to Efim, took him by the shoulders, and sat him down.

"Stepa," repeated Efim in a quivering voice, "I ask of you: on what basis, who gave him the right?"

Iona Ovseich had finally regained his self-control. His color had returned and he began to speak slowly, quietly, as if to himself.

"The entire nation, from one end of the country to the other, has enthusiastically subscribed to the new loan. Only one person in 190 million has said no. And that one person is Efim Granik from our courtyard."

"Stepa," said Efim in a tearful voice, "why he is trying to turn everything around? I subscribed at the Marti factory and he knows that very well!"

"Stop pretending!" shouted Lyalya. "Everyone subscribed where he works, but this is where we live. Even housewives who never earn any money have subscribed, by economizing on family expenses, and you don't have to do that."

"In other words," said Efim, narrowing his eyes as tears emerged from their inside corners, "it's my fault that the Nazis killed my wife and my children, and that Lizochka likes it better at Tosya's than at her own father's?"

Lyalya was about to answer when Iona Ovseich interrupted: "Orlov, what you said was wrong. Guilt is guilt, but calamity is something else. The point is that when Granik, who was in prison for more than two years, returned home and found his apartment occupied by other people, he wasn't left out on the street; on the contrary, he was given living space in the home of an officer, a disabled veteran; he was given a job in one of the leading factories, and now the factory committee is planning to give him a room with all conveniences in the ship repairmen's settlement."

"Degtyar," said Efim putting his arms around himself and drawing his head into his shoulders, "I was born and grew up in Odessa, and all my life, until I was sent to the front, I had my own room, my own little corner. Now they're promising me a room again. Inform the factory that I've refused to subscribe to the loan in my courtyard and let them give the room to someone else who just arrived from Valegotsulov yesterday and deserves it more than I do. I don't care. But don't try to intimidate me, for God's sake, don't try to intimidate me: I don't need anything—I can live, I can die, and I can rise up out of the grave and go to work. Lizochka is doing fine at Tosya's. She doesn't want to be a Jew. She wants to wear a cross, like Tosya. I tell her not to, but she still does it anyway because her father is a nothing now, a nobody."

"Efim," interrupted Comrade Degtyar, "you're missing the point here."

"No, Comrade Degtyar," said Efim, his voice hoarse as if from great exhaustion, "I want people to stop pressuring me and let me live whatever I've got left in peace."

Iona Ovseich was silent for a minute, inhaled loudly, then exhaled. "What can I tell you, Granik? Only the grave can straighten the hunchback. All your life you were a private trader, and today, though you work at a factory, you're still a private trader in your heart of hearts. However, you will live according to our rules, and not by your own: we're not in the Sahara."

The guests rose but Efim asked them to wait: the tea would be ready in a minute, but only Khomitsky stayed for a moment. Degtyar and Orlov left the room without even looking back. Out in the courtyard, when Stepa caught up with them, Lyalya suggested that the entire building declare a boycott on Efim Granik.

"Declaring it is one thing," said Iona Ovseich, "but who'll really carry it out? It's a stupid idea, Orlov."

Lyalya was insulted: why was it stupid? They boycotted her, why not Granik? The two things shouldn't be confused, Iona Ovseich said angrily. It was one thing before the war, and another today.

Stepa said, "Why rack your brains over it? Just leave it as it is: Granik is Granik, everyone knows that."

No, said Comrade Degtyar categorically. It wasn't just a question of Granik: a bad example would be set.

In the middle of the night Iona Ovseich's heart began to hurt badly. He took a piece of sugar, poured some validol on it, and put it in his mouth. It cooled his mouth but brought him no relief and a quarter of an hour later he repeated the process. The result was the same as before, and he had to take a nitroglycerin tablet. The pain soon abated, but his head felt hot, and there was a loud ringing in his ears.

Iona Ovseich fell asleep just before dawn and it was a good thing that Lyalya rang his bell, otherwise he would have been late for work. As soon as Orlov stepped over the threshold, she could feel that something was wrong and insisted that Iona Ovseich get back in bed immediately, saying she'd call a doctor to come to the house. Iona Ovseich refused and sat down at the table to drink a glass of tea. He poured one for Lyalya and buttered a piece of bread for her. While she ate, he asked her to write a report about the pledge drive today so he would have a complete picture of the courtyard's response by that evening.

During the conversation he felt nausea twice rising in his throat. Lyalya again insisted that he go to bed, but was told to stop badgering him.

Comrade Degtyar was at the factory by eight o'clock, and an ambulance pulled up to the gate at ten. The doctor went up to the second-floor party office, and a minute later sent the orderlies for a stretcher. Degtyar asked to be given an injection, saying he'd rest and it would all pass. The doctor gave him the injection, but there was no noticeable improvement. The orderlies spread out the stretcher and helped Degtyar move from the couch. They pulled him up toward the top of the stretcher so that his legs would not dangle, then carried him out the door.

Before leaving for her shift, Lyalya phoned Comrade Degtyar. The party office informed her that he had been taken to the hospital by ambulance two hours earlier. Everything went cold inside Lyalya.

Mechanically she hung up the receiver, having even forgotten to ask what hospital he had been taken to. She had to call again.

Degtyar had been brought to the therapeutic section of the Stalin District Hospital on Yaroslavsky Street, corner of Karl Marx. Lyalya tried to telephone the hospital, but the number was constantly busy. Her heart in her throat, she raced on foot to the hospital.

The first floor of the large gray building (a former high school) was occupied by the district polyclinic, and therapy was on the second floor in an area separated from the staircase by a plywood partition. Usually there was a nurse on duty by the staircase whom visitors could come to terms with, but as luck would have it, she wasn't there now, and right in front of everyone Lyalya clambered over the railing, went up the other side of the staircase past the plywood partition, and had no problem finding the right ward.

She didn't even have to look for it because Lyalya immediately ran into Comrade Degtyar, who, along with the other new arrivals, had been temporarily placed in the corridor, since there were no free beds in the wards. Comrade Degtyar noticed her first and of course could tell everything by her appearance: her disheveled hair, flushed cheeks, breathlessness. Before she could say a word, he had expressed his indignation and annoyance, saying that his pulse had begun to beat faster from the excitement. Lyalya was ready to fall to her knees if only he would calm down; she held her hands clasped together in front of her as if she were in church and the service was about to begin.

The other patients in the corridor could do nothing but observe the scene. Women, men, three or four of them with bedpans in their hands, came out of the wards and also stopped. Iona Ovseich demanded that Orlov leave at once and never set foot in there again, but instead of obeying him immediately, she bent over his bed, tucked in the dangling sheet, tidied the corner of the blanket, and then took his hand and held it in hers. Iona Ovseich was too weak to resist. All the other patients were on Lyalya's side, saying such a considerate wife was a rarity nowadays and he should count his blessings, and not be capricious and grumble.

Iona Ovseich narrowed his eyes in order not to see, the situation was awkward enough already. Lyalya quickly took advantage of this, kissed him on the forehead, then loudly, as if speaking to a child, told him to obey the doctor and in no ease to get up out of bed; she would arrange things with the nurse.

Iona Ovseich was about to quote the saying that a well-meaning fool is more dangerous than an enemy, but he had to remain silent, otherwise this torture might have gone on forever.

Before leaving, Lyalya fluffed up the mattress at his feet to help his circulation, again told him to behave himself, and said that tomorrow morning she would bring him a food package and check up on him. Iona Ovseich's eyes were still closed. Lyalya quickly made a small sign of the cross over herself and quietly tiptoed away.

When Lyalya ran into the courtyard for a minute and told people the news, it caused a great stir: if Comrade Degtyar had agreed to be hospitalized, that meant it was no joking matter. Everyone knew about Granik and the loan pledge, but no one had thought it would have had such a serious effect on Comrade Degtyar. Klava Ivanovna shook her gray head, saying that for thirty odd years everyone had gotten used to thinking Degtyar was made of iron; Degtyar could take anything, withstand anything.

Olya Cheperukha and Katerina were one voice in agreeing that the full responsibility for it all fell on Efim Granik, who had pushed a man to the edge of his grave over fifty rubles; now, of course, Granik was secretly rejoicing. But, on the other hand, Comrade Degtyar was himself to blame: if, five years ago, when Granik was released from the camp, Iona Ovseich had stuck to his guns and not agreed to let Granik have a piece of the outpost, he wouldn't be paying such a high price today.

Iona Cheperukha brandished his fists. "Your mud-slinging makes me ashamed in front of the neighbors."

Olya screamed at her husband in reply that he was an unlucky drayman, he had been born a drayman and would die a drayman, and didn't care about his family or his grandchildren.

Zinovy was just finishing his diploma project. Everything had been arranged at home to free him from any unnecessary cares, and Iona Cheperukha had barely exchanged a word with anyone in his family lately. On Saturday, he had a few drinks as in the old days, and insisted he take Grisha and Misha for the day to the market and the zoo. Olya pressed both her grandsons to her, pointed at their grandfather, and replied that they had no reason to go to the zoo, they had their own zoo at home.

At first the boys stood calmly and watched it all attentively, then suddenly tore free and ran to their grandfather, clinging to him from either side. Old Cheperukha rested a thick-fingered hand on their heads and narrowed his eyes; tears flowed down his cheeks as he said in a drunken voice: "If you only knew how your grandpa's soul aches. Oh, how it aches!"

Efim had not returned home for the third day in a row. No one was particularly surprised, until Colonel Landa began to worry. He said that given Granik's unstable mind, anything could have happened. Gizella told him not to interfere, but not only did he defend Granik, was ready to criticize and blame Degtyar, even though he was in the hospital suffering from a possible myocardial infarct.

Stepa called the ship repair yard and learned that Granik had not been at work for two days. Colonel Landa advised them to call the police, and promised to make inquiries at the morgue. The morgue reported that they had some unidentified bodies, but none fit the description the colonel provided.

On Sunday morning Dina Vargaftik went to the Old Horse Market to buy a lap dog. Recently, especially in the evenings, she had found it impossible to be alone in the apartment. Dina had spent a long time looking around when she suddenly spotted Efim by a cage of green parrots. He was unshaven and dirty, wearing some kind of winter cap with a Red Army star on it. His eyes as he looked at the birds, were enough to drive a person mad. At first Dina was afraid to go up to him, but then she took herself in hand, came up from behind him without his noticing, and called his name softly: "Fimochka!" He trembled all over, as if he had been clubbed on his back. The salespeople and customers standing nearby began to laugh, but Dina could hardly bear the painful sadness of seeing him like that. Without even knowing what she was doing, Dina decided to lie: "Fima, if you only knew how much Lizochka is crying. She keeps asking where her father is. You would not act like this if you knew. Is the child to blame?"

Efim stood next to her for a moment. She waited for him to answer, but he did not utter a single word. Then he turned his back to her and headed for the gate that led to Dukovsky Park.

Dina was so upset by this encounter that she forgot why she was there at the market in the first place, and she left.

When Tosya Khomitsky heard all the details, she said that it was no accident that it was just today that Dina had gone to the market to buy herself a dog and met Efim there. The dog was a good omen.

Dina brushed that idea aside and blushed a deep red. "Tosya, sometimes you say things that are just absolutely sickening."

Now the residents of the courtyard were worried, and almost everyone agreed with Lyalya Orlov that the only one really suffering was Degtyar, who had almost paid with his life. Colonel Landa visited the patient, acquainted himself with the facts of Degtyar's illness, spoke with the doctor in charge, and declared that Ovseich had suffered ordinary angiospasms and had a small stroke. "If you do not wear out your nerves and those of others, a person can last another twenty years with an illness like that," he said to Degtyar.

"Landa," sighed Comrade Degtyar, "listening to you, I'm beginning to suspect myself that there's some kind of sham going on."

"Ovseich," answered the colonel, "don't split hairs. I said you have to take care of your nerves and not create any unnecessary problems for yourself."

"Create unnecessary problems?" said Comrade Degtyar. "Who'd do that?"

Colonel Landa laughed and said: "Right now it's you who creates them, Degtyar, and as a doctor I forbid you to harm the health of a Soviet man."

"Yes, Comrade Colonel of the medical corps!" said Iona Ovseich, narrowing his eyes, the pupils, black as bull's eyes, clearly visible.

The next morning the concierge, Fenya Lebedev, was summoned urgently to the police station to see an inspector. A man in civilian clothes stared at her and asked whether she knew a certain Efim Lazarevich Granik. Instead of answering immediately, Lebedev brought her fingers to her mouth, chewed on them, then cried: "Did he commit suicide?"

The inspector said no, he was alive, then asked her why she had thought he might have killed himself? Fenya replied that she didn't think that, she was just worried about him, that was all. Fine, said the inspector with a nod but she had not mentioned any other possibility, just that one: that Granik had committed suicide. Why?

Fenya was silent for a minute, then replied that all the neighbors had said that Granik was a little touched even before the war, but she hadn't lived in that courtyard before the war. They should go ask the people who had lived there back then. The inspector stared at her as he had at the beginning when she had just come in, and said that Granik was in the hospital, Slobodka, in critical condition. They had found him in Dukovsky Park where he had tried to hang himself.

That same day and the next, the police summoned Orlov, Khomitsky, Dina Vargaftik, and Klava Ivanovna. Each was spoken with individually. The inspector warned them to tell nothing but the truth or else they would be held responsible for giving false testimony. However, no matter what approach the police took, it all came down to the fact that even since he was young Efim Granik had tried to stand out from average, normal people. A day later the police called Lyalya Orlov in for a second time but bothered no one again after that.

Although he felt somewhat better and could now move along the corridor himself, Comrade Degtyar had not, of course, been informed of Efim's latest trouble. On the contrary, Lyalya told him that the entire yard without exception had subscribed to the new loan, and told him a white lie about Efim: Malaya had taken Lizochka by the hand and they had gone to visit Efim together and, finally, his civic conscience had been touched.

However, no matter how much they tried to cover it up, one day Comrade Degtyar was discharged from the hospital and found out the whole truth. He had gone to see Landa to ask for his help in getting a new medicine, pantocrine, which the drugstores still had trouble obtaining. Landa made no definite promises, but said that he would talk with his people, then suddenly switched the subject to Efim Granik, as if Iona Ovseich had been kept completely posted.

Comrade Degtyar said that this was the first time he had heard the real truth; moreover, the entire story said a great deal about all those who were involved. And what was most important, of course, was the action taken by Granik himself: whether he intended to kill himself or not, there could be no doubt about his real motivation.

"I don't understand," said Colonel Landa.

"Sapienti sat, Landa," Iona Ovseich raised himself, leaning his

palms on the table. "A word to the wise is sufficient. You studied Latin, you ought to remember."

"Ovseich," said Colonel Landa in a commanding tone, "please speak with me in Russian. What do you mean about motivation, if a person almost died and we were at fault?"

Comrade Degtyar leaned his head forward and glowered. His lips dropped at the corners, causing creases that ran to his chin: "Sometimes a second can decide a man's fate when he's crossing the trolley tracks. But if a person who has supposedly been persecuted tries to kill himself and immediately finds people to defend him, the only person who can view this as a happy coincidence is someone with a similar psychology."

"Ovseich," said Colonel Landa, turning pale as a sheet, "your illness has done you a good service, but don't abuse it."

"What illness?" Comrade Degtyar was surprised. "You've already made your diagnosis: if I don't get on other people's nerves, you guarantee me another forty years!"

"Not forty, twenty," the colonel corrected him, "but of course I was exaggerating."

Iona Ovseich drew an arc in the air with his finger and said, "It's not for you, Dr. Landa, to grant me an indulgence in matters of my health and life! We can manage without you."

Two days later Colonel Landa called Comrade Degtyar and asked him to come see him at the military hospital on Chicherin Street near Shevchenko Park on his way home from work: he had the pantocrine for him.

When he arrived at the colonel's office, a senior nurse handed Iona Ovseich a bottle, saying that pantocrine was a strong drug, and best taken under hospital conditions. Iona Ovseich was surprised. What did that mean, best?

If he had to take it in the hospital, he would, but if he could take it as an outpatient, then that's what he would do.

The nurse shrugged her shoulders. Appearing slightly confused, she began dealing with other tasks.

A day later Anya Kotlyar and Adya went to Slobodka to see Efim. They were not allowed into the ward, but the patient himself was able to come to the window and lower a rope, to which they attached a parcel. He stood by the window for a while and spoke with his visitors. The conversation with Efim didn't last long. All questions were about his health, and it ended by his simply putting his head out the window, looking silently at Anya and Adya, and smiling a bit crazily.

On Sunday after Lizochka had done her homework for Monday, Anya wanted to take her with her to Slobodka, but Tosya couldn't decide whether that was a good idea and it was postponed for another time. Anya went again with Adya and near the hospital they unexpectedly ran into Zinovy. When they arrived, all the doors were closed and they were completely at a loss as to what to do.

They eventually found an open door and proceeded. As soon as he opened the ventilation window on his door, Efim waved warmly to Zinovy and said that Iona Cheperukha had recently come to see him. Efim said nothing concerning his health, except that it could be worse; they could not drag another word out of him. Zinovy tried his best to rouse Efim, calling on him to behave like he used to when he was a young man. Anya also tried to rouse his spirits but all their efforts were to no avail, which only made them all the more depressed.

They returned to the city on a number 15 trolley and were silent almost the entire way. They began talking on Lutheran Lane near the Lutheran church. Anya said that what she feared most was Efim's discharge homecoming. The courtyard would have a variety of opinions, but Degtyar, of course, would want to prove that he was right and would try to force everyone to think as he did.

Anya was absolutely right this time, Zinovy agreed. He added that Degtyar would still be looking for Granik's accomplices and no doubt would find them.

"Well," said Zinovy, "then he should start with me."

"What kind of stupid joke is that!" said Anya indignantly. "You think because you lost a leg at the front that you can do whatever you want and get away with it!"

Zinovy was about to reply, but Anya grabbed him by the hand and asked him to keep quiet. They were making so much noise that the passengers had begun looking at them. Adya began to laugh, saying that the statistics gathered by the proper authorities have shown that trolley passengers have good eyesight and good hearing.

Anya tapped Adya's lips with her fingers. Zinovy quickly covered his mouth with his hands as if afraid he'd be given the same treatment.

"Boys, boys," Anya sighed heavily. Tears came to her eyes, and she turned toward the window. "I'm ready to die ten times over if only you both could be happy."

Adya grew indignant: "We don't want happiness that costs someone his life!"

They got off the trolley on Tiraspolsky Square. Zinovy resumed the conversation and said: "Anyway, Lyalya Orlov and Dina Vargaftik aren't the only ones in the courtyard. Colonel Landa lives there too."

"And so what?" said Anya with a shrug. "Landa's a big shot in his hospital. He has power—over his patients."

Iona Ovseich had been kept posted from the first about those who paid visits to Granik and he knew how to evaluate the information: it was enough to see who went to visit Granik to draw the obvious conclusion. Stepa Khomitsky and Malaya held another opinion. It was good that people didn't forget their neighbor and were concerned about him. Comrade Degtyar listened closely and said he could only marvel at how willing people were to blindfold themselves if only to have a little peace of mind. They had already had them in their courtyard, Lapidis and Nastya Sereda, and Kotlyar, one right after the other. All kinds of scum like the Mikhoelses, and Katsnelsons were still in hiding today, and people just refused to look past the ends of their noses.

Sometimes Comrade Degtyar would lose all patience and was even ready to compare the activists with animals in harness and said they needed blinders so they would keep to the straight way and not look off to the sides.

The hospital gave notice that Granik would be discharged in a few days. Tosya decided to go with Anya to pick up Efim and take Lizochka along. But everything fell apart at the last moment: Lizochka became hysterical and said that she did not want to go to Slobodka, to that madhouse full of crazy people.

"Liza," said Anya indignantly, "you're a big girl now, but you're behaving like a little fool!"

Liza refused to yield, saying, no, she was not a little fool: everyone in the courtyard—Lesik and Zina and Grandma Biryuk and Grandma Olya and Aunt Katya—they all said that there was a madhouse in Slobodka.

"They're lying!" cried Anya, and stamped her foot. "Your papa had surgery, and they're nasty, unscrupulous people!"

Lizochka's face turned blue and her lips began to tremble. Even though Tosya understood that she should not do this at this moment, she instinctively pressed Lizochka to herself, took her head in her hands, and put her cheek next to hers.

In the end, both women refused to make the trip and decided to entrust the task to the men. Since Zinovy was extremely busy, Iona Cheperukha and Adya went. On the way Iona stopped by the wine cellar on the corner of Degtyarny and Tiraspolskaya streets. He and Adya drank a glass each and grabbed a bottle for Efim. Adya was against it for a man just out of the hospital, but Iona replied that a little wine was always good for a man.

It turned out, as old Cheperukha had predicted: they were barely past the gate when Efim himself suggested dropping by the Slobodsky Bazaar.

"Fima," said Iona, pounding his fists on his chest, "do you think I'd come empty-handed on a day like this! Your best friend wouldn't insult you like that for anything in the world!"

When everyone had drunk his share, Efim and Iona hugged each other hard and kissed, and wanted to do the same with Adya, but he turned aside.

"Adenka," said Efim and began to weep, "you ran and played in the courtyard with my boy Osya. Who could have ever foreseen all this then: where is my Osya now!"

Adya was about to reply: "Where are my mama and my papa now?" but Cheperukha interrupted to insist that they remember only the good, because you didn't get anything out of remembering the bad except more heartache.

They returned from the bazaar to the city on foot. On Frunze Street by the Matrossky Slope, where the narrow, winding road rises steeply, Efim suddenly became capricious and asked that they turn right, toward Dukovsky Park.

Cheperukha was surprised: "Dukovsky Park? For what? Before the Revolution it was a bandit's hideout. The famous thief Vanka Klyuchnik used to hide there in the catacombs with his gang! Anyway, why do you want to go out of your way?"

Efim stood as if rooted to the spot and looked down at the ground.

"Adya," said Cheperukh, seeking support, "am I right or wrong?"

Adya answered yes, he was right, but you could also understand why Efim would want to walk through Dukovsky Park.

"That's a stupid philosophy!" said Iona angrily. "I always thought you were a smart person, but it turns out I was wrong."

Efim didn't want to listen to any more of their squabbling and began slowly following the sewer ditch which ran from Frunze Street all the way to Peresyp. Adya walked beside old Cheperukha, saying that a person needed a safety valve otherwise sooner or later the boiler might blow.

"Son," said Iona, smiling bitterly, "what boiler can take as much pressure as a person."

Dukovsky Park was empty. Transparent vapor rose from the marshy pond. A weeping willow draped its long branches over the black water and a crow was watching them with one eye and with great interest and curiosity, as if expecting that they would do more than they already were.

"Efim," said Cheperukha, "it's time we went home, instead of wandering around like a bunch of tramps."

A freight train rumbled down the railroad embankment. On the bridge it reduced its speed, and it seemed possible to count the cars by the clack of their wheels. Iona and Adya listened raptly until suddenly they noticed, both at the same moment, that Efim had disappeared.

"Fima!" cried Cheperukha, clutching his head. "Fima!"

They ran up to the railroad fence. There was a break at one point in the fence. Adya dashed through and carefully looked around, but there wasn't a soul as far as the eye could see. He came back, clambered up onto the fence, rose to his full height, then onto tiptoe, and finally spotted Efim. He was motionless, resting his forehead against a tree, his cap in his hand. To an outsider he might have just seemed drunk. Adya made a sign to old Cheperukha to keep calm as if nothing special had happened, but Iona was already running like a bear, breaking branches on the way.

"Efim," called Cheperukha with his drayman's voice, "now I can tell you, you're nothing but a son of a bitch! We almost had a heart attack, and you're standing there with your forehead against a tree as if nothing was wrong. Look at people when they're talking to you!"

Efim turned, his eyes blank as a child's who is blind from birth. His brows were raised, his yellow forehead all furrowed.

"I don't want to live in this world. My strength is gone," he said softly.

"Write up a statement," Iona shouted, "and hand it in to the office in heaven. He doesn't want to live, it's too hard for him, but the rest of us are living in clover. You mother-fucker, I'll strangle you with my own hands. I still have strength enough to kill three Graniks!"

Iona went right up to Efim, put his arm around him, cursed him a few more times, then led him down the slope. Adya hung back a couple of steps and, head thrown back, looked at the sky: one after another, white clouds, enormous as fantastic beasts, floated by, all headed for the sea. From the port the wind bore the deep bass voices of steamships, which also seemed to issue from a fantastic beast. Cheperukha stopped for a minute, inhaled, and said: "Anyone who tries to kill himself should be shot on the spot. God, we don't know to appreciate life!"

It was dark when they returned home. They met Stepa at the gate. He said that a celebration was needed for an occasion like this but Iona suggested postponing it for another time since, right after leaving the hospital, Efim had gone for a stroll across the entire city and was extremely tired.

Iona Cheperukha spent the night at Zinovy's. He tossed and turned until morning, listening to every rustle behind the wall at Granik's. Before leaving for work, Iona dropped by to see him. They drank a cup of tea together, walked to Tiraspolsky Square together, and took a number 2 trolley to Peresyp. Iona had to go back to Red Guard Street, and in five minutes Efim was already at the factory.

That evening Comrade Degtyar notified Stepa and Lyalya that at eight o'clock on Saturday there would be a general meeting of all courtyard residents. The agenda was the following: 1) summary of the subscription campaign, 2) other questions. Khomitsky and Orlov were responsible for attendance at the meeting.

Degtyar and the others invited Madame Malaya for a preliminary conversation, but instead of lending her clear, unambiguous support, she began to dodge the issue, then asked that the question of Granik not be raised. Because of his old friendship with Efim, Stepa was prepared to support Malaya, and it took considerable effort on Degtyar's part to convince them that Granik had no enemies here, it was all being done for his own good: no one considered Granik ill or unfortunate, and you had to talk with him normally as with anyone else.

Although no names had been mentioned in the announcement, everyone guessed who the hero of the day would be. Lyalya was chosen to gather signatures on a petition requesting the meeting. On the first evening she encountered no particular problems. Only Marina Biryuk bristled and categorically refused to sign. Lyalya asked what this meant: was Marina against the meeting as such or did she simply not want to sign? But Orlov couldn't get a clear answer from Marina. Iona Ovseich said: "We won't insist—the goat will come home by itself."

However a real conflict broke out the next day when Colonel Landa found out about the impending meeting. The colonel not only refused to sign the list, but took it from Lyalya and headed straight for Comrade Degtyar's. Iona Ovseich had not yet returned from the factory. Late that evening Colonel Landa called on him a second time and this time found him at home. Lyalya Orlov was there, having already informed Degtyar about everything.

Degtyar's first question to Dr. Landa was: who had given him the right to take the law into his own hands—to take an official document away from a representative of the community? Colonel Landa did not reply to the question, but he posed a question of his own: who had given Ovseich the right to blacklist Granik and to make a mockery of a sick, unfortunate man?

"Blacklist!" said Comrade Degtyar loudly, veins swelling on his forehead. "You had to choose an example from the history of dictatorial Rome! Our Odessa cosmopolitans Professor Rosenthal and Professor Zeiliger can be proud. Reinforcements have arrived!"

"Don't try to provoke me!" said Colonel Landa, pounding his fist on the table. "I am a doctor and I will not permit you to torment a person who is hanging by a thread as it is. In 1940 you almost ruined Orlov's life, but today . . ."

"That's none of your business!" interrupted Lyalya. "I got what I had coming. People like me should have been sent to Siberia—"

"Stop talking nonsense!" said Colonel Landa, losing his temper. "As for Granik, I repeat: he's a sick man with a sick mind, and I will inform the Stalin District Committee about the injustice that is about to be committed here! They can send a commission and see for themselves; then we'll speak further."

Colonel Landa tossed the list on the table and left the room, but returned in a second and warned them that if Orlov did not stop going around to people's apartments, he would follow her.

"That's understandable," said Iona Ovseich, "we choose patients who suit us because we have a common disease."

"Ovseich," said the colonel, leaning forward, while Degtyar remained in place as if both legs were rooted to the floor, "you are losing all sense of proportion."

When the door had slammed, Lyalya went over to it and pulled the doorknob with all her might, as if wishing to vent her anger and said: "We've lived in the same building for so many years, and yet I just don't know him at all."

Iona Ovseich turned on the radio: they were broadcasting the latest news. Lyalya sat down on the couch, unbuttoned her jacket to make it easier to breathe, moved her knees close together, and pulled her skirt down. Iona Ovseich watched, but all his attention was riveted to the radio.

A report from Lower Tagil said that the Ural metallurgists were very interested in studying the brilliant work by Comrade Stalin, *Marxism and Linguistic Problems.* A report on "base and superstructure" was given at a recent seminar by the steel worker Fedor Antipov, who had personally made forty-two suggestions on ways to streamline production, seventeen of which had already been put into practice. His innovations had resulted in a net saving of around one hundred thousand rubles. A furnace worker, Khariton Kuzyakin, also gave a report on his own personal contribution to technical progress: nine ideas that had been put into practice with a net saving of seventy-six thousand two hundred rubles.

Lyalya rested her head on the bolster and put one leg on the couch. Iona Ovseich signaled her to put both legs on the couch, otherwise she'd be uncomfortable. Lyalya shook her head. Iona Ovseich waited until the announcer moved from world news to sports, then he took matters into his own hands. Her leg was big, with a large calf and slightly protruding veins, but he lifted it easily and put it next to her other leg. Then he sat by her side, and said: "Orlov, when I listen to the radio, I can't help envying the people in the Urals, Siberia, the Volga. In comparison with us, they're like the three heroes in the painting by the famous artist Vasnetsov."

Lyalya yawned automatically, then immediately ashamed, she tapped her lips and said she did not agree—things always seemed bigger from a distance. On the contrary, said Iona Ovseich with a sly squint, things looked smaller from a distance. But now it was really something else that mattered: petty things were disappearing, and only the grand remained.

"But about the meeting," said Iona Ovseich, "I think we should wait a little."

"Because of Landa?" said Lyalya in surprise.

"Yes, because of him too," said Iona Ovseich. "That's enough games with him for now."

Lyalya shuddered. "He's repulsive, he and his Gizella."

The lights went off. The building across the way also went dark, its windows black, as if it were uninhabited. Then little lights began to appear—candles, kerosene lamps, and pocket flashlights which seemed to scurry by themselves back and forth about the rooms.

Lyalya straightened her jacket in front, rose slightly, and placed her hand behind her back; apparently her bra was too tight. The springs squeaked loudly, and Iona Ovseich said that he would have to have the couch repaired. Lyalya said nothing. Iona Ovseich nudged her thigh with his elbow. For a minute complete silence reigned. He nudged her a second time, then said: "Orlov, you have to be at work early tomorrow—it's time *nach Hause.*"

Lyalya remained silent. Iona Ovseich waited a few seconds, then repeated what he had said, but this time without a bantering tone: "Orlov, it's time for you to go home. I want to go to sleep."

In a flash Lyalya had jumped up, grabbed her coat from the hanger, and left without saying good-bye.

"Orlov," Comrade Degtyar shouted after her, "good night."

At home she went to bed with her clothes on and could not fall asleep for a long time. In the dark colored images floated by in front of her eyes—red, green, violet—her gaze unintentionally followed them; then she felt like erasing everything so that only darkness would remain. Her heart was empty and heavy.

Lyalya did not go to see Iona Ovseich again for the rest of the week. In the evening she sometimes seemed to hear someone knocking quietly at her door. Several times she went to open it but there never was anyone on the landing. On Saturday evening she baked two large pies—one with cottage cheese and the other with apples, to which she added a spoonful of cherry jam. She decided to bring them to the widower, who never thought about himself and didn't take care of himself. As she climbed the stairs to the third floor, her legs were shaky and there was an unpleasant weakness in her arms; she had to hold the plates with all her strength so as not to drop them.

Iona Ovseich greeted her warmly and thanked her for the pies, immediately adding that he was going to have to open his own pastry shop: just yesterday Dina Vargaftik had brought him a pumpkin pie. By the way, it had come out quite well, Lyalya should try it. Lyalya broke off a little piece, put it in her mouth, chewed it, and made a face. She forced herself to swallow it and immediately demanded a glass of water.

"Women, women," said Iona Ovseich, shaking his head. "It's amazing how hard it is to get along with you."

They cut Lyalya's apple pie first. Iona Ovseich took a little piece, then another, and honestly admitted that he had never eaten a pie that good.

Deeply embarrassed, Lyalya blushed, and told Comrade Degtyar to button his lip and not make fun of her.

"Orlov," said Iona Ovseich, "when I look at you, I have to admire you: with your face and your figure you can still find yourself a captain."

Lyalya thought for a second, her eyes becoming deep and sad. Then she answered: "There is one captain, but he passes right by me and never even notices me."

"Who is this blind ass?" said Iona Ovseich in surprise. "Do I know him?"

"You know him," said Lyalya, shaking her head. "Of course, you do, Captain Degtyar."

Iona Ovseich laughed, scratched his chin, and said that they had played a nice scene, like an old operetta.

Lyalya answered yes, it was just like a merry old operetta, and then, quietly, sadly, she began to sing: "Our life is only a play, and you've played out your role long ago."

Comrade Degtyar frowned and said that it was time to change the record, this one was too monotonous.

Lyalya passed her handkerchief over her eyes, shook her hair, and squinting, said: "Yes, Captain, you're right: too monotonous and vulgar."

Iona Ovseich cut himself a little piece of the cheese pie; several crumbs fell on the tablecloth. He picked them up and automatically put them in his mouth.

Lyalya sighed and said: "You're like a little boy. It's impossible to really get mad at you."

Iona Ovseich finished his piece of pie, then praised the cheese pie even more than the apple pie. Unexpectedly he asked why she didn't bring a pie like that one evening to Efim Granik.

"Granik?" said Lyalya, surprised.

Iona Ovseich said, yes, Granik. What was so unusual about that? In the end, he was a lonely man and from the outside it might seem that he had only one patron and protector left in the whole world—Dr. Landa. By the way, there was a nasty story going around about Landa in the hospital: a young man had died of appendicitis. Twenty years old.

"Twenty years old!" Lyalya was horrified.

Iona Ovseich compressed his lips: twenty. They had brought the young man in at night, but instead of immediately operating on him, they postponed it until the next morning, until the peritonitis attack.

"Bastards!" Lyalya whispered. "We're not people to them. To them we're just guinea pigs. The bastards!"

"Orlov," said Comrade Degtyar, "don't generalize. And as for Landa, I have a favor to ask: I don't want this story blown out of proportion in the courtyard."

Lyalya gave her word that she would not utter a word to anyone, but Iona Ovseich objected that a word is a word, but when you hear such things, you should try to keep them quiet.

Two days later, after nightfall, Lyalya went to see Efim with a present: a hot pie right out of the oven. He looked at it in surprise but his guest laughed and said: "Fima, if you are afraid of being poisoned, I can try it first."

There was a knife nearby and she asked him to hand it to her. She cut two pieces, and suggested that Efim pick the one he preferred. Since he showed no sign of initiative, she chose a piece herself, bit into it, and began to chew, squinting from pleasure.

Efim waited until his guest had swallowed what was in her mouth, then asked why she had come to see him.

"Why?" repeated Lyalya, insulted. "Fimochka, how can you ask such questions of a woman who came to see you on her own?"

"No," said Efim, "you're lying: you're not here on your own—Degtyar sent you."

"Degtyar?" exclaimed Lyalya. "A hundred Degtyars could send me here, but if I didn't want to come, they'd be beating their heads against the wall."

"Get out!" said Efim rudely. "Go spread your rumors around the whole courtyard, around the whole city, about Dr. Landa, who cripples and kills people in his hospital. Get out, you're wasting your time here."

"Good God," said Lyalya, clutching her cheeks, "you should rot in hell for talking like that!"

"You Freemason!" screamed Efim. "Get out of here. I can't bear the sight of you. You're always involved in one intrigue or another, as if it wasn't people you were dealing with but pigs: Granik, Landa, Ivanov, Petrov, Sidorov! Get out of here! And take this shit to hell with you!"

Efim grabbed the pie, wound up, and hurled it at the door.

When Lyalya had described the scene in detail, Comrade Degtyar gave no opinion but only asked what Orlov herself thought. Lyalya had difficulty finding the words immediately, but as for Granik's hooligan outburst, she had no doubt that he was simply taking advantage of his recent illness.

"No, Orlov," said Comrade Degtyar, "you're right, but not right enough. This is not just mere hooliganism, it runs much deeper than that: the intellectual Landa and the house painter Granik are together in this, as if they'd been dipping into the same well. At first glance, this might seem surprising, but anyone who knows their family background in some detail, and remembers how they each acted long before the war, won't be surprised."

Lyalya listened carefully, her brow furrowing, but every two seconds she would nod her head in agreement. However, when Iona Ovseich had finished, she admitted that she had not understood everything. One man had returned from the front a colonel, while the other one had been a POW; and it wasn't clear what he'd done to stay alive —how could you equate the two of them?

"Orlov," said Comrade Degtyar, bowing his head and staring at her, "and why don't you ask how it happened that the former Red partisan Joseph Kotlyar ended his days in Kolyma?"

Lyalya unintentionally lowered her eyes. Iona Ovseich ordered her to look him straight in the eye, but though Lyalya tried, she still could not force herself to.

Iona Ovseich bitterly twisted his lips and said, "If the front was a guarantee of how a person would act in peacetime, we would have avoided a lot of trouble in the 1920s, in the '30s, yes, and even today, right now."

After his release from the hospital Efim had visited Dr. Landa twice simply for the pleasure of being with old neighbors. Gizella offered Efim some refreshment, telling him not to be shy, but she didn't sit down at the table herself and went into the other room, leaving the colonel alone with the guest. On his second visit Efim asked Gizella straight out why she wouldn't sit down with them, but her only reply was not to get upset and take it to heart, a housewife always had too much to do.

When she had closed the door, Efim said: "Dr. Landa, your wife doesn't like me."

"Efim," replied the doctor, "you're imagining things."

"I'm not," said Efim. "I understand that a house painter and a military doctor who's almost a general, are not birds of a feather. But why bring it up every time?"

Colonel Landa was about to object again, but then dismissed the idea and poured himself and his guest a glass of vodka. They drank, then they each took a spoonful of pressed caviar, then repeated the process a second time. Their mood improved but their conversation still couldn't get off the ground.

"Dr. Landa," said Efim, quietly and bitterly, "explain something to me: people live almost their entire life in the same courtyard. They even know what kind of underpants the other one wears, if you'll pardon the expression, but when they get together they can't find anything to say to each other."

"Efim," said the colonel, opening a new bottle and pouring some into both their glasses, "what do words mean when the heart says everything. To your health!"

Efim smiled, but the sadness did not leave his eyes. He rose slowly from the table and said: "Dr. Landa, you know how to turn everything into a joke. That's enviable."

When saying good-bye, Efim thanked Dr. Landa for his warm hospitality and the company. The colonel invited him to drop by more often and not to stand on ceremony.

Fenya Lebedev was just finishing cleaning the courtyard. Efim walked by her and she asked if Dr. Landa was home, she had to bring him his rent receipt, that's why she was asking.

After unlocking his door, Efim thought a moment, turned toward the courtyard, and shouted to Lebedev:

"And what the hell business is it of yours where I've been! I go wherever I please and I don't a give a good goddamn about you! You can tell that to everyone."

"You're nuts!" Lebedev screamed in reply, and twirled her finger beside her temple.

When Iona Ovseich spoke again with Orlov about the warm friendship which had suddenly flared up between Granik and Landa, he could only repeat what he had said on the previous occasion: anyone who could remember the past a little would not be surprised. This time Lyalya did not object but even added something of her own: Granik was Granik, and Landa was Landa, but in their attitude toward Comrade Degtyar, they were one pair of shoes.

"Orlov," said Comrade Degtyar, clapping her on the back, "I can see you're beginning to understand dialectics from your own personal experience. Good work!"

The whole next week Iona Ovseich spent night and day at the factory: *Pravda* and the other newspapers reported that the Nineteenth Congress had been scheduled for the month of October. The first order of business was quickly to redo all visual propaganda—slogans, graphs, posters, diagrams—so that not only in every department, in every brigade, but in literally every workplace, people would remember and feel that from now on all life and all work would be part of the preparations for that historical event. At the same time the party bureau, administration, and factory committee called a meeting of the activists in which they reviewed concrete proposals and the entire collective's increased production obligations in honor of the forthcoming party congress. Everyone desired to take on as much as possible, and people frequently had to be restrained and reminded that they needed a real reason to assume new obligations. However, at the general meeting which took place in the factory yard under the open sky after the activists' conference, the workers demanded that their social obligations be genuinely increased, and they set their own figures and indexes.

In his reply, Comrade Degtyar thanked the working class, engineers and technicians, who created miracles and were successfully laying the foundation of communism, thus setting a clear example to the other socialist countries and the proletariat of the entire world.

In conclusion, the participants in the meeting made a decision to send a letter to Comrade Stalin, in which they assumed the obligation of fulfilling their nine-month program by September 20, and their annual one—by Stalin Constitution Day, the fifth of December.

After the activists' and the general meeting, Iona Ovseich invited the department heads to his office several times and posed the problem of their finding supplementary, hidden reserves, since the very first totals demonstrated convincingly that the collective was capable not only of fulfilling but also of overfulfilling the obligations they had assumed.

A similar picture was to be observed at the Krupskaya factory where Lyalya Orlov was now working and at Zinovy Cheperukha's factory, the Kirov. The rank and file knit-fabric and machine tool workers—the cogs without which the most complex contemporary machines could not work or operate—advanced their own plans and figures, by surpassing what had been suggested by the factory and plant management by one and a half, two, and three times. Zinovy had just been appointed department head. He met with his people, and, pencils in hand, they calculated that the third-quarter could be completed no later than September 15, and the program for the year—

by November 30, in other words, starting on December 1, the collective would begin work for the following year, 1953.

On his day off, Comrade Degtyar found a free minute and had a small meeting in his apartment. Orlov, Khomitsky, Marina Biryuk, Dina Vargaftik, Zinovy Cheperukha, and Katerina Cheperukha attended. Klava Ivanovna was also invited. Lyalya herself went to see her, but Malaya was totally out of sorts and kept harping on the same note: that she be told in secret who was in charge of the amateur theatricals and which numbers were included in the program. Lyalya said that there would be no amateur performance, just a business meeting. Klava Ivanovna gave her a cunning look and wagged her finger threateningly.

When Lyalya told those at the meeting what had happened, everyone laughed; on the other hand, it was a little sad—what time did to a person!—and the same thing was in store for us all. Iona Ovseich also smiled, but then immediately called everyone to order and said it was time to get down to business, every second mattered.

"Comrades," said Iona Ovseich, "we are to prepare a worthy reception to mark this great event in the life of the party and the whole nation, and motions have been made in that regard: number one, to organize a group to study the brilliant work by Comrade Stalin *Economic Problems of Socialism in the U.S.S.R.;* number two, to initiate a social improvement project, using the energy of the building's residents, that is everyone from every apartment, all of the courtyard's resources.

There was no need for explanations concerning the first proposal, a study group was a study group, but concerning the second, they could not limit themselves to one, albeit a general, formulation. Comrade Degtyar warned that it would be necessary to go into a certain amount of detail for that reason. Above all, the residents of the building were obliged to guard the premises itself as though it were the apple of their eye. "To be specific: don't knock down plaster in the hallway when moving furniture and other such items; be neat when using the lavatory common in the courtyard and in their apartments; be careful with window frames; be prompt in replacing glass in the rooms, corridors, and on balconies." Further, every tenant was obligated on a regular basis to do repairs on his residence and the communal kitchens and anterooms without waiting for a crisis to develop;

and other conveniences should be repaired together by the residents of the apartment, for which a responsible person should be selected in each commune.

"Now," said Comrade Degtyar, making a slight pause, "in regard to cleaning the anterooms, staircases, and hallways. Until now the building administration has maintained a special cleaning woman paid by the state. It's not difficult to calculate how much money that costs the city. But there is another aspect here, a moral one: can we accept as a norm that on the threshold of communism we need cleaning women to clean our own building? I ask you to speak out."

Lyalya Orlov and Marina Biryuk raised their hands at the same time. Marina had a question, she did not wish to speak, and Comrade Degtyar pointed to her, indicating she should go first. However, it turned out that Marina did not want to ask a question, but to deliver an entire lecture. Not only did she not ask a question but she began to explain to the others that the cleaning women were paid with a portion of their rent money and repairs, again, were apparently financed from that same source.

Iona Ovseich listened calmly and in reply asked a single question: how much personally did she, Marina Biryuk, pay for her apartment?

"How much do I pay?" repeated Marina, as if she hadn't quite heard. "One hundred twenty rubles. Plus sixty rubles for light and five hundred rubles a season for heat, which means, another forty–fifty rubles a month. And in the spring I put up new wallpaper and painted the windows, the doors, there's another fifteen hundred right there."

"Marina," said Lyalya Orlov in surprise, "perhaps you should figure in how much you spend on candy. I know you love sweets."

"I do," agreed Marina. "But what business is that of yours? You don't pay for me, do you?"

Lyalya said that she didn't, but there was no reason for Marina to play the fool and to count light, wallpaper, wood, coal, and her dresses into the rent.

"I don't want to talk to you anymore," Marina answered rudely. "You're not Madame Degtyar yet and you don't have to sign for others!"

Lyalya became furious. It seemed like a fight was about to start, but fortunately Comrade Degtyar was able to forestall it: "Marina Ignatevna," he turned to her, "if I have understood you correctly, you pay one hundred twenty rubles a month for your apartment. I assume your husband makes no less than three thousand, and as a bookkeeper, your take-home is more or less seven hundred rubles. Is that so?"

Marina stared with her usual grin at Comrade Degtyar. He waited a moment, then asked all those present to pool their strength to calculate how much one percent of three thousand seven hundred was and then to divide one hundred twenty by the result, which would be thirty-seven.

Without waiting for them to reply, Comrade Degtyar himself came up with the sum.

"So, it comes to three and two-tenth's percent. But in America, my dear Marina Ignatevna, the worker pays thirty percent for his apartment, that is, approximately ten times more."

"What does America have to do with this!" Marina threw up her hands in despair.

"I'll tell you, Citizen Biryuk," said Comrade Degtyar, raising his voice. "We can imagine how you would weep and wail if we proposed that you pay that same thirty percent, that is more than a thousand rubles a month!"

"When I was with my husband in Germany," said Marina, taking her own tack again, "we visited a German who had four rooms, and he was an ordinary engineer, and his wife stayed home with the children."

"Don't try to frighten us," said Iona Ovseich, raising his voice still higher. It was obvious he was losing his patience. "There are two Germanies: your husband was in the German Democratic Republic, where the power belongs to the workers, and not to John Pierpont Morgan, Jr., and Krupp von Bolen!"

"But why do we all have to waste our time on Marina Biryuk!" said Katerina, jumping up from her chair. "If she doesn't like it here, let her go to Germany or wherever else she wants. But to pretend that she's feeding the Soviet system at her expense—we've already seen these tricks. Enough!"

"Enough!" repeated Lyalya. "I earn eight hundred rubles a month and pay seventy for my room, and I would be ashamed to haggle like certain other people. In what other country would I get a room like that for seventy lousy rubles! A kilo of meat costs thirty rubles at the market. For the price of two kilos of meat a month, you can get an apartment. You could almost say we live free here, but people still find something to yap about! I suggest that the residents of the house themselves clean the corridors, staircases, and the rest, and that we don't need a cleaning woman."

"Does anybody else have an opinion?" asked Comrade Degtyar.

Dina Vargaftik said that everyone there had the same opinion, but other people lived in the building and it was necessary to talk with them too.

"Dina," said Lyalya jumping up, "if you and I go out to clean our own hall, will other people's conscience let them just walk by?"

Dina shrugged her shoulders and said let's see. Right now the only person they could be sure of was Katerina Cheperukha, because her door opened directly into the courtyard and she had no common corridors and hallways with anyone.

Katerina agreed that she had no common corridors or hallways, but on the other hand, she had a neighbor like Efim Granik, who threw cigarette butts and spat on the floor right next to the door.

Stepa Khomitsky got up: "Now as for the toilets. For thirty years now we've been talking and talking, but it's like beating your head against a wall. Yesterday again the trap got clogged up and the stuff plugging it up was the size of a horse's head—carrots, beets, cotton, newspapers, condoms—you might as well open up a department store."

The people at the meeting began to laugh, Marina louder than anyone else, and Stepa warned them that soon they'd call the commission from the epidemic station, then we would see how much laughing there'd be.

"Don't give warnings," Comrade Degtyar interrupted. "Bring people here and let them give fines; one hundred rubles, two hundred!"

Zinovy pointed out that they had digressed, but since they were already on the subject of sanitation, he wanted to bring in the example of Manchuria: the Chinese, especially during the Japanese occupation, lived a life of semi-starvation. Even in the large cities whole districts were without sewers, but things were as clean as they could be under the circumstances.

Iona Ovseich said why go all the way to China for an example if we have Leningrad, Riga, and right close by, Sevastopol.

"Oh," cried Lyalya, "I want to go to Leningrad!"

"We will," said Iona Ovseich, "and we'll see how our people are living so that we won't have to be ashamed before the Chinese; we can be ashamed before our own Leningraders. Then someone's face will be red."

"And someone's will be," said Stepa with a laugh, "but as for the toilets, we've been clogging them up for thirty years and we'll clog them up for thirty more!"

"Khomitsky," said Comrade Degtyar, "your laughter and skepticism are out of place here. However, there is another part to our obligation to work together for the preservation of the premises: we must designate a sanitation representative to the house commission from every floor. As chairman of the commission I recommend Comrade Katerina Cheperukha, who is a senior laboratory assistant at the vitamin factory, with Comrade Marina Biryuk as her deputy."

Although he had not proposed a vote, Iona Ovseich raised his hand, and the others raised theirs after him. Katerina declared that she couldn't do it, she was at work all day, and, on top of that, had children at home, but no one paid attention, not even Zinovy, and they held up their hands until Comrade Degtyar ordered them to put them down.

The next Monday the commission began to do its job. Katerina Cheperukha went around with Stepa Khomitsky to all the apartments, looked into corners where the housewives kept their garbage pails, and found that many of them seemed purposely to be creating ideal conditions for mice and rats. Even at Dr. Landa's they discovered a plywood box which contained a jumble of bread, sausage, and scraps of Dutch cheese. Gizella tried her best to justify herself, arguing that these were leftovers from yesterday which she hadn't had time to throw out yet. Katerina picked up the box which held a kilogram or two of food. She told Gizella that lying was one thing, but there were limits. All of a sudden Gizella began shouting; her face turned red with blue spots like a baboon's backside. She demanded that Stepa no longer bring these Parisians from Ulan-Ude into her home.

"Listen," said Katerina, "it's you who's shouting for half the courtyard to hear."

Gizella put her fingers into her mouth and bit down for what seemed a second, then she became hysterical. Stepa asked them to calm down, they were both just adding fuel to the fire.

The commission continued its rounds on Tuesday. At Dina Vargaftik's and at Marina Biryuk's, where they only found her mother-in-law at home, they also found pails overflowing with garbage, but this time the housewives did not argue with them: on the contrary, they honestly admitted their guilt and promised that it would never happen again.

The commission decided not to check Comrade Degtyar's apartment. However, when they passed by, Iona Ovseich himself caught up with them and expressed his indignation. His room was in perfect order, clearly the home of someone who was very neat. The hallway which served as a kitchen was also beyond reproach. The commission was agreed that it should be given a four plus or even the top mark of five. They were about to say good-bye when Degtyar again expressed his astonishment: what kind of commission were they if they didn't even look at his bathroom!

The bathroom was clean. The iron knobs gleamed as if they had been rubbed with acidol. Katerina said that all the building's housewives should be brought there to see the place with their own eyes and take a lesson from Degtyar. Iona Ovseich asked her not to exaggerate: he was well aware that this was the bare minimum. Anything lower than this could not be tolerated. Katerina persisted in her enthusiasm and praise, until Stepa became interested in where the basket was.

"What basket?" Iona Ovseich asked in surprise.

Stepa laughed, wagged a finger, then said that he meant the wastepaper basket. Iona Ovseich hemmed and hawed, then said that the commission should not go into such intimate details, people might be offended.

"No," Stepa insisted, "tell us where you throw the paper: in the toilet?"

Now Degtyar became genuinely angry and said that he didn't waste any paper and urged the commission not to exceed its limits and to remember its place.

The last to be visited was Efim Granik. On the previous evening they had knocked at his door twice, but both times in vain, though there were grounds for assuming he was home and simply did not want to answer the door. Stepa rang the bell this time; they listened as the sound faded and then heard some kind of noise like a heavy object falling to the floor. They rang again and finally the inner door opened.

"Efim," Stepa shouted merrily. "Are you alive or should we send a hearse for you!"

"What's the matter," asked Efim. "Can't you leave people alone?"

Stepa said he should open up: the sanitation commission was there to inspect his place. Katerina stood off to one side during the negotiations, but Efim caught sight of her and told them that he wouldn't allow her in his place even for a million rubles. Stepa tried to turn it all into a joke and ordered Efim to put on his underpants while they waited, but in reply he slammed the door and no matter how many times they rang, they were not able to get an answer. Finally, Katerina knocked with her fist so hard that the glass shook and she shouted: "If you don't open up yourself—I'm calling the police! Your place is a rat's nest, you raise cockroaches in there. I'll have you evicted from Odessa so fast your head will spin!"

Some kind of racket was going on in Efim's room. They both listened for a minute. Katerina repeated again that Efim's head would spin if they had to leave empty-handed. Stepa only shrugged but Katerina went up to Comrade Degtyar's and described everything that had happened.

"We should have expected it," said Comrade Degtyar. "One time he got away with the loan, and now he thinks he can get away with murder."

Katerina reminded Degtyar that she had warned against giving Granik a place to live here, but no one had listened to her then and now they were paying for it.

At home Katerina repeated the whole story to Olya, but Olya made Katerina swear by her children's health not to tell Iona and Zinovy, or they'd never hear the end of it.

At a small activist meeting—only Khomitsky, Orlov, and Katerina Cheperukha were present—Comrade Degtyar posed the question point-blank: what should we do about Granik? Katerina said straight out that one possibility was to have him expelled from Odessa. Stepa was categorically opposed, especially since Granik was doing good work at the shipyard. Orlov also was against the idea. She did, however, propose that the courtyard raise the issue of Granik's expulsion.

The City Soviet would not, of course, allow it, but Granik would finally realize that they did not intend to joke with him anymore.

"Any other suggestions?" asked Comrade Degtyar.

There were no other suggestions. Silence reigned for a minute, then Comrade Degtyar asked if he might say a few words.

"I've listened to everything," he said. "I kept thinking will one of you try to find the root of the matter or will we keep hopping like sparrows from branch to branch, chirping merrily? And here's the result: none of you did, not a one. But the root of it all is plain as plain can be: would Efim Granik allow himself to act this way if he did not have the direct support of Dr. Landa?"

Stepa shrugged his shoulders: why bring in Dr. Landa here? Landa stood up for Efim after Dukovsky Park and the hospital, after everything had already happened.

"It's like germs!" shouted Iona Ovseich. "Germs fly through the air and transmit infection from one person to another! Formally speaking it was just as Khomitsky said: first Granik, then Landa. But who could doubt that it would be Dr. Landa, no one else but him, who would lend support to Efim Granik when the entire courtyard, everyone, was indignant at Granik and angrily condemned him! Who of you was surprised by that—point a finger at yourself!"

Iona Ovseich stared at them and they each felt his gaze on themselves and instinctively averted their eyes.

"Our country built the Volga-Don Canal, and created the Tsimlyansky Sea, a sea which had never existed before. On the shores of a great Russian river it built the Kuibyshev and Stalingrad hydroelectric stations, the largest in the world. Are we going to sit like frogs in a swamp and wait until they come to us and say: 'We've built communism for you, won't you please come in!' No," Iona Ovseich said, brandishing a fist, "no one will come to us and no one will invite us in: we're going to build it ourselves, with our own hands. And anyone in our way should be tossed aside like a useless weed."

Katerina shouted out Degtyar was right. Back home in Siberia she and her father cut down the weeds with an ax; and those weeds. Stepa stared at Katerina, who shrugged her shoulders and turned away. Lyalya waited a few moments before addressing Comrade Degtyar: "Still, what about Granik?"

"Orlov, Orlov," said Comrade Degtyar shaking his head, "you

remind me of a giraffe: he gets his legs wet on Monday and he gets a cold on Friday."

Stepa laughed and said then the giraffe goes to Dr. Landa—to get himself cured.

"Khomitsky," said Comrade Degtyar, "I don't like your attitude."

As a result of the decision not to employ a cleaning woman, each floor posted a work schedule and hung it by the door of the entrance hall in an obvious place so that there could be no excuses for people who forgot. In addition, Orlov and Cheperukha personally went around to every last apartment and had people sign a work schedule. Some housewives tried to object, saying some days were more convenient than others, that had to be figured in. But Katerina sensibly replied to these complaints: what was convenient for one meant that it was at the expense of another, and there was no way for it to be convenient for everybody. Never mind, we'd get used to it.

And indeed after a couple of weeks people got so used to the new arrangement that no one even felt the need to change anything. On the contrary, since the schedule was drawn up far in advance, it was always possible to arrange things ahead of time and set aside two or three hours for building work.

The complications began when the schedule indicated that it was Landa's turn. First Gizella missed her hours during the day, but perhaps it was more convenient for her to do the cleaning late that evening or early the next morning. But, the evening passed, the morning passed. Katerina made a special trip to the third floor to check up. The corridor and part of a stretch of the stairs were still littered with cigarette butts and as dirty as they had been before. Moreover, the yard cats, as if in cahoots, had been particularly active that week. Gizella had walked past all this with a regal air as if none of it concerned her. Silently at first, then aloud, the others began to voice their righteous indignation: some people here were gentry and the rest were flunkeys and servants! Dina Vargaftik was more upset than all the rest and said openly to Katerina that if she, Dina, had allowed herself to spit in her neighbor's faces even the slightest little bit, they would have made mincemeat out of her. But Colonel Landa's wife could do whatever she wanted because she was the wife of Colonel Landa.

Right after this conversation, Katerina went up to the third floor again. Nothing had changed. She rang the Landas' bell and demanded that Gizella come out into the hall. Gizella opened the door but said she didn't feel like coming out into the hall and invited Katerina to come into her place. Katerina drew herself up and said, "Let's not waste time." Then Katerina asked Gizella how long the cat waste would be left on the staircase to delight people with its aroma.

"Listen," said Gizella, becoming upset. "I haven't been able to bear cats since I was a child, and I won't clean up after them."

"But you'll let others clean up after you?" Katerina asked politely.

"There are only two of us. When my husband and I use the stairs and hallway, we don't leave a speck behind, but the rest of them here live in whole clans—grandmothers, grandfathers, grandchildren."

"Listen, sweetheart"—Katerina suddenly began to speak like a gypsy fortune-teller—"a distant journey awaits you. The jack of diamonds in a blue coat and a cell in a tower!"

Gizella instinctively took a step back. Katerina warned her that this was going to be their last polite conversation, and if the area wasn't clean before morning, she was going to alert the district military staff. They could send a commission over here and find out who the Landas really were.

Katerina made an about-face, military fashion. Gizella asked her to stop, but Katerina was already descending the stairs so quickly it was difficult to believe she was a mother of two sons.

The next day before noon Gizella brought home an elderly woman from the music school, gave her a broom, pail, and mop, and showed her what needed to be cleaned up. The woman worked for about an hour and a half, and was paid ten rubles. She and Gizella thanked each other and said good-bye.

Fenya Lebedev was just finishing cleaning the courtyard. She walked over to the main entrance and blocked the way for a second: "Were you at Landas'?"

"I was," said the woman, "what of it?" Nothing, said Lebedev, she just wanted to know if Gizella was home, she had to bring her the rent receipt. "She's home," said the woman with a nod. "She's resting. She had classes all morning at the school and all afternoon too. She'll be leaving soon."

Late that evening Fenya told Orlov and Katerina that Comrade Degtyar wanted them to come see him.

"Well, how was your day?" asked Iona Ovseich.

"I had a good day," said Katerina.

"Good was it?" said Iona Ovseich. "And how about you, Orlov?"

Lyalya said she had a good day too, adding that the Landas' hallway had been cleaned and there had been no more discussions on the subject.

"So, everything's good here then, is it?" said Comrade Degtyar. "Nothing bothering you then?"

The two women exchanged glances and grew thoughtful. Iona Ovseich observed them intently, a smile both vaguely happy and sad playing on his face. Finally, Orlov admitted that she had some sort of feeling inside but couldn't find the words to express it.

That's right, said Iona Ovseich, she couldn't find the words and she never would if Madame Landa could openly insult the entire courtyard in front of everyone and people just walked on by and accepted it as if they were a lower caste.

"That's not true," said Katerina, "we don't accept it. We forced her to clean the hallway."

"You did?" said Comrade Degtyar, cupping his hand to his ear as if he hadn't heard her right. "On the first All-Russian voluntary work Saturday in May 1919 they also paid ten rubles to have someone else do their work for them!"

Comrade Degtyar paused for half a minute as if anyone might really try to refute him, and then out of the blue he proposed: "Let's all chip in ten rubles and hire people to do our work and cleaning for us!"

Not everyone could afford it, said Katerina, but if someone could that was his own personal business.

"Personal?" said Iona Ovseich. "Katerina, I know you're not trying to excuse Landa, you just want to make things easier for yourself, the hallway's clean and that's that! But you don't seem to care that our building is supposed to be engaged in socialist maintenance."

"What do you want me to do," said Katerina, "pull my hair and scream blue murder like your Odessa women do?"

"Our Odessa women?" said Iona Ovseich, narrowing one eye for a better look at Katerina, who instinctively lowered her head. "And I had thought that the Siberian Katerina was now more one of us than certain people who were born here. And it surprises me when you seek to defend the Landas instead of honestly and openly castigating them."

All right, said Katerina, that was the first time and the last with Gizella, they wouldn't let her get away with it again.

"You're mistaken," objected Comrade Degtyar. "It will be the first and last time on one condition—if the entire courtyard rises up in arms and condemns her. And the initiative should come from the sanitation commission, which bears primary responsibility here."

Orlov asked what that meant in practice—calling a meeting of the women's soviet, the activists, or a general meeting? Iona Ovseich waved away her questions and said they should use their own heads and decide it themselves. And whether it was the activists or a general meeting that was used to condemn her was just a question of form and did not play a decisive role. It was something else that they should be worried about—that events would outstrip them and leave them bringing up the rear.

Iona Ovseich's words began to come true on the very next day. Dina Vargaftik went out with her dog Alfochka for a walk in the fresh air and met Katerina in the entranceway. Dina immediately started a conversation about Princess Gizella who had hired a poor sick, old woman who had to do four hours of back-breaking work for a pittance. But when the other people in the building did back-breaking work, that was considered normal. And yet every day in the newspapers and on the radio we heard that we had full equality, and that everyone had equal rights.

Katerina answered that this was true, but why was Dina appealing to her? There should be a meeting of the entire courtyard; they should all go up to the third floor and tell this to Gizella Landa herself.

"You know what," cried Dina, "there's a reason people say—only the grave can straighten the hunchback."

"That's right," said Katerina, in a fury. "That's what you Odessites are good at: backbiting and gossip, but when it comes time to act, you're all hiding in the bushes!"

"Katerina Antipovna," said Dina, slightly insulted, "if you don't like Odessa, no one's forcing you to stay here."

"I like Odessa," said Katerina, "I don't like the games Odessites play."

"Odessites?" replied Dina. "Do you mean everyone or just a certain type?"

"Fool!" said Katerina, spitting. "In Odessa you divide people into Jews and everyone else, but in Siberia no one thinks like that."

After Dina's walk with Alfochka, she went to see Tosya Khomitsky for a few minutes to unburden her heart. Tosya sympathized with her, but told her it might be better for her to stop interfering.

"Tosenka," Dina moaned, "how can I stop interfering, when people are turning everything upside down right before my eyes?"

Tosya said that then it was necessary to do something and not ask for sympathy.

Dina wiped her tears with a handkerchief and said yes, she didn't need sympathy now. She had her Alfochka, who slept in her bed and ate with her at the table.

"Isn't that right, Alfochka?" Dina kicked off a shoe, and rubbed the dog's fur with it. The dog opened its eyes, whimpered, and half closed its eyes again. "You and I aren't lonely, are we! Our Grisha's moldering in the grave, and no one even cares."

By that evening the courtyard knew all the details of Gizella's gambit. Some were more indignant than others, but they were all agreed on one point: you could hire a woman to whitewash the walls and ceilings in your apartment, but to flaunt your position in front of everybody just because you were the wife of Colonel Landa, that created a bad feeling in everyone. It was like in the old folk tale: I'm the boss and you run the errands.

Only Marina Biryuk alone, from whom it could be least expected, openly sided with Gizella. When Katerina had gathered a group to go see Landa in her apartment, Marina refused point-blank to go with them. Not only that, she began to try to convince the others that a person had the right to spend his hard-earned money as he pleased.

"Hard-earned money!" Dina shouted indignantly. "Gizella and her husband make four thousand, and Katerina has six people, and half the money."

"And my Andrei gets three thousand," said Marina. "If you don't like it, write to Comrade Stalin and tell him that stupid people in the government are throwing the country's money away."

"That's interesting," said Katerina, clapping her hands. "In other words, anyone with money in the Soviet Union can exploit others."

"Exploit!" said Marina with a grimace. "Keep your mouth shut if you don't know what you're talking about. Exploitation is when you profit from someone else's labor."

"But when your health profits at someone else's expense," said Katerina, waving her fist, "that's not exploitation! And to lie on the couch with your behind in the air while the entire courtyard does everything with their own hands I suppose that's not exploitation either!"

Marina shrugged her shoulders and said again that she wouldn't go see Landa. If the others wanted to, let them, that was their business.

When they described the scene with Marina to him, Iona Ovseich first asked Katerina, did she see now that dealing with Landa would be more difficult than it had first appeared?

Katerina did not reply directly, but only nodded her head at Orlov, saying that the two of them could visit Landa together, and if need be, she was prepared to do it alone.

Iona Ovseich shook his head. The lady is going to be told what we think of her, the question is, who is going to do the telling— Katerina Cheperukha or the entire courtyard? I say it should be the entire courtyard to a man!" Iona Ovseich cleft the air with the heel of his hand. "And this will take some work. We've neglected ideological work as if Granik and Landa were our last remaining problems. How much talk has there been about a study group on *Economic Problems of Socialism in the U.S.S.R.*, and now it's here! But just let anyone try to say no to me now. We'll give him the classification he deserves, with all the resulting consequences!"

"What consequences?" said Katerina, shrugging her shoulders. "We'll pour salt on his tail, like we did to Granik."

"Katerina, aren't you ashamed of yourself?" said Lyalya Orlov excitedly. "Iona Ovseich gives all he's got to people, and you criticize him as if our Odessa was your godforsaken taiga where all problems are solved with an ax!"

"Orlov," said Iona Ovseich, "stop insulting her. Katerina did not come here from the taiga, but from the capital of an autonomous republic."

"And even if it was from the taiga," said Katerina with a laugh, "so what?"

"That's absolutely correct," said Iona Ovseich in support of her.

"It means she's healthier in mind and body. And, as for the study group, I'll say it again: I want everyone on board. If someone's attending a study group at his factory, we want a note from the factory, otherwise he attends our study group. The lists are to be on my table on Saturday."

Although it was not her obligation, Katerina took part in the drive along with Orlov. As might have been expected, the first refusal came from Gizella Landa, who said that she was studying linguistic problems at her institute, and had no time for two study groups. Katerina expressed her surprise: no time? And so then what should they say to those women who had children at home, and housework to do, and had to do everything themselves because their husbands didn't earn enough money to pay for a maid?

"Now listen," said Gizella, on the verge of tears, "that's low, to rebuke a woman for having no children!"

"Your tears disgust me," said Katerina. "I don't like people who have abortions because they don't like children's pee-pee and caca, and then cry and say people are heartless."

"Get out of my house," screamed Gizella, "get out immediately!"

Katerina told her to calm down. This was not her private estate here, but a state apartment, adding that she, Katerina Cheperukha, was not there on a personal matter.

"Listen," said Gizella, brandishing her fists. "I am going to call my husband and tell him to send the police here immediately!"

Katerina said no, she'd call them herself.

"Here, take it," said Gizella, grabbing the receiver and handing it to Katerina. "Call wherever you want, whoever you want, but for God's sake, leave me in peace!"

Katerina grimaced in disgust and told Gizella she should take care of her nerves, since they might come in useful, then walked away.

They spoke with Granik that evening. There were no hysterics and shouting. Efim said that his factory had given him a pass to a sanatorium for the month of September and consequently he couldn't make the study group that month. Anyway, he was exhausted after his shift and nothing would stay in his head.

"In other words," said Katerina, "you're refusing?"

"What do you mean refusing?" said Efim in surprise. "I told you in plain Russian that I can't be physically present because of my health."

"Fine," said Katerina, "I'll inform Comrade Degtyar."

"Go ahead," Efim nodded. "If he doesn't understand anything, he should come see me."

Efim slammed the door with all his might. Katerina was boiling with anger and went to see Comrade Degtyar at once. She rang his bell once, twice, three times, and finally he answered the door. Katerina saw Colonel Landa, who was pacing around the table, shouting that Degtyar was intentionally terrorizing people and turning them against each other. As for Katerina Cheperukha, said Landa, wagging a finger threateningly, he'd speak with her in private.

"Cheperukha," said Comrade Degtyar, "answer this question, please: Did I send you to see Gizella Landa?"

Katerina answered no, he had not sent her; on the other hand, Colonel Landa's wife had kicked her out the way a princess kicks out a servant, and threatened to call the police.

"Is that so," said the colonel, becoming aggressive, "She was sitting at home, and you spoke so offensively to her as soon as you had one foot in the door that she almost fainted!"

Katerina replied that that didn't prove anything: Madame Landa was ready to faint every time a mouse ran by.

"Listen," screamed the colonel enraged, "I'll bring you to court for premeditated hooliganism!"

"Don't try to intimidate us," said Katerina. "We live on our own hard-earned kopecks, and we don't have anything to be afraid of."

"What's all this about your hard-earned kopecks?" said the colonel, shaking a fist. "You burst into someone's house and mock a woman who happens to be my wife, and that's what I'll bring you to court for."

"Landa," said Degtyar calmly, "a military man shouldn't make empty threats: we're not judges or prosecutors and we don't pass sentences. And as far as I'm concerned, I can tell you that the entire courtyard is deeply indignant about your behavior, and that's something any prosecutor, any judge, would want to hear about."

"Ovseich," said Colonel Landa, leaning forward, "I see right through you: don't overdo it! Don't overdo it—that's my advice to you. Times have changed."

"I don't understand," said Comrade Degtyar, tossing his head back and tilting it slightly to the side. "What do you mean, times have changed?"

Colonel Landa did not answer. He passed his finger along his jacket, checking the buttons, then straightened his battle ribbons, bowed automatically, and walked out.

"Ugh," Katerina grimaced, and stuck out the tip of her tongue. "A disgusting sight."

Comrade Degtyar looked at the door for a few seconds as if he were expecting Landa to return, then went up to the table, drummed his fingers on it, and said: "Cheperukha, it's very fortunate that you dropped by when you did."

Katerina shrugged her shoulders and said: "Are you afraid he'll really take it to court?"

"Me?" said Iona Ovseich, tapping his chest, "No, Cheperukha, I'm not afraid. Others should be afraid of us."

The first meeting of the study group took place in Lyalya Orlov's apartment. There weren't enough chairs. The neighbors brought some boards, placed the ends on footstools, and made comfortable seats for themselves. Comrade Degtyar said that it wouldn't hurt if there were more room, but as they said, the more the merrier.

Marina Biryuk literally arrived a minute before the meeting began, immediately followed by Gizella Landa. Iona Ovseich surveyed the group and said that he didn't see Efim Granik then asked Comrade Orlov, as the secretary, to make a note of that. Lyalya said she already had and pointed a fingernail at her notebook. Iona Ovseich asked if anyone knew why Granik was absent.

Katerina rose and said that she had reported once already to Comrade Degtyar that Granik was preparing to leave for a sanatorium. His factory had given him a leave, but anyway he refused, saying nothing would stay in his head.

Everyone laughed. Comrade Degtyar called the meeting to order, said that he didn't see anything funny, and ordered the secretary to record Granik's statement. Then he made a motion to inform the ship repair yard. "Are there any objections?"

Stepa Khomitsky shrugged his shoulders. Gizella's face was stony. Cheerfully, like some stupid vacationer at Arcadia or Bolshoi Fontan for the first time, Marina kept looking around.

Iona Ovseich said that there were no objections. He waited a few seconds, smiled pleasantly, then welcomed them all to the new school year. The people responded with applause. At that very moment the door opened and Klava Ivanovna came in. The applause grew even louder. Iona Ovseich asked everyone to rise, and welcome the old activist and community veteran, Comrade Malaya.

"Sit down," said Klava Ivanovna, signaling them all to be seated.

Instead of obeying, they burst into renewed applause. Klava Ivanovna threatened to leave if they didn't stop it at once. Her threat worked, people calmed down and gave their attention to the matter at hand.

The first point was why the courtyard needed to study economic problems, and not, say, questions of Marxism and linguistics. Iona Ovseich began with an episode familiar to all—Efim Granik's refusal to subscribe to the loan. Stepa Khomitsky said that to be more precise Granik hadn't refused to pledge totally but only at home. Iona Ovseich reprimanded Stepa for an inappropriate intrusion and repeated that Granik had refused to subscribe to the loan and had found, as they all knew, an active advocate in the person of Dr. Landa.

Although they were not discussing her, Gizella blushed deeply, and when people turned toward her, she suddenly began to turn pale and become white as a sheet.

Iona Ovseich rapped the table with his pencil and continued: "There's a black sheep in every family, and one swallow does not make a spring. However, the fact that on the one hand, Efim Granik found support, and on the other, did not receive the rebuff due him, forces us to look closely not only at Efim Granik and his protector, but to an even greater degree to ourselves. And the remark made by our respected colleague, Stepa Khomitsky, which you all just heard, should put us on our guard all the more."

Stepa shouted from his seat that it was good that he had put them on their guard. This proved that each one of us was on guard. Someone in the corner giggled. Malaya tugged Stepa's sleeve and told him to shut his stupid mouth.

"Comrades," Iona Ovseich raised his voice, "the great Stalin teaches that under socialism the population's solvency must outstrip production. In practice this means that the workers always have more money on hand than they can spend. Part of this money should be put into a worker's savings bank, and the rest into loans which the state will then spend on those same workers. This leads to but a single conclusion: anyone who refuses to take part in the loan, no matter what his subjective reasons might be, is helping to freeze the nation's wealth, and, in the final analysis, is a detriment to the national economy."

Iona Ovseich stopped. His temples were beaded with sweat. He wiped the sweat off with his fingertips, then took a few sips from a glass of water. When he continued, he did not speak as loudly as he had before: "Of course, there are various ways to measure: however, from the moral standpoint, whether someone has withheld fifty rubles or fifty thousand doesn't matter. Numbers are numbers, but it's who a person really is that counts here."

Iona Ovseich stopped for a second time. Beads of sweat had appeared on his temples again. A cold draft seemed to blow through the room, but in a minute the anxiety passed, and he continued normally.

"And now," said Iona Ovseich, "another example of how money and income can reveal a person's true face. As you may have guessed, I'm referring to a resident of our house building, Gizella Landa. If we'd wanted to, couldn't each of us hire someone for ten rubles to do our work for us?"

"Yes," cried Olya Cheperukha, "but you need ten extra rubles you can spare."

"No, Cheperukha," said Iona Ovseich, and turned to Landa, "not ten spare rubles, but a special kind of morals."

Gizella covered her face with her hands, only her nose protruding. It was clear that her head was quivering. Iona Ovseich did not look aside but asked loudly: "And what kind of morals are we talking about? Where did she get them? Did they fall from the sky? No, they didn't. What we want is an explanation from Gizella Landa herself."

Gizella's face was still in her hands. Iona Ovseich waited a few moments, then asked her to show a little more courage. Finally, Gizella rose, her head lowered like a guilty schoolgirl, and muttered something under her breath.

"Louder," said Iona Ovseich. "Truth should speak in a loud voice."

"It's true that I'm at fault, but I didn't mean to do anything bad."

Gizella thought a moment, then shrugged her shoulders. "I don't understand what I'm being accused of."

"You don't?" said Comrade Degtyar in surprise. "You mean your husband hasn't explained it to you yet?"

"My husband doesn't know that I'm here," said Gizella.

"Well, now!" said Degtyar, even more surprised. "May we assume that he advised you to come here?"

Gizella didn't answer. Everyone was quiet, even the chairs stopped squeaking. Klava Ivanovna mumbled as she dozed. Iona Ovseich repeated his question, adding a new element this time: Or did he advise her not to come?

"I don't want to answer this question." Gizella's voice suddenly rose. "You have not the right to talk to me like this. I don't owe you any explanations, and I don't owe anything to anyone here."

Dina Vargaftik laughed loudly and said: "You might think that we don't live in a courtyard but some kind of a wild forest."

"No," said Katerina, "she doesn't think she lives in a forest, but in her own private home."

"Listen," said Gizella, batting her mascaraed eyelashes, "I came here to study, not to listen to your stupid jokes."

"Why Gizella Landa is here," Iona Ovseich answered calmly, "is something we will establish, not you. And anyone with an objection knows where to complain."

Klava Ivanovna made a soblike sound, then her head lurched forward, her chin resting on her chest. When she opened her eyes, she was somewhat confused at first, then said to Gizella in a tone of reproach: "You're not saying a word. You still haven't learned your lesson."

Marina Biryuk began to laugh. The others didn't find it so funny and only smiled. Iona Ovseich demanded an immediate stop to this nonsense, warned Gizella that people were not obliged to waste so much time on her, and repeated his question for the third time: did Colonel Landa advise her to come here to study the work of Comrade Stalin or, on the contrary, did he try to keep her from coming?

Gizella looked at Comrade Degtyar and every one else as if they were somewhere far below her, dwarfs, Lilliputians. She pushed back her chair with her foot, and headed for the door without a single word and without turning her head. Lyalya Orlov was only able to shout that well-brought-up people didn't act like that, but then the door slammed and Gizella's heels were clicking on the iron stairs.

Now everyone, even those who had been prepared to forgive Gizella, was indignant. Marina Biryuk, as usual, had her own opinion and argued that if anyone else were taken to task like Landa, they wouldn't sit there and take it either.

"Citizen Biryuk," said Iona Ovseich angrily, "if you don't like it here, perhaps you should follow her example!"

"That's my business," said Marina defiantly. "And you don't have to worry about it."

Iona Ovseich compressed his lips, deep creases forming at the corners. Marina looked him impudently in the eye, and nerves of steel were needed not to reply.

Klava Ivanovna intervened: "Biryuk, you're still too young to be acting like this."

"Malaya," said Comrade Degtyar, slamming his fist on the table, "I didn't call on you. Keep quiet!"

Klava Ivanovna folded her hands on her chest and silently moved her lips. Everyone waited patiently in his seat. Comrade Degtyar rubbed his temples with his fingers, then said they would now discuss the next problem: the Soviet economy during World War II.

They finished quite early, before ten o'clock. Iona Ovseich left with Malaya; a minute later Lyalya caught up and joined them. They went out onto Stalin Avenue, toward Alexandrovsky Gardens. Iona Ovseich remembered that under the old regime there had been a market there. A man by the name of Eru, a Karaite by nationality, had lived at number 5. They used to hide literature at his house but then he went over to the Mensheviks. Or, rather, he found his true group. Landa's father used to have a store there.

"That was a hundred years ago," said Klava Ivanovna. "It's time to forget."

"Forget?" said Iona Ovseich in surprise. "I'd think now was just the right time to remember."

The first days of October were unusually lovely. In the evening, when the loudspeakers broadcast reports on the party congress, people could sit for hours in the municipal park, on Cathedral Square or on Stalin Avenue and listen; those who couldn't find a place to sit would stand or slowly stroll by other loudspeakers. The sessions of the congress were not broadcast, and everyone already knew that Comrade Stalin had entrusted the delivery of the yearly report to his deputy Malenkov. Still, people so wanted to hear his beloved voice again with its beautiful, pleasing accent, as if he were the person closest to them in the world, that, despite everything, they continued to hope right up to the very last minute, and kept their radios on at home day and night.

Comrade Stalin did indeed speak on the last day of the congress. That evening Levitan read the speech on the radio, and newspapers published the text in large print. The entire country, the entire world, pondered every word, and could only marvel at the fact that in so few words he could capture an entire historical period in the life of humanity and, literally in a few words, to say what was most important: that the bourgeois had irrevocably and forever tossed the banner of democracy overboard from the ship of history. In practice this meant that the proletariat of the major capitalist countries must, without further delay draw the only one possible conclusion, that is, the bourgeois must themselves be thrown overboard from the ship of history.

The study group's next meeting was devoted entirely to Comrade Stalin's historic speech. Iona Ovseich emphasized that it was a classic example of scientific thought and the art of oratory in which every word spoke volumes. For the proletariat of the United States of America and the entire globe this speech would be the catechism of catechisms, comparable only to the *Communist Manifesto*.

The evening was warm, as if the last days of August had returned. After the meeting people didn't feel like going home. Many remained in the courtyard and continued the discussion there. Iona Cheperukha pounded his chest with his fist and said that now he had a good chance of living a few years under communism: if Comrade Stalin said so, that meant it would happen.

Stepa said that called for a drink, and the three of them—Iona, Efim, and Stepa—set out for Pushkinskaya Street. On the way they ran into Adya, who had stayed late at the factory, and they invited him to join them.

They had a glass each at the wine cellar then Adya bought a bottle of cognac. They used candy with soy filling as a chaser. Iona Cheperukha suddenly began weeping drunkenly and tried to convince Adya not to keep any ill will in his heart—the past was over and done with, you had to look ahead and believe only in the good; when it was time, the bad would come of its own.

After his month in the sanatorium Efim had become very quiet, a bitter grin always on his face. He only drank a little and kept nodding his head.

"Fima," said Iona badgering him and starting to cry again, "Don't be so quiet. Please. Say something."

Efim looked around and made a sign for them to come closer. He brought his thumb and forefinger together and rubbed them twice as if sprinkling something onto his plate.

"I don't understand," Iona said angrily. "Talk like a human being!"

Efim looked around for the second time, bowed his head even lower, and said in a whisper: "Poison. In the sanatorium. They gave it to one guy and he died."

"In the sanatorium?" said Cheperukha, surprised. "Where did you get that crazy idea?"

Efim did not respond. He broke off a piece of candy and held it on his tongue, then, as if afraid of something, began to chew it carefully. Iona said that was disgusting and ordered another glass of Riesling mixed with port.

After they left the wine cellar, Iona stopped by a large plane tree. Old pieces of bark lay at the base of the tree. He put his arms around the tree and pressed his cheek to it. Stepa grabbed him from behind and tried to tear him away, but Iona resisted with all his strength, saying again and again in a drunken voice: "Stepa, my soul is burning, my soul is on fire!"

Adya also tried to convince Iona that it was time to go, before people started watching and it became a real circus. Cheperukha pushed himself away from the tree and shouted: "You snot-nosed brat, in 1930 I carried you in my arms, and now you talk to me like that! I'm in pain! In pain!"

Back home, Iona got it good from Olya, and Katerina added a few remarks of her own. Fortunately, Grisha and Misha rushed to their grandfather's defense, and helped him off with his shoes and clothes, otherwise the two women would have kept scolding him, with no end in sight.

In the morning Iona got up with an aching head and drank two glasses of pickle brine, but it helped as much as incense helps the dead. Olya watched with a certain satisfaction: let the old drayman feel for even a minute the kind of life he had given her.

Adya had a long talk with Anya about what had happened the day before. He bristled at first. She was silent and had tears in her eyes. Then he went up to her, embraced her like a son and kissed her. She lost all control and began openly weeping.

Stepa had not been able to fall asleep until late that night. Early the next morning, at first light, Tosya woke him up and said he should go check on Efim: the man was all alone, he could die, and no one would know.

Stepa rang four or five times. There was no answer. All kinds of thoughts started coming to mind. He examined the glass to see where the putty was weak, then decided to ring one last time. Finally the bolt rattled, and the inner door opened:

"Stepa!" said Efim, frightened. His eyes became glazed for a moment. "Is Lizochka sick? Did she die?"

That took Stepa by surprise: oh, these people, all they think about is death! Bah! Efim explained that he had had nightmares all night long as if something bad was going to happen to himself or someone he loved.

Stepa grunted and raised his arms high above his head in a morning stretch. He hadn't drunk enough yesterday, and had ended up neither sober nor drunk, but he still felt lousy.

Efim took a bottle from the cabinet and put the teakettle on the hot plate. He lay down on his back on the couch to wait for the kettle to boil. Stepa sat at the table, his face in his hands, clearly thinking hard. Efim grunted, and sighed, and sometimes a soft groan would escape him. Stepa instinctively raised his head and cocked an ear: out in the courtyard a cat began to screech. At first it sounded like there was an infant outside the window, but the cry was repeated, this time drawn out and shrill, a sound cats often make after a long night.

The teapot was starting to fill the air with a cheerful whistle. With morning hoarseness in his voice, Stepa said it was time to set out the cups. He poured some wine into their glasses, cut some bread, herring, and onion and told Efim to get up. Efim did not respond. Stepa took the cups, some sugar, and a package of barley coffee from the cabinet. He looked into the teapot. Bubbles were already rising to the surface. He waited a few seconds, the lid still in his hand. He thought of Iona dancing the fox-trot with a tree in the middle of Pushkinskaya Street yesterday and he began to laugh.

Efim looked at the ceiling, and Stepa couldn't tell whether he was listening or not. Again Stepa told him to get up. He turned off the hot plate, filled his cup with hot water, and put the teapot on the floor so as not to dirty a dish for no reason.

Efim sat down at the table and took a glass of wine. Bending his head low, he said: "The factory wants to give me a room. In the settlement for the shipyard workers. I don't want it. I've already lived my life and there won't be any other. Stepa, did you understand me?"

Stepa answered yes, he understood, but if you looked at it with a little common sense a good room was better than a bad one.

"Stepa," Efim sighed, "I can see you don't understand. Good, bad, what difference does it make? Here I can still feel like a human being, like everyone else, but there's nothing for me there but bare walls—I'll have to start all over again from the beginning."

Stepa insisted that a good room was better than a bad one, and whether Efim belonged to a settlement of ship repairers or on Deribasovskaya Street, it made no difference. In the end, he could always come visit.

"Come visit my own home," said Efim with a grin. "In a hearse pulled by black dray horses."

Stepa waved his hand: "We aren't so heavy that we need black dray horses to carry us."

Efim raised his glass, and they clicked their glasses loudly. Stepa wished that things would get no worse. They drank with good cheer and ate with appetite. The only thing to regret was that Iona wasn't there, but at that very moment the doorbell rang. Efim barely had time to get up before there was a tapping outside on the glass, and another ring.

"Of course," said Efim, opening the door, "who else would burst into someone else's apartment except Iona Cheperukha himself!"

Stepa rose to greet him and give him a glass but was stopped in his tracks by Iona's face, which was dark as night.

"Boys," said Iona, "bad news. Landa's been arrested."

"Landa?" Efim's eyes took on a crazed look. His mouth opened, his lower lip trembled. "Landa?"

Iona covered his face with his hand. A tear rolled out from under his finger, and hung at the end of his nose. Stepa looked at Iona, then at Efim, cursed, threw up his hands, and walked out.

Iona struck his chest with his fist and sighed with a deep moan. He said he had to go to work, the horses hadn't been watered since yesterday, and he left too.

Efim left everything on the table just as it was, put on a raincoat, took a box of his new brushes and his stainless steel palette knife, and slammed the door. He slowed his pace in the middle of the courtyard. He looked around, at the windows. As usual the lights were on. Before leaving for work and school, fathers, mothers, and their children were sitting at the table drinking tea. He felt a savage pain, as if his heart had been pierced by a red-hot skewer. Efim clutched his chest with his right hand. For a second his vision blurred. His forehead broke out in a sweat and his whole body felt weak.

The trolleys on Soviet Army Street were crammed. Young men hung from the steps, bumpers, and along the sides, talking cheerfully away. Efim let three trolleys pass, then seeing there was no sense in waiting any longer, he set out on foot. The weakness returned several times on the way. He felt like leaning against a wall or simply lying down on the sidewalk, but time was short. There were only minutes left and it was still a long way to Peresyp.

At first when people learned that Colonel Landa had been arrested, they didn't believe it. Klava Ivanovna was more upset than anyone else and told everyone she met: it must be some kind of mistake. Comrade Degtyar patiently tried to reason with her and finally was forced to say that idle talk was idle talk, no matter who it came from. Malaya responded by attacking him with curses the likes of which he had never heard from her before in his entire life.

Although she had never been a close friend of Gizella, Anya Kotlyar decided to go visit her and lend her support at that trying time. However, Gizella did not even invite Anya to sit down, saying she didn't need any sympathy; the case of Joseph Kotlyar was the Kotlyars' own personal affair, and there were no parallels with Colonel Landa, nor could there be.

Anya clenched inwardly from the insult. She felt like responding rudely, but she got control of herself, apologized, then left quietly, closing the door behind her. In the corridor she turned around without thinking. Gizella was watching her go but immediately pretended to be fussing with the lock.

When Anya came downstairs, the concierge, Lebedev, barred her way with her broom and asked how Landa was feeling. Anya went around to one side as if she had not been spoken to. Lebedev sighed bitterly and said to herself: "It's like a fire: one moment people have everything, and then it's all burned to ashes!"

Comrade Degtyar did not say anything good or anything bad about Anya Kotlyar's visit to Gizella. He only quoted the folk saying: that one fisherman could smell another from far away. Malaya flew into a rage again and threatened to write the district headquarters and the defense minister if Landa wasn't home in three days.

"Malaya," said Iona Ovseich, shaking his head, "that's not the right address."

Malaya shook her fists in response: then she would write to Comrade Stalin personally, he'd look into it right away, and then the people responsible would have themselves to blame!

Three days passed, a week passed, and Colonel Landa did not return. Gizella grew peaked and her eyes dimmed. Her head was always lowered, as if a weight were pressing down on it. Sometimes the neighbors greeted her, sometimes they passed her without a word. Sometimes Gizella noticed them and sometimes she didn't, and gradually they too stopped noticing her.

Dina Vargaftik brought news that sabotage had been discovered in one of the hospitals: instead of narcotics patients had been given a poison, which did not kill them at once, but only after a day or two, making it appear they had not survived their operation. God forbid anybody got sick now.

Tosya Khomitsky brought similar news, but hers was more specific: she was in church and heard with her own ears a cultured, well-dressed woman say that the surgeons in the Jewish hospital had wanted to remove her son-in-law's bladder when he only had a simple hernia.

Olya Cheperukha said indignantly: "Tosya, aren't you ashamed to repeat such nonsense: so now all doctors are bastards, is that it!"

Dina stood up for Tosya: why all? No one said all, but go try and guess which is which.

On Saturday Anya Kotlyar had night duty. When she returned

home that morning she looked so terrible that Adya was frightened and cried out: "Aunt Anya!"

She reassured him and said it was nothing so terrible. It was just that one patient who had to be given glucose intravenously had grabbed the needle out of her hands, thrown it on the floor, and stamped on it. And another fool who was watching also suddenly began to balk even though just two days ago he had one leg in the grave and it was a miracle he'd come out of it.

"Savages," Adya said quietly. "It's medieval."

Anya shrugged her shoulders: some savages, one's from the ship *Dzerzhinsky,* the other one worked at the October Revolution factory.

That afternoon Klava Ivanovna came to see Anya Kotlyar. She told Adya to go out for a walk.

"Will you please tell me the whole truth: did something really happen in your hospital or is it all made up?" asked Klava Ivanovna.

"Madame Malaya, I didn't expect this of you!" said Anya, wide-eyed.

"Save your compliments for someone else," said Klava Ivanovna. "Swear by your life: did something happen or didn't it?"

Anya swore by her life that nothing had happened. Klava Ivanovna sighed with relief: "I thought so. But Landa's still in jail. And they don't keep people for no reason. Something's up."

Sometimes Gizella spent the night at home and sometimes at her sister's on Red Guard Street near the Revolution Theater. Katerina told Zinovy that they wouldn't let Gizella stay by herself in an apartment like that. She'd be moved elsewhere and a World War II disabled veteran with two children had the right to stake the first claim.

Zinovy raised his head and stared at his wife. Grisha and Misha stopped playing with their toys and became quiet. Katerina asked him not to try to hypnotize her and said she could say the whole thing again from the beginning. Zinovy went over to the children, helped them gather up their toys, and told them to go to sleep. As usual, Misha pestered his father to let him stay up another five minutes while Grisha turned without a word and went to get undressed.

At first they both romped around in their cribs, tugging at the bars and laughing. Katerina asked who wanted a strapping to help them fall asleep, and Misha answered no one and they became quiet. Zinovy signaled his wife to shut the door tight, and waited until she had turned toward. Then he said that if what he had just heard five minutes ago were ever repeated again in that house, all Odessa would gasp at what happened to her!

Katerina folded her arms on her chest, and, looking straight ahead, she asked whether this meant that Landa was not guilty and had been arrested for no reason.

Zinovy lowered his head, held it like that for a while, then lifted it again. His eyes were cold as if made of grey porcelain, and in a loud voice that could probably have been heard in the courtyard, he said: "When I was born Dr. Landa was already living in this courtyard and treating people; when I was studying to be a lieutenant, Colonel Landa had been saving the lives of our soldiers and officers for four years, since the very first day of the war. So, mark this and mark this well: I don't know anyone else like Landa! No one!"

Katerina's arms were still folded across her chest as she took a step forward. Now she stared at her husband and repeated her question: "Does this mean that Landa is not guilty, that they arrested him for no reason and that his Gizella should live alone in their mansion?"

Zinovy grabbed a glass, which crunched in his hand, and blood dripped onto the tablecloth; Katerina instinctively narrowed her eyes, her cheekbones turned yellow. She turned slowly around and went off to the children's room. A chair squeaked, then everything was quiet. A short while later he could hear someone sobbing or sniffling. Zinovy took the flannel blanket from the bed, spread it on the sofa and lay down in his clothes.

It was after twelve when Katerina left the children's room. She stopped by the couch, straightened the blanket, put another one on top, turned off the light, and got into bed. Sleep would not come, and she tossed and turned for a long time. A mouse was scratching persistently on Efim's side of the wall. Once again her thoughts turned to Landa: Zinovy was used to him from childhood and didn't want to know the truth, as if that had anything to do with it. But Gizella would definitely be moved out—two large rooms, a kitchen, bathroom, corridor, for one person! No matter what, the apartment would be given to someone, and better it be one of their own, someone from their courtyard.

Katerina sighed. The mouse was scratching somewhere nearby,

almost under the bed. She grew angry at that crack-brained Granik, who spread all kinds of infections around. His factory had offered him a room of his own. But he turned up his nose at it. Bolshoi Fontan is not Odessa, only his courtyard is Odessa. Madman!

The next day the conversation about Dr. Landa's apartment was resumed, but this time Olya started it. Zinovy had finished his dinner and she served him a vermicelli babka with raisins for dessert saying, of course, God forbid that Landa is sent to Siberia, but that's not up to us, and the apartment will fall into a stranger's hands. And who deserved it more than her son?

"Mama," Zinovy had cut himself a piece of babka, but didn't touch it. "It's understandable when my wife says that, but how could you bring yourself to say such a thing!"

"Zyunya," said Olya, resting her head on the palm of her hand. "We've suffered our whole lives in one little room. Now, thank God, you have an apartment of your own. But is this really an apartment? It's an outpost, the old laundry room where the poorest people in the courtyard washed their clothes and their underwear.

"Stop it, Mama," Zinovy said softly.

"Don't stop your mother's mouth!" shouted Olya. "This is the first and last time I can see my son and my grandchildren finally living in a real apartment, but you have to act like a saint who needs nothing in this world but work, work, and more work!"

Zinovy got up from the table and violently pushed his chair away. He tightened the straps on his prothesis, in commanding fashion as if it were a sword belt, and went outside—without his coat or hat. Olya began to cry, then grabbed her coat and ran after him but could not catch up with him. She stood for a while by the gate and then went back in.

The next morning as soon as people woke up and turned on the radio, the whole yard had new cause for celebration: by a resolution of the Soviet of Ministers of the U.S.S.R. the airplane designer Pavel Borisovich Malaya had been awarded the Stalin Prize. Iona Ovseich wanted to go down immediately and personally congratulate Klava Ivanovna and thank her for having such a son, but decided to restrain himself until the mailman brought the newspaper.

When Iona Ovseich went to see Malaya, Orlov, Stepa, and Zinovy were already there, but no one had a newspaper yet. Iona Ovseich neatly unfolded his newspaper, read a few lines about people they didn't know, and then paused with an expression worthy of Levitan himself, finally pronounced the name of Pavel Borisovich Malaya, designer and doctor of technical sciences. Other names were listed and Iona Ovseich read them all since they were all prizewinners. Then he handed the newspaper to the laureate's mother so she could see it with her own eyes. Klava Ivanovna said that she was totally blind without glasses, and couldn't remember where she had left them. So let the others have a look. While her guests read and reread the article, she sat in her armchair, her arms on the armrest, her legs covered with a shawl, and asked herself a question out loud: what did her son need all that money for—one hundred and fifty thousand? She and his late father, Boris Davidovich, had earned seventy rubles a month and managed quite nicely.

"Degtyar," said Klava Ivanovna, "write Pasha in my name and tell him to give one hundred thousand to the child care center; fifty thousand is quite enough for him."

Degtyar said that he could do that but the total amount was to be divided by thc ten prizewinners, which meant they each would receive fifteen thousand.

Klava Ivanovna's eyebrows raised. Stepa laughed merrily. She shushed him, thought for a moment, and said fine, then write Pasha to have a little talk with the other winners: they could each chip in ten thousand and give it to the children.

The door never closed at Malaya's all that day: people were either coming in or going out. Everyone wanted to shake her hand, and no one ever thought that he wasn't the only person in the courtyard or that an old person needs some rest. Later that evening the postman brought a congratulatory telegram from Moscow. After that many people visited Klava Ivanovna for a second time, and everyone asked the same question: was it true that the telegram was from Stalin personally? Klava Ivanovna would reply that, of course, Comrade Stalin had nothing else to do but send her telegrams. They knew that themselves, but it was irritating when you were sure of something then suddenly it turned out a mistake had been made.

On New Year's Eve Iona Ovseich arranged to have the Ilyich Club for the entire evening to honor the courtyard's oldest activist and community worker. Klava Ivanovna had stubbornly refused, but announcements had already been posted in the entranceway and by the club and, like it or not, she had to submit.

Apart from the people of the courtyard, those invited included residents of the neighboring buildings, girls from the shoe factory, the Krupskaya textile factory, and a Pioneer detachment from School Number 68, made up of students who had finished the second term without a single poor grade.

In his short opening speech Comrade Degtyar described Klava Ivanovna Malaya's entire life: from the daughter of a simple worker at the Gen factory, now the October Revolution factory, to the mother of a Stalin Prize laureate. For thirty years, as if it were a single day, through storms and foul weather, frost and heat, this simple woman, worker, and mother, bore her heart like Gorky's Danko so she could give her all to people, to the very last. And people came to her with their sorrows, their joys, and their worries, and never once did the simple door bell to Malaya's apartment ring, and the door remain closed.

"So, dear Grandma Klava," said Comrade Degtyar, opening his arms wide, "let us embrace you, kiss you warmly, and give you our heartfelt thanks!"

As Klava Ivanovna rose to meet him, the Pioneer bugle began to blare, and the drum rolled. Its banner unfurled, the Pioneer detachment stepped into the aisle, clicking their heels military style.

The hall thundered with applause. Klava Ivanovna tried to say a word but the detachment had already lined up along the wall according to rank and, on a signal from their leaders, they began singing Klava Ivanovna's favorite song:

All the world's roads are open to us
And the earth sends us its regards.
The flowers grow and the children are happy,
And the fields are rich with grain!

All right, my girls, all right, my beauties,
Let the country sing songs of us,
Let it praise our names in song,
Like it praises other heroes!

Klava Ivanovna sang along with the Pioneers, and everyone else joined in as well. Those who didn't know the words smiled cheerfully and moved their lips to the music so as not to feel left out at a moment like that.

The leader handed a bouquet of beautiful flowers to Klava Ivanovna and tied a Pioneer scarf around her neck. She kissed him on both cheeks. He made a smart about-face and took his place on the right flank of the detachment. The chairman announced that the floor would now be given to Comrade Zinovy Ionovich Cheperukha, as a member of the engineering and technical intelligentsia, and who was in more ways than one close to being a grandson to Klava Ivanovna Malaya.

The hall reacted to the chairman's joke with great enthusiasm, and when, approaching the platform, Zinovy said, "Not in more ways than one, and not almost, I really am her true grandson!" a storm erupted. People jumped up and began trying to outshout each other: "Right, Zinovy! Bravo! Bravo!"

First and foremost, said Cheperukha, on behalf of the entire collective of the Kirov Machine Tool Plant, he wanted to convey greetings and the warmest congratulations to Comrade Klava Ivanovna Malaya and wish her many, many more hale and hearty years of life! He had frequently spoken with Komsomol members and young factory workers about his good fortune to have been born and to be living in the same building, under the same roof, with such a remarkable person as Klava Ivanovna. As a sign of their love and her unfading youth they had asked him to give her a humble present—an Osoaviakhim badge, engraved on stainless steel, with her monogram.

Before handing it to Klava Ivanovna, Zinovy picked up the badge, which was in the form of book, raised it high above his head, and anyone who could remember Osoaviakhim was struck by how precisely the badge had been reproduced: the gas mask, the corregated pipe, the airplane propeller—all exactly perfect.

Klava Ivanovna was about to head for the platform to accept her gift, but Zinovy was a step ahead of her and began walking toward her, his gait as firm as a man who had both legs, and even the squeaking of his prothesis did not betray the truth. Since Klava Ivanovna was almost a full head shorter than Zinovy, she forced him to bend down, and she pressed him to her breast. They stood like that for an entire minute, as the audience applauded fervently. Many people wiped away tears, a mixture of joy, pride, and delight on their faces. Only the faces of the old people expressed a fleeting sadness or sorrow.

Having returned to the platform, Zinovy concisely described the gigantic technological progress the entire country was making at the present time. Clear proof of that progress, and its powerful inculcation into everyday life, was the fact that the party and government had awarded the Stalin Prize to an Odessite, a former resident of the courtyard, the airplane designer Pavel Borisovich Maly. "The prizewinner's mother is here with us tonight: we take this opportunity to ask her to convey to her son, our remarkable countryman Pavel Borisovich Maly, our warmest regards and our desire that he achieve new success and accomplishment for the good of the nation, for the good of the motherland!"

Zinovy left the platform for the second time, went up to the table where Klava Ivanovna was sitting—this time she calmly waited in her seat—and he shook her hand firmly. The audience applauded warmly. Comrade Degtyar proposed that the applause be viewed as approval of Zinovy's suggestion, then firmly shook the hand of the laureate's mother.

A shoe factory worker, a leader in socialist competition, a shock worker, and Komsomol member, Nadezdha Buzga was now given the rostrum to say a word of welcome. At the rostrum, Nadya took a piece of paper from her pocket, placed it in front of her, frowned cheerfully, and said: "Here is the speech I have written. My comrades should not be insulted but I cannot speak today from a prepared text. I simply wish to say: dear Klava Ivanovna, dear Mama, come to our factory, warm us with your soul, and scold us if need be. It won't hurt our feelings. As a sign of our gratitude and as a pledge of our friendship, please accept our humble gift, these patent-leather shoes. May you wear them for a hundred years and never wear them out!"

Nadya bowed, picked up a box with a red ribbon, and brought it over to Klava Ivanovna, who set the box aside, embraced the girl, kissed her three times, then untied the ribbon and took out the shoes. She put them on in front of everyone and took five or six steps along the stage.

The audience burst into such applause that the chairman had to point to the ceiling and walls a few times, indicating they weren't made of iron or steel, after all.

Comrade Idalia Antonovna Orlov was given the floor to say a few words on behalf of the courtyard and the other neighbors. The hall calmed down a little, though there was still some scattered applause. Lyalya did not wait for total silence; in an excited, resounding, pure voice, like that of a child, bursting with tears of joy and delight, she exclaimed: "Our own beloved Klava Ivanovna! How can I find the words to express even one percent of our love, our respect, and our gratitude! What words can convey the pride we feel from knowing that we have lived all our conscious life side by side with you, breathed the same air as you, and seen the same patch of blue sky above us. Who could forget how, at a very trying time, you were more patient with me than my own mother, took care of me, did not let me go astray. Today, it's painful and shameful for me to remember that I did not fall at your feet and kiss your golden hands calloused from work. So now, my dearest, let me do just that, on this great day, so happy for all!"

Although everyone had heard Orlov's request, they were still surprised when Lyalya ran over to Klava Ivanovna and actually fell to her feet, crossing her hands over her chest. Klava Ivanovna grabbed Lyalya by the elbows and told her to get up at once. She straightened up, then Iona Ovseich came over to help and the two of them forced Lyalya back up onto her feet.

The woman trembled and tears streamed down her cheeks. Zinovy Cheperukha left his place at the presidium table, went to the middle of the stage, and, waving his hands over his head, began clapping loudly. The audience picked up the applause. Row after row, from first to last, rose to its feet to give Klava Ivanovna a standing ovation.

When the storm had abated and people had retaken their seats, a racket broke out somewhere in back. The chairman called for immediate silence, but the racket grew louder and angry voices could be heard as if a fight was about to begin. Those in front instinctively turned around and began to look back. Some young person had suddenly decided to leave, but people were indignant and demanded that he wait until the break. With even greater impudence he continued to force his way out, stepping on people's toes, as if deaf and blind to it all.

"What's going on there in the back rows?" asked Comrade Degtyar.

He received no answer. The voices only grew louder, since the young man had reached the end of the row and was heading straight for the door. Finally Iona Ovseich saw that it was none other than Adya Lapidis. At first he felt a strong desire to shout: "Stop! Where are you going?" but people had already flung the door open and were sarcastically advising Adya to get a little fresh air. Adya stumbled in the doorway. From a distance it looked like someone had tripped him. A cheerful murmur of approval rose from the audience, putting an end to the event. The door closed; the frosty air which had blown in from outside had only refreshed the audience.

The chairman tapped the water pitcher with his pen and announced that the floor would be given to Tatyana Gordeichuk, a worker at the Krupskaya factory, who regularly overfulfilled her quotas by one hundred and thirty to one hundred and forty percent. She would present a valuable gift to Klava Ivanovna.

Tatyana went up on the stage carrying a package wrapped in cellophane and said she could say nothing better than her co-worker Idalia Orlov had already said it, and placed the gift—a knitted silk suit with a monogram sewn on the jacket—in front of the chairman. Comrade Degtyar indicated Klava Ivanovna with a motion of his hand. Suddenly embarrassed by her blunder, Tatyana bit her finger. Klava Ivanovna went up to her, embraced her, and kissed her three times, as custom dictated.

Stepa Khomitsky suggested that Klava Ivanovna try the suit on. What if it didn't fit, and she had to exchange it? Voices rang out in support but Tatyana replied that there could be no mistake since the measurements had been taken beforehand.

Iona Ovseich grabbed his head as if in horror and cried: "Tatyana, why are you revealing state secrets!"

"Doesn't matter," Zinovy shouted, "we're all friends here, and there are no secrets from the people!"

Embarrassed again, Tatyana blushed deeply, but the audience laughed so sincerely that in the end she could only rejoice at this comic turn of events which no one had planned and no one could have foreseen.

Time was needed for the audience to quiet down. However, the uproar was ten times greater when the chairman announced that the celebrant Klava Ivanovna Malaya now had the floor.

Waiting a minute, Klava Ivanovna signaled several times that it was time to be quiet, but this had just the opposite effect, and all she could do was wait patiently until people, who were filled with so much emotion, had poured it all out.

Finally the hall was quiet. Klava Ivanovna looked intently at the audience for a second or two, then, with a nod at the chairman, said: "Tonight you have congratulated me on my thirty years of community service. I should inform you all that in fact it won't be thirty years for another year and a month. But the evening's organizers rushed things a little because in their heart of hearts they were worried that old Malaya might up and die before they got around to it!"

A cheerful murmur arose in the hall. There were shouts of protest and the presidium joined in. Only Comrade Degtyar remained silent, as if accepting her accusation in full.

"As you see," said Klava Ivanovna, "Degtyar himself is not objecting. But I'll tell you a secret: I'm entirely on his side. Why? Because the Stalin Prize, which the party and government awarded my son, is a prize for all of you, and today is a celebration for us all. Allow the old Malaya to bow low and to say: my dear ones, my children, I thank you with all my heart."

Klava Ivanovna bowed to all sides and people applauded. Dina and Tosya took seats in the front row, each of them shedding a few tears despite themselves. There were strangers sitting on either side of them; their eyes also gleamed moistly and they too had to wipe them with their little finger every so often.

"Oh," moaned Tosya softly, "Malaya's had a wonderful life, she's to be envied."

"Dear comrades," said Klava Ivanovna with a sad smile, "time doesn't stand still. The years are passing, we're aging, and we're dying, yes, dying, we mustn't deceive ourselves, and new people are being born to take over for us and we ought to give them everything we have because, as they say, you can't take it with you! We expect our children and grandchildren to thank us for this. And of course it's a bitter thing to be given a reproach instead of gratitude—Grandma, you don't understand anything, everything's different now. There's a grain of truth in that. Sometimes I even feel like a stranger in my own courtyard. Don't interrupt, don't interrupt! And I ask myself—why should I necessarily think that other people are to blame, maybe it's really my fault."

Silence reigned in the room. Iona Ovseich tapped his pen against the pitcher and he seemed to be signaling to the speaker.

"And maybe," said Klava Ivanovna, spreading her hands, "my courtyard, my neighbors, really can't live like one big family anymore—the children have grown up and have children and families of their own. Many people say that it's because of the war. War is war of course, especially the one with Hitler, but after all wasn't there a war three years after the Revolution?"

Iona Ovseich tapped the pitcher again. Klava Ivanovna automatically turned toward him and imperceptibly, as if scratching his hand, he indicated his watch.

"Don't show me your watch," said Klava Ivanovna in a loud voice. "Nobody gave me a time limit."

People smiled. Iona Ovseich smiled too and said that the presidium had been requested that Comrade Malaya speak in specific terms about the community services she had performed in the course of thirty years.

"No," said Klava Ivanovna, "something has changed and it'll never be the same again. Since the evening is in my honor, I want us to think back to the twenties, thirties, to the International Alliance of Supporting Workers, Osoaviakhim, and the outpost. Then everyone will go home and get a good night's sleep and tomorrow they'll wake up and look at the calendar and ask themselves what year it is."

Klava Ivanovna stopped and wiped her tears with her fingertips. Though the room was perfectly quiet, Comrade Degtyar whacked the table twice, rose, and said: "Let's have a round of applause for Comrade Malaya and wish her another thirty years of work and labor for the good of the people and the good of Soviet man!"

Iona Ovseich was the first to begin clapping, followed by the presidium and the audience. Klava Ivanovna stood in confusion for a moment as if she'd been interrupted in mid-sentence. Zinovy and Lyalya walked over to her, took her by the arm, and seated her beside the chairman at the presidium table.

"And as for your misgivings," continued Iona Ovseich in a cheerful tone, "we should dispell them right here and now: yes, Soviet man has changed, meaning, he's grown, matured, and is today a head taller than any representative of the bourgeois world but one thing has not changed and will remain unshakable forever—and that's the monolithic unity of Soviet society which was cemented by the iron will of the Bolsheviks!"

Those words were met with a new wave of applause and this time it was unclear who had reacted first, the presidium or the audience. When the ovation had died down somewhat, Iona Ovseich announced in an excited tone of voice that there had been a motion to send a telegram of salutation to Comrade Stalin on behalf of the entire gathering.

People rose as one, the room ringing with the exclamation: "Long live the great Stalin!" A thunderous cheer rose from all sides as at a May Day parade. Iona Ovseich repeated the greeting to Stalin and the audience responded at once. A person would have had to have had particularly keen hearing to distinguish between the power of the front and the back rows.

The bugle blared at a signal from the leader, the drums rolled, and the Pioneers cried out: "Always prepared!" The chairman announced that the ceremonies had concluded and the movie *The Rich Bride* would now be shown.

As if bursting with joy, women's voices rang out, singing:

All right, my girls, all right, my beauties,
Let the country sing songs of us,
Let it praise our names in song,
Like it praises other heroes!

Efim Granik rang Klava Ivanovna's bell late that evening when she was already in bed. He said that she had been impossible to reach the last few days and he wanted to spend a little time with her alone.

"All right, come in, since you're here. Don't stand at the door like a beggar," said Klava Ivanovna with a sigh.

Efim sat down at the table, unbuttoned his jacket, and withdrew a fairly large package wrapped in parchment. Klava Ivanovna asked him what it was. Efim did not answer and began slowly unwrapping the paper, revealing a large piece of black glass. When she took it in her hands and turned it over, she saw her name, Klava Ivanovna Malaya, in gold letters; there were two gold stars with hammers and sickles on either side of her name.

Klava Ivanovna admired it for a minute or more, then grew suddenly sorrowful and said: "All that's left to do is add the dates."

Efim replied that we all had the same fate in store for us, but Madame Malaya would have to find another painter for that job.

"I don't want anyone else," said Klava Ivanovna with another sigh, but then immediately grew angry with herself. "All right, we'll argue about that another time. An old woman has the right to think about her death but you don't. It is time for you to forget the past, settle down, and start living with Lizochka. Good night."

A few days later, after New Year's, Efim dropped by again but this time he seemed to have a different purpose in mind. He said that Katerina Cheperukha was plotting against him and was going to use the health commission to have him evicted.

"What does that mean—evicted?" asked Klava Ivanovna in surprise. "Your factory is giving you a room of your own with all the conveniences on Bolshoi Fontan."

"So you're against me too?" said Efim, seizing his chest with both hands. "Yes, Landa's gone, there's no one left to stand up for me."

Klava Ivanovna shook a threatening finger at him and said: "Don't pretend to be crazier than you are. The state is giving you a new room in a new building where you can live like a human being and you're acting like some grande dame. I don't have to tell you how beautiful that area is with its trees, greenery, steppe air, and the sea two steps away."

Efim paused for a moment's thought, then exclaimed: "You know, I'm ready to swap with you—you can breathe the steppe air at the seaside and go walking through the trees."

"You think you've caught me there, don't you," said Klava Ivanovna, "but I'll tell you something: if the state ordered me to move there, I wouldn't be capricious about it even though I've lived in this courtyard twenty years longer than you have."

Efim put his arms around himself as if feeling a chill, and gently swayed back and forth in his chair: "At the celebration when you brought up the years before the war, Osoaviakhim, the outpost, I kept telling myself how lucky we are that you're still alive and with us."

Klava Ivanovna sighed deeply: yes, she had indeed said all that but a holiday, a celebration, was one thing, and real life was another, and you shouldn't mix up the two.

"But why," said Efim, "should I who have nothing left in the world have to leave the courtyard for good when outsiders who'd just as soon be living in Cheboksary as Odessa have the right to live here!"

"Efim, I don't like your tone!" said Klava Ivanovna angrily. "You're acting like a landowner who has an estate coming from inheritance. You don't want to understand that times have changed. You never wanted to understand that."

"Madame Malaya," said Efim, narrowing an eye, his face becoming immobile, masklike, "what was it that I was supposed to understand and didn't? Have I won millions and refused to share them? Show me the place where I've hidden my happiness and return it to its rightful owners."

Once again Klava Ivanovna said that she disliked this sort of idle talk but Efim insisted on an answer. Finally she lost her temper and said straight out: "You're a poor devil, it's true, but Degtyar is right when he says that in your heart of hearts you always remained a shopkeeper and, if you'd had the nerve, you would have opened your own shop and not given a damn for anything else."

Efim scratched his forehead with his finger like a simpleton, then placed his hands with their large yellow callouses on the table in front of him.

"Those callouses are from the palette knives and brushes I used when I was young. The war cut me into little pieces and there's nothing left of me now, but still for thirty years running they've been saying I'm nothing but a petty shopkeeper. I'm such a lucky guy!"

That's right, said Klava Ivanovna, he was a lucky man because it was Soviet power that had allowed Efim Granik to become an honest worker even though he caused people plenty of trouble in the meantime.

"But still I'm like a wolf who always keeps one eye on the forest," cried Efim.

"Big mouth," said Klava Ivanovna with a dismissive gesture, "you let your tongue run away with you."

Comrade Degtyar brought an important piece of news from the City Executive Committee: Lvov and Sevastopol were challenging Odessa to a competition to see which city was the best in terms of services and cleanliness. That placed special obligations on the people of Odessa and specifically on their courtyard, which was situated in the Stalin District. From here on in anyone who did not value the honor of his native city and his courtyard would be told good-bye and good riddance!

By decision of the building committee, a three-man team—Lyalya Orlov, Stepa Khomitsky, and Katerina Cheperukha—was to inspect the entire building, every nook and cranny, every cellar and attic. The next Sunday would be a voluntary workday for the entire courtyard: a sentry would be posted by the gate in order to determine who was attempting to shirk and using specious excuses to wriggle out of taking part.

By midday there was such a pile of rubbish and junk in the middle of the courtyard that people keep saying in astonishment that it couldn't be theirs, it must have been placed there on the sly by people from Lvov and Sevastopol!

They had to hire a truck to haul it all away: every family chipped in five rubles. The truck made several trips and its tires mixed so much mud and dust in the snow that it became black as earth.

When people were saying good-bye, Katerina Cheperukha walked over to Efim Granik and, in the presence of Lyalya Orlov, informed him that a mouse had come running into their apartment from his room again. She had made a point of leaving it in the mouse trap to be able to show it to her neighbors, and, if he didn't do something about the situation, he'd only have himself to blame.

Indignantly Efim replied: "And where's the proof that the mouse is mine and not yours? Did he show you his passport?"

"Fima," said Lyalya, grimacing as if she just tasted something sour, "one look at your room is enough."

An hour or an hour and a half after this scene, Efim was sitting in his room sketching on paper with the radio on—there was a report that farm machinery repairs in Turkmenia were experiencing delays and the spring fieldwork was just around the corner. He tinkered awhile with the lid of the washstand, then drove a few nails into the chair so the seat wouldn't wobble, but that did nothing to improve his mood, which was even worse than it had been. He straightened his room a little, then shined his shoes, put on a clean shirt, and went upstairs to see Madame Malaya.

Klava Ivanovna gave him a warm welcome and said that if it weren't for her age someone might think he was her lover, he was calling on her so often, but then she dispelled that notion herself—with a long face like that of people visiting a cemetery, not lovers. Efim did not reply. Klava Ivanovna scrutinized him for a few seconds, then asked: "What's wrong? What's the matter?"

Efim raised his right hand and pointed toward the door with his thumb. "They're after me, they're trying to get rid of me."

"Stop talking nonsense!" said Klava Ivanovna angrily. "Nobody's trying to get rid of you."

Again Efim pointed back with his thumb and repeated: "They're after me. They said they'd get rid of me."

"Those fools!" said Klava Ivanovna with even greater anger. "I'll give them a talking to they won't forget in a hurry. Tell me, have you had dinner yet? Let's have a glass of tea together."

Klava Ivanovna poured the tea from a thermos bottle. The tea wasn't very hot but Efim asked for a teaspoon, which he filled with tea. He blew on it until it was cool, and then smacked his lips with pleasure.

"Fima," said Madame Malaya, shaking her head reproachfully and sighing, "it's time for you to get married. And you should find a wife who'll keep you under control."

She poured her guest the last of the tea in the thermos. He continued to drink it with a teaspoon, smacking his lips.

"Stop smacking your lips," said Madame Malaya angrily. "A person needs nerves of steel to put up with you!"

This caught Efim by surprise. He shuddered and automatically pressed against the back of his chair. Klava Ivanovna walked over to him, tugged his ear as if he were a kindergartner, and said it again: "Fima, it's time for you to get married."

"No, I'm not leaving here!" cried Efim out of the blue. "I can see through all of you, these plots won't work on me! And you can tell Ovseich that I'm not afraid of him, I'm not afraid of anyone!"

"You stupid man," said Klava Ivanovna, entwining her fingers and thrusting her hands out in front of her. "What does Ovseich have to do with anything here?"

"What does Ovseich have to do with anything?" said Efim, jumping up as if he'd been scalded. "I'll tell you—he's standing outside the door right this minute and eavesdropping on every word we say. I'll show you!"

Efim flung open the door and for a second it did seem that something flashed past. Klava Ivanovna looked at the door despite herself but a person would have to have lost his mind entirely to believe in those idiotic suspicions for a single second.

"Listen to me," said Klava Ivanovna when they both were a bit calmer again. "Tomorrow or the day after you and I will drop by Degtyar's together and you'll see with your own eyes that your fantasies and the reality are as different as night and day."

The next day Efim had to work almost two full shifts at his factory—the painting of the cargo ship *Lenin Komsomol* had to be rushed to completion. Then Klava Ivanovna caught a terrible cough that had her blue in the face and, on January 13, the radio and newspapers reported the arrest of a large group of prominent doctors who over the years had risen to high position in the army and health care system, and people were so shocked they couldn't talk about anything else.

Now the incident with Landa came to the fore again and no great intelligence was required to see that it was all one large network—Moscow, Leningrad, Odessa, and all the other cities where those murderers and bandits had had their own agents.

Zinovy's house was genuinely in mourning. Both he and his father were deeply disheartened and Olya clapped her hands ten times a day, saying again and again: "They had everything! Money, dachas, cars, three-room apartments, but that wasn't enough for them, they had to stuff their faces, the greedy bandits, oh, those bandits!"

At first Katerina took no part in those conversations, only looking at Zinovy, expecting him to say the first word, but finally she could restrain herself no longer and said: "Why aren't you saying anything? Did you take a vow of silence?"

For a few days Efim kept apart from everyone and was unapproachable but, even from a distance, it was clear how much he was suffering. Once again people were seized by the fear that he might take his own life; finally Iona Cheperukha forced his way into Granik's room to speak with him.

"Efim," shouted Cheperukha from the doorway, "people have forgotten what your voice sounds like!"

"Go away," whispered Efim. "Get out!"

"Fima," said Iona on the verge of tears from Granik's insulting tone, "after all these years and you speak to me like that!"

"Go away," repeated Efim. "For God's sake go away."

Cheperukha sat down at the table and propped his head on his hands, staring at the black speaker on the wall. Efim groaned loudly as if from an unbearable pain. Iona rose and turned on the radio. They were playing *Tales of the Vienna Woods* by Johann Strauss, which lightened the atmosphere in the room.

"Beautiful music," said Iona. "When you listen to it you can't believe the world we live in is such a mess. Oh, who would have ever thought it about Landa!"

Efim was sitting cross-legged on the couch, his eyes gleaming like black wax under a thin layer of water. Cheperukha shrugged his shoulders and said how could a person ever imagine that there'd be such degenerates and scum among the Jews who suffered the most from the Nazis.

"If it's confirmed," said Efim, lowering his feet to the floor, "if they confirm that it's the truth, then it means not enough of us were slaughtered."

For fifteen seconds Iona looked silently at Efim trying to fathom his gaze but then lost patience and asked: "Who do you mean by 'us'?"

Efim walked over to a pail, filled a cup with water, and drank it greedily, gurgling as it went down. Then he went back to the couch.

"If I didn't know you," said Iona Cheperukha, drawing himself up to his full height, revealing his weather-beaten leathery neck, "I'd say you were a rotten bastard."

Efim sat cross-legged again, his chin resting on his chest. Two tears, huge as summer raindrops, rolled from his eyes.

"All right," said Iona, sitting down beside Efim, "don't be offended. This thing hurts me as much as it hurts you."

The music ended, the next program was on the flowering of ethnic culture in Yakutia. In tsarist times that enormous territory, equal in size to Western Europe, had not had a written literature of its own, whereas now the Yakutsk national epic *Olonkho,* over twenty thousand lines long, had been transcribed in dozens of different versions. More than a million copies of the book had been printed; the number of libraries in the republic exceeded one hundred with around half of them in rural locales.

"Efim," said Iona, "have you ever actually met a Yakut? When my son Zinovy was in Siberia he used to see them all the time: he says they're good people, always smiling, and they speak such pure Russian you can only tell them by their face."

Efim bent forward, pressing both hands to his stomach like someone suffering an ulcer attack. Iona suddenly hit himself on the knee and burst out laughing.

"One time a Yakut came to the Arcadia health resort. He was a famous hunter back home and he won a trip to Odessa as a prize. The doctors noticed that he didn't eat the first day, didn't eat the second day, and didn't eat the third. Finally, they got worried and asked him: what's going on, why are you refusing food? It turned out that, number one, he couldn't eat without drinking some alcohol, because he had gotten used to doing it in Yakutia where it's seventy below, and, number two, he wanted raw meat. Raw meat contains a lot of vitamins and without it all his teeth would fall out from scurvy."

"And so," asked Efim, "did they give him any?"

"What do you mean," said Iona, laughing again, "you can't give a man a prize so he can starve to death in Odessa! The head of the sanatorium issued a special prescription for the Yakut."

The program on Yakutia came to an end and was followed by a concert of songs of the peoples of the Far East—the Luoravetlans, Koryaks, and Niwekhs. Iona listened for a while, then said all the songs sounded the same and he wished Efim good night. Efim asked him to shut the door tight behind him; leaving the radio on, he crawled under his flannelette blanket, placing his jacket on top of the blanket—it could be bitter cold in his room at night—and he fell asleep. He dreamed of Odessa in 1937 when they had just finished building the outpost. His son Osya was reciting his own poems at the celebration. Sonya was beaming with pride for her son and Khilka pressed against her mother's side, staring at her brother, all eyes.

Efim knew a pleasure he had not known for a long time. Once in a while he would suspect that it was only a dream but then he would immediately check by striking up a conversation with Malaya, Kotlyar, Khomitsky, or Lapidis. He walked over to Degtyar to share his foolish misgivings with him. Degtyar replied by ridiculing him: "Efim Granik is not like everyone else, when he has it too good, he says it can't be true, it's only a dream."

The radio resumed its programming at six o'clock. The national anthem was played, then the announcer wished his listeners a good morning and began reading the latest news. Reports were pouring in from every side concerning special feats of labor performed on the eve of January 21. The workers at the Kuznetsk mining complex had assumed the obligation of meeting their monthly quota no later than the thirtieth. Reader demand for the works of Lenin and Stalin had increased to an even greater level in the factory libraries in Makeevka, Dzhezkagan, Tkvibuli, and other industrial centers. Clubs and palaces of culture had organized exhibits and stands displaying a great variety of materials including photos and reproductions of paintings devoted to the close working cooperation between Lenin and Stalin.

The announcer took a short pause in which a rustling could be heard as if he were turning pages, then, in a solemn voice reminiscent of the war years when reports from the commander in chief concerning successful attacks by Soviet troops were broadcast, he announced that by decree of the presidium of the Supreme Soviet of the U.S.S.R. Dr. Lydia Fedoseevna Timashuk had been awarded the Order of Lenin.

Efim was at his washstand and had already picked up the soap but he came to an involuntary halt even though it was perfectly possible to wash and listen at the same time. Then, as if he had been jostled, the soap slipped from his hand, hit the side of the pail, and went flying way off to one side. Efim automatically bent over just as the announcer was uttering the words "for the help she showed the government in unmasking the Doctors' Plot." For a moment his vision blurred and his heart was in his throat and seemed on the verge of flying out his mouth. He picked up the soap, wet it, and worked up a good lather. First he washed his hands, then devoted special care to his ears, face, and neck, even washing his nape and Adam's apple separately, as if he were going to the theater or a concert. After drying himself, he picked up his shaving brush and his "Zolingen" razor with its picture of two fat men standing belly to belly and leaned his mirror against a glass for a better view of himself while shaving. He covered his cheeks with a lather so thick only his nose protruded, making his eyes seem especially dark, two small circles of black marble. After shaving both cheeks, he removed the lather with the palm of his hand, then lifted his chin and compressed his lips, the corners stretched downward. He took hold of his nose with his free hand, his grip resting lightly on his upper lip. He brought the razor up a little above his Adam's apple and slashed his throat from left to right. There was a flash of lightning in his eyes, a crackling and gurgling in his throat; his entire body shuddered abruptly before collapsing to the floor.

After returning home from work, Iona picked up the day's issue of *The Banner of Communism,* which had once been known as *The Bolshevik Banner,* its new name conferred on it after the Nineteenth Party Congress, then he decided to go see Efim: even if he had heard the report on the radio, the newspaper was still the newspaper. Iona rang the bell and, while waiting for Efim to come to the door, he folded the page on which the decree had been printed so that Lenin's portrait was on the lower half. Efim hadn't answered the door yet and Iona rang the bell a second time. He could hear that the radio was on and they seemed to be playing the "Varshavianka," Lenin's favorite song. Iona rang the bell a third time, loud enough to wake the dead, then pressed his ear to the door.

There was a short pause when the song was over but Iona could not hear anyone stirring inside. The announcer said that the symphony's pianist would now play Beethoven's *Appassionata.* Iona's heart skipped a beat unpleasantly and he pounded his fist against the door, but to no avail.

It was possible that Efim had not returned from work yet but it was unlike him to leave the radio on all day. Not only that, there was light coming through the cracks in the door meaning that lights were on inside.

Zinovy had gone to the movies with Katerina and there was nobody to ask if they'd seen Efim today. He went to one door then another in confusion; suddenly, making up his mind, he ran home for his ax.

When he returned he began to fling his ax against the outer door. The force caused the inner door to fly open as well. Iona stopped in the doorway and the first thing to strike his eye was the bed with the jacket on top of the blanket.

"Oy!" said Iona, clutching at his heart. He forced himself to take two or three steps, then cried *"Oy!"* again and thought he was about to lose his mind: hunched up, his head in a pool of blood, Efim was lying on the floor, his glassy eyes looking far past Iona.

Iona knelt down, raised Efim's head, and pressed his lips to it, then burst into tears like a little child. His body shook, his shoulders twitched, and he began hiccuping uncontrollably.

The ambulance arrived an hour later. Iona and Stepa helped carry out the body, having first covered the face with a towel.

There was a crowd of neighbors by the gate: some wanted a better look while others could not bear the sight and turned away.

The next day the morgue sent word to the courtyard that the body could be picked up, but no one went to get it. Iona Ovseich was in favor of leaving it there until the funeral but Malaya, Khomitsky, and Cheperukha disagreed, insisting that the body be brought back to the courtyard first. In the end Iona Ovseich yielded and Efim's body was delivered to the courtyard. A few people from Efim's factory brought two wreaths, one of which was very beautiful, made of fresh conifer branches, and the other was the usual sort with paper flowers and paper leaves. The ribbons were of black cloth with large gold letters: "To Efim Lazarevich Granik with respect from his friends and comrades at work."

The neighbors also chipped in a ruble apiece for a wreath. In addition, Malaya, Cheperukha, the Khomitskys, and Anya Kotlyar each purchased a wreath of their own. Dina Vargaftik brought two potted geraniums, which she placed at the head of the coffin.

Comrade Degtyar said Granik was being shown too much honor, you might think they were burying a person of exceptional merit.

"Degtyar," said Klava Ivanovna, looking at Efim with sadness in her eyes, "a man dies only once."

Efim Granik didn't die, replied Iona Ovseich, he deliberately put an end to his life, and, not only that, he had chosen a special day to make his point.

"So he chose the day deliberately," said Klava Ivanovna, shaking her head. "May our enemies think like he did and make the same choice he did."

"Ovseich," said Iona Cheperukha in a soft voice that was only a step away from a shout, "let's let him rest in peace, at least in his grave, all right?"

Comrade Degtyar closed his eyes and bit his lower lip. Klava Ivanovna assigned Cheperukha to make sure all the doors were open so they wouldn't have to start fiddling with them at the last minute.

The bearing-out was scheduled for three o'clock. At a quarter to three, Tosya brought Lizochka into the room, then walked over to the coffin and kissed Efim on the lips. Suddenly she pressed her face to him, her whole body trembling as she wept uncontrollably. Klava Ivanovna took her by the shoulders and told her to get hold of herself. Lizochka looked at her father and the other people in the room, not understanding what was happening. Tosya told her to kiss her father, that she would never see him again, and then she began trembling again, longer and more severely this time, and had to be given smelling salts.

Lizochka hadn't moved. Klava Ivanovna told her to kiss her father and say good-bye to him, then took her by the hand and led her up to the body. She pressed Lizochka's head forward, mussing her black curls, and held her head in that position for a short while. Then Lizochka raised her head, made the sign of the cross over her father before Klava Ivanovna had time to stop her, and walked away from the coffin.

"Aw, what does he care now," said Iona Cheperukha.

Stepa placed the lid on the coffin, nailed it shut with two nails, then gave the order for it to be lifted. While the men lined up beside the coffin, Malaya and the other women, Lyalya, Dina, Marina, Olya, and Katerina, took turns hugging Lizochka and kissing her cheeks, telling her to love and obey her aunt Tosya, who cared for her and was as devoted to her as her own born mother had been.

The coffin passed easily through the door. The pallbearers lined up in single file and lifted it over their heads. They carried it on their shoulders to the gate where a truck sent from Efim's factory was waiting. A bus, also from Efim's factory, was parked a short distance away, ready to take the mourners to the cemetery. Looking at the large crowd, Stepa said that the men should ride in the back of the truck but, after everyone else had boarded the bus, there turned out to be plenty of empty seats.

The truck with the coffin and wreaths led the procession. Iona Cheperukha sat in the cab with the driver. There was a small hitch with the bus: Klava Ivanovna was saving a seat for Degtyar and asked the bus to wait a minute while she sent Stepa to look for him. When Stepa finally returned, he said that Comrade Degtyar had flatly refused to attend the funeral. It was a long ride. They had to detour through Slobodka because the snow was too high on Frunze Street near Dukovsky Park. The women's hands and feet were freezing and they grew vexed with themselves: why did they have to go? It would have been enough to have paid their respects and seen the coffin to the gate.

Granik had not been given a good place: it was in the middle of nowhere, at the edge of a vacant lot. The ground was strewn with fragments of marble on which there were black Hebrew letters, pieces of granite, broken shells, and empty jars.

The coffin was set down on the ground. The grave-diggers told them to hurry, saying they were behind in their work and it was getting dark already. They adjusted their ropes, lifted the coffin by all four corners, and were about to begin lowering it when an old Jew walked over and offered to recite the muleh. He asked for the name of the deceased. Klava Ivanovna said, Efim Lazarevich Granik.

The old man closed his eyes and raised his head as if he were blind. Then, leaning on his cane, he began reciting the prayer in a thin, cracked voice:

"Iskor elohim nishmas abo mori Chaim ben Lazar sheolakh leolomo, baavur sheani noder tsdoko baado . . . im nishmos Avrum, Istkhok vi'Iakov . . . Amen."

The mourners thanked the old man and everyone gave him a little something. The grave-diggers lowered the coffin into the grave. Klava Ivanovna threw in a handful of earth, followed by Iona, Stepa, and all the others. At first each clod struck the coffin with a thud, but then the sound grew softer and softer. The grave-diggers began using their shovels; a short time later the grave had been filled and a mound rose above the surface whose ends they then evened off. The wreaths were placed on top of the mound. Tosya arranged the ribbons so that the name of the dead man was legible, then they all headed back toward the gates. Adya was the only one who remained behind. He spent about ten or fifteen minutes hanging around the cemetery, picking up fragments and cleaning the snow off them, revealing Russian and Hebrew letters, Arabic and Roman numerals. Then he walked back to the grave, lay down on the wreaths, embracing them and weeping bitterly. From the north, near the New Moscow Highway, a woman's voice cried out, then fell silent for a moment before becoming a hysterical wail of lamentation.

Adya broke off a conifer branch and tore off a black paper leaf, placing them both in his pocket before heading for the gates. Dogs were playing by the gate, one of them black as pitch, the other brown with gray spots; they were rolling in the snow and barking happily. Bulldozers were clearing a small square by the cemetery and, a little further on, earth movers were digging a foundation pit. Trailers drove up to the site from the direction of Zastava, and a mobile crane lowered its cable and hook. Two workers attached the load and shouted, "Up she goes!" The unwieldy mass rose in the air, hung motionless for a few seconds, then, swaying back and forth, was slowly lowered back to the ground.

An enormous white sign with red letters read: "We will fulfill and overfulfill the decisions of the historic Nineteenth Party Congress!" There was also a piece of plywood lower down with the inscription: "Avtogenmash factory, construction by SMU-504."

After the funeral people gathered in Efim's room for a wake. Dina Vargaftik shrugged her shoulders and said it was outlandish, Jews didn't have wakes. Iona Cheperukha replied that the only thing Jewish about Efim had been his bris and his grave in the Jewish cemetery. But the late Granik had liked a glass of Moskovskaya vodka and wouldn't have been against it.

At first they sat for a minute in silence, their faces grim, their eyes unmoving. Then Stepa asked if it wasn't time for a drink. Iona picked up the carafe and poured a drink for Klava Ivanovna, himself, Olya, and Dina, then passed the carafe to Zinovy. When everyone's glass was full, he rose and said:

"Dear neighbors and friends! We have just accompanied Efim on his last journey, a journey from which no one returns. Some people say that no one comes back because things are so good after death. Other people say, what's the point of returning to this world. But no one's in a hurry to get there, everyone puts it off as long as he can, and a person has to have had a life like Efim Granik's to take his own life, of his own free will."

Iona wiped away a tear, raised his glass, and, wishing that the ground lie lightly on the dead man, he drained his glass. The others followed his example and chased their drinks with appetizers. Now conversations sprang up. Lyalya walked over to Madame Malaya and whispered in her ear. Klava Ivanovna nodded in reply, then asked people for a minute of their attention. Still sitting, she said:

"Comrades, we loved Efim with all our heart. It's true that he didn't have an easy life: he lost his family, his wife, his children. But he wasn't the only one, there were millions and millions of others like him. On the other hand, some of our people risked their own lives to save his daughter. And when it was time for him to return to Odessa, he wasn't left out on the street: he was given a room, a job at a leading factory, and recently his factory committee made the decision to allocate him a new room, one with all the conveniences. His comrades from the factory are here and can vouch for that."

Granik's co-workers confirmed the fact, adding that Efim was in everyone's good books and enjoyed his fellow workers' respect, though he did have some odd ways.

"Not only some odd ways, it was more than that," said Klava Ivanovna. "And that was the main reason he committed that senseless act, and not because his fate had been especially tragic as Cheperukha would have it. In his own way Efim Granik did not have a bad life, and our courtyard had a hand in that."

Someone instinctively began clapping at the other end of the table but people shushed him. The room became still again except for the click of forks and the crunch of pickles between teeth. Dina's dog Alfochka whined pitifully under the table; Dina scratched the dog's back with her foot and tossed it a piece of sausage. Then she seconded what Madame Malaya had said: it was true, Efim's life hadn't been all that bad, and some people could find reason to envy him, like her husband Grisha, who had loved life so much, and was killed at the very beginning of the war.

After a half an hour the women had warmed up and their spirits improved. Iona, Stepa, and two of Granik's co-workers pitched in seventy rubles, which they gave to Adya, who added a few from his own pocket and then ran to Tiraspolsky Square and bought three bottles of vodka. There was plenty to eat. Then they took up another collection for more vodka. Olya looked at Iona with a gleam in her eye as he raised his glass, holding it out in front of him, swinging it back and forth. "Listen, everybody," he said, "Fima Granik's gone and he'll never be back!"

Then Iona went over the edge, tearing his new satin shirt, and began shouting that they were all bastards and whores and he was the worst of all because he had seen how Efim was suffering and had left him to the mercy of fate.

His shouting cast a pall over the gathering and Klava Ivanovna told Zinovy to take his father home before he disgraced the family. Iona slumped against his son's chest and began sobbing so bitterly that the others grew teary-eyed despite themselves, even Klava Ivanovna could not hold back her tears.

Her eyes vacant and unseeing, Tosya made a small sign of the cross. Stepa tugged at her arm and told her to stop that, otherwise people would start laughing. Marina Biryuk took Tosya's side: let the fool laugh while other people are crying.

Lesik came running in, saying a telegram had arrived from his father—arriving by plane tomorrow. Marina pressed her hands to her heart in happiness.

Zinovy took his father home and the mood in the room took a turn for the better. Lyalya, Dina, and Olya congratulated Marina and Stepa said a few words on behalf on the men, not stinting on the saltier expressions. Marina blushed and laughed merrily, then immediately covered her mouth with her hand. Klava Ivanovna frowned and said it was time for people to go home.

After she had put the children to bed and was in bed herself, Katerina asked Zinovy: "What are we going to do with Granik's room?"

Zinovy did not reply. He turned his back to her and pulled the cord on the overhead light. For a minute or two neither of them said anything, then Katerina pulled the cord and the light came on again.

She repeated her question: "What are we going to do with Granik's room?"

Zinovy was lying on his side facing the wall. Katerina shook him by the shoulder and said if there was no man in this house, she would take an ax and knock down the partition herself.

"Listen," said Zinovy, raising his head, "the man's body's still warm. How can you talk like that?"

"It's my room," said Katerina. "When Granik came and Marina Biryuk didn't even want to open her door to him, I gave him shelter: I took bread from my children and gave it to him."

Zinovy turned onto his back and looked up at the ceiling. "Twenty years ago this was a laundry room, then they made an outpost out of it. Efim did the decorations and made it so beautiful that the children liked being there better than being at home."

"It's my room," repeated Katerina. "It's mine and my sons' and I don't care what happened here a hundred years ago."

She looked at Zinovy's thin face, high forehead, the slightly hooked tip of his nose, and his freckles exactly like Grisha's. She stretched with pleasure, put her arms around him, and pressed herself to him, whispering: "Crazy people! How long can you cling to the old Odessa! If you don't take the room, someone else will."

Katerina was still harping on the same subject the next morning. Olya had come to take her grandsons to kindergarten but delayed it so she could lend her support to Katerina, who was right this time from the top of her head to the tips of her toes, no matter how you looked at it. Zinovy said not a word, as if he had a mouth full of water. Katerina said she'd go see Comrade Degtyar, the housing department, the City Soviet, and let them try to turn her down.

Klava Ivanovna had the keys to Granik's room. That afternoon Tosya and Lyalya visited Klava Ivanovna and asked her not to give the room away to anyone, it had to be kept for Lizochka. The girl was growing, thank God, she was almost thirteen. Klava Ivanovna thought for a moment, then said: "All right, but it has to go through the City Soviet."

"Why's that?" said Lyalya in surprise. "It's her own father's room."

"Her father's room, her uncle's room, what does that matter?" said Klava Ivanovna. "There's no law that lets young children have a residence authorization in their own name. Especially when the girl is actually living elsewhere."

Tosya sat with her head hanging, while Lyalya's face expressed open indignation.

"What are you making faces for!" said Klava Ivanovna angrily. "Adya was put in an orphanage while his mother was still alive and nobody thought about giving him a room. But a girl's not a boy and of course it's better if she has her own room."

Katerina came by late in the afternoon, exchanged a few words with Klava Ivanovna, then suddenly demanded the keys. Klava Ivanovna had foreseen that turn of events but decided to pretend she was astounded. Katerina flared up like a match: what was so surprising, that room was a part of her place and if she wanted she could just start living there without asking anybody!

"So, do it," replied Katerina Ivanovna heartily, "and show you don't give a damn for Soviet power."

"I'm no Granik!" cried Katerina. "You don't scare me."

"I know you're no Granik," Klava Ivanovna replied calmly, "and I can clearly remember how sweet you made life for him."

Her great excitement made Katerina choke for breath and her voice broke a few times: "You old . . . sick . . . woman! You'll outlive everyone, you'll bury them all!"

Katerina ran straight to Comrade Degtyar from Malaya's, but he hadn't returned home from work yet. When she came back later he had guests, Lyalya and Tosya, and she could tell by their faces that Malaya had already told them the whole story.

Although no one had spoken to her, Lyalya immediately took the tone of the lady of the house as she attacked Katerina: "Aren't you ashamed of yourself to be robbing an orphan! But it doesn't matter, it won't work! Where's your shame, how could your conscience allow you!"

Comrade Degtyar said nothing, observing it all as if he were an outsider. Katerina appealed to him for support a few times, calling herself a fool to have taken pity on Efim and given him half her space. Comrade Degtyar sat as if deaf and mute, and Orlov answered for all of them. The moment came when Katerina was no longer able to restrain herself and asked who was the boss in that house?

"Who's the boss?" Iona Ovseich had finally spoken. "I'll tell you

—truth's the boss here. And justice. But right now it feels like a pack of jackals are tearing their prey to pieces."

Katerina could feel the blood rush to her head; her fists clenched instinctively, and a wild howl escaped her lips. Lyalya gasped from fright. Iona Ovseich automatically shielded himself with his arm but then Tosya jumped and turned the situation around.

"Who invited her here?" shouted Tosya. "Who wants you here? Go back to Siberia and live with the bears."

Tosya whacked the palm of her hand against the back of her head, cursed, and added that for all the pain and trouble Katerina had caused Efim, she should be put on special rations.

"Good lord!" said Katerina, clutching her head. "You people have no shame, no conscience. I did the man a good turn. I was the only one, the whole courtyard turned away from him, and now I have to hear that kind of talk!"

There were tears in Katerina's eyes now and she was clearly suffering. After her flare-up, Tosya had suddenly slumped and become a mass of wrinkles, as if she had aged ten years. Lyalya lowered her head and could not bring herself to raise it again. Comrade Degtyar looked from one to the other, trying to catch an eye.

"You're not saying a word here," he said in a loud voice, "and you're afraid to look me in the eye. I'm not lazy, I can go get a mirror so you can each see your true face."

Katerina rose, started for the door, turned and glanced at Comrade Degtyar, the women, then Degtyar again. Brandishing a fist, she said: "I'll stir up all Odessa, I'll expose all your lousy tricks. I don't want anything that isn't mine, but I won't give up what is mine."

"Troublemaker!" Lyalya shouted after her. "She thinks she can get away with it."

Comrade Degtyar told her to calm down and said that he had a whole evening's work ahead of him, asking her to drop by again in a few days. As for the room, he'd have a talk with the people at the Stalin District Executive Committee. "Let's hope for the best."

The two women left together but Lyalya returned about five minutes later. Iona Ovseich did not invite her in, which caused her to become somewhat embarrassed, but then she at once explained why she was there: the way Katerina had acted had so upset her that she couldn't settle down.

"I can see that," said Iona Ovseich. "But that's nothing to brag about, on the contrary."

Lyalya clasped her hands: you had to be a saint to ask a person to be calm after all that.

"Let's get to the point," interrupted Iona Ovseich. "Do you have a concrete proposal or are you just letting off steam?"

At first his question seemed to have caught Lyalya off guard and she even stood with her mouth open for a second, but then she answered, yes, she had a concrete proposal: Katerina should be brought to court for slander.

Iona Ovseich asked Lyalya to come in. They both sat down on the couch. Snow was whirling softly outside. Then, in a pensive tone of voice, he said that sometimes he found it striking that ordinary people were so quick to seek reprisal. Why was that? What was the source of that intolerance?

Lyalya clasped her hands again: intolerance! Lord, a person was insulted and slandered for no reason at all, and now he was defending the slander!

"My dear Orlov," said Iona Ovseich with a bitter grin, "if I were guided by a sense of personal insult and vengeance, I would have taken half the building to court over the last thirty years, you included."

Lyalya sighed deeply: yes, that was really true.

"Meanwhile," said Iona Ovseich, with a clap of his hands, "you and I are sitting side by side on the couch billing and cooing like a couple of doves."

Lyalya's eyes clouded and her eyelids grew heavy as if she were becoming sleepy. Iona Ovseich placed his hand on her knee, which seemed bare, her stocking was so thin. He rubbed her knee lightly, then whacked it and said: "People must be educated not punished. You're not like Lapidis, and Katerina Cheperukha is not like Kotlyar, or even the late Granik."

The next day showed how right Comrade Degtyar had been. Katerina knocked at his door and it took some talking to convince her to step across the threshold: she kept pressing her hands to her chest, constantly asking him to forgive her and calling herself a fool and a crude and vulgar woman. Finally, Iona Ovseich was forced to raise his voice and insist that she show herself some respect, otherwise it wouldn't make for a very pretty picture: crudeness and vulgarity on the one side, fawning and bootlicking on the other.

Katerina gradually calmed down and said that Zinovy was as much use at home as a fifth wheel on a cart. She had to take care of everything herself and in conclusion she asked Iona Ovseich, as if he were her own father, to stand up for the truth.

"Meaning what serves your interest in the case at hand," said Iona Ovseich.

Once again Katerina began explaining the situation—when Efim returned to Odessa from the camp and the Biryuks were living in his apartment—but Comrade Degtyar interrupted and reminded her that the whole truth would have to include the fact that he alone had been totally opposed to registering Granik. It had been the softhearted Malaya and the friendly Cheperukhas who had wanted to look good, and had even engaged in outright deception.

Katerina hung her head, unable to voice any objection. Iona Ovseich drummed his fingers on the table, rose, and walked around the room, stopping at the window. The frost had drawn long leaves on the glass like those on the palms in Arcadia.

"And how would you have acted if there hadn't been any Degtyar around?"

After a moment of confusion Katerina thought and said that people like Degtyar should live a hundred years.

"Answer the question," said Degtyar, pressing the point. "How would you have acted if there were no Comrade Degtyar around?"

Katerina looked at her hands in her lap, her brow furrowing. Iona Ovseich told her not to hurry but to think her answer through properly.

A minute passed, two, then Katerina spread her hands and sincerely admitted that she couldn't imagine the world without Comrade Degtyar.

Iona Ovseich shook his head, a reproachful look in his eye. There was a tone of censure in his voice, though considerable warmth as well.

"Katerina, you fly from one extreme to the other. It's not everyone who can understand you like that horrible old Comrade Degtyar."

"Oh, how could I have ever called you that!" said Katerina, clutching her head. "I'll never forgive myself for that."

"All right," said Iona Ovseich, placing his hand on her shoulder, "that's water under the bridge. Come see me in a couple of days. I'll have a little talk with the District Executive Committee about the room. We'll see."

"I take your word!" exclaimed Katerina.

"We'll see," repeated Iona Ovseich. "And you should help your father-in-law shorten his tongue, sometimes he loses all sense of measure."

Somehow or other, by the next day, many people in the courtyard knew that Comrade Degtyar was one hundred percent on Katerina's side and that she had spent the entire evening with him.

Tosya and Lyalya went dashing immediately to Iona Ovseich followed a bit later by Klava Ivanovna and they all had the same question on their lips: was it true what they were saying in the courtyard or wasn't it? Comrade Degtyar gave Tosya and Lyalya a good tongue-lashing for lending credence to the gossip and rumors by their action whereas in Malaya's case he answered her question with one of his own: "Malaya, who has the keys to the room now, you or Katerina?"

They all left feeling somehow reassured. It was already eleven o'clock and Degtyar was just about to do some work when Major Biryuk knocked at his door.

"Hello, Iona Ovseich, is it too late to drop by?"

"Hello, Andrei Petrovich," replied Iona Ovseich warmly. "Come in, come in. How have you been?"

The major was in civilian dress with his Gold Star on the left lapel of his jacket; beneath the star were three rows of battle ribbons. Iona Ovseich looked closely at them and counted them. Shaking his head, he said it looked like only eleven, another one and he would have had an even dozen: clearly he'd been shirking. The major laughed, pointed at the star, and said that they didn't give insignias for nothing. Iona Ovseich raised his hands and said: "I surrender."

Though the major refused tea, Iona Ovseich turned on the electric teakettle, then placed a bottle of pepper vodka on the table. He took some dried Gobius fish and two onions from the cupboard but, as bad luck would have it, he'd eaten the last of the butter that morning. He did find a pint bottle of sunflower oil that had a fragrant, dairy-like aroma.

"All right, it looks like we're going to do some real drinking here, so cut up the rest of the pickles," said the major, livening up. He took a small link of sausage from his pocket, then a pint flask of schnapps.

Iona Ovseich reached for the pitcher but the major stopped him, then unscrewed the stopper on his flask, poured each of them a little, and said: *"Freiden und Freundschaft,* as the Germans like to say now."

"To peace and friendship," translated the host, sipping a quarter of his drink, then covering the glass with the palm of his hand.

"Ovseich, you're a sly one," said the major, wagging a threatening finger, "a sly one."

The teapot began whistling merrily. Iona Ovseich added five spoonfuls of tea leaves to make a strong brew. The major poured himself another drink and filled Iona Ovseich's glass to the brim, warning him that he wouldn't let him to wriggle out of drinking again, it was bottoms-up now. At first they chased their drinks with onions and Gobius fish, dipping their bread in sunflower oil, which the major praised, calling it tastier than any black caviar. Then the major began slicing the sausage for Degtyar, keeping a chunk for himself. He poured a third drink, but this time agreed to adopt democratic principles: each of them should follow the dictates of his own conscience.

While drinking tea, they discussed Germany. The major had a number of different things to say about the Germans, a long time would be needed to reeducate them, but he said straight out that Ulbricht was another Telman and there was good reason West Germany was so afraid of him. Germany was well off materially, and living better than the Soviet people, they knew how to watch their kopecks; but simple Russian-style hospitality was as rare as hen's teeth over there.

Andrei Petrovich laughed and waved his hand dismissively. Iona Ovseich opened the bottle of pepper-flavored vodka, poured his guest a glassful and himself half a glass, then proposed a toast: "To Russian hospitality!"

The major liked the pepper vodka, calling it primo deluxe. The Gobius fish had left a thin film of oil on his fingers. The major sniffed it, half closed his eyes in pleasure, and said he could eat like this seven times a week and start again on Monday!

"Petrovich," said Comrade Degtyar, jestingly wagging a finger at him, "I can see that you're an expert at courtesy."

The major did not reply, becoming pensive for a moment, and from his eyes it was clear that he was thinking of something else. Then, out of the blue, he asked about the late Efim Granik's apartment: what is going on? Granik's daughter is his legal heir, but the old women in the courtyard are gabbing away saying all sorts of different things.

"Andrei Petrovich, how long are you here for?" asked Degtyar in reply.

The major shook his head in reproach: look at that, you asked a person a question and he answered by asking you another question.

Comrade Degtyar sipped his tea, dipped a piece of bread in salt, and took a few bites and another sip of tea, then said: "Andrei Petrovich, do you think you have a better idea there in Germany of the decision-making process that's going on here?"

The major frowned and said that there was no reason to quibble over words but, as far as a room for the orphan was concerned, he was prepared to put on the pressure.

"You're *prepared* to put on the pressure?" said Iona Ovseich with surprise. "It seems to me you've already started. You come in here and start dictating terms right off, give this back, give that back, though you did, of course, first consult with the old women in the courtyard."

"All right then, Ovseich," said the major, unbuttoning his collar and loosening his tie a little. "I can see that you have a real way with words. As our General Kapusta says: you can turn shit into bullets."

Comrade Degtyar lowered his head, veins rising in relief on his temples: he forced a cough, then said: "I don't follow you."

Andrei Petrovich placed his hands on the back of the chair and leaned forward; his small green eyes, exactly like those of a forester, stared at Degtyar, seeming to bore through him. Iona Ovseich was about to shift his position but suddenly the major burst out laughing, freed his right hand, and thumped the table amicably: "All right, Ovseich, we got started on the wrong foot."

Comrade Degtyar rubbed his chest, smiled, a slight melancholy in his eyes, then said in a friendly tone of voice: "You're right, Andrei Petrovich."

They came to an agreement about the late Granik's room: if the major was needed for anything, everyone knew where he lived and he would be ready to see people day or night. His leave was over in March.

Back home the major quarreled with his wife: Marina, in typical fashion, called him spineless to his face and said that for all the good he was doing, he should have stayed in Germany. Andrei Petrovich objected, arguing that Iona Ovseich was a practical man and they had seen eye to eye on all points; however, deep down, in his heart, he was not deceived: Degtyar had openly given him to understand that he was just a soldier home on leave, while Degtyar had boasted and bristled and made much of himself.

Marina was unable to calm down, her own words fueling her anger. Now Andrei Petrovich also lost his temper and shouted angrily that his conscience was eating away at him because she had moved into the Graniks' apartment; she shouldn't have done that!

"Apartment!" said Marina, clasping her hands. "You call this an apartment? Would Kurt Ausdorf, that unlucky mechanic, that frozen fish, have agreed to live in an apartment like this?"

"What does Kurt Ausdorf have to do with anything!" said Andrei Petrovich indignantly.

"I'll tell you," said Marina, losing the last of her self-control. "You're a major with the Gold Star and your family is all huddled together here like a bunch of miserable slum dwellers and your poor old mother has nowhere to rest her head!"

"Listen," said Andrei Petrovich, "Degtyar and I didn't talk about us. I went to see him about Lizochka."

"Good lord," said Marina, exasperated, "you don't understand anything. What does it matter who you went to see him about!"

The next day a representative of the Stalin District Housing Office appeared at Madame Malaya's door accompanied by the concierge, Fenya Lebedev, and demanded the keys to Granik's apartment. Klava Ivanovna replied that she had no keys and said that he should speak with Comrade Degtyar. The official replied that she would bear criminal responsibility for her irresponsible actions. He pasted a sheet of paper stamped with a seal on Granik's door and went to call the police.

Klava Ivanovna called the factory at once; fortunately, Comrade

Degtyar happened to be in his office. He listened intently, her tension audible on the phone, and ordered her to surrender the keys.

"How can I do that?" asked Klava Ivanovna, taken aback. "That means they'll come and move some stranger in there."

There was a click at the other end of the line. Klava Ivanovna tried Degtyar's number a few more times but his line was busy. She could see she was wasting her time and ran to Andrei Petrovich's.

Major Biryuk had just returned home and was in full dress. Klava Ivanovna said it was a stroke of luck, now the housing department and police would see who they were dealing with. Marina backed up Madame Malaya but then, for no apparent reason, the major obstinately objected, saying the District Soviet was in charge of the district and knew what it was doing.

"The District Soviet is made up of ordinary people," said Marina, "and they can make mistakes like everybody else."

They can do more than make mistakes, added Klava Ivanovna, they can do worse things than that, she'd seen that in her time.

All right, said the major, giving in, he agreed, but he wasn't going to speak with a policeman or any small fry from the housing office, but with the chairman of the District Soviet.

"You're naïve," said Klava Ivanovna with a clap of her hands. "Once they've moved someone in, you can talk yourself blue in the face for all the good it'll do!"

"So then what do you think I should do!" said Andrei Petrovich angrily, "stand guard by the door?"

"Why do that?" said Klava Ivanovna in surprise. "They should be back any minute."

No, said Andrei Petrovich, this was no time for partisan action.

"Klava Ivanovna," said Marina, pointing a mocking finger at her husband, "Major Biryuk thinks he's knows life! He lives there in Germany with everything he needs and people waiting on him hand and foot, and he thinks it's like that everywhere else."

Marina was about to say more, for she was enjoying herself, but, glancing over at her husband whose green eyes were growing brighter and brighter as if igniting from within, she restrained herself.

The two women went downstairs, waited about ten minutes, then went their separate ways. It turned out that Klava Ivanovna had sounded the alarm for no reason: no one else came there that day, with a policeman or without. Only once did the Cheperukhas' door open; Katerina peeped out, then slammed the door shut.

When Zinovy came home from work, Katerina met him at the door and told him that that old hag Malaya was up to some tricks with her crowd.

"Don't let it get you crazy," said Zinovy.

Katerina served dinner in silence. A few minutes later Olya arrived with her grandsons followed by their grandfather, who had clearly found time to do a little celebrating on the way home. He said "Hi, kids," to them all and Olya replied by calling him a shiftless bum. Zinovy cast a glance of reproach at his mother but old Cheperukha paid no attention; he unfolded a fresh copy of the newspaper *The Banner of Communism* and read the headline aloud: "Zionism's Dirty Face."

The adults grew momentarily quiet while the children continued squabbling by the faucet. Slowly, and with feeling, Iona read the article about a gang of criminal doctors who, it had now been established, were connected with "Joint," an international Jewish Zionist organization—and a branch of American intelligence. According to the article, the doctors were paid from "Joint's" coffers.

Olya covered her face in horror. Iona said that wasn't all. He had come to a passage about the recently deceased prominent Zionist statesman and former president of Israel, Chaim Weizmann, who was living in England in 1915 and, in his capacity as a chemistry professor, had carried out military assignments for the English government. At one point another Zionist leader, Zhabotinsky, had formed a Jewish legion and taken part in the war on the side of the Entente.

"The Entente?" said Olya in even greater horror. "I remember them coming to Odessa in 1919 and gunning people down!"

"She remembers!" said Iona with bitter mockery. "All Odessa remembers! Let's read on."

The article also spoke of Abba Eban and Reuven Shiloach, who had worked for years for British intelligence, the latter having subsequently founded Israeli intelligence.

Katerina shook her head and said there was a reason people said you scratch my back and I'll scratch yours.

"That gang, oh, that gang," Olya muttered to herself. "They should be cut into little pieces and hung on every tree."

Iona was sitting at the table. Olya told him to go wash his hands. He replied that he hadn't been handling anything dirty but she was unrelenting.

Zinovy picked up the newspaper and forgot all about his dinner even though he was reminded to eat ten times. He read the article through to himself, thought for a while, then said: "The article makes sense, it takes in a lot of history, and you can feel that the author knows a lot more than he's saying, but he should have quoted some specific examples."

"No matter how good something is," said Katerina with a shrug, "you always find something wrong with it."

Iona Cheperukha finished his dinner, then drank a glass of cold water and sighed bitterly: "Efim is lucky to be resting in peace, while we're here finding out about things that make your hair stand on end."

Zinovy was reading the back page of the paper—there were reports from Warsaw, Budapest, Sofia, and Prague concerning the arrest of enemies of the people, many of whom had succeeded in worming their way into high positions in government and finance; bloody terror was still raging in Yugoslavia, the entire country had become nothing but one huge concentration camp: tens of thousands of partisans and heroes of the struggle for national liberation had been killed by Tito's executioners.

"They had a good teacher in Hitler," said Olya.

"What a world," said Iona, whacking his knees. "What a world, who can you trust now! You pick up a paper and everything in it upsets you."

Turning the newspaper front page out, Zinovy demanded that everyone be quiet and then ceremoniously intoned: "Comrade voters, I would like to inform you of the following: Comrade Stalin has given his consent to be placed on the ballot, and has filed as a candidate for deputy to the Odessa City Soviet."

Katerina did not believe it, saying that Zinovy was pulling a trick on them. She grabbed the newspaper from his hands and read the notice herself. Olya too wanted to read it with her own eyes and be certain that no one was fooling her: in the Gorky Sailors' Palace concert hall, and on Customs Square in front of the Odessa Port Administration Building, as part of the joyous event, large rallies had already taken place whose speakers included Churbakov, a well-known crane operator and deputy to the Ukrainian Supreme Soviet, the outstanding crane operator and port mechanic Turlenko, and many others.

"That means," concluded Olya, "that Stalin must be coming to meet with the voters."

Iona Cheperukha replied that if Comrade Stalin had to meet with all the people who voted for him, he wouldn't have enough time to button his tunic and pin on his medals.

Katerina took exception to her father-in-law's remark and said that, number one, even though Stalin was a generalissimo, he wore a tunic like an ordinary marshal, and, number two, it was only in his portraits that he wore all those medals, he didn't wear them in real life.

That was right, agreed Zinovy, that was really true; many years ago the French writer Henri Barbusse wrote that Comrade Stalin had the mind of a scientist but wore a simple soldier's greatcoat. Iona Cheperukha began justifying himself, saying that was not what he had meant at all, it was just that he'd expressed himself poorly; everyone knew of Comrade Stalin's modesty, may God grant even one percent of it to the other people in charge. Now Katerina attacked him with a new reproach: why had he come home and begun by telling his family the bad news instead of the good!

For a second the old man was taken aback; an evil gleam flashed in his eyes, then he said calmly, but with a calm that could give a person the chills, that if he heard accusations and criticisms like that in his son's house one more time, he would never set foot in there again.

He left the room, slamming the door behind him. Zinovy told Katerina to call him back but she didn't so much as stir. Not only that, she justified herself entirely, referring to Comrade Degtyar, who had been right to say that old Cheperukha's tongue could stand to be a little shorter.

"Listen," screamed Zinovy wildly, his gray eyes and especially their expression exactly like his father's, "You can all go straight to hell! And you and Degtyar know what you can do with all that gossip of yours!"

Katerina tore off her apron and began changing her clothes. The boys started crying and asked their mother not to go away. Olya wrung her hands and cried that her husband, that drunkard, had taken the best years of her life and now was destroying the family and ruining his son's life. Katerina had already taken her coat off the hanger when Olya grabbed it by the collar, swearing that she would kill herself if Katerina took one step from the room.

Katerina looked twice at Zinovy as if waiting for him to leave too or at least say something, but he stood there like an idol gazing hypnotically at her.

Olya carefully took the coat from her daughter-in-law's hands and brought it into the other room. When she returned she suddenly began scolding her grandsons: bad boys, they sat there listening to all sorts of nonsense when they should be drawing with a red pencil or studying their ABC's; they'd be starting school that year and should make their parents proud and happy like all the other children.

Misha brought his mother a chair and Katerina sat down. Her face in her hands, she wept softly and whispered: "Why, why is everything so complicated here, why is there so much pain and suffering here!"

Late that evening Iona Ovseich invited the concierge, Lebedev, to come see him: he told her to go to Malaya's and get the keys to Granik's apartment. Lebedev said that it would be better to summon the old woman there but Iona Ovseich's response was to repeat what he had said: "Go to Malaya's and get the keys."

Lebedev returned about ten minutes later but without the keys. She twirled a finger beside her head and said that the old woman had gone out of her mind. Iona Ovseich listened carefully, his right eye narrowing, his left eye round and unmoving as if made of glass.

Klava Ivanovna brought Lebedev the keys the next morning. Lebedev flatly refused to accept them, saying that now Malaya should go run and bring them to Comrade Degtyar. Klava Ivanovna told her to shut up, saying she could have her evicted in no time flat. She started to slip the keys back into her pocket but Lebedev snatched them away from her, hurled them to the ground, and shouted nastily that everyone here thought he was a big shot but people should be patient and keep quiet. For effect, Klava Ivanovna covered her ears and went back through her own front door. Still furious, Lebedev cursed her own life twice out loud, then suddenly burst into laughter and began singing, rolling her r's: "Oh, you beauties, oh, you girrrls!"

That same day a mechanic from the building administration arrived, accompanied by someone whose appearance and gait were that of an official; they tore the paper with the seal off the door and unlocked it; the mechanic left after a moment and the official took a hammer and gimlet from his pocket, nailed two rings to the door, hung a lock on them, and tugged at it three times before leaving.

That evening, after work, Katerina walked by Granik's and spotted the large, heavy lock, as if the apartment were a barn containing kolkhoz property. The children weren't back from kindergarten yet and as often happened Zinovy would stay at work until midnight. Katerina began pacing her apartment; something had to be done, Comrade Degtyar had to be informed at once, but the suddenness of it all had her completely at sea.

A minute later her mother-in-law came flying in like a madwoman and began wailing hysterically: "Katerina, have you seen what they've done!"

Katerina did not answer but ran out into the freezing cold without her coat and then up the three flights to Comrade Degtyar's even though she realized it was completely pointless—he'd never be home at that time of day. Then she dashed to Tiraspolsky Square where there was a pay phonc which turned out to be broken and gobbled coin after coin. It was the same story with the phones on Stalin Avenue and Karl Marx Street; as the saying goes, it never rains but it pours.

Returning home, Katerina found Tosya in her apartment and she made the same stupid remark that Olya had: "Have you seen what they've done!"

"No, I haven't!" said Katerina, shaking her head. She suddenly attacked poor Tosya, cursing her up and down while Tosya sat there in silence, listening to it all.

Several times Olya tried to appeal to her daughter-in-law's sense of shame: "Katerina, Katerina, what does Tosya have to do with it!" but Katerina was unable to stop herself until she had said her piece.

Katerina went by Iona Ovseich's three times before eleven o'clock, ringing his doorbell as if it were a fire alarm, and then finally went outside to check if his lights were on, but they were not. The next day she tried several times to reach him by phone but either there was no answer or else a woman answered and haughtily informed Katerina that Comrade Degtyar was very busy and that she had no idea when he'd be free, but if it was something urgent, she could pass word on to him. Katerina said, yes, it was urgent, and angrily slammed down the phone.

Finally, on the fourth try, she succeeded in finding Iona Ovseich at home. Katerina was still seething but had not had time to begin talking with Degtyar when three more people arrived: Major Biryuk, Lyalya, and Tosya. Degtyar welcomed his guests warmly, apologizing because he had nothing to offer them, and then voiced his suspicion that they were all there because of the same reason, Granik's room.

"Degtyar, you're a real clairvoyant!" said Major Biryuk in surprise. Degtyar made no objection to this and, in turn, addressed his guests with a joke of his own: "Shall we elect a workers' presidium or not bother this time?"

Lyalya and Tosya said nothing but Katerina rudely replied that she didn't know about other people but she was in no mood for jokes. Comrade Degtyar frowned and was clearly about to call her to order but Katerina was a step ahead of him and shouted: "Aren't you ashamed of yourself for this deception!"

Everyone was confused and clearly ill at ease, especially Andrei Petrovich. Only Comrade Degtyar retained his composure and calmly asked: "Whom have I deceived?"

"Me, them, everyone in the world!" cried Katerina, her voice even louder now.

"Katerina Cheperukha," said Comrade Degtyar, raising his voice slightly, "I could kick you out of here, or I could call the police and these three people could be my witnesses, but I prefer to tell you publicly, in front of other people, that you are a barefaced liar!"

"Me, a liar?" said Katerina, pressing her hands to her breast. "Me, lying?"

"That's right," said Iona Ovseich, "you're lying. And I demand that you repeat what you said about Granik's apartment, and what I said, and I want that done here and now in the presence of these people, one of whom is an officer in the Red Army and a hero of the Soviet Union."

Katerina's eyes bulged as if suffering from memory loss; she swallowed two or three times, a grimace of pain flashing across her face. Finally, she replied that Degtyar had said he would go to the Stalin District Executive Committee and talk with someone there.

"And what else?" said Degtyar, urging her on.

"I asked you if you promised."

"And what else?"

"I said that I believed you."

"And what did I say to that?"

Katerina thought for a moment, gnawing on her baby finger; she grimaced with pain again but then suddenly her face lit up as she exclaimed: "Now I remember! You said that my father-in-law could do with a shorter tongue."

"Don't try your tricks on me," said Iona Ovseich angrily. "Answer the real question."

"You're the one trying tricks!" said Katerina, on the verge of tears. "I said that I believed you and you said that my father-in-law . . ."

"Enough," interrupted Iona Ovseich. "Now I'm going to ask another question: who was it that beseeched me, saying I was like a father and a protector, who beat her breast for having once insulted her dear Iona Ovseich! But then even all that didn't seem sweet enough to you and you went whole hog, and said you couldn't imagine the world without Comrade Degtyar, people like him should live a hundred years!"

Katerina turned pale as a sheet and it was clear to all that Iona Ovseich's version did not contain a single unnecessary word. The bridge of Andrei Petrovich's nose furrowed and he carefully smoothed out the tablecloth several times though it was not wrinkled in the least.

"Bah!" exclaimed Iona Ovseich. "What a disgrace—to sink so low as to forget yourself entirely and flatter an ordinary person, your neighbor, as if he were the very Lord of the Sabaoth!"

"In the heavens," whispered Lyalya.

"And how!" said Iona Ovseich, twirling a finger in the air. "But it was here in the courtyard."

They all sat in silence for a while. All thoughts had fled Katerina's mind with a single exception—she had to get an ax, knock down the partition, and smash down the door which Efim had made from the window. They could come after her but she'd show them. Katerina pressed the palm of her hand to her cheek as if suffering from a toothache and a heavy moan escaped her lips.

"I'll tell you what Katerina Cheperukha regrets," exclaimed Comrade Degtyar. "She could have grabbed a little something from the state and now she's ashamed of letting the chance pass her by!"

Andrei Petrovich defended her, saying that it was just the other way around, she was suffering because of the way everything had turned out. Katerina, however, denied that herself: no, she was a fool, a perfect fool, who had hoped and believed that someone would do something for her. But it had taught her a good lesson, one she would remember for the rest of her life.

"That's right," said Iona Ovseich. "And the bricklayer Fyodor Pushkar, who has a wife and two children, is supposed to spend the rest of his days in a workers' hostel so Katerina Cheperukha can have her own dancing school and gymnasium!"

"Really," said Lyalya, grinning, her lips extending into a red strip, "the very idea."

"And these two," said Iona Ovseich, pointing a finger at Lyalya and Tosya, "while pretending to care about the orphan who now has an excellent living situation—everyone should have it so good—were trying to obtain her an apartment of her own ten years ahead of time. It didn't matter that people are living in cellars, it didn't matter to them that some people don't even have a little corner to call their own!"

It cost Lyalya some effort to listen until Ovseich was done. Then she entwined her fingers and assumed a guilty expression, like a naughty schoolgirl: if she had known that they'd wanted to move a whole family into Granik's, they wouldn't have heard a word against it from her!

"You poor thing," said Iona Ovseich pityingly, "you couldn't have figured that for yourself!"

Lyalya twisted her lips, lowered her head, and said, "That's the way the world is, when you're healthy, you think everyone is."

Katerina was stunned and the conversation seemed to be passing her by. Andrei Petrovich tapped her on the back and she shuddered, looked at each of them in turn as if they were strangers to her, and rose heavily to her feet. She said good-bye, her voice as hoarse as if she had just caught cold the minute before, and she walked out.

Tosya started to the door after her. Iona Ovseich tried to stop her and Lyalya grabbed her by the arm, but to no avail: Tosya tore free and slammed the door behind her.

For a minute they stayed seated and silent. Major Biryuk was noticeably ill at ease, as if he wished to speak with Degtyar but with no one else present. Iona Ovseich gave Orlov an assignment for tomorrow—to drop by her new neighbor's and see how he was doing—and then saw her to the door. Lyalya was reluctant to go and automatically stopped in the doorway. Comrade Degtyar joked: "If you're so interested, you can put your ear to the keyhole."

When they were alone, Major Biryuk placed his hands on the table. His fingers were still deeply tanned and looked strange there in wintertime. "Degtyar," he said, "I don't want to meddle but I don't like any of what's going on."

Degtyar did not reply at first, as if deciding whether to answer or not, then asked: "Just what is it you don't like?"

"I don't like any of it," said the major, "the way you talk to them, and the way they talk to you. But the main thing is, if you knew beforehand that the executive committee was going to take the room, why did you make promises that couldn't be kept?"

"Promises?" said Iona Ovseich. "But you heard it with your own ears, I didn't promise anybody anything. They just gave the meaning they wanted to what I said."

"But that means," said the major, pressing his point, "that what you said was vague enough to give people hopes when you should have given them a loud, clear 'no.' "

Iona Ovseich rose from the table and walked over to the window. The moon was shining, silvering the snow on the roof of the building across from him, dark blue smoke hovering over chimneys as it did in Andersen's fairy tales. For a second or two he admired the view in spite of himself. Then he sighed gently, and said: "When a sick person goes to the doctor, the doctor can simply listen to him and write out a prescription, and *sei gesund.* But a true doctor presses and squeezes in places the patient thinks are perfectly healthy. And then suddenly the patient cries out, oh, that hurts! That's a real medical diagnosis. When people come to see me, I can just say yes or no too. But first I want to poke and squeeze a person, to poke a person from every side until he cries out, oh, that hurts! And then that person will see for himself that he's not as healthy as he thought he was. That's a form of diagnosis too, ideological diagnosis, and one a bit more complicated, I'd say; those diseases are more dangerous and harder to treat."

Major Biryuk peered intently at Degtyar, his green eyes flaring. Iona Ovseich went back to the table, put his hand inside his jacket, and rubbed the left side of his chest. He shook his head in reproach and said: "Where would you ever find a doctor who could install a new motor!"

"Time for you to get some rest, Ovseich," said Major Biryuk.

Degtyar waved his hand dismissively: "Rest, what's that!"

"Ovseich," said the major, "it's time you got some rest, not for yourself, but for other people's sake."

Comrade Degtyar raised his head and narrowed his right eye. Blue veins had swollen on his temples.

"For other people's sake," continued the major, "so that they can breathe in peace and not have to keep trying to figure out where Degtyar might squeeze them next to provoke a pain and make another diagnosis."

"Major Biryuk," said Iona Ovseich—he was using all his strength to restrain himself but his hands and lips were out of his control—"think what you're saying, Major Biryuk."

"I'm a soldier," said Andrei Petrovich, drumming his fingers on the table, "and I'm talking to you like a soldier. Save the shouting for your women and your courtyard."

"I don't have any women or any courtyard," said Iona Ovseich, "and I'll say it again: I don't like your tone."

"Listen," said Major Biryuk, "listen closely and make a mental note of this: you've tricked me for the last time like you trick those women. I can make it plenty hot for you—"

"Get out," said Iona Ovseich, jumping up to stand in front of Major Biryuk, who was clearly a head taller than he, "Get out, or else we'll continue this conversation elsewhere!"

The major cursed him and said, "And I thought you were a regular guy!"

Iona Ovseich walked over to the telephone, picked up the receiver, and dialed 02, the number for the police. Andrei Petrovich burst into loud laughter as if from genuine mirth, grabbed the receiver from Degtyar's hands, and hung it up. Iona Ovseich recoiled automatically as Major Biryuk tapped him on the shoulder and wished him a good night.

At around five o'clock in the morning Iona Ovseich was awakened by a sharp pain in the pit of his stomach. The pain spread to the small of his back and his spine. He felt nauseous; a wave of fear spread from somewhere in his stomach which made him gag for a minute or two before it receded. Still, he could feel that it would come back again soon, and indeed it did. Iona Ovseich took a lump of sugar and sprinkled a few drops of validol on it, then placed it under his tongue. It quieted the pain a little. Now he had to lie without moving, to relax his arms and legs as much as possible, until they became heavy as lead, and wait patiently.

Ten minutes later his breathing was freer and Iona Ovseich could feel himself falling asleep when he suddenly remembered his talk with Andrei Petrovich. The memory caused an inner tremor that reached to his throat, and all thought of sleep vanished from his mind. The pain was greater this time, spreading through his back to his elbow. Iona Ovseich put another piece of sugar with some validol under his tongue, turned his back to the window, and ordered himself not to think about anything. At first he succeeded: the window frame receded into the darkness, a light frost on the lower frames, but then, all by itself, imperceptibly, the vertical and somewhat foreshortened horizontal frames emerged in the form of a large cross that seemed made of iron. Iona Ovseich looked to the right, but exactly the same sort of cross stood out from that window as well.

Of course, it was stupid nonsense, he shouldn't give a damn about any of it and just pay no attention, but the crosses loomed insolently from the windows and at times he even had the idiotic feeling that they were flickering closer, then away.

Iona Ovseich closed his eyes; the sensation seemed to have passed but then another idiotic idea came into his mind: closed eyes reminded him of corpses. He felt that he should turn over and shake all that madness right out of him. Iona Ovseich had mentally begun to turn over when suddenly he could see himself lying outstretched, his legs straight out, his arms straight out, a genuine corpse—and he felt such a spinning violence within him that he thought the end had come.

His shirt was soaked through, his body ached as if he'd been clubbed, and tears flowed down his cheeks. Iona Ovseich thought of Polina Isaevna—the poor woman, she had suffered for so many years! —and against his own will he began weeping loudly, moaning and sobbing. He wanted some love, some human compassion, to hear a kind, affectionate word. Once again he thought of the scene with Andrei Petrovich, and he couldn't understand how he could have treated a guest like that. He swore aloud that he would throw all false pride aside and go to him and openly tell him where he had been wrong and where Andrei Petrovich had also been in the wrong.

Iona Ovseich rose with difficulty the next morning and for a moment it occurred to him to spend the day home in bed, but he walked around his room a little, drank a glass of strong tea—he didn't feel like eating anything—then automatically put on his jacket, scarf, and his cap with ear laps. Now all that remained was to take his coat off the hook.

When Iona Ovseich said good morning to the militia guard at the front door of the factory, she told him that he looked very pale today, he was probably coming down with the flu, and she advised him to take aspirin and put mustard plasters on his legs at night. In the hallway, as if in cahoots, both his secretary and one of the planners looked fearfully at him and reproached him for allowing himself out of bed in his condition, and threatened to call a doctor if he didn't start taking care of himself. Iona Ovseich nodded as if in agreement and then went into his office.

He had a mountain of pressing tasks, especially in connection with the elections. You could count the days now, and some people weren't coping so well with their responsibilities; workers had to be taken off the job and sent out to do propaganda work in the factory itself and among the populace. In addition, he had to supervise the construction of the voting booths personally, and not delegate that task to anyone else, because carpenters were capable of dragging things out to the very last minute.

He spent the first half of the day going from one department to another and talking with people; he didn't feel any worse but there was an unpleasant weakness throughout his body. At times it seemed that all he had to do was make a single decisive move and some inner screw or valve would snap back into place and he'd feel hale and hearty again, but Iona Ovseich knew from experience that this was a false sense of well-being which arose precisely when there was the least reason for it.

After lunch he locked himself in his office and allowed himself to curl up on the sofa in the corner for thirty or forty minutes. Two or three times he felt a strong desire to go to sleep, to take off his shoes, his clothes. But he caught himself before that tricky idea could take hold and got up at once. Basta!

At the end of the shift, Iona Ovseich asked the canvassers to stay another ten minutes. In fact they stayed about an hour; they turned out to have a mass of questions and each one had to be answered. In the course of the conversation Iona Ovseich warned them all several times of a very widespread error—thinking that elections to the local soviets were not as important as elections to the Supreme Soviet and for that reason didn't require much effort. Some of the people at first pretended that this was not a problem for them but then they found the courage to admit that they too had been guilty of that failing.

Having seen the canvassers off, Iona Ovseich dropped by the cutting department. There was a narrow area there where waste material was piled, sometimes achieving enormous proportions. He spoke with various people, asking them if they had any complaints against management. He jotted everything down in his notebook, but then in turn warned them that no allowances would be made for loafers and idlers, and that, beginning tomorrow, even though it would spoil the holiday mood a little, they were going to start posting a list of idlers for everyone to see. The foremen and the workers were entirely in favor and proposed themselves that a three-man committee be selected to check and supervise this. They nominated candidates and voted on the spot.

A fine snow was falling and there was a nip in the air. Iona Ovseich took a deep breath. He had begun to feel a little nauseous and his legs were wobbly again but that passed quickly and his whole body felt stronger and seemingly even younger. He thought of the old song "We Are Little Children and We Love to Work." Iona Ovseich began singing it softly, quickened his pace, and, thinking back over this day, saw once again that he had been right not to yield to his desire to stay home in bed but to force himself to get up and go to work and put in a normal day as if he were absolutely healthy and fit.

His plan for the evening was to restudy Comrade Stalin's thesis on the base and the superstructure, in particular, the section on reverse effects, the influence of the superstructure and ideology, on the economy. However, he had to put that off because Major Biryuk arrived a second after he himself had gotten home. It even seemed that Biryuk had been lying in wait for him in the corridor and had only allowed Degtyar enough time to take off his coat; in other circumstances that would have been no joking matter but, after yesterday, a different tone had to be taken of course.

Major Biryuk was wearing lounging clothes, a flannellette jacket with a silk collar, which he had clearly brought back from Germany, brown pants with black cuffs that looked like a band of moire; his hands were plunged into his pockets and there was a friendly smile on his face, in short, no one would have even thought these two men had engaged in a bitter dispute the night before.

"You look like a burgher straight from Dresden or Weimar," said Iona Ovseich with a sly smile.

The major waved away the remark, took a chair, and sat down at the table, pausing to think for a moment. Degtyar sat across from him and rubbed his temples and eyelids. Andrei Petrovich reproached him for being so unsparing of himself. "Look how pale you are, like you just came out of a dungeon."

They remained silent for another minute or two, the major looking at Degtyar in the expectation that he would begin the conversation. Degtyar, however, did not begin it and so Andrei Petrovich decided to launch it himself.

"Ovseich," he said, "forget what happened yesterday."

Degtyar was still silent and it wasn't clear whether he was listening or not. Major Biryuk fidgeted a little in his chair, scratched the back of his head, and coughed before adding: "I've already forgotten it. Believe me, there was all kinds of nonsense going through my mind all last night. I tossed and turned all night. But it's all behind me now. Bah!"

The major laughed. Iona Ovseich peered at him, his lips twisting with what was either mockery or pain, then said: "Forget it, you say? All right, let's forget it then."

Andrei Petrovich frowned, the dark spots on his nose becoming more evident, larger, and his skin appeared glossy, as if smeared with grease. He shook his head: "You're like our Colonel Poluyan, a good guy, but don't ever step on his pet corn or you'll wake up dead."

"Your Colonel Poluyan is of no interest to me!" said Iona Ovseich, suddenly raising his voice. "Let's dispense with the comparisons, Major Biryuk! I like things clear, day is day, and night is night."

"What's with you?" said Andrei Petrovich, taken aback. "Are you starting up again?"

Iona Ovseich leaned back and looked at Biryuk with an unflinching gaze; Biryuk in turn lowered his head, his green eyes staring hard at Degtyar, and they sat like that for half a minute or more until finally the major couldn't stand any more, averted his eyes and said laughingly: "You're a hard-hearted man, Ovseich."

Degtyar's gaze remained unchanged, though there was a little more life in his eyes now. Biryuk sighed and shrugged his shoulders.

"Who the hell knows about you civilians, everything's upside down with you. A person comes to make up and he gets it in the neck from you, and that's your fault too."

"In the neck!" said Iona Ovseich with emphasis. "That's just how it is, *right on the neck*!"

"Listen," said Andrei Petrovich, half rising and pushing back his chair, "I didn't come here to get lessons from you in the Russian language. If you want to get to the point, fine, let's do it, and, if not, *alles guten* and *auf wiedersehen!*"

Iona Ovseich automatically leaned forward and was about to tell his guest to sit down, but instead he stood up himself, came out from behind the table, stopped by the couch, fluffed up the pillow a little, and straightened the blanket. At first Major Biryuk observed all this in silence, then spat vigorously on the floor, turned around, and slammed the door behind him. Iona Ovseich stood sunk in thought for a moment. His heart was making itself felt again, as if there were a needle sticking out from under his shoulder blade. Just to be on the safe side, he took a few drops of validol, spread out his notes on Comrade Stalin's work on linguistic problems, and was at once absorbed in them. At first, his thoughts adhered closely to the subject but then by association he recalled that well-known poor excuse for a linguist, Academician Meshchaninov, of whom Comrade Stalin had said in all sincerity that if he hadn't known him personally, he might have thought he was dealing with a deliberate enemy. Suddenly the image of Andrei Petrovich was before his eyes and it was as if Comrade Stalin's words had not been addressed to Academician Meshchaninov but to Major Biryuk; that if he didn't know him personally, he would have thought he was dealing with a deliberate enemy.

"Nonsense," said Iona Ovseich aloud, but the thought had left its residue: you never could tell.

Polina Isaevna had hung an oilcloth by the pantry to keep the steam from the teakettle from ruining the wallpaper; the oilcloth's pattern was of large green squares connected in sections that were like bars, and there was something red along the sides, carrots or radishes. For a minute or two Iona Ovseich examined the oilcloth calmly but then began growing irritated by that absurd combination, prison bars and radishes! He went back to his notes, wishing to lose himself in his work but could not. He rose from the table to pace the room a little and had taken a few steps between the window and the door and then, before he knew what he was doing, he suddenly went back to the pantry, tore the oilcloth from the wall, threw it on the floor, and trampled it with his feet.

That was somehow a relief, and he could only marvel at the trifles on which a person's mood can sometimes hinge; he kicked the oilcloth into the corner as if it were a soccer ball and laughed with pleasure at the accuracy of the kick.

A large dark purple rectangle had formed on the wall during all the years the oilcloth had hung there, or rather, in that spot the wallpaper had retained its original color but, since all the rest had faded greatly, that spot seemed unnaturally bright. It was the usual story: everything had to exist under the same conditions and change at the same rate, otherwise differences would inevitably arise. Things were like people; just take that Major Biryuk: an officer in the Red Army, a chest full of medals, but he'd spent a few years in Germany, even if it was in the Soviet Zone, and there was something different about his character, his ideas, his temperament.

"The Iron Curtain! They're still claiming there's such a thing as the Iron Curtain!" said Iona Ovseich aloud, the words escaping his lips. He sighed deeply and poured water from the thermos bottle into the teakettle, which he then brought to a boil. He drank a glass of tea without sugar, then sat back down to work.

He went to bed quite late, around two o'clock, but he could not fall asleep: the argument with Biryuk would start up on its own all over again; Biryuk had put on airs and gotten up on his high horse but, in the end, he had taken it all back. That would seem cause for satisfaction, and yet it had left an unpleasant aftertaste. He remembered the twenties—a kulak with a sawed-off gun under his shirt, secret supporters of the kulaks, malicious old man Kiselis, and that anti-Soviet big mouth Lapidis. Iona Ovseich tried to drive off all those uninvited guests but the memories had a snowball effect. Lapidis was followed by the memory of the poor fool Efim Granik; then came Joseph Kotlyar; then Dr. Landa, not as he was now but as he had been during the first years of Soviet power when he still had a private practice in venereal and dermatological diseases.

"Some company!" Iona Ovseich exclaimed unwittingly.

The next morning it cost Iona Ovseich an enormous effort just to lift his head: all night long he had dreamed of people in shapeless, bloodstained garments, like American Ku Klux Klansmen. They were moving in even ranks, an endless procession, their eyes gaping terrifyingly through the narrow slits in their hoods and, since every pair of them looked like every other pair, it seemed that the same eyes were reflected and repeated in thousands of mirrors.

Following the advice his mother used to give him for forgetting bad dreams, Iona Ovseich looked immediately out the window but he understood that it was all quite simple, without any mystery to it: Moscow Radio was just broadcasting a report on the Doctors' Plot, and, before he had awoken, his ear had caught the words but his mind had not fully processed the information. Iona Ovseich could not forgive himself for having overslept and missing such an important report but an hour and a half or so later he read the full text in *Pravda* at the factory: "Esteemed Comrade Editor. I have received numerous letters and telegrams expressing patriotic sentiments in connection with the unmasking of the Doctors' Plot. Unable to reply to each individually, I would like to use your newspaper to pass on my heartfelt gratitude to all the organizations, institutions, military units, and individual persons who have congratulated me upon my being awarded the Order of Lenin for the aid I provided to the government in the unmasking of the enemies of the Soviet people. Lidiya Timashuk. February 9, 1953."

It was the February 11 edition and Iona Ovseich was somewhat surprised that the letter had been published after a delay of two days. He carefully examined all the other pages but found no other mention of the subject. Actually, one such letter was entirely sufficient: in the last few days it might have seemed that people had already begun forgetting those murderers in white coats but today's papers had provided a new shock and fifteen minutes later people began coming to the party office from various sections and departments to discuss the issue personally with Comrade Degtyar because they were so agitated and upset. They were certain that Comrade Degtyar knew more than had been printed in the papers and each of them aspired to his special trust. Iona Ovseich looked each person intently in the eye, then spread his hands and said with all possible clarity: "The papers print everything that needs to be known, now all we can do is wait for what the prosecutor's office and the court have to say."

That seemed like new information in comparison with what the newspaper had printed and people left flattered and doubly satisfied: first, because Comrade Degtyar had been open with them, and, second, because news was news.

That evening Iona Cheperukha dropped by Degtyar's place. Iona reeked of alcohol but he was steady on his feet and coherent. He said straight off that he had an indelible stain on his conscience for not sending Lidiya Timashuk his own expression of gratitude. Comrade Degtyar said that it was never too late. Cheperukha replied by shaking his head like a horse, beating his breast with his fist, and shouting: "I'm rotten and don't try to talk me out of it! I'm a rotten bastard!"

Degtyar tried to calm him down but Cheperukha was distraught, cursing himself for allowing doubts to creep up on him and to wonder whether this unmasking was the genuine article or not. And indeed a few minutes later it all became clear when Cheperukha mentioned the name of Dr. Landa. Of course, Cheperukha did not deny that all those Kogans, Vovsis, and Vinogradovs were out-and-out enemies of the people but there must be some innocent people among them too, like Dr. Landa.

"Cheperukha," said Comrade Degtyar, closing his eyes tight, "let's say that you didn't drop by here tonight and that we had no conversation."

No, protested Iona, he had dropped by and there had been a conversation, but he was ready to risk his neck that Dr. Landa, whom he knew personally, like he knew the palm of his hand, was not guilty and had been arrested by mistake. Guilt by association.

"Guilt by association?" repeated Iona Ovseich.

That's right, confirmed Cheperukha, and then went even further, demanding that the courtyard write a collective letter to Lydia Timashuk, who knew the whole truth, to ask her to stand up to the government for our Dr. Landa.

"What? Have you gone out of your mind," said Comrade Degtyar taken aback, "or are you just pretending to?"

No, said Cheperukha, and his voice was stone sober. He had not gone out of his mind and he had already written the letter: Comrade Degtyar and the others should read it and sign it.

The letter had been typed and was quite literate. As he read it, Iona Ovseich could not believe his eyes: this was something completely new for Cheperukha, the only other possibility was that some more experienced hand was at work here.

"All right," said Iona Ovseich, neatly folding the sheet of paper and placing it in his side pocket, "you can go."

Pausing to think, Cheperukha had not moved when the doorbell rang. Degtyar opened the door and in came Major Biryuk.

"Oh, Ovseich, give him the letter," said Cheperukha happily. "He should sign it and he has to mention that he's a hero of the Soviet Union."

Comrade Degtyar replied that he would decide in what order people would be shown the document, but Major Biryuk displayed such interest and persistence that Degtyar was forced to yield.

As he read, the major's eyebrows rose higher and higher, finger-thick folds forming on his forehead.

"But, Degtyar, this is a provocation! This is outright provocation!"

"A provocation?" said Cheperukha, pretending not to understand. "What kind of provocation?"

"I'm telling you," Major Biryuk shouted shrilly, "this is a typical provocation!"

"And I'm telling you," said Cheperukha, adopting the same tone as the major, "that you're a putz! A perfect putz!"

Andrei Petrovich's eyes flared with green fire and he seemed about to attack Cheperukha with his fists but Iona Ovseich stepped in between the two of them and reminded them they were in his home, demanding they go elsewhere if they wanted to fight.

"You're right," said the major, quickly taking himself in hand, "you're right, Iona Ovseich. But I won't forget this provocation."

Cheperukha was motionless, as if his feet were rooted to the spot where he stood; his swarthy wrinkled face had paled noticeably but it showed no sign of fear or confusion; on the contrary, he was clearly up for a fight and had made a point of clenching his drayman's fists.

"That's good," said Degtyar calmly, "now you can talk."

Now, when the situation had become more or less normal, Andrei Petrovich declared that there was nothing to talk about because things couldn't be any clearer: it had turned out the authorities had made a mistake, innocent people had been arrested, and Cheperukha was writing protest letters and inciting others to do the same.

"Listen," said Cheperukha, whacking his sides with his hands, "I lived my whole life in the same building as Dr. Landa, the man served in the war from the first day to the last, and so how could there be anyone who knows Dr. Landa and can judge him better than me!"

"And so that means," parried Major Biryuk without a pause, "that if you lived in the same building as the Kogans and Vovsis, you'd be better able to judge them than the government agencies that deal specially with this sort of problem?"

"And so they're saints and can't make a mistake?" said Cheperukha, raising his voice again.

"Stop with those Odessa jokes—answering a question with another question," said the major, wagging a threatening finger.

"Did he really answer a question with another question?" said Comrade Degtyar. "In my opinion, he's restating what he said in the letter: that, yes, government agencies have made a mistake and are arresting innocent people."

"Ovseich," said Cheperukha, cleaving the air with the heel of his hand, "don't try to pin anything on me. I've always stood for the truth and I know where Moscow is and I know where the Kremlin is and I know the right people to go to."

"All right," said Comrade Degtyar, nodding his head, "and the people who helped you type the letter, you know their addresses too, of course?"

"I won't tell you their addresses. But I'll tell you who typed it. I did," said Cheperukha, raising his index finger, "with this finger right here."

Comrade Degtyar and Major Biryuk both stood in silence for a moment, scrutinizing this crude and insolent man who was trying to wriggle out of the situation by joking.

"And who's going to believe you!" said the major, taking his hands from his pocket and crossing his arms over his chest. "You can't say two words in Russian without making a mistake."

Cheperukha brought his thumb to his teeth, bit at his fingernail as if it were annoying him, but then replied quite amicably: "Pigs give birth to pigs, elephants give birth to elephants, and my son is an engineer with a higher education."

"Stop it!" cried Iona Ovseich unexpectedly. "Stop this farce!"

Andrei Petrovich automatically drew himself up and, though he was in civilian dress, it was clear from his bearing that he was a professional soldier. Cheperukha, on the other hand, now let himself go entirely, giving Comrade Degtyar the finger. Then he bent his right arm at the elbow and crossed his left arm over it, showing it to both men in turn.

"You'll pay for that!" Iona Ovseich reacted at once. "You'll be eating soup at forty below!"

Andrei Petrovich was so incensed that he was on the verge of grabbing Cheperukha by the arms, twisting them behind his back, and kicking him out, but Degtyar stopped him in time, saying that all they needed was a fight and the police.

Cheperukha demanded his letter back but Iona Ovseich turned his back on him. Cheperukha clucked his tongue, walked to the doorway, and stopped, saying loudly with reproach and threat in his voice: "You're a fine bunch of citizens!"

He slammed the door with such force that the glasses rattled in the pantry.

"Now I understand you, Ovseich!" exclaimed Major Biryuk.

Iona Ovseich covered his mouth with his hand. His eyes had become glassy. Andrei Petrovich took him carefully by the shoulder and asked him for the letter; he'd bring it to the Ministry of State Security, the MGB, tomorrow. The comrades there could deal with it. Iona Ovseich did not respond and might not even have heard what was said to him. Andrei Petrovich repeated his question and patted Degtyar on the back.

Iona Ovseich raised his head, his eyes heavy with many days and years of weariness, and said hoarsely: "What for? You're on leave. There's still time."

"No," objected the major, "there's no such thing as leave when you're dealing with something like this; the alarm has to be sounded right away, everyone has to be alerted."

"You're right," agreed Comrade Degtyar, but said again that he would deal with it himself and would be keeping the letter.

Andrei Petrovich shrugged his shoulders, the expression in his eyes unclear—it was either a mixture of surprise and mistrust or simple confusion.

When the major had left, Iona Ovseich reread the letter, and mentally reviewed all the scenes and conversations of the evening. He had the distinct impression that they had gotten too carried away and discussed things that should not have been discussed.

The next day Iona Ovseich was caught in the election campaign whirl and inadvertently forgot all about Cheperukha and his letter. Returning home late that evening, he found a note from Major Biryuk in his keyhole, asking him to call him as soon as he came home. As he read the note, Iona Ovseich's first impression was that someone had been lying in wait for him around the corner and had struck him on the back of his head with great force. His heart missed a beat but then he grew irritated and ashamed of letting himself be frightened by such a trifle.

It was still early, a little after ten. Iona Ovseich removed his hat, scarf, and coat, then smoothed his hair on the sides with the palms of his hands and set off to visit Major Biryuk. In the hallway, however, he came to a stop, shuffling his feet for a few seconds, starting one way then the other until finally he decided that there was no reason to go running to his neighbor at that hour.

Back in his apartment, household tasks helped his unpleasant inner agitation to pass—he put the teakettle on, sliced some bread and sausage, and cleaned an onion, sprinkling it with salt to absorb the water. Iona Ovseich thought that in another ten or fifteen minutes he'd be back at work on his outlines and notes, but Major Biryuk arrived before he had even finished his meal. Greeting Degtyar, his guest quoted the Eastern proverb that if the mountain would not go to Muhammed, Muhammed would go to the mountain, and informed

Degtyar that he had already dropped by there once and left a note in the door.

After a short pause Comrade Degtyar nodded and said that yes, he'd found it. Andrei Petrovich frowned: "So if you read it, why didn't you come by?"

"Well," said Degtyar, pouring his guest tea and bringing the sugar bowl over, "in my opinion it was an invitation, not an order."

"You know what," said the major, immediately raising his voice, "I don't like all these klein shtetl tricks you people use here—my opinion, your opinion, their opinion! Did you go by the MGB?"

Degtyar hastily sliced a piece of bread, buttered it and sprinkled it with sugar, placed it on a small plate and handed it to his guest: "Try this, Andrei Petrovich, it's very good. My late mother taught me how to make it."

"So," said the major, drumming two fingers on the table, "it's clear you haven't been to the MGB."

Degtyar sliced a piece of bread the same size as Andrei Petrovich's, broke off one corner, and chewed it slowly, his face expressing his pleasure. Then, after a sip of tea, he said: "And why is it that you're so sure I didn't?"

"Listen," said the major, growing genuinely angry, "give me a straight answer—I was there, I wasn't—and stop beating around the bush!"

"Why should I give you an answer," said Iona Ovseich in a tone of surprise, "when you already know everything anyway."

"I don't know anything," said Andrei Petrovich. "I just assumed that."

Iona Ovseich wiped his chin with his fingers and said in a thoughtful tone of voice: "An assumption is a hypothesis, and hypotheses aren't built on sand."

Major Biryuk placed his elbows on the table and propped his head on the palms of his hands. His small green eyes peered intently at Degtyar, his puffy eyelids even more swollen from tension. Once again Iona Ovseich had the impression—not so much an impression as a memory—that he had encountered those small green eyes and that hostile gaze before, sometime at the end of the twenties or the beginning of the thirties when he had been sent out to the countryside to take part in collectivization.

"Listen, Andrei Petrovich," said Comrade Degtyar, suddenly changing the subject, "where were you born?"

The major continued to regard Degtyar in silence as if no one had spoken to him. Iona Ovseich could feel some mounting hostility in that gaze, though he could not understand why it was there or where it was from. All sorts of nonsense kept occurring to him, including the memory of a kulak family of Russified Germans from Tsebrikov, a father and three sons, all strong as horses.

"Ovseich," Major Biryuk finally said, "don't stare at me. Two can play that game and I would win."

Iona Ovseich shuddered as if a chill had shot through his body but he quickly overcame the sensation and asked the major to give him a list of the rules they should play by. The major changed position, half turning in his chair so that he now faced the window. A snow-capped streetlight was swaying in the wind, and it was surprising that the snow had not fallen off. The major sighed deeply and said: "We don't get on, you and I. Whose fault is that?"

"Major Biryuk," said Iona Ovseich hoarsely, "what was the point of your remark about playing games? What did you mean by that?"

Andrei Petrovich turned his face toward Degtyar again, spread his hands, and said with a smile that he hadn't meant anything in particular.

"Nothing in particular?" said Comrade Degtyar. "All right, you meant nothing in particular then."

The major spent another few minutes fidgeting on his chair, then pulled back his sleeve for a glance at his watch and was surprised that they had been sitting there so long.

"It doesn't matter," said Iona Ovseich, reassuringly, "you have something important done."

The major was about to bring up the subject of the letter but Iona Ovseich was a step ahead of him: "Shall we check with the MGB as to whether or not I've been by there?"

"Ovseich," said the major, his feelings hurt, "don't try to make a fool out of me. I trust you like I trust myself."

Comrade Degtyar thanked him for the kind words and said in an amicable tone: "People can find a common language when they want the same thing."

When the door had closed behind the major and Degtyar could

hear his footsteps on the cast-iron stairs, he went back to his room where he paused pensively in front of his bookcase, whose top two shelves contained works on politics and philosophy; he shook his head and, in a loud voice, uttered: "Oh, that son of a bitch!"

The night passed calmly: his heart caused him no special problems and only once did he take a piece of sugar with five or six drops of validol on it. Still, his entire body somehow felt uncomfortable—no matter which way he turned, the position was wrong. It would have been better to have a pain in one spot.

Like his feelings, Degtyar's thoughts were also confused—first he sought to mend fences with Biryuk even though they hadn't actually quarreled, then, he would go to the other extreme, and accuse him of wrongdoing, though not everything he had done was so wrong. It was only at daybreak when he had risen to wash and walk around his room to limber up that he grew distinctly irritated with himself for having been spineless with Biryuk, essentially allowing him to control his acts and behavior.

Recalling the whole to-do about the MGB added to the stock of Degtyar's irritations: it could appear that he had been afraid of Biryuk and had acted like a coward; the major had been a hair's breadth away from actually questioning him, but Degtyar had dodged the question and wriggled out of answering. But there was no reason at all he should have answered, he should have immediately called him to order: it's none of your business, Citizen Biryuk, you're no one to be telling us what to do and checking up on us!

Quite unexpectedly, Cheperukha was waiting by the gate, and seemed to have the patience to remain there until nightfall. Comrade Degtyar walked by him without stopping. Iona lingered behind for a second, but then caught up to Degtyar at once and, without even a hello or a good morning, demanded his letter back. Comrade Degtyar continued walking, but a drayman is a drayman and Cheperukha grabbed him by the sleeve and began shouting loud enough for the whole street to hear that it was a lousy trick to take a letter from a person and then use it like it was your own property. People looked back over their shoulders and some stopped and began to observe the scene. Softly, and through his teeth, Iona Ovseich gave Cheperukha a friendly warning to stop his vulgar clowning, but Cheperukha grew even hotter and ended up shouting like a hoodlum that he would wring Degtyar's neck like a mangy chicken. There was a moment when Iona Ovseich had already put his hand in his pocket to pull out the letter and throw it in the troublemaker's face if only to put an end to that sickening scene but, fortunately, he did not; Cheperukha had fired his last round and now spat on the snow; the saliva was pale red, his gums must have been bleeding. He said that he was going straight to the MGB where he'd tell them everything himself. "Our Chekists can tell the difference between real enemies and real friends."

"So, go," shouted Iona Ovseich with anger, "go, before they come for you!"

At the factory, the carpenters had finally gotten a real move on; the frameworks for six voting booths were already up and finished. The foreman said that the rest of the woodwork could have been finished today if the warehouseman hadn't held up the plywood.

"The plywood will be here," said Comrade Degtyar. He called the warehouseman at once and gave him a piece of his mind; he promised that he would personally be watching to see if the carpenters building the booths received all the material they needed on time.

The carpenters came to see him with another complaint that afternoon: the red cloth they'd been given had been cut so close it tore as soon as you nailed it up. The carpenters needed more red cloth in order to do their jobs well, but no one was bothering to listen.

Comrade Degtyar called in the chairman of the factory trade union committee for a second time, and, in the presence of other people, made it so hot for him that the chairman literally left the room sweating and searching his pockets for a handkerchief to wipe his face. This pleased the people there in Degtyar's office; they were completely on Degtyar's side because as soon as those factory trade union committee bigshots started feeling a little of their power, they forgot whether the workers were there for them or they were there for the workers.

Cheperukha was forgotten in the commotion of the day but in the late afternoon, when things began winding down, Iona Ovseich remembered Cheperukha threatening to go to the MGB himself and tell them everything. It wasn't turning out very well at all: of course he should keep the letter, that was the right thing, but still that was no way for a person to talk to him. And now if Cheperukha really had carried out his threat, that would make for a fine kettle of fish. Of course things always ended up in their place sooner or later, but he had to find the key here, especially since Cheperukha was far from being a Dr. Landa, whom he so zealously defended. It was just that the man's brain had broken down for a minute.

Iona Ovseich decided to visit Zinovy that evening and, if the man hadn't done anything in the heat of the moment, they could still discuss the problem and come to some sort of terms. And, as for Biryuk, he had to be told what was what.

Finally, things quieted down; the awful pandemonium was over —like a funhouse mirror it made the large seem small and the small large. In the factory's front hall Iona Ovseich felt the radiator to check if it was good and warm, put on the watchman's large gloves, whacked his hands a few times, then returned the gloves to their owner, remarking in jest as he said good-bye, "The weather's so warm it makes you drowsy."

He went into a grocery store on Lenin Street and bought two hundred grams of sausage but they were out of butter. The salesgirl told him that some wonderful lard had just come in that day. Iona Ovseich thanked her anyway, saying that he had liver problems and people with liver ailments were advised to stay away from fats. The salesgirl just laughed: "Don't pay any attention to that, you'll go when your time comes; if you're always trying to protect yourself, you waste your life and spoil other people's." "All right," said Iona Ovseich, "weigh me out a hundred grams." The salesgirl advised him to take two hundred, his wife could fry up some onions in it and they would taste as good as if they had been cooked in butter. Iona Ovseich half closed his eyes, raised his brows a little, and shook his head: "I don't need two hundred, a hundred is plenty." The salesgirl looked to the left and the right, then bent forward and whispered rapidly: "Come by tomorrow, I'll keep a pound of butter for you."

The salesgirl had beautiful white hands and clean nails, a pleasure to look at. She was wearing small gold earrings with red stones that looked like rubies and a freshly starched smock that was fitted tightly over her breasts. Her smile was pleasant and friendly. Iona Ovseich thanked her, not wanting to go back out into the cold. The cashier had already started looking at the two of them, it was becoming too obvious, and so he asked for another piece of paper to wrap the lard a little better. The salesgirl told him to put the package on the counter and rewrapped it herself in one second. Taking the package, Iona Ovseich found himself gazing at his own hands: they were stained by ink and other things, and it was high time he cut his fingernails. Quickly, like a schoolboy, he pulled his hands inside his sleeves, assumed a severe expression, and left the store. Outside he stopped in front of the shop window where he could appear to be reading a sign or examining the goods on display, whereas in reality he simply wanted another look at that woman who emanated all the warmth and comfort of home.

On his way up Roza Luxembourg Street, Iona Ovseich began thinking of that woman again but he was facing some urgent tasks and they quickly gained the upper hand over idle dreams.

Iona Ovseich had barely opened his door when the phone rang. He couldn't imagine who would be calling him at that hour. It turned out to be Lyalya Orlov, who said that she'd been trying him at the factory and at home. There had been no answer either place, but now finally she'd had some luck.

"Get to the point," interrupted Iona Ovseich.

Lyalya replied that it wasn't something to be discussed on the phone and that she would stop by in fifteen minutes. No, said Comrade Degtyar, he wouldn't be there in fifteen minutes, because he was on his way to see Cheperukha and he couldn't tell beforehand when he'd be through.

"So you already know everything!" cried Lyalya.

Iona Ovseich's heart skipped a beat unpleasantly—so that meant the old man had already gone and done it—but his outward reaction was calm: all right, she could drop by, he'd wait for her.

He couldn't delay it any longer, he needed to work out a concrete plan of action to respond to the foolishness that foolhardy drayman had committed out of fear. But what proved to actually have happened could not have occurred to anyone; not only did old Cheperukha not stay quietly at home like any normal person would while no one was bothering him, not only did he not run to Bebel Street as could have been expected from his threats, he had started going around to apartments on his own and was collecting signatures in defense of Landa! It was one of two things: either the man had gone completely off his head or it proved that Biryuk was right and steps should have been taken at once and he, Degtyar, had messed up. It was true that not a single tenant had given his signature and that of course was a very positive development, but, on the other hand, no one apart from Dina Vargaftik had gone running to Orlov, Malaya, Degtyar, or even just to a neighbor, to express his outrage and plan a rebuff to that foul blackmail and provocation.

Iona Ovseich paced rapidly around the table, his face so exhausted that it was painful to behold, and Lyalya reviled herself for being in such a hurry; she should have let the man get himself a good night's sleep first. Finally, he came to a stop and asked her if Major Biryuk knew of all this. Lyalya shrugged her shoulders and said, "What difference does that make?" Suddenly Comrade Degtyar attacked her, shouting that she shouldn't be sitting on the stove and warming her fat butt, she had to know what was going on here and should be peaking in every corner.

Lyalya almost burst into tears from this insult and wanted to repay him in kind, but she was able to get a grip on herself and said that if it was her job to find out, she would. Iona Ovseich began pacing around the table again, his eyes betraying the intensity of his thoughts. Lyalya sat quietly on her chair, afraid to stir.

"Orlov," said Comrade Degtyar, "are you familiar with Gizella's sister's apartment where she goes to spend the night?"

Lyalya answered that she wasn't but that they could call in Dina Vargaftik. She'd been there once or twice. All right, said Comrade Degtyar, bring her by.

It wasn't even ten o'clock yet but Dina and Alfochka had already gone to bed. Lyalya asked her to hurry so as not to keep Iona Ovseich waiting. Dina threw a bathrobe on over her nightshirt and a topcoat over the bathrobe, then told Alfochka to behave herself, she'd be back soon. In the hallway Lyalya pointed out that only the top button of Dina's bathrobe was buttoned. Dina grabbed the middle button and used both hands to close her coat, but their rapid pace prevented her from buttoning it below the waist. Lyalya said that her coat needed to be well buttoned, or else she'd look cheap. Dina replied that with the life she lived she could walk around naked and no one would dare point a finger at her. Lyalya twisted her lips in distaste and grabbed the hem of the coat to cover Dina, even if only a little. Without warning, Dina pinched Lyalya's hand painfully, and said that it was disgusting to be touched, especially by certain women. Lyalya could feel the blood rush to her cheeks; at another time she would have smacked someone in the face for a remark like that but that was all they needed now, to bring their women's squabble to Comrade Degtyar.

Seeing Vargaftik, Iona Ovseich automatically took note of her clothes but said nothing. He stared in silence at Dina; and it was only Dina's stupidity that prevented her from noticing the mockery and contempt in his eyes.

Sitting down on the couch, she opened her thick and dwarfishly short legs, whacking her thighs after every two words, whether from envy or pleasure it was difficult to say. She liked the room where Gizella's sister lived, saying it was fit for a lord, with ornamentation on the ceiling, and statues of elegant women in the corners. You could make two rooms out of a room like that, but her husband and son had been killed at the front, she was a mother alone with her daughter, they didn't need any more than what they had. Comrade Degtyar asked if the apartment had all the amenities. Dina half closed her eyes in pleasure and replied that it had everything you could want: steam heat, central gas, hot water in the bathroom, shelves: "We should only have a quarter of what she's got."

"Dina," Lyalya suddenly interrupted, "close your legs, you're not home."

"Orlov," said Iona Ovseich with a frown, "this is my home and if any remarks need making I'll make them."

Dina had already flushed a little but, after receiving Degtyar's support, she quickly took heart and said with a nod in Lyalya's direction: "There's a good reason people say that manners are everything."

Lyalya's entire body tensed like a circus horse. Looking from one woman to the other, Iona Ovseich proposed they postpone their quarrel until their day off and wished them good night. This was so sudden that both women were caught completely by surprise. They continued to sit where they were, and Degtyar was forced to wish them a good night for a second time before they finally got up and left.

Dina stopped by the landing, laughed bitterly, and said to Lyalya: "Lyalya, you and me, we're a couple of old fools."

It was dark on the second floor, the bulb was out. Dina asked Lyalya for a hand, saying she was blind without her glasses. Lyalya took her by the arm, well above the elbow, expressing surprise that Dina could stand being touched by a woman like her.

"Oh, Lyalya," sighed Dina Vargaftik, "you're too good at keeping grudges. They're supposed to deliver kerosene tomorrow. I'll get up at five o'clock and save you a place in line. That way you'll be near the head of the line."

Orlov returned to Comrade Degtyar's fifteen minutes later, bringing him presents for Red Army Day: a green-spotted muslin necktie, a bottle of men's eau de cologne, and the book *The Knight in Tiger Skin* by the Georgian poet Shota Rustaveli. It cost Iona Ovseich some effort to restrain his anger; in the first place, it wasn't February 23 yet, and, in the second place, the necktie and the eau de cologne were overdoing it. On the other hand, he accepted the book with pleasure, especially since it was a great classic work of Georgian literature, and immediately recited from memory: " 'Everyone thinks himself a strategist if he's looking on from the side.' " Then he grew thoughtful, his eyes becoming tense; after close to a minute, he finally remembered the lines and joyfully exclaimed:

"Better glorious death in battle,
Than the shame of inglorious days!"

Lyalya said the poem was so beautiful and intelligent, you just couldn't believe it had been written eight hundred years ago.

"You know what, Orlov," interrupted Iona Ovseich, "since you've come to visit a solitary bachelor at such a late hour, let's you and I go for a stroll down the boulevard."

Lyalya clapped her hands and laughed with happiness, then asked for ten minutes to get herself together. Iona Ovseich replied that wasn't necessary, she'd be noticeable enough as she was, even though it was dark outside. Lyalya said sulkily that she wouldn't allow anyone else to make jokes like that. Degtyar let her reply pass and raised his hand as if about to give her a whack on the behind.

"No, don't!" exclaimed Lyalya, covering herself in back with her hands. "Please don't."

Iona Ovseich shrugged his shoulders; when someone made such a fuss to convince you not to do something, you could almost think it was exactly what they wanted.

A cold wind was blowing in from the sea. As long as they were walking down Bebel Street, they felt it only at the intersections, but it blew directly in their faces all the way down Pushkinskaya Street and they tried to shield themselves from it with their collars. Lyalya grew mischievous and covered Iona Ovseich's cheeks with her gloved hand, which had an unwintery smell of lilacs about it. He became angry and asked her to put a stop to her inappropriate jokes but Lyalya had gone too far to stop now. At Lanzheron Slope it suddenly began blowing from every side as if half a dozen winds had joined forces. Lyalya automatically pressed her entire body to Iona Ovseich, who unbuttoned his topcoat to shield her better, and, though it was quite uncomfortable, they walked like that to the Pushkin monument. There were a few isolated pedestrians coming from the direction of the opera, but there wasn't a soul near the City Soviet, the policeman on duty was obviously inside. The cannon from the English ship *Tiger* loomed up ahead, motionless as a museum piece, its black muzzle pointed toward the sea. Iona Ovseich and Lyalya walked past it and stopped by the railing at the cliffside.

Although it was late February, it was business as usual in the port. Various sounds reached them—the clang of iron, a switchman's horn, the hiss of electric welding, rapid bell sounds from a vessel, and sometimes just a human voice, so clear they could distinguish every word. They stood for a few minutes in silence, then Iona Ovseich pointed toward Peresyp and said that there had been an enormous pier there until it had been burned down during the uprising of 1905. The detachments of insurgents, mostly workers from the Gen plant, had built barricades on Moskovskaya Street and near the bridge, while the port's bums had rushed to loot the storehouses; they rolled out the wine barrels and drank so much that many of them fell into those barrels and drowned. In the movie *The Battleship Potemkin,* Sergei Eisenstein showed Cossacks shooting people down on the steps, but that was poetic license: in reality, it was impossible even to approach the boulevard that was called Nikolaevsky back then, because mounted White Guards were ranked everywhere and firing into the lower part of the city around Primorsky Street. The paving stones literally ran with blood and there were many children among the dead, twelve- and thirteen-year-old boys. Then the tsarist authorities held a trial and among the defendants were a hundred and forty teenagers. He hid with relatives on Koblevsky Street and it had been a miracle he avoided arrest.

Lyalya took Iona Ovseich's arm and they walked over to the cog railway where they stood for a short while—the rails were covered by snow, two narrow black lines which emerged arcing left and right and disappeared underground somewhere down below; actually they were hidden from view by a large overhang where the terminal was located. They continued on their way, walking past the Richelieu monument and the Potemkin Stairs. Lyalya removed her gloves, rubbed Iona Ovseich's numb fingers between the palms of her hands, then brought them to her lips and blew warm breath on them. Iona Ovseich smiled sadly and said that back when he had been a little boy and his fingers would freeze in the icy weather, his mother used to warm them that same way. Oh, Mama, Mama!

"My God," whispered Lyalya, "you're so gentle and tender."

"Orlov," exclaimed Iona Ovseich in a friendly but ironic tone, "I can see you'll be proposing in another minute."

Lyalya did not reply but only unbuttoned the top of her coat and was about to place Iona Ovseich's hand on her breast but people were now approaching. He carefully extricated his hand and said that he would keep it in his pocket.

"Good lord, what do we care about them!" said Lyalya vexed.

They chose a more comfortable direction by the colonnade of the Vorontsov Palace, with the wind blowing from behind them now. Far up ahead, an enormous column of fire rose from Shkodova Hill: it was the waste products from the oil refinery that burned day and night. Lyalya asked if there wasn't some way of using all that for people's benefit. Iona Ovseich peered intently into her dark green eyes, which were all pupil, and answered a question with a question: "Orlov—if we could have done something else with it, do you think we'd be heating the sky for no reason?"

Lyalya stood motionless as if in anticipation. Iona Ovseich made a half turn away from her and pointed a finger toward the ship repair yard, then with a long arching movement indicated a sweep of coastline, saying it was a military harbor and off limits, from Platonovsky and Austrian Beach all the way to Lanzheron. The Vorontsovs were no fools, he said, they chose a good place for their palace. Lyalya suddenly grabbed his shoulder, yanked him back toward her, and whispered in a breaking voice, as if she were panting for breath:

"Come on, say a few words about something else! Can't you talk about anything else!"

Without waiting for his answer, she took Iona Ovseich's head in both her hands, pulled it right to hers, and pressed her lips to his with such force that he could taste salty blood in his mouth. Iona Ovseich tried to tear free but at first could not. Finally free, he spat to clear his mouth, otherwise he would not have been able to utter a word. Then he automatically wiped his lips with the palm of his hand, took a step forward, and began shouting angrily: "Orlov, have you gone mad, or what!"

Lyalya's head was lowered and her shoulders were trembling slightly. Iona Ovseich could not regain his composure and repeated his reproach, adding this time that she was acting like she was seventeen instead of three times that. They stood facing each other in silence for a few moments, then Lyalya turned and began walking quickly toward the boulevard.

"That's right," Iona Ovseich shouted after her, "but you should run and make it really theatrical!"

Lyalya, on the verge of tears, stopped, placed her hands on her chest, and said: "Why are you shouting at me! For God's sake, don't shout at me!"

They returned to the city by Vorontsov Lane and it was dark all the way to Karl Marx Square. Small lights under tin shades were burning by the gateways and it seemed that someone could come flying out of one at any moment. Several times Lyalya clutched instinctively at Iona Ovseich's sleeve. He would quicken his pace as if finding this burdensome or unpleasant; finally, Lyalya could restrain herself no longer, admitted she was frightened, and took his arm. At first her fingers barely touched him, but then they began squeezing more tightly and convulsively with every sound and every shadow in every gateway; he could feel her fingers even through the thick wool of his topcoat. Iona Ovseich shook his head reproachfully and asked with a hint of mockery: "I wonder why you're so nervous and frightened." Lyalya did not answer but two or three times pressed herself closer to Iona Ovseich, as if not quite meaning to. He did not protest. Then Lyalya raised her head, looked slightly off to one side, and said: "Don't be angry. It was all my fault it happened, but there was nothing else I could do."

Iona Ovseich did not reply. They crossed the square and turned onto Sabaneev Bridge. The sea was visible again—huge cranes in the port, the silhouettes of ships, red and white lights on their masts; it all seemed to be at the end of a long corridor lined with buildings two, three, four stories high. Lyalya sighed, nestled herself against him again, and said softly: "You're special. You're not like other people at all."

When they were saying good night by the front door, Iona Ovseich had a coughing fit, then said that he had a stitch in his left side. Lyalya was worried and offered to put cupping glasses on him, God forbid he was coming down with pleurisy or pneumonia. Iona Ovseich dismissed the offer with a flick of his hand—women always needed to have a patient of their very own! They wished each other good night and went their separate ways.

The following evening Iona Ovseich dropped by the Biryuks, hoping they'd give a "lonely traveler" a cup of tea with some raspberries, which people say is good for a cold. Andrei Petrovich frowned, and said they had nothing to eat themselves, but then immediately offered Degtyar his hospitality. Marina brought out a stack of dishes and the table was soon covered with a great variety of food, as if an important general had arrived with his entire retinue.

"Well," said Degtyar, lowering his eyes and squinting cunningly, "it's not hard to be the wife in a house with a husband like this."

Marina shrugged her shoulders; it was probably the other way around—it was not hard to be the husband with a wife like that.

They sat down at the table. Iona Ovseich congratulated Biryuk on the two upcoming holidays. First, on the elections, in which he'd be voting at home, in his own country, not somewhere in Germany, and, second, on Soviet Army Day. They each drank a glass of vodka, chasing it with little salmon sandwiches. The major opened a jar of crabs but Iona Ovseich flatly refused any, even at the risk of offending, saying that he'd be willing to put those nasty things in his mouth only if there were nothing left to eat in the world. Andrei Petrovich did not insist and said only that the Germans considered them a great delicacy. Iona Ovseich retorted that "The French eat frogs and the Koreans eat dogs, so are you going to tell Russians to eat them too!"

They refilled their glasses and drank again, this time to the Biryuks. Iona Ovseich looked around and saw that they had screened off one corner of the room for Andrei Petrovich's mother and turned the front hall into a little bedroom for the children. All that could be seen in room was Andrei and Marina's sofa bed. He rose, and walked around the room, counting his paces to himself so that no one else would notice what he was doing, then sadly shook his head, saying there was no room there for a billiard table. That surprised Marina: Really? To listen to her husband, they should be the envy of half of Odessa. Andrei Petrovich frowned and bristled, the conversation clearly not to his liking. Degtyar, however, attached no significance to this and continued: like it or not, in this case the lady of the house was right.

"Yes, and so?" asked Andrei Petrovich in an angry tone.

Degtyar walked around the room again, listening carefully; he could hear the old woman turning and wheezing on her bed. He stopped by the window with his back to the street and pointed to the courtyard.

"In our courtyard there is an apartment with two large rooms, a good-sized kitchen, and a separate toilet and it's occupied by one person. You know who I mean."

Marina was the first to guess. "Gizella Landa."

"That's right," answered Iona Ovseich loudly, "Gizella Landa. She hasn't actually been living here the last two months. She's been staying with her sister on Red Guard Street. According to our information, the sister has a room fit for a king and big enough to turn into an entire apartment."

Once again sounds came from behind the screen whose fabric was indented in one spot as if a person had pressed his face against it there.

"Mama, are you going to lie still or not!" cried Marina irritably.

Andrei Petrovich shifted his gaze from his guest to his wife. Iona Ovseich squinted an eye cunningly and said, "That's what they call a dumb scene in the theater because a character is very much present but doesn't speak."

"Ovseich," said Andrei Petrovich, "are you proposing that I force a person out onto the street so I can take over his place?"

"That's not it!" said Marina before Degtyar could answer. "Iona Ovseich didn't say the person had to be driven out into the street."

"Ovseich," said Andrei Petrovich, placing his hand over the back of his chair, his green eyes fixed on Degtyar, "Landa is under investigation but there hasn't been a trial yet."

"That's right, there hasn't been a trial yet," said Iona Ovseich, walking over to the table and resting the palms of both hands on it. "But I assume that Major Biryuk, unlike Cheperukha, has no doubts on this score."

"What does Cheperukha have to do with it!" blurted Marina. "This is strictly a question of fairness: there's five of us, and I'm not even going to mention the fact that this is a hero's family, and Landa is alone, no children, no husband."

Andrei Petrovich placed his hands on the table and leaned forward. His bright green eyes grew yellow as he distinctly enunciated his words, which contained an undertone of warning: "She's not alone, Marina Ignatevna, she has a husband."

Marina shifted in her chair, clearly needing all of her strength to refrain from replying. Wishing to cool her fury, Degtyar calmly placed a hand on her shoulder and said: "Major Biryuk, I thought that you were able to look ahead a little, but obviously I was mistaken."

"Look ahead!" said Marina with a forced laugh. "My husband only knows how to look at behinds!"

Andrei Petrovich bit his upper lip, pulled the vodka bottle over, and poured himself a half a glass, downing it in a single gulp. Marina called her husband a drunk, grabbed his empty glass, and poured herself some vodka, which she also downed in a single gulp. "All right, let's compete, let's see who can drink more."

Andrei Petrovich lowered his head. His wife said that he looked like a menacing bull. Iona Ovseich watched for a second or two in silence, then shook Marina's hands, then Andrei's, and said it was only a lover's quarrel. He promised to stop by tomorrow or the day after. Better still, they should come by and see him. Marina accompanied Degtyar to the stairs and was even more worked up when she returned ten minutes later. She demanded that her husband go to the District Executive Committee first thing the next morning. Andrei Petrovich did not reply, a look of long-suffering on his face. Marina said that his expression was disgusting, then threw a sheet, pillow, and blanket on the couch, making the bed sloppily. She lay down facing the wall and warned her husband not to touch her or she'd scream blue murder.

Andrei Petrovich looked in on the children, who were both fast asleep. He shut the door halfway, lined up four chairs, put on his flannellette pajamas, and got in his uncomfortable, make-shift bed. "Who's going to turn out the light? Pushkin?" shouted Marina. He got up to turn off the lights, grabbing his topcoat at the same time.

Marina laughed in the dark: "Comfortable, darling?"

Cheperukha was driving Andrei Petrovich crazy, people were organizing in support of an enemy of the people, so how was he supposed to think about his own family? "Shut up!" ordered Andrei Petrovich.

"I won't shut up!" cried Marina. "You poor schmuck."

Light fell through the window; the chandelier cast a long shadow across the ceiling, its crystals clinking softly in the darkness. He felt an urge to take a stick and smash that absurd chandelier to smithereens. Andrei Petrovich turned onto his side, causing the chairs to creak. Marina said that he should come into bed with her and, after waiting a minute, she got up, walked over to her husband, and took his hand. He asked her to let go but she squeezed his hand all the tighter and said that if he didn't get into bed with her right now, she would lie down on the floor and stay there until morning when the children woke up. "Fine," replied Andrei Petrovich, "let them wake up and see you there with their own eyes, they're not little any more, they'll understand what it means." Marina clasped her hands: "Oh, you criminal, turning your children against their own mother!"

The old woman gave a drawn-out moan behind the screen as if suffering severe pain. Andrei Petrovich rose, tossed his coat neatly over the back of a chair, and walked to the couch. As soon as they were together in bed, Marina put her arms around his neck, paused for a moment, then stirred, lifting her nightshirt to her shoulder, baring her stomach and breasts; she pulled off his underpants and whispered in his ear: "Make love to me! Make love to me!" Then she whispered more insistently, "Harder, harder than that!"

When they were spent, Marina told her husband to move away from her a little, it was hard to breathe so close. Finding a more comfortable position, she placed her hands outside the blanket and laughed quietly: "I'd like to imagine Ovseich doing that with Orlov, but I just can't."

Andrei Petrovich replied that that was of no interest to him. His wife was offended—go to sleep then, go to sleep, you got what you wanted. Then she rested her face on his shoulder and a second later was asleep herself. He opened the ventilation window and sat down on the windowsill. Stray snowflakes drifted into the room. He lit a cigarette and in his mind's eye could see that evening in all its irritating detail, like the acts of a play. Everything had been wrong—the wrong questions, the wrong answers, the wrong words; he should have come right out and said, "Listen, Degtyar, what the hell business is it of yours? What are you giving away other people's apartments for!" Then they would have seen who could look ahead and who couldn't.

"Oh, you shit," said Andrei Petrovich, swearing out loud, "I can see you're looking ahead: you smell of mothballs!"

Marina moaned in her sleep, her right hand groping for her husband. Andrei Petrovich closed the ventilation window, lowered his feet into his slippers, and quietly moved back to the couch. Marina reached out again, her fingers, like a sleepwalker's, groping blindly, until they felt the elastic band of his shorts; she slid them down his belly, closing her hand on him as if feeling a pear, then stopped moving. Andrei Petrovich stretched with pleasure, then began thinking about Degtyar again; the son of a bitch didn't hestitate to go mucking around in other people's lives but this time he did not feel such great anger; then he buried his face in Marina's hair and fell asleep.

After returning home, Iona Ovseich had sat at his table for a long time underlining Central Statistical Board reports on the fulfullment of the economic development plan for the year 1952. Then, when he was in bed, he mentally reviewed his entire conversation with the Biryuks. He had liked Marina today, you could feel she was a woman of character who wouldn't back down, whereas the major had proved quite green in matters concerning civilian life. Iona Ovseich turned off the light and in the darkness pictured Andrei Petrovich's confused and angry face. A smile came of its own to Degtyar's lips. Then his thoughts turned to old Cheperukha, all creased and calloused, a real Peresyp drayman, but that memory somewhat spoiled his mood. After thirty years he had to start all over from the beginning with Cheperukha. Then once again he recalled Biryuk with his eyes sharp as that muzhik at the fair. "Green eyes, that's right, green, but the kind of man who, if you yield him the road, will run over you like a tank, and you just try and stop him."

He felt a sudden stitch in his left side, he mustn't be lying in the right position. It passed quickly, however, though his hands had become somewhat sweaty and his body unpleasantly weak. Before dawn, he had another stitch and he dreamed that he was in danger from without. Iona Ovseich woke up; his anxiety lasted for another minute or two, then he tore off his blanket and tightened the laces on his long johns, which, otherwise, would be dangling all day. He took a little exercise, then rubbed his neck, throat, and forearms with a wet towel, and started the teakettle so as not to waste time while he was getting dressed. A button fell off while he was buttoning his cuffs and his first impulse was just to turn up his sleeve, get through the day like that, he could ask Orlov to sew the button back on later. An unpleasant thought flashed through his mind: it was little things like that which built up a dependency on a person. He took a needle and thread and sewed the button back on himself.

The teakettle was whistling. Iona Ovseich sprinkled the tea leaves right into his cup; he'd need a clear head to look through the Central Statistical Board reports again. He began sipping his tea, a pencil in his right hand. And he had indeed missed something of importance the previous evening: he remembered reading that rail and sea transport had increased nine percent in comparison with 1951 but the fact that trucking had increased by fifteen percent had eluded his attention. It was the same story with river transport where twelve percent more cargo had been shipped. Iona Ovseich shook his head—that's how you could miss the important things sometimes. He circled in red the information concerning the growth in workers' real income, seven percent for the year, eight for the peasants, with a total increase in national income of eleven percent. He made a note for himself in the margin: use the city for an example, the factory, the courtyard.

Before leaving for work, Iona Ovseich looked in on Orlov. She was just having breakfast and had clearly not had her robe on because she was still tying the belt at the door. The bed had not been made yet and he remarked, "It's a good thing it was me who dropped by, but what if it had been someone else!" Then he instructed her to make an announcement that there would be a general building meeting tomorrow. At the same time, someone had to go around to all the apartments and inform everyone individually that it was his personal responsibility to attend. Marina Biryuk, Katerina Cheperukha, and Dina Vargaftik could be drafted for that task. One other thing: they'd need two or three women to speak of how their standard of living had risen in the past year, using their own family as a case in point. Lyalya had just opened her mouth to ask who should handle that but Iona Ovseich was a step ahead of her and said that Idaliya Orlov should handle that.

"Oh!" exclaimed Lyalya.

"Stop the oohing," said Iona Ovseich, "and get to work! You've got two whole days."

Lyalya clasped her hands: two days, that was practically nothing! And after Granik's room was taken away, Katerina hadn't wanted to do anything at all.

"Don't worry," replied Iona Ovseich, "she'll want to."

There wasn't much time left for talking, Degtyar was already reaching for his coat. In no time at all Lyalya had made him a sandwich of peasant sausage, which had an appetizing aroma of garlic, wrapped it in a newspaper, and tried to stick it in his pocket. Iona Ovseich refused it, saying that it was disrespectful to speak with the workers and engineers with garlic on your breath.

"Oh, then I must smell of it too!" exclaimed Lyalya in fear, covering her mouth with the palm of her hand.

Iona Ovseich was already becoming angry at being detained by such trifles. Lyalya pressed her hand harder to her lips and there was a suspicious gleam in her eye. He looked reproachfully at her then said: "All right, unwrap the sandwich so it doesn't go bad. I'll drop by this evening and eat it along with a cup of hot tea."

The day went well at the factory in all respects: even the suppliers, who usually caused most of the trouble, came through a hundred and five percent. The upcoming elections were in the air and the holiday mood was reflected on people's faces, as if a bright May sun had been shining since early morning, though in reality a light gray snow mixed with drizzle was falling and sloshed unpleasantly underfoot outside and in the hallways. Standing by the conveyor belt, a young woman who looked seventeen or eighteen was humming a song from a movie: "December seems like May to me, and I see flowers in the snow." Iona Ovseich walked up behind her without her noticing and put his arms around her; taken by surprise she shuddered and blushed.

Addressing everyone in the section, Degtyar said in a loud voice: "Comrades, let's congratulate Vera Bogachuk on her very first election!"

The people nearby began clapping. When Iona Ovseich offered Vera Bogachuk his hand, she grew even more confused and he had to take her hand himself. All the women laughed and shouted: "Here's a husband for her, go get married you two!"

The booths for the secret ballot were already completely equipped and Iona Ovseich checked each one separately to make sure that both halves of the curtain overlapped so that when the voter took ballot and pencil in hand, he could be certain that no one was observing him. He asked to see the ballot box for the absentee balloters and ordered it decorated with red cloth—it was a holiday for everyone. He examined the tables and chairs for the electoral commission and, just to be on the safe side, made sure they had a half dozen extras in reserve. Then he ordered the voting area closed, no unauthorized persons to enter before the twenty-second, and instructed the factory trade union committee to see to it that the floors were given another good washing by Saturday evening.

Before the second shift started, Iona Ovseich called a meeting of his canvassers for the last time before the elections; quoting from memory, he presented them with the figures from the Central Statistical Board reports, which they hurriedly wrote down, impressed by how much the man could retain in his head. Degtyar insisted that each of them personally revisit all of his electors and check to see that they had all received their voting instructions and knew their number on the list. In conclusion he repeated that his door was always open, and no one should feel bad or be afraid to interrupt him at any time, day or night. "This old horse won't break," he said as he pounded himself on the chest. Not everyone understood his joke, but many of them caught his tone and expression, and the room filled with lively good cheer. Suddenly, Iona Ovseich got another stitch in his side as he had that morning and his vision blurred for a moment. It was a miracle he remained on his feet. Some people noticed and watched with fear in their eyes but Iona Ovseich regained control of himself and wished them all success, concluding the meeting with a battlefront command: "Forward, comrades! Attack!"

No sooner had they left and he had sat down on the couch than Orlov called to ask when he was coming home. She absolutely had to see him, it was urgent. Either from weariness or ill health, Iona Ovseich grew suddenly angry and shouted how much was he supposed to worry over meaningless details, he'd be home when he was home. He slammed down the receiver. For a minute or two he seemed to feel a certain relief and even a sense of greater strength, but soon enough however his heart grew heavy. He had begun to feel human compassion for that woman, who genuinely wanted everything to be good but was still far from being able to tell what was important from what was secondary. She must still be standing out in the cold by some telephone, her tears streaming down her face from that undeserved insult.

Iona Ovseich glanced at his watch. The passage to Deribasovskaya Street was open until nine; he might still make it, he thought, rising with difficulty. Outside the gate, he began heading toward Pushkinskaya Street where he waited a few minutes for a trolley bus, but there was none coming in either direction and he continued on foot. At first his legs were heavy as logs but he gradually limbered up, quickened his pace, and now his only worry was that he might be late. He arrived just in the nick of time, the cashier had begun counting her day's receipts and warned the customers that her supervisor was waiting for her and she couldn't spend much more time there. Iona Ovseich walked up to the counter and chose the taller and heftier of the two salesgirls and asked to see a pair of kapron stockings for a woman approximately her size. The salesgirl shook her head: there were no kapron stockings. Iona Ovseich became indignant: what did that mean! Everyone in Odessa was wearing them and she said there were none! Clearly a bit tired from the day, the salesgirl let her eyelids half close heavily and shook her head a second time: "There's no kapron, but there's lisle." Iona Ovseich asked which was better. The salesgirl shrugged her shoulders. "Depends on your taste." She placed two pair on the counter, both of them almost a dark chocolate brown. The stockings looked quite decent, even rather dressy, with a silky gleam to them, but he wanted something in a lighter color. The one waiting on him cast a quick glance at the other salesgirl and smiled: "They're just right if they're for your wife, they shouldn't be any lighter." No, said Iona Ovseich, he wanted them lighter, closer to flesh tone. The salesgirl doubted that they had any but as soon as she opened the drawer, almost without looking, she found another two pair, a yellowish chestnut leaf color, the shade a blond woman's legs will sometimes turn toward the end of summer. Iona Ovseich examined the tops of the stockings carefully and asked if they wouldn't be too tight for a full-thighed woman. No, said the salesgirls, these lisle stockings would stretch well, at worst they might be a little short, but the dress would hide that. All right, said Degtyar with a nod, he'd take both pair and wanted them in a box with a greeting card. There were no boxes, but the salesgirl found a pink ribbon with an inscription in red: "A happy day is wished for you," which looked quite elegant. Iona Ovseich thanked her and the salesgirl said she hoped he enjoyed his holiday on February 23, and he in turn congratulated her on the elections and the upcoming March 8 holiday, wishing her success in her work and her personal life.

As he headed for the door, both salesgirls and the cashier continued to follow him with their eyes as if they were somehow sad for him; then they bolted the door behind him.

Orlov was waiting for him almost right at his door, but, despite his expectations, she advanced no complaints about being insulted. On the contrary, she admitted she had been at fault for not making herself clear on the phone, then went right to the point: that evening, it was six on the dot, she had dropped by to see Katerina, who seemed glad enough to see her. Old Cheperukha had started up, drunk as usual, shouting loud enough for the whole courtyard to hear that on election day he was going to tell all the voters how Degtyar had silenced him, stolen a letter from his pocket, and threatened to have him sent to Kolyma. Katerina had told him to shut up but in response he had roared all the louder, and said that only lowlife lived in that courtyard and that included his wife and daughter-in-law and he didn't give a good goddamn for any of it, and let the people who were afraid be afraid, personally he wasn't afraid of anything.

They sat for a minute in silence, then Iona Ovseich rose, took the package from his coat, and placed it on the table. The ribbon with the inscription was in view and, when Lyalya read it, she automatically reached for the package then caught herself and blushed deeply.

"Yes," said Iona Ovseich loudly and with emphasis, "maybe Biryuk really was right."

Lyalya did not even have time to ask what Biryuk had been right about because Iona Ovseich was seized by such a coughing fit that it seemed he would be turned inside out or burst some vessels in his brain. She grabbed him by the shoulders to still his shaking a little and pressed him to her, his face against her breasts as if he were a child; still, the attack grew worse, he jumped up from the couch, and lay stomach down on the table. He opened his mouth a few times, a hoarse gurgling sound emerging each time, then he ran over to the washstand and jumped up and down twice. Lyalya felt that she was gasping for breath herself but Degtyar was clearly feeling better now, the cough subsiding. She poured him a glass of water but had to hold it with both her hands because they were trembling so badly. He rinsed his mouth and took a few swallows. Finally, he could breathe freely and he said: "What a life."

Veins had swollen on his temples, as it sometimes does with horses; his eyes were so weary and exhausted and, at the same time, so intent and so understanding, that Lyalya wanted to fall to her knees, throw her arms around his legs, and remain there forever.

"Orlov," said Iona Ovseich, threatening her with a finger, the smile on his blue lips somehow detached from the rest of his face, "put all those thoughts out of your mind. You're not the same person you used to be."

"Oh, I'd die if something happened to you," exclaimed Lyalya, covering her eyes with her hands and turning around.

Iona Ovseich pressed his left side with the palm of his hand and said that he had a constant stitch there, it might be dry pleurisy. It started that night they went walking on the boulevard and an icy cold wind was blowing in off the sea. Lyalya uncovered her face; her eyes were full of tears and once again she said that she'd die if anything happened to him.

"You'll die!" said Iona Ovseich, wagging a threatening finger again. "I'll give you die. You're just looking for a way to wriggle out of working!"

Lyalya smiled and wiped her eyes with a handkerchief. Iona Ovseich asked her to go at once to Zinovy's and bring him back there. "If he can't come right away, regardless of the reason, tell him that Degtyar will be sitting at home specially for him and will wait up until three o'clock in the morning." No, said Lyalya, waving her hands, no, it had to wait until tomorrow: in his condition a person had to get into bed and not deal with party business.

"Orlov," repeated Iona Ovseich, "go to Zinovy's and bring him back here. Let's not waste time over nothing."

Lyalya returned five minutes later alone, and told Degtyar that Zinovy had wished him a good night and said that they'd see each other tomorrow, God willing. After a moment's silence, Iona Ovseich asked: "Does he know what's up?" "He must," answered Lyalya. "What does 'must' mean?" said Iona Ovseich, raising his voice. "Facts are what's needed here, not guesswork." Orlov answered, "It is not guesswork; if Zinovy didn't know, he would have asked what it was all about, but he didn't ask." Iona Ovseich tilted his head to one side and said: "All right, it can wait until tomorrow."

Lyalya turned out to be right: Zinovy was up on everything. Not only that, he gave his own account of everything that had happened, beginning with the old man making the scene on the street. Iona Ovseich asked what conclusion should be drawn? Zinovy thought for a moment, his eyes expressing everything but condemnation of his father. Iona Ovseich opened his hand and whacked his other hand with it, and said: "Zinovy Cheperukha, I'll make you pay dearly if that old drayman—I won't even call him your father!—causes any trouble on election day."

Zinovy rose, adjusted the strap on his prothesis, and stared insolently at Degtyar with his icy grey eyes: "I don't owe you anything and you won't make me pay dearly for anything."

"Zinovy Cheperukha," said Iona Ovseich, gathering all his strength to overcome his lack of breath, "I give you my word of honor that I'll make you pay dearly if that drayman . . ."

Seized by another coughing fit, Iona Ovseich grabbed his sides, which reduced the pain; he nodded to his guest, telling him the conversation was over and it was time for him to leave.

Iona Ovseich barely made it through the next day at the factory and left earlier than usual; he still had the building meeting ahead of him, but at home he fell completely apart; his entire body felt made of cotton. He tried to force himself to exercise, inhaling and exhaling deeply as the yogis of India advise, but that made him feel even worse:

he became dizzy, his vision blurred, and he was lucky to be able to grab onto the bedstead. When Lyalya learned that after all that he still intended to run the building meeting, she was horrified; she took him forcibly by the arm, laid him down on the couch, and told him to take an aspirin, which would make him sweat. That should bring him some relief.

He took the aspirin with a sip of water and told Lyalya to pay careful attention to what he was about to say: whether he was healthy or not, the meeting had to go on. He would show her the places he had marked in the papers with the totals for 1952, which should be read aloud to the audience. At the conclusion, after the women had spoken, there should be a final summing up so that people would take the most important fact away with them: namely, that our people and our whole country were now genuinely closer to completing the task assigned by Comrade Stalin in February '46—creating the material and technological basis for communism.

Iona Ovseich was lying on his side and now turned over onto his back. His face was so pale that Lyalya could not bear to look at it. She said she should call an ambulance but his reply was an ironic grin: tomorrow is election day and he was supposed to call an ambulance today. Very interesting!

"Good lord," said Lyalya, entwining her fingers and turning the palms of her hands out, "this isn't the last election there'll ever be. Think of yourself for once!"

The long conversation had tired Iona Ovseich and he signaled Orlov to calm down, then told her to go, or she'd be late. Lyalya bent over him, wiped the beads of sweat from his forehead, and said that she was going to send one of the women to sit with him until she came back.

"Orlov," whispered Iona Ovseich, "go, please go."

Lyalya returned an hour and a half later and Iona Ovseich was surprised that she had been so quick about it. Lyalya answered that for her it was just the other way round, it seemed to take forever.

"All right," he said, turning toward her, his eyes opening and closing, "you didn't forget to sum up, did you?"

No, said Lyalya, she hadn't; she had summed things up, then Marina Biryuk and Dina Vargaftik had repeated it in their own words. Iona Ovseich opened his mouth part way, his lower lip drooping somewhat, "They shouldn't have done that! The summing up was supposed to be the last word, *that* was what people should have taken home with them."

One corner of the blanket was dangling on the floor. Lyalya picked it up and tucked it under his legs, which were cold as ice. Once again she said that an ambulance should be called: the polyclinic took calls until noon but tomorrow was a holiday for everyone, not a workday.

"Listen to me, Idaliya," said Iona Ovseich. "At five, five-thirty, before the polls open, go see Zinovy and warn him again about his father; tell him that if he doesn't take all the necessary steps, what I promised would happen will. Then go see Fedya Pushkar; he complained to me that the partition's too thin and he can hear every word the Cheperukhas say. Maybe you can spend a little time with him until he stops feeling like a stranger in the courtyard. He has to be drawn gradually into helping us."

Lyalya replied that she would definitely drop by and see Fedya Pushkar and spend as much time with him as needed. She took the pillow from Polina Isaevna's bed, laid it on the windowsill, pulled over a chair, and rested her head on the pillow. At first Iona Ovseich paid no attention to this, perhaps dozing off himself, then he was wide awake again as if shocked from within; he demanded that Lyalya go home and go to bed like a normal person. She rose without a word and left the room; he could hear the sound of the lock clicking shut but, opening his eyes fifteen minutes later, he again saw her resting on the windowsill and this time ordered her to lie down on Polina Isaevna's bed. Lyalya said, no, not for anything in the world, and even put the pillow back on the bed; for a second time Iona Ovseich ordered her to lie down on the bed or return to her own apartment and now she had no choice but to yield.

She woke up a few times during the night, seeming to hear someone calling her, but it couldn't have been Iona Ovseich, because it was a child's voice. She would get up, walk over to him, and listen closely to his breathing, trying to discern his face in the dark: his jaw was hanging open and a bit back, and in profile he reminded her of a bird; a stream of saliva trickled from his mouth and this was very frightening the first time, she thought it was blood. She wiped his mouth carefully with the edge of her shirt and for a moment was seized by a premonition that made her want to shout and wake him. She restrained herself with some effort and returned to her bed where she lay for a long time with her eyes open, not allowing herself to fall back to sleep. Even when she finally drifted off, she remained anxious and alert in her sleep.

A little after five o'clock Iona Ovseich called out to her, saying it was time to get out of bed, the voters would already be up. Lyalya washed quickly and was about to start making Iona Ovseich breakfast but he flatly refused it; he ordered her to go down to see Cheperukha at once, those old Odessa draymen were in the habit of starting their day at four o'clock in the morning.

Iona Ovseich's guess had been quite close: by the time Lyalya arrived at the Cheperukhas, Zinovy was already gone and the old man was at the table, still hung over from the night before. Katerina set a glass down in front of him; he drank it, wheezed, and rose to leave, but his daughter-in-law barred his way, saying she wouldn't let him out of the house looking like that. The old man grew indignant and shouted that he was in the habit of being the first one at the polls in all elections. Katerina responded by locking the door and hiding the key in the pocket of her apron.

"It's a trick! It's a trap!" he shouted, stomping his feet. "Look, look, my grandsons, look what they're doing to your grandfather!"

Cheperukha drank the rest of his glass, lay down on the couch, opened the newspaper, and began snoring. At nine o'clock, when nearly the entire courtyard had voted, Katerina and Olya notified the commission that old Cheperukha had taken sick and asked them to send a ballot box to his apartment.

The ballot box and an envelope containing the ballots was brought by a young girl. Cheperukha ground his teeth and sobbed in his sleep. The girl wanted to wait until he woke up but Katerina said that he had just fallen asleep and so there was no telling how long she might have to wait there, and there must be other people needing her help at the polls. Olya took the envelope from the girl, removed the ballot, opened it, then folded it in half and placed it in the ballot box.

When Lyalya had informed Iona Ovseich of all the details, he said that a gross violation had taken place and if he were Cheperukha he'd lodge a complaint immediately. Lyalya was very distressed by this, having been certain that Iona Ovseich would be pleased and praise her for the report. She asked what she should do now, suggesting that she go to the chairman of the election commission and make a clean breast of it.

Iona Ovseich said nothing, his nose blue as its own shadow. Lyalya wrung her hands—why, why had she told him everything! He told her to hand him his shoes and clothes but she shook her head, saying, no, she wasn't going to help murder him. She swore she'd die before she let him get up. In reply, Iona Ovseich demanded that she stop her hysterics; he sat up at the edge of the couch, propping himself on his hands. Her eyes were frantic now. He asked her to help him, he still had to go down and vote. She took him by the arms to stop him and, when he made an effort to free himself, they both fell. She was afraid that her weight would crush him and turned aside just in time and they ended up on the couch side by side and face to face. The stench of his sweat made her hold her breath and, for a minute or two they lay there without moving, as if they were lying in wait for something. She shuddered, a chill passing through her entire body although her head was flushed with heat. Iona Ovseich stirred a little and moaned; she wanted to put her arms around him and press him to her but could not bring herself to do it. Then, all of a sudden and against her own will, she got up, full of irritation and anger, though at whom she did not know. Lyalya said that it was time for him to go to the polls, they must be looking for him by now. She told Iona Ovseich to lay back on his bed and she'd have the ballot box sent up to him.

Bitter as that was to swallow, Iona Ovseich was forced to agree: ninety-eight and six tenths of the voters had already cast their ballots and they were close to first place for the Stalin District, which was leading the entire city, and so now every vote counted. Zinovy made a point of coming home to vote even though he could have had his name taken off the register like a traveler and voted at the Kirov factory.

Since the chairman of the commission was urgently needed at the executive committee, his deputy brought the ballot box, accompanied by Madame Malaya. In the doorway she said that she wanted to see that rare sight with her own eyes—Degtyar sick—and ordered the lights turned on. She sat down by the head of the bed, frowned, and asked in a loud voice: who started that stupid rumor that Degtyar was sick?

"Degtyar," said Klava Ivanovna, leaning over him and patting his cheek, "believe me, a woman could only envy your complexion."

Iona Ovseich smiled, squinting from the bright light. "Malaya, I'm not deceased yet, so it's dangerous to praise me so highly."

"All right, enough pretending," said Klava Ivanovna, clapping her hands, "get up and get dressed. I want you to be with everyone for the holiday."

Iona Ovseich yanked back the corner of the blanket like a soldier and turned jauntily onto his side, a miracle, like the one in the movie *St. Jorgen's Holiday* in which the young Igor Ilinsky played the part of a swindler who threw down his crutches and began dancing. Suddenly, however, Iona Ovseich grabbed his chest with both hands and was seized by a fit of coughing that frightened Lyalya Orlov and the deputy from the commission. Only Klava Ivanovna's face remained stony as she whacked Degtyar on the back at ten-second intervals, insisting he get hold of himself. He pressed his hands to his mouth trying to suppress the coughing but it didn't help at all, on the contrary. Klava Ivanovna ordered that he be given ephedrine. Lyalya shrugged her shoulders as if she had never heard of it before. Klava Ivanovna shouted that all everyone wanted to do was to bleed Degtyar white and there wasn't even any ephedrine on his table!

Lyalya suddenly swayed on her feet and seized her fingers in her teeth. Somewhere deep inside her, near her heart, she felt a pleasant pain. She quickly bent close to Malaya, and rested her head on her shoulder, so great was her shame. Malaya pretended to dodge but in fact brought her shoulder up closer and into a more comfortable position.

Iona Ovseich cleared his throat a few more times, wiped his mouth with his fingers, mechanically examining them as if expecting to find blood but saw only traces of phlegm and saliva. He shook his head reproachfully and said that he felt like he'd been turned inside out. Klava Ivanovna replied that it didn't matter, he'd be back on his feet before the wedding. She signaled the woman from the commission to hand her the ballot and the ballot box, and ordered everyone to look the other way. Lyalya placed a fountain pen beside the ballot box. Iona Ovseich read through the ballot closely; on the left were the names of the candidates for deputy and on the right the names of the nominating organizations. He paused for a few seconds, it was the last chance to make any changes, then he placed the ballot decisively in the box. The deputy chairman of the election commission warmly congratulated Comrade Degtyar, wished him a speedy recovery, and then in the presence of witnesses rechecked the seal, two strings in wax. Everything was in place. For his part, Iona Ovseich heartily thanked the commission for its care and concern, then reminded them not to stand idle, there was still plenty that needed doing before midnight.

The deputy left. Lyalya sat closer to Iona Ovseich while Klava Ivanovna told him of the wonderful canteen they had this year at the polls; they'd brought in butter by the crate and people were taking two kilos apiece, and the Moskovsky sausage was as good as the ones they used to sell at Dubinin's, on Deribasovskaya Street, corner of Preobrazhenskaya. "Degtyar, do you remember that sausage!" Then she went on to praise the records that were being played at the polls: Lemeshev, Klavdiya Shulzhenko, Rashid Beibutov, and an entire set of Soviet Army songs and dances.

Iona Ovseich was lying on his back with his eyes closed. Suddenly Malaya whacked her knee: what an old fool she was, why didn't she think to tell them earlier to turn up the loudspeakers full force so that Degtyar could have also enjoyed the music.

"Malaya," said Iona Ovseich, turning to his left side, then to his right, and finally onto his back again, "there's something the matter with me."

Klava Ivanovna looked intently at him and said that he'd probably be better off sitting up than lying in bed and that she'd send for her rocking chair right away. Iona Ovseich grinned bitterly in reply and pointed toward the door: they should go, he wanted a little sleep. Lyalya refused but Klava Ivanovna took her forcibly by the arm. Lyalya made such a long-suffering face that Klava Ivanovna felt like slapping it. In the hallway Lyalya suddenly pressed her forehead to the wall as if she were some prim and proper young lady; now Klava Ivanova was seriously angry and she threatened to have Orlov sent to the insane asylum at Slobodka, they'd cure her good there.

As soon as the two women had left, there was a phone call from the factory. Iona Ovseich had to identify himself twice, either he hadn't been heard or hadn't been recognized. He was told that ninety percent of the voters had voted at the factory polling place and was then asked if the canvassers who had turned in a hundred percent of their courtyards could go home now. Iona Ovseich asked what place they were in for the district. Not that near first—third or fourth. Iona Ovseich allowed some of the canvassers to go home, with the rest to stay and help out: no matter what, the worst they should do is second place.

The song "Broad Is My Native Land" could be heard from outside. Iona Ovseich sighed automatically as he recalled 1937 when the movie *The Circus* was playing everywhere in Odessa: the Frunze, the Postyshev, the Korolenko, the Utochkin, all of the major cinemas. People saw the film five times and each time they suffered again for Lyubov Orlova and her little black son. Her singing voice was a little nasal and she had an American accent, as she sang "Mary, Mary, you're going to heaven!" while at the top of the circus tent. And any second she could have fallen from that dangerous height to the ground. At the end of the film, a joyous smile on her face, she walked in a column of Soviet people, the handsome Martynov beside her, everyone wearing white sweaters as in an athletic parade, as they all sang in unison:

Broad is my native land,
Many are its fields, forests, and rivers!
I know of no other country
Where a man can breathe so free!

When the record was over, Iona Ovseich wiped his tears with the palms of his hands. His room was seized by stillness, as if the holiday had suddenly ended while in full swing. He had an agonizing desire to hear the song again from the beginning, to bring him back his youth, the thirties, when they had started building communism and no one was thinking about a war with Hitler which would set communism back fifteen and maybe even a full twenty years. Iona Ovseich groaned aloud; it was painful to think how many millions of people had died, not to mention those who were killed, and how many more were yet to die without having seen communism with their own eyes.

A call came in from the factory at eleven. More than ninety-nine percent of all the voters had voted, they were in second place for the district. Iona Ovseich said that a few more canvassers could be sent home, people with families first, and the rest should be sent out to the addresses of those people who had not voted; the canvassers should stand guard by their gates, their doors, their entrances, wherever, but by twelve o'clock there had to be a one hundred percent turnout.

The abrupt movements he made while talking on the phone caused him another stitch in the side and he wanted to stick a finger between his ribs to determine the exact location. While he was poking and prodding himself, Orlov came running in panting for breath and red in the face, and, without pausing, shouted: Hundred percent! Iona Ovseich raised his head, took his watch from the table; the second hand was making circle after swift circle, as if it were being pursued and urged on. As he replaced the watch, a sharp pain above the bridge of his nose furrowed his brow and he said in a hoarse voice: "We're an hour and twenty minutes ahead of last year."

An ambulance arrived thirty minutes later. Major Biryuk and Khomitsky helped carry Degtyar down, followed by Klava Ivanovna and Orlov. Iona Ovseich was looking up—at the ceiling, the staircase, a stretch of sky—and everything streamed together and swayed. His body felt unusually light, as if it had no weight, as if the earth which had always held him in its grip had now suddenly released him and he was suspended somewhere in space.

Malaya wanted to get into the ambulance but the doctor said that was not allowed. He slammed the door and they drove away. Karl Marx Street, at the corner of Yaroslavsky, was dug up, new asphalt was being laid, and they had to detour down Bebel and Lenin. It felt like they were going to another city, it was taking so long. Black tree branches, and black wires, a startling amount, flashed by overhead as Degtyar glimpsed the February sky. Somewhere down below trolley cars were ringing, cars were honking, and suddenly the stretcher bearer cried shrilly: "Watch out!"

The Stalin District Hospital was overworked that day. Iona Ovseich was admitted without much ado, but the doctors' displeasure was palpable. They had had to place cots in the hallway and a long winter evening and night lay ahead of them all. The duty physician took Iona Ovseich's papers, registered him in admissions, ordered a nurse to take his temperature, and then went off to his office. Even though twilight had not fallen yet, Degtyar still had the distinct sensation that it was late evening outside and dark, while there in the reception room, a yellow bulb shed a cozy light and the Dutch tile stove emanated a homey warmth; he had the feeling that any moment his mother, his own mother, would come in and say: this isn't real, this is only a dream, wake up, son.

Iona Ovseich shuddered. The nurse removed the thermometer from under his arm—thirty-eight point one celsius. It was pretty high, but saying it would rise even higher by that evening, she made a notation on his temperature chart, then went to deal with her syringe. The water in the sterilizer was boiling over, spiraling onto the electric hot plate and the parquet floor where it left a brown stain.

As the nurse had predicted, his temperature did indeed rise that evening and his breathing became labored. He was put on oxygen and given an injection. Iona Ovseich tried to fall asleep and, two or three times he had no sooner succeeded than he was shocked awake, his mind a confusion of policemen, Polina Isaevna, Germans in green helmets, the one-legged Kotlyar, the madman Granik with his smile. There was a ringing in his ears, a whistling, a roaring, like a street play, an orgy; an ugly hunchback whose face was painfully familiar fell off a horse, his feet stuck in the stirrups, as he cried: "A horse! My kingdom for a horse!"

The crisis lasted three more days. Degtyar was put on antibiotics and fed glucose intravenously; there wasn't a vein left unpricked. His comrades at the Stalin District Committee called every day and inquired if there were any medicines that were in short supply and might be of help. Degtyar was moved into a semi-private room whose second bed was temporarily empty. High officials offered a place for Degtyar in the Province Committee Hospital on Peter the Great Street that was especially for the elite members of the party, old Bolsheviks, pensioners of national importance, and people of merit. The head of the ward and the physician in chief replied that at present Comrade Degtyar could not be moved, and, moreover, was already receiving all the care modern medicine could provide. He was allowed visits twice a week, from five till seven in the evening. Malaya and Lyalya Orlov were issued special passes which gave them the right to visit Degtyar every day. Lyalya was unsparing of herself and visited him before her shift and after, sometimes even managing to run over on her lunch hour.

Some improvement seemed to occur on his fourth day in the

hospital and for the first time Iona Ovseich asked for a glass of tea with lemon. Overjoyed, Lyalya squeezed in half a lemon but Degtyar refused the tea, saying it was too sour. He told her just to put in a slice so that it would float on the surface. She cut a piece from the center, the thickest part of the lemon, and tossed it in the glass. The tea grew somewhat paler in color. Iona Ovseich took a few sips and rested for a short while on his side, then drank almost half the tea. He set the glass down beside him on the blanket and closed his eyes. It was clear from his face how deeply tired he was. Lyalya bit her lip and shook her head. Iona Ovseich moaned pitifully like a little boy. You had to have nerves of steel to listen to that moaning. A deep and terrible premonition in the pit of her stomach made her want to scream. She fought to overcome that urge, then opened the night table and began arranging things in the drawer.

The first of March was a made-to-order spring day; sparrows hopped merrily about the tree outside the window, their chirping so loud it sound like an aviary. Iona Ovseich asked that both shutters be opened and the doctor gave his permission for ten minutes and no more. No sooner were the shutters open than a fresh breeze, cool with the last traces of winter, blew in, the branches of the trees began waving by the window, and the wires between the posts swayed as if made of rubber. Iona Ovseich opened his mouth wide, closed it, then opened it again, wanting to gulp the air endlessly. A bell rang, there was a school nearby; the bell rang for a long time, but apparently the children were playing and didn't notice. Two large tears streamed from his eyes. My God, how beautiful life was, people didn't appreciate it, life was so short, over before you knew it. Iona Ovseich raised himself up onto his elbows. He experienced the certainty that everything would be all right; all that was needed was to want it in the right way, the human will was capable of performing miracles. He threw the blanket off him, first grabbing hold of the bed, then the back of a chair. His legs would not obey him; in just a few days they had almost forgotten how to walk, and it cost him a great effort to make his way to the windowsill. His heart either would beat softly or suddenly leap into his throat. A disgusting nausea with a sweetish aftertaste arose in him as can happen in a room where a corpse has lain too long. For a moment he was seized by the mad fear that any second now his soul would go flying out of his body, his soul just a piece of the blue sky, fastened somewhere within him, beneath his breastbone, on a thread, a web. Again Iona Ovseich took a deep breath; his head spun and his vision blurred. It was a miracle he stayed on his feet. Just then a nurse entered the room and helped him back into bed.

Late that day he took a turn for the worse and he was given injections of camphor and cordiamine, and put back on oxygen. Once again he had the sensation that the earth had relaxed its grip on him and his body was sailing through space. Malaya held his hand, read his pulse, and kept saying that with a pulse rate like that Degtyar should feel better than he looked. At first Iona Ovseich did not respond but when the pain had abated a little, he said: "Malaya, when it's bad, it's bad."

The next day a girl from the factory bought Comrade Degtyar a bouquet of snowdrops and a basketful of tinned food and oranges, as if he were preparing for an expedition to the North Pole. Iona Ovseich put a few oranges in the nurse's pocket, telling her to give them to her children. He ate two of them himself, wrapping the peels in paper and placing them in his night table drawer: they'd come in handy for tea.

He had a visitor from the District Committee, Comrade Artyukhov, who brought greetings from everyone and the desire that Degtyar would soon stop pretending to be sick, bad examples were infectious: Kogut had already come down with the flu and his temperature had been over forty Celsius for two days in a row and the doctors couldn't get it down. Iona Ovseich replied jestingly that he was ready to swap his double pneumonia for a single one of Kogut's flus. His visitor laughed and leveled a threatening finger at him: "We know your tricks, Degtyar!" Degtyar smiled bitterly and spread his hands. All of a sudden Klava Ivanovna attacked the visitor: if he was going to say such lousy things to a sick man, he shouldn't have come there at all. Artyukhov blushed and said perhaps he should not have come, but then added that if he had said anything wrong, he wished Comrade Degtyar would forgive him. Iona Ovseich said no apologies were necessary, he and Klava Ivanovna had a love that went way back and she was just jealous. Klava Ivanovna looked from one man to the other, rose from her chair, and went out into the corridor.

"A strong woman," said Artyukhov. "If she was five years younger, we might find a guy for her."

The guest stayed a little while longer. They spoke of province business, the sowing campaign was just about to start, and Konup, Zanoza, and Patsela had already been sent out to the countryside. The people there were working full time on repairing equipment and the overall picture didn't look bad. Food was a little on the tight side, and of course there were some bastards who were slaughtering their livestock and selling it on the sly, but they were a minority. They'd get their just desserts in time. The visitor winked merrily, making a thumb's-up sign. Iona Ovseich gave a protracted sigh: the kolhozes were almost twenty-five years old but the kulaks could still find places to hide.

"Let 'em try!" said Artyukhov, amicably whacking Degtyar on the shoulder. A raid was planned for tomorrow or the day after on a shoe operation. While Degtyar had been ill, the District Committee had put things under increased control. At the door, he remembered the chocolate in his pocket, took it out, and placed it on Degtyar's stomach, ordering him to get well.

Klava Ivanovna returned to the room when the visitor had gone; she sat down on one corner of the bed and whacked her knees: "Artyukhov! Can you imagine! Who the hell is he?"

Iona Ovseich said nothing. There were deep circles under his eyes, the size of a five-kopeck piece from tsarist times. As if blind and deaf, Klava Ivanovna raged all the more: why had he allowed some Artyukhov to speak with him like that!

"Calm down, Malaya," Iona Ovseich uttered with difficulty. "He's not just anyone, he's the head of the industrial department. And he's a good guy."

"A good guy. Oh, Degtyar, Degtyar!" she said, shaking her head.

He turned onto his other side and moaned softly: "Malaya, why do I feel so bad? Those antibiotics should have helped a long time ago."

"Be patient," said Klava Ivanovna, bending over him and stroking his stubbly cheeks, "just a little more patience."

Iona Ovseich tossed and turned until the middle of the night. Twice he asked for luminal or barbamil and after taking the tablet, there was an empty heaviness in his head as if it were weighed down from every side but hollow within. He would doze off after ten or fifteen minutes, then wake up in anxiety, the palms of his hands covered in sweat. During the first few seconds he could not remember where he was and wanted to call out for help. There was a blue bulb burning by the door. He would grow a little calmer and doze off again and the whole process would start from the beginning.

A hideous anguish welled up in him just before dawn. The sky was still black, but the stars had lost their brightness and were twinkling faster and faster, as if they were burning out and in a hurry. He had a sense of immense solitude and hopelessness, as if he had never exchanged a single word with another person during his entire life, had never heard a human voice, but had just flown through life and left a trace in space for half a second before being extinguished. Iona Ovseich tried to summon pleasant memories, something from his childhood, but everything kept converging at one and the same point, time was not divided into events, the beginning was the end, the end the beginning, and the past, present, and future were all behind him now.

"I'm dying," whispered Iona Ovseich. "Mama, I'm dying."

A wave of icy cold coursed through his entire body as if he had been smeared from head to toe with ether in one second. He lost his breath: his heart became enormous, reaching from his stomach to this throat, becoming more compressed and swelling at the same time. The ribs were no longer able to withstand the pressure and all they could do now was explode, the body breaking up into millions of particles flying off in every direction! He gathered the last of his strength, pressed one leg against the other and his hands against his torso. His head was rooted to the pillow, then suddenly he was crashing, reeling, and spinning inwardly; the bed went flying from under him and he barely managed to grab hold of it with his hands and feet. The little hammers on innumerable alarm clocks began ringing, ringing, ringing, until Iona Ovseich burst into tears, crying freely and without shame as he had long, long ago in his childhood.

It began growing light and someone turned on the radio in the room next door: Moscow was broadcasting excerpts from the latest news. The Kalinin kolhoz in the Tedzhensky district, Maryisky province, had been the first to finish the spring fieldwork in Turkmenia. The workers of the Hero of the Soviet Union Kurban Durda agricultural artel were one day behind and now both kolkhozes were competing to fulfill their obligations to the state ahead of schedule. Despite severe weather conditions, the builders of the hydroelectric power plant in Kuibyshev were continuing to speed up their work; new progressive methods were being used for the pouring of cement in the foundation pit which would permit the completion of work eight months ahead of the projected deadline. The machine tool makers of the Kirov plant in Odessa had bestowed on the motherland a wonderful gift: they had built an automated machine tool machine which could produce parts accurate to a thousandth of a millimeter.

Iona Ovseich shuddered as if he had suddenly been called by name—the Kirov plant was literally a fifteen-minute walk from there. His mouth had filled with a sweetish saliva. He wanted the commentator to repeat the item but he was already reading a report just in from Kazakhstan—having completed their February assignment ahead of schedule, the miners of Karaganda had shipped dozens more trainloads of coal than called for by the plan. Iona Ovseich seethed inwardly with a feeling of indignation and protest—why was he lolling in bed when everyone else was busy working. The past night now seemed strange and alien as if it had not happened to him but to someone else, some stranger. Lyalya came to see him and there was fear in her eyes; she had been plagued by nightmares all night, right up to the morning; she'd be afraid to repeat them. Iona Ovseich waved his hand dismissively—she should take her dreams to a gypsy fortune-teller. Then for the first time since he had taken ill he asked how things were going in the courtyard. Lyalya automatically replied that first he should recover, courtyard business could wait. Iona Ovseich disregarded her reply and posed a specific question: how had old Cheperukha been acting? Lyalya hesitated, and from her eyes it was clear that she had completely forgotten Cheperukha lately. Iona Ovseich drummed his fingers on his bed and asked a follow-up question: had she been staying in contact with Fedya Pushkar, he must be better informed than she was. Things had come to a standstill on that as well: not only had she had not been in contact with Fedya Pushkar, she had even forgotten that he existed.

"Good Lord," said Lyalya, entwining her fingers and making them crack, "I'm to blame. Punish me, but I couldn't think about anything else all this time—you were so sick!"

Iona Ovseich raised himself up onto his elbows, a mocking glint in his eye: what good was all that sympathy and emotion if it made her lose heart and sit back waiting to see what would happen; meanwhile, Iona Cheperukha was no doubt exulting to himself that Degtyar had taken ill and now he could carry on to his heart's content! No, said Lyalya with a start, that wasn't true, the whole courtyard asked about his health ten times a day and Katerina Cheperukha had promised to get some special vitamins at her factory that were worth their weight in gold now.

"Orlov," said Iona Ovseich, licking his lips to moisten them, "I'm not talking about Katerina Cheperukha, I'm talking about Iona Cheperukha."

Lyalya lowered her eyes, plucking at a ribbon on her dress in silence. What could she say: that Katerina Cheperukha and Iona were from the same family? Yes, but a family and a person were not the same thing. Even a person was not always the same, he was one way today, a different way tomorrow, and yet a different way the day after tomorrow. Lyalya raised her head and now her eyes looked right at Degtyar without evading his gaze. She had clearly come to some realization. All right, she would visit Fedya Pushkar today and the two of them would listen to what the Cheperukhas were saying on the other side of the wall.

The nurse looked in and asked the visitor to leave, rounds were beginning. Iona Ovseich was just thinking about the Biryuks and wanted to inquire as to their progress in the last week but it was difficult to formulate the question since he had not informed Orlov of what had been going on. The nurse reminded them a second time that rounds were beginning and they had to break off their conversation at that point.

The doctor arrived about forty minutes later and, still in the doorway, ordered the patient to remove his robe. She sat down on the bed, examined him back and front with a phonendoscope, then spent a long time squeezing, pressing, and sounding him, took his blood pressure twice, once on the right, once on the left, finding only a small difference. Finally, she allowed him to lie back down, helped cover him with the blanket, and said: "Good work, Degtyar. Today I'm satisfied with you."

"You are?" said Iona Ovseich. "But I'm dissatisfied with you."

The doctor automatically stepped back; a look of fear flashed in her eyes and her face paled slightly. Iona Ovseich took her hand tenderly and hastened to reassure her: he was dissatisfied that they had been willing to give him so much of their time when he was just taking the opportunity to loll around like a slugabed. The doctor removed her glasses and wiped them on one corner of her smock. Her nearsighted eyes squinted almost to the point of closing and she looked completely different now, just a woman with her own cares, family, children.

"You know," she said softly, "Sometimes people do take advantage. The worst time for this is in January. February. God forbid."

There was an unpleasant aftertaste in Iona Ovseich's mouth and he automatically tried to swallow. He let go of the doctor's hand. The right words were swirling through his mind and all he had to do was utter them aloud but he restrained himself, feeling somehow sorry for her. He switched the subject—roughly when would they release him. The doctor put her glasses back on and her usual expression appeared in her eyes, as if she knew more about the patient than he knew about himself, but was obliged to keep that a secret, and the patient did not even have the right to guess what she knew.

"Degtyar," she replied in a firm tone of voice, smiling with only the corners of her mouth, "we're not shamans or witch doctors here. We're medical people."

Iona Ovseich turned his head, tilting it somewhat; out of habit he narrowed one eye and said: all the more reason—like any other science, medicine should be able to fix time limits scientifically and make prognoses.

"Degtyar," she said, the same smile on her face, and Iona Ovseich once again felt that unpleasant aftertaste in his mouth, "medicine is not like mathematics or chemistry. Or even like agriculture."

"Or even like agriculture," said Iona Ovseich in surprise. "Why did you choose agriculture?"

"I could have just as easily said physics, astronomy, geology," said the doctor with a shrug of her shoulders.

"Of course," agreed Iona Ovseich, "who could doubt that, agriculture just happened to occur to you, that's all. I understand."

In the pause that ensued, the doctor grew thoughtful and a shadow crossed her face. She rose from Degtyar's bed, crossed her hands over the belt on her smock, and said in a loud and confident voice: "All right. I'd suppose that we can release you in a week's time."

"Thank you, Doctor," said Degtyar, placing his hands on his stomach, "you're spending too much time on me as it is."

"Yes," repeated the doctor, "you can be released in about a week's time and then you should rest at home for three days or so; the hospital will do the paperwork for putting you on the sick list and then you have to spend some time in a sanatorium, preferably a cardiac sanatorium. I'll call the factory myself."

Iona Ovseich was about to say that there was no need to call the factory, now was no time for him to be resting, but the doctor had already opened the door and slammed it quickly behind her. She stood in the corridor for a few seconds without moving, her eyes having become sharp and small. Seeing her there and fearing the worst, Orlov came running over and asked what had happened, was he feeling worse? Startled, the doctor shuddered, then said, no, on the contrary, he was doing considerably better. Oh good, said Lyalya, clapping her hands, that meant he'd be coming home soon!

"That I don't know," said the doctor with sudden anger. "You may know but I don't."

Feeling somewhat confused, Lyalya thanked the doctor and was about to enter Degtyar's room when the doctor stopped her and informed her that it was no longer necessary for her to be constantly at the patient's bedside. Lyalya pretended to obey those instructions and began heading for the exit but she hid by the staircase, waiting there two or three minutes before tiptoeing nervously back to Iona Ovseich's room. Certain that she had left quite some time ago, he was pleasantly surprised to see her. He poured her some tea from his thermos bottle, opened a fresh package of biscuits, and took the chocolates with the white filling which the women from the factory had sent him yesterday. He asked about Gizella Landa—where was she living now, in her own place or at her sister's? He took a special interest in the Biryuks and Marina in particular, who was supposedly engaged in a mounting conflict with Landa on the question of housing. Lyalya took a sip of tea and a bite of biscuit and was about to answer the questions when the door flew open revealing the doctor, who attacked her at once: "Aren't you ashamed of yourself for deceiving a doctor! You're a grown woman but you act worse than a schoolgirl; you hide in the stairwell and then slip back in here at the first chance you get!" Iona Ovseich looked in confusion from one woman to the other, unable to understand what was happening. Lyalya mumbled something in reply and opened her pocketbook; her fingers wooden, she had trouble finding her pass. The doctor grabbed it immediately from Lyalya and tore it in half, ordering her to leave the room at once: the patient needed rest and visitors like her only aggravated him and delayed his recovery.

Lyalya jumped up as if she had been scalded and even forgot to say good-bye. The doctor slammed the door and told Degtyar in detail how that woman had cunningly tricked her. Indignant, Iona Ovseich condemned Lyalya as well, but added that the doctor could have found another, more humane way of dealing with Lyalya.

"Degtyar," said the doctor with a stammer, clearly hesitating whether to say something or not, "I didn't want to say this but now I have to: many of our patients here are outraged that certain other patients have special privileges. I've had to explain to them that you're in critical condition."

Iona Ovseich paused, needing time to collect his thoughts. The doctor waited patiently, placing her hands on her belt, her overstarched smock making a crinkling sound. Finally, he rose halfway, his elbows somewhat in back of him, his veins swelling from the great effort, and he said in a hoarse voice: yes, they were right, he should have figured out for himself that he was receiving special treatment there. The doctor removed her eyeglasses, blew on the lenses, wiped them thoroughly with her handkerchief, and put them back on. The pupils of her eyes were now minute, the size of a pin head. "Well," she said, "you don't have to tear your hair out over it. Ultimately we did what we could, no more."

"Doctor," said Iona Ovseich, "I have a favor to ask of you: tell your superior that the patient Degtyar asks, no, not asks, demands, that he be transferred immediately to the general ward, the ward for everyone."

The doctor shrugged her shoulders: "That's impossible, there's not a bed to spare right now, we have patients out in the corridor." In the corridor! said Iona Ovseich in astonishment, while there was an empty bed right there in his room! The doctor shrugged her shoulders again: it wasn't empty, it was reserved for especially critical cases, the physician in chief was the one who assigned patients to that bed. All right, said Iona Ovseich, then the patient Degtyar demanded that he be given a bed in the corridor and, if he wasn't, her superior should come see him, he wanted to speak with him personally. All right, said the doctor with a nod, she'd pass on the message, but it was, of course, a favor he was asking, not an order he was giving, patients didn't give the orders there.

He had to wait quite some time for a response. Iona Ovseich was about to ask the nurse to remind the doctor but then the doctor herself returned and informed him that the department director and the physician in chief would not be there today, they both had been summoned by the District Committee.

"Both at the same time?" said Iona Ovseich, finding it difficult to believe in such a coincidence.

At the same time, said the doctor, emphasizing the point. The senior nurse was here now, she could send her there to confirm it. No, said Iona Ovseich, she didn't have to send anybody: he could wait until tomorrow. The doctor continued to stand by his bed and then asked if she could go. There was a familiar tone to her voice that reminded him of Landa, no, rather of Lapidis—he had been especially fond of irony. Iona Ovseich felt a sudden heat in his stomach, near his ribs, and his heart began beating wildly. All his muscles tensed, especially those in his arms and legs. He was about to jump to his feet and slam his fist on the table but a second later he was seized by an eerie weakness, and cold sweat snaked down his spine. Instinctively he pressed himself against the mattress. The doctor's face became runny and flat as if seen through murky water, then it receded quickly and finally came to a stop. Once again he heard her voice, deliberately polite: "Degtyar, I have to go, the other patients are waiting for me. Please rest calmly and don't get yourself all worked up."

About five minutes later the nurse came by, a syringe, whose tip was covered with cotton, protruding from her hand. She ordered him to turn over on his stomach. Iona Ovseich asked what kind of shot she was going to give him and the nurse replied analgine with dimedrol. Iona Ovseich was surprised—how did he know it was analgine with dimedrol, where were the ampules? The nurse grew indignant and replied rudely: "Listen, Degtyar, I've got thirty patients besides you. If you want the shot, let's see your ass, and if you don't, that's all right too."

"Whether I want it or not is none of your business," said Iona Ovseich angrily. "Bring the ampules and open them here!"

"You know what," said the nurse, "if you can talk like that, you can give yourself the injection."

Iona Ovseich did not reply but stared into her eyes. The nurse withstood this for a few seconds, then burst out laughing, squirted out the contents of the syringe into the air and went to get the ampules. So as not to waste time while she was gone, Iona Ovseich lowered his long johns to his knees and turned over on his stomach. The door opened a minute later but it turned out to be Malaya.

"What's this," she exclaimed from the doorway, "why are you lying there like that—are they going to give you an enema?"

What do you mean, an enema, replied Iona Ovseich angrily. He was waiting for the nurse, she was supposed to give him a shot. Malaya helped him pull up his long johns, then said that since he was awaiting the nurse in that seductive pose, things must have taken a turn for the better. She sat down on the bed, placed her purse by her feet, and took out a pot of broth which she had just made; it was still hot, he should drink some right away. Iona Ovseich literally shook: "Are you trying to disgrace me in front of the whole hospital, first one comes, then the other, and you both stay for hours on end. No wonder the other patients are outraged!"

"Outraged?" said Malaya in surprise. "They just don't know who's in here, that's all. They need to be told."

"Malaya," said Iona Ovseich, closing his eyes, "please get up and go, and come back during regular visiting hours, from five to seven, like everyone else. And hand over your pass."

Klava Ivanovna did not even ask why but automatically handed the pass to Iona Ovseich, who tore it into small pieces. "All right, go," he said, "good-bye."

Klava Ivanovna stopped by the door for a second: "Do you think your rudeness has offended an old woman? No, I'm happy that you're becoming your old self again."

The nurse brought the analgine and dimedrol, placing the ampules on Iona Ovseich's night table so that he could check them but he refused. He turned obediently onto his side, groaning and shuddering slightly when the needle penetrated his flesh. He thanked the nurse and, when saying good-bye, added: "Don't take what happened earlier personally. It was directed at someone else."

Iona Ovseich felt relatively good for the remainder of the day and evening; he even wanted to get up and go for a walk down the corridor. This was of course the usual symptom of a patient who had begun to feel slightly better and already thought that his recovery was proceeding too slowly. Iona Ovseich took a few steps toward the window and back, then looked out into the corridor. There were four beds along the wall with small white stools at the head of each one. It did not seem as terrible now as when the doctor had told him about it earlier in the day. Men were playing dominoes near the marble staircase and two of them were slamming their pieces down with such vigor that it was hard to believe they were sick and he found himself envying them. On the other hand, they needed to be reminded where they were. Iona Ovseich automatically looked around but unfortunately no staff people were nearby. The effort had made him dizzy and he became slightly nauseous; he had to go back to bed.

He lay with his eyes wide open until twelve o'clock, reviewing tasks at the factory and in the courtyard that he had been unable to complete. The factory, however, caused him less anxiety because the District Committee had taken it under its control. The courtyard was essentially adrift. Brag though he might, Biryuk would only be in the courtyard a short time. Something would certainly go amiss with Landa's apartment if it weren't handled properly; Gizella would end up being evicted and some outsider given her place. There were always plenty of people in and around the executive committee ready and willing to take a good apartment. Tomorrow he must inform Marina to come by the hospital—she'd understand what was what right away, and she knew how to restrain the major. But there was probably no hurry to deal with Cheperukha, that was more than one day's work.

"Oh, Cheperukha, Cheperukha," said Iona Ovseich aloud and with pain, "what kind of a bug has gotten into you!"

His memory now turned to the more remote past, the twenties, then it hopped to the forties, the war, the years right after the war, then went back to the thirties. He recalled some of the old drayman's wilder escapades, rows with his wife, shouting for the whole courtyard to hear, drunken debauches, and finally his friendship with

Granik, but who could have ever thought that all of a sudden the man would go as far as he had gone now!

"Degtyar," said Iona Ovseich to himself, "it's your fault, there's no getting out of that."

There was some sort of noise out on the tin window cornice, as if someone were scratching, trying to enter. Iona Ovseich turned on the light and peered out into the darkness. It must have been a bird, though the birds were usually asleep at that hour. He felt pity and compassion for that living creature, which was unable to find a place for itself and wanted shelter and affection. He whistled a modulated sound and the noise outside quieted for a few seconds. Iona Ovseich laughed in spite of himself; a bird was a bird but it knew what was good. Tomorrow he'd sprinkle some bread crumbs for it. He turned onto his left side facing the wall and fell into a deep, sweet sleep as he used to when he was young. He dreamed that he was chewing something resilient, a little salty, sweetish, like a finger or a piece of a living body.

He woke up in a good mood the next morning and picked up the bedpan to urinate but he put it down at once and then, for the first time since he'd taken to bed, he walked to the bathroom under his own power. He suffered a little shortness of breath on the way back to his room but that was normal enough: it would have been surprising if he hadn't been short of breath. He lay quietly for a few minutes. Everything was back to normal. He touched his cheeks with the palms of his hands and felt the stubble as thick as if he'd been wandering in the forest for a month. As soon as the nurse made an appearance he asked about a barber. It turned out that the barber was already there and was seeing ambulatory patients in the shower room. The nurse suggested that she have him come to Degtyar's room. At first Iona Ovseich agreed but then a second later changed his mind and shouted after the nurse that it wasn't necessary, he'd go there himself.

There was only one man in line. Iona Ovseich realized that he had been longing to see new faces. He took a stool and sat down. There was a pleasant smell of aftershave lotion in the air. The barber clearly loved to chat as all barbers do. He was telling the man in the chair some silly story about the woman a friend of his had married. When they became intimate it turned out that the woman was a little bit a man too. Things turned nasty and now his friend was filing for divorce. On the other hand, as bad luck would have it, she was a fine person and they could have had a decent life together. In the end, what was the difference.

Iona Ovseich's turn came. He seated himself in what had formerly been a dentist's chair. The barber was surprised that they hadn't met earlier; judging by his beard, the patient had been in there some time. Degtyar explained that he had been suffering from double pneumonia, they said he was in critical condition, today was his first day out of bed. The barber lathered Iona Ovseich's cheeks, raising a good froth, and said that ever since penicillin had been invented, pneumonia was no longer the disease it had once been when it killed people one after the other. Cancer, that was a disease, but pneumonia wasn't a disease anymore. Iona Ovseich was sitting with his eyes closed, smiling to himself; for a moment he was about to explain to the barber what real pneumonia was but then he was seized by a pleasant lassitude, the lather felt prickly on his skin, and a smell of cleanliness and health wafted into his nostrils. Now the barber's small talk seemed even more soothing. When the shave was finished, Iona Ovseich made a movement to rise but the barber stopped him, picked up his scissors, and neatly evened Degtyar's sideburns. He trimmed Degtyar's neck with his clippers and cut the hair that was growing in his ears, then took a step back and sprayed him with an atomizer. Iona Ovseich half closed his eyes. Then, the flower-like taste of aftershave lotion in his mouth, he automatically turned away. There was a sudden sharp pain in his chest that went to his spine, he must be tired, but, all in all, he felt elation, as if he had grown younger. The barber paid him that very compliment, saying now he could see that he was a young man. Then he set up two mirrors, one in front and the other in back so that his client could have a full view. He accepted the five rubles from Iona Ovseich, placed them in his pocket, and expressed the wish that the next time they met it would be near the opera, in Aunt Utya's café.

When Iona Ovseich had left, the barber seated his next customer and signaled the people waiting in line to set the door ajar. He shook his head and said: "I don't like the way he looks."

There was a black traveling kit, whose leather was worn clear through in places, on an iron table. The barber opened the bag, its clasps clicking. The customer joked that he must have a Spanish garrote concealed in there. The joke fell flat apparently because no one there knew that a garrote was an iron collar used to execute people in Spain.

Though his first impulse on returning to his room was to go immediately back to bed, Iona Ovseich forced himself to sit by the window for a few minutes. The street with its traffic, voices, and noise could be bracing and indeed it was a pleasure to watch people hurrying on their way, unaware they were even passing a hospital. His hand moved instinctively forward and opened the window a crack. Fresh air came in and he had the feeling that it was traveling with his blood to every cell of his body. He wanted to stay there and keep gulping that air but, as they say, there can be too much of a good thing. Iona Ovseich closed the window, went back to his bed, took off his pajamas, folded them neatly, and lay down. He felt like a nap even though he had just woken a little while ago. He closed his eyes, turned his face toward the wall. For some reason that was uncomfortable and he turned onto his other side, then onto his back. That didn't help, it still didn't feel right. He turned back toward the wall and seemed to doze off. For a minute or two bright specks of color flickered before his eyes then vanished, replaced by a soft velvety darkness. No sooner had he felt some relief than a searing pain flared near his heart, accompanied by the fear that it was impossible either to inhale or to exhale. Fortunately, a nurse came by and immediately called a doctor. The doctor raised Iona Ovseich's hand, took his pulse, then ordered him to lie perfectly still. The doctor left for several minutes, returning with the department head, who pressed his fingers under Degtyar's shoulder blade. Iona Ovseich groaned deeply, feeling he had been cauterized from within with a red-hot iron. The department head told him to calm down, calm down, it was nothing terrible, probably a minor spasm. "We'll send an electrocardiogram machine here right away and take a cardiogram, then we'll have a complete picture. In the meantime the patient is to be given a cube of morphine and a cube of strofantin."

Iona Ovseich could hear every word distinctly, but the voices sounded as if they were coming from a deep darkness and he couldn't understand who was speaking or whom they were addressing and even the words themselves were borne away, like a belated echo of the attack of burning pain inside his breastbone and stomach. The nurse had brought the ampules but had not yet had time to insert them in to the syringe when the patient emitted a gurgling sound and seemed to be choking. Large, pea-sized beads of sweat emerged on his forehead, his face became sallow, and his blue lips chattered. "It's all right, my good man, it's all right," said the doctor reassuringly as Degtyar was quickly given an injection of morphine. Tying his arm with a band of rubber to help with the strofantin injection, the nurse felt one place, then another, finally saying that the veins were bad. They had to do the injection intramuscularly but beforehand gave him five cubes of novocaine to reduce the pain. Iona Ovseich opened his eyes, which were filled with inexpressible suffering. The doctor stroked his arm, wiped the sweat from his brow, and again said, "It's all right, dear, be patient, it'll get better, it has to."

The nurse brought in two oxygen tanks and the doctor placed the mask on Degtyar's face. He did not have time to inhale properly, for he was already exhaling by then. His arms were dangling like whips, his legs looked waxen. They placed hot-water bottles under his calves, close to his feet. The doctor signaled the nurse to take over for her, then sent the orderly to fetch another cylinder of oxygen. She left for the other wards: the patients had been waiting for her rounds for a whole hour.

A technician brought the electrocardiogram machine before lunchtime. He placed the electrodes on the patient's wrists and chest, having first wiped the contact area with a swab. He turned on the machine, which ran at an even rate, its sound somehow reminiscent of a child's toy. Chattering, it began extruding a narrow strip of paper with a long series of blips on it that were either large with flattened peaks, like that of a volcanic crater, or quite minute, in some places forming an almost straight line. The nurse called the doctor, the technician tore off the paper and said it was a textbook rear-wall myocardia. He turned off the electrodes, wound up the wire, closed the lid on the box, and took the cardiogram with him. His office would send them their interpretation, the chief was in until two today, so they'd have it tomorrow around ten or eleven. He cast a passing glance at the patient from the door, then closed the door behind him.

When the oxygen cylinder was delivered, the doctor ordered that it be left out in the corridor for the time being: sometimes patients overreacted. Either hearing what the doctor said or somehow intuiting it, Iona Ovseich asked that the cylinder be brought into his room. The doctor said there was no special need to, but ordered it wheeled in and placed close to the head of the bed. When they attached the mask, the hose proved on the short side and they had to bring the cylinder even closer. Iona Ovseich bore all the noise and commotion patiently until they finally had everything in place. The department head looked in again and tested Iona Ovseich's blood pressure and pulse himself, after sounding him thoroughly. Then, in a loud voice, he said that, objectively speaking, the patient should be feeling better.

"Listen, Degtyar," said the department head, addressing the patient directly, "You should feel better now."

After leaving the room, the department head beckoned the doctor with the slightest motion and told her to detain one of the nurses at once and have her stay at the patient's bedside.

Relief came to Iona Ovseich late in the afternoon, his breathing grew more even, and the nurse allowed the mask to be removed. He felt no worse for that, on the contrary, he had a definite sense of liberation. Only mute echoes remained of his recent fear and he felt like exchanging a few words with the nurse, finding out what the weather was like outdoors, the signs of spring were everywhere. He remembered that only that morning he had left his room under his own power and gone for a shave. He had sat by his open window enjoying the sight of the street but all that seemed to have happened an eternity ago.

The doctor came at around ten o'clock, her unscheduled visit motivated by the need to write up the patients' case histories; there was an enormous amount of paperwork and it was physically impossible to get it done during the day. Iona Ovseich smiled sadly in response to say that he understood perfectly and explanations weren't needed. The doctor smiled too, her eyes were kind and a bit preoccupied. She ordered the nurse to give Degtyar an injection of promedol instead of morphine so as not to hamper the diuretics. She wished him a good night, smiled again, then finally said good-bye, see you tomorrow.

The nurse gave him the injection and left the room, and Iona Ovseich was alone. He could hear the patients clacking their dominoes out in the corridor. The door to the women's room slammed closed, footsteps shuffled quickly down the corridor, a metal cup clanked—apparently, they were scooping boiled water from a small tank. A hoarse male voice shouted, "who's spilling the home brew?" Then he could hear the clack of dominoes again, a whole machine gun burst of them this time. All together these sounds formed a strange image of well-being, as if people had been bored at home and had decided on their own to spend a little time here, then return home again. He wanted to doze off but at first something within him resisted, as if sleep were not merely sleep. Finally, his body took over and he was asleep.

Iona Ovseich woke a few times during the night, experiencing his usual reaction: he could not immediately tell where he was and his heart sank in fear. After a few seconds of agony, he would grow a little calmer. The nurse was sleeping on the other bed and he could hear what sounded like snoring. One time she raised her head and asked what was the matter, why wasn't he sleeping? He said he was all right and she should get some rest. Once again he could hear the young girl's soft snoring, a pleasant sound. For some odd reason it reminded him of stale hay and he visualized a small hill with a tractor rumbling peacefully in the distance, cows with enormous udders, filled to overflowing with milk after the day, roaming the hillside, the evening sun casting its parting rays, everything as fine and beautiful as a painting. Then, with no transition though it was already light outside, the anxious voice of a newscaster began speaking, mentioning the name of Stalin before reading:

"On the night of March 2, 1953, Comrade Stalin suffered a sudden brain hemorrhage, affecting important areas of the brain, suffering as a result the paralysis of his right leg and right arm, as well the loss of consciousness and speech. On March 2 and 3, the appropriate medical measures were taken but have as yet to cause a significant turnaround. The treatment given Comrade Stalin is under the constant supervision of the Central Committee and the Soviet government."

"Nurse," cried Iona Ovseich, "did you hear what they just broadcast on the radio?"

No one answered and it was only then that Iona Ovseich saw that he was alone in the room, there wasn't even anyone to share the news with. He made an automatic movement to rise from his bed and go find people but he immediately clutched at his heart with both hands and cried aloud. A patient looked in from the corridor and was about to call the physician on duty at once but Iona Ovseich stopped him, beckoned him closer, and said: "Did you hear what they just broadcast on the radio!"

The other patient sighed bitterly, lowered his head, and whispered: "God forbid, God forbid!" Degtyar's heart was burning with pain, pressing against his chest like a horse's hoof. He had to put on the oxygen mask again but it brought him no relief. He was about to begin screaming wildly when, thank God, the doctor came and gave him an injection. The pain subsided a little but a minute later he felt a nausea that was even worse than the pain.

"Ooh!" groaned Iona Ovseich, tearing off the mask. "Oh, I feel awful!"

The doctor tenderly told him to calm down, that was what he needed more than anything right now, but Iona Ovseich wouldn't listen to her. The doctor ordered the nurse to put the mask back on, then shouted in a rude voice: "Stop it, Degtyar! You're not the only patient here, there's a hundred more besides you."

Iona Ovseich narrowed his eyes, and tears appeared at their corners, as he whispered: "Doctor, I feel so awful, why don't you believe me?"

The doctor adjusted the mask and loosened the straps a little so it would be less confining. She increased the flow of oxygen from the tank and asked Degtyar if his mouth was dry. She took his arm and squeezed it with her fingers in a few places, then ordered the nurse to get a large ampule of glucose, we'll try it intravenously.

The vein slid under the needle. The doctor froze for a second as if rooted to the spot, then quickly pushed the syringe down. A dark brown layer of blood appeared at the bottom; at first the amount of blood increased rapidly as the plunger lowered, then it gradually vanished, leaving only a transparent fluid which, moving from one mark on the syringe to the next, gradually entered the patient's body.

For lunch the orderly brought a bowl of semolina soup, meatballs with mashed potatoes and a glass of kissel. The orderly was lingering in the doorway and the nurse ordered her to put everything on the night table. The orderly looked around the room for a clean towel to cover the table but, having no luck in finding one cast a glance at the patient, waved her hand in dismissal, and quietly left the room.

His condition remained on the same level until that evening, becoming neither better nor worse. Klava Ivanovna arrived at five o'clock and the first thing that caught her eye was the oxygen tank. His meal was still on the night table untouched. The nurse placed a finger to her lips but Klava Ivanovna had already sat down on the bed, taken Iona Ovseich's hand, and asked in a loud voice: "Degtyar, what's the matter with you? It's me, Malaya."

Iona Ovseich turned his head. His eyes looked out from between his eyelids, narrow strips, whitish like cataracts. Klava Ivanovna peered into his face for a second or two, then asked: "Your heart?"

The nurse waited until the patient closed his eyes, then she mouthed the word "infarct." Klava Ivanovna shuddered, as if hiccuping, straightened her back, and then froze in that position, only her jaw moving slightly. Iona Ovseich half opened his eyes and it was clear from his gaze that he was perfectly conscious and understood everything. He raised his hand to remove the mask and say something but they stopped him in time.

"Degtyar," said Klava Ivanovna, taking charge, her wits back about her, "lie still. I'll be here with you now."

The door flew open and there was Lyalya, a crazed look in her eye, a good thing the patient couldn't see it. Klava Ivanovna rose to meet her, took her by the hand like a little child, and brought her out to the corridor where she categorically forbade Lyalya to enter the room.

"Oh, mama," wailed Lyalya, "he's dying!"

"You fool!" said Klava Ivanovna angrily. "You perfect little fool!"

"Oh, he's dying!"

"Orlov," said Malaya, becoming even angrier, "leave, and don't bother people when they're working. Either you leave nicely or I'm calling the orderlies."

Lyalya went downstairs. There were long, backless benches beneath the staircase. She sat down on one, leaned against the wall, and fixed her gaze on the cement floor, sitting there like that until seven o'clock. Visiting hours were over, said the cloakroom attendant, time to go. Lyalya jumped to her feet, slipped a ruble in the attendant's pocket, and, without saying a word, dashed back upstairs. She paused outside Degtyar's room to catch her breath, her legs literally trembling in fear. Finally, she regained a semblance of self-control but no sooner had she opened the door than she saw that horrible oxygen tank and the mask on his face. She fell to her knees like a half-crazed woman, seized Degtyar's hand, and began covering it with kisses. It was all too sudden for Klava Ivanovna to be able to react. Iona Ovseich tore his hand free himself and signaled them both to leave at once. It cost Klava Ivanovna some effort to compell Lyalya to rise from the floor. Several times she repeated that this was disgraceful, the whole country was grieving, Stalin had taken ill, and everyone, the healthy and the sick, even the children, were exerting all their strength to retain their self-control while Lyalya Orlov was letting herself go entirely and making hysterical scenes!

Iona Ovseich groaned loudly, he must have heard every word. Lyalya was no longer resisting and asked only to be given an assignment of some sort, she was ready to sacrifice her own life. Finally, Klava Ivanovna managed to get her out into the corridor, then brought her to the main door. Lyalya said that she would wait there all through the night. The bolt clanged shut behind her.

"Call me if that woman tries to force her way back in," said Klava Ivanovna to the watchman.

Iona Ovseich was given two injections during the night, promedol and strofantin, which afforded him some relief and he began falling asleep. Klava Ivanovna pulled the bedpan out from under the bed and said: "Wait, don't fall asleep. First take a piss, you haven't pissed in a long time."

His urine was scant, almost brown in color, and had a very sharp odor. Malaya brought the bedpan to the bathroom and poured the urine into a clean jar: it should be sent for analysis tomorrow.

Iona Ovseich began to fall asleep again. Klava Ivanovna sat by his feet, tucked in the end of the blanket, straightened the hot-water bottle, and sighed softly: "Degtyar, I'm thinking about Orlov again. When you have your health back, you really have to get things straight with her. You had it easier with me."

It was not a good night for the patient, who woke frequently, panting like a locomotive. The physician on duty was called in a few times. Klava Ivanovna asked that the patient be given an injection. They tried one but it did no good. Right before their eyes, Iona Ovseich's face grew pinched, his nose became sharper, and the bone began showing through his forehead as if his skin were being pulled tight at the back of his head. At certain points it seemed the worst had come but, thank God, his organism rallied its forces and his condition would return to its previous state. He asked for something to drink often but the doctor said the less fluids the better, so as not to overwork his heart. At first Klava Ivanovna spoon-fed him water, then dampened his lips with a moist cloth, repeating again and again: "If you mustn't, you mustn't. That's what you always taught us."

He seemed to take a turn for the better toward the morning and he insisted that Klava Ivanovna lie down and get herself a little sleep. When the light was off the room grew hushed; voices could be heard outside, someone seemed to be calling Malaya, Degtyar, but perhaps that was only an illusion. Gradually sleep began to overcome him again, more a drowsiness than actual sleep. With his eyes closed Iona Ovseich could still distinctly see that it was gradually growing light outside. People were hurrying to work, at first just individuals then larger groups until there were crowds of them. Factory whistles began wailing desperately, covering the sky with clouds of black smoke. People opened their mouths to cry out but no sound issued from them, as in a silent movie. The black smoke settled on the ground. Thousands of tentacle-like hands began chaotically clutching at heads, chests, throats, no one could breathe, and finally an insane voice cried out: "Breathing! Breathing!" Iona Ovseich opened his eyes. It was quiet outside and he had to listen intently to hear what the loudspeaker was saying:

"On the night of March 3, there continued to be disturbances in the breathing and the blood circulation. The greatest changes were observed in the respiratory functions: the appearance of periodic breathing malfunctions increased in frequency. The degree of oxygen deficiency increased. The systematic use of oxygen as well as medical measures gradually caused a slight improvement in the condition and by the morning of March 4 the degree of respiratory insufficiency had declined somewhat. Further, during the day of March 4, the critical respiratory disturbances resumed. Blood pressure was a maximum of two hundred and ten and a minimum of one hundred and ten. No changes of significance in the lungs or in the abdominal region were determined during the course of the past twenty-four hours. The urine proved to contain the normal amount of protein and red blood corpuscles. Blood analysis revealed an increased quantity of white blood corpuscles (up to seventeen thousand). Oxygen-assisted breathing and penicillin treatment were continuing. The patient was in a soporific profoundly unconscious state. Breathing under the control of the nervous system and heart function continued to suffer sharp disturbances. Tretyakov, Minister of Health of the U.S.S.R. Kuperin, Chief of the Kremlin Hospital. Lukomsky, Chief Therapeutist of the Ministry of Health. Active Members of the Academy of Medical Sciences Professor Konovalov, Professor Myasnikov, Professor Tareev. Corresponding Member, Professor Filimonov. Professor Glazunov. Professor Tkachev. Assistant Professor Ivanov-Neznamov.

There was a short pause filled with soft static followed by a click, then the announcer moved to other news.

"Malaya," Iona Ovseich called out, "did you hear that?"

Yes, said Klava Ivanovna, she'd heard it all, even the deaf could hear that. Oxygen, urine, protein, red corpuscles, white corpuscles, who'd have ever thought we'd be hearing such things about Stalin.

"Malaya, all the doctors were academicians and professors, but there was one assistant professor—Ivanov-Neznamov. Malaya, what does that mean—Assistant Ivanov-Neznamov?"

Klava Ivanovna sat in silence on her bed: the announcer's voice could be heard again: yesterday thousands of workers visited Comrade Stalin's native city of Gori.

"Malaya," said Iona Ovseich, panting for breath and signaling for oxygen, "Stalin is a Georgian, and Georgians live to be a hundred and twenty years old."

He closed his eyes. Klava Ivanovna sat down beside him and helped him put on the mask. She could hear the hiss of the gas. Iona Ovseich's arms were outside the blanket; they were long, thin, and pale, all skin and bones. She bent over him and kissed him, the first tears appearing in her eyes: "Oh, Degtyar, how am I supposed to bear all this!"

By midday the patient's condition had taken turns both for the worse and the better. One time he opened his eyes and stared so long and so intently that his gaze was unendurable.

"Degtyar," whispered Klava Ivanovna with tender affection, "it's me, Malaya, do you recognize me? You're going to live."

Iona Ovseich smiled. She knew that mocking grin of his all too well and it tore her heart to pieces. She took his hand and then suddenly a mad idea occurred to her—she could transmit some of her life into him, she only needed to desire it with all her might. She sat up straight, squeezing his fingers firmly. He looked at her and smiled. She squeezed his fingers even tighter and once again said: "You're going to live."

Soft, warm waves like morning mist coursed through his arms and legs. His entire body was filled with a sweet sensation, mixed with a touch of alarm and puzzlement, a feeling he knew from childhood. And there was a sense of traveling—up ahead the sun seemed to be shrinking behind smoke-darkened glass, a yellow spot in the darkness, becoming smaller and smaller until it finally disappeared. For an instant the darkness was cut by a band of milky light. Iona Ovseich shuddered, wheezing heavily, a gurgling in his throat; veins thick as rubber tubes swelled on his neck, one eye turned up while the other looked directly at Klava Ivanovna but the pupil was not reacting. She pressed her cheek to his forehead, which was warm and moist with perspiration.

The doctor came and drew back the eyelids, took his pulse, and examined his stomach. After sitting quite still for a moment, she got up and left. Five minutes later the nurse arrived with a bottle of iodine and daubed the brush. She asked Klava Ivanovna to leave the room, then flung off the blanket, moved closer to the dead man's foot on which she painted a number in large lines. Then she covered him with the blanket again, pulling it up to cover his head. Klava Ivanovna wanted to come back in but she was not allowed to and was told she would no longer be allowed to enter the room. A rolling bed arrived two hours later. The body was transferred from the bed to a stretcher, then placed on the rolling bed and taken away.

The funeral took place the next day. Iona Ovseich's coffin was set out in the factory yard, a military band played a funeral march, and the men and women workers, the technicians, engineers, and clerical staff paid their last respects to the dead man. The women wept openly, the men held out the best they could but still their tears began to flow too. The eulogies were given by comrades from the City Party Committee, the Stalin District Committee, and the District Executive Committee followed by people from the factory staff, the factory party committee, and the workers. The band began to play again as a truck whose bed and sides were decorated with red bunting drove into the yard. Garlands of spruce and a wreath of thuya hung from the sides of the truck. The procession went out to the street, the people in front carrying crimson pillows with the deceased's medals and decorations. The pallbearers carried the coffin on their shoulders for an entire block, then the command was given to place the coffin in the truck. There were buses for those wishing to accompany Iona Ovseich and they began heading for the last time to the building where the dead man had lived.

Those who had organized the funeral intended to spend the customary two or three minutes there but things took a different turn. An enormous crowd was waiting by the gate, not only the residents of the courtyard but hundreds of people from the neighboring buildings. Klava Ivanovna led a detachment of Pioneers who had been excused from school especially for that purpose. Major Biryuk, Stepa Khomitsky, Zinovy Cheperukha, and Klava Ivanovna were all wearing mourning bands. Lyalya Orlov was dressed all in black and many people took her for the widow. Despite the raw March weather, old Cheperukha came out wearing only his suit, a dark blue cheviot made to order for him before the war. Dina Vargaftik had on a cashmere shawl with fringe and tassels that was tied tightly under her chin, bordering her face in black like an obituary. Anya Kotlyar was in regular clothing, a light spring topcoat whose sleeves were trimmed in beaver-lamb, and a man's hat with earlaps since she had to protect her injured jaw from chills; the only unusual item was a black silk scarf which she wore around her neck. Adya was standing beside her, capless as usual, his hands thrust in his pockets. He examined people's faces intently and many people came to an automatic stop, expecting he would speak to them or ask them a question. He frowned, his eyes darkening, glowering with anger. Anya tugged at his sleeve twice and whispered a reproach to him but in response he turned his back and continued to stare. Zinovy too reprimanded him but Adya did not obey, he only made an inept remark about Zinovy's mourning band, saying that Zinovy should cut it in two, give the red half to his old man and keep the black half for himself. Zinovy gave Adya a look of surprise and sorrow for he was clearly suffering greatly that day. Now Adya felt awkward, raised his head, revealing his thin neck with its prominent Adam's apple, and stared up at the sky, maintaining that foolish posture until Zinovy had walked away.

The funeral director wanted everyone to say their farewells right there by the gate but this made people indignant. Major Biryuk, Zinovy, Stepa Khomitsky, and old Cheperukha hoisted the coffin up onto their shoulders, carried it into the courtyard, and placed it on a table covered with rugs. Now no one would have to rise up on tiptoe to view the body. At first the crowd was dense and there was shoving and pushing, everyone trying to surge ahead. Little children started screaming in fear. Klava Ivanovna ordered the men to exert some crowd control. Andrei Petrovich proposed that everyone line up single file and move in a circle around the body. Most people lined up at once while others needed a tug or a push. Some people wanted to linger by the body. Stepa Khomitsky and Zinovy hurried them up, saying they could get back in line if they wanted, but since that could have dragged things out for hours, old Cheperukha was sent to the back of the line and no one else was allowed to join.

Major Biryuk announced that the viewing of the body had concluded and that the parting words would be spoken by one of the courtyard's oldest residents and a longtime assistant of Iona Ovseich Degtyar, Comrade Klava Ivanovna Malaya.

The concierge, Lebedev, brought over a wide stool and helped Klava Ivanovna climb up on it. Some people were still talking but their voices quickly grew still until finally the silence was complete.

Klava Ivanovna's grief-stricken voice rang out in the courtyard:

"Comrades, we are accompanying on his last journey our dear and beloved teacher, friend, and neighbor Iona Ovseich Degtyar. Our courtyard is an orphan now. For thirty straight years, day and night, we constantly felt that Comrade Degtyar was side by side with us, in life and work. We have been through crisis and hunger with him, hardship and war, and no matter what problems arose along the way, he was always first to meet them, he always raised our spirits, always had a warm, heart-felt word for a friend while at the same time he taught us to hate the enemy, and not to spare ourselves, our energy, our life. What benefit did he derive from his superhuman labors, what sort of sanatoriums and palaces did he expect in return! Go have a look at the furniture in his apartment and you'll get a clear answer to that question and it might even make some of us ashamed of ourselves. We were illiterate and ignorant, he helped us get an education, he forced us to study because anyone who doesn't study cannot help build communism."

Klava Ivanovna raised her head and surveyed the crowd with a long intent stare. She extended her hand forward, her finger stopping in one place then another before she continued: "Here, right here, I can see people to whom he gave a part of his own heart in all generosity, happy as a little child when he was able to say: 'Malaya, something's been accomplished but there's still a lot of work to do before the job's done.' He didn't have time to finish."

A sudden cry rang out as if someone were suffocating. Lyalya Orlov fell onto the table, grasped the corpse's head, and pressed her lips to it with such force that she could not be dragged away. Andrei Petrovich and Stepa Khomitsky took her by the arms, and for a second they were able to break her grip but then she immediately seized hold of the coffin. The crowd had begun to grow restive. Major Biryuk pressed down on her elbow from behind. Lyalya groaned mournfully as she let go of the coffin. A bottle of smelling salts was passed forward from the back row and held to Lyalya's nose. Olya and Katerina took Lyalya by the waist from either side, forced their way through the crowd, and led her up to her apartment.

"Dear Comrade Degtyar," said Klava Ivanovna, her eyes fixed on Iona Ovseich's body, "you'll live forever in our hearts. You will be a shining example for our children and our grandchildren as you were for their fathers and their grandfathers. You never left the ranks when you were alive and you will stay in the ranks forever. Farewell, our faithful comrade, our friend in battle! Rest in peace, my dear Degtyar!"

Klava Ivanovna began to cry. Sighs of sorrow could be heard from the crowd where someone now began sobbing loudly. Andrei Petrovich announced that the funeral meeting had concluded. Klava Ivanovna kissed the dead man, then was followed by the others. Tosya Khomitsky was about to cross herself but they stopped her in time. The men lifted the coffin and the strains of a funeral march rang out magnified twice, three times by the stones of the courtyard and was all the more magnificent for that. At a slow pace, swaying slightly from side to side, they carried the coffin to the gate. They were forced to slow their pace at the front door because people were pressing and crowding from every side, even posing a danger to the coffin at various moments. The people near the coffin raised a heart-rending cry which was not even drowned out by the sound of the band. The front rows quickened their pace as much as possible whereas the people in back slowed theirs and finally the coffin was through the gate and in the truck. The driver started the motor and was about to pull away when old Cheperukha suddenly clambered up onto the truck, raised both hands, and, in a loud voice, called for silence. It had all happened so suddenly that no one had time to stop him or order him down from the truck. Iona beat his breast with his fist and addressing the coffin cried out: "Dear Ovseich, today you were at home with us here in the courtyard for the last time. Tears can't tell of the pain in my heart and the wound that you've left there! I was used to knowing you were nearby for all the years of Soviet power. Whenever I came up to the gate of my building, I was always well aware that you were here and could watch every step. Not every family is alike, some are better than others; a father can strike his son, a son can reply with a rude word, but still the father is the father and the son is still the son. Having lost your own children, you built an outpost for our children: you worked unsparingly to make sure we all had a good place to live. Not everyone liked you all the time, and you rubbed some people the wrong way, but in his heart of hearts everyone knew that Degtyar never wanted anything for himself, all he wanted was to build communism for all of us. He spared no efforts to bring that day closer, and to see it with his own eyes. How can one heart be so big! He died in harness. He has left us forever and taken a piece of our lives with him, a piece that will never return. Rest in peace, dear Ovseich, and remember us kindly."

Leaning against a stone pedestal by the gate, Gizella Landa stood motionless, an unhealthy feverish gleam in her eye. A bitter grin played on her lips. When the elder Cheperukha had finished his eulogy and hopped down to the pavement to stand in the ranks with everyone else, Gizella followed them automatically for a few seconds. The band began playing again and the procession moved onward until the block was deserted and the ground was strewn with broken spruce branches and pieces of paper flowers. Gizella went into the courtyard, which had a cemetery-like hush about it. There wasn't a soul there, everyone had gone to see Degtyar off, even the children. In the hallway she leaned out the window and looked down at the courtyard again, then she turned away and opened her door. The room had an unlived-in air, a thick layer of dust on the piano's black lid. She ran a finger along it. Without removing her coat, she sat down on a round chair, a screw squeaking under the seat. She closed her eyes and pressed her head to the wall where the wooden bas relief of Mozart dug into her forehead, then she began weeping bitterly, covering her mouth with the palms of her hands.

Those accompanying the coffin walked as far as Stalin Avenue on foot. The band began to play "You Fell in the Fateful Battle." The familiar words rose in people's memories and they followed along, moving their lips in silence. All of a sudden the band fell silent in mid-note and the procession came to a halt. A policeman walked over to the funeral director and word was passed back that people should now board the buses. The musicians were allowed on first, then everyone else found seats. The truck with the coffin drove up in front. Some of the wreaths had already been placed on the coffin, the rest were taken on the bus. Ten minutes later they passed Chumka and the railroad bridge, then arrived at the second Christian cemetery, formerly the international cemetery. Iona Ovseich had been given a good place, not far from the main gate. The coffin was placed beside the grave. Out of sheer momentum the people in back continued to press forward and had to be restrained. The wet snow sloshed underfoot and got into people's shoes. The younger people clambered up onto the monuments and trees. People were getting restless. Finally, a representative of the factory's party organization opened the funeral meeting, saying a few words himself. The next speaker was a comrade from the District Committee and he was followed by Andrei Petrovich Biryuk, who would say the final words on behalf of the people of the courtyard and their neighbors. "First and foremost," said the major, "we are saying farewell to a Bolshevik, a Communist, and a soldier who in word and in deed gave us an example of how to live—not for oneself but for other people. Today we can say loud and clear that Iona Degtyar lived a remarkable life and here at his graveside we vow and promise to serve our people and our party, giving our all unstintingly as he did. Rest in peace, dear Comrade Degtyar, your memory will remain bright in our hearts forever!"

The grave-diggers picked up the coffin, lowered it to the bottom of the grave, and began shoveling. Those who were close by were able to toss in their handful. A little hill-shaped pile formed on the coffin. The grave-diggers quickly flattened it out, tamping it down. The band began to play the "Internationale." People drew themselves up to their full height and stood like that until the final note had faded.